The PRINCE'S PSALM

Eric Shaw QUINN

DSP PUBLICATIONS

Published by

DSP PUBLICATIONS

5032 Capital Circle SW, Suite 2, PMB# 279, Tallahassee, FL 32305-7886 USA
www.dsppublications.com

The Prince's Psalm
© 2016 Eric Shaw Quinn.

Cover Art
© 2016 Paul Richmond.
http://www.paulrichmondstudio.com
Cover content is for illustrative purposes only and any person depicted on the cover is a model.

Author Photo by Adam Robitel.

ISBN: 978-1-63476-835-1
Digital ISBN: 978-1-63476-836-8
Library of Congress Control Number: 2015918978
Published June 2016
v. 1.0

Printed in the United States of America
∞
This paper meets the requirements of
ANSI/NISO Z39.48-1992 (Permanence of Paper).

For Anne and Christopher Rice, without whose encouragement and support this book simply would not have been written. And for my father, Ron Quinn, whose tolerant faith led him to discover the verse in 1 Samuel that inspired this work, to see those poetic words as testament to the divine and universal truth of love, and to share that truth and his faith with me.

ACKNOWLEDGMENTS

THIS BOOK was a labor of love with the accent on labor. The work was demanding and difficult, but my burden was lighter for the love, support, encouragement, advice, and hours of hard work from so many others.

Anne Rice, my beloved friend and colleague, who always encourages me to write the book I want to read, learned that this was my dream project and did everything in her power to make that dream come true. She would accept no excuses or delays, opened her heart and her library to me, and shepherded me through an unimaginably arduous process by sharing her enthusiasm for the story and her limitless and considerable experience with the task at hand. Her faith, wisdom, and guidance are the reason this book is more than just a dream.

Christopher Rice, my best friend and business partner, not only kept me going through the process of writing this opus; he never gave up on the project and, in the end, took on the job of agent and got *The Prince's Psalm* published. Without his unwavering friendship, you would not be reading this book. If you're looking for the definition of best friend, I'd say you'll be hard pressed to find a better example than Christopher. I have never met his equal and hope I am half the friend in return that he is to me.

My sweet, dear, scholarly father, Ron Quinn, whose example of faith, tolerance, and persistent, progressive liberalism in the face of overwhelming odds have inspired me all my life, found the verse on which this novel is based in the Book of Samuel. He shared with me those few couplets, a testament to the love and sacred commitment between two men, in an effort to soften the blows of those who tried and failed to use his faith as a weapon against my civil rights. Dad's simple, personal act and his desire to tell his gay son that he and God loved all His creation unconditionally—even me—was the beginning of my journey. My father's generous act opened my eyes and inspired me to tell this story of true love from the Bible, an ancient book too often quoted as containing so many hateful lies it does not and used to justify so much ugliness that it does not espouse.

Gregg Hurwitz and Marc Glick are my cavalry, who rescued Jonathan and David when all seemed lost. Their belief in the story and this novel gave me the tools and the encouragement I needed to help me transform my expansive historical novel into a dramatic work, worthy of its heroes.

Nicole Galland offered up her time and talent to aid and encourage me to tell this story with a voice as confident as my conviction of how important I believe it to be.

To this constellation of bright stars, I add the names of those who helped me make this novel more than a Word file in a folder on my backup drive and deliver it into your hands. Beckett Giotto, and his patient and enlightening reads, Anne Regan and her most excellent cadre of indefatigable editors who keep me on course and kept the story true without ever forgetting the story.

And Elizabeth North who built a home where my warriors could find refuge as she took their story out to the world, a thousand thanks to Elizabeth and all her Dreamspinners, for where would the world be without dreams?

*And it came to pass… that the soul of Jonathan
was knit with the soul of David,
and Jonathan loved him as his own soul….
Then Jonathan and David made a covenant,
because he loved him as his own soul.*

1 Samuel 18:1-3

PART ONE

FIVE SMOOTH STONES

And he took his staff in his hand, and chose him five smooth stones out of the brook, and put them in a shepherd's bag which he had, even in a scrip; and his sling was in his hand: and he drew near to the Philistine.

1 Samuel 17:40

Chapter One
The Book of Elah

And there went out a champion out of the camp of the Philistines, named Goliath, of Gath, whose height was six cubits and a span.

1 Samuel 17:4

"God, do you believe in me?" David whispered his prayer softly.

The Elah Valley echoed with the call of the Philistine trumpets. His blood ran as cold as spring water. The warm sun of summer morning filtered through the myrtle leaves in the bushes where he hid.

The trumpet call again split the air.

He knew what would follow the braying. He had witnessed it for the first time only the day before. King Saul himself told David that it had been the same for forty days. Day forty-one would begin no differently, David knew. How it would end, only God knew.

Alone, he hid in the brush on the north side of the valley, nearest the massive Israelite army encampment. In the hills south of the valley, so near David could easily have walked to them before his shadow grew shorter by half, camped King Achish with thousands upon thousands of Philistine men-at-arms. Their fearsome iron machines of war sat gleaming in the sun, waiting to cut him and all the men of the tribes of Israel to tripe for the carrion birds that swam in the drafts overhead.

"I believe in you, God," David sang softly under his breath as he waited for the inevitable. "How could I not? One has only to look into the sky at night or witness the birth of a new lamb or be lost in a storm to feel your presence. What would you have of me? I have followed you to this place, and I will follow you as far as you will lead me. If this be the end of my journey or my own folly, then I pray that you will know I came here this day seeking your glory, not my own. I seek only favor in your eyes and in the eyes of those whose faith in me I would restore."

The shouts of the Israelites aroused him from his psalm.

Day forty-one had begun.

He dared a look through the leaves of the myrtle thicket where he hid to gain a view of the Philistines' ultimate weapon. David's heart danced with fear.

The warrior was called Goliath. A man, and not a man, the Philistine was larger than life. His height cut a shadow that stretched too far into the morning sun. Even the day before when David, safe amid the army of Israel on the ridge above, first beheld Goliath, the scale of the man had struck David cold with fear. Viewed from David's hiding place upon the plain, he was still more fearsome to behold.

Swathed in gleaming bronze, Goliath towered over the flat grassland around him. Though he had heard it said that the Philistine champion was a man of the tribes of Moab and hence a distant kinsman of David's, the resemblance ended there. Six cubits and a span from sandals to his brow, what parts of the man that weren't sheathed in armor showed Goliath to be swarthy, dark, and dusted with black hair. David, fair, smooth-skinned and golden-haired, could only have met his opponent eye to eye were he seated on horseback.

The two could not have been more opposite. Though David had faced down wild beasts of prey, Goliath was the more terrifying for possessing animal prowess and the wits of a man. His size spoke but half his malice. Every span and cubit of the giant bore witness to the ill he represented to all the tribes of Israel. Still, the lofty peak of Goliath's helmet did not reach by half the height of the threat intended by the vast Philistine army he stood before.

Higher still were the stakes David faced. He had come to defend the honor of his God and his country before an audience that numbered in the tens of thousands, kings and princes counted among them. Above these lofty goals, still higher were the yearnings of David's own heart: to be a man in the eyes of his brother and to win favor before the one he loved most.

David's only protection that morning were the deep green leaves and crisp white blossoms of the myrtle bushes that surrounded him. The king's armor, so generously offered, had been so generous, in fact, it had swallowed David whole and so it had been left behind more of necessity than valor.

He watched Goliath move onto the plain, his every stride three or more of David's own.

David felt naked in his slight linen tunic. Anxious, he slipped his hand into the pouch of the small shepherd's scrip that hung at his side. He fingered the five smooth stones selected from the nearby brook when the sun was new in that morning's sky. These, and his faith in the God of his fathers, were the only weapons he carried that morning.

The sun glinted in David's eyes from the fine polished armor of the massive warrior, as Goliath took his place just out of range of King Saul's archers. He stood alone in his arrogance, his head bare, his helmet and his shield well back with his armor carrier.

"Cowards of Israel." The giant's voice traveled farther than the arrows of the ten tribes and reached easily into the hills above David's head. "I come to you again today. My offer stands as true as I do, here before you. If any man among you can defeat me, the great army of the Philistines will lay down their arms and swear themselves your slaves. But if I prevail, then you will submit to us and be the slaves that you were born to be."

The valley then shook with the roars of the armies on both sides of the gulf above them. David could feel the voices of fifty thousand men raised in oaths to and against gods. It swelled within him. It gave him courage. It terrified him. He saw the enormity of what he knew he must do for his God, for his family, for his king and, most of all, to prove himself to his prince.

"Is your one puny god too weak to prevail here?" Goliath taunted. He strutted up and down in the dirt. Clouds of dust rose at his massive feet. "If you are afraid of us, why have you bothered to come all this way? Is there not a man among you?"

Taunts and curses answered. The Philistines began to drift back into their own camp, bored with the daily spectacle. The answers, shouts, and shield-pounding stayed strong along with the numbers on the side of Israel.

"The battle is yours, Lord," David said softy. He moved, as boldly as he could manage, onto the field of combat. "It is already won. We are only here to reveal your will in this and discover who you have already chosen as the victor."

As he made his way onto the plain, David was so small that at first no one on the Philistine side, including Goliath, took note.

David drew nearer to the giant of a man than any in the army of Israel. Cold stabs of fear pierced his chest. Goliath was made more fearsome still by the unequaled iron weapons that he and the Philistines alone possessed. Had David the king's own sword, it would truly be as a willow wand compared to the giant's iron blade.

"What is this?" the Philistine's voice boomed out as he, at length, realized David's approach. His laughter echoed scorn off the hillsides around them. "Am I a dog that you come at me with sticks?"

David clutched at the water-polished stones. Goliath seemed to rise up from the plane as David drew nearer. Still he advanced toward his foe.

"Is this the best that the army of Israel can do? Is this who you send to fight?" Goliath mocked. "I thought we faced an army of men, but I see I am mistaken. Do your mothers know you boys are this far from home?"

David, clad only in the brief robes of youth, looked small and fragile from where circumstance alone forced Prince Jonathan to watch. David's legs were as bare as his head of coppery golden curls that flashed in the sun more brightly than the most highly polished helmet. The Prince's heart stopped as he watched David make his way awkwardly through the weeds and brush that populated the valley floor. Transfixed and powerless to help, Jonathan bargained silently with the god of men's fate. He wished with all he had to offer in exchange that his final words to David had spoken his true feelings instead of the hurtful sentiments he'd pretended.

"Come here, little boy, and I will make your pleasing flesh into food for vultures and jackals," Goliath challenged David.

David stopped. He held his ground. His gaze fell on the javelin strapped to the behemoth's back. He knew he must get no closer until he had separated man from spear.

"Let me have one more chance," Jonathan pleaded softly as he watched. His words were lost in the angry shouts of those around him as they answered the giant's jeers.

David took a deep breath. It was time to seek the inspiration he had prayed for in the darkness of his tent the night before.

He ran straight at the giant.

A cheer went up on both sides. Goliath reached to draw his spear. Before the weapon was at hand, David turned and dashed back a safe distance away. He bounded atop a rock outcropping to bring himself nearer eye to eye with his adversary. Stillness fell over the crowds. The two—warrior-giant and boy—regarded one another.

"All is at the ready, Your Majesty," the general said to King Saul. "The army of Israel awaits the signal."

"Ah, Abner, it is a shame that one so brave and so fair of visage and heart must die to give us this victory," Saul said, shaking his head sadly as he watched the spectacle unfold.

Goliath grasped the spear from his back and hefted it. He tested the weight as he judged the distance to this boy who dared challenge him.

David tried to breathe. He fought against his fear to keep his balance atop the boulder where he stood. Searching the crowds above, he spotted the prince's standard and found the strength to speak on behalf of all he loved.

"You come against me with sword and javelin, but I come against you in the name of the God of Abraham and of the armies of Israel, whom you have insulted and defied," David called back in answer to all Goliath's rebukes. "This day the Lord will deliver you to me. Today I will give the carcasses of you and all the Philistine army to the vultures and the jackals, and the whole world will know that there is a God in Israel. All those gathered here will know that it is not by sword or spear that the Lord saves; for the battle is the Lord's, and he will give all of you into our hands."

The roar vibrated the valley like rolling thunder. Israel spoke with one voice. They cheered David's words and bravery, answering Goliath, at last, as they all would wish.

"He speaks well," Abner said as David's words still rang in the valley.

"He roused me from death with that voice and those words." Saul spoke with a fatherly pride, as though he'd expected such eloquence once the boy faced his mortal task.

The tumult caught the usually tepid interest on the other side of the valley.

The Philistines had fallen into the habit of ignoring the ritual bullying. This new challenge seemed to promise a morning's brief sport. They began to take up places to finish their meals, view the outcome, and witness the death of Goliath's first challenger. They roared with anticipation as David dashed down from his perch and were answered in kind.

Spurred on by the courage he gained from the cries of support, David again ran toward the giant. Then, just as before, he reversed course. He paused just beyond the javelin's range.

Goliath waited, the hunter poised, amused by what he thought the boy's fear and timidity.

David judged his opponent's intent. He balanced himself, taut as bowstring, ready.

Goliath shifted his weight onto his right foot. He tensed to charge the boy and bring an end to it.

Sensing, David ran down toward and to the left of his towering enemy. Again he froze, still just beyond the javelin's reach.

Goliath turn, pursued, and again drew within range.

David awaited Goliath's approach. Once more he ran toward and to the side, forcing the great tower of a man to redirect the momentum of his massive frame.

Goliath stumbled back, found the boy in his sight, and poised to pierce David with his spear. His arm tensed. He drew back.

David's heart beat like hooves on cobbles, his intuition raised by the hot blood in his veins. He could feel the giant's moves in the air as one feels a coming storm. Not a breath before it was too late, David doubled back. He darted in front of his deadly adversary, across Goliath's path to the far side.

The Philistine grunted in frustration. He pivoted, shifted his weight back onto his mighty calf to put all his heft behind a powerful launch of his spear, anticipating David's next move. David changed his course and moved out of Goliath's range. Goliath roared with anger. Subtly, David took command of the field as his tactics nettled the giant into action.

"Are you afraid to fight me?" Goliath taunted in response. "Does your God of cowardice instruct you to run?"

David laughed as he made sport of the great ox. He was the youngest and smallest of eight brothers, and so undaunted in response to the bully's words. His throat was dry, more from fear than exertion. His mirthless laughter was strangled, but he knew that, however forced and joyless, it would provoke anger in his rival—and with the anger, carelessness. Again and again he dashed across Goliath's path. He laughed louder, taunting as Goliath struggled to keep pace with the erratic course. He passed within range and temptation as the Moabite drew back and then hesitated again and again.

The crowd joined in the laughter at the big man's expense, provoking and enraging Goliath further.

Eliab took no joy in the spectacle. Those around him cheered as David made a fool of their hated tormentor. He found no cause for laughter, though it filled the air around him. All Eliab could see was his youngest brother literally flirting with death on the field below. All he could hear were the words of blame he had heaped on David, echoing in his head. On their last meeting, Eliab had accused David of hurting his military career. The great general, Abner, had that morning assured Eliab that his move to a field command was a promotion earned from respect for Eliab's abilities as a lieutenant. Like Jonathan, Eliab too longed to take back his words to David for fear they would be his last.

David kept up the torment of his oversized adversary. The response grew on both sides.

The Philistines shouted words of encouragement to Goliath. They called for him to use the spear and finish the boy. Goliath only just managed to keep his head and his own counsel. Though he seethed with anger, he was a serious and battle-forged soldier. He knew that to attempt to hit a moving target at such a range would only waste the spear, for which he had no replacement near at hand. He cursed himself and his complacency. In truth, he had only worn the javelin down to the field for show. For forty days he had come down to the plain. For forty days there had been no sign of challenge from Israel. There had been no reason to believe that morning would be different. One spear and one sword were all he'd brought. So confident was Goliath that he'd even left his helmet with his shield carrier.

Rather than waste the spear, Goliath waited and focused. He was still and alert as David's taunting sprints drew within range.

Nearer and nearer David teased Goliath like a dog on a tether. Goliath bided his time. With each pass David came closer to the Moabite, who tracked his prey with practiced persistence. On one such pass from David, Goliath turned and pursued. David led him on a mad and circuitous dash through the brush, wheeling, turning, and doubling back. Once in the chase, Goliath, unaware, was caught by his prey. His lumbering pursuit earned him more laughter. Goliath tried repeatedly and unsuccessfully to close the distance. His attempts to take aim at a full gallop were futile.

Frustrated and tiring, Goliath shouldered his spear. Leaning into it, he fell to his knee to add momentum to the mighty vault. David was near enough to hear Goliath's grunt of effort. A gasp went up. The spear was airborne.

To the horror of those in his camp, David froze beneath the projectile as if waiting to be skewered. Only at the last did David step aside. The deadly iron tip of the beam-sized spear buried itself harmlessly in the firm valley earth only a few paces away. Running back, David plucked the spear from the ground.

Struggling with the weight of the massive shaft, he took aim at Goliath with the Moabite's own weapon.

Cheers accompanied David as he upended the odds. Carefully he sighted his target. Running to add as much force as his small frame could compound, he hurled the spear with all his might. The acclaim of the crowd turned to derision and laughter. The spear not only missed Goliath, it so overshot the mark as to be lost in the tangle of trees and brush in the foothills far beyond the reach of either combatant.

"I am a tall man and in need of a shave," Goliath bellowed, joining the laughter on both sides at David's seeming incompetence. "But I am not Mount Seir," he laughed, playing to the crowd. The ruddy ridge of mountains that earned Edom its name was often jokingly called "Mount Hairy" for its dark, stubbly tree line. "How tall do I look from down there, little boy?"

Jonathan's heart broke with despair. He lost all hope for David's life and his own happiness. He fought his own heart, longing to hide his face away from the inevitable tragedy upon the field. Unable to bear to see what surely must be. Unable to resist his last glimpses of David, no matter how bleak. At last his heart gave him courage to turn and face the truth.

"I am mistaken," Goliath bellowed. "I took you for a beautiful youth. I see from your skill with a spear that you must be a girl child. Come, allow me closer, the better to take in your beauty and your charms."

Goliath called out the compliments a suitor might pay in court to a woman as he drew his sword and resumed the chase. David only smiled at such mocking as he was used to from even his mother and his sisters. He remained focused and sure as he led Goliath on an erratic chase.

Believing David's fate sealed, all on both sides watched in growing quiet, waiting only for the giant to cut him down and end the valiant and laughable tragedy. For his part, David gave the Philistines a bit of their own. They laughed as Goliath slid and stumbled. He struggled to keep up the dizzying pace as its course twisted across the valley floor like the trail of a desert adder in the sand. First this way and then another, then turning at full speed and doubling back, David offered up their tormentor as a morning's entertainment of a different sort. Goliath fell behind briefly following each change in course, then closed the distance between them until David reversed directions and the process began anew.

The race might have gone longer, though the larger combatant was clearly tiring from the exertion. Fit though he was, Goliath was a massive man in full armor, and they had been running all morning. Then, in one false step, David was down, clutching his ankle and writhing on the ground.

With pride and finality, accompanied by the moans and cheers of both sides, Goliath stalked deliberately and in no great haste toward his fallen prey.

He withheld his final act of victory, wresting from it all he could, confident of what all had known from the start would end this tragic morning.

The Israelites braced for the loss of one so brave as the Philistines cheered for the petty victory, their abandoned morning meals grown cold. The scene before them seemed decided to all. David remained on the ground, unmoving save for his lame thrashings even as Goliath, sword drawn, slowly approached.

Jonathan froze, unable to look away from the inevitable. He cried out, finding his voice and his grief as Goliath closed the distance grandly.

David was oblivious to the cries and noise of the armies. The crowds could only see the valley below them. David saw the ridge above the Wadi Asad, at the boundary of his father's grazing land. He reached into his tunic and clutched the sling that hung around his neck. He fingered the lion's tooth that adorned the lanyard. The tooth had been plucked from the mouth of the very lion whose fate had inspired David that morning. He had made the sling for Micah, who inspired him in everything else.

"Micah," David said quietly. "It's the camels all over again."

He saw Micah's face as clearly as he'd seen it that first morning when they were both but boys, playing in the streets of Bethlehem.

CHAPTER TWO
THE BOOK OF MICAH

What is man, that thou art mindful of him? And the son of man, that thou visitest him?

Psalm 8:4

DAVID'S MOTHER, Nitzevet, wished their home in the countryside above Bethlehem free of men for a time, so that she might tend her daughter's illness and her grief. David's sister Abigail had miscarried after a long illness that took not only the child in her womb but her prospects for motherhood. Only David, Nitzevet's youngest, still summered at home, so Nitzevet had simply banished him to spend that summer in Bethlehem with his father.

The seven brothers David's senior had long since abandoned tending orchards, vineyards, sheep, or any of the work of running the family karmel. They preferred the thrill of politics, the talk of war, the intrigue of trade, and the company of the sort of women town afforded the sons of Bethlehem's revered elder. David was left at home with his mother and two older sisters. His summers were spent attending to the herds of goats and sheep, the vineyards, the groves of olives, the orchards of dates and pomegranates, the fields of barley and winter wheat, and managing the small village of slaves and retainers that comprised the substantial karmel.

Though he knew to be sad for his sister, David was delighted to discover he had been freed of a summer of toil and his mother's watchful eye to run wild in the streets of Bethlehem with his older brothers. David loved the city, and owing to the complete distraction of his busy and important father and the carelessness of his brothers, he spent most of that season on his own. Wandering the markets, visiting with traders, and tasting the many flavors of the world outside his small and very controlled piece of it, he sampled just enough to whet an insatiable appetite.

But for all his adventures, that summer was memorable for David only because it was the summer he met Micah.

Their paths had crossed one morning a few days into David's stay. Once established in his father's summer residence, he fell into the easy habit of sneaking out early, while his brothers slept off the effect of too much wine from the night before. He found he could adventure and explore all morning and be home, bathed, and at table for the midday meal without anyone taking notice. One morning, after eluding his father's head servant, Baji, David decided to explore the nearby market. He arrived at the busy square just as a band of camel-mounted traders arrived from well east of the Arabah. They were the color of burnt sugar and festooned with gold. David was most intrigued, not only by their strange beasts of burden, but because they did not unload their wares. The traders paused only to water the animals and to buy provisions.

Curious, David drew nearer to one of the strange creatures while their masters haggled for food and supplies.

He knew that traders favored camels for a number of reasons. They could travel long distances without food or water. They had a tremendous strength and capacity to carry great quantities of cargo as well as the traders themselves. Their eyes and noses were well suited to blinding desert storms. Even their feet seem designed by the god that made them to walk sure-footed across the shifting liquid sands.

What David did not know was that their hideous dispositions also made camels an excellent defense against thieves, rivaling even the best-trained dogs.

David approached the gawky, peaceful, unfamiliar animals with friendly curiosity. Their smell starved him for breath, but he was otherwise undaunted as he drew nearer. He reached out to reassure one of the huge hairy beasts as they began to stir. Instead of making a new friend, he found himself on the receiving end of a hissing, spitting, braying assault that would have made the most unruly donkey seem serene. He was too horrified to move as the foul-smelling creatures bore down on him and defenseless when the attacking camels were joined by their masters. Their sharp curving knives were drawn, ready for attack, heedless of David's youth.

"What are you doing there, boy?" one of David's sunbaked assailants demanded, his long knife making whishing sounds as it cut through the air like a willow branch.

"Turn out your hands," another ordered, grabbing him. "Let's see what you've stolen."

All the while, the insane beasts were still at their deafening caterwauling. David stood rooted to the spot. Silence his only answer, he was ready to face his doom. He was certain Nitzevet would stand over his lifeless body, clicking her tongue and shaking her head in a silent "I told you so." His fate would only confirm her oft-stated conviction that little boys who go out in the city alone are either abducted and sold into slavery or cut to kabobs by bandits.

"A thousand pardons, Your Worship," a tall, surprisingly self-assured boy said, appearing seemingly out of nowhere. He stepped directly between David and his would-be executioners. "You must forgive my little brother. He is simple. He means no harm, but he hasn't the wits of a monkey."

With that, all eyes turned expectantly to David.

The tall boy's dusty curls shook as he nodded to David with an ease more suited to signaling that his was the next prayer at Seder than a plot to defy a band of armed men. David could only stare amazed. He was even more confused by the rescue, certain his own older brothers would never have stood in harm's way for him. With his back to the traders, the boy winked at David and pulled a foolish face.

Without thinking, David issued forth with a shrill and maniacal laugh. Then to the amazement of all present, including himself, he spit on the nearest camel. Still more amazing, the camel reared and fled, taking its masters with it in pursuit. One of his accusers, perhaps the leader, remained behind to admonish the tall boy to take better care of his addled brother.

"You must be more careful. The touched are a responsibility, but also a blessing, for they may have the divine sight," the man said, shaking his finger in the boy's face, his knife still drawn. "Thank you for saving us from harming him. Such a curse it would have been to us had we harmed one of the chosen." He clasped his fist to his chest and gave a solemn little bow.

The boy nodded gravely, echoing the gesture, reverently bowing in return. He turned and gently took David under his arm.

"Come, brother," the boy said loudly. "You went out without eating. Mother will be so worried. You must not wander off on your own." Then, under his breath as they neared the corner, he hissed, "Run."

It was as though they discovered wings they had not known they possessed. They ran until they were in a field on the other side of town. David's sides ached. He fell down laughing uncontrollably. The boy fell down beside him. They laughed themselves dry in fits and starts, thinking the laughter was done and then dissolving into a new spasm. As their breathing became steady and they regained the power of speech, Micah rolled onto his side. Still lying on the ground, he offered his hand formally, like men greeting one another to show they were unarmed.

"I'm Micah," he said in a gasp.

"David," David said, taking the hand and holding it firmly.

They regarded one another for a heartbeat. Then Micah, with surprising strength, drew David to him. Their noses only a breath apart, they stared into each other's eyes, their chests still heaving, suddenly serious.

"Did you see that camel run?" Micah demanded at last. They had been laughing together ever since.

Theirs was a perfect kinship.

It came at a time in David's life when boys decide without knowing it what kind of man they are to become. Though many were the powerful and adoring forces in David's life, only Micah offered him the mirror in which he could see his true potential.

The youngest of his nine brothers and sisters, David was younger even than his nephew Joab, eldest son to David's sister, Zeruiah. But it was more than age that separated him from his brothers. Where his brothers took after their father, Jesse—tall and broad, powerful and dark—David favored their mother, Nitzevet—slight and beautiful, graceful and fair. Still, it was not just that he looked like the son of a second wife or a pilegesh brought in to bear a child for a barren one.

There was no second wife in the house of Jesse ben Obed, and no need or want of the pilegesh or concubine that many men of Jesse's stature might have had just for propriety's sake. David's father Jesse had been a wealthy and promising young man, the only son of the largest landholder in Bethlehem and most of Judah. He could have chosen many wives. No one knew for certain the reason he'd only ever taken one. Many thought it was because he was a progressive man with modern views who did not hold with the old and primitive ways. "Do we still live in tents?" he often asked when arguing against the backward views of some zealot or babbling son of Belail.

Those who knew his wife knew better.

Nitzevet was as formidable as she was beautiful. She was a woman not to be trifled with. Serving women often fled her presence in tears when the house didn't run to suit her. The thought of junior wives was fearsome indeed. Jesse himself was quoted often enough as saying that "a quarrelsome wife is like a constant dripping. What man of even mere passing wisdom would choose to fight the same battle on two fronts?"

In truth, there was simply no more room in Jesse's heart for another wife. Such was his love for Nitzevet. She had given him eight sons and two daughters—and it wasn't for want of trying that there weren't more.

David was Nitzevet's favorite, though she'd never admit to such a thing. But that wasn't what set David apart. David was Jesse's favorite. He was the favorite of his elder brother Eliab and all the rest of his older brothers and sisters. Indeed, David was everyone's favorite.

As a child David seemed charmed. It was told that his first words were sung in a voice haunting and beautiful even in the cradle. He played the harp like it was part of his hand. There had never been a lesson; he had simply taken up the small stringed demilune his sister Abigail had discarded in frustration and played it like a master. He danced as soon as he could walk. He leaped and cantered to some unheard melody at an age when his brothers and sisters had still been negotiating remaining upright.

Psalms poured out of him as soon as he found words. He scratched his lyrics and poems in the wet clay when the other students were struggling to form the letters.

More than anything, there was that voice. Clear and beautiful like a woman's, with the depth and richness of a young man. Jesse proclaimed that David's voice could make an angel weep with jealousy.

Nitzevet had called him David. It meant "beloved" in their tongue, and it had become as much a prophesy as a name.

Beloved.

That was what set David apart. But like those most cherished of treasures, David was set apart from everyday life. Like a jewel too prized to be worn, too valuable to be taken from its strongbox, David found himself isolated and alone. No family occasion was complete without the latest psalm written, sung, and accompanied by David alone. No festival could conclude without at least one dance solo from David. Yet when the festivities were at end, David felt locked away with all the feast day ornaments.

When the time came that David might join his brothers as they followed in Jesse's footsteps, again he was set apart from the others.

"But, Father," David pleaded when Jesse and the older boys were to go hunting. "Why can't I come along?"

"You are too young yet," Jesse answered, sweeping the boy into his arms, unable as always to resist holding and protecting his youngest.

"But Ozem was hunting with you when he was my age," David argued, unswayed by fatherly affections.

"Darling boy, you are not Ozem." Jesse sighed, planting a kiss atop David's head. "What if you were to fall from your horse or be gored by some beast?"

"But Ozem has fallen off his horse as often as he's outgrown his sandals," David insisted.

"Yes, beloved, but I have six more sons like Ozem," Jesse said, holding David closer at the thought of it. "I have only one David."

"Oh, Father." David relented, embracing Jesse.

So he stayed behind, safe and alone. It broke his heart a little each time he waved good-bye, yet he felt selfish whenever he tried to find his own path.

"But, Eliab," David begged, pursuing his oldest brother down the road to their father's great house. "Why can't I come with you to train? I want to be a soldier too."

"David, David, David," Eliab said, turning and catching David around the waist. He vaulted his younger brother easily onto his shoulders and retraced his steps to the house. "Father forbids it. You know that."

"That's a terrible reason, Eliab," David said, pulling Eliab's hair. "How will I become a man if I don't learn to parry a sword, wield a bow, vault a javelin, defend myself and my home?"

"Why would you need to do that?" Eliab laughed. He took the boy down off his shoulders and tossed him playfully in his arms.

David tried not to laugh but failed.

"I will defend you always," Eliab said, tickling his brother mercilessly. "You are safe in our father's home until it is mine, and then you must remain with me."

"But, Eliab," David gasped. "Won't I ever move away on my own?"

"No, you never can," Eliab answered, suddenly serious and holding his brother out at arm's length, his feet dangling well above the dust. Their eyes met. "You must stay with me always. Who else would take care of me?"

"But when you go to war, what then?" David asked, as bright and quick as dawn in summer. "Won't you want me to come with you? Who will take care of you?"

"No, then you must stay here where I know you are safe." Eliab had chuckled. "If you were with me, I'd be too distracted to fight, too worried about you. I'd be watching out for you when I should be watching out for Philistines. You wouldn't want that, would you? Your dear old Eliab, run through while he was checking over his shoulder for his favorite brother?"

"No, Eliab," David said. "I'm sorry."

"So you see," Eliab said, perching David on his shoulder like a prized fowl as they came once again within sight of the house, "you've no need to learn to fight. I will do that for you, and my sons after me. Now go help Mother while I go train to keep you both safe. I will bring you a surprise from town if you do a good job."

Eliab set David on the path and propelled the wispy youth homeward with a playful swat.

"Yes, Eliab."

Safe and alone, David remained within the sound of his mother's voice long after most boys had taken up the spear and struck out on their own, at least until suppertime.

His life, until that fateful and singular summer of his liberation, had been lived as a beloved prisoner. The bonds of expectation and fears of disappointing held him firm.

Starved both for company and adventure, David met Micah.

To Micah, David was just another boy and not much of one at that. Insofar as Micah could tell when they first met, David possessed no useful skills whatever. He could not throw. He could not wrestle. He was too small to be an ally and too fragile to use as a weapon. In Micah's eyes David was, for the first time in his life, nothing special.

David adored it.

It seemed to David that they remained together, at first, only because he followed Micah like a hungry stray. But what began as a generous impulse in Micah that morning at the market grew in his heart. In the end David was less the foot soldier recruited to the cause than the standard to which Micah pledged his loyalty—if not by spoken oath, by his every action.

Micah's family lived in town in modest circumstances, though neither boy noticed, as such is of little consequence to boys. As the years passed, Micah became more a regular at Jesse's table than David became at Micah's family table, for save for that singular magical summer in Bethlehem, David's life was lived mostly within the protective confines of the family karmel's boundary stones. The boys grew up together running its fields, scaling the heights, and exploring its forests. Together they found as much life as it was possible to find in the small city and the surrounding hills of Judah.

Micah dreamt of being a soldier. There was nothing for him to inherit and still less in the way of opportunity for a young man of his means. His choices were limited to shepherding or, with luck, he might find himself apprenticed, little more than a slave, until he'd learned his skills. Only then, once he'd paid back his master in labor, earning only room and board in exchange for his youth, would he be free to labor for his own benefit, trapped within the walls of Bethlehem. It wasn't the laboring that bothered Micah. It was the trap. Micah would have wanted to be a soldier even if his prospects had been better.

Micah saw soldiering not only as a chance for advancement and to seek his fortune, but as a grand adventure. One for which he had been training, with anyone he could get to teach him, since he was a boy.

David had never really considered what he wanted to be. No one had ever asked him. He could read and write. He could sing, play, and compose for the harp. He was swift with figures and good at managing a staff. He had a skill for tau and other dice games. He was good at all this but because it was expected of him. His true talent was for being good at whatever he tried. He had simply never tried his hand at soldiering skills.

Had it been up to Nitzevet, David would never have gone outside at all. Jesse was not much more inclined. Between Jesse and Eliab and all of David's older brothers, David had been discouraged and later forbidden to pursue the combat training in which David's older brothers had been amply and professionally schooled.

So David taught Micah to read and write, and Micah taught David to fight.

Together they would spy on his brothers' lessons. After, they would practice their purloined combat skills on one another on the Bethlehem common or in the karmel's sheep pastures.

To Nitzevet's horror David scraped his knees, twisted his ankles, and cut his fingers. His fair skin honeyed in the sun. His hair burnished white over the gold. In Micah's presence David no longer felt as though he'd tripped and fallen to Earth from the moon. He felt as though he did not need to apologize for or live up to anyone's expectations except his own. He was just a boy growing into a young man. Though there was opposition at first to this "rough boy from town," their names were soon joined as one.

"Where are David-and-Micah?" "David-Micah, come inside at once." "David-Micah, not one more word."

Micah was a year and a summer older than David, but his experience often made the difference seem greater. In the absence of David's busy father and his bigheaded older brothers, Micah became David's teacher as well as his student and most constant companion.

David proved an apt pupil, often exceeding the teacher in his zeal to win favor in Micah's eyes. David would practice for whole mornings on his own when he was supposed to be studying or tending the sheep. His aim with a spear became as fearsome and accurate as the strike of an adder. He could ride as well as an officer, and though the bow proved too broad for his grasp and the sword too heavy for him to do much more than defend himself, with a sling he could pick a feather out of the tail of a roosting dove without awakening it.

As always, Micah pretended not to be impressed, but he was good at keeping his own secrets. Though David never suspected, Micah grew to be as awed by his companion as everyone who had ever met David. Secretly Micah was always at pains to protect David—as much or more than any of David's brothers.

Beloved.

In the meadows, the wilderness, and the gardens of Jesse's karmel, the two boys created a world of fantasy where they grew into men.

Often they would ply Nitzevet for just enough permission to get away with more than the leave they'd begged and vanish into the woods, free and alive.

They would promise to tend the sheep, tormenting Nitzevet into letting them stay the night in the shepherd's hut in the hills above the grand family home. Then they would bribe the shepherds to keep their confidence before stealing away into the wilderness.

It had been on such a summer journey that they'd had one of their most secret adventures and begun their greatest. The weather was cooler that year, following a winter drier than any the most ancient among the elders could remember. David and Micah had convinced Nitzevet that they were going to help out by tending the sheep together for a few nights. They did watch the sheep over their shoulders while they played at their true purpose: being the king's soldiers on their phantom campaign. They had a stash of crude weapons they kept hidden at the shepherd's hut, certain that none but their small order of two, plus the shepherds who tended Jesse's flocks, could locate the little structure, let alone anything concealed there.

They'd gone off with the sheep and their weapons of war. They skirted the boundaries of the ancient stones that marked the farthest reaches of the lands all agreed were Jesse's by right from his own father. Owing to the spare rainy season, the forage was lighter that year, and the sheep grazed higher and farther into the Judean wilderness. That night their army of two made camp deeper than they'd ever been into the hills.

Stripped near naked, they smeared each other with clay to conceal themselves from their spectral Amalekite foes. They stole through the brush just short of a thick stand of trees. Micah scouted out their vaporous enemy. David acted as lookout, disguised most convincingly as a shepherd. The sheep munched contentedly on the provender of a nearby clearing, and the sun drooped lazily in the summer sky. David's attention wandered from one charge to the others.

"Hey, David," Micah called. "Did you hear that?"

David turned to answer but never got the chance.

Just past his friend, a she-bear reared up out of the brush. The scarce forage that had brought them into harm's way had drawn her farther south than was her provenance, into that hillside clearing. Micah looked back toward David, smiling, his back to the first true enemy they'd ever faced. He stood guard just within the borders of the little patch of open ground. By the time Micah heard her, it was too late. For years after, David heard her angry cry in his worst dreams, like the sound of a tent ripping on a still night.

David became a fearsome thing when he saw how near to danger Micah stood. His heart swelled. It was as though wings sprouted on his back. The distance between them dissolved like mist at daybreak. The spear he held became an extension of David's hand, his will, and his mighty anger at anyone or anything that threatened Micah. David invested the crude wooden shaft with an energy born of a need and fear he could scarcely understand.

The javelin found its mark. The bear came down so near to Micah that her claws tore the back of his calf as she fell. Like a lightning strike, David knew the strength of what was in his heart for Micah. As suddenly as the earth disappeared beneath his feet, he was weeping in Micah's arms. Despite his wounds, Micah found himself comforting David.

"Shhhh," he whispered into David's ear as he stroked his hair. "All is well."

Though he didn't say it, David wasn't weeping for himself. It was the thought of losing Micah that brought water to his eyes. Even once the threat was gone, just thinking of Micah, of what might have been, made him weep, made his heart ache as it stirred his body.

They agreed they could never tell anyone of their conquest for fear they would surely never be allowed out of Nitzevet's garden again. They skinned the bear and burned the carcass—both as an offering of thanks, and to keep from drawing jackals or the threat of other scavengers near to their bleating charges. It was dark by the time they'd finished with the bear, gathered a full count of the terrified flock from all the directions to which they'd scattered, and made a fire. The cool mountain air made huddling up with their blankets on the bearskin the best place to tell and retell the story of their secret adventure. Under the thousands of stars in the black sky above them, they whispered in awe, retold, and embellished the legend of David's clandestine heroics.

"I'll tell you, David ben Jesse," Micah said in a serious tone, taking David's hand in his and drawing their faces near together. "I have not been that struck by your skill as a hunter since you spit on that camel and started a stampede."

They laughed until they fell into each other's arms. Micah's arms were around him. David nuzzled his head under Micah's chin like a nursing kid. His hands explored Micah's chest. Micah's fingers found David's chin. He drew their faces together for their first kiss, gentle and then more urgent. And then more.

It was easy and natural between them.

The bearskin hung on the wall of the shepherd's hut. It bore silent testament to the consummation of the bond between them.

Their summers passed as did their youth. Their secret quests held secret new adventure, but little else changed between them. From the start they had been their own tribe. David knew no greater joy than the complete acceptance of Micah's company. Micah was never happier than knowing that David slept safe in his arms.

CHAPTER THREE
THE BOOK OF ELIAB

He looked on Eliab, and said, Surely the Lord's anointed is before him.
1 Samuel 16:6

DAVID AND Micah impatiently grew older. Each in turn attained his thirteen summers and stood at temple to say the prayers of manhood. Still their names were as one word in the mouths of all who knew them, brothers more than the seven nature had provided David. Despite their best efforts to hold fast to what they shared, the two who were one could not defeat time. The magic of youth began to steal away from them with each new sunrise.

At last they grew restless with dreaming about life and yearned to live it. Micah, already David's senior, was around less and less. David, left in the world of his father's karmel, was surrounded by those whose feelings toward him had not aged since his childhood. Though he knew every blade of grass and olive branch for a hundred yokes in any direction, without Micah's company David felt more and more a stranger in a strange land. Micah's absence was sharpest in summer. During their youth Micah had lived the whole season on the karmel, returning to his family in Bethlehem only for direst emergency and official family obligations. Each successive summer saw Micah at Jesse's table a few suppers less than the season before.

Then, in David's sixteenth summer, Micah did not come to the karmel at all.

"The Brothers," as David's seven older brothers were collectively known around the karmel, were summering in town. They had, as always, departed following Shavuot at the end of the counting of the forty-nine days of Omer between Passover and the barley harvest. They would remain in town until the last meeting of elders, returning for the yoreh season harvest and the holy days of the autumn months.

In the days of Micah-and-David, the annual migration of "the Brothers" had been a joyous time. David truly ruled the house and farms that everyone tacitly acknowledged he already ran. His talents for managing his father's estate were proved with each year's greater yield and market price. David's secret was that he relied on the women. In so doing he found time to devote to David-and-Micah. As their summer days together ebbed and finally, that sixteenth summer, receded altogether, the season found David like a man lost on a night without stars.

The farm thrived under his undivided attention, but summer had lost its luster. Though he spent those long days in the company of his mother, two sisters, and the extensive staff, he felt Micah's absence deeply. His heart ached. His prayers were filled with a longing he could not understand. Micah's company became the most familiar subject of David's psalms and prayers, but even attaining that no longer felt as though it would fill his empty heart.

"*As the deer panteth after the water brooks, so panteth my soul after thee,*" David sang in a high, sweet voice.

His sisters exchanged a look. Nitzevet's eyes were raised to heaven. The three endured yet another evening's mournful serenade in silent suffering. David insisted they hear another new psalm that night after their supper. It was his fourth new psalm that week. It was also the fourth evening of that week. Nitzevet secretly longed for Eliab's return so David could once again sup with the men and quarrel with his brother after.

"Mother, it's too hot…," Abigail began.

Nitzevet sighed and raised her hand to silence her daughter.

"*My soul thirsteth for God, for the living God: when shall I come and appear before God?*" David sang on, oblivious to his audience's growing restlessness.

David was always prone to his moods. Nitzevet had grown to accept and even to love the garment-wringing of her youngest. That summer, though, the moods reached a pitch that tried even her most motherly patience. She longed for Micah's return as much or more than David but fought to keep her peace on it for fear that she would only make matters and moods worse.

"*My tears have been my meat day and night, while they continually say unto me, 'Where is thy God?'*"

"David," Nitzevet said, her voice quivering as much from amusement as irritation. "Could you not play something of a lighter spirit?"

David paused and regarded her pensively.

Nitzevet held his gaze, smiled, and nodded hopefully.

"No," David sighed. "I cannot. There is no joy left in my life."

Slowly summer waned.

At last the evening was at hand that Jesse, along with brothers Eliab, Abinadab, Shammah, Nethanel, Raddai, Shimea, and Ozem, were due to return from town to resume residence in the country. David looked forward to their return and dreaded it. He loved his father and his brothers, but he knew their homecoming would increase his workload.

Summers were always easier. Though David had to staff two houses and see to both tables at every meal, for three months he had only to do his work once. When his father and brothers were in residence, David often had to undo what they had done before he could do what he knew needed doing.

Everyone knew—none better than Eliab—that David ran the karmel in truth if not in name, though he'd only yet seen sixteen harvests. His brothers, his nephews, and even his father were too busy with politics, soldiering, and the self-important activities of men to tend to the family fortune.

Eliab, as eldest, was Jesse's natural heir. David and the Brothers would be little more than the retainers who worked Jesse's lands. Unlike David, the others were unconcerned. Each, in his own way, planned to seek his fortune in the king's army or the wide world beyond the gates of Bethlehem and the stones at the boundaries of their father's lands. Each was confident of the continued support the family estate provided.

There was the rub between eldest and youngest. Beyond the simple rivalries implicit in being brothers, Eliab and David were at odds over the strained "marriage" that fortune imposed on them both.

Eliab could ill afford to seek his glory and part with David's brilliance at managing the extensive plantation. David found he could not leave the karmel he would never own without forsaking his family's welfare and his own fortune. Eliab needed to assert himself as master, that he might take the reins from Jesse one day. David would have no master, but he was indentured to the interests of his beloved family. Eliab was anxious to captain his own fate abroad in the world. David yearned for the freedom to follow Micah, that they might seek their fortunes together.

As brothers David and Eliab loved each other. But as men each longed to be master of his own fate. Each knew that no household could endure two masters, yet neither could bear the yoke of the other.

It was on this flint that the sparks were struck between them.

Their conflicts grew into the stuff of family lore. Eliab's departure earlier that year, after David's sixteenth Shavuot, had been marked by a discord between them that had left the household silent for days. Eliab had slammed the great front door and David fled to the shepherds' hut in the hills.

The day of Eliab's return with the Brothers dawned heavily. As the fateful evening approached, David's sense of anticipation and dread grew.

The imminent return threw the day into a distracting welter of activity and excitement. The barley was long since harvested. The wheat had been ground. Still, there were vineyards to be tended, olive groves to be groomed, cows and goats to be milked, sheep to be herded, linen and wool to be carded, spun, and woven, date palm fronds to be pruned, and orchards of pomegranates and terraces of fruit and melons to be irrigated. Even then, the work animals needed feeding and watering to accomplish it all. Not to mention there was a house to be cleaned, beds to be made, and supper to be prepared for the considerable and expanding household. David, along with his mother and his sisters, had been up since before the sun.

Practicing his music in the pleasant chill of the growing eastbound shadows was the first time he had taken a seat all day.

Their small party sat on cushions on the cool tiles of the floor in Nitzevet's sewing room. David played as the women spun wool and flax into thread for the winter weaving. The sun drooped lazily under the eyebrow of the thickly overgrown arbors that shielded the rooms of the large house. A breeze blew in from the central courtyard.

David's voice and music were like pale wine. Sharp at first and then soothing. The pure sweet notes took away the late summer heat of the month of Elul and eased the drudgery of the mundane tasks the karmel demanded.

"Oh God, do you believe in me?" David sighed as he plucked absently at the strings of his lyre.

His mother looked up at him from under a disapprovingly arched eyebrow and then back down at her work.

"I know I believe in you, Lord," he went on. *"One has only to behold the night sky or feel the heat of the Hamsin winds or witness a streak of light fall from heaven and split an oak to feel your presence. But what would you have of me?"*

"David," his mother scolded gently without looking up. She sighed wistfully but remained intent on her task, twisting wool onto her distaff. "You mustn't say such things."

"Does the Lord know of me or care about me?" David continued as though his mother hadn't spoken, making a song of it as he accompanied himself on his lyre. *"Though I have many blessings from him, he's never answered a single one of my prayers. Can he not hear me? Or does he just not care? How do I find comfort in either answer?"*

"David, you are such a terrible boy," his sister Abigail giggled, more amused than disturbed by her younger brother's regular proclamations on such grand topics.

"Yes, it is most fortunate that he can play the harp and sing so well. God would surely frown on such presumption otherwise if he didn't make it sound so pretty," his eldest sister, Zeruiah, confided loudly to Abigail.

"The Lord could not frown on such a *gamila*," cackled Maha, the serving woman attending the three ladies.

"Little girl?" David translated Maha's Arabic slang indignantly.

"Pretty little girl," Abigail corrected with a prim smirk.

"I may be the eighth of eight brothers," David threatened, striking an ominous cord on the lyre strings. "But I am still a man in this house."

"And you look better in a silk tunic than any of the women who live on your father's karmel," Maha sniffed as she refilled the water cups.

"Maha," David said sternly, plucking two dissonant notes to echo his tone. "You forget yourself."

"Indeed," Nitzevet said sternly, still not looking up. "My son has the best legs in *all* of Bethlehem, not just the karmel."

Even David had to smile as the roomful of women dissolved into a musical chorus of chirping laughter.

"Is it not bad enough that I must be treated this way by my father and all my brothers?" David moaned, resuming his playing with a doleful tune. "Sisters, even your sons regard me more as their aunt than their uncle. I was doomed by the Lord's malice to be a servant of my brothers before I even learned my prayers."

"David, practice your music," Nitzevet said sharply, looking up. She tired of her son's all-too-familiar verses. "It's too hot for all this again just now. Play something soothing if you're going to stay in here."

With a respectful nod to his mother, the only person from Dan to Beersheba and all of Israel in between who could command from him more than a haughty head toss, David resumed his playing. He began an amusing song of a shy young shepherd extolling the virtues of his great love, who turned out in the final verse to be his finest sheep. Nitzevet only rolled her eyes at the clever lyrics and their implications. It was a little coarse for the company but easier to hear than David's endless poetic writhing against his fate.

Though she knew there would be little for David at the time of inheritance, she took some measure of comfort in the certain knowledge that there would always be a place for David at Eliab's table. Nitzevet gave thanks that her most precious one would always have a fine home and a comfortable future in his brother's house. *If only David could be more at ease with his place in the world*, she thought in her own silent psalm.

As if in answer, David took up a bittersweet love song. His voice drifted out with the light breeze that cooled the fine limestone house. Set high in the hills above the city, Jesse's imposing home commanded a fine view of the sprawling farm. The large open rooms inhaled the steady sea breezes that coursed in a heartbeat the three-day journey across the plains of Philistia. Ruffling the sycamores and scrub in the rugged shephelah and climbing into the hills of Judah, they arrived cool and calm in Nitzevet's sewing room.

The music, the summer day, and the hard work lulled everyone into a drowsy repose. Nitzevet alone saw Eliab. She smiled in response to Eliab's pleading sign behind David's back. He stole in through the courtyard garden.

The house was at peace and in order. Then, David's legs were flying through the air as his benevolent but unseen assailant tossed him over his shoulder kicking and screaming. The disturbance spread as Eliab ran away with his little brother.

David wasn't startled for long. He knew his brother's playful grasp all too well.

David had passed the days of his youth stuffed into oil jars, stranded on tree limbs, and tossed into every body of water large enough to get him wet and muddy. He had also had the best seat at every festival, sacrifice, and trip into town: his brother's broad and sturdy shoulders.

Though three summers had passed since David had stood up as a man to read from the scroll, they had neither of them outgrown this, their traditional greeting. Eliab was of age to marry. Only his desire to go adventuring in the king's army kept him single. His stay in town was filled with as many women as there were nights in his visit.

Still each year it was the same. Eliab abducted David; David screamed and struggled like a virgin being captured by Amalekites to be sold into slavery.

The custom was well kept that evening. David shouted the house down as Eliab bore him on a wild and circuitous ride to the mule trough. There, as always, he dangled David above the murky water until the pleading and threatening brought the intervention of ultimate authority—Nitzevet.

"Eliab, you put me down this instant or I will poison your wine at table," David howled, swinging wildly and without much malice toward his brother, his arms too short to afford his fists any serious purchase.

"Ah, little brother," Eliab teased, splashing water onto David with one hand and dipping him dangerously close to the water's surface with the other. "Is that any way to welcome your loving older brother home? Besides, you look as though you could use a little mikveh, and the mule trough is so refreshing."

"Eliab." Nitzevet's voice rumbled from the distance like thunder coming over the hills before a summer storm. Her determined stride drew her quickly nearer to play her part in the ceremony. She tried not to smile as she approached, happy and relieved at replaying the old fun and not the old fight.

"What about my welcome home?" David demanded. Still upside down, he folded his arms and looked up into his tormentor's face. "Why not come home with a casket of jewels to show your affection for your favorite brother rather than this primitive rite to prove your manhood? I'm hardly challenge enough to be much of a trophy."

"I think you'd make an admirable trophy," Eliab said, holding his brother up for inspection. "In fact, I think I'll have you dipped in bronze and mounted on marble like a little Canaanite god. We could keep you in the kitchen to scare away evil spirits, or at least vermin."

Eliab laughed loudly and alone at his own joke, though it was an effort for David not to join in.

"Put your brother down at once," Nitzevet shouted as she arrived, breathless. The contest always and inevitably ended at the stables. There were only fields, orchards, and hills beyond.

"Now you've done it," David said, checking his nails for dirt and evenness as casually as if he was standing upright.

"Where is your father?" Nitzevet demanded, smacking Eliab on the back of the head as she caught up to them. "You two will turn me into stone one of these days, carrying on like a Philistine invasion."

"I rode ahead so I could surprise my brother," Eliab said, upending David and crushing him to his chest like he was hugging a Canaan shepherd pup. "And why scold me? You might have warned him when you saw me coming, if you're so concerned about the state of your delicate nature and our refined household."

"Mother!" David accused, joining his brother in shifting the focus of torment to her. "How could you?"

"Oh, throw him in, then," Nitzevet called over her shoulder. Turning her palms heavenward, she raised her hands above her head as she stalked back toward the house. "Your father will be home soon. I need to speak with him about disinheriting you both."

"Well, there goes nothing for me, though a sad loss for you." David sighed. Eliab stood him upright before again crushing him in an overzealous embrace. "Let go of me, you big oaf."

"Oh, little brother," Eliab said, putting an arm around David's shoulder and dragging him back up the hill toward the house. "You're too pretty to worry about such practical matters as inheritance."

"That's easy to say when you're the eldest and the ugliest," David groused as he feigned a struggle against his brother's iron grip.

"Perhaps you'll marry a rich husband?" Eliab said, pinching David's cheek. "Your sisters haven't done so badly."

"Neither have their husbands," David said, managing to tuck the back of his brother's robe into his sash unnoticed.

"Speaking of which," Eliab said, freeing David enough to allow him to walk alongside, "I ran into your betrothed, Micah, after Rosh Chodesh at temple last new moon." They paused as they came into the small, fragrant kitchen garden fringing the side of the house.

"You are such a simple beast." David groaned, trying to hide his excitement about news of Micah. "Just because you were born in the country is no reason to act quite such the son of Belail."

"Oh, so sorry to waste your time with my like," Eliab said with a humble bow. Picking up his stride, he easily left David behind. "I guess you don't care to hear any message Micah sent for you by such as me," he called back over his shoulder.

"No, Eliab," David said, doubling his shorter stride to catch up and trying not to plead. He pursued Eliab into the thicket of fig trees that sheltered Nitzevet's kitchen garden from the wind. "Micah's a good friend, and I have hardly seen him since we were in town for Passover worship."

"Well, which is it, little brother?" Eliab demanded with a devilish gleam in his mahogany eyes. He wheeled so suddenly that David collided with him and was once again in the vise grip of his brother's arms. "Do you want to hear the message from your sweetheart or don't you?"

"Eliab," David wailed.

"Which is it?"

"Micah's off to join King Saul's army for the spring campaign," Abinadab said, emerging suddenly from behind the fig trees and smacking Eliab's bare backside. His delight in spoiling Eliab's torment of their younger brother was unconcealed.

"You jackal," Eliab said, dropping David into a bed of coriander in the confusion. He struggled to untangle his robe from his sash and cover his naked ass as he attempted to capture Abinadab.

Eliab found this brother's capture and punishment a more formidable task than the previous round. Abinadab, only a year Eliab's junior, was almost as tall and more stalwart. They were as much in league as men as they had been as children. Nitzevet called them the twins, as one was always to be found about the same designs and mischief as the other. They were as evenly matched. Their battles grew titanic as they grew into men, splintering furniture and shattering crockery with their struggles to resolve whatever argument brought them to blows. The best anyone could do or hope for was to stay out of their way until they'd reached some truce or agreement or were just too tired to battle on. Most simply fled their clashes. Their father Jesse laughed helplessly. Only one possessed the bronze to still their storms like rain on a brush fire.

"Abinadab, David, Eliab bin Jesse," Nitzevet bellowed, emerging from her kitchen like a she-bear from her lair. "Get out of my garden and stop that at once."

The men scrambled like boys as they scattered and made to deflect the wrath of their beloved mother.

"Go and get yourselves cleaned up for supper, and don't let me hear any more of this nonsense until after the harvest is in," she said, striking Abinadab with the wooden spoon in her hand, simply because he was the nearest.

Eliab snatched David out of the coriander before his mother could see the damage. They all filed past under her withering glare. Each son kissed her check as they went inside. They left her to find water, oil, and linens and make ready for the homecoming feast they'd smelled all the way up the hill from Bethlehem.

And Saul blew the trumpet throughout all the land.... And the people
were called together after Saul.

1 Samuel 13:3-4

THE NEWS of Micah's decision to join King Saul's spring campaign set the
tone for conversation at supper that evening. It also disturbed David far more
deeply than his brothers knew or he was willing to admit. He tried not to let his
anxiety show. It did not aid his efforts that talk kept returning to war. His feelings
grew harder and harder to ignore. He longed to leap up from the table and run
into town. How could Micah have made this decision without discussing it with
him? How could he send such important news as a mere message to David and
by means of Eliab, of all people?

David tried to change the subject to talk of the farm, of music, of local
affairs and affairs of the heart, but it was like convincing the Jordan to flow
north. Talking about war had become the favorite pastime in all the tribes of
Israel. David could not change that in an evening.

The Philistines were again raiding the Israelite villages nearest their
stronghold along the coastal plain. United under the pentapolis of their five great
Philistine city-states, their assaults demanded the attention of Israel's king and
begged his response. King Saul was at pains to try to repulse them with limited
forces and resources. Outnumbered by Philistine armies and outmatched by
Philistine command of the secrets of iron, the king pulled a double yoke. The
Israelites were a loosely knit band of tribes scattered throughout Canaan. They
rarely tried to accomplish anything together.

Occasionally, inspired by circumstance or common threat, a judge—
typically a high priest of the Levite tribe—would arise to unite the tribes to face
their enemy. Once each victory had been achieved, though, each man returned
home to his own tribe with no thought of the rest. Samson, perhaps the greatest
of the judges, had been killed by the Philistines only a few years before. The
judges since had been plagued by corruption and bad sons, all the worse as the
title often passed down from father to eldest.

The current high priest, Samuel, was a fine man and gifted prophet
who had assumed the title after the demise of his predecessor's sons. Their
intemperate character had led them into looting shrines, keeping company with
temple whores, and one too many ill-advised fights with the Philistines. Along
with their final battle, they lost not only their lives but the Ark of the Covenant,
their most sacred trust. Their epic demise killed their father, the Judge Eli.
Many said he died of a broken heart on hearing the news. Eli's death left his
apprentice Samuel more or less keeper of the faith.

Samuel managed to be worthy of the trust, securing the return of the
ark and victory over the Philistines at Beth Car. Still, Samuel's own sons had

proved a disappointment when their day arrived. The time for change had come. The tribes were no longer content to trust their future to the old system of judges. Jesse joined with the other leaders of all the Israelite tribes to insist that Israel be as other nations, and to implore that God grant them a king to rule and unite them.

Samuel feared offending God and argued against the idea, but the elders were set on a king. In the end Samuel relented and petitioned God on their behalf, in time anointing Saul God's chosen king.

As a result, the two principal occupations of all the tribes of Israel had come to be warring with the Philistines and criticizing the king.

The supper table that night at the house of Jesse was no exception.

Nitzevet rolled her eyes. The volume of the discussion grew so loud that she could hear them in her dining room off the kitchen, which she shared with the other women. Though tempted to treat for peace, she left her husband to rule over his house. Nitzevet would rule over Jesse later in the privacy of their bed. There she could banish political discussion to the townhouse, where the men could have it their own way and she was not around to hear.

Eliab and Abinadab were particularly worked up that night. They had been lobbying their father all summer for permission to join King Saul's ceaseless campaign to rid the country of its enemies once and for all.

"You are fine, strong men," Jesse said for the thousandth time as he had for the many months since Ziv had breathed the last cool breath of spring. "And while I think you would be an asset to King Saul's armies, I think you will be more help to your people here at home."

"David and the women can run the house well enough," Eliab moaned as though wounded.

David ground his teeth in silence. He disliked being dismissed with the women.

"Yes, but who will rule Bethlehem and Judah?" Jesse asked sagely. His dark bushy eyebrows, frosted with the white born of age, wisdom, and eight sons, rose toward his hairline. He knew he had years left in him. He knew too that he was not as strong as he once had been. More than that, though, he had ambitions for his sons. He was accustomed to rule and to power, albeit on a smaller scale than their new king. Still, he knew it was the authority of men like himself who invested the king with what power he had. Jesse wanted his eldest sons to command that power and take part in what government Saul and his heirs sired.

"But, Papa, what will there be to rule if we don't do something about the Philistines?" Shammah argued. Two years younger than Abinadab, he had a stake in winning an argument he would make to Jesse soon enough. "The fight needs our strength. It takes a strong back to move the stubborn stone."

"So it is said, brother," Eliab agreed, heartily patting his younger sibling's shoulder.

"It is also said that it's better to meet a bear robbed of her cubs than a fool in his folly," David said, silencing the table with his unexpected voice. He speared another taste of the veal, carved from the fatted calf for the occasion.

Jesse choked slightly on his wine and his laugher.

"What's that, little brother?" Eliab asked, turning sharply on David. He was far from amused by his brother joining the discussion against him.

"It isn't strength that's going to defeat the Philistines," David said with the calm of certainty. "They outnumber us three to one, if not more."

"What then, little general?" Abinadab demanded mirthlessly. "What do you think it will take to vanquish these primitive savages? More flower arrangements? The table is well set, by the way—a thousand compliments."

"We are the primitives in this fight," David said, ignoring his brother's attempt to move his influence back to the kitchen. "We cannot even sharpen our own plowshares, let alone forge them. How are we to fight an ironclad enemy with bronze weapons? Or worse yet, stone? We might as well use these copper ewers in which our mother arranged the flowers for the table tonight."

"I'm not sure you know from which you speak, little one," Eliab said with a stern and final air.

"I'm the only one at this table who's ever been to the plain of Ono," David continued, undaunted by his brother's dismissive severity. "Why do you think they call it the land of the craftsmen? I could not run this farm without their abilities. Iron—their iron—makes possible our way of life today. Yet we do not command its secrets and must depend on the very people we call enemies to put food on our table. How is a strong back going to defeat that?"

Even the women's dining room went quiet.

Eliab and David regarded one another silently. Dismissed by a brother still in his sixteenth summer, only the sound of Eliab's labored breathing revealed his rage.

All eyes but David's were on Eliab. David continued to eat as calmly as before he'd spoken.

"I thank you, David, for your thoughts in this," Eliab managed, fighting to control his anger and focusing it into a more dangerous force as a result. "You see the world through the eyes of a boy. You forget that it was the God of Abraham who gave Samson the strength to pull the temple down upon the heads the Philistines, not the god of iron."

"It killed Samson too, didn't it?" David asked with a coy baiting tone.

"So, now you would mock the Lord and the army of the king as well as your own brothers?" Eliab bellowed, his fury taking him. "I think, boy, you have forgotten your place, which is here keeping my house in the company of the women. They are more your equals than the men at this table where you are allowed to sit. You are a fine ornament with your songs and your poetry and your garlands, your beautiful face and fair hair. But you are as much an asset in war as the fancywork on the hilt of a fine sword; little help in battle but pretty enough to be worth fighting for."

They glared at one another, filled with a silent and consuming fury.

David held the tears that threatened to betray him. He treated Eliab to a dagger-sharp glance of parting. Then, unable to dam the flood and unwilling to let the torrent be seen, he fled the room, overturning his bench in his haste.

Eliab sighed, disgusted. He loved his brother, but more and more of their exchanges came down to this test of wills between them. Eliab longed for David simply to take his place at the table where they both knew Eliab would one day preside. He welcomed David as a continuing part of his life. *Why always this struggle?* he wondered. Why could David not be happy with the plan God had so clearly laid for them both?

Nitzevet snatched at David's hands as he wrapped some cheese and bread in a piece of linen, bundled his harp in lily leaves, and tossed it all into his worn, leather scrip. He eluded her comfort and dashed out into the night to seek refuge from his own anger as much as Eliab's. He knew he would find peace on the remote hillsides of the estate, where the sheep grazed on wild grasses and barley stubble in the company of the silent men keeping watch. David sought to be alone with his thoughts and bitter prayers to an indifferent God. He made his way up into the cool of the hills to take refuge at the shepherds' encampment.

"Where are you?" David howled at the night sky, falling to his knees. "Oh God, why do you fill me with such fire and then throw cold water in my face at every turn in the road? It is not that I lack the talent or the keenness to be regarded as a man and an equal. It is only because you gave me the wits to be aware that I know enough to see and lament my fate. Perhaps it would be better if you'd made me to see no farther than the flowers on the table, if you are to keep me always in the kitchen." Trailing off, he angrily wiped the tears he hid in the darkness. He rose and made his way deeper into the night.

David knew they could do without him well enough until harvest, if he stayed away that long. He could send word of duties that needed attending with the shepherds. Some few returned from the flocks each day, at the ends of their shifts, to their homes in the small village clustered between the fields and barns.

The shepherds only just looked up from tending the fire outside the rustic but watertight hovel. Little more than shelter where the shepherds slept when not in the fields, it often served as David's second home. The young master's fights with his father and his brothers were many and storied. It was David's habit to retreat to the distant hut following their clashes.

The men around the fire that night were aware that Jesse and the brothers had returned that evening after their summer's absence. None were surprised to see David. One among them grinned, five *gerah* richer for having guessed that the brotherly truce wouldn't last the night.

They nodded in silent greeting as David joined them. Though his visits were frequent, none would venture a *gerah* guessing his mood. Sometimes the words poured out of him like the ceaseless waters of the Jordan. More than once David had kept them up so late that they slept through shift change and were met with harsh words by the shepherds still in the meadow, overdue for relief. Just as often David was sullen, brooding, and emotional, laughing with the fleeting madness that comes after too long a shift in hot weather. Whatever his state of mind, David came to the shepherds' hut to heal the unseen wounds of brotherly battle.

That night David only grunted in greeting. He climbed the ladder on the side of the hut, taking the rungs two at a time, nearly falling as he struggled to keep his tears out of sight. He wished vainly that Micah would magically follow him up the ladder, to comfort him and to make him feel as he always felt with Micah.

He lieth in wait secretly as a lion in his den.

Psalm 10:9

DAVID WOKE to the smell of supper cooking. The men who had slept at the encampment that night made ready for the return of the men who had spent a wakeful night out in the fields with the various herds.

"Good morning, Master David," the man tending the pot of spicy lentil soup called up to him as he climbed down from the roof.

"Good morning," David said, descending the ladder into their midst, looking sleep worn and distant. His mind was on neither his appearance nor his company.

He declined to share their hearty repast and sipped at an infusion of hot water, herbs, and dried fruit essence he prepared for himself. David had discovered the drink from eastern silk traders whose acquaintance he'd made at market. He favored it in the morning over the heavier fare that most on the farm took at the start of their demanding day.

He found a seat on a rocky ledge. From there he could see the main house. The smoke rose from the fire of his mother's kitchen. He knew she and Maha would already be sweating over the domed terra-cotta ovens in the late summer heat. Flatbreads for the day were baking against the smooth clay walls inside as Nitzevet roasted grain to be served with fruit, sweet cakes, honey, and yogurt for the morning meal.

The rhythm of the day, usually soothing, made him feel trapped and restless.

"I will tend one of the flocks today," David announced to the men as they made ready to depart the camp to relieve the previous shift. "Where will I find them?"

"They are on the grassy sides of the bald hill near the Wadi Asad," one of the more senior members of the party said with a tone meant to discourage. The isolated, forbidding ridge was separated from the wilderness of the surrounding hill country only by a steep chalky wadi named for the lions that hunted there. Cut into the hills by a thousand years of flash floods, melted snow, and the annual mountain rainfall, the wadi was a thin defense against the creatures that kept shepherds employed.

"You've grazed over that far?" David mused aloud, as he considered how early in the season it was to be grazing in such a remote part of the karmel but neither heeded nor acknowledged the warning in the man's voice.

"It's all dried up now. So, no worry about visitors coming by for a drink and a bite." The man shrugged, trying a different tack to discourage his experienced but youthful and brash employer. "The grass is good. You can get them to water easy enough and still be back in daylight."

David knew the "visitors" were wild mountain predators, always game for the easy feast of slow-moving sheep. The senior man's worry and warning were wasted. David had been tending his father's flocks since before he'd been seated with the men on holy days. Younger even than when his older brothers had taken their first turns. In fact, David had made a point of it, to prove to his brothers that he was their equal. His pride had doubled back on him, though. He had earned the task in perpetuity as there was no one younger to slough it onto.

That late summer day, David was heedless of the possible threat even next to the ominously named wadi. He was more interested in a chance to be alone with his thoughts. He gave instructions to the men, sending them to the house to be his hands in his absence, to convey his instructions at a distance, and to run a few errands. The shepherds gave in easily, glad of the diversion from their endless vigil over the same ungrateful sheep.

David slung his scrip over his shoulder and struck out in the direction of the high plain through the familiar hills of his father's ancestors. He felt as though he were off on one of his quests with his absent coconspirator Micah.

Those times were much on David's mind, as his old friend Asad left his post to greet him. Asad, the little Canaan shepherd dog who, like the nearby wadi, was called "lion" for his regal fierceness, held a special place in David's heart. He leapt and chattered in his delight at seeing his old friend and savior. Born a runt, Asad's future held only a sharp blow to the head from the master of all Jesse's flocks. When David had first held the tiny whelp in one hand, he felt a kinship and spared the animal. Naming him Asad as a joke at first, he trained the pup himself. Had it been up to David alone, Asad would have spent his days in the house at David's side, not in the fields. Nitzevet would have none of it and banished Asad as soon as he was able to earn his keep with the other dogs. In the field Asad had more than lived up to his name. He became the best of the pack that tended Jesse's many flocks.

There was still a strong bond between them. David kept Asad out of service more often than he would an ordinary work dog. Their reunions were always those of old friends, and the shepherds made sport of their affection.

Well met, David and Asad took charge of their keep. They sent the night shift back to the hut for lentil soup and sleep, ending their day at its beginning on their backward shepherd schedule. The two guided their small flock up to grazing land high in the hills, at the edge of the wadi far from the others. There they settled in for a breath of the quiet David sought. He had brought an awl, a few strong bits of hide, and stout leather lanyard to fashion a present he had in mind for Micah. The gift was part of a plan he had for meeting with Micah again soon. The counting of the days of the harvest month had only begun. David was certain that, before they'd done, preparation for harvest market would take him to Bethlehem. Though the bounty was still on the vine, he schemed to meet Micah following the holy days and before the Sukkot harvest festival.

The sheep at their ease, David set about making a sling for his old fellow warrior. He would present Micah his handiwork as token of their long neglected summer campaigns in the hills, when no more sophisticated weapons could be had.

The day was warm. Despite the shade David had found under a gnarled old tamarisk, the heat and the daydreams made him heavy with drowsiness. The sheep were content, lazily stripping the clearing bare. Their easy sounds lulled David into a quiet reverie as he focused on his leatherwork and imagined presenting it. He looked up occasionally to survey his charges.

It was just what David had in mind when he chose to while away the day tending. He made a meal of some cheese and flatbread he'd tossed into his kit as he'd fled his mother's kitchen the night before. Asad got the lion's share. David hadn't much appetite, perhaps because of the heat or, more likely, because the argument with his brother still stuck in his craw.

Each time he repeated the quarrel in his head, he held his temper. He said all the things to Eliab that were in his heart, each time better than the last, each time closer to his brother's respect. Each time he came back to his retreat in the fields, high in the hills above the fine home he feared would always be his easy and comfortable prison.

Micah was his defense against thoughts of his argument with Eliab. He would return from the angry words at Jesse's table to the sling and the fond memories he intended it to evoke.

Once completed, David could not decide how best to adorn it. He wanted it to be like no other. He wanted it always to remind Micah of its origin. He wanted immortality, at least in Micah's thoughts. Setting the work aside, he leaned against the tree to ponder the ideal ornament.

The flock ruminated complacently. A light breeze rippled the leaves above him. The tall grasses bordering the clearing hissed in a gentle wind, a thick buffer between the little basin and the upswell of brush and hills beyond. To his back was the steep and impassable wadi. At the far side of the clearing was the mouth of the narrow passage that wound down the hill to the brook and on to the hut and home.

David debated whether it was too early to drive the herd down to water. Asad dozed in the shade nearby, one eye open, his head resting on his paws.

The dog's calm offered excuse enough for David to delay the effort. He unwrapped his harp and invented a breezy psalm of summer and the coming harvest. The instrument fell against his chest. His eyes closed, for just a breath it seemed, and yet the dream of Micah and Eliab, off to join the king, stretched epic before him. He watched their great adventures, returning home to cheers and accolades as David tended to their supper in his mother's kitchen.

He awoke suddenly. The air around him was charged as when the Hamsin winds dried and tortured the air so that he could see sparks fly from his fingers at night.

Asad bristled silently, frozen still like a bronze figure.

David followed Asad's gaze.

At the far side of the clearing stood a lion, blocking the only means of escape from the boxed-in pasture. Sleek and golden in the late day's sun, the creature was poised, taut as a bow, ready to strike. The feast was spread in the field before him, bleating and unsuspecting as, well, sheep.

David drew down, concealed by the same tall grass the lion used for cover. He signaled the dog to hold. As he crawled forward, his hand fell on the little sling he'd made for Micah. He realized he had a weapon. Keeping his eye on the lion, he fumbled in the dust under the tree for a rock or gravel with which to load the pouch.

Suddenly, from the whispering grass, a rabbit broke cover. It dashed across the clearing to safer ground, little more than a flicker. Instantly the lion was on him, so fast it was hard to remember where he'd been before. Relieved that the lion was hunting rabbit and not sheep, David peered through the grass tips to watch what he thought would be but a brief pursuit. He leaned back to get a better view. His hand came to rest on a piece of granite, sharp-cornered and of enough heft to make the sling really count for something.

Without thinking, David loaded. He wound the cord around his arm as much from habit as preparation. Though a lion was a foe he'd prefer not to face, he was little concerned. He knew a predator would stop the hunt once it had a meal.

But as David watched, the meal had a lesson for the hunter. Rather than a short chase, the rabbit made good sport of the big cat. Sprinting, the would-be supper almost flew. Then abruptly it doubled back with blinding velocity in the opposite direction. The evasion repeated with dizzying frequency, the rabbit often running straight at its fearsome foe. The lion, though fast and agile, was a great lumbering beast by comparison. The cat faltered and even fell as it attempted to match the erratic course of his fleet adversary.

In the end the heat and the rabbit took the day, as the lion grew hot and tired of the chase. One last diving lunge sent the lion careening and tumbling into the tall grass at the far side of the field. The false step afforded the rabbit the time and space it needed to vanish into the brambles and down into the wadi.

It was quite a show. David smiled as the rabbit eluded seemingly certain fate.

The lion was neither sated nor down for long. Frightened, the sheep had knotted themselves tightly against the hill, forming an easier banquet for the hungry and frustrated hunter. Flattening itself to the ground, the lion moved so slowly that David had to look away and back to see its progress. He watched as the cat made its way toward the increasingly panicked sheep.

Tightening his grip on the sling, David came to his feet. Asad rose to back his master but held his ground, awaiting David's call.

"Hey," David shouted, his heart like a bird trapped in his chest.

Startled, the lion turned. Their eyes met. It sprang.

David only had time for three smart turns overhead. He let the stone fly.

A friend loveth at all times and a brother is born for adversity.
Proverbs 17:17

ELIAB WAS with Jesse and his brothers Shammah and Abinadab, debating the latest news from the battlefield and the impending confrontation with the Philistines. It had been a hot day. The men had cooled themselves with a taste too much of Maha's chilled beer. Their arguments had become little more than swagger and declaration.

They were in fact shouting too loudly to hear David, absent all day and briefly forgotten, as he entered. He stalked over and threw the lion's carcass onto the table before them. Platters and goblets shattered on the tile floor. The brothers themselves overturned benches and chairs rushing to get away from the huge cat before they were only just realizing it was dead.

"There's tonight's centerpiece," David said before turning and stalking back out.

Eliab's laughter echoed in the hall, music to accompany David's departure.

A man's gift maketh room for him.

Proverbs 18:16

DAVID FINGERED the lion's tooth nervously as he made his way down the dusty winding road into Bethlehem. Asad sniffed and chattered at his heels. The sling he had made for Micah was draped loosely around his neck. The tooth hung from the sling's leather strap. The gift seemed imbued with good fortune. It had already slain a lion. The talisman made it a lucky amulet and gave it a story to remind Micah of David always.

As he made his way down the road, David rehearsed the fine speech he would make as he presented Micah the revered token. Officially David's reason for going into town was to get etrog. The strange fruit was needed to complete the ritual lulav for the Sukkot thanksgiving feast. He had spent the days since Yom Kippur making ready for the annual harvest festival and hoping to hear from his friend. He built a thatch-roofed sukkah in the garden to accommodate the mighty banquet that such a prosperous household as Jesse's must serve, as much a sign of their thanksgiving as a celebration of their bounty. He had thought it would be a distraction, but it only served to remind him of Micah's silence.

By tradition the family was supposed to live in the sukkah as a tribute to the days when their tribe had possessed no permanent dwellings. But David and Micah had been the only residents in years past, another adventure. The sukkah had, in more modern households, become a decorative awning over the outdoor harvest feast. That year the sukkah held only sad memories.

His brothers had been little help in the process, for which David was already mightily thankful without benefit of a festival. If asked, his brothers would have said they were still in solemn reverence for the high holy days. In reality, they were too busy arguing about politics and refighting all of King Saul's battles to help with the preparations. Their negligence meant David had been able to direct servants already in the easy habit of his instruction, without having to make it appear that the orders came from Eliab or Jesse.

All was in readiness. Aside from preparing the harvest feast, a task his mother was jealously supervising, the lulav was the only item left undone.

A kind of wand, the lulav was wound together with palm fronds, the branches of willow and myrtle along with a small citrus fruit called etrog. In the ceremony, the wand of four species was waved in all six directions to symbolize that God was everywhere. It was an old-fashioned tradition, rather primitive, David thought, but the ceremony and the sukkah in the garden gave the day a familiar and festive air that he always loved.

He smiled as he remembered past joyous celebrations and sleeping out under the thatched roof of the sukkah with Micah.

In truth, the etrog was not so important that a houseman might not have been dispatched to fetch it home. It was also true that David wanted—needed—an escape from Eliab's overbearing presence. Eliab had not wept to see his brother off. There were a few other items to be acquired and even a few shekels' premarket business to be transacted prior to bringing the karmel's yoreh harvest to market in the coming weeks. Still, there was nothing that couldn't have waited or been managed by messenger.

The real reason David was going into town was Micah.

Since Eliab's announcement of his beloved friend's imminent departure at the homecoming supper weeks before, David had been able to think of little else. His frustration at Micah's growing absence from his life was already a source of anguish. Just the idea of Micah departing on campaign left him sleepless.

"And so I made this for you as a remembrance of a friendship that once was in our lives and which will always be in my heart." David practiced his little speech, pausing to extend the pouch of the sling, still hanging around his neck.

Imaginary Micah was so moved by the sad reminder of the bond of friendship he had forsaken, he at once proclaimed his devotion to David, vowing to stay on at David's side until the day David could come away with him. Both were moved to tears. Their true feelings came out and they fell into each other's arms. David reached out to embrace the air where daydream Micah stood making the declaration David so longed to hear. Asad, forgotten in the reverie, growled and advanced. He barked at the evil spirit that had brought water to his master's eyes and against whom David now raised his arms in defense.

David laughed as the little shepherd leaped up. Asad stood on his hind legs as if to embrace and comfort David, licking the tears from David's cheek when he knelt to stroke his loyal companion.

"Oh, Asad," David said, ruffling the fur on the dog's head and then stroking it back into place. "Too bad Micah isn't more like you. Come on," he said, rising and slapping his thighs. He crouched slightly before his adoring constant comrade. Asad sprang into a stance of readiness, his legs spread wide, his center of gravity lowered so he could leap or run in any direction David might chose. He watched David intently, his eyes bright with fidelity and affection.

"Race you to town," David called over his shoulder.

It was mostly downhill from the point where their race began. The two had an easy run of it, though David knew it was more a tribute to Asad's loyalty than David's prowess at their contest that kept the little shepherd at David's side.

David did not break stride as they came into Bethlehem. They dashed through the city's gates and down the broad main street. Startled, residents and fellow travelers leaped aside as they passed in a cacophony of dogs and children who had joined the field in their race for home.

Jesse's townhouse was one of the finest in the city. It held a place of honor on the main street, just off the central plaza in front of the temple. Aside from the formal and religious occasions like sacrifices and public meetings held there, the plaza was also the site of the best well in town. As a result people gathered there for living water and news. Kiosks were at hand to sell to the plaza crowds, though the larger market was just to the west. The selection was better at the market, but the gossip was juicier at the well. One could rely on company there during daylight and often long after darkness fell.

Across the square from the well was David's family home. Only a small staff attended the imposing, flat-roofed limestone residence once Jesse and David's brothers returned to the karmel for the harvest and winter months. When the master was not in residence, those servants who remained in town spent most of their time in their own homes on the meaner avenues of the busy little city, returning each day to make sure the place was clean and secure.

David and Asad and their boisterous retinue were their own welcoming committee at the dark and quiet house. Asad reached his familiar home first, barking out his victory from the top step. They bid their entourage farewell as David unfastened the latch and entered.

Tossing aside his pack, he bounded through the house. He threw open the doors into the courtyard and drew water from the cistern there to wash and make himself presentable for his visit to town. If he had looked like a dusty wanderer upon his raucous entrance, he emerged a young gentleman.

"Guard the house," David answered Asad's barking before latching the heavy wooden doors.

Business first, David made his way across the plaza in the direction of the market. He nodded in greeting, recognized as Jesse's son by many unknown to him.

"Young David," called the heavy but spry older man near the well. He rose from his place and hurried across the plaza. "I did not know you were to be in town, young master."

"Bahija," David said, pausing to properly greet his father's head servant in the city.

"The house is not ready—there is nothing there—how long will you stay? Sukkot is only just—"

"Baji," David said, laughing and calling the florid, voluble man by his pet childhood name. Though Baji meant happy, he was as easily distressed as he was quick to laugh. David spoke in soothing tones. "I'm just in town for etrog and to speak with Korah about market business. Probably just the night."

"What will you eat?" Baji continued in a tone to suggest there had been a death in the family. "The beds are not made up. Why did you not just send to me? I could have brought you etrog and carried any messages you might need sent to the likes of that Edomite."

"Now, now, Korah's a good man," David said, trying and failing to calm him. "And I will manage just fine for the night."

"Is there anything you need?"

"No," he said firmly. "I'm off to the market to speak with Korah while he's there."

"I will look to the house while you are out," Baji insisted, stroking David's arm as if he needed comforting.

"It's not necessary," David tried again to assure him, but there was no dissuading the devoted man.

"I will make you a bed, put oil in the lamps, and lay in some food for you," Baji insisted. "It's the holiday so there is no one in residence after dark. Do you want me to stay the night to see to you?"

"No," David said firmly, dismayed by the prospect. He'd actually looked forward to having the place to himself. "Thank you, but no, I won't hear of it."

"Is there nothing I can do for you?" Baji almost pleaded, twisting the loose fabric of his robe.

"I'm fine, really," David assured him and then realized, "There is one thing, though. Have you seen Micah? I'd hoped to meet up with him on this visit."

"Oh, well now," Baji said, his eyes sparkling, suddenly mischievous. "Your old playmate. I'd have thought that sixteen summers would have been enough time playing. That sister of Korah's is still a beauty and more than willing, I hear. If you're looking for a playmate, she might be more fun for you now."

"Baji," David scolded, blushing. "Eliab says Micah is off to join the king's army for the spring campaign, and I wanted to see him before he left."

"Well, as it's not yet winter, I don't think you're too late to make your farewell," Baji teased, laughing the musical laugh that had earned him his name. "I'll see what I can do. Perhaps I should make up a couple of beds, just in case you have a guest for the night? Or perhaps just one big one?"

"Baji," David moaned, hiding his face. "I can stand it no more. I'm off to market where I belong. I'm not up to the skills of conversing at the plaza."

Baji's laugh again rang out as David fled west to the peace of the noisy market and the ease of talking shekels and gerah with Korah and the other traders there. Baji had made David feel suddenly as though he'd come to temple without a robe. Were David's feelings that transparent? How much did Baji know? Or was he just being a tease? Had it become plaza gossip? Was that why he'd heard so little from Micah?

His head swam with worries and unanswered questions as he wandered adrift in the crowded and familiar market.

Was he too old for a boy's infatuation? Had Micah outgrown the feelings David still nurtured in his heart? Was he making a fool of himself?

"David ben Jesse," Korah called out, his voice rising above the din of the preholiday marketplace. "An honor. Please sit in our tent. Allow us to serve you. It would be a tribute to my household."

"I'm not buying anything," David said firmly. He smiled. The Edomite's wheedling flattery cleared his head and put him on his guard as well as on familiar turf.

"Of course you are not," Korah went on, leading David to a worn but comfortable goatskin stool. "You cannot buy anything here, for what is mine is yours. Anah, fetch our esteemed guest some pomegranate nectar."

"This is not my first trip to the market," David said, eyebrow arched.

"So suspicious of your old friend Korah," the trader said, taking a seat on an upended crate. "Now, what brings you to our humble tent today? Here's your nectar. You have of course met my sister, Anah?"

"Of course I have," David said, looking up as he reached to take the cup. It slipped in his nervous hands and he almost dropped it. Anah caught the cup and restored it to David's grasp, taking and holding his hand suggestively. "And yet I must say that each time is like the first. Such beauty is always refreshing."

David knew the way of the market. He had grown up with the customs and rituals of the stew of humanity that frequented the busy souk. He could ill afford to do business with only Israelites and make the most from his father's yield. In trade he embraced Arabs, Edomites, Amalekites, Egyptians, and even Philistines, buying and selling in their many tongues.

Quick wit and ease with foreign custom made him as much ambassador as salesman. Thus had he made Jesse's karmel one of the richest in all of Judah, though in truth it had been so on the day of David's birth.

Korah laughed heartily.

"You are right, brother, he is very beautiful," Anah said, stroking David's cheek, forward as no respectable woman could be. When she was still very young, death had taken Anah's husband in an Amalekite raid. Though necessity soon took her virtue, her beauty endured. Korah was a practical man who made his living from trade. He saw Anah as a fellow trader.

David felt trapped in the tent. The blood left his legs and rose into his face.

The trader only laughed harder at his guest's obvious discomfort.

"Such pretty hair," Anah said, twirling one of David's reddish-gold curls in her fingers.

"You are redder than Mount Edom at sunset," Korah croaked—half laughter, half cough. "You had best leave us before you kill him, Anah."

"Will he be at the festival tonight?" she asked with a small bow as she turned to leave.

"How could he refuse such a sly invitation, vixen?" Korah said, laughing. Clapping David's shoulder in a comforting, brotherly way, he shooed Anah out. "It's hard to tell who's the girl and who's the boy."

"Why, which are you?" David asked, finding his tongue at last.

"I'm too hairy to be a woman," Korah said, stroking David's smooth cheek.

"Not, I'm told, in Edom," David said with an evil grin. "Is your great red mountain not named Seir for all your furry beauties?"

"There now, that's the David I know," Korah said heartily. "Your fear gone as soon as my sister leaves the room."

"There is nothing more fearsome than a beautiful woman," David said with an easy smile.

"True, true," Korah said, nodding broadly. "Except maybe you, when it's time to argue the prices for the harvest market."

"We are all afraid of the things we want the most." David smiled distantly, no longer in the conversation with Korah. "Because they are the only things we cannot bear to lose."

"Then I am right to be afraid that I'm getting ready to lose my money?"

"Most of it," David said with a shrug. "Unless you choose not to buy from me. Then you will lose it all."

"Yet I fear for my sister at the festival tonight, for it seems that she is not what you are most afraid of losing," Korah said, catching David's attention and his eye.

David felt naked at first, as though all his fears on the way to the market had been realized and his secrets had become the topic at the well. The two men stared at one another for what seemed like an eternity, their eyes locked. At last Korah erupted into his rich, coughing laugh.

"Why so serious all of a sudden?" Korah demanded jovially, shaking David by the shoulder. "I have only to mention my sister and you look as blank-eyed as an Egyptian sculpture. You must come to the festival; my sister may save me a fortune if she can catch your favor, if not your eye."

I will go into thy house with burnt offerings: I will pay thee my vows.
Psalm 66:13

DAVID WAS whistling a tune he had been inventing as he made his way back to the house. His purse hung heavy from the sash of his tunic. It struck his thigh prosperously as he walked. The leather pouch was pregnant with coin, early payments from Korah and several other merchants. The fall harvest market was always more interesting to him than the summer grain market. Grain traded like gold: it sold at pretty much the same price for everyone. More grain meant more profit for a farmer, but the more there was, the less it was worth. Good grain harvest meant low prices. Bad harvest meant high prices.

But the yoreh market was more about the salesman than his wares. Fruit and vineyard harvests were more about the quality than the quantity of the product. David was better at negotiating the deal than he was at making sure his produce was the best in the marketplace. The karmel made more money from staples like wine, flour, and oil, but the fine points of a good deal made for a more interesting day at market.

"*You crown the year with your bounty,*" David sang, trying out some words to the tune in his head. "*Your carts overflow with....*"

The blow caught him unawares and nearly knocked him off his feet. It took a heartbeat for him to realize that the purse had been snatched from his belt. The brigand was making away with enough to pay the karmel salaries all winter. Without thought David took flight. He closed fast on the heels of the thief. A cry, a flying leap, and the two went tumbling into the street. Dust rose up in clouds. David quickly felled and pinned his adversary, bringing them face-to-face.

"Pretty good," Micah said, panting hard and laughing harder. "But the idea is not to get robbed in the first place."

"I'm not robbed," David crowed, giving his assailant a firm shake. He was still smarting from the start Micah had given him but elated at seeing his beloved at last. "I have both my purse and a new slave, so I've made a profit as I see it."

"Is David among the profits?" Micah joked, making light of an old song that was sung about the king.

"Very clever, slave," David said sternly. He pinched back the grin that flowered just from being in Micah's company after so long an absence.

"Oh, you think I am your slave now, do you?" Micah asked, still cocky.

"I'm the not one with my back in the dirt." David shrugged.

"So that's all it takes to make a slave?" Micah posed with a sly edge to his tone.

"It's a good star—" David began. Abruptly he found himself flying through the air and just as suddenly staring up into Micah's face. His beloved nemesis lay on top of him, looking down into his eyes.

"Then I guess that makes you my slave," Micah asserted, holding David fast even as he put up a minimal struggle. Micah leaned down to whisper in David's ear. "You'll be mighty pretty at my table each night, slave, and attending me in my chambers."

"Master David," Baji cried out in alarm, running across the square toward the two.

Micah leapt to his feet, startling Baji to a halt.

"Here, Baj," Micah said, tossing the servant David's heavy purse. "Keep this safe for your master. He has a slave to catch."

"Master Micah? Master David?" Baji said, only just managing to catch the purse without spilling its contents in the dirt. "What's going on?"

Their backs were his only answer.

Bethlehem's two main avenues met just at Jesse's door to form the temple square. The road that crossed the plaza led to the souk in the west and the trader's gates in the east. Both were broad and straight, befitting their service and their residents. Just off the main roads, the streets turned narrow and winding, as likely to end in a flight of stairs or a blind alley as a new street around each corner. David had some passing knowledge of the city, but he was after all country gentry. Whereas Micah, save for the nights he'd spent with David, had lived his whole life within the walls of Bethlehem.

As the chase progressed, two things became clear to David. First, that he had best keep up with Micah because he was no longer sure he could find his way out of the maze of streets. Second, and more humbling, that after Micah had taken David's purse, he had clearly allowed himself to be caught. The best David could do was keep sight of the soles of Micah's feet, eventually losing even that.

Rounding a corner, David found himself staring at a blind alley. Three houses came together where the little path met their walls. Micah had vanished. The street ended. David looked foolishly into the surprised and wary faces of the people who lived there. They stared back at him suspiciously from where they hovered over the cooking fire outside their front door.

With a nod of greeting, David turned to take stock of his position. He searched for a sign that he might guess not only where Micah had gone, but how to get home from wherever he might be. Behind him he found three narrow and remarkably similar streets, each of which offered little in the way of clues. With a sigh he realized his only course of action.

"Micah ben Joseph, I am your slave," David said with a disgusted sigh.

"So you are," Micah said, dropping down from the low roof of one of the small houses that had interrupted their chase. "I think you should bear me out to the grazing field," Micah said, making as if to hop onto David's back. David was very much the shorter of the two, and Micah's feet were still firmly planted on the ground.

Those around the nearby fire laughed at their antics.

"Well, that will never do," Micah said as if considering it. He stepped back and paced around David as though assessing a mule for purchase. "I suppose that since you are my slave, that makes you valuable property, and valuable property should be well cared for."

"Oh no," David managed to say before he was hanging upside down over Micah's shoulder like a sack of flour. His short robes fell unflatteringly up. They were treated to the laughter of those they passed on their way to what turned out to be the common grazing ground. The grassy patch was used by the city's goats for forage and the rest of Bethlehem, particularly the young, as open space safe within the city's walls.

"There we are," Micah said, unceremoniously depositing David on the grassy ground, grown cool in the long shadows of the coming autumn evening.

The goats were all long gone to milking. The last of the meadow's young habitués were making their way toward home for the evening meal. No one was near the spot where Micah had laid David to rest.

"What are we doing here?" David asked, not bothering to get up and be knocked down again. He looked up at Micah and the darkening blue skies behind him.

"This is where we used to train," Micah said, extending his arms to include the whole field around them. "This is where I learned be a soldier and tried to teach you."

"I know where we are," David said with an overacted bit of irritation. "What I don't know is why we're here."

"And now I'm off to be a soldier and your training is at end." Micah shrugged, a malicious little twinkle in his eye. "So, just like when our lessons were done and we'd copied our letters on fresh clay to test if we'd learned them, now it's time to see if you learned your lessons here."

"So this is my final test?" David asked with a smirk.

"You can win your freedom, slave, if you can pin me," Micah said, throwing his arms wide and backing away. He took up a stance familiar from the beginnings of the many matches they'd set themselves on that very ground.

"Are you serious?" David asked, half sitting up.

"So you are content to be my slave?" Micah demanded, smacking David's head as he danced in and then away again to avoid David's wild swing.

"Stop it," David said, shaking it off.

"Stop what?" Micah asked, dancing in again to tap David's head playfully once more before bounding away.

"Micah, stop it," David warned, less amused.

"Stop that?" Micah said, skipping in for another slap. He missed.

David leapt to his feet and onto Micah.

The two went tumbling across the grass, Micah laughing as always. They'd fought more battles in that field than King Saul and the Philistines had in all of Canaan.

With surprise on his side, David started the match with a slight advantage. Though Micah was larger than David, that had not always decided the outcome of their battles. David could give as good as he got, excelling in areas like swordplay where his size and grace were more an advantage. But wrestling was not his forte, and David's advantage soon turned to rout as he struggled to keep from being pinned.

Micah was on David's back. Relentlessly he tried to turn him over. Their legs twined together like vines on the arbor. Their hands locked. Micah's breath was hot on David's neck. His body ground against David's. At first it was just a wrestling match. But it had been months since they'd last seen one another. The absence soon began to be felt between them as proximity and friction took their course.

Micah stopped trying to turn David. He held David firmly in place as he rode up on his back. David felt Micah's response, hard against him. He replied in kind rather than trying to get away. They kept up the appearance of the struggle in the darkening field until David could stand the exquisite torture no longer. At last David's longing overcame him. He simply gave up.

Without his resistance to hold them in place, David flipped easily onto his back. Micah, surprised, was suddenly looking down at David. Their faces were only inches away from one another. Hard and panting they froze, staring into each other's eyes. They said nothing. Slowly Micah's face drew nearer to David's, their eyes locked.

Then Micah was up.

"You win," Micah said to fill the awkward silence that followed. "I grant you your freedom, on condition that you accompany me to the Harvest Market Festival."

He extended his hand to David, lifted him off the ground, and set him on his feet.

"Festival?" David asked, still panting, unfinished, confused.

"It's the best food and wine in the world," Micah said, throwing an arm over David's shoulder and leading him. "You know why?"

"Why?" David asked softly, stung and bewildered by the cheerful rejection.

"It's free," Micah said, laughing too loudly at his own joke.

They washed each another by torchlight in the courtyard of Jesse's empty house. Baji, true to his word, had made up one huge bed in one of the sleeping rooms on the upper floor, filled the lamps, heaped bowls with fruits and nuts, and spread the table with bread and cheese and wine enough to feed David and all seven of his brothers. David and Micah dressed in clean linen tunics, tied fashionably at the waist with leather thongs. They stood facing, inspecting each other as they made ready to go out for the evening.

They had hardly spoken since their match on the common. Though they were familiar enough to be easy in their silence together, there was something unspoken between them that night.

"Micah," David said softly, coming up behind his friend. The sling with the lion's tooth was wrapped in a square of silk and clutched behind his back. "There is something I want to say to you."

"Not now, David," Micah said heartily enough to drown the quiet. "We'll be late, and all the best food and the prettiest girls will be taken. Come."

David set the prize aside for later as he followed. His heart sank as the evening and the truth unfolded before him.

Micah took his leave almost as soon as they arrived at the brightly lighted market plaza. The booths of the merchants were laid with tempting bits of roasted meats, fresh-baked breads, cheeses, fruits, vegetables, and all the bounty the harvest market promised in abundance.

Musicians played enticing music in accompaniment to the wild, whirling dancing of the many cultures brought together by the commerce of the thriving souk.

Bethlehem's was a jewel, second only to the Jebusite city of Jerusalem along the Road of the Patriarchs that ran along the ridge of hills from Beersheba in the south and Jezreel in the north connecting all the tribes. The trade routes that crossed the ridge road in the two cities led to Damascus in the north, the great sea in the west, the strange Arab lands and beyond in the east, and to the great prize of Egypt to the south and west.

The rituals and customs of the festival were as foreign as those who traded there. Unlike David's sisters, the girls of the market could dance with men and ply their own form of trade. Micah lost no time in stepping into the arms of one and then the next, whirling and then writhing in time to the exotic, untamed music that grew wilder with the night.

David was left on his own. Between longing looks in Micah's direction, he nibbled at the kabobs and exotic delicacies. He spoke with the merchants offering them, many already familiar. The market was abuzz with the news of Prince Jonathan's single-handed rout of the massive Philistine armies. David was soon lost in the stories of the tribes' great new hero.

"What's the matter? Don't you know how to dance?" Anah asked, suddenly standing at David's shoulder. Her husky voice sent a shiver through him.

He turned and regarded her. She stared straight into his eyes. Even David's own mother was not so bold with him in public. The experience was unaccustomed but not unpleasant.

"Are you afraid?" she asked, coy and enticing.

Without a word David took her hands and spun them into the area that had been cleared for dancing. Swept up in the unbridled rhythms, he danced with Anah until she could no longer keep up. Drawing cheers from those who stepped aside to let him have the circle, he leaped and twirled, lost in the music, seeking release of his joy and frustration. Inspired by his abandon, the musicians, too, became more and more liberated, stirring David to greater heights until both peaked in an inspired conclusion. A final shrill note was blown and David threw himself to the ground, spent and exhilarated.

The crowd shouted praises. Anah rushed into his arms. Micah embraced them both as the three turned gently together on the dance floor. Everyone closed in to touch David like those who dipped their cloths in the blood of a sacrifice to carry a stain of the blessing with them. From there the three made a feast of it, dancing and reveling in the spirit of the night of wine and merriment. They danced together, with Anah between them. They made a joke of feeding one another. They eschewed cups, spraying wine into each other's mouths directly from the skins.

After enough wine, David was convinced to sing, though he was never shy about it and would have sung sooner had anyone asked him. To the surprise of all but one present, he chose a decidedly mournful psalm of unrequited love. It was a fitting end to the party, like the closing scene of a bittersweet play. All were content to wander to their tents and homes, arm in arm, happier for the warmth of present company because of the thoughts of loss the song evoked.

"Come, David," Micah urged, Anah clutched under his strong right arm. "Let's go back to your father's house. There is wine and food there, and the night is yet young. Look how high the moon is still."

"Yes, David," Anah urged, rushing to him. Taking his hands in hers, she dragged him toward the arch that led back into the streets.

"Why not?" David agreed, a shade ruefully. His bitter tone was lost in the sweetness of the wine. Anah nestled against him. The three made their way, singing and dancing.

"You are a very good singer," Anah said as they drew near the house. "And you dance like a street performer from the market at Damascus."

"Yes, all he needs is a jewel in his navel," Micah teased, reaching through David's robes as he tried to keep himself included.

"And finger cymbals." David laughed at the idea of it, having seen some rude version in the smaller trading towns in Philistia on the road to Megiddo. "Here we are. Welcome to my father's house." David held the door and helped Anah up and over the high threshold.

"Such a fine home," she purred silkily as David and Micah set about lighting the lamps.

"My mother would be pleased you think so," David said with a gracious nod. "Wine? Some food?"

"Just you," she said, drawing close and touching his lips with her finger.

He pulled back without thinking and laughed as though it was only a jest. "Well, wine for me. And you, Micah?"

Anah was stung. She took David's inexperience in such things as rejection. Only Micah saw Anah's hurt. Unlike his childhood friend, Micah knew just what to do.

"Certainly, David," Micah said, accepting David's offer. He stepped up beside Anah, placing his hand at the small of her back. "Wine would be most welcome. And I've got a tooth for some of Baji's olive conserve and some bread to dip in it."

"I'll see what I can find," David said with a servant's bow. "And Anah, I'll bring you a cup just in case you change your mind."

He hummed to himself as he put together a tray of food and cups. Reaching up, he tore a sprig of fragrant summer jasmine, still blooming, from the trellis above the kitchen door to the courtyard. He breathed deeply of the rich summer perfume before adding it to the tray. His feet were light. Returning to the main room, he danced a few steps to the unheard music from his memory of the festival.

He froze in the shadows. The song he was humming stuck in his throat. The joy left him, taking with it the rhythm of his steps. Unobserved, he watched the two standing in the light, locked in their embrace, their lips pressed hungrily together, each lost in the other.

Quietly David set the tray on the table. His hand brushed against the silk of the small bundle that contained the treasured gift he'd made. He had come to town to present it to the friend who'd forgotten David was even there. He took up the gift and withdrew. He moved hurriedly to the upper floor. Grabbing a wool blanket off the sumptuous bed Baji had made for him, he climbed to the roof garden.

The harvest moon blurred through the mist in his eyes. He lay on his back and bundled himself against the night chill.

"Oh God, why don't you believe in me?" David asked, lonely, full of wine, and very jealous, though he hardly knew of whom.

He looked up into the stars expectantly, as though God might answer him if he waited long enough. In time sleep overcame his heartache, and he dozed fitfully.

"There you are," Micah said, spreading another blanket over him.

David stirred but said nothing. He did not turn to face his friend.

Micah lifted David's head and slipped a pillow beneath. He slid under the covers and up behind David like two spoons in a chest. He drew the blankets over the two of them. "What are you thinking? It's getting too cold to sleep up here."

Their bodies fit easily together, as much from habit as from everything that had passed between them.

"I was just thinking about that night on the bearskin," Micah said softly. "It seems so distant now, but we are not old enough for it to have been that long ago."

"Or for the feelings to be gone between us," David said breaking the silence with something finally worth saying.

"Those feelings will never be gone," Micah said, tightening his hold on David meaningfully. "The joys of childhood fuel the laughter of life. But we must grow up just the same."

"And leave."

"Yes."

"I brought you something," David said, turning slightly, thrusting the bundle into Micah's hands.

"What is it?" Micah said. Sitting up, he unwrapped the present under the light of the pregnant harvest moon that hung low above the western horizon.

"Something to remind you of me and summers and that bearskin," David said simply, his big speech forgotten. "To bring you luck. To bring you home."

"I will carry it with me into battle," Micah said, tying the sling around his neck. "What is this? A tooth?"

"A lion's. I killed it with this very sling while I was making it for you in the pasture by the Wadi Asad."

"You killed a lion with a sling?" Micah asked, his voice hoarse with disbelief.

David shrugged.

"The Lord has always favored you, David ben Jesse."

"And yet he breaks my heart like a twig snaps under my foot."

They stared at each other in silence for a time, familiar enough with one another to understand all that needed to be said. A sad smile creased Micah's face as he looked into David's eyes, bright with tears in the moonlight. Lying back, Micah reached up and drew David down beside him as before.

"We cannot always be boys, David," Micah said softly into his ear. "But I will always love you."

David knew their secret adventure was over forever, but he was happy to fall asleep in the arms of his first love one last time before their paths diverged. The Lord alone would decide when and if they crossed again.

Though hast also given me the shield of thy salvation: and thy right hand hath holden me up, and thy gentleness hath made me great.

Psalm 18:35

"PRINCE JONATHAN came running out of the hills shouting like a man touched, raving at unseen demons, 'Flee before the God of Israel,'" Joab said, acting the part. His rapt audience lingered around the Sukkot table in the house of Jesse, following a meal that had made the massive cedar table groan. "The prince alone charged straight at nearly ten thousand Philistines with only his armor-bearer following at a safe distance behind. The king and what was left of his armies stood opposite on the hill of Gilgal watching, helpless. You could almost see the color drain out of King Saul's face as he bore witness to his son's bravery and almost certain doom. Prince Jonathan is the favorite of all the king's sons, as you know."

"What does the prince look like?" David asked, trying to picture the story in his mind, dreaming of glory and worried for Micah in battle.

"Don't be such a boy," Eliab said, giving David a loving cuff. "Go on with the story, nephew."

"He's as tall as his father," Joab said. He looked into David's eyes, ignoring Eliab's boorishness, and indulged the beautiful boy. David's nephew Joab, eldest son to Zeruiah, was actually quite a bit older than David. He stroked David's reddish-gold hair as he replied. "As you know, the king stands a head or more above the tallest of men. In that, and in all things, the prince is the opposite of you, David, dark where you are fair. And just then, we all thought we were about to witness his death.

"Suddenly, like one of the stories they tell of the days of the patriarchs, a miracle occurred before our eyes. As if in answer to Jonathan's call to the God of Israel, the ground shook so hard under our feet that it nearly knocked us down. Across the valley in the Philistine camp, tents fell, horses shied; fires broke out from overturned lamps and the like. A great cry went up among them. 'Flee before the God of Israel,' they screamed to one another in terror. Their wailing echoed across the nahal from their hilltop to where we stood."

"The Philistines?" Jesse asked, a grin of satisfaction spreading over his face.

"My hand raised before the God of Abraham," Joab said, nodding vigorously as he did. "If I had not been there in the ranks behind General Abner, I would not have believed it myself. The Philistines actually took up the prince's chant, 'Flee before the God of Israel.' They turned as one and fled west, toward home and the protection of their own gods. We had but to pursue and take them down as they ran. In your seats I would be hard pressed to believe it. Yet we all saw it with our own eyes and knew it in our hearts. Our Prince Jonathan, the man the king himself the next day proclaimed his heir and our next king, single-handed routed nine thousand Philistine men at arms. I do not expect to see anything so amazing again in my life."

"And they've made you a lieutenant for your own bravery in the battle, your mother tells me, Grandson," Jesse said. He placed his hand over Joab's. The young man sat up proudly in his place of honor at Jesse's right.

"Well, I did my best to follow Prince Jonathan's lead." Joab shrugged with a practiced humility. "His was an irresistible force. Not only did every single deserter from the army return, but many more joined the fight on our side to follow such a man."

"It seems the council's wishes for a king are to be the first step in realizing our dream of achieving the promises of Moses." Jesse sighed, not yet taking his hand away. He stared into the distance at a sight only his heart could see.

"There's sour milk in Samuel's beard." Eliab croaked with laughter.

"Mind your tongue," Jesse warned, back from his reverie.

"What an old fool he has become," Eliab went on despite his father's tone and warning. "To denounce the king before a battle, endanger our men, and then be so dead wrong about the outcome, which he divined in our enemy's favor."

"I am a witness it is true." Joab sighed. "Men deserted and fled into the hills, fearing that God no longer fought at our side."

"Yet was it not Samuel who chose Saul as king?" Jesse demanded sternly.

"Father, you cannot defend the actions of a man who is clearly still sore that the council demanded a king in the first place. He was clear enough about his objections at the time," Eliab insisted. A chorus of agreements from the younger members of the party accompanied him. "I think he fancied himself another great judge like Gideon."

"I am not called upon to defend the actions of the Lord's most esteemed servant Samuel," Jesse growled, less than amused by the casual way in which the young regarded such matters. "Nor are you elected to question God's will."

"How can you say that the Lord is acting through Samuel?" Eliab scoffed, warming to the argument.

"Who else could have known that Prince Jonathan, who was not yet born at the time of Saul's investiture, was to be the brilliant and worthy successor to the king? Or that King Saul would raise an army, vanquish our enemies, and make us more prosperous than ever before?" Jesse asked with a wry smile.

"Samuel certainly didn't see Jonathan coming when he warned that the battle was lost before the prince had won it," Eliab blustered.

"Yet if he had not, would we still have won?" Jesse answered easily. "Who do you suppose it was who made the ground give way under the feet of our enemies? King Saul? Prince Jonathan? If the king had attacked when they'd originally planned, would the outcome have been the same? Who's to say that the delay Samuel's actions brought about didn't win the battle?"

Eliab's face reddened in response to the laughter that precluded his argument.

"*In our distress Prince Jonathan called to the Lord; he cried to God for help,*" David sang, taking up his harp and improvising a peaceful end to the argument. "*From his temple he heard the voice of his chosen; the cry came before him, into his ears.*

"*Then the earth shook and trembled; the foundations also of the hills moved and were shaken, because the Lord was wroth.*

"*The Lord is my rock, my fortress and my deliverer;*

"*God is the rock in whom we take refuge. He is the shield and the horn of our salvation, our stronghold.*"

"Bravo, little brother," Eliab bellowed with harsh laughter. Wounded by Jesse's rebuke, he was a bully looking for someone weaker so that he might salve his pride. "You make poetry of the prince's bravery, even as you take away the credit for his valor."

"Such was hardly my intention, Eliab," David said, setting aside his harp, disgusted. "I wanted only to bring harmony to the thanksgiving table, but I see you prefer sour notes."

"Always my better, aren't you, David?"

"I leave that to the audience to decide, though I hear no applause for your performance tonight," David said, his voice trembling. His ears were hot with anger and embarrassment.

The gentle laughter soothed David's anxiety as it further inflamed Eliab's resolve.

"Well, cousin, I think you are not on the turf best suited to your shoes," Joab chortled, pounding Eliab's back.

"Yes, I admit I do not possess the skills of the courtesan," Eliab answered Joab by striking out at David. "But how much singing was there on the battlefield at Gilgal? Was it the high notes that earned us the victory, or the harmony? I wonder what my little brother would do were he taken out of the banquet room. Would you fire an arrow at the Philistines with your harp?"

The laughter was on Eliab's side this time. David's breath was short as he rose.

"It seems you are too modest, big brother." David smiled. "It looks as though you are the courtesan after all. You administer your poison like a true lady. It is too bad you were not with me in the hills last week when that lion was threatening one of Father's flocks. Perhaps you could have brought him down with your feline wit and guile. Are these the weapons you plan to employ on the king's behalf, when you join his forces this spring?"

Even Eliab laughed.

"I fear you are lost," Joab said, his face red, again pounding Eliab's back.

"I fear you are right, cousin," Eliab said, hoisting David onto his knee and kissing his cheek. "I am no match for you, my prince. I am thankful for many things this harvest. But most of all, I am thankful that you, little brother, despite all outward appearances, are on my side."

"Hear, hear," Abinadab declared, raising his cup. "To our little brother David. Praise be to God that once we leave him here at home, we have only the Philistines to fight."

They all drank a hearty toast to a blushing David.

"Would you not want me fighting at your side then, brothers?" David asked in the quiet as they drained their cups of harvest wine.

"You are far too valuable to make you fodder for the Philistine archers," Eliab said with a warm embrace before tossing David easily into Abinadab's arms.

"If you came along, what reason would we have to go away to war?" Abinadab asked with a shrug, passing him off onto brother Shammah's knee.

"Should we also bring Abigail and Zeruiah?" Shammah laughed, smacking David's backside as he set him back onto Eliab's lap. "They're both taller and older."

"And neither as pretty," Eliab echoed. "So we leave you behind for reasons of safety, little brother."

"Both yours and ours," Abinadab added, the joke almost too big for David to bear.

David managed a smile as Eliab crushed him in a one-armed embrace.

"Cowards, all," Jesse said, laughing with his sons and capping the joke as he reached out to stroke David's hair.

And Saul gathered the people together, and numbered them in Telaim, two hundred thousand footmen, and ten thousand men of Judah.

1 Samuel 15:4

"WE ARE only taking what we need," Eliab said, fighting to control his voice and his anger.

"I simply do not understand why you need to take three of the best men on the karmel," David answered petulantly. He did not look up from packing baskets of food to sustain his brothers while they were on campaign with the king. "Why haven't you trained your own body of men to attend you? Is that not a part of the preparation to become a charioteer in the king's army?"

Chaos reigned. Eliab, Abinadab, and Shammah prepared for departure. The household was engulfed in the storm. Their orders had arrived only a week before. They had spent the intervening time toasting their courage in battles yet to come rather than preparing for their mission.

Officers commissioned in the king's army, and their families, were expected to provide not only the soldier, but his sword and his supper. Israel was more an idea than a country. The treasury of the king was accrued largely from the spoils of war and the control of trade royalties. There was little in the way of taxes to arm and feed those who fought in the army of Israel. The battles were fought and funded by those with something to lose. In this way the taxation was paid by those who could best afford it.

Rations were offered to foot soldiers who volunteered their service for lack of other opportunities. Their allotments were meager and often only what could be scrounged from the land around where the army was camped. Officers, cavalry, and the elite new charioteer class provided not only their own food, armor, tents, aides, and weapons, but also their own horses and chariots. The king paid them in lands or royalties. In return, if the wheel fell off a chariot or a horse threw a shoe, the officer was on his own to mend the situation.

Jesse had paid to train Eliab and his brothers. He had outfitted them with the armor and weapons they needed to fight at the king's side. Still inexperienced in the responsibilities of leadership at home or in the field, it had never occurred to Eliab to consider what was involved in feeding himself and his brothers for the six months or so they would be away. People and provisions were not a part of his dream of glory. It came as a shock when he awakened to the reality of his commission.

When the day came for Eliab to embark for the Negev and points south to join in the pursuit of the Amalekite King Agag and his forces, the truth was all too clear. Just getting ready to go to the king's encampment at Telaim had already exceeded his knowledge of soldiering on campaign.

David was beside himself with anger at his brothers—not for their requests, but for making no preparations. Eliab simply appointed the strongest-looking men who worked on the farm to join him on his dangerous assignment. He then began emptying the food stores into baskets and assembling whatever else from the household he felt he and his brothers might need or want while they were away.

Not only had the house been thrown into confusion, but David and Eliab had been having at one another since sunrise. They bickered over each item they packed.

"We are only cavalrymen." Eliab sulked at David's harsh tone. "We are hardly charioteers."

"Did you bother to get and train horses, then?" David asked, wrapping wheels of cheese in spruce-wood skins, bound together with thick coarse twine.

"Well, of course we did," Eliab answered irritably.

"Yet it never occurred to you that you'd need footmen to tend the animals while you were away from Father's stables?" David accused.

"I don't see what difference a few hands more or less will make around here...."

"That is because you are a selfish, spoiled beast who has never once even tried to take part in the running of this karmel," David said, slamming the lid on the wicker trunk he was packing. He locked his blazing glare with his brother's. "You just sit down to the table and expect to be fed. You never once consider where the food comes from or what it takes to get it to the table. You may be an officer by right of being the eldest, but you are no more than the lowliest foot soldier in your preparation for the job."

Eliab slammed his fist down on the thick wood of the kitchen table, raising a small cloud of flour into the air. "You will not speak to me thus in front of these men," Eliab shouted, his temper taking charge of him. "How are they to respect and serve me if they hear a boy in my home redress me as you do?"

"Respect you?" David demanded, laughing as he rolled an urn from the pantry. He righted the urn alongside the stout silver chest that stood opposite the kitchen's massive hearth. Sputtering, he set about filling the crock with wine from the tap of the basswood barrel resting on the tile-covered lid of the chest. "Brother, I can make food mysteriously appear on the table before you and put together a mule train in the time it takes to prepare supper. I can even outfit it with what it will take to sustain you for months. But you will have to do more than treat your youngest brother to a tantrum to earn the respect of men who have been working daily as you yourself never once have done to enrich, feed, and clothe you."

"That is it," Eliab said, grabbing David and throwing him over his shoulder like a bag of grain. "We will have an end to this conversation."

Wine spilled from the open tap. One of the servants, who was trying to be invisible during the contretemps, rushed to close the wooden valve.

"Put me down, you Philistine," David wailed. He pounded Eliab's back as his brother carried him up the stairs.

Even Nitzevet was too terrified and distressed over sending her sons off to war to say anything. She and the rest of the women only observed the struggle out of the corners of their eyes as they continued, silently, to make ready for the imminent departure of the three eldest brothers, packing food and linens into baskets and trunks.

The six other brothers whistled and shouted. They cheered for either David's or Eliab's victory with a mocking seriousness that only further served to inflame both men.

"Now you boys," Jesse shouted, emerging from his study just as Eliab and David disappeared up the stairs. "Abinadab, do something. Don't just stand there carrying on like some simpleton in a mob. See to your brothers."

"Yes, Father," Abinadab said, spoiling to get in on the fight. "Come on. Shammah, Nethanel, come and help me."

Eliab slammed the door in concert with the three oafish farm boys lumbering up the stairs. The very house shook under their feet.

"Oh my Lord, what sons you have," Nitzevet said, hiding her tears in Jesse's shoulder.

Eliab pulled the latch. He shoved a heavy trunk in front of the door to ensure that they were not disturbed, though he needn't have bothered.

"Eliab," Abinadab called out, pounding on the door.

"Go away and leave us in peace to talk, or I'll come out and thrash you and anyone with you and throw you back down the stairs."

The house was quiet save for the sound of the three brothers filing softly back down the stairs and out the big front door.

"There's an end to that," Eliab said, turning.

David braced to defend himself against the beating that had been offered to his brothers.

Instead he was surprised to find himself locked in Eliab's embrace.

"David, David, David, my beloved little brother," Eliab said, rocking him in his arms as he had so often in their youth. "I will miss you so much when I'm gone. And the food that magically appears on the table wherever I happen to be. And the clean linen robes that always seem to be hanging on the back of the door in whatever room I sleep. I will miss your sweet voice when it's screaming at me for some imagined wrong I've done you or singing me my favorite songs. But David, as I've told you since you were a pup, it gives me the strength I need to face this fight knowing that you are here safe, singing my favorite songs and making the success that only you can make of this place. Your labors will care for us all long after our petty squabbles with the Amalekites are settled and forgotten. Look after our mother and father and my best interests at home. That is the important work. Mine is the just the brute force needed to allow that to continue undisturbed.

"Little brother, you give me something to fight for."

"As well as someone to fight with?" David asked as his brother released him, touched by Eliab's words but far from at peace.

"Yes, even that I will miss," Eliab said, affectionately tapping David's chin with his fist.

"Why can you not see me as a man?" David sighed, defeated but still angry and confused about his feelings. "Why do you suppose that I'm someone who needs to stay here safe so you can defend me? Do you not think it selfish to expect to be provided for on your grand adventure by those who labor on your behalf...?"

Eliab came down on top of his brother with all his might, pinning David's much smaller frame firmly against the wooden floorboards, holding him there effortlessly. He secured both David's hands with one of his. With the other he tweaked David's nose. He ran his fingers through David's hair as one might play with a baby.

"There now, mighty warrior," Eliab taunted. "Throw me off as you would an angry Philistine who decided to take you for his prize. Show me what you would do."

"Get off of me, Eliab," David hissed, trying to turn his face away from his brother's torment.

"That's how you plan to defeat the Philistines, is it? Girlish fits?" Eliab asked, laughing at his little brother's pointless struggling. "You see? You expect to be regarded as a man just as you say I expect food to appear on the table before me without ever concerning myself with how it got there. You have earned your place here. You are a good steward who I hope will live here with me all the days of my life. I must earn my place now. You mistake what it is to be a man."

"Let me up," David growled fiercely.

"Have you learned your place?" Eliab asked patiently. "Do you see why it is that I am glad you will remain here?"

"Get off."

"The person who does not see the man you are, David, is you," Eliab said. He released David's wrists and rose to leave. "Good-bye, little brother."

David watched his brothers depart from the roof terrace. He was ashamed to go and say good-bye, and then more ashamed that he had not, for he could not know whether he would see them again.

And Saul came to a city of Amalek, and laid wait in the valley.

1 Samuel 15:5

BY THE time Eliab and his party caught up to the king's forces, they were massing just outside the enemy stronghold of Amalek, home to the Amalekite king, Agag. On the way, Eliab and his brothers had passed through the smoldering ruins of the Amalekite cities of Havilah and Tel Masos. They followed for days in the scorched and lifeless wake of King Saul's wrath as he scourged the Amalekites from the land.

The charred wreckage along their way was a sobering reminder of their mission. They were a somber and quiet party by the time they reached the camp of the army of Israel.

The sound reached them before they gained sight of the massive force. The ground vibrated beneath their feet as they mounted the final hill before descending to the plain of the Amalek Nahal. They froze, struck dumb by the sight of more than 200,000 men and the thousands more camp followers spread out across the valley below.

"Whose son are you?" the guard demanded as they approached the fortified perimeter.

"I am Eliab, son of Jesse, uncle to Joab, lieutenant to King Saul. My brothers and I are here on orders from his most excellent person," Eliab said, trying to sound confident. He rode to the fore and held out the parchment that granted his commission, trembling in his unsteady hand.

"Joab's cousins," the guard exclaimed. "Finally. We were beginning to wonder if you'd been captured by bandits in the hills."

"We have been trailing you since Telaim," Eliab said, dismounting. He struck his chest in salute to the guard, who returned the tribute with a perfunctory listlessness. "You have done your jobs well, for we have seen not a living soul between there and here."

"Our king is on orders from the God of Abraham, and we have spared not so much as a dog in our path," the guard said, shaking his head, his face drawn and hollow as a man in mourning. "You will find Joab's tents there, below those rocks that look like a pair of jackal's ears." The guard pointed out the direction and the landmark. He stood aside to allow Eliab and his party to pass.

The three brothers and their attendants spoke hardly a word to one another. Gathered there in that one remote and desolate spot were more people than they had seen over the course of their entire lives. Silently they made their way through the sights, sounds, and smells, overawed.

"I wonder that they even need weapons," Shammah ventured at last. "If I saw this coming toward me, I would simply run away."

"I might yet," Abinadab suggested, laughing but not entirely in jest.

"Stay a minute, brothers," Eliab said, raising a hand. "We are a band of country bumpkins, and there is no concealing that. Still we need not confirm it. Close your mouths, pick your chins up off your chests, and hold your heads up like the sons of Jesse, who helped choose the king we come to serve. Bethlehem is Damascus compared to the campsite that was Gibeah before Saul was king."

"Damascus?" Joab repeated, overhearing and roaring with laughter. He shared his mirth with the officer who walked at his side.

"Joab, I am sorry," Eliab said, dismounting quickly and taking a posture of deference toward his nephew. "I meant no disrespect. I was only encouraging my brothers to be proud of whose sons they are in the face of this, this overwhelming place. We do not want to disgrace you."

"Fear not," the officer answered with great good cheer. "All here are from humble hearths and rustic villages—including the king, as you wisely point out. Individually we are at the mercy of the powers that surround us. But this—" the officer proclaimed, throwing his arms wide to include the vast force surrounding them. "This is what we can be when we come together as a nation."

"Thank you, sir," Eliab said with a respectful incline of his head to the young officer. "Are you one of Joab's men?"

"I am indeed," the officer laughed. "Or at least, I hope I may count myself as such."

"Eliab," Joab said, both laughing and blushing. "This is Prince Jonathan."

"Oh, my Lord," Eliab said, falling to one knee in awe and admiration. "It is an honor to meet a man of such legend."

"Well met, good friend," Jonathan said, clasping Eliab's hand and pulling him to his feet.

"This is my cousin, or rather in truth, my uncle, Eliab," Joab said, rushing to explain and introduce them, as much to avoid any further embarrassment as to keep common courtesy. "These are his brothers, my uncles Shammah and Abinadab, all sons of Jesse of Bethlehem."

The two brothers scrambled down off their mules to get their heads below their prince's.

"Ah yes." Jonathan nodded warmly. "A fine man, Jesse. My father speaks well and often of Jesse of Bethlehem and his support. One of our bravest new men is from Bethlehem. He has only just joined us this season and already he has proved his mettle and resolve in battle. You would do well to look him up. Perhaps he can help you to make as good a start of it. You could certainly do no better than to have such a man at your back. Perhaps you know Micah. His father's name escapes me at the just now."

"Perhaps," Eliab nodded, reeling at the thought that a friend of David's could be his better. "We have an old family friend whose name is Micah."

"It is the same Micah." Joab nodded in agreement with Eliab's unspoken thought. "Though old is not really the word to describe him."

"Excellent," Jonathan said enthusiastically. "Joab, we will conclude our business later. You must conduct these men to their confederate with haste. We will soon march on Amalek. You would do well to follow in such footsteps as Micah's for your first battle. It will help you, getting started, to take the lead from his experience. We await only word from the Kenites of their evacuation before we move on the city. It is an honor to serve at the side of the sons of Jesse," Jonathan said, striking his chest in salute as he turned and walked briskly away. "Joab, I leave you to help make your uncles ready."

"Yes, sir," Joab said, striking his chest and encouraging the others, still dumbstruck at meeting the prince, to do the same.

"Perhaps we can write 'rube' with ashes on our foreheads," Abinadab suggested, climbing back onto his mule.

"Be easy with yourselves, brothers," Joab said, taking the reins of Eliab's mount and leading the group toward where he knew Micah and others from Bethlehem to be encamped. "I find that silence serves me best in this strange place."

"Don't sell yourself short," Eliab chided. "The prince was walking with you as your equal."

"Such is his way." Joab shrugged modestly. "But I am from Bethlehem too, don't forget. I was new here once. I do have to say, our ranks have never been so swollen as this. The story of the prince routing the Philistines with only a bow and the word of God has inspired many to believe in the destiny that the seers have been prophesying since Moses crossed the Sinai. Now that we're invincible, what's to fear?"

"It's true," Abinadab said, nodding. "I know of more than five men from home who were skeptical of the king's ambitions just last Rosh Hashanah. All are now training to come and join in."

"Good thing we were already in training to come this spring." Eliab chuckled. "Though I guess people will think us opportunists, and well we might be, but this way we can lose ourselves in the crowd."

"Speaking of lost, where have you been?" Joab asked, smacking the flank of Shammah's mule and giving him a start. "I've worried all the sentries till they hate to see me coming, asking after you and warning of your arrival. We didn't know whether to send out a search party or take up a collection for your ransom."

"We got a rough start." Eliab snorted, remembering. "I thought David was going to lock us all in the pantry and make us eat naught but grain for supper. He was vexed that we were leaving and taking his best bondsmen to come and tend our camp and horses."

"I'll bet," Joab said, laughing. "Well, you have only the fury of the Amalekites to face here."

"Eliab ben Jesse," a youthful voice cried out playfully. "Joab said you were coming, but I thought sure your mother had changed your mind and enticed you to remain at home to spend your father's shekels."

"Ah, Micah," Eliab said, smirking. He pulled his mule up to a halt. "Still the impudent young cur who insinuated himself into our family, I see. I hear from the prince that you've made quite a name for yourself already. Should I tell him some of the names you made for yourself back home?"

"Well, it's true I don't have my father's name to ride in on, so I've had to make one for myself," Micah said, grasping Eliab's wrist heartily in greeting.

"Perhaps one day when you find out who your father is, you'll have a name worth repeating," Eliab said, clapping Micah painfully on the shoulder.

The others began to clear off, and the bondsmen to unload, as everyone made room for what they assumed was coming between the two young titans.

"You two have not come all this way to fight with each other," Joab said sternly. "Let's have no more of this, even if it is only in jest. Eliab, Micah is your senior here. I'm sure he has much to teach you."

"You'll be surprised how much," Micah baited.

"Micah," Joab said, turning on him and bringing him up short. "You have no formal training and could learn a lot from Eliab and his brothers."

"Oh, I doubt it," Eliab said nastily.

"We'll see how smug you are once you've tasted your first battle," Micah said. His lips went white as he pressed them together, no longer amused by Eliab's refusal to give him any of his due.

"You seem pretty smug to me," Eliab said with a shrug.

"You can't stand it, can you?" Micah snorted, giving Eliab's shoulder a provocative shove. "You can't bear the thought that I might be your equal, let alone your better."

"Little boy, I assure you no such thought has ever occurred to me," Eliab said, patting Micah on the head.

"Little boy?" Micah answered him contemptuously, lowering his voice and stepping in so that their noses almost met. "I'm as tall as you and better equipped to be a man." He grabbed himself suggestively between the legs. "If you don't believe me, ask your pretty little brother."

Like a strike of summer lightning, Eliab was on him. The dust clouds rose. Joab rushed to separate the two. The crowd closed in to enjoy the spectacle. It promised to be a close match until the trumpets sounded.

"Joab, the prince bids you come," a young soldier said, rushing to them. "The Amalekites are on the move and will attack before midday. The time is now."

"Tell the prince I am there," Joab said, yanking at Eliab and Micah's belts. "You two need to save this rage for the enemy. Later in the tent, you boys can lift your robes to compare. For now there are real battles to be fought and the true measure of men to be taken. So cover your feet. Get ready for a battle, and don't make me ashamed to call you kinsmen. Eliab, Micah will bring you to me when you are ready."

Chastened by the rebuke and the impending gravity of the occasion, the two slunk back. Joab took his leave, disappearing into the swirling crowd.

"Get your armor and your weapons together and meet me here," Micah said over his shoulder as he ran for his own tent.

Panicked and terrified, the three brothers struggled to unpack and to arm for battle at the same time. Around them the constant din of 200,000 men and their seconds grew to a roar. Trumpets sounded. Orders were shouted in what seemed chaos. The uninitiated trio felt smaller, more boys and bumpkins than ever.

"Ready?" Micah demanded. He swept past without waiting for a reply. "This way."

"Make camp," Eliab shouted to the bondsmen. He and his brothers turned and ran to keep up.

The men of Amalek clearly knew what awaited them and preferred to die on the battlefield than be slain in their beds. The news of King Saul's vengeance had preceded their arrival. Vastly outnumbered and outarmed, they threw themselves against King Saul's line and were laid waste, almost by their own hand.

Eliab and his brothers were steeled by their first trial in battle as they advanced with the king's forces into the city. They were sickened by the slaughter, cutting down row after row of the charging Amalekites. They advanced their line easily into the city, their only obstacle the bodies they were forced to step over.

Micah had indeed shown his mettle. The corps with whom they fought got separated from the larger force. They quickly found themselves surrounded and would have been overwhelmed but for Micah's encouragement that they fight back-to-back. They held without losing a man until the main body of the army caught up, crushing the Amalekites between. Eliab was silenced in his dismissal.

"We are victorious," he said to Micah as they marched, their differences forgotten.

"We have only begun," Micah sneered at Eliab's greenness. "The true test of your stomach for war is now to come. We'll see what you're made of— or maybe just what you ate this morning."

Nothing that Micah or Joab said or did could have prepared the brothers for what came next. No lesson from their fight masters included any insight into the horror that followed on the heels of what had seemed like victory in the battlefield. On orders from the king, in keeping with his mission from the Lord, the great army took to the streets of Amalek, slaughtering all that they found there—be it woman or child or ox. No life was to be left, no trace of the Amalekites to remain. Every structure was put to the torch; every vestige of the city and its people was to be obliterated from the valley.

Eliab and his brothers found themselves doing things of which they would never speak even with one another. Their supper-table bravado and vaunting of war was gone. They became soldiers. They understood that the romantic talk of battle and bravery was but the conceit of youth and nothing to do with the true work of war.

Separated from Micah, they made their way through the streets of the city, covered in blood and ash and gore from the travesty they had helped impress on Amalek. By the time the blessed horns blew and the cry went up that the battle was at end, all three had left the contents of their stomachs far behind. It would be a long time before thoughts of food would again come to them pleasantly.

Criers passed through the ranks with word that the Amalekite King Agag had surrendered to King Saul. Victory was undisputed. Spoils could be taken and the killing could stop. Thoughts of plunder had no appeal to the sons of Jesse. They understood the bleak, hollow look on the faces of the soldiers they had seen when they first arrived at camp.

Equally jarring was how sanguine Micah had been, earning his place in such a brutal campaign.

Dazed and splashed with the blood of soldiers and innocents alike, Eliab walked down the small winding street. The burning, empty homes had burgeoned with life only a morning before their arrival. He took care to step over the hacked bodies of those who had lived under those fallen and flaming roofs.

They look so like us, Eliab thought. His heart was wrenched by the thought of such a fate befalling the family he'd left back in Bethlehem. He knew that these same people had been raiding the villages of southern Judah. That they had wrought a similar fate on those of his countrymen who had lived there. He was at once thankful that his family was safe and horrified at the cost exacted for their safety.

A cry roused him from his waking nightmare. He awoke to find himself borne down upon by a man with a spear. He charged at Eliab from the smoldering wreckage of one of the ruined homes.

Eliab felt as though he moved underwater. He tried to raise his shield, too late to deflect the javelin's tip before it pierced him. His own death rose up before him, a certainty, fallen in his first battle. In an instant the sadness of what he would leave behind swept over him, even as he struggled to defend himself against the inevitable mortal blow.

Then the man was lying dead on the stones at Eliab's feet and Eliab was alive. Micah pressed his foot on the throat of the still-twitching corpse as he struggled to pull his sword free from the man's chest where it was lodged. Abinadab and Shammah were just as suddenly at his side. Relieved, they were filled with praise for Micah's quick thinking and reflexive action on their brother's behalf.

"I am alive but for you Micah," Eliab said, extending his hand. "I am your servant and your foot soldier, sir. It is an honor to follow you into battle."

It was as though Eliab saw Micah with new eyes. Humbled, he thought of his own words to David: *You mistake what it is to be a man.* He wondered if he too had missed the mark.

"Eliab," Micah said simply. A smile spread across his face. He abandoned his sword where it remained wedged between the ribs of the fallen Amalekite. Here at last was the respect he'd sought from the men of the house of Jesse and their like, all his life. Here on the battlefield, all men were equal at last. Here a man's merit was his true worth—not the name of his father, the count of his flock, or the measure of his lands.

No one saw the boy as he emerged from the same house from which Eliab's attacker had appeared. He seemed too young for battle. His tears for the father he'd only just watched slain before him washed tracks in the soot that stained his face. Silent but for the catch in his breath, the boy stole across the yard from the burned remains of the house where he had hidden from his father's murderers.

Eliab only saw a boy, when he looked up from where he stood holding Micah's wrist in his hand as Micah clasped his own. He did not see the revenge that was the only true progeny born of the violence of war. Eliab did not see the dagger when the boy pulled it from the folds of his tattered and muddy robes. None of the brothers noticed the knife until the boy thrust it into the back of his father's killer. The boy fled, leaving his dagger where he had planted it. Micah fell forward, caught by the hand he had extended to take Eliab's. Kept from falling into the dust by the firm grip of the man whose life he'd only just saved.

"Micah," Eliab cried out, catching Micah in his arms. "Abinadab, get his sword and follow me back to camp. Shammah, run ahead and see to his care."

"Save your strength," Micah moaned into Eliab's ear. "It is done."

"Don't say that, Micah," Eliab said running as best he could as he carried the full weight of the other man over his shoulder.

The distance back to the line seemed much farther than it would have had the task been less urgent. The litter bearers were carrying the fallen back to carts already laden with bodies. Others heaped the bodies of enemy casualties onto the huge fires they fueled.

"We need help," Eliab cried out. "He is wounded."

"Over here," Shammah called to Eliab from under a nearby awning. Hastily erected, the goatskin shelter offered little more than shade in which to tend to the injured and make the dying more comfortable. Micah was not yet gone as the three brothers settled him onto a litter. Shammah tried to get the attention of those skilled at helping the wounded, as Eliab and Abinadab stayed with Micah.

"Eliab," Micah said, his voice a whisper.

"Yes, Micah, what can I get for you?" Eliab asked, drawing nearer, his ear next to the boy's mouth.

"I ask your forgiveness," Micah managed hoarsely.

"You saved my life," Eliab said, shaking his head. "What would I have to forgive you?"

"I spoke crudely of your brother, and I was wrong to do that." Micah gasped out the words, fighting to stay conscious long enough to speak them.

"Men speak such in jest and with each other," Eliab said, waving it off. "It is nothing."

"David is more to me than my life. I would not have him know that I spoke so of him. It hurts me that you, his brother, know," Micah said, finding strength in his resolve. "Here," he said, reaching up and pulling the sling from under his tunic. "This is the last gift that your beautiful brother ever gave me. Return it to him for me."

"You shall do that yourself, though I know he will not take it," Eliab said, trying to refuse the offer in an effort to encourage Micah, unable to accept what Micah knew was inevitable.

"Tell David that it was not as lucky for me as it was for him. He should never part with it," Micah said, placing Eliab's hand on the sling, too weak to remove it himself. "Let him know that it gave me great comfort to feel him next to my heart during the time we have been parted. Tell him that the only disappointment I feel now is that I know I will not see his face, hear his voice, kiss his lips again."

There was a small gasp that Eliab took to be Micah taking a breath, but there was no more. As he drew back to look, he saw the life leave Micah's eyes. He held the boy's body next to him, refusing to let him go. It was as though he held his brother David in his arms. It was a thought he could not bear. For the first time in his life, Eliab wondered if the cost of battle was worth the gain. It was on that day that Eliab became a man.

And Eliab his eldest brother heard when he spake unto the men; and Eliab's anger was kindled against David, and he said, Why camest thou down hither? and with whom hast thou left those few sheep in the wilderness? I know thy pride, and the naughtiness of thine heart; for thou art come down that thou mightest see the battle.

1 Samuel 17:28

ELIAB STILL felt Micah's lifeless body against him as he looked down upon David standing against Goliath that morning in the valley of Elah, years later. He despaired to see his beloved youngest brother fallen, unable to rise and run as the giant closed on him. Though the thought of facing the great Philistine warrior turned his guts to water, Eliab wished with all his heart that he could trade places, take the blow, die in his brother's place.

Eliab knew in his heart that David, in his faith and his courage, was more a man than he would ever be. He braced to witness his brother give his life in such a selfless cause.

Was this the will of God? As he had at Micah's side, Eliab again felt small and helpless in the face of a world so vast and unexplainable. He needed the God of Abraham to allow him the courage to stand upright in the light of day. As he had when he bid farewell to Micah, Eliab learned from David what it was to be a man.

Chapter Four
The Book of Samuel

But the Lord said unto Samuel, Look not on his countenance, or on the height of his stature... for the Lord seeth not as man seeth; for man looketh on the outward appearance, but the Lord looketh on the heart.

1 Samuel 16:7

"How LONG, O Lord? Will you forget me forever? How long will you hide your face from me? How long must I wrestle with my thoughts and every day have sorrow in my heart?"

David's voice echoed mournfully through the hills above his father's house. Following his brothers' return from King Saul's legions with their news of triumph and tragedy, he took refuge in the hills.

"His last words were of you," Eliab had said, his voice breaking. He held out Micah's sling to David. No more needed to be said.

The full impact of the return of the token struck David as swiftly as death. He rubbed the smooth enamel of the lion's fang against his thumb and tried to understand that he would never see Micah again.

He fled first from the company of his family. He refused to participate in the Passover celebration. He remained in his room as those he loved celebrated, with special significance, the traditional rites venerating their escape from slavery to the promise and prosperity of their little land at the crossroads of the world. He could see no freedom and feel no promise.

Nitzevet ached for her son, unable fully to understand his loss, yet longing to bring him comfort for it. Though she tried to tempt him with familiar pleasures, she was unable to rouse David from his lethargy. He could not be coerced into his favorite dice game, tau. He showed no interest in the rituals and ceremonies in which he had always taken as much delight in preparing as participating.

"Why should I celebrate a God who cares so little for my happiness?" David scoffed, refusing even to get out of bed.

Nitzevet urged his brothers to try. But where Nitzevet's attempts merely failed, their halfhearted ploys were disastrous, yielding more fights and hurt feelings than solutions. Nethanel became so convinced by David's sad and faithless arguments in favor of the hopelessness and futility of life, he too refused to partake in the retelling of the story at the Seder table. Ozem and Shemia got into such a bitter fight with Raddai over David's reaction to Micah dying a hero's death that none of the three was speaking to the other two. They sat silent around the table until called upon to speak their part.

Those returning from the battle, which had added such special meaning to that year's Passover, had their own demons to face.

Abinadab had left a girl behind in the city. He was too busy seeking his own comfort in their reunion, after the rigors and horrors of battle, to attempt to wrest David from his wallow of sadness. He understood David's remorse. Shammah hardly spoke. He joined in the official ceremonies of family as a silent supplicant. Though seated at the table, he was not yet home from the war. Without taking leave of their company, he slipped away again and again to another place as though entranced by music from another room.

Eliab tried as earnestly as possible to face David. Though he had bravely faced his own death, his nerve took him only as far as his youngest brother's door. Once there, he was always overcome by his own fears of David's demise. He saw his little brother dying in his arms in Micah's place. He stole away from David's door silently, unable to face either the living brother he loved so dearly or the thought of losing him.

Jesse simply held David and allowed him to cry. He was unable to find words of comfort to speak.

David was grateful for his silence.

In was only in David's loss of Micah that his family understood the truth of what had been between the two adventurous boys. Their love was not uncommon. Though with most boys it passed as they became men, many kept youthful lovers as one might a concubine. Eunuchs were as popular as courtesans in the harems of royal courts, and the tradition of warrior-lovers stretched back farther than the ancient tales of Gilgamesh.

His family's surprise at the strength and depth of the bond between the two was more that they had not known. And not knowing, they did not know how to speak of it to David. The two had always seemed as brothers. How to comfort David for the loss of a lover he had never named? Their efforts, however well intentioned, only made it worse.

At last the company of his family became more torture than cure. David escaped them. He returned to the mountainside shepherd's hovel to seek comfort in his music, the silence of the black nights, and the wordless companionship of Asad and their charges.

"*Look on me and answer, O Lord my God. Give light to my eyes, or I will sleep in death,*" David's newest and oft-repeated psalm yearned plaintively to a God who could not seem to hear his prayers.

David's dreams were at end. All he had hoped and planned for his life was buried with Micah in the wild and distant Negev. There was nothing for him but to stay on, one of the indentured servants of the sprawling estate. He would trade one master for the next at his father's death, tending the fields, the orchards, and the flocks on behalf of his brother and his brother's children. Until such day as his blood would serve as nourishment for the earth, he would devote his body and his life to the cold indifferent land. His existence would mean no more or less than any of the others who labored beside him.

When he dared, he dreamed of the time that had still been possible only a few days before. Serving at Micah's side, conquering the world, following his beloved leader in the grand adventure of life. Who would he follow now? Where would his life take him but from harvest to harvest?

"My soul is in anguish. How long, O Lord, how long?"

And Samuel said, How can I go? if Saul hear it, he will kill me. And the Lord said, Take an heifer with thee, and say, I am come to sacrifice to the Lord. And call Jesse to the sacrifice, and I will shew thee what thou shalt do: and thou shalt anoint unto me him whom I name unto thee.

1 Samuel 16:2

SAMUEL AWOKE with a start. He listened intently in the silent darkness of his rooms in the temple at Ramah. Had he heard someone crying out to him?

It was not the first time the high priest had awakened with such a feeling. The sacred shrines at Shiloh and then at Ramah were the only homes he'd ever known. His mother had offered him in service to God as thanksgiving for her own fertility.

Raised as a servant to the great judge Eli, Samuel's future changed one night in his youth. He awakened hearing his name called. He had rushed to the bedside of Eli to hear his master's bidding. The priest was sound asleep and less than spiritual in his feeling toward being awakened in the night by his young apprentice. Dismissing Samuel, the old man sent him back to his own bed.

Twice more Samuel came to his master, certain he had heard his name called, and twice more Eli sent him back to bed. On the third occasion, Eli realized that Samuel might be awakening as a prophet, able to hear the call of the God of Israel. He advised his young charge to remain in bed the next time he heard his name and answer the Lord.

Just as he had done on that night in his room in Shiloh so many years before, Samuel sat up, hearing his name called, and answered.

"Speak, Lord, for your servant is listening."

Samuel knew his own life was in danger. He had rebuked the authority of his king. King Saul had killed scores of men without flinching in his absolute faith in his mission. What difference would the neck of one more old man make?

Samuel wondered if he had chosen his own executioner when he chose Saul as king. In so doing, he had made it clear that he alone had the power to anoint Saul's replacement. Samuel's death would serve to secure the succession of Saul's line. It was a fact lost on neither man and deeply unsettling to both, though for vastly different reasons.

A peace settled over the old priest as he listened, alone in the stillness. As he heard a voice that no one else in the room would have heard, Samuel felt at ease.

"Jesse," he said aloud, nodding. A smile spread across his face.

He arose without lighting the lamp and made his way easily in the darkness. He called for his serving man to make ready for their journey.

"Select the finest heifer from the sacred herd. We will make sacrifice in Bethlehem so that the king's spies may find a purpose in our journey that is easier for the king to hear," Samuel explained to the confused and startled man, who wondered only why they were making ready for a journey in the middle of the night. The acolyte had spent enough time serving Samuel not to bother trying to decipher the old man's meanings. He listened only for his instructions and followed them to the letter. *The king's spies?* he thought, chuckling to himself as he stumbled through the shadows from the stable to make ready for their trip—unaware that those spies were near enough to hear him had he spoken aloud.

Samuel needed no more sleep. His way lay clear before him. He hardly knew his destination, but he knew his purpose.

He took down the sacred horn. Fitted with gold at its tip and sealed with a hinged golden lid at the opposite end, it was worked and encrusted with crystals and stones cut to sparkle in the light. He had used the horn only once before, to anoint King Saul. He hummed the prayers as he filled the horn with blessed and scented oil from the jar on the altar.

As he bathed and dressed for the journey, Samuel sang as though he was in the temple on a holy day. Certainty made the journey before him a chance to enjoy the scenery along the way rather than searching the horizon for his happiness.

The sun rose on his small party as they departed. They followed the Road of the Patriarchs as it wound along the ridge of the mountains of Ephraim and Judah, from Samuel's home in Ramah, straight and true to the gates of Bethlehem.

Once underway, their destination certain, Samuel paused to reflect on the winding path that had brought him and all of Israel to this destiny.

Because thou hast rejected the word of the Lord, he hath also rejected thee from being king.

1 Samuel 15:23

THE BATTLE of wills between Samuel and the king had begun almost without either man noticing. Saul, a mule trader from an insignificant village, had been a reluctant king at first. Without the clarity of the still small voice, Samuel would not have believed it himself. Saul, who was not privy to Samuel's most intimate counsel, did not believe it. It had required that Samuel use his gifts of prophecy like a vulgar market performer. He had first to convince Saul of his powers of divination, that he might have faith in the priest's claims on behalf of their shared God. Only then had Saul been willing to allow Samuel to choose him, publicly, as the king demanded by all the people of the tribes of Israel.

Using their gifts, the two men began to build a country where none had existed before. Saul had a surprising talent for military strategy and for leading men. As with all great leaders, he could think three moves ahead and guide men to their destinies by inspiring the best and the worst in them. Samuel brought his divine sight to bear on the decisions of statecraft and warfare. They made the armies of Saul a dreaded and undefeated force for a score of years and ten and made Israel profitable and formidable.

At first Saul had depended on Samuel for insight and guidance, as Samuel depended on the God only he could hear. Samuel, though he was reluctant to acknowledge it, was dependent on Saul's mule-trader skill with people and his charismatic leadership, both in the field and in their new capital of Gibeah.

Samuel laid out the will of God as it was communicated to him from on high. Saul put those divine visions into action and made them a reality.

Over time, as men do, and encouraged by the flattery of others, both forgot God's grace. They came, more and more, to believe in their own personal greatness as the explanation for their success. The oversight that undid them was to miss the greatest gift God had given either man: each other.

Together they had forged a new nation from naught but the dust of Canaan. Pride drove them apart.

Saul sought the autonomy of being king. Though he was dependent on Samuel and his visions and prophecies, Saul was swayed by his own popularity. He fell in love with the growing worship of his seemingly invincible reign. He came to believe in the songs sung about him. He took to heart the stories told of him around the fires.

People turned from Samuel and his God, his traditions and his worship, in favor of their own power, as reflected to them in their shining king. The more they slipped away, the more Samuel tried to tighten his grasp on the king. He had felt choosing a king was a mistake. He had foreseen this turning from the authority of God. What he had not foreseen was his own fear of the people turning from him as God's representative. The more he tried to assert himself, he seemed less God's messenger and more a man trying to take power for himself.

Saul was torn between two forces. His faith was strong, but the needs of his countrymen were real, tangible, and growing.

There were many small skirmishes and border disputes between the two as each sought to assert his own authority. The battle lines were drawn, and the first open aggression between the two great men came just after Yom Kippur, the fall before Micah joined the king's army.

Following a campaign of raids on a series of the villages of Israel, the Philistine armies were massing at Micmash, threatening to strike at the very heart of all that the two had given their lives to build. Saul took his armies to Gilgal to face them. There he awaited Samuel. The priest was to bring the Ark of the Covenant from the Yom Kippur ceremonies to the valley between Micmash and Gilgal. There, the ark would be carried before the army of Israel into the battle against the Philistines.

Samuel was not at all certain of the battle. It had been forced on them by the Philistines. He reluctantly agreed to meet Saul at Gilgal, to bring the ark, and to make sacrifice before the battle. In this much Samuel could see his way forward with the divine sight, but no further. As was his practice, he sought the will of his God at Naoith, the source of his most restorative spiritual practice. There he dared call the name of Yahweh as he had at Yom Kippur, seeking divine guidance. For days he prayed and fasted, but no sight came to him. He was seven days late by the time he emerged from Naoith and found his way to Saul's camp at Gilgal.

Troubled by the silence that his entreaties to God had yielded, he despaired when he arrived at camp to find that Saul had made the sacrifice already. The visions that Samuel had sought at Naoith rushed up to meet him, black with death and failure.

"Saul, what have you done?" Samuel railed as his party drew near to the king.

Attacked in front of the men he had sought to rally when they despaired of Samuel's arrival and God's blessing, Saul answered sternly and with the royalty learned in years of ruling.

For the first time, Samuel denounced his beloved Saul, speaking the words of his inner voice even as he heard them, unaware of their full implication and meaning until he had finished speaking. "Now your kingdom will not endure; the Lord has sought out a man after his own heart and appointed him leader of his people, because you have not kept the Lord's command."

Both men stood shocked by Samuel's words. Each wished the judge could take them back. Both knew that their days of ruling together were at end.

When Saul answered him in kind, Samuel struck him, for he knew in his heart that Saul was no longer his king, though he did not know more.

Leaving the ark to Saul with the curse of his denunciation, Samuel left the king and his troops to their fate. He returned to Gibeah to await the news of the king's defeat.

Word of Prince Jonathan's miraculous victory, through the intervention of the God of Israel, shocked Samuel to his core and threatened to destroy everything he believed.

"Why do you mock me?" Samuel wept and cried out to the Lord when he heard the news of the battle. Tearing at his robe, he fell to the dirt, smearing himself with the soil like a man in mourning.

Samuel's rage was born from years of confusion and frustration.

Forsaken by his own mother as a fertility offering to the priest at Shiloh, he had lived as little more than an indentured servant at the temple there, a slave to the priest Eli and his corrupt and wicked sons. After years of humble servitude, he had risen to power only at the demise of those sons. Perhaps this explained the series of personal sacrifices that had been his life. Perhaps his mother had offered him up for greatness.

Given his chance at last, he showed himself to be up to the challenge. He led his people to victories at Mizpah and Beth Car and fancied that maybe his fate was to be the tribe's next great judge.

Still the people had cried out for a king. The Lord answered, passing over Samuel and putting his power into the hands of a rude and uneducated Benjamite. Samuel became the new king's proclaimer and his servant, Saul's holy messenger.

The visions that began when the Lord first called Samuel as a boy had led him to be the servant of yet another man.

When the people first demanded a king to make Israel like other nations, Samuel scolded the elders who levied the request.

"To ask for a king is to turn your back on God's rule," Samuel protested.

Most saw his protestations, even then, as an attempt to maintain his own power. Samuel was certain of the Lord's voice and, through his unfailing guidance, Samuel had helped to move the tribes of Israel ever closer to their dreams of nationhood and sovereignty over all of Canaan.

An old man by the day of the battle at Gilgal, Samuel had followed the infallible voice in his heart. From the day he was led to choose Saul as king on the Lord's behalf, to guiding his king in each victory, Samuel had been led true by his faith in the voice of the God of his fathers.

With the news of victory, Samuel's certainty crumbled. As he looked back on that day, raging at Saul at Gilgal, he feared it had been his vanity and not the Lord's word. His late arrival, his own wounded pride and childish resentment of Saul's growing popularity with the people, was it God's will or his pride that guided his actions? The victory over the Philistines, despite his pronouncements of doom, called his ability as a prophet into question in the eyes of the nation. Worse, it brought doubt upon their God.

"Oh Lord, forgive me for being a man." Samuel wept at the altar in the temple he had built near his true family home at Ramah. He feared he'd lost what influence he had with the king and forsaken his God in his anger. Sobs of grief racked Samuel's body. He made sacrifice in penance for his blasphemy and lay prostrate in the blood before the altar.

"Surely I have taken your name in vain by bearing false witness against your chosen king as I claimed to speak for you," he gasped. "Take me if it is your will. Bring Saul a better and truer counselor than me, but let no one but me suffer for my treachery."

Then, as it always happened, a great peace came over him. He saw and understood how those before him had been similarly destroyed by the same gift of sight that had been given him. He understood that he was but a man and could not understand the Lord's will no matter how deeply he might be allowed to gaze into tomorrow. And he knew he was forgiven. He saw the wisdom in keeping the domain of God in the temple and the domain of men in the palace, that neither would become too careless of the true source of all power. He glimpsed again the Lord's divine plan.

"Help me to be a better man," Samuel said, his sobs replaced with tears of joy.

It was a humbled Samuel who returned to Saul.

He sought to do the will of the God he served as he sought the king's rapprochement.

The two men again met when Saul made his annual pilgrimage to Ramah to make a thanksgiving sacrifice for his summer victories and the yoreh harvest, the last David and Micah would celebrate together.

A breathless tension preceded their meeting. Their parting at Gilgal had been fearsome to all who beheld it or heard the story repeated by those who had. Theirs was the struggle of the country made flesh. The tribes of Israel were a people united by their faith. But their faith had only taken them so far. Just as it had taken Moses to lead them out of Egypt and into Canaan, it had taken a king to help them find the answers to their prayers.

If this balance could not be achieved by these two men, how was the dream of a nation, united by its faith in one god, to be made whole?

And so it was that not only were king and priest anxious of their reunion, but so too were those who looked to both men to lead them.

After Gilgal, Samuel regained his footing as God's servant and recommitted himself to that service. But the battle at Gilgal had made Saul only too aware of his own mortality. Prince Jonathan's victory had offered Saul the opportunity to end the Philistines and wipe them from Canaan. But without Samuel's sight, he could not decide which path was best and missed the opportunity God had placed in his hands.

As Saul approached the great stone of sacrifice before the temple, Samuel in his finest linen came from behind the altar and fell on his knees before the king.

"Forgive me, my king," Samuel asked reverently. "My pride has made me forget my duty to you and to God."

Saul lifted the old man up in his mighty grasp, a powerful hand on each of Samuel's shoulders. Without a word he embraced the old priest, relieved and thankful to have Samuel's counsel restored. It was as though God had returned to his table.

The cheering of those in the square of Ramah was the perfect expression of the joy and relief both men felt.

Each man saw in the other the gift that God had given. For a time they saw God's wisdom in dividing power between them. Saul returned to the palace at Gibeah for the winter, and Samuel spent his days awaiting the will of his God and his king.

The rainy season came. No battles or raids arose to challenge their return to cordiality. Spring followed. The Amalekite raids began in the south. The plague of invaders burned their villages and slaughtered the men, women, and children of Israel in their homes. Saul was called on to act. As was their custom, he sought Samuel's council as he prepared for campaign.

In answer to the king, Samuel spent his time in prayer and fasting. He sought the will of God and the wisest course for his king and his people.

God's answer to Samuel's prayers was swift and severe. He was sickened by the visions of herem he saw and feared that they were born not of his God but of his rage at those who slaughtered his people. Again he petitioned God. His visions in answer were more disturbing still, for he was shown what the future held should the terrible commands of his first visions not be realized. With a heavy but certain heart, the priest carried God's words to Saul on the eve of the battle that took Micah from David for all time.

God decreed to Samuel that the Amalekites be punished, not only for the raids, but because they had waylaid the children of Israel as they escaped from Egypt and Pharaoh. That punishment was to be severe.

"Go now, attack the Amalekites and destroy everything that belongs to them," Samuel told Saul and his most trusted advisors. "Do not spare them; put to death men and women, children and infants, cattle and sheep, camels and donkeys. So says the Lord who sent me to anoint you king over his people, Israel."

Samuel had been clear. He had taken the very word of God to Saul as it had been revealed to him. He fought to keep his own pride and to convey only what had been imparted that he might serve his God, his king, and his country; that he might be a better man.

Still, he was a man. When he returned to Saul's tent on the day of victory, he found the Amalekite king very much alive and the king feasting on the flesh of Amalekite cattle he had been commanded to destroy. Samuel was blinded by both rage and grief.

"Samuel," Saul called, raising his goblet in salute. "Author of our victory."

Samuel struck the goblet from the king's hand, dashing the wine into Saul's face. The celebrants were stunned silent, their goblets still raised in the priest's honor.

Samuel too was frozen in his rage, unable to speak or to act. His heart broke as he saw again the consequences he had been shown. He knew that his vision was the truth of not only Saul's future but his own. A king cannot be king and ruled by the visions of his priest. And God cannot rule man through his priest, no matter how clear his word.

In one final, desperate act to avert the future that had been revealed to him, he tore the sword from Saul's scabbard. Goblets tumbled into the dust as those nearest the king reached for their blades. Before any might act, Samuel turned on the Amalekite king and struck his head from his shoulders.

Even as the blood fell upon him, Samuel knew it would do no good. The future had been cast, and neither he nor anyone else could avert it. Weak with despair, he dropped the sword and fell to his knees, facing the tent of stunned faces. His eyes met Saul's.

"The Lord now turns from you. He no longer chooses you as king." Samuel's final words to his king and his friend broke both their hearts and spirits. He rose and, with a low bow, left Saul's tent, never to return.

Trembling with rage and fear, Samuel was certain his head would be cleft from his shoulders before he left the king's camp. Yet, to his astonishment, it remained where God had placed it. All during the winter that followed, Samuel prayed for God's guidance as he watched over his shoulder for Saul's spies and assassins. There at Ramah, he awaited spring and either the word of God or the will of man, never once guessing that his destiny lay in Bethlehem.

Peaceably: I am come to sacrifice unto the Lord: sanctify yourselves, and come with me to the sacrifice. And he sanctified Jesse and his sons, and called them to the sacrifice.

1 Samuel 16:5

ABINADAB WAS in fine spirits. The horror of the battle of Amalek was briefly forgotten, lost in the arms of Sarah. The daughter of an Ephraimite merchant who lived in Bethlehem with his family, she was the woman Abinadab intended for his own. He met Sarah first when both were children and had little use for one another. They met again many years later when youth was not gone but burned brighter as it neared its end.

By chance he saw her across the plaza outside his family townhouse. Concealed behind a low wall at the side of the house, he observed her in the square each day when the shadows turned eastward and the heat began to subside. By the fourth day, when he saw she had returned to the shade of the tamarisk trees near the well to drink pomegranate juice and gossip with her friends, he found courage enough to scheme.

On the pretext of gathering living water, Abinadab took an amphora across to the well. As he waited to fill the huge urn with water he did not need, he stole glances at the beautiful girl. Their eyes met. She blushed, giggled, and looked away from his hungry gaze. She spoke of him behind her hand to those with whom she shared the shade that day. The amphora was filled before Abinadab had yet managed the courage to speak to the lady. Trapped, he had no choice but to maintain his charade. It was then he discovered that the crock, when filled with water, weighed far more than he could easily lift. It was a fact for which he'd not accounted, never having fetched water before. Yet proving his nascent manhood before her would not allow him to quit the labor.

His struggle reached epic proportions. He tried tilting the urn against his shoulder but only succeeded in pouring water down his back. Efforts to get a handhold beneath the vessel proved a more efficient means of crushing his toes and fingers than of lifting the urn. His best efforts produced more laughter than results, though he did secure the attention of most everyone in the plaza that day, particularly the little knot of girls surrounding Sarah.

"Lift with your legs," suggested one of the servants waiting for his turn at the well.

Delighted with the advice, Abinadab squatted by the urn and wrapped his powerful arms around it. Though the task was unfamiliar to him and the urn unwieldy, Abinadab's training and life on a working farm had built him into a young titan, the equal of his mighty brothers and any other young man of Judah. In short, he wanted for ingenuity, not force, in his battle with the storage urn. Using his legs and the motivation of his growing embarrassment, he launched the jug briefly into the air, onto and then, sadly, over his shoulder. As quickly and with as much force as it had taken to raise it, the huge storage jar slipped from his hands. Shattering into a thousand shards, the great vessel crashed to the stone pavers that comprised the plaza, drenching and terrifying Sarah and her friends.

The laughter died. All seemed lost. Abinadab froze to the spot, unable to speak or flee.

Slowly a soggy Sarah rose and crossed to where Abinadab stood in the water line. Wordlessly she passed him. Without warning she grabbed a bucket from the hands of one of the serving girls returning from the well. Turning back, she bore down on him, emptied the bucket over Abinadab's head, and burst into laughter. The scandal of the water fight between boy and girl that ensued was the talk of the village for days after. Abinadab left the plaza soaked but with the name of Sarah's father and directions to his house managed from Sarah, before she was dragged away home by her mother's angry and protective serving woman.

Their courtship of several months had been fueled by the certain knowledge of Abinadab's imminent departure for war. The intensity of each kiss, sunset, and time together heightened their youthful spirits and their innocent understanding of love.

Their farewells when Abinadab departed to join the king's army had been thick with the sugary sentiment of youthful ballads and heroic odes to war. The intensity of their reunion was fueled by the genuine travesty of what Abinadab had witnessed in his brief time on campaign. He was only home for a short while to observe Pesach with his family, and later, with hers. He had returned to her a man aware of the fleeting and ephemeral gifts of life and love and time.

Sarah, who'd seen no more than a girl could see from the gates of the city, was overcome by her lover's passion and seriousness. In the embrace of their reunion, she found that she preferred the smooth and easy kisses of youth. Though she welcomed him home dutifully, her heart began to slip away even as her arms held him fast.

The midday meal with Sarah's family long over, Abinadab had lingered until he had been shooed from their courtyard by her mother and sent on his way. The ease of her company was still with him as he trod the dusty ridge road's twisting course north toward his family's estate and beyond.

He hardly noticed the old man and his small party as they passed him on the road into town.

"Young man?" called the elderly traveler. "Can you direct me to the house of Jesse?"

The question's aim brought Abinadab up short. His hand found his dagger in his sash. He turned to take in the source of the inquiry.

"Good day to you, father," Abinadab said formally. His eyes roamed over the ephod that the holy man wore, better suited to a holy day temple than a dusty mountain road. "Why do you seek the house of Jesse?"

"I am Samuel, judge of Ramah," the old man called, dismounting his mule with the help of his serving man. "And you are Abinadab ben Jesse, I see now. I seek to meet your family. I would ask your father to join me in making sacrifice for the grain harvest in Bethlehem."

"Most holy," Abinadab said, startled that the old man knew his name. He knelt awkwardly in the dust. "I did not recognize you at first. I have only seen you briefly and from a distance at Amalek, when you visited the king there after battle."

"A blessing upon you, boy," Samuel said, placing his hand on Abinadab's head. He left it there for a long time as he spoke. "Do you fight with the king, then?"

"It was my first battle," Abinadab said, trying to nod with the old man's hand roaming his head as if examining him for an unseen wound below the hairline.

"Not him?" Samuel said enigmatically. He removed his hand and helped the boy up. "You have other brothers?"

"Yes, there are many of us," Abinadab volunteered, not really understanding the judge, but not really expecting to. "You have passed the turning to my father's karmel. It would be my honor to lead you to my father's table, where I'm sure you will be most welcome."

"Thank you, good son," Samuel said, allowing the boy to help him back onto his mule. Nodding to his serving man, he bade the acolyte surrender the animal's lead to their new guide. "I look most forward to meeting your whole family."

"All were still there from Passover when last I left to see my beloved in town," Abinadab said, bragging, happy and proud to return home with the judge of all of Israel on a tether.

"Make haste; we have work to do before the sun sets," Samuel urged.

Jesse made seven of his sons to pass before Samuel. And Samuel said unto Jesse, The Lord hath not chosen these.
And Samuel said unto Jesse, Are here all thy children?

1 Samuel 16:10-11

"HAVE YOU no other sons?" Samuel demanded with an odd tone of irritation.

Jesse was unsure what to make of the disconcerting little man. He'd arrived only a few minutes before, explaining that he wanted Jesse to join him in making sacrifice in the city the following morning. Jesse had heartily agreed. To make sacrifice with the highest holy authority in all the tribes would deeply enhance Jesse's already august standing in the village and elevate him above even the other elders in the eyes of the community.

As soon as he gave his assent to join the old man and asked him to stay the night, Samuel demanded to see Jesse's sons, before they could pause for a mouthful of food or a cup of wine. Baffled, Jesse complied.

Samuel was delighted to see the impressive silhouette of Eliab. More striking still than Abinadab, he was a fine figure of a man, much like the king, head and shoulders above those around him. "There is a king if ever I saw one," he thought, extending his hand to take Eliab's measure. Grasping Eliab's hand, he searched his face for signs. He awaited the confirmation of the inner voice.

"A fine man," Samuel pronounced, shaking his head. "Good and true, but not the man I seek."

"You see," Abinadab said quietly to Eliab, as they stood back and watched their brothers presented to the judge. "He said something of the same thing to me on the road. Perhaps he seeks a companion? Someone to tend him at night?"

The two laughed rudely at the idea.

"You have a base mind," Eliab snorted, equally baffled by Samuel's strange behavior.

One by one Samuel dispatched each of Jesse's sons with the same praise and rejection.

"Have you no more sons?" the old man asked Jesse when the line was exhausted. His eyebrows were drawn together in worry and despair.

"Well, yes, as a matter of fact," Jesse answered, remembering to think of David as merely a son. Jesse rarely considered him in the same barn with the rest of the herd. "My youngest is in the fields tending to the sheep."

"You must fetch him to me at once," Samuel declared, striking the ground with his staff resolutely. "The future of all the tribes of Israel depends on it. We will fast until he has been brought before us."

"Yes, most holy," Jesse said, inclining his head respectfully. He was as confused as Abinadab by the man's behavior but keener to understand. "I will send a servant to summon him to us. May I make you more comfortable while we wait? Some food or perhaps something to drink?"

"I thank you for your hospitality, but I prefer to wait and meet your son before I break my fast," Samuel said, removing himself from their company. Mindless of his hosts, he knelt in prayer in the shade of a stand of trees.

Exchanging a shrug and looks of confusion with his elder sons, Jesse dispatched a servant to fetch David down to meet the judge. Mindful of their duties and with regard for the station of their guest, Jesse and his sons took up postures and at least the appearance of prayer as they awaited David's arrival and some possible explanation. The sun sank westward.

Nitzevet threw up her hands, frustrated that none would take food or drink in deference to their visitor's abstention. By the time the servant finally returned, tempers had grown with appetites. Samuel kept his place in prayer under the oaks. Jesse made his way to meet the servant, who returned running.

"Is all well?" Jesse asked, alarmed that his son was not in the servant's company.

"Master, I found young David with a flock in the meadow near the little pond where we often water the sheep," the servant said. He feared the real question, feeling he had failed.

"I see, but why is he not with you?" Jesse inquired, keeping his voice low so that his guest might not notice.

"David preferred not to come down just now," the man explained, shifting nervously from one foot to the other.

"Did you tell him that the judge of all of Israel has asked to see him?" Jesse hissed.

Eliab and Shammah had drawn nearer to discover, if not what was going on, at least when they might expect to eat.

"Yes, well, it is of note that such was the reason he refused to return," the man answered with excessive formality, staring at the ground near Jesse's feet.

Shammah let out a short blast of a laugh that caught Samuel's attention. The old man rose, helped by his staff and his serving man. The high priest began slowly to approach the little knot of men who were no longer paying attention to their esteemed caller.

"What do you mean?" Jesse demanded hotly, his brows nearing above flashing eyes.

"The young master says—you should forgive me for repeating—that he has no use for a representative of a God who would treat him so ill," the servant relayed, backing away as if to avoid a blow.

"Is your youngest coming?" Samuel asked, surprising the little cabal.

The brothers coughed and snickered.

"There seems to have been some confusion," Jesse explained, in the musical and surprisingly high-pitched voice he used to calm himself and others during heated debates over town laws and local judgments. "I will send my eldest son on this important task. Perhaps while we wait, we could share some wine. You could explain your urgent interest in my sons…."

"I am on a mission from the Lord," Samuel said as if he had not heard. "We must pray together for his guidance while we await your son's arrival."

"All right, Eliab," Jesse said, shooting his eldest son a meaningful look. "Make haste. Bring your brother here to meet the judge, that he may complete his urgent mission from the Lord."

"Yes, Father," Eliab answered with stiff words the occasion demanded but the tone of one sharing a private joke. "I shall make haste."

And Samuel said unto Jesse, Are here all thy children? And he said, There remaineth yet the youngest, and, behold, he keepeth the sheep. And Samuel said unto Jesse, Send and fetch him: for we will not sit down till he come hither.

And he sent, and brought him in. Now he was ruddy, and withal of a beautiful countenance, and goodly to look to.

1 Samuel 16:11-12

DAVID TOYED with a reed in the waters of the stream as it flowed past. The sheep drank from where it pooled nearby. Fed by a spring, the living water was always fresh and cool, even in the summer. The meadow where it was situated was actually high in the hills. It provided excellent grazing and a place to water the flocks without having to herd them down into the vale.

"David," Eliab called, spotting his brother and quickening his pace.

David did not respond or even look up from the ripples he was painting on the smooth surface of the pond. Even Asad kept his peace as if in reverence to his master's feelings.

"David, did you not hear me?" Eliab asked when he was at his brother's side.

"I did," David said without looking up from his brother's reflection beside his own in the water that had grown still before them.

"Why did you not reply?" Eliab asked. "Or come down when our father called for you?"

The hollow look on his brother's face was Eliab's only answer.

"He meant a lot to you, didn't he?" Eliab asked gently, taking a seat on the bank beside David. "More than we knew."

David only nodded.

"When he gave me the sling you had made for him and asked me to return it, he said it must be that it was only lucky for you and that you should wear it always," Eliab said, knowing not what else to say. "He said he loved it and never took it from around his neck, because it kept you close to his heart. With the last breath he took, he told me that his only regret in death was that he would not be with you again; to see your face, to hear your voice, to hold you, and to kiss your lips."

David's body trembled with sobs. His tears became a torrent as the question that had torn his heart was answered. He fell into Eliab's arms.

Eliab held his little brother for a long time, the silence broken only by sobs. They held on to one another even as David subsided. Micah's absence made them keenly aware of the gift and how easily it could be lost.

"David, there is something I must ask you," Eliab said solemnly, breaking the quiet after a very long time.

"What is that?" David answered, matching his tone. He drew back and looked into his brother's face, fearful of what he might find there, what he might want to know. His heart opened by Micah's dying declaration, he could deny nothing that Eliab might care to ask.

"Why exactly is the holy judge of all of Israel demanding to see you?"

They regarded one another for a breath or two. The flood of their laughter came in scale to the tears before it.

"I have to tell you that I am as surprised by this news as you," David said at last when their mirth had eased their pain.

"The best part was you sending word that you had nothing to say to him," Eliab exclaimed. He clapped David powerfully on the back and roared once again. "You are some piece of work, little brother. The king himself cannot refuse an audience with Samuel. But my little brother dismisses the Lord's very voice on earth like he was a presumptuous housemaid called too early with the water."

"My faith was low," David said with a sad smile. "Your words from Micah have brought me the strength I came up here seeking. I will come with you to meet him, if you wish it."

"Between us, brother, I couldn't much care less, after his dismissal of our king and our victory at Amalek," Eliab said, chuckling. "But he will not let anyone at the house eat or drink until he's met you."

"Oh, really?" David said, reaching for his scrip and emptying its contents of bread and cheese and a skin of wine onto his lap. "Then you must be most hungry, brother. Forgive me for not offering sooner."

David blew a horn to summon relief to tend the flock. As they waited, the two ended their respective fasts, Eliab's imposed by their odd company, David's by his grief. Both chuckled at their deviousness, starving their brothers while they ate their fill.

At length, when the shepherd had taken up David's watch and the two brothers had finished eating, they began their walk home, the sun sinking behind the hills.

The talk between them was easy and free as it had not been recently, if ever. There was a new appreciation between them. Both were more aware of the brevity of life and seized the opportunity of that day.

Cheers went up from their famished brothers as they came into sight of the house. Smoke began to rise from the oven chimneys as Nitzevet brought the kitchen to life and made ready to have food on the table as soon as their illustrious guest would allow.

"David," Jesse exclaimed, rushing forward. He took his son's arm and more or less dragged him across the garden to where the judge lay prone, chanting as he had most alarmingly for quite some while. "I know your brother must have told you, we have a most important visitor who has insisted on meeting you.

"Most holy," Jesse began, drawing David near to where the old man lay with his face in the dirt. "May I present my eighth and youngest son."

Samuel roused himself enough to get to his knees. But when his eyes met David's, he threw himself to the ground once again.

"Beloved one," Samuel cried out, to the amazement not only of David but his father and his brothers, the servants, and even those in Samuel's party. "David, you are a man after the Lord's own heart. He has sent me here to meet you and to anoint you.

"The horn," Samuel shouted to his man as he scrambled to his feet. Hardly pausing to brush the dirt from his robes, he embraced David as though he were one long lost and only just returned. Taking the jeweled horn from the hands of his servant, Samuel tipped the strangely scented oil onto David's golden, glowing locks and cried out. "I anoint you, David ben Jesse. You are the Lord's chosen. Through you his will shall become manifest on this earth. He will deliver your enemies to you. But you must be wise as you decide how you wish to deal with them. Such are the actions of great men judged."

All were too astonished to speak, save for Samuel. He called out to Nitzevet, who stood in the shadow of the house awaiting some development.

"A feast," he shouted, throwing his arm around David and sweeping him triumphantly toward the house. "We must celebrate David the chosen one, the beloved of the Lord."

And the Lord said, Arise, anoint him: for this is he.

1 Samuel 16:12

THEY LEARNED little more of the purpose of Samuel's visit. The following day, after leading them in sacrifice, the old priest departed for Ramah.

He had become a most entertaining and welcome guest following his strange and ambiguous behavior upon his arrival.

At the table the old man regaled his hosts with tales of being raised in the temple at Shiloh and called by the Lord in his youth. He told tales of Ibzan, the judge from Bethlehem who had thirty sons and thirty daughters and ruled the tribes of Israel for seven years.

Samuel insisted that David sit beside him at table. Despite his show of preference, if not outright affection, all he would say in answer to David's questions was that the Lord would make himself clear in his own way and his own time.

"Have faith," Samuel said genially, grinning from the good food and ample wine. "The Lord has sent me to anoint you, but your path is your own to discover. The Lord will reveal himself to you and his way will be made clear before you."

"But how will I know?" David asked, confused and fearful of the pronouncements.

"Look at that sunset," Samuel answered, pointing through the arches and across the courtyard.

"I cannot see the sun from here," David said.

"Yet you know it is there," Samuel said quizzically. "You know it is sunset?"

"Well, of course," David answered, uncertain of the question.

"How?" Samuel asked simply. "How do you know?"

"Well...." David mused as he considered it. "I can see the quality of the light reflected on the walls of the courtyard."

"So too will you see and know the signs of the Lord," Samuel said with a mischievous smile. "Have faith. The Lord made the sun to set; can he not make himself clear to you?"

CHAPTER FIVE
THE BOOK OF SAUL

Now the Lord had told Samuel in his ear a day before Saul came, saying, Tomorrow about this time I will send thee a man out of the land of Benjamin, and thou shalt anoint him to be captain over my people Israel, that he may save my people out of the hand of the Philistines.

1 Samuel 9:15-16

"YEA, THOUGH I walk through the valley of the shadow of death, I will fear no evil."

Saul chose David's own words as he prayed softly for the boy's swift and merciful dispatch. He watched, at once mighty king and powerless man. Goliath narrowed the distance between the gleaming edge of his sword and the delicate neck on which the king's weary head had rested.

Theirs was an unlikely friendship, the rude unpolished king and this poised and graceful boy. David was as beautiful as a memory of youth, his voice that of an angel. His songs and his nature had brought comfort to his king and done as much to save Saul and his kingdom from ruin as any of Saul's generals or ministers. Now, in an act of selfless and youthful bravery, David would once again ransom the king's fortunes and save his throne.

"Oh, Samuel, where are you when I need you?" Saul prayed aloud. His words, raised to heaven, were hidden under the cries of those around him as they cheered the hopeless sport unfolding in the Elah Valley below. "Why force this crown upon me and then desert me when I try to be the king you insisted I become? Can it be God's will that I sacrifice this boy in exchange for another year on the throne? What will he ask of me next year? My son?"

Saul searched the crowd for his son's face and found him, silent amidst the cheering mob.

"Lord, what price do we pay to be king?" Saul said. The images of all that he had sacrificed to be king were suddenly upon him, even on that crowded and noisy morning.

And he had a son, whose name was Saul, a choice young man, and a goodly: and there was not among the children of Israel a goodlier person than he: from his shoulders and upward he was higher than any of the people.

1 Samuel 9:2

"MY DARLING, I will be back to you before you have time to miss me," Saul said, embracing the beauty whose company was all he could think to ask of God. "Ahinoam." He whispered the name into her ear again and again like a chanted prayer.

"You are too late, my love," she beamed, pulling away to look up at him. "I miss you already."

"Yet I still must leave you, my life," Saul said, smoothing her dark, glossy hair. "I curse my father's donkeys for running away."

Ahinoam made a hissing noise, breathing in through her teeth to scare away the spirits of the curse. "My husband, you mustn't." She grinned, standing on her toes to twirl one of his dark curls around her finger. "You and your father would have no mules to trade with no donkeys."

"Then I pray to meet them returning as I leave town, so that I might be back at your side the sooner," Saul said, crushing her in a mighty embrace even as he knew he would have to let her go.

Saul ben Kish was a simple man with a simple life. His days were made of uncomplicated pleasures and filled with the joys of a young man coming into his own. His family was a poor one. The clan of Saul's father, Kish, was among the least of the tribe of Benjamin, the smallest of the tribes of Israel. The clan of Kish owned no property, but they had built a good life for themselves as mule traders. In the small village of Zela, in the hills above Gibeah, their stables prospered. The new iron plowshares brought abundance to the farms of the fertile hills and valleys of Judah. The sturdy donkeys and fine horseflesh of Kish's stables produced excellent mules to draw those miraculous new iron blades deep into the hard earth of the hills.

Though theirs was not a rich family, they did better than many. They were fed and sheltered and thankful on the holy days and all the rest of the days of the year.

So, when his father's donkeys went missing, the family faced ruin at the loss of the source of their livelihood.

Saul was a physically remarkable man, taller by a head than those around him or any he had met. He rose above others not only in his physical prowess but also in his character and devotion to family. His wife, Ahinoam, was the most beautiful daughter of the wealthy merchant Ahimaaz. It might have been said that she married below her prospects, had Saul not been such an exceptional man, handsome, strong, and true of heart, favored among men, including his father-in-law.

Saul was then, of course, the son on whom Kish most relied. It was to his most favored son that he turned to find the lost donkeys and save the family.

"I have asked my cousin Abner to look in upon you while I am away," Saul said, releasing Ahinoam and letting her feet come to rest again on the floor. "You may rely on him and should tell him if you need anything. I trust him above all men."

"Then why not take him with you?" she asked playfully, laying her head against his broad chest.

"Because I value you above all things." Saul chuckled at her flirtatiousness. He was a man of thirty. Though their wedding bed was many summers behind them, their love was as new as the day Ahimaaz had first tried to chase the young mule trader from his threshold.

"Master," Mahli, Kish's stable man, beckoned discreetly from the doorway of the simple mud brick house. "All is in readiness."

"I must leave quickly so that I might be back sooner," Saul said to Ahinoam with a sudden and intense embrace.

"Papa," his son Jonathan called on hearing his father's farewell, struggling up onto two coltish legs. "Come with you."

"Not this time," Saul said, vaulting Jonathan into the air above his head. He would be as beautiful as his mother and as tall as Saul was himself, Saul thought as he drank in the sight of his laughing son, already as long as one twice his age. "You must look after Mama while I'm out playing with Old Pa's donkeys."

"I want play with donkey," Jonathan commanded, kicking and looking cross.

"Then I shall fetch them back to you, my prince," Saul said, embracing his son. His heart was filled to breaking with the joy he felt for the life God had, in his generosity, given. "But only if you take good care of Mama. Promise."

Jonathan nodded as he put a hand on his heart solemnly.

"Good man," Saul said, handing Jonathan to his mother.

He shared one last smile with Ahinoam and left without saying good-bye.

One last look over his shoulder, and Saul rode away from a life that he loved perfectly, never to see it again.

There were hoofprints from the missing asses leading into the hills of Ephraim, but even those faded away as they crossed onto the hard and unyielding summer earth. The search stretched on for days. It led them through the districts of Shalisha and Shaalim and back into the territory of Benjamin and beyond.

It was Saul's love of his family and his concerns for their well-being that kept him at the search for so long. Finally worries over his family's prospects for winter were outmatched by his concerns at being so long absent from them.

When at last they crossed into the area known as Zuph and neared the holy city of Ramah, he had not the heart to go farther. They paused for living water at a well on the roadside. Mahli refilled their skins and saw to the horses. Saul gazed into the lands beyond, stretching on into the distance until they met the sky. His eye fell upon the city atop a nearby hill.

"Mahli, we must return," Saul said with a gusty sigh. "My father will stop thinking about the donkeys and start worrying about us."

"Master, stay a breath," Mahli said as he too looked upon the city surrounding the grand temple before them. "Forgive me if I speak above my place. We are come to the sacred city of Ramah. I have heard that there is a seer here, a man whose vision has never been wrong. Many from your tribes put great store by his word. Let us go to him now. Perhaps he can tell us which way to take."

Both were plain men of the hills, with little education and much superstition. The idea of asking a seer seemed a reasonable suggestion to both. The notion of the great judge of all the tribes of Israel was too big for their village, and so they considered asking Samuel as they would consult a seer in his garish and tasseled tent at market.

"Yours is wise counsel, Mahli," Saul said, nodding as he weighed the man's words. "But I fear that we cannot earn his audience. If we go, what can we give the man? The food in our sacks is gone. We have no gift to take to this wise man."

"Good sir," Mahli said, "I have a quarter of a shekel of silver that I have been saving. I will give it to the man of second sight so that he will tell us what way to take."

Both men knew that the donkeys would not be lost if Mahli had secured the gate as was his duty. Though Mahli felt certain he had, he could not be sure, and his heart was heavy. A quarter shekel of silver was dear but a small price to pay for an easy conscience. Saul knew the reason for the generous offer, and though he never doubted that Mahli was blameless, he knew that accepting Mahli's offer would do more to ease the man's mind than a thousand pardons.

"Good man," Saul said to his servant in a serious tone. "Come, let us to Ramah."

Dusty and smelling of the road, the two rode into town to find the seer of legend. More than the clouds that rose from their robes unsettled those from whom they inquired after the soothsayer. As Samuel was the judge of all the tribes of Israel, they wondered if Saul was mad when he inquired in such a manner of the great man whose name was as one with the city.

"Is the seer here?" Saul asked a couple of serving girls, at the well to gossip and draw living water for their mistresses. The two eyed the stranger.

At first the girls only giggled, thinking he was teasing them. Saul held his ground and gave them a serious if puzzled look for their odd behavior. From his manner they understood that Saul was in earnest, and they laughed all the harder.

"He is," one girl answered, giggling at Saul's dirty clothes and foolish questions.

"He is ahead of you," the other girl added, better able to contain her amusement at the imposing country oaf who asked so commonly after the city's most prominent citizen. "Hurry now; he has just come to our town today."

"Yes, hurry," the other advised, finding her tongue and wishing a little fun at the stranger's expense. "The people have a sacrifice at the high place. As soon as you enter, you will find him before he goes up to the high place to eat. The people will not begin eating until he comes, because he must prepare the food. Afterward those who are invited will eat. Go up now; you should find him about this time."

"I thank you, ladies," Saul said with a stiff and old-fashioned bow that earned him a hail of new giggles. He tried to overlook their odd behavior as he made his way toward the high place, thinking them a bit simple, perhaps.

Further inquiries were met with similar responses from the locals. Still, their mission was of grave importance to the family. Saul and Mahli pressed on toward the holy place.

"How strange the people are here," Saul remarked to Mahli as they left a group of youths sputtering with laughter behind their backs after seeking further directions.

"Theirs are city customs." Mahli shrugged. He was a man from Arabah and found the customs of one tribe of Israel as odd as the next. "I wonder how we would greet them if they were to come to Zela."

"I hope with more hospitality than we have found here," Saul said. He thought to take special care of strangers from then on, in light of his own experience as one.

As Saul and Mahli sought him, Samuel made ready for the sacrifice of which all Ramah had spoken. The priest had been in prayer and fasting in honor of the holy rites. He, too, sought divine guidance, an answer to the growing public demand for a king of all Israel.

The private voice that guided him had answered his fervent and reluctant prayers. It was foretold to Samuel that a man from Benjamin would come seeking him that day. This the priest knew was God's intended. He was to anoint the man king over all of Israel to deliver the people from the hands of the Philistines.

With great anticipation Samuel set out from his dwelling to the temple high place for the sacrifice that day. He recognized Saul even before he knew who he was, even before he spoke to him. Saul stood tall, impressive, and unmistakable among all those around him in the crowded temple square.

Saul searched the crowd for one who looked as he expected a seer to look.

Samuel made his way straight and true to the man he knew had been sent to him. Before he had spoken, he knew with the certainty of the still small voice that filled him, *This is the man who will reign over Israel.*

Samuel approached with an expression so welcoming that Saul, who had tired of his reception thus far from Ramah, was inspired to greet the old man.

"Good sir," Saul said, inclining his head as he had observed others do in this city, though it seemed curt to him. "We have come seeking the seer known to be of this place. I wonder if you could direct me to him."

"I am the seer," Samuel answered with a puzzled smile, wondering at the simple and gentle nature of this impressive and powerful man. "Go ahead of me to the high place," Samuel instructed, indicating the temple beyond the square. "Today you are to dine with me. I have been awaiting your arrival along with all the people of the tribes of Israel. To your father's family are all the desires of Israel now turned."

Saul was baffled and suspicious of the seer and his grand words.

"I am a Benjamite, a stranger here, from the smallest tribe of Israel," Saul said, eyeing the old man with some concern. He had heard stories of the trickery of city dwellers and the pleasing ways they had of separating a man from his property almost before he knew it was gone. "My clan is the least of all of the clans of Benjamin. Why do you say such things to me?"

"All will be explained in time," Samuel said, gently taking Saul's arm and guiding him toward his own servants. "For now, you should know that the donkeys you lost have been found and are already returned to your father. You need worry for them no longer. They have served their purpose and brought you to me."

Saul was stunned silent by the seer's prescience. He could dispute him no further.

Samuel commended Saul to his servants, "Take good care of this man and his servant. See that they are cleansed, robed, and ready to join me at the head of the table when the service is complete. Tell the cook to prepare the special meat that I gave him. Our honored guest has arrived as promised."

Though he was good-natured, Saul was not a man easily led. That day, though, he was so overwhelmed by Samuel's knowledge and hospitality that he allowed himself to be bridled as easily as a good mule. He found himself wearing finer clothes than he had ever seen, perfumed with oils, and seated at the head of a massive table crowded with men easily his betters.

By the conclusion of the ceremonies, it was clear to Saul that Samuel was far more than any market seer. He worried that the quarter silver would be too humble an offering for a priest so august. Before he could offer Samuel any tribute, the priest was serving him a roast the like of which had never graced even Saul's most bounteous holy feast table. Those present looked on Saul with interest and admiration. They were too polite to ask the name of a man so great that he not only sat at Samuel's side but was served by the priest himself.

"Enjoy," Samuel said, setting the roast before Saul. "This was set aside for you, for this occasion, as this meal has been planned in your honor."

Though overwhelmed by the surroundings and the generosity of his host, Saul was also hungry from the road. He ate his fill and heartily enjoyed Samuel's company at table. The two men spoke of Saul's family, his wife and son. Samuel seemed little interested in Saul's business or property. He laughed out loud at Saul's suggestion of tribute.

"Saul, it is my honor to sit beside you," Samuel assured his guest, liking the man more and more for his lack of deceit or guile. Samuel's life was filled with men who sought to gain something from him. It was like an ocean breeze in the hills in summer to meet a man who expected nothing, was grateful for what he got, and sought to repay the unasked favor.

After the banquet the fine guests all bid Saul farewell. Though his other guests were still curious about Saul, Samuel did not yet disclose his identity to them. Saul returned with Samuel to his home, and the two men spoke together as they enjoyed the cool of the night on the roof of Samuel's house.

"We have much to discuss, you and I. You must stay the night with me. My servants have prepared rooms for you and your servant," Samuel said, not wanting to overwhelm his guest with too much at first. He knew that he would need more than just the news of the donkeys to convince this good-hearted man of the enormity of the task for which he had been divined.

"I thank you for your hospitality," Saul said, with the deep and formal bow that was his custom, forgetting the curt nod that passed for manners in the city. "I cannot impose on you for the night. My servant and I have tents with our horses and can easily make our own comfort without asking more of you, who have been so generous to us both."

"Then stay as a favor to me," Samuel asked with a twinkle. "I have told you I expected you. Tomorrow I would like the time to explain why. But I am an old man and am tired from the ceremonies. Would you do me the courtesy of staying the night so that we may speak in the morning before I begin yet another busy day?"

"I can deny you no request after your many kindnesses," Saul said. "Though it still seems to me that I am the one on the receiving end. I will call it a favor to you only if that, too, is your request."

"It is, Saul," Samuel assured him. Putting a hand on the man's broad shoulder, he rose to take his leave. Samuel's heart was at peace, for he could easily see in Saul what the Lord of Israel must see. Saul's kind and generous spirit spoke of the sort of man who would view the duty before him as a trust from God and not as a means to realize his own ambitions. This man could never see greatness as a goal in itself. Saul was the one that Israel needed, and Samuel said prayers of thanksgiving until sleep overtook him.

At daybreak the old priest went to awaken his guest and found him packed and ready for the journey home.

"Ah, Saul, you make ready to leave me so soon," Samuel said, again charmed. "I will send you on your way in good time, but first another favor, if I may ask it?"

"Anything, good sir," Saul answered with another deep country bow. "Though I know I have naught fine enough to repay you for your hospitality."

"I think you will be surprised," Samuel said with a sad smile. He knew how much he would ask in return for a good cut of meat and a night in a clean bed. "Send your servant on ahead. Stay here a while and speak with me. I have a message for you from God."

Saul was astonished at the idea of it.

At once his mistrust of the clever city dwellers rose up in him again. Yet Samuel had been so kind. He had not asked Saul for anything more than his time. Though Saul longed to return to Ahinoam, he could not calculate that a morning's delay would cost him.

"I am your servant," Saul answered. He was still concerned, but he was content in the certain knowledge that if this were a swindle or trick of some kind, he had the upper hand. He owned nothing worth stealing. "Mahli, go to my father and see to the donkeys and his stables. I will not be far behind."

Mahli placed his hand over his heart and bowed to Saul. He turned, climbed upon his horse, and rode away. He wanted nothing more than to see for himself his master's donkeys again safely in their stalls.

Samuel led Saul to the altar at the temple. There he had Saul kneel before the God of Israel. The priest draped his own shoulders with a holy shawl embroidered with golden thread, which he had never worn before nor would he again. He took down a jeweled horn, newly minted into service for just this purpose, fitted with gold at its tip and a hinged golden lid at the broad end. Samuel opened the horn with his thumb as he prayed over the man before him.

Then, with a sense of loss and of relief, he anointed Saul with the horn of sacred oils, in God's name as king over all of Israel. He kissed Saul on both cheeks and held the chin of the astonished man in his hand, looking deeply into Saul's eyes. "The Lord has anointed you leader over his inheritance.

"When you leave me today, you will meet two men near Rachel's tomb, at Zelzah on the border of Benjamin," Samuel said, holding Saul's rapt attention and his gaze. "They will say to you, 'The donkeys you set out to look for have been found. And now your father has stopped thinking about them and is worried about you. He is asking, "What shall I do about my son?"'"

Saul's heart beat heavy in his chest. He knew not what to make of any of this. He wondered how to escape the old man without seeming ungrateful.

"Then you will go on from there until you reach the great tree of Tabor. Three men going up to God at Bethel will meet you there. One will be carrying three young goats, another three loaves of bread, and another a skin of wine.

They will greet you and offer you two loaves of bread, which you will accept from them.

"After that you will go to Gibeah of God, where there is a Philistine outpost. As you approach the town, you will meet a procession of prophets coming down from the high place with lyres, tambourines, flutes, and harps being played before them, and they will be prophesying. The spirit of the Lord will come upon you in power, and you will prophesy with them; and you will be changed into a different person. Once these signs are fulfilled, do whatever your hand finds to do, for God is with you."

Saul was almost too overwhelmed to stand. How could he believe such a thing? How could he be chosen to be king? "Samuel, how can I believe this?"

"How could I know all that is to unfold for you today without the certain knowledge of the Lord?" Samuel answered. "Go from here. If all does not come to pass as I have foretold it, then return home to your wife as is in your heart to do. But if, instead, it is as I have said to you here before God, then you must search your heart for God's will for you."

"Samuel," Saul said, still kneeling and clutching the sleeve of the old man's robe. "I cannot be king. I am a mule trader from the hills of Benjamin. What do I know of being king?"

"The Lord will come to you and make your way clear to you," Samuel said, taking Saul's hand and helping him to his feet. "I will see you again soon. All will be clear by then. Go now and find your way. I must go to Mizpah to meet with the council of elders."

Saul found Samuel's servant holding his horse for him just outside the temple. Filled with fear and wonder, he vaulted onto the animal's back and rode for home, through the crowded streets of Ramah as though across the open plain. The road home took him to Zelzah. There, near the tomb of Rachel, he was astonished to be hailed by two friends of his father. Too afraid to speak, he drew up his mount near to these men.

The two seemed genuinely glad to see him. They called him by name and clapped him on the back and shoulders heartily.

"It is a good thing to see you, Saul," said the elder of the two.

"Yes," agreed the other. "It was with much concern for your father that we thought he might have lost you in the confusion."

"I am well," Saul managed hoarsely.

"And we are glad to hear it, as well as your father will soon be," said the old man. "The donkeys you set out to look for have been found. And now your father has stopped thinking about them and is worried about you. He is asking, 'What shall I do about my son?'"

The two family friends laughed warmly, delighted for their friend Kish and the prospect of the return of his favored son.

The perfection of the priest's visions stunned Saul. He tried to share in their good humor, but was too troubled by the prospect of Samuel's claims.

"I had best not keep my father waiting," Saul said, bowing deeply. He was relieved at least that they bowed deeply in return. The customs of home were a comfort to a man so lost.

He rode on with greater haste toward home. Thinking to thwart fate, he took a road he knew would bring him nowhere near the tree of Tabor. He found the road blocked by great boulders. He was forced to follow a string of strange and unfamiliar detours, wandering through the hills of Ephraim and Benjamin with no idea where he might be. He followed the directions of strangers, hoping that he would find himself in Ahinoam's arms by nightfall.

The sun was well past its height as Saul wound his way down a narrow path along a deep wadi. He had to dismount and lead his horse through the tricky terrain. It slowed his journey, but Saul was relieved. By his reckoning he had passed by Tabor on the far side of the hills and would soon find himself almost to Gibeah and home in the hills well beyond.

As the path wound around the steep hillside, it turned back and gave Saul a view of the land beyond. There in the distance, not far from where the path rejoined the main road, was the great tree he had come so far to avoid. Approaching him from the other direction, heading toward Bethel, were three men Saul knew in his heart he would have missed had he arrived at this turning in the road at any other time.

As they approached, he saw that one in their party led three goats. He knew he was on the path God had chosen.

"Good fellow," one of the men called to him as they drew near. "Have you eaten?"

"No, good sir," Saul answered. "Not since I broke my fast this morning."

"We are in luck, then," said the man leading the tethered goats. "We are pilgrims, on the way to make sacrifice at Bethel. And we must offer two of these loaves that we carry to the hungry on the way to make ourselves ready."

"We have seen not one soul, hungry or not, on the road today," said the man carrying the loaves. "Would you take these two loaves? The third is for the priest at Bethel. You could make a meal and have plenty for later, and we could make ready according to our tradition."

"It seems that God has brought us together for this very purpose," Saul said softly, taking the loaves and bowing deeply to his benefactors. "I thank you and bless you for your kindness."

"And a blessing upon you," called the men as they hurried on to their sacrifice.

Saul tucked the bread into his pack, too filled with anticipation and fear to eat. He resigned himself to his fate as Samuel's prophesy seemed to be unfolding before him with the certainty of sunrise.

The road home led through Gibeah. Saul made his way there directly to meet his fate head-on. His hunger turned to a kind of hollowness, unlike any he had ever experienced. Not the pain of hunger, but a giddy openness that gave him feelings of lightness and clarity. So pleasant was the sensation, he did not take even a little water or a sip of wine to wet his palate for fear that he would frighten it away.

When he arrived at Gibeah, a procession of prophets met him, joyous and making music with their instruments. They made their way to him, as foretold.

Saul stood as they approached.

"We have found you, Saul," they sang. "It is as we have seen."

They sang and circled him, dancing and playing as they ringed him round and round. Saul began to follow them, turning with them. Faster and faster they turned until they were no longer on the road outside Gibeah.

Saul was swept away. The world around him seemed to change, and God changed Saul's heart. He saw it all before him. He saw his way. In his rapture he knew the answer to all that would be asked of him. Nothing changed and yet nothing was ever the same.

As their little band made their way into the town of Gibeah where he was known, many were startled to see Saul in the company of the prophets.

"What is this that has happened to the son of Kish?" one began to ask another.

"Is Saul also among the prophets?"

The refrain was taken up by the musicians with him. They made a song of it.

"Is Saul also among the prophets?"

It was the first of many songs that were to be written of Israel's new king.

And Samuel called the people together unto the Lord to Mizpeh.
1 Samuel 10:17

IT WAS with a heavy heart that Samuel made his way to Mizpah, even as Saul was returning to Gibeah in the company of the prophets. Both men knew that the king had been chosen, but Samuel alone knew the price that would be exacted for the choice. He felt that the people had turned from God in asking for a king, and he meant to make clear the terrible consequences of turning from the Lord.

Jesse was a young man still and proud to represent Bethlehem at Mizpah. He had only recently taken his father's place as the head of the family. With his fine new wife, he looked forward to building a family in the promising new age he saw dawning in Israel. The tribes were more prosperous than ever before. Trade soared, and the sons of Israel seemed at last on the rise in the world. Jesse could see no limit to what was possible. God's long awaited promise, he believed, was about to be fulfilled.

Jesse's youth allowed him a vision of the future undimmed by the shadings of disappointment and sorrow that experience brings. As he made his way to Mizpah, the sacred city of Benjamin, it was with a hopeful heart. All anyone could talk about was the council's call for a king, to make a single kingdom of their tattered tribal allegiance. Jesse was hopeful that there would finally be answers from the great Judge Samuel.

The time honored tradition of being ruled by superstition and priests was a quaint relic of the past that Jesse and other like-minded young men felt should be relegated to legend. Samuel opposed them, but how could he not? It would mean an end to his line.

In truth, Samuel's sons had been given and lost the chance to succeed him, as had the sons of Eli, the judge before Samuel. All had failed, succumbing to all manner of corruption. As the men of Jesse's generation assumed their place at the head of their family tables, they were united in their desire for a country modeled on and strong enough to defend themselves against those that surrounded and overran them at will.

Samuel warned them, with the words of their unnamable God, of the consequences of choosing to be ruled by a king over God. The old man's words fell, not on deaf ears but on young ones, for "elder" was a title that connoted birth and property more than age and wisdom. It was not that they could not hear him. It was that they heard only what they longed to hear.

When he warned that a king would conscript their sons from their fields into his army, the elders of this new age cheered, for they wanted a strong army to unite and defend them. The wonder of iron had freed their sons from laboring on their family's farms, and they were eager for the power and glory of officers.

Their judge cautioned the elders that a king would take a tenth of their grain and vintage for his officials and attendants, but they were rich and did not fear taxes. They were willing to pay for a better life and could afford one. Moreover, they were certain that the king's attendants and officials would, like his army officers, be their second and third sons. The priest railed against daughters swept up into servitude as perfumers, cooks, and bakers. They were delighted that unmarried daughters would be able to find respectable work in the growing towns and cities rather than being forced to choose between spinsterhood and harlotry. Samuel said that a king would make them slaves, and the young men only laughed at the idea that they could be made servants to someone they themselves had appointed.

As they made their way to the meeting at Mizpah, Jesse and the other elders were light of heart and high of expectation, where their judge, Samuel, was pensive and concerned for their future. Still, the priest was on orders from God. While he was concerned, he was in no way uncertain. His call that they gather at Mizpah in Benjamin brought the elders of every city, town, village, and clan to the sacred place, hopeful of an answer to their petitions.

All the greatest men of the tribes of Israel gathered in the plaza before the temple of Mizpah, revered but too small to hold their eminent body in comfort. A hush fell upon them. Samuel came out. He stood on the high place of sacrifice before the temple to address them.

"This is what the Lord, the God of Israel, says," Samuel declared, his voice echoing off the faces of the gleaming limestone buildings that surrounded the square. "'I brought Israel up out of Egypt, and I delivered you from the power of Egypt and all the kingdoms that oppressed you. But you have now rejected your God, who saves you out of all your calamities and distresses.' And you have said, 'No, set a king over us.'"

Jesse's heart sank as he heard these words. He feared that Samuel had but found a new way to deny them their rightful claims to take their place as men in the world.

"Your God has seen fit to answer you," Samuel declared. "Now present yourselves before the Lord by your tribes and clans. You may expect his answer then."

Samuel stepped down. He went back inside the temple and closed the doors behind him. Jesse was almost afraid to hope. Was it another trick? Was it an answer? Would he reveal God's choice for king at last?

"I say we call him to account," cried out Joshua, the powerful elder from Ephraim. "Let us call the tribes, clan by clan, to stand here before God. If this judge cannot find a king from among the men of God's chosen, then I say let us see if we cannot find one for ourselves."

There was resounding agreement. Messengers rode out from Dan to Beersheba to call the heads of every clan to stand before the Lord at Mizpah.

With great dispatch, the vast crowd of the most worthy of each clan and tribe were brought before the temple at Mizpah. So great was the gathering that the food and wine of the small city ran short.

Saul had not yet returned to Ahinoam's arms before he was called to join the men of his clan at Mizpah. On his way home to her, Saul encountered Abiel, his uncle, on the street of Gibeah, preparing to leave for Mizpah.

"My nephew?" Abiel called out, uncertain even then that it was Saul.

Still dazed from the visions he had seen during his time with the prophets, Saul looked upon his uncle like a stranger.

"Saul, it is you," Abiel said, embracing his nephew. "Where have you been? My brother has been tearing at his hair in worry."

"I have been abroad," Saul replied, much comforted by the sight of his uncle. "I was looking for my father's lost donkeys. When it was clear they were not to be found, I consulted Samuel, for I was near Ramah."

"Samuel?" Abiel said, stunned by such news. "What said he to you?"

"The priest assured us that the donkeys had already been found," Saul said. He omitted the rest of what passed between him and the great priest. His visions had shown him what he must do to earn the crown, and bragging to a relative on the street was not among his appointed labors. "I have sent Mahli on ahead to make certain that the old priest spoke true."

"Oh, he spoke true," Abiel said. The donkeys had walked back into their stalls almost as soon as Saul was over the horizon. "But though Mahli may find the donkeys in your father's stable, he will not find your father at his table. We have been called to Mizpah by your friend Samuel. It is good that our paths have crossed, for we have no time to spare."

"Mizpah," Saul said, recognizing the name and its meaning even as he heard it. "Yes, this is it, then."

"It is indeed," Abiel said, grasping Saul's elbow and guiding him toward his train. "I have been detained, but you must accompany me there directly. It is a blessing, for your father will already be there to greet you. I am certain he will be especially glad of your company."

They made their way to Mizpah with the others from all the tribes.

It took seven days for all to find their way to the holy city of Benjamin. Once gathered, their camp encircled the little town like an invasion.

"My son," Kish cried out with joy, seeing Saul with Abiel as they approached his humble camp. "I thought I had lost you for the sake of a few stubborn beasts."

"I am well," Saul said. He embraced his father as though bidding him farewell, for he could see beyond their embrace. "I am here."

Saul kept to himself as they awaited the arrival of the more distant clans. He was helpful in what ways he could. Using his family's fine pack animals, he hauled water and food. Theirs was a humble clan, and he was regarded by most there as little more than a servant. Saul took no notice, even of the arrogance of Joshua of Ephraim, who had called the clans together in answer to Samuel's challenge. Certain of Joshua's appointment, many there thought it a waste of time to make the journey. Saul kept his own counsel and awaited a sign.

On the evening of the sixth day, the call went out. All at Mizpah would meet at dawn before the little temple where Samuel had remained in refuge.

The sun was halfway up the sky by the time they were assembled. They called for Samuel.

The old priest emerged. He resumed his place on the great altar.

"You are here, I see," Samuel said. "The Lord has already chosen a man from among you to be your king."

The cheer of relief and exaltation shook the little square.

Tribe by tribe, Samuel called the men forward, ending with the smallest, Benjamin. When the tribe of Benjamin came forward, Samuel began to call them clan by clan. At last Matri's clan, to which Kish and his kin answered, was called forward. But when Samuel named Saul as God's chosen, he was not among his kinsmen.

There was shock that God had chosen a man from such an undistinguished clan of so small a tribe.

"Has the man come here yet?" asked one of Joshua's indignant clansmen.

"Yes," cried out a noble member of the tribe of Judah. "Does God know where he is?"

There was laughter in the crowd.

"He is among the luggage," Samuel answered with certainty born of his oneness.

Saul had remained behind with his father's pack animals, helping to organize the food and water for the assembled throng. There, among the luggage, he was found and led forward through the crowd.

A hush fell over those assembled as Saul passed among them. His head above all those men present, he passed through the crowded plaza as visible as a boat upon a lake.

"Behold, there is none among you like him that the Lord has chosen," Samuel said, finding satisfaction in the choice of such a man, if not the necessity. "There is no man like him among all the people."

"Long live the king."

The shout began small, from only a few in the crowd. It grew.

Before Saul could pass through the people to take his place beside Samuel on the high place, voices of most in the crowd were raised as one.

"Long live the king."

The words shook the town to its foundations that day and resonated throughout the country from that day forth.

Saul felt the roar in his chest like a living thing. He prayed silently for the strength to be a man worthy of God's choice.

At last he stood beside Samuel. He nodded to those who had come there from the farthest hills and hamlets of Israel to know his name.

Samuel raised his hands to bring quiet to the joyous crowd.

He led them in a prayer for their new king. His words blessed Saul and all his endeavors on behalf of all those who had called for his anointment. Then he spoke from his heart the words he felt from God.

"I have heard you and have set a king of God's own choosing over you," Samuel said, laying a hand on Saul's shoulder. "Now you have a king as your leader. He is a fine man, above all others and worthy of his charge. Perhaps most because he has not sought to be king and is not yet certain he is worthy, as some men might have been."

Samuel's eyes found Joshua's. The two men regarded one another tensely. Joshua's camp had not been among those chanting for their new king.

"As for me," the priest went on, "I am old and gray, and my sons are here with you. I have been your leader from my youth until this day. Here I stand. Testify against me in the presence of the Lord and his anointed. Whose ox have I taken? Whose donkey have I taken? Whom have I cheated? Whom have I oppressed? From whose hand have I accepted a bribe to make me shut my eyes? If I have done any of these, I will make it right."

"You have neither cheated nor oppressed us," answered a man from the tribe of Dan. "You have not taken anything from anyone's hand."

"The Lord is witness against you, and also his anointed is witness this day, that you have not found anything in my hand," Samuel bellowed, waving his staff at those present.

"He is witness," the crowd shouted in answer.

The crowd was still giddy with victory and their new king.

"It is the Lord who appointed Moses and Aaron and brought your forefathers up out of Egypt. Now then, stand here, because I am going to confront you with evidence before the Lord as to all the righteous acts performed by the Lord for you and your fathers.

"After Jacob entered Egypt, they cried to the Lord for help, and the Lord sent Moses and Aaron, who brought your forefathers out of Egypt and settled them in this place.

"But they forgot the Lord their God; so he sold them into the hand of Sisera, the commander of the army of Hazor, and into the hands of the Philistines and the King of Moab, who fought against them. They cried out to the Lord and said, 'We have sinned; we have forsaken the Lord and served the Baals and the Ashtoreths. But now deliver us from the hands of our enemies, and we will serve you.' Then the Lord sent Jerub-Baal, Barak, Jephthah and

Samuel, and he delivered you from the hands of your enemies on every side, so that you lived securely.

"But when you saw that Nahash, king of the Ammonites, was moving against you, you said to me, 'No, we want a king to rule over us'—even though the Lord your God was your king. Now here is the king you have chosen, the one you asked for; see, the Lord has set a king over you. If you fear the Lord and serve and obey him and do not rebel against his commands, and if both you and the king who reigns over you follow the Lord your God—good! But if you do not obey the Lord, and if you rebel against his commands, his hand will be against you, as it was against your fathers."

Many in the crowd were not moved by Samuel's words. They thought they were the sour notes of a singer who had been asked to leave the stage. They revered Samuel, but they knew him to be a man as they were men. They knew that they would be aggrieved in Samuel's place.

"Now then, stand still," Samuel said, as if he read the thoughts of the skeptics and nonbelievers. "Witness a sign from the Lord that you may know he is here with us today; that you may know what an evil thing you did in the eyes of the Lord when you asked for a king. Is it not wheat harvest now? I call upon the Lord to speak in thunder and rain. And you will realize."

Samuel raised his arms to heaven.

Clouds boiled in the clear sky, turning day into night. Lightning split the darkness. Thunder rolled across the heaven. Rain fell upon those gathered.

The people stood like livestock, too amazed by what they saw to speak or move.

The spirit moved Saul. He fell to his knees before Samuel. Awestruck, the crowd fell to their knees with him.

"Pray to the Lord your God for your servants so that we will not die," Saul asked of the priest on their behalf. "Forgive us if we have added to all our other sins the evil of asking for a king. Take back the crown and let me follow."

"Fear not," Samuel replied, deeply moved by Saul's words. The rains subsided as quickly as they had come. The sun broke through the clouds and all was as before. "You have done all this evil, yet do not turn away from the Lord, but serve the Lord with all your heart. Do not turn away after useless idols. They can do you no good, nor can they rescue you, because they are useless. For the sake of his great name, the Lord will not reject his people, because the Lord was pleased to make you his own. As for me, far be it from me that I should sin against the Lord by failing to pray for you. And I will teach you the way that is good and right. But be sure to fear the Lord and serve him faithfully with all your heart. Consider what great things he has done for you. Yet if you persist in doing evil, both you and your king will be swept away."

None was more moved than Saul by the power of the Lord and the importance of the royal yoke that had been placed upon his shoulders.

Jesse and the others left solemnly. Their victory was banked by the harsh truths that Samuel had spoken. Though many did not yet accept Saul as their king, Saul vowed to himself to keep the laws of God, that neither he nor his people should be swept away.

After the events at Mizpah, Saul returned to the home of his family in Gibeah, troubled and uncertain. Alone at last after the feasting and celebrating that followed his acclamation, Saul lay with his face in the dirt and prayed to God for guidance. Though he was king, there was no army to lead, no palace to occupy, no treasury on which to draw. Sleep overcame him at last. With sleep came dreams.

When he awoke, he knew.

And the Spirit of God came upon Saul when he heard those tidings, and his anger was kindled greatly.

1 Samuel 11:6

IN THE days that followed, news came that the Ammonite king had invaded Jabesh-Gilead, a city belonging to the tribe of Gad. Though the men of Jabesh sued for terms of peace, the vindictive king set terms to disgrace all of Israel.

"Their king says he will accept surrender only if he may gouge out the right eye of each man of Jabesh," the messenger repeated to Saul as they sat at the table in the home of Ner, Saul's uncle in Gibeah. Saul received his first messenger as king, his cousin Abner seated at his side.

"He seeks to disgrace us," Saul said, looking at the floor in his disgust. "But he disgraces himself by the asking such an atrocity."

"What shall I tell the elders of Jabesh?" the messenger asked, the idea of a king still so new that the man spoke plainly to Saul.

"What of the other tribes?" Abner asked the messenger.

"The elders have been given a stay of only seven days to consider their answer," the messenger replied. "They have sent messengers to the other tribes, but there has been no reply. They thought to ask of you to intercede on their behalf with the elders for support, since you are the newly chosen king."

All eyes turned to Saul. He paused for a breath, looking at those around him in disbelief. He had dreamed of this meeting. He knew the course he must take.

"Abner," Saul said, placing his hand on the shoulder of his childhood friend and longtime confidant. "I ask that you accept the commission of general over the army of Israel, though you have not one man yet to command."

"I am honored to serve you," Abner said with a gentle smile. He too knew the height of the task that stood before them, though he did not yet have Saul's faith. "I will be your army until such time as Israel shall provide one to their king."

"Good man. Now, for your first commission," Saul said without hesitation, "send for two oxen. Slaughter each and send the pieces to the elders of each tribe, saying that this is what will become of the oxen of any who do not follow Saul and Samuel."

Those present were unsettled by such a bloody message to their own people, but each felt the resolve of Saul's certainty, so none questioned it.

"It shall be so, Your Majesty," Abner said, striking his chest in salute to his king, setting an example for those around to follow.

"Call Samuel and ask him to come to me," Saul said to the messenger.

"As you say, Your Majesty," the messenger said, mirroring Abner's tone and salute.

It was thus, by little ways and great acts, that Saul earned their respect and created what it was to be king of all Israel.

Following Samuel's thunderous demonstration of the Lord's willingness to intervene on their behalf, the elders responded with alacrity to the summons of their new king.

Samuel, too, was moved to respond to Saul's call. He had thought himself set aside by the will of the people. He gave thanks that the will of the new king was that he take part in ruling the lands and the people. It was a good sign and one for which he had hoped.

"Greetings, my king," Samuel said with a respectful country bow on entering the house of Ner in Gibeah. Saul had remained in his uncle's house as he prepared for the liberation of Jabesh. "The messenger from Gad brought me word of the trouble in Jabesh and that you would seek my counsel?"

"Ah, Samuel," Saul said, looking up. Abner and a few other men had been assembled from among their kinsmen to help command the forces that Saul had called forth. Saul knelt at Samuel's feet, his head bowed. "I thank the Lord that you have come. I seek your blessing, your divine sight, your wisdom, and your guidance in this."

"How may I help you?" Samuel asked, warming to his part in the new government. Only once the priest had placed a hand on Saul's head and intoned a prayer of blessing did the king look up. The other men knelt out of respect for Samuel and, more so, their new king.

"I thank you," Saul said, rising. He guided the old priest to the table. There was spread a map, drawn by a resident familiar with the territory around Jabesh. "The right thing to do is clear to me. I seek God's will in this that we may also do what is best for the people of Jabesh, of Israel, and most of all, the men whose lives we will risk in the doing of it."

"I see, yes," Samuel said. The voice spoke to him even as Saul asked. "You must gather your men here at Bezek."

Saul could hardly contain his feelings of relief. Without explanation of the map or the circumstances, Samuel had placed his men on a plain above where the Ammonite armies were encamped, prepared to overrun Jabesh. "This is a good sign," Saul nodded. "My plan was to break the men into three forces and to attack here, here, and here."

"The first blows must fall just before the cock crows three days hence," Samuel said, his heart swelling as their partnership was born. "It will be over before the sun is down. God will bring you victory."

"It shall be so," Saul said, clapping the old man heartily on the shoulder. "Gentlemen, we have our orders from on high. Let us make God's will a reality on the plains of Gad."

And they said unto the messengers that came, Thus shall ye say unto the men of Jabeshgilead, Tomorrow, by that time the sun be hot, ye shall have help.
                                                                    1 Samuel 11:9

HIS LEGEND had been born in just this way.

Saul raised an army of three hundred and thirty thousand from the tribes of Israel and Judah in less than seven days. Under his command they wiped the Ammonite force from the plains and hills of Gad.

There had been dissent about Saul's idea to invade during the last night watch, particularly from Joshua of Ephraim and those who had supported his ascension reluctantly. By the heat of the day, Jabesh was liberated and the Ammonites laid waste. Those who survived scattered so that no two were left together. Dissent among the ranks of the tribes was at end. There was even a call for the heads of the dissenters.

"Who was it who asked 'shall Saul reign over us?'" Abner demanded, even before the victory celebration began that night in the streets of Jabesh. "Let these men step forward, if they be man enough, and dragged before us if they be cowards. Let us cut off the heads of these snakes, that we may hear no more of these questions of the legitimacy of our great king."

A cry went up both for the king and for the blood of those who did not support God's choice. Saul had only to raise his hand and silence fell over the crowd.

"No one shall be put to death today," Saul declared. "For this is the day that the Lord has rescued Israel. As his instruments, we are as one now, as we have never been before. Let us celebrate our victory, and let us be one people starting today. Let us be the nation that God has given us the chance to be. Let us earn the blessing that is the gift of Israel."

The celebrating continued all the way back to Gibeah, where Saul was reaffirmed as king. Samuel presided over fellowship sacrifices and laid the cornerstones of Saul's new palace even before the days of the celebration were at end. Gibeah was from that day forth called Gibeah of Saul. It rose mighty on the hill, high above the plain of Benjamin.

Ahinoam was sent for, and Saul began life anew. Anointed by the Lord, Saul sacrificed the joyous life for which he had been so thankful. He dedicated himself to the God of Abraham and the work for which he had not known he possessed a gift. He had left home only to find his father's donkeys and returned the first king of Israel.

Though I walk through the valley of the shadow of death, I will fear no evil: for thou art with me; thy rod and thy staff they comfort me.

Psalm 23:4

"*FOR THOU* art with me," Saul intoned, as he prayed for David's swift dispatch on the field of battle against Goliath. The thousands around him drew and held a breath, silent as they watched Goliath raise his mighty sword to strike.

The psalm died away on Saul's tongue.

It had all begun so well, with such promise. As God's instrument, all fell before him. How had he lost God's favor? How had he lost Samuel? Where was God as this innocent was led to slaughter to further the plans of a king? "God, do you believe in me?" he whispered hoarsely and then fell silent, awaiting his reply.

CHAPTER SIX
THE BOOK OF JONATHAN

And the Philistine said to David, Come to me, and I will give thy flesh unto the fowls of the air, and to the beasts of the field.

1 Samuel 17:44

JONATHAN WAS bereft. He stood watching, unable to help, unable to look away. His gaze shifted from David, who lay defenseless against impending slaughter on the valley floor below, to his father, whose ceaseless ambitions for his country and his house crowded out even the least of his humanity. Jonathan loved his father, yet he hated the king.

Their differences had grown from the disappointments of a hero-worshipping boy discovering that the father he idolized was mere flesh and blood, into a growing rift between prince and king. His earliest memories of his father were of the great and mighty man who sheltered and protected Jonathan in his powerful arms. He had only vague memory of the father who was not also king. By the time he understood, the father was lost and only the king remained.

Jonathan had spent the rest of his life trying to find him. He had followed his father to war before he'd even said the prayers of manhood. There he tried to capture his father's eye on the field of battle, where Saul's gaze remained transfixed for all the years of Jonathan's youth.

Saul grew ever more obsessed with uniting Israel, defeating her enemies, and in so doing, fulfilling God's will. As a boy Jonathan could not understand his father's focus on their great unnamable God and his representative, Samuel. To the boy it seemed merely that he had lost his place of favor in his father's heart. His younger brothers and sisters had never known the father that Jonathan had known.

Though he had devoted his every endeavor on the battlefield and at court to earning his father's pride and grace, it seemed to Jonathan that he could never attain it, never be good enough. Blinded by his quest for favor, he had risked losing what he treasured above all else. He had dismissed David as his own father had turned his back on him. It was the prospect of loss that made the value clear.

As he could but stand and watch that morning at Elah, he looked back and forth between David and Saul, across the divide of the hills and valley that separated them. He saw such faith in both men, yet it all seemed too late. He feared he could never bridge the gulf that kept him apart from either man. He knew he could never believe in Samuel's cruel God, who had taken his father and would surely take David from him, in exchange for another forgettable victory in service to a country that didn't exist.

As for Saul, he was yet in Gilgal, and all the people followed him trembling. And he tarried seven days, according to the set time that Samuel had appointed: but Samuel came not to Gilgal; and the people were scattered from him.

1 Samuel 13:7-8

"IS THIS the Lord's will or Samuel's?" Prince Jonathan shouted, his patience at end. They had been awaiting Samuel's arrival at Gilgal for seven days, and Jonathan feared further delay would cost them the battle if not their very lives.

"Jonathan, you mustn't speak so," Saul said with a weary sigh. *I may be king of Israel, but there is no ruling over Samuel or my children*, Saul mused as he regarded his son with a well-hidden smile of pride.

"Father, we cannot wait much longer," Jonathan pressed. "There are nine thousand Philistines over that next hill. They've begun attacking our villages and eroding our defenses. Our men are deserting as we wait for, for... what? What exactly are we waiting for?"

"The Ark of the Covenant and the blessing of the high priest of Israel," Saul said, and not for the first time since the sinking sun had risen that morning.

"Well, if we're going to set him on fire and hurl him onto the other side, he might be of some use to us," Jonathan said, rising to look out of the open tent flap. He searched the horizon once again for signs of the priest's long-awaited party. "What do we need with a self-important old man?"

"Jonathan, that is enough," Saul said sharply. "The men will hear you. I can't command you to believe as I do, but I can have your tongue cut out to stop your dissention if I must."

"I'm sorry, Majesty," Jonathan said sincerely, more concerned with his father's censure than his threats. "I will be quiet if it is your will. But it is for your part that Samuel angers me so. I don't think he respects you or the crown he himself gave you."

"My son," Saul said, stroking the hair on Jonathan's bowed head. "You must be patient with Samuel and me. We are old men. We are trying to change with this modern age, but it is not easy. There has never been a king over Israel before. We must invent the path we follow, in accordance with the will of the God of our fathers and the beliefs and traditions of our people."

"Yes, Father," Jonathan relented. He was unwilling to risk Saul's renewed wrath, and glad enough of his father's forgiveness, that he did not say all that was in his heart. "With your leave I will return to my own tent until you need me."

"Stay, there is food and drink," Saul said, gesturing at the low table laid with what would have been the feast on a holy day for any home in the kingdom.

"I need some rest," Jonathan said with a hint of a bow as he stepped back to leave.

"Very well, my son," Saul said, taking a seat on one of the richly embroidered cushions surrounding the table. His top advisers were already seated, awaiting what had been intended as the midday meal. "I'll send for you as soon as Samuel arrives. I want you with me for the sacrifice."

"Yes, Father," Jonathan said, struggling to keep his temper as he fled. "Uncle Abner, gentlemen." Jonathan nodded a respectful good-bye to the men at his father's table as he went. He exchanged a look of resignation with his Uncle Abner, long his closest advisor.

Abner nodded in silent reply, acknowledging his appreciation for Jonathan's attempts.

Jonathan left the great tent and made his way hastily through the dwindling camp.

"Prince Jonathan? When do we move?" a nearby lieutenant called to him.

"After Samuel's blessing," Jonathan called back as genially as his rage permitted. He made his face a mask, showing no sign of how he felt. It was not the first time. He had spent most of his twenty-seven years on his father's campaigns. There had been little time and less privacy for such luxuries as the personal feelings of the king's son.

Saul had been at war almost since the day he'd been anointed.

Jonathan was a young man of a new age. Raised in the palace, bright and well educated, to him the ways and beliefs of his father's generation seemed more like the superstitions of their enemies than of an enlightened people. Jonathan's views made him skeptical of the myth and ritual of his father's devout beliefs. He had always thought Samuel chose his father in the hope that he would be able to continue to rule Israel by ruling her king.

It seemed to Jonathan that Samuel took credit for Saul's every success and gave his father his due only in failure. With the devotion of a son, Jonathan saw that Saul had turned out to be a brilliant tactician. He had led a country with no army, no treasury, no taxes, and no borders to prosperity and victory over some of the most fearsome warriors in the world. He'd won the respect of his people and the consternation of Samuel.

Jonathan's frustration and anger grew as, again and again, Samuel set his father up to fail. He gave Saul impossible tasks and made unreasonable demands—always, according to the priest, the very instructions of the Lord. Again and again his father rose to the occasion and foiled Samuel's plans for his father's failure.

What Jonathan did not see, could not believe, was that Saul had become more and more dependent on Samuel's unfailing prescience and prophesy to guide him to military success. Uncertain of his own talents, in Saul's heart the credit for all his victories belonged to the Lord. He grew unable to act without divine guidance through Samuel.

To Jonathan's eye it appeared Samuel's influence grew in direct proportion to Saul's indecision. Though Jonathan kept his relations with the priest cordial, out of respect for his father, there was tension between the two. Despite his father's reassurances, Jonathan could not believe what his father believed. He simply found it too hard to believe in something he could not see or account for on the field or in his battle plans.

"Well, Palti, the old man is at it again," Jonathan called to his armor-bearer as he stalked into the tent.

"Which old man?" Paltiel asked without looking up from polishing the prince's breastplate.

Paltiel ben Laish had been with Jonathan all his life. His father, Laish, was an elder of Gallim, a small village near Saul's childhood home in Benjamin. Assigned as a boy to be the prince's companion, Paltiel and Jonathan had been trained and educated together. Palti, as Jonathan called him, looked forward to a bright future in the kingdom, which would one day be ruled by the man who most confided in him.

"The priest who would be Samson," Jonathan snorted derisively.

"Your father would slap you with an open hand if he heard you say that," Paltiel said, managing to smile and click his tongue.

"Sadly more to defend Samuel than the true hero," Jonathan said, flinging himself facedown onto this cot.

"So, what exactly is the high priest of all the tribes of Israel up to today?" Paltiel asked, setting aside the breastplate. He rose and filled a cup with water and a taste of wine.

"As always, the man's object is known only to him and the private God who speaks so no one else can hear," Jonathan said, leaning on one elbow. "My guess would be that he's trying to feel powerful by making the king wait. But who ever knows what that old sorcerer is up to?"

"Here, calm yourself," Paltiel said, offering the cup to the prince.

"I wish that I could find the calm in a cup of wine that my father does," Jonathan said, taking it. "I can at least end my thirst, if not my mood."

Jonathan stared through the open flap of the tent as he lay back on his bed cushions. His mind wandered as he drank. He felt trapped. Not by the Philistines who outnumbered him, three men for Israel's every one. He felt mired in the will of the Lord—*or more likely*, he thought, *the will of Samuel*. Whoever chose his father as king had chosen his life as the king's son as well. Was it God's will? Was it Samuel's ambition? Either way, Jonathan had been offered a life of legend before he was yet a man, as unchangeable as the words etched in a monument.

Surrounded by enemies in a land that was occupied when their ancestors arrived generations before, Jonathan's life had been all about fighting because his father's life was all about fighting, because Samuel and his God told them so.

Jonathan was thankful in many ways to be freed of the servile life, scratching for food and deferring to others, shared by most of his countrymen. But he bridled at the bit that duty put in his mouth. What good was it to be king when it took away all choice?

"Do you want something to eat?" Paltiel asked, as much to break the silence as to serve.

"No, but feast yourself," Jonathan answered, handing him his empty cup. Paltiel was at once friend and servant. "They've put out food in my father's tent. Go and get yourself a plate of what you like and tell them it's for me. I'm going to try to rest."

"Thank you, my prince," Paltiel said with a genuine smile. Despite the difference in their rank, Jonathan had always treated him more as a brother than an attendant. "I'll bring back a little something extra just in case you change your mind later. We must be ready for battle."

"Should there actually be one," Jonathan said with an angry snort. He turned on his side to try for the peace of sleep.

"By your leave," Paltiel said, backing out of the room. Jonathan was never one for form, but Paltiel felt it was important. He took great delight in the status he derived from his proximity to the prince. The little nods and respectful salutes he received as he passed through the camp. The way that officers made way for him and the guards held the flaps of the king's tent open for his unquestioned entrance. The little tributes of power swelled Paltiel's ambition.

That day at Gilgal, Paltiel entered King Saul's tent more unnoticed than usual.

"Your Majesty, we simply cannot wait for the man any longer," the king's general declared, pounding the table as he shouted. "We've had reports of extensive desertion in the ranks. We are down almost five hundred men since this morning, and we'll lose as many more before the sun sets. We can ill afford this...."

"Abner, you forget yourself," Saul shouted back at him.

"I have not forgotten you or your men," Abner said, uncowed by Saul's legendary rage.

"Yet you would have us go into battle without the ark or proper blessing?" Saul demanded.

"We've been in battle without the ark as often as not." Abner shrugged reasonably. "You are the Lord's chosen. Who better than you to make the sacrifice?"

"It just doesn't seem right," Saul said, his brow furrowed. Unsure of the path, he wavered in his argument. "Is Saul among the prophets?" He thought of the little song ruefully. If only the gift would return to him. He counted on Samuel for his vision but still had to rule as king. He walked the blade's edge, both king and subject.

Samuel had grown more and more impossible to work with over the years. More than once the priest had made Saul's life a misery for the smallest slight and the least departure from his God-given instructions.

"Perhaps something has happened to him, Your Majesty," Abner suggested soothingly. "He is an old man. Anything is possible. He was supposed to be here seven days ago and still we wait. Samuel himself could not want you to sacrifice this battle or the lives of these faithful men." Abner's words were from his reason, not his heart, since neither he nor any man could predict what bloody or monstrous request the priest might next make.

"I suppose you are right." Saul sighed, wishing for the fleeting prophetic vision that had shown him his duty so clearly. "Make ready for the sacrifice. If, by the time the preparations have been made, Samuel has not arrived, then we proceed without him."

"Yes, Your Majesty," Abner said, bowing as he all but ran from the tent, his staff in unbidden pursuit.

Paltiel took the two plates he'd filled generously while he listened and followed. He balanced the dishes as he made haste for his master's tent, certain that Jonathan's appetite would return upon hearing the news.

And Saul said, Bring hither a burnt offering to me, and peace offerings. And he offered the burnt offering.

1 Samuel 13:9

THE SACRIFICE had been hastily made. The smell of burning ox flesh still filled the air. Saul stood on the hill and called his men to arms. A cry went up that made the hair on Jonathan's neck bristle with emotion and pride. His father, for all his faults, was an admirable commander. Without education or training, he had built the army of Israel from a band of badly armed villagers into a formidable fighting force. It was Saul's conviction the men followed, Jonathan thought, his father's absolute faith. They believed that he believed.

It was a trait Jonathan admired, though not one he felt he would ever possess.

A trumpet blast fell on the ceremony like water on coals. The long-awaited Samuel crested the hill. A hush fell over the crowd as Saul turned to defer to his priest.

"Great Baal," Jonathan snarled under his breath, fortunate that his father did not hear him invoking the Philistine god of storms and thunder.

"Saul, what have you done?" Samuel demanded. He descended on the king like an angry mother on a troublesome child rather than a subject speaking to his king.

Jonathan's hand unconsciously found the hilt of his sword as the old man began raining abuse on his father.

"You come before the Lord with pride and arrogance and presume to make the sacrifice?" Samuel demanded, closing the distance between the two men.

"Samuel, we thought something had happened to you," Saul began to explain. The king he had only just been evaporated as Jonathan watched. "We have awaited your arrival and your blessing for seven days and nights."

"It is not bad enough that you would bring battle so soon after Yom Kippur," Samuel shouted, playing to his audience. "Now you blaspheme by making a false sacrifice to support your unholy war-making?"

"In truth it was the uncircumcised who chose the time and place of battle, not I," Saul argued.

Jonathan looked at the ground. He could not bear the sight of his father flailing and stammering.

"What sort of king are you to take your orders from infidels, rather than waiting upon the word and the blessing of the Lord?" Samuel demanded, striking Saul's breastplate with his staff. "You have turned your back on the Lord, and now the Lord will turn his back on you."

That was it.

It was all Jonathan could do not to draw his sword and strike the man dead.

The troops, fired for battle only a few words before, ran into the hills.

"The Lord will choose another man to be king," Samuel railed, no longer even speaking to Saul but addressing the crowd directly. "This battle is lost, and you have lost your kingdom. I leave you to your will, since the will of the Lord no longer suits you. The Lord will find a man after his own heart to take your place."

Samuel turned to leave without asking for so much as a crust of bread or a drink of water. Jonathan thought it a calculated insult to Saul's hospitality and his authority and proof the old man had not traveled far. The prince could only guess that Samuel saw the battle as a lost cause and was scheming to save his "prophecy" from the tarnish of either predicting a failure or a victory that did not come. This way, Jonathan reasoned, the priest could predict the failure he had surely caused.

Saul fell to his knees to beg for Samuel's forgiveness. "Please, Samuel, leave us the ark to bear before us as protection."

Jonathan watched, his heart breaking.

"It is the Lord who is your shield," Samuel called over his shoulder. "The ark has not protected those who've not been worthy to carry it before you. Keep it. The Lord will return it to the holy, washed clean of your blood."

It was a terrible curse. The king collapsed to the ground, stricken by it.

The ark had been lost only once before, by the ill-fated sons of Samuel's predecessor, the last hereditary judge, Eli. Their demise had brought Samuel to power. The priest damned Saul by the comparison to the two. Had the old man crafted the same scenario to secure the return of the reins of power to his own hand? The similarity was too terrible to contemplate yet too evident for Jonathan to deny.

It was the end, worse than the outcome of the worst battle they had ever faced. Jonathan helped his father to his feet and led him toward his tent.

"No, no, leave me here in the shade of this tamarisk tree," Saul said before they could reach the royal pavilion. "I must speak to my generals and determine a course of action. Perhaps we must leave the field to our enemies today."

"Father...," Jonathan began but could not offer comfort without also offering offense.

"Here, let me help," his Uncle Abner said, lending his arm to the king.

"Yes," Jonathan said, stepping back. "Thank you. I... I must seek my own counsel." Jonathan's rage permitted him to say no more to comfort his father just then.

As Saul began to assemble what was left of their forces, Jonathan sought the privacy of his own tent.

"The monster has defeated us more handily than our own enemies," Jonathan bellowed. He kicked over furniture and broke the dishes and jars

Paltiel had so carefully packed to preserve their palace way of life even on campaign.

"Your Majesty, I implore you," Paltiel pleaded on behalf of the crockery. "How will we live if you destroy all our possessions?"

"Live?" Jonathan said, bursting into wild laugher. "The instrument of our immediate demise is just the other side of that wadi. Those cliffs are the only reason we are still alive now. Both armies keep their high ground. But geography will not protect our few against their thousands when they decide at their leisure to attack us.

"We don't even have sharp swords without our enemies' skills to put an edge on them," Jonathan went on, his laughter bordering on hysterical. "You are looking at a dead man, Palti. Who cares for the dishes of the departed? Destroy it all or make a present of it to the Philistines, for it will be theirs in either case by the dawn of the new day."

"Oh, well then, if we have nothing to lose," Paltiel said, tossing an armload of bowls that he'd managed to rescue from his master's onslaught.

"Hold there," Jonathan said with such force that Paltiel thought he referred to the pottery that now lay in shards at his feet. "We have nothing to lose," Jonathan echoed, suddenly as joyous as Palti had ever seen him on a feast day.

"Yes, Majesty," Paltiel nodded solemnly.

"Don't you see?" Jonathan said, his enthusiasm undimmed by Paltiel's dark mood. "We're already dead. We'll see whose god is in the field with us today, by God. Get my armor together. We're going on campaign."

"On campaign?" Paltiel asked, as concerned for his prince's sanity as their precarious situation. "Should I notify the men?"

"No, just you and I," Jonathan said, his voice dropping to a whisper. "If we tell them, they'll only try to reason with us, and there is no place left here for reason."

"It is to be a campaign of two?" Paltiel asked fearfully as he began threading the straps into Jonathan's armor.

"Just so," Jonathan crowed, gathering up his sandals and lacing the bronze greaves onto his calves with them. "If we're already dead men, who cares where they find the bodies? What difference if we meet our end here or in the Philistines' teeth? Get my sword and burn the tent; we're going out in a blaze of glory, Palti."

Paltiel was unable to convince Jonathan to take along a few other soldiers for moral if not military support. He was able to persuade Jonathan not to torch their lodgings with flakes of reason from the prince's own pastry of logic. "If we burn the tent, the others will come to see to us, and your plan will be discovered."

"Good man," Jonathan said, smacking Paltiel smartly on the shoulder. Then, turning, he made for the rim of the nearby wadi that separated the two forces. "Come along, then."

With a sigh and the resolve of the truly desperate, Paltiel followed his lifelong master out of camp and into the wilderness. He rarely accompanied Jonathan into battle. After preparing the prince for combat, Palti most often stayed behind to see to Jonathan's comforts upon his return. Still, he reasoned, there seemed little in the way of choice. Given the day's disastrous turn of events, the only question left to him was where he wanted to die. Despite his unctuous and slightly pompous nature, Paltiel was, in the end, loyal to his prince. When the sun set on their ruin, he preferred history find him at Jonathan's side in the field to burned in the tent.

"Majesty," Paltiel said, after they were a few paces outside of camp. He had regained some of his wits during Jonathan's silent, steady progress toward their objective.

"Yes, Palti?"

"We are headed in the direction of the wadi," Paltiel pointed out respectfully.

"Exactly," Jonathan replied with conviction.

Burned with the tent was looking better all the time.

Though the Philistines' massive force and the king's armies were formidable, thus far the wadi had defeated both factions. Neither group had yet been willing to surrender their respective high ground. The narrow and rocky wadi had been the greater force by keeping them apart.

The plan became clear to Paltiel. They were in fact going to scale down the smooth cliff face, dangling above razor-sharp rocks into a basin no wider than the footpath there, completely vulnerable to the least attack from above. Then, with little more than their grit, teeth, and fingernails, they would ascend the steep rock face opposite in order to hoist themselves directly into the middle of the Philistines' camp. As he looked down into the breach, he knew that not only was his master mad, but that their end was at hand. Whether the fall or the Philistines took them, it would be swift.

"Mark this," Jonathan grunted as they neared the upper edge of the Philistine side of the gorge. "When we get near the top, I'll call out to them that we are arrived."

"So much for the advantage of surprise," Paltiel muttered under his breath.

"What's that, Palti?" Jonathan hissed back over his shoulder.

"Right behind you, sir," Palti said, his voice low in hope they might die on level ground.

"Right," Jonathan went on, kicking dust into Paltiel's face as he ascended. "If they call out 'Come on up,' then the Lord is with us, and no one can stop the righteous. If not, then Samuel is right. God left with him, and good riddance to such a fickle and faithless deity."

"Right you are, sir," Paltiel said, trying to spit out some of the dust as quietly as possible.

"Softly now, crawl up here beside me," Jonathan instructed as he came to the upper edge of the cliff without breaching the top. "Let us go up together and present a united front."

"Yes, our numbers should make the difference," Paltiel said, coming up beside Jonathan on his left.

"You are a good man, Paltiel ben Laish," Jonathan said, clapping him on the shoulder, almost dislodging him from his precarious fingerhold. "It has been an honor to know you."

"It has been my honor," Paltiel said. Tears stung his eyes from the glare of truth near at hand. He knew these words might be the last he ever spoke. "You are a good man and great leader. I am with you, heart and soul, to the end and beyond."

Jonathan smiled and nodded, still grasping Paltiel's shoulder. Unable to speak more, he too felt the enormity of destiny upon their two lives. "Ready?" he asked at last.

Paltiel nodded with as much conviction as he could muster.

"Now."

The two men vaulted themselves over the crest of the wadi and onto level ground with as much grace as possible.

"Lay down your arms before the army of the God of Israel," Jonathan bellowed to the twenty or so men. The Philistines were loosely scattered around the largely unprotected and, only just before, seemingly unbreachable line of defense.

Surprised and startled at first, the Philistines there at the rear of so massive a force began to laugh at the audacity of two men to attack their twenty, let alone ten thousand.

"Come on up and we'll teach you a lesson," the captain called out, still laughing.

Jonathan loaded his bow from one of the two quivers strapped to his back. Like his father he was a head taller than even the tallest of men. Prince Jonathan made a formidable sight as he cried out and charged the small band of men. He fired his first arrow on the fly. It clipped the ear of the captain before striking a small tree just over the Philistine officer's shoulder. As the arrow found its target, the ground became like water under the captain's feet. The tree fell. The boulders, strewn along the edge of the chasm from which the wailing Israelite had emerged, began to tumble down the hillside. Gathering speed and debris, they crushed everything in their path.

As the massive earthquake continued, so too did Prince Jonathan's charge. Heedless of the pitching earth beneath his feet, he got off shot after shot, taking down ten men with as many arrows. "Flee before the God of Israel," he cried as he kept up his deadly barrage of arrows.

Rather than taking up arms against the prince, the Philistines present did just as he asked. They fled.

"Flee before the God of Israel," the Philistines shouted as they tumbled down the hill with the boulders and trees.

Terrified and overwhelmed, the cry spread through the Philistine force as they began to retreat. Jonathan and Paltiel pursued the retreating Philistine forces out of the hills and onto the plain below Gilgal, where King Saul and Abner were drilling up the six hundred or so men who had remained loyal. As Saul's forces tried to keep their footing despite the massive quake, their attention was suddenly captured by the movement on the plain before them.

"Flee before the God of Israel," the Philistines cried out as they ran, terrified, from their hillside fortifications into the valley. Many were wiped out by the enormous avalanche the temblor had triggered on the Micmash side of the basin.

Saul and his men stood stunned, as much or more by the sight of their rout as the quake.

"Look," one of the scouts shouted. "It's the prince."

As the king looked on, his son chased the Philistines out of the hills, raining arrows down on them and leading the cry "Flee before the God of Israel."

A cheer went up. The king's call to action was trumpeted and met almost before it was made. With the Ark of the Covenant borne before them, they plunged into battle and fell upon the Philistines. Deserters from Saul's thinned forces, hidden in the wooded hills above, came down into the basin like winter rains, sweeping the Philistines from the vale and back toward Philistia.

By nightfall the Philistine army had splintered and been pushed back nearly half the distance to their own land. Most had not stopped running even when the Israelites made camp for the night at Beth-Aven.

"We must fast in observance of the Lord's deliverance," Saul decreed, ever mindful of his duty. "Let it be known that we will show our thanks to God by fasting between now and sunset tomorrow. Praise be to the Lord for our mighty victory."

And the men of Israel were distressed that day: for Saul had adjured the people, saying, Cursed be the man that eateth any food until evening, that I may be avenged on mine enemies. So none of the people tasted any food.

1 Samuel 14:24

JONATHAN AWOKE with a start. He was uncertain at first where he was. The ground was cold beneath him. His body was sore and stiff.

The pursuit of the Philistines had taken him a long way from camp and the princely comforts of his tent. The prince and the few men who had caught up to him followed until the sun deserted them. They needed to return to camp for weapons and supplies before they could resume the chase. This meant that, though the prince had harried the Philistines to within reach of bearding them in their lair, they would live to fight another day. They too returned home for rest and supplies. Once the rainy winter season ended and spring baked the mud into roads again, the Philistines would have regained their strength, and the cycle would begin again.

"What day is this?" the prince groaned, sitting up.

"What day, sir?" Palti asked, confused. "It is the seventeenth day of Bul."

"Is it some day of holy punishment or divine retribution?" Jonathan asked, rising painfully to his feet.

"Not officially, no, my prince," Palti answered, smiling at the prince's bitter wit.

"Yet there are no smells of a meal being prepared or warm tents over our heads or a privy dug for the officers," Jonathan groused. He tried to compose himself with as much dignity as a man might after spending a night on the ground.

"Yes, as you know, my lord, the leader of our little band insisted that we pursue the enemy well past the point of no return and the help of the king's main forces. So we stopped here unsupplied for the night." Palti and Jonathan exchanged smirks. The bit of impudence was the sort of jest they often shared out of the hearing of others.

"Well, he must need new advisors to have stayed such an unwise and cursed uncomfortable course," Jonathan answered back over his shoulder as he pissed against a tree at the edge of the clearing.

"It does seem that after winning the battle for the king single-handed, they could have sent something out to you."

"Single-handed?" Jonathan roared with laughter. "Is that to be the legend?"

"It is what the men are saying," Palti said with a certain air. He offered the last half skin of water as the prince came near the smoky little fire he'd managed.

"The men won the battle. I just started the fight," Jonathan said. Taking the skin, he squeezed and swallowed a prudent taste of what little remained.

"We would have been in a bad way if, when the Philistines looked over their shoulders, they had seen only you and I in pursuit."

"Still, I was very proud to be at your side," Palti said quietly as the two men stood by the sad fire. "After I got over thinking you had completely taken leave of all your senses."

They laughed together, two men proud enough that they needed no recognition.

"All right, you insolent upstart," Jonathan said, cuffing his friend heartily. "Wake up whoever's left with us and let's get our fleas and stink back to camp."

"Yes, my lord," Palti said, signaling to the sentry on watch to sound a call.

"Oh, but stay," Jonathan said, raising a hand. He took up his spear and moved purposefully toward the tree line.

"What is it, my lord?" Palti asked, wary as he made to follow, waving off the guard just before he sounded the call. "Philistines?"

"I shall be a true hero now," Jonathan called back, picking up his pace to a trot. "And I'll have your job, too, I think."

"What is it?" Palti asked, running after him.

"Nourishment," Jonathan shouted joyously, driving the spear into the side of an old tree. The bark splintered and fell away. Honey oozed down the skin of the dead husk of the oak. A few bees, too drunk with cold to be a threat, took to lazy flight. Jonathan raised his spear tip to his mouth and ate the honey, comb and all. He looked to Palti with a broad grin and extended the spear to his servant. "Sweets to break the fast, and Mother not here to scold us."

"Wait," the sentry called out running toward them. "Stop where you are."

Both men turned and drew their swords. The spear and its sticky sweetness fell to the dirt.

"Where?" Jonathan demanded, pivoting and waving his sword with dire purpose.

"There," the sentry said. He pointed at Jonathan's spear as he came up beside them and slid to a halt in the loose dirt and leaves underfoot.

"My spear?"

"Your father," the man panted, breathless from running.

"He's an older man," Jonathan scoffed. "Broader too."

The jest was lost on the sentry. Paltiel cackled appreciatively.

"He decreed a fast until sunset to show thanks to the Lord for our victory," the guard managed. Lifting the spear, he cleaned the sharp metal cap of the honey and handed it back.

"A fast?" Jonathan bellowed. "In the middle of a battle? Is the Lord a general for the Philistines, that he would ask us to fast during battle?"

The guard fell to his knees, his head bowed.

"You did right to tell us," Palti assured the terrified man, helping him to his feet. "Now go and wake the others. Tell them it is time to make ready to return. Speak of this to no one. The king's word is law."

"Yes sir, thank you, sir," the sentry said, backing and then running away.

"Plague and famine," Jonathan swore, throwing his sword. Striking with such force, the blade stood upright in the soil, trembling. "How are we to win a war when my father cannot stop looking to the old gods and old ideas that got us into this mess in the first place? Samuel calls down this God's curses upon us all before the battle. Then my father wants to pay homage to the same God by starving me and the men who gave him the victory despite this petulant deity."

"Your father was chosen king by that same God," Palti said sharply. He hoped to help rein in the anger, which he more than shared, before the men drew too near.

"How are we to win a war looking behind us?" Jonathan seethed.

"We must win the battle together," Palti advised, taking Jonathan by the elbow. He guided his prince toward the rest of their clothes and armor.

"You are right, I know," Jonathan said. He breathed deeply, trying to slow his racing heart. "I just so often feel that we have to fight two battles on every field. We must first overcome Samuel and his God before we can begin to face whoever has showed up to raid our villages and kill our people. Where is this God when the villages are burning?"

"Sire, all this will change when you are the king," Palti said, placing Jonathan's breastplate against his chest. He raised the prince's hands and placed them against the cool metal to steady it, then began to secure the straps. "To be a king, you first need a kingdom. Just now you must help your father to get you one to inherit. Meantime it's worth remembering that Samuel, more than the Philistines, is empowered to take it from you."

"Help me lace my sandals," Jonathan said, turning away. He was both chastened and chilled by Paltiel's cold-bloodedly exacting answer. "We've a long walk home on empty stomachs."

"Yes, sire."

Then Saul went up from following the Philistines: and the Philistines went to their own place.

1 Samuel 14:46

"SIRE, THE Philistines are within our grasp," Abner pleaded. "We can strike them down if we but catch them running away."

"Can the Lord want us to put arrows in the backs of our enemies?" Saul said to his cousin, rubbing his throbbing temples. "I cannot think that is the right thing to do. If only Samuel was here to pray for guidance that we might know."

"Majesty, Samuel was not here for yesterday's victory," Abner said, refilling Saul's cup with wine. "Yet our men have wiped out Philistine camps and villages halfway from here to the sea. Already they are driving home plundered herds that would have taken them three years farming to build. Bounty and a blessing fall to us, despite Samuel's curses."

"Do not speak ill of Samuel to me," Saul said, smashing his cup to the ground. "He spoke as he did because I provoked him. I must win the people's hearts as well as their lands and loyalty. I cannot do that without the Lord on my side."

"I do not speak ill of Samuel, but I do think that it is time for him to keep to his temples and his prophesying and leave the battlefield and the palace more to you," Abner said. "Perhaps this victory is a sign of just that."

"But what are we to do now?" Saul said, drinking directly from the wine ewer. "How are we to know our next move—what is right—if we do not consult Samuel?"

"My lord," a young lieutenant said urgently from the flap of the tent. "The sun is going down. The men have set upon the plundered livestock, eating the flesh with the blood still in it."

"You see, cousin," Saul said, turning to Abner. "This is how it begins. If we can win the battle without Samuel, then why obey any of the very Levite laws that made us a tribe to begin with? This is why all the leaders before me were holy men."

"Why then are the lands promised us by the Lord still in the hands of our enemies?"

"Enough," Saul said. He downed the last of what remained in the small pitcher and slammed it onto the table, a final punctuation. "Lieutenant, send word out to the men that they are to bring their prizes here for proper slaughter and for a sacrifice to give thanks for our victory. Sukkot has come early to the battlefield.

"Get some men together and bring a stone here to this spot from the hills yonder so that we might do this thing according to the law and before God,"

Saul concluded, surveying the unruly encampment. "Bring a priest to preside if one is among us."

"Yes, sire," the lieutenant said, striking himself on the chest in salute to his king. He ran to follow his orders, calling out instructions as he went.

Saul watched for a breath as the camp came to order and moved toward a single purpose at his word. A proud smile crossed his face. He had done better at this job than he'd ever thought he could.

"And Abner," Saul said, softly, when no one was nearby. "Just so you know. I could have strangled the old man with my bare hands when he pulled that stunt yesterday. He is the most impossible citizen in my kingdom, but he has never, until yesterday, steered me wrong. We shall seek the Lord's guidance on our own. But we shall speak of Samuel as we would wish to be remembered— for his virtues and not his vitriol."

Then said Jonathan, My father hath troubled the land: see, I pray you, how mine eyes have been enlightened, because I tasted a little of this honey. How much more, if haply the people had eaten freely today of the spoil of their enemies which they found? for had there not been now a much greater slaughter among the Philistines?

1 Samuel 14:29-30

THE AIR was redolent with the smell of burnt flesh as Jonathan led his small raiding party over the last hill into camp. The sun was long set. The only thing preventing him and his men from ending their absurd thanksgiving fast was their complete lack of food.

Their legs grew weak beneath them as the smell of roasting meat rose up to greet them. The wadi between them and the next hill seemed to pull away, stretching ever wider as they traversed the vale. The gentle swell crowned with the king's encampment rose mighty and insurmountable before them.

At last they fell into camp. Their journey at end, their bodies were spent as much from the fasting as the pursuit that had taken them so far from their beds and the cooking fires.

Around them a feast was in progress. The men fell onto all that was offered them to slake their thirst and hunger.

The prince made his way to his father's tent, his mouth watering for the banquet he expected to find laid there. Instead, as was all too often the case, he found only wine and discord around his father's table.

"He has deserted us," Saul was lamenting, his voice thick with the wine that comprised the royal feast. "Jonathan," he cried out, rising. Staggering a step or two, he dropped heavily back into his chair. "You are returned to us safely. There is blessing in that at least."

"Hello, Father," Jonathan said, his brow knit with concern over his father's condition as much as the somber tone that filled the tent like the smoke from a badly made fire. "Who has deserted us in our victory?"

"The Lord has left me," Saul wailed, waving his arms in a broad gesture, spilling wine on his robe.

"We defeated our enemy, wiped his villages from our lands, and lost only the time it took to do it." Jonathan soothed what he assumed was the demon of his father's drunkenness. "The Lord is surely on our side as never before. You should eat something to celebrate our victory."

"I have no appetite, my son," Saul sighed sadly. "You see, not only has Samuel deserted me, but the Lord will not answer. We sacrificed three great bulls to appease him for our disobedience."

"I'm sure he appreciated it," Jonathan said, his tone patronizing. He lamented the loss of so much good meat when he was so hungry.

"But the Lord was silent in answer to my prayers for his guidance," Saul said, tears coming to his eyes. "I thought in my arrogance that perhaps our victory might mean the Lord had chosen me over Samuel—that I was to be the recipient of his word as well as the instrument of his will. And so we fasted in thanksgiving and made sacrifice. Still there is no answer, and our enemies have escaped us."

"Our enemies have escaped us because our men were starving from fasting in the midst of battle. Instead of acting to catch them, we have wasted the day in foolish obeisance to a God who'd already answered us with victory," Jonathan bellowed, his hunger and his anger outmatching his judgment.

"Jonathan, you forget yourself," Abner said firmly. He rose and took his nephew's arm.

"I hope I live long enough to forget what fools we have been today," Jonathan shouted, snatching his arm from the general's grasp. "I thought when that overreaching, power-mad priest had at last left our midst that we might finally proceed as men of good judgment in a modern age, instead of the primitive and superstitious fools that he makes us into."

The tent cleared of most of its occupants as they scurried to escape the storm they could see reigning so clearly on the king's brow.

"You will not speak to me, or of the God of Abraham, in such a manner," Saul raged, upsetting the table and hurling his wine cup at his son. "I have been winning the battles of this country all your life with little more than this primitive God and superstition on my side. I was a mule herder before this rude God you speak of made me king."

"You are a brilliant man who earned those victories by the sweat of your brow and the blood of all of Israel," Jonathan answered back, too hungry and frustrated to be mindful of his place. "That pretender to the title of judge took you for a country fool. He has been playing you for one, taking credit for your victories and blaming you for his own failure to do what you have done. Perhaps now, without the trickery of that market-day faker, your genius will prevail over our enemies, and we can get on with the business of making Israel a country and put an end to the endless wars that Samuel has brought you."

An anxious silence crackled in the air. Chest-to-chest, they towered above the wreckage of the tent and the heads of those brave enough to remain.

Saul was silenced by his fury but compelled by his son's passionate defense. In many ways, with Samuel there, he'd never believed himself to be the author of his fate or his good fortune. Like his wine, the king needed the comfort of his old advisor to absolve him of the terrible responsibilities of making war and choosing death for so many on both sides.

"Perhaps there is a reason for the Lord's silence other than the king," one of the camp priests spoke up. He had been called up for the sacrifice and since been unable to extricate himself from the royal party.

"What do you mean?" Abner asked. Ever the peacemaker in the king's tent, he sought any solution to the insoluble and long-standing argument between father and son.

"Perhaps there is one among us who has sinned against the Lord and eaten the flesh with blood in it, or broken the fast before sundown," the priest offered, attempting to provide a scapegoat to take their sins into the wilderness so they might at last eat.

"And if there is?" Saul asked.

"Oh, blood and thunder," Jonathan shouted, throwing the shield he still carried to the ground. "Are we to take the word of any rube who wears a priest's ephod? I broke the fast. I ate honey I found in a hollow oak by my campsite this morning. The army at our backs was too weak from hunger, or just too weak-minded, to resupply us so that we might make an end of our enemies once and for all. Instead we dull our swords and our wits on the implacable leaden laws of the Levite priests."

"Then you must be put to death," Saul said, dropping to his chair. "Seize him and take him to the altar that we might appease an angry God and regain his will and favor."

"Father, you cannot be serious," Jonathan said as the guards present reluctantly approached the prince and stood on either side of him.

"It is not for me to say," Saul mumbled, hanging his head. His heart was heavy at the thought of losing the Lord's favor and breaking at the thought of losing his most favored son.

Paltiel had stood in the darkness just outside the tent to listen without being swept up into the battle between father and son. On hearing the death sentence pronounced, his mind raced. He moved casually into a group of soldiers milling nearby, oblivious to the dire events unfolding only a few steps away. Helpless, he watched as the soldiers led a stunned Prince Jonathan away. He was terrified that he would be put to death with his prince if the king's eyes were to fall on him. Uncertain and confused, he rushed to the prince's tent. The king's actions seemed like those of a man taken leave of his senses. Paltiel thought seriously of abandoning the life he'd built, getting his things, and heading into the hills to see how the night unfolded.

Blind to his surroundings, he stumbled toward the tent. His mind raced. What could he do? All his power came from the prince. How could he, a mere servant, help?

A young officer looked up from his feast by the fire just outside Jonathan's tent.

"Paltiel, where's the prince?" a young officer asked heartily. "We have been waiting to salute him for leading us to victory yesterday. Is he returned?"

"Yes," Paltiel said, suddenly clear on his course of action. "They are taking him to the altar to pay tribute to him for his actions. Gather as many men as you can and go there quickly."

The officers around the fire were on their feet, their platters forgotten, lighting torches off the fire. They struck their chests in salute and hurried to rally their men to pay tribute.

"Tell the other officers," Paltiel called. He grinned at his deviousness and then hastened to pack a bag, just in case.

The trumpets sounded throughout the camp. Soldiers by the thousand fell into formation. They poured toward the altar in force to honor their beloved prince and hero. None were aware that Jonathan was being taken there for slaughter and sacrifice.

Saul was in agony. He was torn between his love for his son and his loyalty to a God who had made him a king and victorious in his campaigns. It was right to honor the law of the Levites, but it was his son. Salty tears fell into his wine as he tried to drink up enough courage to order Jonathan's execution.

"Oh Lord, what is your will?" Saul begged. "What would you have me do? Answer me," he wailed.

"Jonathan, Jonathan, Jonathan," the shouting began. It grew louder as more joined the crowd just outside the tent. Saul paused and listened. He wondered at the noise. Cheering and trumpeting mixed with singing and the chanting of his son's name.

He set aside his wine. Smoothing his hair and robes, he gathered himself into the figure of a king and emerged from his tent. There he beheld an amazing sight. The field surrounding the altar was filled with torch-bearing men calling out for his son and singing his praises. "Give us Prince Jonathan. We want the prince."

It was his answer.

"Thank you, beloved Lord," Saul shouted into the deafening acclaim. He ran toward the altar like a boy homeward for supper. "Thank you."

Jonathan stood quietly with the guards, awaiting the king's arrival. Catching up to them, Saul threw his arms around his son. The two men nearly toppled, spinning in place from the momentum.

"Father…," Jonathan began, determined to forgive the old man for doing what he knew his father thought to be his duty.

"Not another word out of you," Saul said, taking Jonathan's arm and dragging him onto the altar. The king raised his son's hand high above their heads clasped in his own.

"I give you my son, Prince Jonathan, the hero of the battle of Gilgal and my true and rightful heir, chosen just now by the Lord," Saul proclaimed. The crowd responded with a joy equal to their king's and a voice large enough to express his thanks.

And the people said unto Saul, Shall Jonathan die, who hath wrought this great salvation in Israel? God forbid: as the Lord liveth, there shall not one hair of his head fall to the ground; for he hath wrought with God this day. So the people rescued Jonathan, that he died not.

1 Samuel 14:45

"I GIVE you the bravest man in Israel, my son, Prince Jonathan," Saul said, raising his goblet yet again. The harvest feast crowd filled the palace banquet hall with their reply.

"Prince Jonathan," the crowd echoed.

Jonathan winced at the tribute. His father had ordered his death with the same conviction only a few days before at Gilgal. Since their return to Gibeah, Saul had hardly ceased with the tributes, or the wine.

There had always been an understanding that he would be the heir to Saul's throne, but it had never before been said officially. While Jonathan was proud of the tribute and the accolades, the notes of the praises being sung were a shade flattened by the fact that, only a heartbeat before his acclamation, his father had slated him for execution to avoid offending Samuel or his God.

He nodded graciously to the crowd as they drank to his health, to his bravery, to his archery, to his unborn children, and to excess. Saul was drunk more and more of late. The excuse of toasting his much-vaunted son at a festival that was all about excess was the ideal occasion for his father's wine consumption.

Jonathan smiled sadly. He knew that a festive king tonight meant a morose and remorseful king for at least the next day and possibly longer. His father's moods, always powerful and unpredictable, seemed to worsen with each passing year. The wine helped at first. Then it became as much a part of the problem as the solution. With the rains of winter beginning, so too would begin the long dark moods of the season. These combined with days and weeks of the king barricaded in his chambers with only his wine to comfort him.

He could find no blame for his father. It seemed manifest, given the burden and sheer bloody brutality of the life for which he had been "chosen."

"The next king of Israel, Prince Jonathan."

"Prince Jonathan," the cheer went up again. Jonathan was no longer even paying attention. He was certain no one present would remember much if anything that passed that night. He rose and embraced his father warmly. The drinking, the moods, the rage, even the death sentence did not temper his love for his father. In fact, none of it would have hurt Jonathan so deeply had he not felt so strongly about the man.

"Father," he said into Saul's ear as he drew him into the embrace. "I've had too much wine I think. I must return to my apartments and get some rest."

"I've seen thirty more harvests than you, boy, and the celebration has just begun for me," Saul said with a slight tone of redress.

"That's why you are the king," Jonathan answered lightly, breaking the embrace but holding his father still at arm's length.

"And how will you be king?" Saul demanded laughing.

"Earlier in the day," Jonathan joked, grasping his father's shoulder affectionately.

Saul laughed heartily in reply.

"Good night, Father."

"You have no idea," Saul said, a strange twinkle in his eyes.

Jonathan marked it down to the new vintage, and with a formal public bow he withdrew to the family's private rooms.

The palace of Gibeah had been built for his father by the people, in homage, after his first major victory at Jebesh. The people were not only grateful to him but proud of themselves. The palace they built was an expression of their pride and their gratitude to their king.

In the lifetime that had passed since Jebesh, Saul had defeated Edom, beaten back Moab and the kings of Zobah, vanquished the Amalekites, the Ammonites, and held the Philistines at bay. As the kingdom had grown and prospered under Saul's rule, so too had its capital. The city of Gibeah had grown into a sprawling center of government with the ever-expanding palace at its heart. A substantial share of the palace was devoted to public spaces. There was a massive banquet hall. The throne room had been built large enough to accommodate all of those needing an audience with the king. Beyond were offices, treasuries, counting rooms, armories, and accommodations for a standing guard and a sizeable retinue of officers and staff, courtesans, eunuchs, servants, and concubines.

As grand as the public portion of the palace, the private quarters surpassed them. They were as fine as the country could afford for the king they held so dear. In addition to the private dining rooms, drawing rooms, baths, gardens, and quarters for servants and the high-ranking, there were luxurious apartments for the members of the royal family.

Jonathan's rooms were second only to those of the king in their luxury and grandeur, a compensation for spending almost as much time on the battlefield as in residence. Jonathan had been on campaign since the previous spring. The harvest festival marked the beginning of winter, a time when the weather forced even their enemies to remain at home. Crossing the courtyard and gardens, an ease came over him. He was particularly pleased to avail himself once again of the extravagant comforts of home. As he approached his own private oasis, the massive carved wooden doors swung wide.

"Good evening, my lord," Palti said, taking Jonathan's cloak as he entered the large main room. Flames from a central pit flickered on the painted wall panels. The hangings rustled softly in the breeze from the open doors. "How was the banquet?"

"It gave me something truly to be thankful for," Jonathan joked ruefully. "The peace and quiet of returning to my rooms."

A twittering of laughter and sounds of splashing water drifted into the main room from beyond the hangings that separated the sitting area from the prince's private baths.

"Who is…?"

"A present from your father," Palti said in answer to the unasked question. He drew back the richly embroidered silks to reveal a selection of women, in various states of undress, preparing his bath.

"Good evening, my prince," said one with fiery copper hair, who was adding another steaming pitcher of water to the substantial pool at the center of the room.

"Prince Jonathan," trilled the giggler, a dark beauty who emptied the remainder of a basket of flower petals into the pool. She rushed to his side to help him off with his clothes.

"Hello," Jonathan said with a grin. He allowed himself to be disrobed and led into the bath by the three women.

"We are a gift from your father, my lord," explained the third. A flaxen-haired lovely from the exotic north with her strange lilting accent, she alternated between pouring perfumed oil into the steaming water and rubbing it into his skin. "He sends a message with his present."

"Sorry about the execution," the three said in harmony, unaware of the meaning of the words they had been taught. "Forgive a superstitious old man."

Jonathan's laugh came up in bubbles as he slid beneath the surface of the water. The delicate hands played over his body as his companions joined him.

Samuel also said unto Saul, The Lord sent me to anoint thee to be king over his people, over Israel: now therefore hearken thou unto the voice of the words of the Lord.

1 Samuel 15:1

"PUNISH THE Amalekites for what they did to the children of Israel when they waylaid them as they came up from Egypt," Samuel railed, pounding the table and his breast. He preached in a frenzy of conviction, as he so often did when he conveyed the word of God to King Saul and his elite commanders.

"Lord, give me patience," Jonathan said, rising to leave. Saul shot him a stern look that cooled his resolve and returned him to his seat.

It was not the first time he had heard some version of this rant from Samuel. It was the reason they were gathered in the wretched tent outside Telaim in the bleak and inhospitable Negev of southern Judah. Once his father and the holy seer had made peace following the incident at Gilgal, it had been just as though no one had been rebuked and publicly humiliated.

Following their miraculous victory there over the Philistines, for which Samuel was somehow managing to take credit, their forces swelled. Two hundred thousand foot soldiers from the tribes of Israel and an additional ten thousand from Bethlehem, Hebron, and other cities and settlements of Judah were united as one behind their king and his blessed prince. Moreover, the armies were not just the young, the poor, and the late-born looking for opportunities taken by the burgeoning population and job-stealing iron. The first families were sending their eldest sons, trained and outfitted, to join the growing campaign to take all of Canaan for the Israelites and fulfill the prophecies of Samuel's predecessors.

"We will pursue them into Egypt if we must," Saul declared, rising and then kneeling before Samuel for his blessing. "God's will be done."

Samuel placed his hand upon the king's bowed head. He closed his eyes and moaned the singing words of prayer. Everyone kept still and tried to look appropriately serious and reverent.

Saul rose and motioned for Jonathan to take his place.

Reluctantly Jonathan crossed to stand before Samuel.

The two regarded one another.

Samuel offered Jonathan a kindly smile. Despite the animosity between them, Samuel saw Jonathan as a great salvation. He had publicly been most supportive of Saul's decision to name Jonathan as heir following the young prince's breathtaking heroics.

"May the Lord fill you with the same genius and bravery that inspired you to triumph at Gilgal, my prince," Samuel said, grasping Jonathan firmly by the shoulders. "May he move heaven and earth, as he did on your side there, to keep you safe and grant you victory over the enemies of Israel."

Only Saul's firm hand on Jonathan's shoulder convinced him to kneel before Samuel. He had not forgiven the priest for the risk he had caused at the battle he now claimed as his God's victory. Out of respect for his father's faith, Jonathan knelt. Samuel again sang the prayers. His voice sounded old and pleading to Jonathan.

The process was repeated for each of the generals. The party then moved outside the tent to make the formal sacrifice before the vast troops gathered there.

Jonathan stood at his father's side during the ceremony. He harbored doubts. He was following his father into an ill-advised campaign at the behest of a priest he did not trust, on behalf of a God of whom he was, at best, uncertain. Samuel's insistence on the brutality of their tactics, killing the women, children, and livestock of the Amalekites as they razed their villages, was as abhorrent to the prince as the necessity of righting an old slight that had happened in the time of Moses.

The bull's blood ran across the stone slab before them.

At last the ceremony was over. Samuel returned to Ramah, and the troops made ready to march the next day. Jonathan returned to his tent to be free from the stifling public obligations of rank.

Palti and several servants were packing and making preparations.

"Prince Jonathan, how was the sacrifice?" Palti asked him as he entered. "Do you require anything?"

"What goes on in here?" Jonathan demanded irritably as he began removing the armor and ceremonial cloak.

"I'm packing what we won't need tonight to make an early start of it tomorrow," Palti said, rising to help the prince unlace his armor. "If it disturbs you...."

"No, but perhaps they can take what's packed to be loaded up and leave us in peace while I change," Jonathan suggested with a weary sigh.

"Take those things out and load them on the prince's cart. Then see to the horses and livery," Palti directed the men who were packing the crates with the prince's plate. He hurried them away before he returned to attending the prince. "I take it the ceremony was not to your liking."

"Oh, I don't care about all that superstitious nonsense one way or the other," Jonathan said, struggling to unbuckle a leather strap on his side. "If it helps people to believe and to feel better about going into battle, then more's the better. Lord knows I have my own reservations."

"You don't approve of making war on the Amalekites?" Palti asked distractedly, shooing the prince's hand away from the buckles and the straps so that he could undo them. "They have raided a goodly number of Judean villages."

"Yes, I know," Jonathan said. He raised his hands into the air as much in surrender as in an attempt to stay out of the way, as Palti worked to free him from the elaborate formal attire. "But what we need to be doing is establishing and defending a border. If we are to be a country, we should decide what and where that is, exactly. We can hardly ask that our borders be respected if we ourselves have no idea where they are."

"Very wise, sire," Palti said, removing the breastplate and setting it aside.

"Otherwise every spring of my life will be spent in battle," Jonathan said distantly. "All I have ever known of life is fighting and war. I wonder if I will ever know the softer pleasures of life, if I'm am always either on the battlefield or recovering and resting up for more."

"You had a pretty good winter at the palace," Palti said with a knowing chuckle.

"Concubines are not lovers," the prince said, though he laughed at himself. "I could have brought them with me if I chose. But a man needs more than that. My father has fought every season of my life. I'm lucky to have been born at all."

"You have two brothers and two sisters besides," Palti said. He shoved the prince back onto a stool so that he could unlace his leg armor and remove his sandals.

"My father is a very lucky man," Jonathan said, laughing heartily.

Palti smiled, joining him in the laugh, pleased to have helped remove the burden from his master's shoulders along with his mantle. "Perhaps some supper while there is still yet time?"

"Enough, Palti," Jonathan said, holding up his hands again. "You win. Supper will give me ease and strength. And, send word for the pale one with the flaxen hair…."

"Orit?" Palti asked genially, teasing the prince about his embarrassment of riches.

"If you say so," Jonathan said, falling back onto the cushions of his bed.

"You prefer the fair-haired?"

"Jealous?" Jonathan teased back, tossing a cushion at his childhood companion.

"Maybe after I've gotten you fed and packed and prepared for tomorrow, I'll have time for such fancy. Though in truth I'd rather the company of your sister, Michal, if I have a choice."

"Really?" Jonathan said, batting his eyes as he held a pillow over the lower half of his face like an imaginary veil. "If it's her company you miss, I could nag and argue with you while cutting off your balls."

"What a way to speak of your sister," Palti said, hanging the prince's cloak.

"Should I tell Father of your intentions toward the princess?" Jonathan asked, lying back.

"But who would fetch your dinner with my head on a pike?"

"It'll be our secret, then."

For rebellion is as the sin of witchcraft, and stubbornness is as iniquity and idolatry.

1 Samuel 15:23

THE VICTORY banquet in King Saul's tent was in its second day.

King Agag, the guest of honor, was tied, spread like an eagle in flight between stout wooden posts driven deep into the ground, a sign of complete victory over the Amalekites. The surrender was absolute. Survivors were taken as slaves, to be sold or used as the victors saw fit. The best of the livestock was lowing and bleating in makeshift pens just outside, ready for transport back to Gibeah along with the contents of the Amalekite treasury.

The wine flowed. The table was heaped with food. The celebration continued.

Prince Jonathan had only just returned from his tent to find the party he'd left the night before still going on in his father's. Jonathan laughed to himself, amused and amazed at his father's stamina for this and in all things.

"The prince," Saul shouted, raising his cup in salute as Jonathan entered the tent.

"The prince," the party joined, toasting him.

"Father, you need rest," Jonathan chided.

"Son, you need wine," Saul shouted, laughing at his own drunken humor.

"Oh my." Jonathan chuckled, taking a place at the table. "Yes, clearly I have much catching up to do before I can join this party."

"That's my boy," Saul bellowed, embracing his son.

Though there was much wine involved, there was much to celebrate in his son. Many lives had been saved and many, including the king, said that the day was won by the prince's cool acumen in the panic of the Amalekites' unexpected attack.

Jonathan took up the cup brought to him. Getting to his feet, he raised his wine high.

"I give you my father, the King of Israel," Jonathan said, drunk more with the occasion than the spirits. "King Saul."

"King Saul," the party echoed.

"What is this?" Samuel's voice cut through the joy of the occasion. He stormed into the king's tent, tearing the flap aside, dusty and sweating, fresh from the road.

"It is a celebration, most holy," Saul said, coming from behind the table, jubilant at the prospect of sharing his victory with Samuel. "We are victorious. The Amalekites have surrendered. I give you Samuel, the author of our victory."

Samuel snatched the cup from Saul's hand and dashed its contents into the king's face.

Jonathan was on his feet, his hand on the hilt of his sword before he had the chance to consider. His Uncle Abner's firm grasp stayed him, but only just.

"The Lord has commanded you to lay waste to the Amalekites, to wipe them from the face of the earth in retribution for their refusal to help Moses and his people as they returned to the Promised Land from the slavery of our Egyptian masters," Samuel railed.

Saul fell to his knees, helpless.

"He bid you destroy them and all that they possess. He commanded that you kill them, their children, and their livestock. And yet despite the victory the Lord has brought you, this camp teems with their cattle and sheep, their people, and here stands their very king."

In a rage Samuel reached down and drew the sword from Saul's belt.

"As your sword has made women childless, so shall your mother be childless among women," Samuel railed, raising the sword above his head.

Jonathan drew his sword in Saul's defense, as did many others, when the priest turned and hacked off the head of the Amalekite king where he stood.

"You have turned your back on the Lord and his commandment to you," Samuel pronounced, tossing the bloody sword on the ground before Saul. "The Lord now turns from you. He no longer chooses you as king."

With a dramatic bow, Samuel turned to go. Saul, devastated and weeping, threw himself to the ground. He grabbed and kissed the hem of the priest's flowing robe. He begged him to stay, begged for one more chance.

Samuel never turned back, even as a part of his robe tore off in Saul's hand.

Jonathan could contain his fury no longer, even with his uncle's assistance. Overturning the table, he rushed to his father's side.

"Father," Jonathan said, embracing and helping the older man to his feet. "You are the king of Israel by right, not at the behest of that superstitious old fool."

The stinging blow silenced the prince as he fell back against his uncle. His cheek burned, as much from shame as the slap. His eyes blurred with tears, but he could still see Saul chasing after Samuel, pleading for forgiveness.

And Samuel came no more to see Saul until the day of his death: nevertheless Samuel mourned for Saul: and the Lord repented that he had made Saul king over Israel.

1 Samuel 15:35

"THE PRIEST stopped the night at the home of Jesse, the village elder there," the soldier reported, in awe of the throne room where he stood. The spy was still dressed in the robes of a simple traveler. The king sat brooding in the shadows, listening to the report. "The next day in Bethlehem, he made sacrifice to the harvest. Then he returned with his servant to Ramah. He has remained there since, under observation, carrying out his normal duties and no more."

"Bethlehem?" Saul said, turning the word over, searching for any meaning he might wrest from it. "Bethlehem."

"Yes, sir." The soldier nodded. "Just a small Judean farming community and trading center south of the Jebusite city of Jerusalem. No real significance."

"What is he about?" Saul hissed to no one. Massaging his temples, his eyes closed, he puzzled over the priest's every move. He knew Jesse. The man was one of his earliest supporters, or of the monarchy at least. Saul had passed through Bethlehem a time or two. Neither man nor city seemed important. Still, with Samuel's vision, things were rarely as they seemed.

"Sire?" the soldier asked, wondering how to proceed.

"I know he is plotting my ouster, but how? And why there?" Saul continued, arguing with someone the soldier could neither see nor hear. "It makes no sense to you, but you mustn't underestimate his powers."

"That will be all," Abner said, stepping in to dismiss the scout and return him to his duties. "Keep me posted as to all you find out. I'll see that the king gets the information."

"Yes, sir," the young man said, looking from Abner to the king for confirmation.

"Why have you forsaken me?" Saul screamed. Drawing his dagger, he flailed wildly in the air. In tears, he fell in a heap on the stone floor.

"I will rely on your discretion," Abner said.

In answer the soldier backed, terrified, from the chamber.

"Sire," Abner said gently, approaching as one might draw near to a wounded animal. "Saul, why don't we get you something to eat? Come, my cousin. Just come with me—"

"Don't you touch me," Saul shouted, fending Abner away with the dagger he still clutched. "You're just trying to poison me." Saul's voice echoed along the stone walls as he ran from the throne room.

Abner stood watching after his cousin, helpless.

"It's worse than I thought," Jonathan said, stepping from behind the screen where he had observed the proceedings. "Is there anything that can be done?"

"I'm at a loss," Abner said, his voice heavy with fatigue. As the king's condition deteriorated, more of the responsibilities of governing fell to him, compounding his own duties.

Jonathan tried to contain his heartbreak. The two left the grand chamber. They made their way through the halls of government outside the doors to its seat. His father's recent absence had made it urgently clear just how much responsibility did rest on the king.

Saul had not wanted to be king or even believed in his ability to master the job. Samuel had believed. It was Samuel's absolute belief in Saul that had given him the confidence to rule. Without it he seemed unable to believe it himself.

Jonathan could only see Samuel as a puppeteer, using his father as a means to rule. That was but half of the truth. Saul clung to those strings, keeping a firm grip on Samuel, not letting go. He needed Samuel's certainty to accomplish and endure the brutal and horrific costs of wresting a kingdom from a land already occupied by many others.

Without Samuel's blinding faith, Saul could see, with unflinching clarity, the unbearable price he had exacted from all around him—family, friend, and foe—in order to become the king he had been called to be. He could no longer sleep. Food reminded him of the slaughter. The comfort he sought in wine only heightened his growing mistrust of all around him. Delusions of plot and persecution fueled the nightmares that kept him sleepless.

He ran amuck through the private rooms of the palace, both king and madman. Yet his authority made it impossible to question his actions, no matter how disturbing.

In his absence, as Abner ran the affairs of state, Jonathan became his father's public face.

"His doctors don't seem to be making any progress." Abner sighed as they made their way to the meeting hall to get on with the business of running the kingdom. "It seems clear that, for now, you'll need to lead the troops on patrol. Praise be to God, no attack is imminent. Though I have reports you should see that the Philistines are massing under command of King Achish at Gath. For now, just a show of force to reassure our own people, and enough arrow sharpening to remind our enemies that we're still here. Perhaps by Shavuot he will be well enough to take part in public for the Feast of Weeks, but you had best prepare just in case."

"I am not the king," Jonathan protested, keeping his voice low as they made their way through the public rooms and passages of the palace. "My father is alive. I don't feel right about usurping his place, either at the head of the army or the table, whatever our reasons."

"You did an excellent job with the First Fruits ceremonies," Abner assured the young man he was already prepared to serve. "The kingdom is only just coming together behind your father. It could be disastrous to all his work, all he has accomplished, if we tell people that their government, their king, is unstable and cannot be trusted. This is something you must do for your father. There are forty and seven days left until Shavuot and the feast. Let us trust in the doctors to do their work, as we trust in the Lord to bring in the barley harvest."

"General," Eliab said respectfully, keeping his distance from the two great men and their quiet words together. "All is in readiness. The meeting with the king's advisors can begin when you will."

"Thank you, Lieutenant," Abner said, nodding formally. He was glad of an interruption to the pointless argument. "Prince Jonathan, this is Eliab ben Jesse of Bethlehem. My newest lieutenant, promoted on the battlefield at Amalek."

"Yes, we have met," Jonathan said, smiling gently at the memory and then darkening as he recalled the outcome of that day. "Captain Joab's uncle, I recall. My sympathies for the loss of your tribesman Micah. He was a good man with much promise. Too young to lose."

"Thank you, Your Highness," Eliab said, bowing his head politely. "It is kind of you to remember. I would not be standing here were it not for Micah's bravery. My family was much distressed at the loss of such a dear friend and constant presence at our table."

"We had best get to work," Abner suggested, leaning against the great doors to the council chambers. "We've the king's business to attend."

"His Highness, Prince Jonathan," the chamberlain announced, calling the assemblage to order.

Behold, I have seen a son of Jesse the Bethlehemite, that is cunning in playing... and a comely person, and the Lord is with him.

1 Samuel 16:18

"TO MY son, the lieutenant," Jesse said. He raised his cup in tribute to Eliab, home from service to the king to celebrate the Feast of Weeks with his family.

"Eliab," echoed the other men, raising their cups to join in Jesse's tribute to his son.

"Tell me, brother, does this mean Abinadab and Shammah do as you tell them?" Nethanel asked jovially in the relaxed mood of the family feast. They had only just come from temple for the offering of the loaves and the elaborate sacrifices of atonement in honor of the harvest. The family had contributed the bull, one of the rams, and the goat for the proceedings. It was an honor, but all were glad for the ease of their own company at home.

It had been a good year for the farm. The family's standing had been much enhanced by being asked to sacrifice with Samuel, as well as having him as a guest in their home. More was expected. The community looked to the house of Jesse for leadership. Joab's standing with the king, and Eliab's promotion, furthered their position and tore at David's heart. While he was happy for his nephew's and his brother's success, it deepened his feeling of being left behind as others passed him by for opportunities he would never know.

"Yes," Eliab agreed good-naturedly. "Thank goodness that it's only those two and not David for me to manage."

David tried to look more amused than he felt. Though he did not join in the laughter, he mustered a convincing smile to reflect the pride he did share for his brother's achievement.

"Well, lieutenants do not manage warlords," Jesse said, noting David's discomfort despite his youngest son's efforts. He tried to make a joke of it, promoting David from shrew to dictator, though really only making it worse. "Thank goodness David is on our side. A toast to him, his mother, and sisters for this fine feast, which we all now enjoy without lifting a finger."

It took more than dinner to assure no work would be required, as was tradition following the ceremony. It was ironic that though a feast was expected work was forbidden.

"Yes, I suppose it's nice to have a day off," David said, bowing his head in his own behalf. "In truth, it only means we have to do two days' work at once to make it possible. Perhaps if I had brothers to boss around...."

"And when did you stop?" Abinadab scoffed at the notion.

"Well, I suppose that's true," David allowed, topping the joke. "I guess what I really need is the army of Israel to back me up when I ask for your help."

"Little brother, I have seen the army of Israel." Shammah chuckled. "It is not nearly so fearsome as our mother and sisters, the soldiers in your army here."

"I hear you, Shammah." Nitzevet's voice echoed from her dining room to prove his point.

David laughed at last, a trace more at ease. Though no matter how much of the wine he took, his brother's success still stuck in his throat. He was as ashamed of his selfishness and envy as he was angry at his fate. Had it not been a feast day, he would have taken to his rooms or the hills to spare the others his foul mood. As it was he kept silent, which only attracted more attention as the table of men prodded him for a reaction.

"How fare the crops? The flocks? The market? Does the harvest compare to last year's?" they asked him. "What of town? Any gossip? What fun have you got up to?" All only elicited one- or two-word responses from their little brother. They persisted, still, in their belief that his silence was grief for his loss of Micah. There had been tears for Micah that day. But it was not just the loss of his friend and companion he mourned. It was the link to the world Micah provided that he missed all the more. The loss ached in him as he listened to tales of his brothers' conquests at court.

"You have hardly said a word," Eliab finally said, cornering him in the garden as the party broke up. The men had moved outside so that the gentiles from Nitzevet's staff could come to clear away the remains of the day unseen. "Are you troubled?"

"I am… not my best today, brother," David said, trying to avoid the ugliness of the jealousy in his heart.

"You look well enough," Eliab reassured him. "The feast and the day went off perfectly, as always. Everyone knows that is mostly your doing."

"Great." David sighed.

"Perhaps a song?" Eliab asked, trying to think of something to cheer his brother. "If you feel up to it, I'm sure we'd all enjoy hearing you."

"Perhaps," David said, turning away. Each suggestion only deepened his feelings of being relegated to a status little more than that of the women. "Not just now."

The larks filled the silence between them. Eliab stared helplessly at David's back. David fixed his gaze on the horizon.

"Is it Micah?" Eliab ventured at last, summoning the courage.

"In a way," David said, nodding, the bitter tears returning.

"He was a good friend," Eliab said, trying to comfort his brother, placing his hands firmly on David's shoulders. "And a good man."

"He was just a man." David shrugged.

Eliab took the movement as a rebuff and took his hands away.

"But he was a man," David continued. "And he saw me as his equal. I miss that. I miss being seen. I miss the respect."

"David," Eliab said gently, drawing near without touching. "We see you. We respect you."

"When you're here," David snapped, turning back to face his brother.

"Well, there's my work," Eliab said, startled by the ferocity of the response, stepping back. "I've a career to think about now."

"And I've no hope of anything of the sort," David said. "You go off to do whatever you choose in the world, to spend the money I'm earning for you here to buy yourself a place at court. I'm stuck here with the women to tend to the table and perhaps sing a pretty song to entertain you when you come home to trumpet the triumphs that are only possible because you are not mired here supporting yourself."

"Well, from what Micah had to say about how often you'd seen his feet, perhaps you are better qualified for the job of wife than you let on," Eliab said, lashing out in anger. He regretted it instantly. He had overshot the mark, destroying David's loving memory to win an argument.

"Even Micah," David said before he turned and ran from the garden.

Eliab would have pursued him, had he had any idea what to say.

David hid in the shepherd's hut until he was certain his brothers had left. His bitter prayers, to a God who had sent the judge of all Israel to anoint him and then ignored him as he languished on his father's farm, lamented his fate.

"Don't you want to say good-bye to them?" his sister Abigail asked when she came up to bring him food. "Soldiering is dangerous work."

"How dangerous can court be?" David snorted.

But the Spirit of the Lord departed from Saul, and an evil spirit from the Lord troubled him.

1 Samuel 16:14

"HE THREW a spear at the serving man who brought his food." Jonathan's mother sobbed, her face buried in his shoulder so he could barely understand her. "When I went in to try to calm him, he struck me."

Overcome by the memory, she was unable to support herself. Jonathan lifted her off her feet to lay her on one of the many red silk divans sprinkled throughout Ahinoam's sitting chamber. His sisters rushed to comfort her.

"It's true," Michal said distastefully. "The spear is still stuck in the door of Father's chamber. Everyone is afraid to go in to remove it."

"I will see to it, Mother," Jonathan said, stroking Ahinoam's hair.

"He's never struck me in all the years we've been married, never once," Ahinoam said, dissolving into a new fit.

"Michal, Merab, stay with Mother," he instructed his sisters. "I'll post a guard at the door to keep you all safe."

"Thank you, brother," Merab soothed, stroking the back of his hand.

"They will deny entrance to the king?" Michal demanded, incredulous at the idea that a mere guard could protect them from Saul.

"If I say so, yes," Jonathan said, irritated by her tone. He loved his sisters, each in their own way. But Michal spoke as no other woman ever spoke, more with the tone and expectation of a man. It was both refreshing and abrasive. Like a cold bath, it invigorated but required the right state of mind to be fully appreciated. "I will see to Father. I think there is no fear he will come out of his rooms for now. Just avoid going to him, all of you, until I tell you that it is safe."

"He thought I was trying to poison him," Ahinoam wailed.

"It is that fear, however unfounded, that will keep him behind his own doors," Jonathan said, trying to reassure her. Jonathan had been raised on the battlefield and was inexperienced with the tears of women. Though he loved his mother and sisters, he was unable to deal with their emotional response to this. His mind raced to find an excuse to cover his retreat. "I will go find Uncle Abner and the doctors and see what can be done for Father."

Jonathan closed his mother's chamber doors. He leaned against them to catch his breath. When he looked up and saw himself in the faces of the two young soldiers stationed there, he had to laugh. He was the man who had chased ten thousand Philistines out of the hills with nothing more than a spear, a few arrows, and his good diction, and he was afraid of his sisters.

"Don't let anyone in, particularly my father, without my permission," Jonathan said. He struck his chest in salute before departing, without waiting to see the tribute returned.

He made his way to the doors of Saul's chambers. A small crowd was already gathered there. The injured servant was being tended to along with several others who were scuffed and bruised, though none seriously wounded.

"You've heard?" Abner asked as Jonathan approached. He guided the prince aside so they might speak more privately.

"He hit my mother," Jonathan said by way of answer.

Abner drew a sharp breath through his teeth.

"She is my mother and, if did I not know him to be sick, I would be in there with my sword drawn," Jonathan said, shaking his head. "What are we to do? What ails the man? It is as though he is possessed by evil spirits from some fearsome fireside tale. Is it the drink?"

"He has hardly drawn a sober breath since we returned from Amalek," Abner agreed, nodding at the possibility.

"Forgive me, sir, for overhearing," Paltiel said gently. "You should know, Ahinoam has seen to it that his wine is mostly water or just grape juice. Still this state persists."

"The doctors have tried all that they know to do," Jonathan said, throwing up his hands in despair for his father. "Are we to put him down like a lamed horse? Or let him ruin his life's work and all of us in the process?"

"Perhaps some time away?" Abner suggested, mystified by the king's continued madness. He was not a superstitious man, but Saul's behavior was like a man filled with demons, his own will and good sense lost.

"Where are we to go?" Jonathan scoffed with a snort of laughter. "Philistia, to take in the sea air? Or perhaps a mountain retreat with the bandits of the Negev?"

"Excuse me, Majesty, sir," Eliab said, approaching. "The doctors say the serving man and the guard's wounds are not serious, no permanent harm. They will all be tended in private until they are well enough so questions might be avoided. They are good and loyal men. I think we may depend on their silence."

"He is like a cornered beast." Abner sighed. "The spear is still in the door. I fear that if the guards had not gone in, he would have killed the man."

"I've heard it said that music is the charm for a man possessed by his savage nature," Paltiel suggested. He spoke to the prince as humbly as he might make menu recommendations, mindful of his place in such a conversation.

"I have heard that as well," Abner said, his brow knit with his troubles. "I know that music can have a calming effect on me at the end of a stressful day."

"In truth?" Jonathan scoffed derisively.

"The doctors have tried all their herbs and potions, the finest care," Paltiel pointed out. "Priests have prayed over him. He's had nothing but wine and time to relax. Still he cannot sleep. At least the music might aid him to rest."

"Agreed." Jonathan nodded. "I am forever nodding off during those infernal concerts my sisters will arrange after dinner. Perhaps if he got some sleep, he could recover himself."

"Excuse me, Majesty," Eliab said, still there and unable to keep his own counsel a breath longer. Joab's advice to remain silent had served him well, but his burning desire to restore his relationship, however volatile, with his youngest brother outweighed even his own ambition. "I know of a fine musician and singer. He plays and accompanies himself on the harp and is the author of a hundred pleasing melodies."

"That is most thoughtful of you," a surprised Abner said, a polite dismissal of a young lieutenant who had overstepped his bounds in an effort to please. "We have many fine court musicians who I'm sure will suffice."

"I have heard them, sir," Eliab persisted, as much to his own surprise as that of his general. "None can compare to the troubadour of whom I speak. What's more, he is a beautiful youth, as well-spoken as he is fine featured and brave enough to have killed a lion on his own and a bear, I hear, which, if you'll forgive me, might come in handy in this situation."

"I must say, that does not describe any musician of my acquaintance," Jonathan said, giving Abner a playful wink, thinking he understood the young soldier's desire to bring his pretty boy to court. "It does seem the sort of artist that this particular engagement requires."

"True indeed, my prince," Abner said, playing along, not feeling strongly enough to put up an argument. "How soon can you have him here?"

"If I send out a rider now, I can probably have him here by morning," Eliab said. He beamed at the thought of David's face on hearing of his invitation to court at his brother's behest.

"Make it so," Jonathan said, patting Eliab's arm and giving him a knowing smile. "Palti, see if we can't find some finer rooms than servants' quarters to accommodate the lieutenant's boy."

"That's most kind, though I'm sure it's more than required," Eliab stammered, surprised by the prince's generosity. "I'm certain he'd be most pleased to be quartered with the rest of the palace guard."

"Nonsense," the prince said with as much generosity as dismissiveness. "Nothing but the best for your boy, Eliab. He can hardly attend you in the officer's quarters, and the guard's barrack is little more than a barn. See to it, Palti."

"It will be done." Palti nodded with a tight smile. Always jealous of any who might be of more service to his master than he, he was proud still that he was the author of the idea itself.

"Thank you, sire," Eliab said, still confused but afraid to say more to the prince.

"Now I must see to my father," Jonathan said softly. He took his leave of their company. With a deep breath, he swung open the chamber door. "Father, I hear there is a spear stuck in your door. I wonder if I might borrow it to go deer hunting?"

Let our lord now command thy servants, which are before thee, to seek out a man, who is a cunning player on an harp: and it shall come to pass, when the evil spirit from God is upon thee, that he shall play with his hand, and thou shalt be well.

1 Samuel 16:16

DAVID'S BROTHER Ozem was closest in age, but that was all they had in common. Ozem and Shimea, the next oldest of Jesse's sons, were inseparable friends. They followed and emulated Raddai, who was just older than Shimea and just younger than Nethanel, whose word was law among all the younger boys. Well, all except David.

With Eliab, Abinadab, and Shammah—the three eldest brothers—away at court, Nethanel was the oldest and largely "in charge" in the way that the oldest in any family are held accountable for the behavior of their younger siblings. They are granted a certain authority in payment for their liability. It was an arrangement that was understood and accepted among all the brothers and all who worked on Jesse's karmel. Except, of course, David.

So it was, when word came by messenger from Prince Jonathan requesting the pleasure of David's presence at court, there was a great stir in the house. Typically delivering news of a message from the prince to a brother, even one who remained cloistered in mourning at the shepherd's camp high in the hills, would have been a coveted task—except, of course, when that brother was David.

"Nethanel, go and tell your brother that a message from Prince Jonathan awaits him here," Jesse instructed, once the messenger had been offered food and drink and made comfortable.

"But, Father, what of the messenger's horses? If they are to be ready to return to court by morning, they'll need proper tending."

"True enough," Jesse agreed, stroking his beard thoughtfully as he took up a place at the table beside the king's messenger. "You had best send Raddai, then, or get him to tend the horses. Tell David that, on Eliab's recommendation, he's been called to court by Prince Jonathan."

"Yes, Father," Nethanel said, too relieved of his burden to consider the weight of the news. He promptly surrendered the dining room for the barn. He knew as well as anyone the kind of mood that had taken David into the hills. Having experience of his brother's moods, he had no interest in disturbing him.

He found the balance of his younger brothers in the stables, admiring as much as caring for the horseflesh newly arrived in a barn full of mules.

"He's a beauty," Ozem said, taking the stiff-bristled brushes to the glossy coat of the fine animal. "I expect he could make it the length of the Jericho road in a day's ride."

"Don't be a donkey," Raddai said, squeezing the cool water out of the cloth onto the sweaty trembling flanks of one of the other horses the messenger had brought with him. "Do you see wings on his shoulders?"

"Well," Ozem demurred to Raddai's seniority. In truth neither boy knew a thing more about horses than it took one to sire a mule. "I suppose he'd still leave more ground behind in a day than we've covered in a lifetime."

"He's here from Gibeah isn't he?" Nethanel asserted, taking the cloth from Raddai's hands. "Brother, Father desires that you should go up to the shepherding hut and fetch David down. Eliab has gotten the prince to call David for duty at court."

"I would, of course," Raddai said with a humble gesture. "But you see, with Father busy entertaining the king's messenger, you will need to see to Father's duties. That leaves me to do your bidding and to see to this lot getting the horses ready for their return." Raddai had already heard the news and was far more concerned with the fate of its messenger than the content.

"True," Nethanel said, easily susceptible to Raddai's considerable flattery. "Very responsible of you to consider it such. I suppose it would be best to send Shimea to conduct our little brother safely down from the hills."

"And on any other day, I'd be glad to do it....," Shimea began.

"Oh, leave it off," Ozem said, tossing the brushes to Nethanel. "I know it'll come down to me in the end. I always get stuck because no one can tell David to do anything he's not already of a mind to do. Even Eliab barely got him down the hill to see the judge of all of Israel. I don't mind so much. Only you never know how David's going to take a thing, do you? I'm as likely to get a browbeating as a kiss on the cheek."

The stable door banged shut on his brothers' laughter as Ozem struck out on his errand. The long hike gave him plenty of time to dread the encounter, and Ozem managed to work himself into an anxious state by the time he found David.

Following instructions from the nightshift shepherds he heedlessly awakened to inquire after David, he found his younger brother perched on a rock outcropping. David swung his legs over the cliff above a dizzying drop as he played and sang his mournful and plaintive songs into the abyss.

"*My God, my God, why have you forsaken me? Why are you so far from saving me, so far from the words of my groaning?*" David sang out, his voice clear and piercing, his golden hair turned to fleece in the sun, his tunic laid aside, his skin baked to bronze. Stroking his harp, he looked to Ozem like an angel out of one of the stories he'd heard at the temple. Yet his words were so sad. "*O my God, I cry out by day, but you do not answer, by night, and am not silent.*"

David was as a man possessed since fleeing the house and his brother's accusations. He was not shamed by Eliab's words so much as illuminated. He knew his heart. His songs and his prayers became one. He beseeched God for mercy and understanding.

"Oh Lord," David whispered, letting the small harp fall away, his head bowed. "What is your will for me?"

"Brother," Ozem said gently when David paused in his playing.

It was all Ozem managed to say before he found himself pinned to the ground. David looked down into his brother's face, still panting from the fear and exertion Ozem's unexpected arrival had evoked.

"Moses's staff," David swore, recognizing Ozem as no threat but still too angry to let him up. "You scared me so bad my foreskin grew back."

"Maybe you're just cold," Ozem said, resisting the urge to fight back, as he could easily have upended his little brother. "Perhaps if you put on some clothes?"

"What do you want with me?" David demanded, exasperated by the interruption of his precious bad mood.

"I came to bring you a message," Ozem began, still lying in the dirt. He spoke as though they were seated across the table from each other. David's small frame barely covered his chest.

"I'm not coming back down," David declared, pounding Ozem's breast with one hand and shaking a warning finger in his face with the other.

"Shall we send word to Prince Jonathan, then, that you are not interested in coming to court?" Ozem asked with a mocking tone to match his smirk.

"What are you talking about?" David asked desperately, grasping the front of Ozem's robe and pulling their faces closer together.

"There is a messenger from the prince at our father's house," Ozem explained patiently and slowly. He took his time to enjoy the torture and to gauge the response. "He has asked that you come to court. Eliab has apparently recommended you for duty."

"Eliab? The prince? What duty?" David insisted, his head too light to make more sense.

"I expect that you can ask the prince," Ozem said. "They've sent a horse and an escort for you. You are expected by morning."

"I am?" David shouted, flinging his arms around his brother's neck and kissing him about the face.

"All right then, get off me," Ozem said, standing with David still hanging from his neck. "I've instructed the shepherds. Someone will be here to take your watch. I'll wait here for him. Get your things and your wits together and get down to the house."

"It's the Lord's will that I go to the palace," David shouted. He grabbed his tunic, his scrip, and his harp, hugged Asad, and cheering ran, without bothering to dress, down the hillside.

"We shall have peace here at last." Ozem laughed to himself. He took up David's seat on the rocks and admired the view of his father's lands as he awaited the arrival of the shepherd.

And Jesse took an ass laden with bread, and a bottle of wine, and a kid,
and sent them by David his son unto Saul.

1 Samuel 16:20

THE MULE train that bore David to Saul's palace was also laden with gifts
from Jesse in tribute to his king. He managed to hide his emotions from David
as he bid him good-bye, but Nitzevet was sweetly surprised to find tears in
Jesse's eyes when she brought supper to his study.

"My beloved husband," she said, setting his tray on the table with his
scrolls and tablets, plans for the city's security against bandit raids from the
Negev. "What ails you, sir?"

"It is not the same here without David," Jesse said softly, his voice choked.

"It is much quieter," Nitzevet said, her eyes twinkling.

They held each other as they laughed.

"I love all my sons," Jesse said, holding his wife at arm's length for a
heartbeat. "Thank you for my sons and my daughters. I am a man much blessed.
My riches are increased tenfold by each of my children. Thank you, my wife."

"You are so sentimental today," she answered him sweetly, taking his
face in her hands.

"I never thought to say good-bye to this one—to David," he said, bowing
and shaking his head.

"You said good-bye to Eliab and the others easily enough," she said
without accusation.

"And they will be fine on their own." Jesse sighed. "But our David,
he is a little rare for the world. Sometimes people destroy what they do not
understand; what they haven't seen before; what they are not expecting."

"No one who's ever met David has failed to love him," Nitzevet said,
hugging Jesse's head to her breast. "He will be well taken care of wherever the
will of the Lord leads him."

Jesse began to cry softly again.

DAVID SHED more than a few tears, as well, as he departed that morning.
Still, he was too excited to be sad for long. The Hamsin winds of late summer
blew away the dust of home and made his fingertips crackle with sparks at
everything he touched. It filled the world with a sense of magic and change.
Along with the dust, the hot desert wind swept away the pangs of nostalgia.
Asad followed him down the road barking and leaping, unwilling to let David
go. He watched the little shepherd and his father over his shoulder until they
disappeared. Then, turning from home, he truly began the trek toward Gibeah
and the morning's sunrise.

Mostly David was too afraid of what lay ahead to be sad for what he'd left behind. He touched the sling around his neck, just under his robe. He felt Micah with him, watching over him, as he made his way behind the silent and forbidding messenger who'd been sent to fetch him back to the king.

As the hills of Judah rolled past, David dared to wonder if his summons had to do with Samuel's strange prophecy, or if the Lord had simply answered his prayers at last—or if both were the same. He wondered at his mission for the king and imagined all sorts of daring duties: spying on the king's enemies or following the heroic Prince Jonathan into great, decisive battles.

The journey was surprisingly brief as they made their way into the thick forests and over the rust-colored terra rossa soil of Benjamin. It was adjacent to and yet a world away from the sleepy farmland of the northern regions of David's home province of Judah.

As the sun reached its height and morning came to an end, the city rose into view.

Gibeah simply meant "hill," a most descriptive title for a city built on the side of a mountain. At its peak stood the large and impressive palace. The masonic skills learned in service to the master builders of Egypt and handed down from father to son were brought to bear in the execution of this monument.

David fell easily under the spell cast by those master builders, intended to strike awe into the hearts of approaching strangers. The city and the palace loomed high in the hills above, appearing that day, as they often did, to be floating in the clouds. The haze burned away to reveal a very different reality. David was glad the reins of his mount were held in other hands as they came into town. The capital teemed with people and activity, bursting with the vitality of a city at the heart of a thriving new nation. While David had been to market in strange cities before, it had typically been on the back of a produce wagon, to trade fine wine and oil for iron tools in some dusty Philistine market, not on the king's business, and certainly not at or near a palace of any kind.

A gleaming metal grill was lifted away as they approached the arched entryway to the courtyard of the king's grand residence. It was more overwhelming in person than it had seemed balanced in the clouds. David felt at once strangely important, completely at home, and frozen with fear.

"Here we are," the messenger said, speaking his first words to David since they had made their way down the little road that led through the hills from Jesse's house to the Way of the Patriarchs. David could feel the thinly veiled contempt in the words of his escort as he helped David down from the king's horse.

"David ben Jesse," the tall hawk-nosed man said to him. His was a tone at once official and dismissive. He made David's name sound like an item called out from the manifest of some shipment of baskets from the country. "I am Paltiel ben Laish, personal aide to the prince, who bids you welcome. Come this way, please." Paltiel turned wearily and led the way without so much as a greeting or pause for reply. David grabbed his harp, still wrapped in lily leaves. Abandoning the rest of his belongings, he dashed after his host. He tried to keep up in the confusion and activity of the main palace courtyard.

It was like the first market day following harvest, there at the king's very door. David wondered what occasion had created such a stir, unable to know that such was the state of the king's doorstep each day. His little caravan, so grand in the scale of Bethlehem, hardly warranted a glance in Gibeah.

Before David had had the chance to get a good look at the throng of activity unfolding in the forecourt, Paltiel disappeared through a huge archway. David followed him down a long colonnade with polished stone floors leading to a central courtyard, embellished with gardens. It was populated with a better-dressed, better-smelling group of people than had been in the welter of humanity that had greeted him just inside the front gates.

Once again, before David could take his bearings, his guide and their path led them away from the grand and beautiful garden. They passed through a series of smaller colonnades, courtyards, and passageways, each finer and more beautiful than the last.

"Here we are," Paltiel said, pausing just outside a large set of heavy doors beautifully carved, rich and dark with oil. "I will leave you here to make ready. Your things will be brought to you. I will notify the prince and Lieutenant Eliab that you are here."

"Thank you, sir," David said, baffled and confused. "Is this where the soldiers are quartered?"

"You are anxious to get to work." Paltiel laughed, knocking on the heavy door with a large metal ring hinged in the mouth of a great bronze lion. "But you will not be expected to tend to the needs of the soldiers here. The prince will explain your duties. You and Eliab may make whatever arrangements between you that suit."

"Yes, sir," David said quietly, his brow wrinkled in confusion and concern.

Was he to serve Eliab here as well? Was the army to be no different than home?

David's thoughts were interrupted as the huge doors opened. The light from within poured into the shadowy passageway where David stood. The scents of perfume, incense, flowers, and spices, the rustling of silk, and the birdlike chirping of female laughter seeped out into the passage where he stood with his brusque guide. Silhouetted in the doorway stood the statuesque form of the most amazing creature David had ever beheld. Tall as a young olive tree, thin as a river reed, pale as milk, and hung with more ornaments than a gentile temple deity, it was unclear to David if he beheld man or woman or some seraphim out of myth.

"Salaam," their extraordinary host addressed them, bowing deeply.

"Eliab's boy," Paltiel said by way of introducing David, as though he had left his name in the courtyard with David's clothes. "Prepare him for presentation to the prince and find him an oda. His things will be brought here, but from the look of him, you'll need to have the court draper see to something more worthy of royal presentation."

David felt small and shabby in what he had thought his finest robe.

"It shall be so," the creature sang in its odd nasal voice. It squinted its kohl-rimmed eyes at David and leaned down to him for a closer inspection. "Now that he's at court, he can't just simply lie down and raise his legs."

"Not at first, anyway." Paltiel laughed. The two spoke of David as though he were not present or did not understand what they were saying—which, in truth, he did not. Well, not entirely. "I'll leave you to it, then. I know your expert skills."

"Indeed you do," the living statue said, extending a bejeweled hand and beckoning David inside. "Come with me, boy. We shall make you fit for a king, or a prince at least."

Tentatively David extended his hand. He was firmly grasped and dragged inside as the door banged shut noisily behind him.

"Pig," the idol said of Paltiel, then put a protective arm around David. The harp was taken from David's hands, and he was guided gently across the glowing inner court. "I hope that he did not hurt you or take advantage of you, my dear one," his host cooed, stroking his hair maternally. "My name is Eliakim. What may I call you?"

"I'm David ben Jesse," he replied distractedly, taking in their surroundings.

A cloud of laugher as delicate as the beating of birds' wings echoed off the polished stone walls and caught David up.

Women, who could be seen and known only by their eyes, richly made up after the Egyptian fashion, observed him. They gazed safely from behind their veils and the heavy curtains. Their laughter echoed as though inside a great cave. The draperies hung between columns and arches that separated the roofless antechamber from what seemed to David, from the resonance of the place, to be vast chambers beyond.

"Shoo, shoo," Eliakim hissed playfully. His host set the harp aside and pulled up David's tunic to reveal his manhood as casually as one might pass the bread at table. "He is not here for you. He is a real man."

Eliakim's strange words were met with another thrill of feminine giggling. The eyes flickered away amidst the sounds of rustling silk and bare feet on polished stone. Those who had stared at him in his embarrassment retreated into the rooms beyond the curtains. Too stunned and humiliated to move, David made as if to smooth the front of his robes still held aloft.

"You must never go beyond those curtains," Eliakim said, grasping David between his legs gently and inquisitively, but firmly as one tests fruit for ripeness, "so long as you have these."

David only nodded, still uncertain whether to address Eliakim as a man or a woman or in any way how to react in this upside-down world.

"Such is the sole province of the king," Eliakim said, stroking David's face with the fingers of the other hand. "It would mean your death. And you are too beautiful to die."

"What is this place?" David asked, trying not to react to his host's familiarity. "Who are you?"

"Come, boy," Eliakim said. His host released the intimate grasp and smoothed David's tunic. Eliakim then took up the harp and led David to another set of doors at the far side of the little court.

David hesitated, resisting the firm but gentle pull of Eliakim's hand, which enfolded his.

"Don't be timid, my jewel," Eliakim cooed musically. "I am here to serve you, not to harm you. I am sultan, but only within these walls. I am the king's chief eunuch."

"Eunuch?" David repeated the unfamiliar word

"It means I have none of these," Eliakim explained, again grasping David where his legs met.

Eliakim laughed at the look of horror upon David's face.

"Only in this way may I be trusted to be among and to serve the king's pilegesh and even his wives. For a king must be more certain than any man of the lineage of the offspring of his wives and concubines."

"Am I to lose…?" David trailed off, frozen still just outside the doors.

"No," Eliakim laughed gently. He put a comforting arm around David's shoulders as he soothingly led the boy through the doors and into the equally luxurious chamber within. "I am here to serve you as well. You are most fortunate. Most soldiers' boys sleep in the stables when they are not wanted. Musicians and performers must sleep outside the walls of the city in their wagons, if they are lucky enough to have them," he added, holding up David's harp.

"I see." David nodded, not really seeing.

Eliakim set aside the harp on the gleaming marble surface of a bronze-legged table. He led David to the edge of a great pool of steaming, richly scented water, covered with a mosaic of floating petals and aromatic leaves.

"Eliab must be very well thought of by the prince that you should be accommodated here," Eliakim purred as he guided David to sit on an exquisite cushioned bench. The sound of his voice calmed David as he began to unlace the sandals from David's feet, still filthy from the road. "We shall make you beautiful for him and for your presentation to the prince and his family. Then you will stay here with me and those like me that we may serve you until Eliab has need of you."

Before he fully realized what was happening, Eliakim began to slip the tunic over his shoulders. Surprised, he gasped slightly and caught the fabric in his hand.

"Oh, you are shy," Eliakim said. Notes of delight came into his strange soothing voice before he snatched the tunic away playfully and tossed it aside. "Tahir, come and join us," he called, clapping his hands together.

A young man, closer to David in age, came from behind one of the room's many richly embroidered hangings.

"This is David. Help him to feel more at home," Eliakim said softly, warming oil in his hands before smoothing it into David's skin. "Tahir serves as I do. Tahir, this is David, Eliab's boy, here at the invitation of the prince."

"I am Tahir, first eunuch of the baths," the youth said. He dropped his robe to the floor with a practiced ease that was more startling to David than the man's nudity. "Greetings and welcome. Come, let me bathe you," Tahir went on, stepping into the water and extending his hand to David.

"Tahir tends the baths," Eliakim said softly, easing David onto the uppermost of the stone steps that led beneath the surface of the water. "His skills will take away both the tension and the dust of your journey."

"You like what you see?" Tahir laughed, taking note of David's stare and giving his hips a toss.

"I, well, I…," David stammered.

Eliakim took his hand and, with Tahir, guided David into the water. They seated him on the stone steps half submerged in the fragrant waters.

"You are a bashful one," Tahir said, giggling. He began to rub salt crystals into David's skin to prepare and smooth it. "It's hard to believe you are a soldier's boy and yet so modest."

"A soldier's boy?" David asked, relaxing into the insistent kneading of the strong and skilled hands.

"Are you with him always or only on campaign?" Tahir asked, pausing to catch David's eye. "Has he wives at home yet?"

"Eliab," Eliakim added as he lifted David's foot from the water and began to smooth the sole with a coarse stone. "Is that not his name?"

"Yes, Eliab," David said, not fully grasping the conversation and its context.

"He sent for you on behalf of the prince," Eliakim said with an admiring little humming sound. "The prince is a beautiful man. Shall you be entertaining them both?"

"I have no idea what I'm doing here," David answered sincerely. He could not have felt more completely a fish on the shore had God swept him up, like a character out of some primitive myth, and set him amongst the stars above.

"Well," Tahir said, leaning in, his face near David's ear, his large hand sliding up the inside of David's thigh. "Let me know when you find out if you are to serve only the prince and your master Eliab. We are allowed to choose our own company when we are not in service."

He smiled. Like a stranger on the road ahead becomes a kinsman as one draws nearer, David's circumstance suddenly came into sharp focus, and he laughed.

"Yes," David said, leaning back, still chuckling as he started to enjoy the bath he was getting. "I am anxious to hear what Eliab has to say."

I cried unto the Lord with my voice, and he heard me out of his holy hill. Selah.

Psalms 3:4

"SO, BROTHER, have you sold me as a dog priest?" David hissed at Eliab. He was unable to speak to him in full voice, as they stood just outside the prince's chambers awaiting their announcement.

"Dog priest?" Eliab laughed at David's use of the common slang. The male attendants who bore the disdainful title served at the temples of the Canaanite god of Baal. There they offered their sexual favors in exchange for tributes of gold. The favors and the gold were believed to solicit the fertility blessing of the god of the seasons, weather, and harvest. Though strictly forbidden to the people of Israel, many went to seek the favors of Baal, as well as the priests and priestesses. "Such language. What would Father say?"

"Shall I tell Father, who thinks I'm here to fight at your side, that you've signed me up as a boy whore at the king's court and put me up with the courtesans?"

Like the fine palace, the court of King Saul was modeled on those of the old kingdoms around them. David had discovered, during the seemingly endless preparations for his presentation, that Eliakim had been bought from a northern kingdom. The eunuch brought with him the traditions of the harem so that the king might be like other kings in his practices and customs. Though he had been a plain man from a small village in Benjamin, Saul came to enjoy the privileges and pleasures of being king. His harem was not as large as many, but it was well-appointed and regularly attended.

The tradition of keeping concubines and pilegesh had come from the time of Moses and before, but outside the palace it was more often the gift of a barren wife to her husband. For a king, though, it was a sign of his power and his country's standing to maintain many pilegesh only for pleasure and entertainment. Though pilegesh and concubine alike were no less worthy than a wife and their offspring no less legitimate, because they had come without title or dowry there was no assumed privilege of inheritance, though it was often designated.

David was not shocked by the fact of the king's harem so much as he was by being included in it.

"You smell like flowers," Eliab teased his little brother, who was draped in white silk and garlands. His harp had been replaced by one gilt and gleaming in the dull light of the antechamber. "Actually, you've never looked better."

"Enough," David growled, taking a cut at him with the harp.

"Perhaps I should tell Father that you have found your true calling at last."

"The prince will see you now," Paltiel said, slipping out without fully opening the door and closing it quickly behind him. "Stand up straight. Don't look directly into the prince's eyes. Speak only when he speaks to you. Answer as simply as possible. It is only out of respect for Eliab that Prince Jonathan speaks to you at all. Be still and I will announce you."

"I love it here," Eliab said.

"That's good," David managed to squeeze between gritted teeth. "Because you had best never come home."

The door opened. David left a shocked Eliab and Paltiel in his wake. He made his way to the prince, bowing low as he announced himself.

"Prince Jonathan," David said with authority to his much-surprised host. "I am David ben Jesse, Eliab's younger brother, son of the noble Jesse ben Obed, elder of Bethlehem, elector and member of your father's council. I want to thank you for a most unusual welcome."

"Boy, you may not—" Paltiel began, grabbing David's arm.

"Never touch me or speak to me in that fashion again," David said, shaking Paltiel off. "I have been polite to you so far because I am a guest here. As I see you are merely a servant, you will address me as the son of Jesse of Bethlehem. Speak to me only when I call for you or to ask after my comfort. Is that clear?"

There was a shocked silence during which Eliab and Paltiel each held their breath, unsure of what would happen next.

"You are most clear, my prince," Jonathan said, suddenly rocking with laughter. He dropped to one knee before the breathtakingly self-assured and beautiful young man who stood before him. "We are honored to have you here."

The prince could not resist taking David's fine hand and planting a small kiss on his palm. Their eyes locked. David, the heat of his anger turned to steam by the bracing welcome, was able to see the man before him for the first time.

The prince's hair was like oiled black lamb's wool, hanging in glossy ringlets around his face, gathered partially back by a gold band. David met the prince's stare. When kneeling the prince was almost David's full height and taller than Eliab when he was not. Dark and gleaming with flecks of gold, the prince's eyes seemed to devour as they beheld him. David shivered, slightly chilled as though the insubstantial robes he wore had fallen from his shoulders.

In turn, Jonathan was much pleased by the sight of the flashing gold hair. Wound with jasmine, it toppled over David's soft, bare shoulders, smooth and honeyed by the sun. His green eyes were alive with the light of the room and David's fiery mood. More than his beauty, Jonathan was taken with the boy's spirit. Fearless and uncowed by his first meeting with a man who could have had his head flicked from his shoulders as easily as a beetle from a leaf, David met the prince man to man, both subject and peer.

Jonathan smiled at the boy. He rose, holding David's hand still. It was a wistful smile, for as compelling as Jonathan found his little invader, David was only dressed as a courtesan. He was in truth a noble son of Israel. The inclinations the prince felt would have to remain his private fancy.

"Jonathan?" Princess Michal's voice broke the spell between David and the prince. She closed in on the pair from the door of the adjoining royal apartments. "Who is our guest?"

"Ah, sister," Jonathan said with an easy laugh. "This lovely bauble is the son of noble Jesse and brother to our friend Eliab. He has come here to play his healing harp for Father to help him sleep."

David wanted to run from the room. He understood the purpose of his royal summons. He was to do and to be no more here than he was at home. Still, he was to be and do it at court, so there was that. What of Samuel's words and prophesies? Was this to be his destiny? A musical balm to the king, that he might be better rested? His smile was a sad one, and at his own expense. His pride had led him to forget that his talents were the Lord's gifts. To suppose himself something far above his station in the Lord's purpose was his folly, not the Lord's trickery. He was a singer. Well-spoken and pleasant to look at, he had the skills to run a farm, to play, and to sing, but nothing more. What had he supposed God would have him do?

"Ah yes," Michal said, boldly taking David's arm like a new doll brought for their amusement. Grinning over her new toy, she called back to Merab. "Sister, this is the wonderful singer come to soothe Father's spirits."

"You must give us a sample," Merab said, taking David's other arm as they escorted him back toward the family chambers.

"Mother, we have another guest for dinner," Michal called to Ahinoam, who was only just emerging into the more public meeting room where David had been received.

"Come along, Jonathan," Merab called back to her brother and his attendants. "We shall earn a fine concert with an excellent dinner and the best company that the court of Israel has to offer. Come and see how it's done."

"Yes, sister." Jonathan nodded with a loving grin. "My prince, would you like your brother to join us, or is he to be kenneled with the dogs for allowing us to receive you as we have?"

"No kennels for him," David said sternly, fixing Eliab with a withering glare. "I would not wish that on Your Majesty's dogs. Let him sit with us so that we may keep an eye on him."

"Your wish is my command, my prince," Jonathan said. He winked at Eliab and then whispered, once David and his sisters had left them briefly behind, "We'll get you out of this before your father hears of it."

"I have already sent word," David called back.

Jonathan shrugged his shoulder, his palms to heaven. The two men laughed together like brothers as they followed David's retinue in to supper.

The evening of David's presentation at court was a triumph for Eliab as well as David. Ahinoam was as smitten with the boy as were her daughters Michal and Merab. His songs, after the fine dinner the women served them, held all present in thrall. Abner, to whom Eliab had first recommended his brother for the duty, was duly impressed. The prince dismissed Paltiel from the dinner to prepare David quarters in nearby royal apartments.

"So that he may have easier access to my father," Jonathan instructed his aide. In truth he thought it would not be unpleasant to cross paths with the beautiful youth as he went about his day. Certainly there was nothing that could pass between them; still, he reasoned, it was pleasing to have a peacock around even if you couldn't eat it. One could appreciate the plumage without plucking it.

Jesse's gifts were brought at David's insistence, presented, and well received, particularly the excellent wine. The evening was a late one, as no one could bear for it to end. David was exhausted to the point of delirium when Eliab helped him to his new quarters.

"Well, you have now officially been promoted to prince after only half a day at court," Eliab said with a low coarse whistle as he looked around at the large, well-appointed quarters his little brother had been assigned. David's were far superior to his own officer's billet.

"You think this is nice? You should have seen my room in the harem," David teased, full of enough of their father's fine wine to laugh about it.

"I am sorry about that," Eliab said, unable to stop himself laughing.

"Yes, you sound most repentant."

"No, in truth, I am," Eliab said, still laughing. "Once I had told them about you, your story took on a life of its own."

"Well, I cannot guess what you said of me," David said, throwing himself back onto a sofa heaped with silken pillows. "Everyone was convinced I was your lover."

"What?" Eliab said, only just beginning to understand fully.

"Yes," David said, nodding sleepily. "They put me up with the eunuchs and the concubines because they thought I was your 'soldier's boy.' I didn't know there was such a thing. Have you one already? Will he be jealous of me?"

The two brothers ended the perfect night with laughter and the pleasure of each other's company. With the dawn came the harsh reality of the duties of a new day.

And it came to pass, when the evil spirit from God was upon Saul, that David took an harp, and played with his hand.

1 Samuel 16:23

"THE LORD is my shepherd; I shall not want." David sang the song he'd written for Micah's funeral for the king. His voice, quavering and uncertain at first, grew in strength as the words evoked the comfort of his lost friend's presence. *"He maketh me to lie down in green pastures: he leadeth me beside the still waters. He restoreth my soul: he leadeth me in the paths of righteousness for his name's sake. Yea, though I walk through the valley of the shadow of death, I will fear no evil: for thou art with me; thy rod and thy staff they comfort me. Thou preparest a table before me in the presence of mine enemies: thou anointest my head with oil; my cup runneth over. Surely goodness and mercy shall follow me all the days of my life: and I will dwell in the house of the Lord for ever."*

The king was still, silent in his bed.

David continued to strum out the melody, improvising and keeping up the tune. He had no idea what he was doing. The enormity of what his brother had promised from him had not fully taken root until that morning, when he was first escorted to the king's chamber doors.

A cacophony of shouting and shattering crockery emanated from inside and echoed throughout the private rooms of the palace as the servants tried to bring the king his morning meal. Frightened and bloodied, they ran from the room where the king continued to storm and quake with rage. Only Ahinoam was able to quiet her husband, daring to go into the room and put the king to bed.

"Come," she said softly, taking David's hand and leading him to the doors of the dreaded room. "He is in bed, but he is not yet asleep. He has not slept for days, no matter how much wine he has drunk. Don't speak to him or look at him. Take up your place in the chair I have set for you just inside the door and play. The Lord guide your hands and fill your voice with his notes to take away the evil spirit that is upon our king."

"The Lord's words?" David asked, unsure of what to do. "Perhaps something from temple?"

"Something soothing," Ahinoam suggested.

"Soothing?" he echoed, too terrified even to remember his manners.

"Something that makes *you* feel better," she advised.

Thus, he chose the song he'd written to assuage his own grief after Micah's death.

There was no sound from the king, who was partially concealed from David by the draperies around his bed. After what David had heard and witnessed before his arrival, he was thankful that the king had not taken a sword to him or chased him out of the palace.

As he played, his thoughts wandered to Micah and their times alone in the meadows and hills of home. He thought of a future that would never be and wondered where his life would take him. He sat in the king's bedchamber, playing his harp, a human sleeping draught, dismissed as a courtesan, respected only because he was thought to be his brother's catamite and still not really rating much higher in the estimation of those around him, despite his change of quarters.

He was at court, but nothing else had changed. Despite the strange visit from Samuel and his odd promises, David's life and his prayers seemed undone, unanswered, like leavened bread unbaked. Perhaps this was the answer, he thought, and the fault was his. Perhaps all that was wrong with his life was his own pride, expecting, hoping.

So lost in thought was he that he missed the sound at first. He played on and on, contemplating his life and his place in the world. At last, tired, he dared to pause. He wondered if he would be killed for the affront, uncertain of what was expected of him.

Just then, in the silence, he heard the ragged breathing and the soft snore of a sleeping man behind the king's bed-curtains. Silently David rose and made his way out of the chamber. He was most surprised to find the sitting room filled with the most august and powerful in all of Israel. They looked to him with anxious anticipation, as if the fate of the nation rested upon his shoulders, and he alone could save them. Jonathan the prince of Israel, Abner the general of Israel's armies, Ahinoam the queen, the princesses, the other princes, ministers, advisors, officers, and officeholders, all hung in expectation of David's pronouncement.

"He's asleep," David said with a shrug, unaware of the enormity of the statement. "May I be permitted to take my leave now?"

David was overwhelmed by the answer. The little crowd surrounded him and swept him silently out into the great hall. Once away from the bed where the king at last slept, they rejoiced and gave thanks to David and to God. He was embraced, rewarded, bowed to, and shaken by the hand by all present, all whose lives and futures rested with the success or failure of their sick and troubled king.

David was thankful to have brought so much happiness. More so, he was glad to have a break after playing all morning. He could see God's will for him in their grateful faces and found a measure of his own peace there.

When the king awoke, late in the day, he was able to take food and to receive his wife and his son Jonathan. He had little to say and was still easily agitated. David was summoned again at night and played the king once again into peaceful sleep.

The king was still asleep when the servants brought his food the following morning. When they returned they were able to serve him without incident, though the king did not speak or respond to their presence. After he had eaten, David returned to play for Saul that morning. Again that night he came to ease the king's troubled mind with the gift of his music and the pleasure of his company.

David found a kind of joy and gave thanks to the Lord that the gift that had been given him might help the king. He saw that he had taken his talents for granted and found time to make sacrifice and ask forgiveness. Contentment and gratitude filled him. He found value in his ability to be the Lord's instrument in the king's recovery if not consolation. His sadness did not lift. Micah was still gone. David's own dreams seemed as ill-fated.

The schedule evolved as the miraculous cure continued, surprising none more than its practitioner. For weeks David played for a silent and distant man he knew only through the respect and reverence of others to be the king of Israel. Saul remained lost in his shadowed world of fear and unseen demons. The family was pleased that Saul was at least getting some rest and eating. They began to despair of the king, their husband and father, ever being as he was before, ever truly returning to them and to the nation that needed him.

"The day is coming, Jonathan," Abner said earnestly. They were in the privacy of the prince's quarters, alone but for Eliab and Paltiel, their most trusted aides. "The Philistines are massing at Gath for their most sizeable attack so far. My scouts bring ever-worsening reports daily. Rumor has it that King Achish has some deadly and mysterious weapon brought from Moab. The time for decision is almost at hand."

"And yet it is not at hand," Jonathan snapped, fatigued by this, Abner's favorite theme of late. "I will not usurp my father's power one breath before the need is dire."

"But the king himself chose you as his successor," Abner argued.

"The king is not dead." Jonathan spoke with an authority that brought all present to their knees before him. "I'll thank you to remember that, lest people get the idea that you are guilty of treason to his crown."

"Forgive me, my prince," Abner said, his head bowed to the floor. He was secretly proud to see the young man risen into the great king he would one day be. "I meant no disrespect to your beloved father, my cousin, and my king. I speak only of my concern for his kingdom and my desire to return it to him intact when he is restored to us, fully recovered, on the day the Lord wills it so."

"Well answered, my uncle." Jonathan chuckled, prodding Abner's shoulder with his toe. "Your skills may be wasted on the battlefield. You'd be a fine ambassador to the court of some malevolent eastern potentate. Forgive me if I sounded like one. Give your wicked nephew a hug."

"No umbrage is taken, Your Highness," Abner answered, rising and clapping Jonathan warmly on the shoulder. "You spoke only like the prince it is my privilege to serve."

It was a brief respite from the prince's ill humor. As the weight of his dilemma rested heavier on his shoulders each day, Jonathan's natural good humor grew more strained. Those around him—family, friends, soldiers, and subjects—all began to dread and even to avoid his stern company. He grew snappish and short with his mother and sisters, ill-tempered and impatient with his brothers, and harsh and demanding with those who served him.

The only person at court who seemed exempt from the prince's stormy mood was the new court musician, David. His miraculous cure for the king was credited for his startling relationship with the prince.

Where others simply became quiet and deferential around Jonathan, David was at ease and as sharp-tongued as he was with his own brothers. Their spirits were as twins. David too was wary of his fate. Was this the man he was meant to be? His happiest times at court were in the company of the prince. The two shared a bitter humor, born of their mutual dismay over their unwitting and unchosen destinies.

Israel's was a court ruled by three unintentional tyrants.

Though the king's condition was less critical, it remained grave enough to keep him in his apartments, the draperies drawn against the light and the world outside. Adding the mercurial moods of Jonathan and David kept the court on tiptoe amidst hen's eggs.

David kept mostly to himself when he wasn't attending the king. He emerged to sate the demand for his presence only at court functions where the prince was in attendance. This was most welcome, since it was only in David's company that the prince became bearable, returning to his old self and pleasant enough to be around.

"David, how much longer do you expect the king's treatment to take?" the prince asked David at a dinner for the visiting king of Edom. King Hadad's people had been subdued by King Saul. Brought into alliance with Israel, his was a growing and important presence at Gibeah.

"Do you expect rain during the Counting of Omer?" David asked, carving lamb from the bone.

"It never rains in the summer months, brother," Eliab said, trying to deflect David's typically disrespectful tone.

"It has," David said, tearing a tiny piece of the bread and dipping it as casually as if he were at his father's own table. "Can our prince not predict the future?"

"I am a prince, not a seer," Jonathan said, smiling at David as though he'd paid him tribute in gold rather than mockery.

"And I play the harp, great prince," David said with a dismissive tone. "I'm just a singer."

As others gasped, the prince laughed well and heartily. He was blinded, as always by David's wit and company, to any fault others might perceive.

Eliab sighed, relieved that once again his brother would not be losing his head and the family lands to an angry monarch for his insubordinate tone.

Like the others present, Eliab assumed David owed his grant of tolerance to Prince Jonathan's gratitude for his father's recovery in David's care. So, too, did many assume that Jonathan's distemper was due to his concern over his father's health and the dilemma of his own succession. While both truths certainly contributed fuel to the fires that burned unseen within the prince, there was another blaze in his heart that David stoked.

As winter came on, Eliab returned home, as did most of the men at arms. The palace guard remained, but the rains and muddy roads provided Israel better protection than all the iron in Philistia.

Bored in his winter prison, anxious for his father, and freed of the chaperone of David's older brother, Jonathan was more relaxed in his manner toward David each day.

"Thank goodness we have you at court, young David," Jonathan said, using the excuse to stroke the back of David's hand as if in jest. "If you supped with the Philistines, we would surely be ruled from Gath and not Gibeah."

"You are too generous, my prince." David smirked, looking up from his meal irritably. "If I was to take a meal with the Philistines, it would be at my own table, and both you and they would be ruled from Bethlehem."

Jonathan only laughed. "I suspect, Prince David, that such may one day be true. For I have heard your playing and smelled your perfume. I too know that you possess the power to charm into submission all who behold you."

"So then you think that the nation should be ruled by a courtesan?" David asked, tossing the bread aside, his appetite spoiled by the all too familiar assertion. "Would that be better or worse, do you suppose?"

There were actually gasps in the room as all eyes turned to the prince.

"Don't sell yourself short, my prince," Jonathan answered, oblivious to the company or their reactions as he dragged the back of his index finger across David's downy cheek. "I think you would do as well or better than I will do, should I have the privilege of following my father's footsteps, and his are mighty sandals to fill indeed. No, David, while my father will one day unite and rule all of Israel, you could command the moon to bow down and make the sun blush."

Now the laughter was at David's expense and the relief palpable.

"Will you favor us with a song?" Jonathan pleaded, daring to take David's hand. "The kingdom is yours for the taking tonight."

As he sang, David felt something new in his heart. Rather than feeling dismissed by the prince, he felt more alive at their engagement. His heart beat more quickly. There was more passion in his psalms. It was as though he was more awake somehow. Like a familiar refrain, sung as if to a different tune. If he were to be no more than a decorative addition to the prince's court, so long as the prince was Jonathan, it would be enough.

David soon found himself promoted from court bauble to demigod.

He fell into a routine in his care of the king. Each day, following the king's morning meal, David would play the king to sleep and sit with him until midday. He would leave the king sleeping in his eternally darkened world and return that evening after Saul's supper to play him to sleep once again. Never did a word pass between them. David sometimes spoke soothing words of prayer and encouragement to his sleeping king. Otherwise theirs was a silent and morose routine.

The morning of David's elevation occurred like many others. The king had been disagreeable, throwing his plates and food at those who served him and creating a disturbance that called for Ahinoam's return to minister to the situation. That morning even his queen could not calm her king. As David waited outside, the disturbance between the two grew in intensity on the other side of the door. He waited patiently for his invitation until he heard Ahinoam cry out. Then, with the confidence of his growing familiarity with the royal family, David simply burst into the room.

The king froze, holding Ahinoam roughly in his large hands. David stood in the doorway. Their eyes met. A smile spread across the king's face. He was instantly at his ease. Gently he released Ahinoam and moved to take up his bed again. The queen fled, leaving David behind with only a thankful glance in parting.

The king kept to his bed, silent and unseen as always. David began to play. He sang many psalms of his own invention familiar to them both.

At last David grew tired. The time had come when the king was typically asleep. David ended his last psalm. He sat quietly for a bit, as was his habit, to observe whether or not the king was sleeping.

"Come here, boy," the king said. He extended his hand outside the bed-curtains to summon David nearer.

The words, the first David had ever heard the king speak, struck terror into his heart.

Warily David drew nearer the king's bed.

"Be not afraid of me," the king said gently. "You have driven the demon from my heart. I want to embrace you as my own son."

David took the great man's hand. Saul, like his son Jonathan, greatly exceeded David's stature and easily overpowered and drew David to him, even in his weakened state. With tears of joy in his eyes, he held the boy for a time. He stroked David's hair as David knelt on the floor beside the king's bed.

"WHERE IS David?" Jonathan asked when he arrived to take his midday meal and found an empty place at his table.

"He has yet to return from the king's chambers," Paltiel answered absently as he fussed over the details of the prince's repast and the important men who attended him that day.

Alarm swept over Jonathan. He startled those present when he bolted from the room. Knocking serving men aside and toppling the trays they carried, he ran through the passageway that connected the royal apartments. He burst into his mother's dining room where David, in his typical defiance of convention, often scandalously supped with the women, as had been his habit at home.

"Have you seen David?" he demanded, giving fright to all those present with the despotic tone of his panic.

"Not since last night at supper," Michal answered him back in kind, irritably looking up from conversation.

"Perhaps he is still in your father's rooms," Ahinoam said. Her hand flew to her mouth as she realized. She rose and moved quickly in the direction of the king's apartments. "Your father was in a temper this morning. David actually stepped in on my behalf when Saul was rough with me."

Before she finished speaking, both were running back along the passage, through the king's sitting rooms and into his bedchambers. Jonathan's heart ached, as he feared that his father might have harmed the boy. Chastising himself that he'd not set a guard outside the door to protect David from the king's occasional violent outbursts, he burst in unannounced.

Gasping from exertion, he surveyed the room. His anguish turned to astonishment. Catching up, his mother joined him. They stood together silent in amazement. The room was brightly lit for the first time in many months. The shades over the windows were thrown open, the bed-curtains pulled aside, the bedclothes scattered and empty. David's harp sat on his chair by the door, unattended. Neither he nor the king was in evidence.

Laughter trickled out and found the prince and his mother where they stood. They followed its sound through to the king's bathing chamber. There in the glow of the late autumn sun, they found David grooming the king's hair and beard with olive oil and a sharpened blade. The old man sat before him in a tub filled with steaming water.

"There you are," the king said easily, as though they'd only just seen one another. "When do we sup? I'm famished. David has been playing and tending me all morning and must be ready to eat an ox."

Ahinoam fell to her knees and wept. Silent prayers of thanks moved her lips.

Charging across the room, Jonathan, devoid of all inhibition in his complete joy, swept David into his arms and whirled him through the air. Circling in a dance of joy, he kissed him on the face.

Surprised and startled at first, David struggled against the effusive assault. But as it continued, the fight went out of him. David relaxed into the impassioned embrace, eyes closed and head lolling back. He welcomed the show of affection for which he had, unawares, been so long starved.

"Jonathan," the king insisted. "You must put my personal armor-bearer down at once."

Stunned and embarrassed, the prince dropped David gently to his feet. Their bodies slid against one another. Saul's voice drew their two soaring hearts back to their true surroundings. Each grinned furtively at the other over what had passed between them.

"I can hardly sit at table as king of all of Israel with my beard a different length on either side," Saul laughed, oblivious of their discomfort.

The prince filled with joy at the ease he heard in his father's tone. He gave David's hand one last squeeze before letting him go to his father. David let go of the prince's hand with a reluctance that gave him pause. He returned to grooming the king.

Though he remained thereafter at court to play for and serve as Saul's most personal and trusted servant, he never again saw the prince in the same light. No one at court regarded David as before. His music was officially deemed divine, by royal decree and by all who had witnessed the miracle.

Despite their private feelings for one another, David and the prince's public relationship continued as before. Their shocking and familiar banter delighted and pleased the king, who found favor in David's every word, thought, and gesture. He sent to Jesse pleading that he spare him David.

"He must clearly be your greatest treasure," the king's messenger conveyed, when he arrived at Jesse's home with a mule train laden with Saul's rich gifts. "I offer these humble tokens only in tribute that we may lease David from you for as much time as you may permit us. Your David is the light of the court and the salvation of his king and country, who owe both him and you, his father, a great debt of gratitude."

"Is this a message from a king or a smitten youth?" Jesse jested privately to his wife, though their pride was ill-concealed beneath their mirth.

Saul sent to Jesse, saying, Let David, I pray thee, stand before me; for he hath found favor in my sight.

1 Samuel 16:22

THE KING'S cure irrevocably changed David's life at court.

His duties to the king thereafter were largely ceremonial. He found himself with time to take his leisure and no idea how to do that so far from home and in such unfamiliar territory. At first his newfound attention at court captivated and intrigued him. But the ways of court life became as quickly apparent. His applause for the king's recovery was all too soon replaced by those who found guile in the gift he'd given so freely.

The king was the government and Saul was the king. His illness had thrust many, less reluctant than Jonathan, into positions of temporary power. Upon his recovery those less reluctant to assume power were more reluctant still to give it up.

Jonathan's brother Ishvi, usually content running the family's mule farm in Zela, came to court on hearing of his father's illness. Though his motive for coming was genuine, once there he was persuaded by supporters of Saul's old rival, the Ephraimite Joshua, to take a more active role in the family's other business: running Israel.

More adept on the battlefield than in the council chambers, Jonathan's focus was on the king's recovery, and before anyone noticed, Ishvi was too much used to spending the king's treasury. Flattered and courted, he hired many of Joshua's supporters to accomplish public projects, and in so doing made a host of new friends.

When Saul returned to his duties and discovered what Ishvi and his new friends were up to, his younger son was quickly banished to Zela and his many grants and contracts rescinded.

Ishvi, Joshua, and their supporters were powerless to argue their grievances, and they were far from the only ones aggrieved. Jonathan's brother Malki had been given free rein at the farm in Ishvi's absence and was most displeased to find he was back to working for "that tyrant" Ishvi. His supporters at court, many in General Abner's family, searched for ways to express their disfavor as they found themselves suddenly out of power in the original family business.

Many more who had thought themselves on the rise in the king's absence were shy to admit their disappointment at his recovery and their corresponding decline.

It was unwise and potentially fatal to show such resentment to the king.

Jonathan was an easy target, but after a lifetime's experience, largely impervious. That, coupled with the facts that the king's health was far from certain and Jonathan their future king, kept the prince shielded from much of the pettiness of court life.

David became the focus for those who felt their powerlessness most keenly. His favor with the king and heir was obvious. His acclaim for the king's restoration made him a target, and his inexperience made him vulnerable to any whining courtier with a quiver full of complaints.

It began almost as soon as the king was on his feet.

Esau, the chancellor of royal projects and an ally of Joshua's, threw a party to celebrate the king's recovery. In an elaborate slight, the most celebrated musicians throughout Israel were called to court to play for the event.

When Jonathan found that David was not invited, he dispatched Paltiel to discover Esau's reasons.

"They already have musicians hired," Paltiel was only too happy to report. Before he could take a seat, Paltiel was once again dispatched to explain to Esau's aides that neither Jonathan nor the king would be able to attend if David was not invited.

David, blissfully unaware of the intended snub, was delighted to be invited to the grand fete. He was still more thrilled to discover that he would not be expected to play.

The hall at Esau's fine home was as beautiful as any David had seen outside the palace. He made his way through the colonnade that led to the gilded entryway.

"What business have you here, boy?" the tall, balding servant demanded, blocking David's way. With his shiny head, hooked nose, and downy fringe of white hair, the man looked like a vulture to David, who found him comic at first.

"I am David ben Jesse," David explained patiently. "I am a guest of your master, Esau."

"Indeed," the man said with a snort of laughter. "I understand Prince Jonathan insisted that you be present. You know we do not want for musicians tonight?"

"I have left my harp at home gladly," David said, annoyed by the man's tone and implication.

"If you'll come with me, then," the servant said, turning and leading the way. "You've come to the wrong entrance, but no matter. None are yet present who might take umbrage."

The room was laid out with a long table at one end, raised above the others. Draped with the king's colors, laid with golden plates, and decorated with blossoms and bejeweled urns, it was a splendid setting for the king, David thought.

Those tables nearest the main one were decorated in similar fashion, though lighter on the jewels. The rows of tables were less and less opulent in declining succession until one neared the back of the room, nearest the serving entrance. There a single long wooden table with benches had been set up for the servants of those attending the party.

"Here you are, boy," the vulture said with a dismissive wave of his hand. "It matters not where you sit. There are wooden bowls. The kitchen is through there and down the stone path if you get hungry. My best to the prince."

Stunned, David stood watching the man walk away. He had not been to the house before and was not well acquainted with Esau, so he did not wish to be rude, but felt that if he so decided, his would not be the first volley. Deciding instead to make the best of it, David took a place at the table.

The hall filled quickly with the richest and most powerful of Gibeah and Israel. The return of the king was a big celebration, and people found their way to the city despite the season. Their servants, many damp and muddy from the road, soon crowded around the table where David sat. He tried to be friendly but found himself rebuffed or, at best, treated with the dismissively deferential manner at which Paltiel was a master. "Rudely polite" was how David described it to Eliab when they commiserated about court life. Isolated at that inhospitable table, he wished his brother were not in Bethlehem.

Paltiel arrived with Prince Jonathan and was soon in conference with the vulture. The two spoke with great animation to each other, shooting David meaningful looks as they took more of his tablemates into their confidence. Polite rudeness was soon replaced with frosty silence. David could get little more than nods from those around him.

He was reminded of his brief stay at the harem and Eliakim's bleak description of a musician's lot. The singers and players arrived through the kitchen entrance at the back, as did most of the servants. But when they weren't performing, the musicians sat outside the hall, many in the dirt, waiting to be called.

When they played their music was excellent, though not easy to hear from where David sat. He thought the food provided those forced to take their own wooden bowls to the kitchen was not as good as the yeoman's fare at the shepherd's hut at home. His delight at being invited dimmed considerably as the evening progressed.

Then things got worse.

Bored, David watched the party to which he had clearly not been invited. He noticed the prince looking distractedly about the hall as he talked with the guests nearer his glittering table. David was eyeing the nearby exits and contemplating escape when Jonathan called for Paltiel. Paltiel made his way swiftly to the prince's side and, as David watched, he saw Paltiel pointing back to where David sat in the shadows at the servants' table.

Not content to simply send Palti to fetch David, Jonathan made his way through the crowd, ignoring those who attempted to speak. He marched in a straight line to where David sat. The guests made way, forming a conspicuous corridor through the crowd that led directly to David. By the time the prince reached him, every eye in the hall was turned to look.

David considered running for the nearby door.

"Come, David," Jonathan said, beaming as he extended his hand. "A thousand apologies. There seems to have been some sort of mistake."

Too dazzled by the prince's attention to remember his escape plans, David took the strong hand he offered. Jonathan lifted him over the trestle and led him back through the crowd to the front table, loudly calling Esau's name as they went.

"Yes, Highness?" Esau said, scurrying to the prince's side.

"Esau, you are a lucky man," Jonathan said, putting a powerful arm around their host's shoulders and dragging him to the front of the hall.

"I thank you for saying so, Highness," Esau said, confused and humiliated. "It is an honor and our great good fortune to have you at our humble table."

"You can save that for the spring crops," Jonathan said, drawing Esau's ear near to his mouth but not speaking more softly. "Had the king arrived and found young David here, the man who saved his royal life, seated in the back with the dross and eating provender from a wooden trough, this house would soon enough have been David's and you his servant, if your luck held."

"A thousand pardons," Esau said, motioning the vulture over with violent hand gestures. "I'm sure it must be some oversight."

"Zeev," Esau hissed at the vulture as he approached.

"Yes, master," Zeev called, scurrying to his aid.

"You fool," Esau said, smacking Zeev on the shoulder. It wasn't a serious blow but one intended to show Jonathan how upset he was. "Find the king's musician a place nearer the main table."

"At the main table," Jonathan demanded, tightening his grip on Esau and again speaking loudly into the man's ear. "And, for your health, remember that the king considers David as a son. He is not to be referred to as the king's musician again unless you are seeking a brief but powerful thrill."

"Yes, Highness. Of course, Highness," Esau said, almost falling as Jonathan abruptly released him.

Zeev caught his master and was cuffed for his trouble. The two fled to usurp others and make room for David.

"What seems to be the trouble here?" Joshua demanded in a loud, hearty tone.

"Do I look like the majordomo?" Jonathan snapped, his eyes flashing. There was no love lost between their families since that fateful day at Mizpah.

"You have much better hair." Joshua laughed, making a joke of it.

David wished for death.

"Perhaps you don't recognize me?" Jonathan asked seriously. "For though you might not think me your better, I would suppose that, out of respect for he who *was* chosen as king, or perhaps he who chose him, you would greet me with, at least, the respect of a bow before addressing me like a servant."

"Your Highness," Joshua said, bowing, then rising and raising his goblet. "Prince Jonathan. Long live the prince."

"Long live the prince," the crowd answered in chorus.

David could not suppress a smile.

Needless to say, no one was looking at anything else going on in the hall.

David looked longingly toward the exit as Jonathan, still holding his hand, led him to the place next to his own, unseating its previous occupant. Thankfully the king arrived. Trumpets sounded and the crowd, briefly distracted, moved to be seen offering personal greeting to King Saul as much as to welcome him and celebrate his return to good health.

David considered hiding under the table. He decided it would only cause the prince to seek him out again, attract more attention, and result in possible bloodshed.

The talk at family feast meals at home sometimes got heated, but David was unprepared for the idea of conspiring to dine or scheming to celebrate. Though he had been a hero only a few days before, no one, other than Jonathan and the king, spoke to him that night beyond greetings and the barest pleasantries. David figured the other guests probably feared for their lives should they not offer him the proper respect in the royal presence.

The excruciating evening ended with Saul demanding a song from David. His talent was undeniable, and his performance of a simple psalm of thanksgiving was received warmly. A chill settled by the time David returned to his seat beside the prince. Jonathan proudly crushed him in a great hug. David could not miss the looks he earned. Though uncertain of the meaning behind the bold stares, to him none seemed friendly.

The party ended. The snubs continued.

David was neither fish nor fowl, neither nobleman nor servant.

Though, after the prince made such an example of Esau, David was accorded the trappings and show of greater respect at formal events, the only friends of whom David could be certain were the prince and the king. He began to long for Eliab's return, if for no other reason than the open show of hostility a brother could offer. Returning to old habits, he took refuge with the women and found great affection from Ahinoam, Michal, and Merab.

People stopped speaking when David approached, staring at him silently until he departed, never rude but never inviting.

Once, when seated behind a screen waiting to perform at a banquet for the king, David overheard a couple of men talking.

"Well, at least that little singer isn't here tonight," one said with a derisive laugh.

"Do you suppose he's catamite for both of them?" his friend answered him.

"I know he was kept at the harem when he first arrived," offered another.

"Whatever the case," said the first, "it's clear that he'll do anything to keep the royal favor. Perhaps we can all have a turn when they're finished with him."

David ached as they drifted away in a cloud of coarse laughter. He was not deaf to the words of his critics, nor was he immune to their sting. His lessons in life at court were mostly bitter ones. More often David took to his rooms. He appeared in public only when summoned.

On one such day of self-imposed exile, David sat in the small private garden that adjoined his chambers, idly strumming his harp for his own entertainment. He sang of home. He had missed harvest and the fall market, in fact and in his heart. Though he kept up a healthy correspondence managing his affairs in Bethlehem, he did it to keep himself occupied at court as much as to keep the karmel in good order. He was surprised and chastened to find himself pining for the drudgery and confines of what he had considered a prison so very recently.

As the winter months came on, there was less and less to be managed at home. So long as the Lord watered the wheat with winter rain and the servants kept the livestock fed, there was little else to direct. With nothing more to occupy him than to pray for rain, court became a new kind of prison. His prayers were filled with pleas for an end to his loneliness. His secret wish was that Micah could somehow return to his side.

A knock at his door disturbed his mournful refrain.

Arising, he rushed to answer. He expected it to be a summons from the king, who was on the mend but still glad of David's company and psalms.

David's heart danced when he found the prince at his door like a visiting neighbor.

"My lord," David answered, unable to contain his smile. It was the first such visit since David's arrival, and he was at pains to keep his dignity.

"My prince," Jonathan said with a gracious bow of his head. "I was wondering if you would be able to attend a small celebration that I'm hosting? I'm having a dinner for some of my captains, and I thought you might play for us."

"Certainly, my lord," David said, his smile frozen, his mood fading.

"I am most pleased," Jonathan said stiffly, unable to read the boy's mood. David had seemed at first glad to see him and then disappointed. Still, he was determined. "I'll have Paltiel apprise you of the particulars, if you promise not to kill him when he calls on you."

"Must I?" David sighed, a degree of warmth returning to his smile.

"I do rather depend on him," Jonathan said with a grave nod.

"If I must, then." David relented, turning his palms heavenward in surrender.

"I will look forward to your company," the prince said with a tight little bow before turning to depart.

True to his word, David merely took down the details when Paltiel managed to come to him at the last possible opportunity on the day of the party. He rattled off David's instructions for the evening and escaped with his life. David arrived outside the prince's apartments according to the prince's wishes and rapped at the great, carved doors.

Paltiel answered, opening the door only enough to lean out and face him. David could hear the sound of men laughing. The clatter of plate and goblet seeped from inside.

"Good, you are here," Palti said officiously. "He does not need you yet. Please wait here. I'll call when the prince is ready for you."

Paltiel closed the door without pausing for David's reply.

He regretted not killing Paltiel when they'd been alone in his rooms and he'd had the chance. Still, a promise was a promise, he thought with a smile. Settling in on a nearby bench, he waited more briefly than he'd expected. Paltiel emerged again, closing the door and crossing to him.

"The prince regrets that he is not certain when he will need you," Paltiel said with a poisonous delight. "He begs that you wait upon his pleasure in your rooms. We will send for you there."

Stung by the prince's careless treatment, David nodded only once. He was careful not to show his hurt lest he hear about it for days after, swirling on the tongues of the court gossips. Wordless, he rose, bowed, and departed.

By the time he reached his own doors, he was ready to escape the palace and run away home. His anger blazed at his temples. He spoke the words and curses owed another to himself on his solitary walk. Flinging open his door, he stalked inside.

"Camel's breath," he shouted, slamming the door behind him in a rage.

Asad, his little Canaan shepherd, jumped up on him, barking.

"Stay down, boy," David ordered before remembering he'd left Asad tending the flocks at Jesse's and had not seen him since his departure in midsummer. "Asad," he cried out, dropping to his knees to embrace the little shepherd. "What are you...?"

"I thought he might remind you of home," Jonathan said, stepping from the shadows and frightening David so badly that he fell over screaming. Asad erupted into a torrent of snarls and barking. He ran growling past Jonathan into the garden to defend his master, who lay on his back, laughing. "It pleases you, I take it?"

"Yes, thank you," David said, gasping for breath and trying to regain himself. Asad dashed back in and toppled him with another enthusiastic greeting. "How did you know?"

"I asked your mother what we could do to bring some small measure of home to you here at court," Jonathan said, taking a seat beside David on the floor. He placed an ornately embroidered silken sack between them. "She sent Asad as our first court ambassador from Bethlehem. Your father sent word that there was only one way to keep you from turning ugly when you were imprisoned by the rainy season."

Jonathan pushed the bag toward David.

"What is this?" he asked.

"Open it and find out," Jonathan exhorted with a mysterious grin.

David undid the braided and tasseled silk rope with which the bag was tied and emptied the contents into his lap. He could only gasp as he turned the treasure over in his hands.

"Your father says that no one in Bethlehem can beat you at tau," Jonathan explained as David marveled at his gift.

"I could not bring myself to play with such a grand twenty squares set," David said, running his fingers over the princely game board. Crafted of dark wood and ivory, it was inlaid with gold and silver. The playing pieces and dice were crusted with precious stones. "This is too fine a thing to be a game."

"Nonsense," Jonathan said, taking the board from him. "Also, you will not find me so easy to defeat as your mother and your little sisters."

"My littler sisters are bigger than me," David said, mocking his own stature. Lighthearted in the prince's company, he warmed to his kindness. "Yet I doubt you could have defeated them or that you offer me any real challenge."

"My little sisters are bigger than you too," Jonathan said with a deep laugh. "In fact, everyone I know is bigger than you. We shall see who challenges who."

"Such an elaborate ruse. Why have you gone to such bother for me?" David asked, suddenly aware that this was the first time they had ever been alone together. That they were in David's room made it sweeter.

"You've seemed so sad lately, no matter how grand the tributes," Jonathan answered with a shrug as he set up the playing pieces and the board. "Then it occurred to me that you had never been away from home before."

Jonathan looked up, and their eyes met.

"Besides," he went on without looking away, "we must find some way to pass the winter months trapped here. Now, what shall we play for?"

"Hmmm," David mused, leaning back against Asad. "What would I like?"

"So you just assume you will win?" Jonathan asked with an indignant snort as he arranged an armload of cushions on the floor to accommodate their play.

"Only as sure as I am spring follows winter," David answered, taking a place opposite.

"Oh, I almost forgot," Jonathan said, clapping his hands.

Servants entered bearing trays of food and drink. They began laying the feast out around them. "Your mother sent a list of your favorites and instructions for their preparation. I passed them along to the cooks in our humble kitchens. I hope it will suffice."

"If it does, we must never tell my mother," David said with a grateful and joyous smile. He had admired the prince and his achievements before he'd ever met him. His beauty left David breathless from their first meeting. He had seen that the prince was a gracious and dignified ruler.

To discover that such a man was possessed of such a kind and generous heart seemed almost too much to expect of a mere mortal. He was, it appeared, as fine a companion as anyone could choose, an obedient son, and a noble prince. Best of all, there they sat on the floor of David's room, eating his favorite lamb in yogurt sauce wrapped in hot flatbread, playing his favorite game, while Asad begged bites of their supper.

Thoughts of Micah and the joy absent since they had been parted filled his heart. His hand rose to his breast. He touched the lion's tooth on the sling that hung there still. "Thank you," David said. Though he spoke to Jonathan, his thanksgiving was also made to Micah for guiding him to a new friend in such a lonely and crowded place, and to the Lord for finding a way to answer his prayers.

"A pleasure, my prince. I thought you needed a pleasant surprise for a change," Jonathan said, dropping one of the pyramid-shaped dice into David's hand. "Ready? Cast your lot with mine. We'll see who goes first."

"Fate is with me already," David said with a sly smile as he took up the three silver pyramids and tumbled them onto the carpet. "What shall we play for?"

"The winner gets to choose what we do tomorrow?" Jonathan suggested, stroking Asad's fur as he lay back on the heap of cushions he had assembled.

The prince's words made David feel that he had already won. He readily agreed, confident that he would soon be choosing a day filled with all the idylls of home he'd missed since arriving at court.

Thou hast put gladness in my heart, more than in the time that their corn and their wine increased.

Psalm 4:7

AND IT came to pass that Prince Jonathan was much better at tau than David had anticipated. Even given best two games out of three and then three of five, David found himself out for a day of falconry with the prince, early the next morning.

"Excellent, my two princes together," Saul said with delight as he excused David from his morning playing duties. "I could not aspire to better friends for either of you." They left the palace with the king's blessing just after sunrise.

"This is Adalia," Jonathan said, holding the hooded bird aloft as it clutched his gloved hand with its fierce-looking claws.

"Doesn't he mind the hood?" David asked, reaching to stroke the bird and thinking better of it as he got a closer look at Adalia's talons.

"Not a bit," Jonathan said lightly. David followed as they made their way to the top of the hill to begin hunting. "He trusts me. This way he isn't bothered by things that might frighten him. Or distracted with things that might waste his time."

"Waste his time?" David asked with a wry smile. Amused, he fancied how much work he could accomplish on his father's karmel with the number of men who pursued them as they tromped out into the hills to watch a bird do their hunting.

"Yes, exactly," Jonathan continued patiently, glad of David's company under any circumstances. He was glad of his father's recovery and gladder still that it freed David and allowed them the opportunity at last to spend time at leisure together. "He is trained to bring down birds for me. If some were to fly by, he would strike out at them, for he knows it is his duty. But I would then have to call him back. It would delay our progress and waste his time and mine. When he was young, he wore jesses—leads—on his legs to keep him close. Now he flies free. The hood lets him know that he is to stay on my fist, where he'd rather be."

"I see," David observed. They made their way up to the ridge.

"How do you know that he'd rather be there on your fist?"

"Because he always returns," Jonathan teased, tousling David's hair with his free hand. "Here we are," he announced as they crested the hill.

The view of the broad, spare, rocky vale below was dizzying. Other hawks circled there already, hunting without falconers to guide them.

"Now watch, David," Jonathan said, gesturing for the men who accompanied them to fall into position. He then unhooded the bird. Thrusting his fist upward, he gave a single shrill whistle. Adalia launched himself aloft, circling overhead. Jonathan led the expedition down into the rocky vale. "This is called 'waiting on,'" Jonathan explained softly. "We are in waiting."

As they walked Adalia kept watch and followed from up above.

Suddenly, as they drew near to a stand of brush, birds erupted into the air. Jonathan gave a sharp two-note whistle. The falcon fell from the sky. Swiftly, Adalia grabbed one of the pigeons from flight. Surrendering its prey into Jonathan's waiting hands, the bird took flight again and again, taking down game birds until they dispersed and hid themselves in the brush.

Again Jonathan signaled with the single shrill whistle as before. Adalia resumed his place in the sky above them.

Before the day was much older, the leather pouch Jonathan carried was filled with small game birds.

"Here, Palti," Jonathan called, extending the bag to his aide. "Take these back. You and the men head home. David and Adalia will walk with me for a time."

"My lord," Paltiel said, taking the bag with a perfunctory nodding bow for his prince. A suspicious look was all the farewell he offered David as he parted. David still found the man troubling, though he was willing to try for cordiality on the prince's account.

"Would you like to try?" Jonathan asked, taking another leather glove from his belt and offering it to David.

Gamely, David took the glove. It swallowed his hand and arm as he slipped it on. He made a fist as far from his face as possible, his eyes squinted.

"He will not come to you if you show him you are afraid," Jonathan said with a laugh he tried to conceal with a cough.

"He has a hood on," David pointed out, trying to make light and not to flinch but not really succeeding at either.

"We'll see," Jonathan said. He placed his fist next to David's and eased Adalia over.

As soon as the bird was on David's fist, he began to flap his wings and cry out in distress. Unable to fly away, Adalia became more and more agitated. David, in turn, was more afraid and skittish.

After letting the two go on long enough to make his point, Jonathan placed his fist next to David's. The bird stepped easily back onto his master's forehand. At once he grew quiet.

"He seems to know," Jonathan said, laughing.

As they walked along, Jonathan worked with him. David came to trust, just as Adalia had. He did not become a master that day or even remove Adalia's hood as he held him, but he got the idea. He grew easier with the falcon and the prince.

"Thank you for a fine day," David said as they returned to the palace. "It was nice to be out in the countryside." He was too shy to say that what he had enjoyed most was Jonathan's company. It made no difference where they had gone, though he would always remember every detail of their day.

"You must sup in my rooms tonight," Jonathan said, catching David's forearm insistently. "I'm sure the spoils of our hawking will make a fine pie."

"I would be honored," David replied with a formal bow that got a laugh from Jonathan.

"It would be better that you were hungry," Jonathan said, his eyes sparkling. "Come at lamplight?"

"I will not fail to," David said, starting to bow. Catching himself, he laughed nervously. "May I bring a guest?"

"A guest?" Jonathan asked, a shade of alarm playing across his face. Wanting to be a good host, he only nodded. He was determined that they should be friends and fought to keep his feelings from getting in the way. "But of course, I'm sure it will be a grand pie."

"We will see you there," David said with a nod as he turned to go.

Bathed, perfumed, and clad in his new palace finery, David scratched at Jonathan's door in the darkling twilight of early evening.

"Come," Jonathan's voice called out from within.

"Wait here," David said as he eased the door open. He was most surprised to find the prince plainly dressed and very much at ease in anticipation of his company.

"Look what I have for us tonight," Jonathan called out. He held up a game board. It was similar enough to the board for tau to make it clear it was a game as well, but the resemblance ended there.

"What is that?" David asked, examining the board.

"It's a game called senet," Jonathan said. "I thought we could play to see who decides what we are to do tomorrow."

"Tomorrow?" David asked, delighted at the prospect. "But I don't know how to play."

"Excellent, then I can begin winning at once," Jonathan said, guiding David to take a seat. "Your guest decided not to join us?" he asked, a little too pleased to be gracious.

"Oh no," David said with a nod. "He's outside."

"Ah," Jonathan said, his smile slipping ever so slightly. "Ask him in before he thinks we are from Sodom."

David gave a whistle. Asad dashed and leaped into the open arms of his delighted prince.

"Asad," Jonathan cried out, hugging the little shepherd. "The perfect guest. I'm so sorry that I did not think to invite you myself." With a playful swipe and the toss of an old slipper, the chase was on. David laughed as the two dove behind tapestries, vaulted chests and tables, and generally tore through the grand rooms, ending when Jonathan tumbled into the bathing pool, Asad barking victoriously from the edge of the water.

Thus they began their first winter together.

Each night they would play tau or senet or dice or just argue to see who would choose what they would do the following day. One of their favorites was a dice game of their own devising that they called Camel Trader. Each in turn would roll the dice in secret and then announce the unseen tally. The object was to guess if the tally was the truth or a lie. Both men became masters at reading the other.

So long as the weather held, their days were spent outdoors in the hills around Gibeah.

Jonathan was known to be the finest archer in Israel, and they spent days at target practice. The prince's long, powerful arms and clear-eyed aim made the bull's-eye more a certainty than a goal. David became a passable shot but never Jonathan's equal with a bow.

The king gave David a horse, and Jonathan taught him to ride it. The two soon began to vanish into the wilderness together, borne away by their steeds.

They camped and hunted, sometimes in elaborate parties and sometimes on their own, on private expeditions that reminded David of his days with Micah.

As the weather turned, they moved their days indoors. Jonathan chose to have David train with him at swordplay and hand-to-hand combat when the dice favored him. David chose music and dancing as their pastimes when he was the victor. Neither cared.

They were happy simply to be at each other's side. Each man had found the friend he needed. Both were happier than they'd been in many days and moons prior. David came to trust Jonathan just as Adalia did. And, like devoted little Asad, Jonathan found joy in David's company and a peace he did not recognize. As spring came on, they were speaking one another's words, and each had long since given up knocking at the other's door.

David learned what it was to be a prince, and Jonathan learned how to forget.

"The two princes," Michal called them one night at dinner. The name stuck.

"My sons," Saul called them, for he felt a father to both.

Their joy with each other made them irresistible to all who encountered them. Even Palti found himself smiling around them. Though he longed for the day David would return to Bethlehem, he loved the prince enough to delight in his happiness.

The more time they spent together, the less likely it seemed that the day of David's departure would ever arrive. Though Saul was long recovered, the subject of David's return home was not just deferred, it was forgotten.

Jonathan managed to bank the coals in his heart so well that David came to believe in them as friends and brothers alone. As good as they had become at Camel Trader, neither could yet see completely into the other's heart.

David's rising influence with the prince, and the devotion of the king, served to fan the flame of the ill will already alive and well at court. It mattered less to David than before. The king's esteem granted David the rights and privileges of the royal family. Jonathan's friendship gave him the life of a prince.

When celebration of David's birthday at court nearly eclipsed the concurrent observance of Shavuot, the king dismissed all criticism and warnings. He was ever grateful for the gift that David was credited with restoring to him—his health. Still, when in a few days less than a year, the singer who'd been bunked in with the eunuchs was feted at the king's table like a member of the royal family or a visiting prince, tongues wagged outside the king's hearing.

Publicly David was vaunted as the man who'd saved the king, no matter what was said privately.

Now the Philistines gathered together their armies to battle, and were gathered together at Shochoh, which belongeth to Judah, and pitched between Shochoh and Azekah, in Ephesdammim.

1 Samuel 17:1

THE BLESSING of the king's recovery was soon doubled. Even as joy reigned at court, Abner was relieved to have the king back on the throne when reports from his scouts worsened. The Philistines were again on the march, gathering for a massive assault. Stories of a secret weapon were everywhere.

David was of two minds as the talk at court turned to war. He was troubled by the development for Israel. It meant destruction and bloodshed for the innocent and those in the military alike, as the invaders moved into the hills from the coastal cities of Philistia. It also meant that David would, at last, join his brothers and the men of his country in battle at the king's side, and he was quietly thrilled. Eliab had returned to court and his service to Abner in the spring. Abinadab and Shammah had arrived with the recent news of impending war.

"*You give me your shield of victory, and your right hand sustains me; you stoop down to make me great,*" he sang himself a little psalm of triumph as he made ready to accompany his king and his prince into battle. His role as the king's armor-bearer would not put him on the front lines, but he would be there, taking part as he and Micah had dreamed and practiced on their mountain campaigns.

God's will was at last clear. David's gifts, used in service to the Lord, had led to the fulfillment of his dreams. Though his heart was still heavy that Micah would not be with them in body, he had only to touch the lion's tooth on the sling he wore always around his neck to restore the spirit of his absent and beloved friend. Jonathan, in many ways, had come to fill that void in David's heart. Though the prince could not replace his old friend or everything they had shared, the bond David felt for Jonathan dulled the edge of his fears of facing battle.

Paltiel arrived at David's quarters, joyous in the duty that had been assigned him.

"I'm here to help you prepare for your journey," Paltiel announced.

"Oh, that's hardly necessary," David said politely. He did not relish the idea of tainting this joyous preparation with Paltiel's special form of smiling aggression. "I've only a few things to put together before I go to assist the king."

"Nonsense," Paltiel said. "The king has been most generous with you and your family in reward for your service. You'll be returning home with quite the treasure train."

"Home?" David asked, confused by Paltiel's words and wary of his court trickery. "I won't be returning home just yet."

"But the king has ordered it," Paltiel said with a pretense of concern and confusion.

"Why?" David asked, distressed by the possibility that Paltiel might, this once, be telling the truth.

"Well, you know, David, the king does not actually discuss his decisions with me," Paltiel said nastily as he began to drag David's belongings together. "That said, if I were to hazard a guess, it would be that he decided that since he's planning to fight the Philistines and not entertain them at a court banquet, he won't need you to sit in the enemy's laps and squirm appealingly."

Had there been a weapon at hand, David would have struck Paltiel down with it.

As it was he simply turned and ran to the king's quarters. He managed to make his way through the chaos of the king's retinue as they prepared for departure into battle. Saul was with Abner and his advisors when David found him.

"My king," David said, kneeling at Saul's feet. "A word with Your Majesty?"

"David," Saul said, placing his hand gently on the boy's head. "Not just now, my son. I've much to attend."

"May I not help you?" David pleaded, catching the king's hand and holding it. "Why do you send me home?"

"My dear boy," the king said, cupping David's face between his two hands. "The battlefield is no place for the likes of you. We will send for you as soon as we return. Meanwhile, I'm sure your father misses you greatly. You will have time with your family."

"But, Sire," David appealed. "I am your armor-bearer. I have come to court to serve you and to help you as you make a nation for us all. How can I help you if I am at home during the most difficult parts of your journey?"

"What a loving and obedient heart you have," Saul said affectionately. "Jonathan is right about you. He is also right when he says that we will not be able to focus on the rigors of battle if we are worried about your fate. It is why we leave our wives and daughters behind as well. Not because we don't care, but because we care about you most. So you see, you are helping me. Go to your father. I will send for you soon. You have the king's word."

"The prince wants this also?" David asked, stunned, rising.

"Yes, it was his suggestion, but I am in full agreement," the king said, ruffling David's hair indulgently. "Now run along and get packed. I've ordered many fine gifts for you and your family. I must return to the concerns of the battlefield now."

"May the Lord fight at your side and bring you home safe," David said, striking his chest in salute as the soldiers did, even as he fought back tears of rage.

Delirious with anger, David could not remember a single footfall that led him from the king's side to the prince's apartment. Yet there he was. He burst through the doors to find a scene not unlike the preparations underway in the king's quarters.

"What are you doing here?" Eliab asked, pausing from his work, stunned by David's arrival. "I thought you'd be on your way home by now."

"What are you doing here?" David asked, surprised to find Eliab in service to the prince.

"The prince sent his own man, Paltiel, to help you make ready for your journey even though he himself is preparing for a long and dangerous campaign," Eliab said with a tone so snide that it bordered on anger. "So the sooner you get your kit together and get your jewelry box on the road, the sooner we may all return to the life-and-death work that we are about."

"Where is the prince?" David demanded, surprised and infuriated by Eliab's tone.

"Preparing for battle," Eliab sighed disgustedly. "Now run home to Mama."

"I would be preparing to go with you had it not been for the prince's order that I be sent back to Bethlehem," David snapped. He judged, rightly from his older brother's reaction, that Eliab had not known of the order. Before they could discuss it further, the prince came in.

"David, I... sorry. I didn't..." was all Eliab managed before the prince strode in with a buzz of people and activity.

"Greetings, sons of Jesse," Jonathan said heartily. "Do I intrude on family business?"

"The king informs me that you counseled that I should be sent home to sit out the war with the women," David said to his prince without so much as a by-your-leave. Eliab grabbed at David's shoulder.

"David, please try to understand," Jonathan said, unruffled by the accustomed familiarity he would have tolerated from no other. "It is a selfish choice. I make it on my behalf alone. I simply could not concentrate on battle were you there and at risk."

"What are you saying?" David demanded hotly. The games of Camel Trader were forgotten as he thought only of himself. He was too blinded by his pride and anger to see the prince's true meaning.

"Why, that you are too valuable to... my family to be put at risk," Jonathan said, unable to express his true meaning even were they not surrounded by servants and officers. "Your service to the country is not performed on the field of battle but is no less important to Israel."

"Well, my lord," David said with a low bow. "You are right."

"Thank you." The prince nodded, astonished by the unprecedented admission.

"It is a selfish choice," David snarled, rising and facing Jonathan as an equal. "You make it without regard for the lives or wishes of others and with no consideration for anyone other than you and your—"

The prince's slap brought an end to the tirade and a stunned silence to the room.

The blow hurt both men more deeply than a mere slap could be felt.

Undaunted by the comeuppance, David found new words of insubordination. "I am as worthy as you or any man. I demand that you allow me to go."

The two regarded each other for a breath. All present tried not to move or breathe in the hope that they might simply disappear. Eliab was immobilized by his rage, unable even to speak words of consolation to his prince or drag his insolent brother from the room, as he felt obligated to do just then.

Jonathan broke the tensions and the staring contest when he laughed.

"David," Jonathan said, shaking his head. He adopted a crippling and poisonous tone for the benefit of those around them. Lifting David easily from the floor, he carried and set him just outside the door as he spoke. "Do you propose that we have a singer defend the nation? I do believe that you are a man of considerable talents. But rather than earning us a victory, they would more likely earn you a place in King Achish's harem. Now go home and count your new rings and gold bracelets before I send you home with only the spanking you so richly deserve."

Though it broke his heart to be parted thus, Jonathan closed the door in David's face. The stout oak planks from which the door had been hewn could not contain the hearty laughter that accompanied David's dismissal.

Humiliated, David fled the palace, Gibeah, and the prince the instant Jonathan set him outside the door of his chambers. The jewelry, the presents, his clothes, Asad, and even his harp caught up with him at Jesse's house many days later. David never so much as looked at the gifts. He knew the treasure he most wanted was not among them.

And the three eldest sons of Jesse went and followed Saul to the battle: and the names of his three sons that went to the battle were Eliab the firstborn, and next unto him Abinadab, and the third Shammah. And David was the youngest: and the three eldest followed Saul. But David went and returned from Saul to feed his father's sheep at Bethlehem.

1 Samuel 17:13-15

THE RIDE home to Bethlehem seemed a long one, even galloping on the back of the fine horse the king had given him. The ride and horse only reminded him of Jonathan. With his help David had become a formidable warrior, particularly on horseback.

At this same teacher's bidding, the only foes David faced were the legions of gnats and the forces of boredom he battled on the journey home. David had time to think and to see his life for what it was. He had come as close to his dream as a man might ask. He had been found wanting by those best suited to decide. It was a bitter and heartbreaking admission, but David could see it as sharply as the view following a strong rain. God had answered his prayer. He had been given the opportunity for which he'd asked. The opportunity revealed that David was not worthy of his own highest aspirations.

"I thank you for your grace," David prayed over and over again as he retraced his journey of barely a year before. He had often heard it said that blessings granted were most often the source of the greatest sadness. He had not truly understood until that day.

God had prepared the perfect life for David, and he had been ungrateful. So the Lord, in his wisdom, had blessed David with the answer to his prayers, not to hurt him, but to allow him to see the truth. Samuel's prophecy had been fulfilled. David had used his gift to heal the king, and in so doing dispatched the enemies of all of Israel. Now, it was time to resume the life for which the Lord had prepared and intended him.

"Thank you for your grace."

His spirit broken and his dreams dashed, he returned to his father's house resigned to his fate, if not content with it. With a humorless zeal that stunned even his family, more than familiar with his nature, David poured himself single-mindedly into the business of running the farm and family enterprises.

By new moon in the following month of Bul, the karmel was ready for harvest and running as smoothly as a stream slips past the rocks. There was no joy in it, only hard work. David drove the staff like a dog herds sheep.

"What troubles you, my son?" Jesse asked him on the journey home from the Bethlehem temple, after the Rosh Chodesh sacrifices for the new harvest moon.

David did not answer right away. It was not out of disrespect for his father. He had not stopped to try to put his feelings into words since his arrival home.

"I am finding what it truly is to become a man," David said, when he did speak at last.

"What is that truly, my son?" Jesse asked, with a tone of mild amusement at the thought of life lessons from one so young.

"That dreams are the inspiration of youth. Becoming a man means awakening from those dreams. A man finds his way in life by accepting his limits and making the most of what he is offered, rather than wasting his time dreaming of that which he is not and cannot be."

"That sounds very sad," Jesse said, his brow wrinkled with care.

"I suppose that accounts for why one so seldom sees a man playing as boys do." David shrugged. He clicked his tongue and flicked the willow wand to hurry the mule so that they might be home for the family meal sooner.

Dust gathered on David's harp. The dice and the tau set remained unplayed in the cedar box on a shelf in David's room. He spoke and thought only of work. Not Jesse, his sons and daughters, his wife, nor any of his many servants, all of whom loved David above all others, could find anything to bring back the light into the eyes of the one who had brought so much life and light into their lives.

Occasionally, when he thought no one was looking, David would reach into the breast of his robe and touch the lion's tooth on the sling. A tear might course down his cheek, tribute and bitter memory of what might have been and what was. Then he would tuck the memories away with the sling and return to the task at hand.

In time he felt he had escaped his dreams and killed the pain that only hope can bring into a man's heart. He lived instead in the cold reality of harvest, trade, and commerce. It was joyless but painless, in the way that the juice of the poppy makes one numb to the ache of a wound. David traded the empty hope of happiness for the dull comfort of tangible success.

It was in this prosperous fugue that David found himself in a state of ease, following a heated haggling with his old friend Korah.

"For the love of Baal," Korah wailed, throwing up his hands. "I surrender. I need no profit, only peace from this assault. David, my friend, you learned to be a harder man at court."

"I learned a lot at court," David said distantly.

"Anah, bring us something cool to drink," Korah shouted to his sister, who still tended him as he had not yet found a man to take her. "It is too bad you are not with the king still."

"Do you not enjoy my company?" David asked, an eyebrow raised.

Korah gestured to a stool. David sat before his host would take a seat beside him.

"Yours is company of a different sort now, my friend," Korah said without really answering. "I simply meant that if you were with the king still, he might not be in stalemate with the Philistines."

The fate of the king and his army was all the news of which anyone spoke.

Saul had met the enemy. They were twenty thousand strong and equally matched across the valley of Elah. Both forces had taken to the hills on either side of the paltry stream that ran across the plain between them. So nearly matched, neither would surrender the high ground to venture an attack on the other.

"Surely such a hardened warrior as you have become, in your short time in the king's court, could wrest a resolution from such a tangled situation," Korah said, taking a cup from the tray Anah held out to them. "Thank you, my dear sister."

David accepted his cup but said nothing to Anah. He was still ambivalent in his feelings toward her. Their last meeting at his father's townhouse had been his last night with Micah. He spoke stiffly with Korah about harvest business matters, avoiding questions about life at court and any dalliances court life might have afforded him. David excused himself before either man had finished his wine. He bid Korah a formal farewell and left his baffled companion behind.

"What has become of my friend?" Korah asked no one in particular. He watched David make his way across the market. David did not speak to another soul between Korah's tent and the archway that marked the entrance and the exit to the bazaar, though he passed many whose names he knew.

"David, stay please," Anah said, catching up to him. Boldly she took his arm as he crossed under the arch and back onto the streets of town.

"Anah," David said, extracting his arm. "What are you doing? It is not proper for you to accost me on the street like this."

"So you are still a boy, I see," she taunted, her voice playful but with the glint of a sharp edge. "I mistook your manner at my brother's tent. I thought perhaps that you had shaved your whiskers, but I see you have none still."

"A boy?" he said, stopping full. He turned to face her. "Do you seek to insult me?"

"I seek, as I have always sought, your company," she said, stepping close to him. She spoke softly that they might not be overheard. "But there is always something between us."

"As I recall the last time we met, it was my best friend who was between us," David said.

"Are you jealous of him or of me?" she asked, naming the old ache, her words sharp enough to bring back the fire to an ill-healed wound.

"What would you have of me?" he asked flatly.

"I would have all of you as a woman has a man," she said with startling frankness.

"You are the widowed sister of an Edomite trader," David said with the unflinching accuracy of a well-aimed arrow. "Only so much of me is available to the likes of you. I believe that, in truth, is all of me that you want."

"What about what you want?" she asked, not flinching from his efforts to hurt her. "Do I have anything that you want, or are those parts not available from me?"

"Come, I will show you," David invited coldly, turning and walking away.

A bemused smirk spread across Anah's face. She watched him walk away without so much as a single backward glance. As he neared the corner, she hurried to catch up to him. She kept always a few paces behind. When he reached the door of the townhouse, unoccupied just then by any but a few servants, he turned to open the door for her, confident that she was there. He held the door, but he did not look at her.

Wordlessly they made their way inside. She followed him to the upper level of the well-appointed dwelling.

"Here," he said, standing outside the door to the room where he slept, the bed well-made and comfortable.

She stepped inside and stood as he closed the door behind them.

They regarded one another for a heartbeat. They were more combatants in some unnamed struggle than lovers.

"What have you brought me here to show me, little boy?" she asked provocatively.

In a single move, he dropped the tunic he wore to the floor around his feet. He stepped easily out of it, kicking away his sandals. The sun and rigors of his farm work, his longstanding habit of a soldier's training, kept up in tribute to the memory of his fallen friend, as well as the generous gifts of God and his father, had shaped David's body into something Anah found impossible to resist.

"That will do," she said. Tearing away her own clothes, she leaped onto him, knocking him back onto the bed.

Their kisses were so filled with passion that David tasted blood and did not know or care if it was his or hers. She fought him for it, but he was able to climb on top of her as the two grappled for the position like wrestlers.

This they reversed several more times. They continued their bout, filling their hands with one another's flesh until, at last, he entered her. He thrust powerfully, violently, her hands clasped behind him urging him on.

When both were spent, he fell away. The two separated as strangers who have accidentally brushed against one another on the street and make way out of politeness rather than any real feeling for the other.

"You still miss him very much," she said at last.

He did not answer. He rose and began to dress.

"You are still in love with him," she said, sitting up slightly, her naked breasts drooping, her elbow crooked behind her.

He froze, unable to look at her. The tunic fell from his hands.

"That night, nothing happened between your friend and me," she said to his naked back. "I wanted it to, but he said that his heart belonged to another. That as much as he wanted to, he could not be untrue."

David's legs gave way beneath him, and he sat on the edge of the bed. The force of his sobs shook them both. With a tenderness they had not shared, she held him as he cried. She soothed him with her hands, humming tunes as one would to a child.

Horrified to be so transparent, he was unable to keep it inside any longer. He was glad of the comfort. He was glad to know that she thought it was for Micah alone that he wept. Though Micah's place in his heart was forever inviolate, the angry words that had passed between him and Jonathan were foremost in his mind as he cried himself to sleep in her arms.

And Saul and the men of Israel were gathered together, and pitched by the valley of Elah, and set the battle in array against the Philistines. And the Philistines stood on a mountain on the one side, and Israel stood on a mountain on the other side: and there was a valley between them.

1 Samuel 17:2-3

"WHY HAVE we come to Elah, if not to engage the enemy?" Jonathan asked sincerely as he and his father walked along the perimeter of their encampment, a rare chance for privacy. "We have been here for thirty-seven days, staring at one another across this valley."

"I know it is frustrating, but I will not give up the high ground," the king said with a sigh. "We do not have Samuel here to tell us the outcome. I will not risk running the men into range of their archers and impale them on Philistine spears if I do not know it will succeed."

Jonathan only sighed in response. He did not wish to bait his father into another argument over his continued faith in Samuel and his capricious God.

"You look here, now," Saul said sternly, taking his son's arm and turning him so that they faced each other. Their eyes so alike, his son's sharp young visage so like his once had been, it was as though he was looking into polished metal and seeing a reflection of the past. "I forbid you any more heroics like in Gilgal. You can't count on an earthquake every time."

The two men laughed easily together as they resumed their walk. They nodded genially and received the salutes of those they encountered.

It was cool that morning, a pleasant change. Their stroll was agreeable, for a time.

A trumpet brayed from across the valley, shattering the early calm.

"Oh Lord God, please, no," Jonathan moaned. "Not him again. If for no other reason than to silence that great ox, I would fling myself on our enemy's spears. Even death would be preferable to this."

"Good morning, cowards of the ranks of Israel," the booming voice echoed across the narrow plain as it had each morning, when the sun was halfway up the sky, for the last thirty-seven days.

A chorus of groans came in answer from throughout the massive camp of the army of Israel.

King Achish of the Philistine city of Gath, who led the combined forces of the five cities of Philistia, had ordered his men into place in the southern hills above the plain of Elah. There they awaited the arrival of Saul and his armies. By the time the king and his men arrived on the scene, the Philistine position was so formidably established that simply to charge them would have been to waste lives and the resources. The only appropriate response to the forbidding

Philistine encampment on the south of the valley was for King Saul to establish an even more unbreakable line on the northern ridge.

There they might have stood staring at one another in tense and angry silence but for what had been revealed as the Philistines' secret weapon: Goliath.

Dwarfing King Saul and his Prince Jonathan, who stood head and shoulders above most other men, the flesh and blood Goliath was more intimidating than any iron machine of war. Standing more than six cubits high, his shoulders broad enough to match, he rose above the plain. To look Goliath in the eye, one man would have to sit on the shoulders of another. Clad in an array of magnificent bronze armor that weighed more alone than any other soldier and his armor together, Goliath stood gleaming in the summer sun each morning to mock his enemy with his words and his confidence. Armed with sword, shield, and spear made to titanic scale and accompanied by his muscular armor carrier, each day he made his way out onto the plain that separated the two camps. Leaving his shield with his servant, and standing just beyond the range of Jonathan's bow, he began his quotidian harangue.

"Am not I a Philistine, and you servants to Saul?" the giant demanded, as he had done in some form for more than a month. "Choose you a man for you, and let him come down to me. If he be able to fight with me and to kill me, then will we be your servants, but if I prevail against him and kill him, then shall you be our servants and serve us."

The words of the challenge varied slightly, but the terms were always the same.

When no one answered his challenge, as King Saul had forbidden each man in his army to do, Goliath would then torment and provoke Saul's troops. He called them out as cowards. He impugned their families, their mothers, and their single puny God. He asserted relentlessly that they were men of such little spine that none among them would come down to face him.

The daily taunts were as demoralizing as they were infuriating. The king had been forced to issue strict regulation on the wasteful expenditure of arrows in response. It not only depleted and disarmed them, it marked the field for their enemy to know the exact limit of their reach.

"I'll take an axe and chop him down," Jonathan demanded, pleading with the king, itching to silence the great brute. Wisely Saul would not hear of it from the prince or any man.

"I cannot stake the fate of my armies on the outcome of a single battle," Saul explained to his advisors, as he cautioned them against allowing any man to face Goliath's challenges. "Nor do I suppose would King Achish or his cohorts on the other side. A defeat would only be a moral blow to my men, and victory would do nothing to help our cause."

Galled by the order and the repeated taunting, Jonathan took delight in leading the men in creating their own response. They pounded on shields and pots while shouting all manner of curses on the offending Philistine. But the challenge was relentless, and their threats and curses grew stale in their mouths for want of action.

After a few weeks, Goliath's morning rants simply became a part of their billeting. They took it in stride, though it cut a bit more out of every man's heart who heard it each day.

More than the torment of the giant's derision, though, was the grind of the passing days of inaction and the deadening routine of drilling and preparation as they waited. All longed to be home again. Harvest was coming and with it, the new year and the festivals that followed: times of celebration, of family, and of home.

None longed for home more than the prince himself, an unfamiliar feeling. The prince was more at home on the battlefield than at court. There were no manners or protocols to be endlessly debated in the field, no visiting foreigners save for the ones he had come to kill. Jonathan was free to be a man among men when the army was on campaign. Though he much preferred uneventful spring and summer patrols, he would gladly have chosen the bloodiest battle over moldering at the palace during the rainy months, tormented by every trivial detail and imagined offense.

That season the campaign, or perhaps the prince himself, was different. The Philistine forces were no more formidable than usual. The army was well armed and well numbered to face them. It was not the fearsomeness of the assignment that made him long for hearth and home. Yet the nostalgic ache grew with each day spent waiting. Each dawn brought a new opportunity for Jonathan to restate his final argument with David. He longed to apologize for striking him. For want of other occupation, each day was plagued with yearning to make his reasons clear. Every night brought fevered dreams filled with desire to express in greeting what he wished he had said in parting.

Every day the wait became ever more maddening.

When it wasn't Goliath's voice ringing in his ears, it was his own, shouting at David and dismissing him like some servant. More maddening still was that there was no way to tell David what he truly felt in his heart. Perhaps he would find peace if he could at least make clear what he did not feel. As it was, the only peace available came in the knowledge that the enemy was in sight and David was safe at home.

His walk with his father cut short by the nettling Philistine, they made their way back to the king's tent for a meal.

"Father, how long do you see this going on?" Jonathan asked, hungry for an end to the punishment of their days at Elah.

"It depends upon their cooks and their quartermasters," Saul said with a shrug as he held the tent open for his son. "We will fight when they begin to run out of supplies. It's as simple as that. They are farther from home, but they came knowing this as well as I. We simply have to wait them out. I have no idea how much is in their larder. Keep your troops drilled and ready. The time of our victory will be chosen by our enemy."

"Yes, I see." Jonathan nodded, smiling to himself. He was proud as always of his father's great wisdom in these matters. "I will take my men out on patrol, then. We could use the break from this, and we need to get on our horses and hone our swords."

"Wise, but stay within a trumpet's call," Saul said in agreement as he took up his place at his table. "The prince and I would eat."

And Jesse said unto David his son, Take now for thy brethren an ephah
of this parched corn, and these ten loaves, and run to the camp of thy brethren.
1 Samuel 17:17

THE ENDLESS days of waiting depleted not only their enemy's larder but also that of the king's men. Each, save for the lowliest foot soldier, was accountable to bring supplies enough to sustain him on campaign.

David and Eliab had come near to blows when Eliab stripped the pantries of their father's house with an eye to feeding and supplying the brothers, their men, and animals.

Well-supplied as he had since learned to be, he was unprepared for the drain on his reserve over the weeks stalled at Elah. There had been no opportunity to raid or plunder as they advanced or even to buy what they needed at friendly markets along the way. As they began their second month mired in inaction, Eliab wrote to his father asking for fresh supplies. Wisely, Jesse saw the letter as an opportunity and an answer to a question he had not yet thought to ask.

Since returning from his last visit to Bethlehem, David had been at once frenzied in his pursuit of work and distant, morose and reluctant to partake in the simplest of human interactions. He had driven the staff to near exhaustion, pushing them to harvest and yield record crops and vintage. But when his mother asked him to play a song of celebration when the family was dining, he took to his room and wept uncontrollably long into the night.

The house became as if in mourning. In truth, it was as though the David they had all come to know and expect around every corner had died. Jesse could think of nothing to stem his son's secret grief. Even Nitzevet had no suggestion to offer when consulted.

"My wife, he is lost," Jesse said when they were alone in their bed. "I fear that he will make a fact of it and fall on his own sword or take himself over a cliff. What are we to do, to bring him back from the ledge where he has paused for so long, contemplating the abyss?"

"I cannot tell you, husband," Nitzevet said, cleaving more tightly to Jesse as if to ward off a chill. "I despair for him. It is as though he has lost his way, and yet he has never seemed more driven. Nothing that used to give him pleasure seems to interest him anymore. The grooms must exercise the horse that the king gave him, for he will not ride. His harp is out of tune from disuse. He only goes to the shepherds' compound when he has instructions for the men and never stays the night. I know losing Micah was hard for him, but that is more than a year ago. He seemed joyous when he was at the palace. Perhaps it is that he misses?"

"But he is to return to court when the king does," Jesse said, shaking his head. "Surely this is not enough to break his spirit, and that is what I fear has happened. He is like a loving dog beaten until it will not look up for fear of another blow. In truth, it has only been just over a month since his return, but it has felt like a lifetime. Perhaps it will pass. Perhaps he will find his way again."

"Is there nothing you can tell him?" Nitzevet said, lifting her face to look into his. "Is there nothing you can do?"

Eliab's letter seemed a prayer answered when it arrived.

As if a further sign, Jesse had no sooner read the letter and understood than David passed just outside his study doors. He was on his way out to the barn to supervise the preparations for the storage and disposition of their harvest, due soon at market.

"David," Jesse called out to his youngest through the open door.

"Yes, Father?" David answered dutifully, pausing to look in.

"Can you arrange to be away for a few days?" Jesse asked. "I have a task that I need to entrust to you."

"It is not the best time," David answered with an honest shrug. "But we can make anything possible if you think it is important, Father. What do you require?"

"As you know, the king's army has been stalled at Elah for some time now," Jesse began. He rose from his desk and came from behind it to face his son.

"So I have heard." David nodded expressionlessly.

"Your brother writes that their supplies are running low. Since they have not moved, they have not had a day of plunder or tributes," Jesse went on, half sitting on the edge of his desk. "Such is the way that an army manages."

"Yes, it has always seemed primitive and haphazard to me, but so I am given to understand," David said with an irritable roll of his eyes.

"Well, this means that your brothers are nearing the end of their supplies. They have not had fresh bread or meat since they left home." Jesse sighed, lacing his voice with more worry than he truly felt. "I am concerned for their health and their well-being."

"As are we all, Father," David said, a small scowl crossing his face as he remembered his last encounter with his brother.

Jesse grinned at the petulant twitch of life in the corners of his son's mouth.

"It is our duty to your brothers and to the king to send fresh provisions to sustain them in their quest to make Israel a single nation for us all," Jesse went on seriously, laying the mortar on thick to wall out as much argument as possible.

"Certainly, sir," David said formally. "Shall I put together a shipment for them?"

"Yes, my son," Jesse said with nod and a tone to match. "And then you must deliver it."

"I cannot," David said, physically recoiling from his father and the idea as he stepped backward toward the door.

"But you must," Jesse insisted firmly. "I can trust this important job to no one else."

David could think only of Jonathan's stinging rebuke at their parting. He could not bear the thought of even a chance of having to face the prince again. Though far from a certainty at such a massive encampment, even the possibility was more than he could countenance.

"Father, harvest is at hand," David fumbled, searching for any reason but the truth with which to defer. "The grapes are already coming in. The wine is going into barrels. There are fruit and dates to bring in, preparations for the winter planting to be made. And the market...."

"My son, this farm was here when you were born, was it not?" Jesse asked, amused at the life that the request had breathed into his son. "Do you not suppose I might have learned something about running it?"

"Father, I did not mean to—"

"And you have four brothers here, each one's back broader and stronger than the next, to help me to accomplish that which age no longer permits," Jesse said, enjoying the animated discomfort and the distinct prospect of one of David's long-absent tantrums.

"But why not send one of them?" David suggested, valiantly trying to evade being drafted into facing, at best, Eliab. When they last parted, his brother had literally picked David up, slung him into the saddle on the back of his horse, and struck the animal's flanks to rid himself of his younger brother at a gallop. At worst there was the prince and his reproach. David's reputation had doubtless been reduced to tatters when word spread of his disgrace with the prince. He doubted his welcome at court or in the king's presence.

"David, I love all my sons," Jesse said, shaking his head seriously. "But none else who are now at home could I trust with a task so important. Too many temptations and detours between here and Elah."

"How are they to gain our trust if not given the chance to earn it?" David stammered, almost making his father laugh.

"Surely, you'd like to see your brothers and your friends from court who are there?" Jesse asked, more to probe for David's reaction than in a belief that David would answer him honestly. Jesse did not know the source of his youngest son's troubles, but he knew they flowed from court, for no other course made sense. David's reactions only deepened his suspicions.

"It would be.... Father," David said with a heavy sigh, unable to contrive another false argument without lying to Jesse's face, a practice he was not about to begin. "It is too painful for me to make this journey."

"But why, my son?" Jesse asked tenderly. He put an arm around David's shoulder and guided him to a chair. "Your time at court has enriched this family more than ten seasons of the finest harvests. Clearly you found favor with the king and his court."

"Perhaps so," David said sadly. "But I also found my place. There is much I would aspire to in life, but the truth is that when the time came for the men of Israel to face our enemy, I was sent home to mind the hearth. I have at last accepted this as my lot. It would hurt me too deeply to return and see who… to see what it is that I can never have, who I can never be."

"Oh, my son," Jesse said, kneeling to embrace David as he might have a small boy. "Only the Lord knows your future. This is your place today, but it may not be tomorrow. It is only in not knowing what each day may hold that each day holds promise. We were all slaves in Egypt, and Moses's place was as the son of Pharaoh. Yet here we are today."

"I cannot be any taller than I am," David said. Tears streaked his face.

"But you can have faith that the Lord made you the perfect height."

"What other path is there for me, Father?" David pleaded, grasping Jesse's strong arms with both his hands. "I can see no other way. Hope hurts too much to keep it in my heart."

"David," Jesse said, wiping the tears from David's face with his broad flat thumb. "Sometimes the only way to find your way is to be willing to be lost."

"Thank you, Father," David said, embracing Jesse by falling into his arms, grateful for his father's answer to a question he did not know to ask.

"I'm glad at last to be able to help," Jesse said, stroking David's hair as he rested his head on his father's shoulder. "You have never seemed to want or need anyone's encouragement, so I never thought to offer it."

David only smiled as his father held him. He resolved to take his father's advice to lose himself in the task. He would set out to deliver the supplies to his brothers at Elah and trust in the Lord to help him to find his way.

*I will not be afraid of ten thousands of people, that have set themselves
against me round about.*

Psalm 3:6

PRINCE JONATHAN awakened earlier than his men.

He was much fatigued by the constant company of others and craved
some time alone. Quietly, he put together his pack and guided his horse
away from the small camp of the patrol he had led into the hills above Elah.
Once a safe distance from his sleeping comrades, he mounted the horse. His
objective was a clearing on a high ridge he'd noted during reconnaissance the
day before. He sought the view and the peace he knew he would find there.
He could survey the valley below to report to his father's generals and eat his
midday meal in silence.

At least, that had been his plan.

His long inactivity, and the lethargy of the dispiriting days of standoff he
had endured with his men, had lulled him into a false sense of place. For want
of a battle, he forgot he was on the front lines of a battlefield and took himself
into the open.

In the fullness of time, even Jonathan saw his folly as laughable. When
the Philistines arrived, he had been sharing his meal with a curious hawk,
dropping bits of bread onto the narrow ledge where the bird perched just below
the ridge where Jonathan sat. Cornered between the spear tips of the Philistine
patrol and the cliffs at his back, only the thrill of engagement and the possibility
of letting his father down were foremost in his mind. He startled his would-be
executioners by bounding over the breach to join his lunch companion on the
unseen ledge.

When the hawk flew off, unwilling to share its roost with the prince,
many of the superstitious Philistines believed that Jonathan had transformed
himself into the fowl and taken flight. Frightened by such powerful magic,
they began to back away and to flee the scene. Those valiant enough to remain
behind in the face of such powerful spells challenged one another to dare a
glance. At last one soldier was selected to venture to the ledge and braved a
look. Jonathan was ready for the invader and pulled the soldier into the void.
The prince nearly shared the fate of the hapless Philistine as the man struggled
to save himself before plummeting to his death on the rocks below.

His cries as he fell saved the prince's life. Jonathan's men, already
searching the hills for him, were alerted by the Philistine's screams. They
easily outflanked the small scouting party that had cornered their prince and
struck down those they did not drive over the precipice. In their zeal they nearly
dispatched the prince along with their enemies.

Glad of his rescue, he felt more a worthless son of Belail than a prince for having risked himself and his men on an errand of such folly. Jonathan spent the balance of the day scouting deeper into the hills in silence and shame, well ahead of men who forgave him more readily than he could himself.

The false step was forgotten by all when, near sunset, the king's messenger reached them with news that Saul had chosen a champion to fight the giant and recalled them to camp. Initially furious at not being chosen himself, Jonathan's rage turned to horror when he discovered the name of the champion the king had chosen for almost certain death.

"David." He whispered the champion's name. The name spoken so softly was the most important the prince had ever uttered. In less than a breath, he understood his course.

He was decided.

Jonathan could no longer deny his heart. He was overwhelmed by just the thought of losing David, of never hearing his voice raised in song or, as it so frequently was, in discord. The idea that he might never again see the light flashing in David's pale green eyes or push the unruly gold curls from his face brought a coldness into the prince's soul. An agony grew in his chest that made it hard for him to breathe. He spurred his horse wildly forward without a word. His men followed, startled by their prince's urgency to witness the battle, unaware of the king's choice. His vision blurred, Jonathan led the charge back to camp. Uncertain of what he would do when he arrived, he was certain that he would do anything to be with David once again.

And Saul said to David, Thou art not able to go against this Philistine
to fight with him: for thou art but a youth, and he a man of war from his youth.
1 Samuel 17:33

JONATHAN COULD not sleep that night.

He and his men had stopped to make camp when it was too dark to continue. Sleep was impossible, and Jonathan was soon leading his horse through the darkness along unfamiliar mountain trails. Though the distance to camp was not far, finding his way doubled the distance. The darkness doubled it yet again. His men followed even when the moon failed to light their way, as true to their prince as they were confused by his errand.

They arrived at camp just at daybreak. Jonathan made his way at once to the king's tent, leaving his men with the barest civilities in parting.

"I must speak with my father," Jonathan instructed his ragged and exhausted men as they made their way into the encampment.

The camp was alive in a way that Jonathan had not seen it since their arrival, so many days before. Men moved with purpose but in a strange silence.

So too did he find the king's tent, looking settled and sleepy outwardly but filled with a blaze of activity on the inside. The king and his commanders made last-minute plans for the long awaited battle.

"Father, you must let me fight this Goliath," Jonathan proclaimed as he swept into the king's tent.

"Jonathan, my son, good, you're back," Saul said, looking up from the wet clay where he sketched and resketched his plans for the day as he described them to his commanders. "I am grateful for your bravery, my son, but I need you for more important tasks. I cannot waste so much talent on such a fool's errand."

"But, Father," Jonathan persisted, taking Saul's arm and attempting to pull him aside. "If you want to rally the troops, sending your own son and heir would show your commitment and your resolve."

"Have you been about the camp this morning?" The king laughed. Resisting his son's pull, he rose and put an arm around Jonathan's shoulders. "The men are like children getting ready for a feast day. No, my son, I do not have a morale problem. If anything, our challenge is to keep the men calm enough that we don't tip our enemies to our intentions."

"Even so, Father," Jonathan persisted, a desperation in his voice that his father misunderstood, and which made him proud of Jonathan's bravery and willing self-sacrifice. "What message does it convey to send a courte—a court musician to fight this monster? But if you sent me...."

"Exactly," the king said, steering Jonathan toward the door. "If I send you, they catch the scent. By sending the boy, it could simply be a drunken youth, overreaching, taking the field on his own. Surprise, my boy, surprise is the gift that the Philistines' arrogance has given us."

"But what of David?" Jonathan asked softly as they stood apart from the others, near the tent's entrance. "He will surely die."

"And it will be a sad loss to me and to his own father," Saul said, giving Jonathan an embrace with his one arm still across the prince's troubled shoulders. "But his father will remember David proudly, as will I. For he will save so many more lives by his brave death and may well give us the day by his folly."

"His? His folly?" Jonathan asked. The enormity struck him. The slap, his own words that had parted them so harshly, echoed in his ears. He had meant to frighten and discourage David. Had he challenged him to this very act instead?

"Yes, son, it was David, not I, who suggested this plan," Saul said, realizing. "I would never order a man to certain death, at least not without offering him the choice. You will have to make such difficult choices when you are king. In truth, my plan was built on David's foundation, not the other way round. He volunteered for this duty. I saw our opportunity in it. He will die a great hero."

"A singer defending our country," Jonathan said flatly, repeating and mocking his final words to David.

"Well, yes," Saul said with a tight shrug, too aware of the seriousness of the task to laugh at the prince's jest. "Now you must go. Ready yourself and your men to take up the charge. David's fall provides the army with the signal. Even that gift is unique. The entire army can be engaged with a single sign."

"I would speak with him," Jonathan demanded.

"It is generous of you, my son," the king said, mistaking Jonathan's intent. "But he is already in position on the valley floor. Look to your own duty so that you might pay tribute to David's sacrifice with your own valor in the coming battle. Ready your men."

Jonathan found himself outside the king's tent. His chest ached. He wandered like a ghost through the strangely quiet camp. Men with battle armor under their robes ate around their fires, as though it was any morning. Horses were corralled with saddles on; their riders milled nearby in disguised battle gear. Mostly the camp was empty. The great mass of foot soldiers had taken up their places, concealed since before daybreak, in the brush and woodland that bordered the plain.

The prince took little note of the strangeness. His mind reeled as he wandered aimlessly about. He was unable to decide on any course of action with which his heart might know peace. Could he see David? What could he say to him? He could neither change places nor suggest that David abandon his mission with an easy heart. In the end the decision was made for him.

"There you are, my prince," Paltiel said, spying him. He hurried to guide Jonathan into his tent and get him into battle armor out of the view of their enemy. "You must be famished." Paltiel found his charge strangely silent as he fed, cleaned, and armed him, preparing him for the harvest-season battle they had been spoiling for since summer. Paltiel plied the prince for information about the plan but learned little more than any foot soldier might already know. Jonathan only answered yes, no, or nothing at all.

Like a specter, Prince Jonathan led his men. They moved toward the bathing tents, loose robes swaddled around their battle gear.

They took up their place in a line that never moved to await their turn for a hot bath they did not need, while servants boiled water for naught but show.

The vain and vulgar cock's crow of Goliath's trumpets awoke them. This day it was the call to battle all in the king's camp had too long awaited. The men made their way as if to view the valley and Goliath's daily show as cover for taking up their positions to attack. They watched for their signal to charge an enemy they could see gathered around their fires across the valley, grown complacent in the impotent response of the Israelites.

David looked small and fragile from where Jonathan was forced to watch. Bareheaded, his coppery golden curls flashed in the morning sun more brightly than the most highly polished helmet. David made his way awkwardly through the weeds and brush that populated the valley floor. Clad only in a tunic, he advanced against his armor-plated foe.

He was so small that at first no one on the Philistine side, including Goliath, took note of his arrival on the field.

Jonathan led his men into position for battle. As he took up his post, he tried to prepare himself to watch what he loved most in all the world struck down before him, sacrificed to win victory in a valley that was home to no man.

*The Lord that delivered me out of the paw of the lion, and out of the paw
of the bear, he will deliver me out of the hand of this Philistine.*

1 Samuel 17:37

PRAYERS WERE too bitter on the prince's tongue. In lieu, he silently cursed the
God who had brought him this day. How cruel was Samuel's nameless deity,
who would allow him to love so deeply and then force him to watch, helpless,
as it was taken away. Was this punishment for his faithlessness? Or had he
placed this curse on himself when he hadn't shown the courage to speak his
heart when he'd had the chance?

He forced himself to watch, hating God and himself, blame enough to
go around.

The giant raised his sword. The end would be swift.

Perhaps, Jonathan thought, *this will be my last battle as well*. That he
could pray for.

CHAPTER SEVEN
THE BOOK OF DAVID

And David spake to the men that stood by him, saying, What shall be done to the man that killeth this Philistine, and taketh away the reproach from Israel? for who is this uncircumcised Philistine, that he should defy the armies of the living God?

1 Samuel 17:26

"THE PRINCE is away on patrol," the soldier said. David felt great relief and disappointment. He had dreaded and prayed for just this answer as he found his way to the king's camp. To bring a swift end to his agony, he enquired of the first guard he met.

"Do you know of Jesse's son called Eliab?" David asked next, facing his second demon full on and secretly hoping to find him on patrol with the prince.

"Oh yes, the lieutenant," the man nodded. "Whose son are you, who asks after Eliab?"

"I am Jesse's son, Eliab's brother David," he said, striking his chest in salute to the soldier. Though not much older, the guard was physically more imposing, even though David was still astride his horse. "I am come to bring my brother bread and meat."

"Oh, are you now? And have you something for my trouble if I direct you to his tents?" the soldier asked with the presumptuousness of an empty belly.

"I am sure that my brother would welcome you at his table if you lead me to him," David said, bartering for peaceful passage to his brother's campsite, fingering the hilt of his dagger just in case.

"Why wait to celebrate your arrival?" the soldier asked. He ran his hand up David's leg. Several of his compatriots closed in around them, laughing crudely. David tensed. Was this good-natured, or would he be called to defend himself against his own countrymen?

In seeming answer, trumpets echoed in the valley below. The soldier and his friends turned away.

David feared and hoped that the battle with the Philistines had begun. It was as if the onset had awaited his arrival as its call to arms. He dreaded it, as any man might, yet he hoped that it was begun. He prayed that he might be there to take part without time to be asked to account for his presence or discovered and sent away. David dismounted his horse. He followed the men as they moved in the direction of the clarion call.

"Cowardly armies of Israel." The voice boomed up to them from the valley floor beneath. Every man of the army of Israel answered as one, drowning out the challenge. With a word to his man to watch the horses and their cargo, David pushed to the fore.

He squeezed through and found a spot nearest the ridge that overlooked the valley. What he beheld as he stared made David doubt what his eyes told him. The source of the noise and shouting seemed to be a man, but one who looked to be strangely distorted, oddly out of scale, as though closer than he could be. Like a picture painted with no regard for nature, the gleaming armor-clad soldier appeared as tall across the valley as men just a short way down the ridge.

More curious to David than the giant who addressed them were the words he spoke.

"Is there no man among you who would face me?"

"What is this?" David asked a soldier nearby, a member of the party who had menaced him only shortly before. The man paused in his shouting and shield-banging long enough to hear David's question.

"It is said that his name is Goliath," the soldier answered, panting still from all his exertion. "He is a Moabite who fights on the side of the Philistines."

"I did not realize Moab was the land of giants." David laughed. "I have been told that I have Moab blood in me."

"Clearly, then, that is not so, little man," said the guard, David's guide from his arrival. He tousled David's sweaty ringlets as he laughed at his diminutive companion.

"Is this familiar to you all?" David observed as the giant continued to assail them with insults and taunts.

"It is too familiar," one of his new friends answered. "There's a bet on how long he keeps it up. This makes forty mornings straight that we have been treated to this little performance. And each day it is the same."

"Send you down a man to fight me," Goliath shouted up at them in the relative quiet. The soldiers were quickly bored with shouting, and the noise in King Saul's camp died down. "If he defeats me, then we will lay down our arms and swear an oath to serve you. But if he loses, then you are honor bound to serve us. What say you?"

There were scattered catcalls and flatulent hisses in reply. None took the field in answer.

"He has made that offer each day passing two new moons."

"Will no one challenge him?" David asked.

"Yes, it is sad, but no man has come forth as yet," the soldier explained, bored with baiting the giant. "The king has promised the man who defeats him great wealth. Half his kingdom and his daughter's hand and a tax exemption to the victor's family. Yet the army is made up of cowards, as you well know, and none will fight this puny man."

"I see you make me the butt of your jest." David smiled.

"In truth, the king has forbidden it," another soldier volunteered, to spoil his buddy's fun.

"But why?" David asked, perplexed, in his youthful zeal, by the wisdom of one more experienced.

"Perhaps it is your one tiny God who makes you weak," the Moabite called up to them. His laugh boomed as it echoed against the stony cliffs. "Our gods are many and powerful, and we fight fearlessly knowing they are on our side."

"He defiles the God of Abraham and we do nothing?" David asked with a tone of righteous indignation that made those near him laugh.

All but one.

"David ben Jesse," the familiar voice cried out to him. "Why have you come here to this place? With whom did you leave our father's poor sheep? Though in truth, perhaps the sheep are safer without the like of you around."

The laughter grew.

"It is our father who has sent me to you," David tried to put in. Eliab grabbed him by the upper arm and attempted to drag him away from the hearing of others.

"What lie have you told our father so you could come down to watch the battle?"

"I have come here at the behest of our father and his concern for your well-being," David said under his breath, humiliated both by the task and by his brother's treatment. "A concern, I assure you, I do not share."

"An easy tale to spin without Father here to unravel it," Eliab bellowed, mocking David and hustling him backward in hopes of sending him packing as quickly as possible, as fearful for his safety as he was still angry from their last parting.

"You mistake me, brother." David spoke up in his own defense, wanting to dispel the impression Eliab was giving. "I have come with the bounty of our father's harvest to grace your table. I could just as easily give it to your fellows here, if you don't believe me. Who can I interest in bread, meat, and cheese fresh from my family's farm?"

"Temptation, eh? That's your game, is it?" Eliab boomed, laughing. "Perhaps the sheep are safe with you after all. Have you come here in search of a ram?"

Had he slapped David, it could not have stung more. His fair face became crimson with shame and rage.

"You've found me out, brother," David hissed, a viper cornered. Eliab and the others fell silent. "Do you want to know what I'm doing here, brother? Do you want me to tell all your comrades why it is I've come?"

"Tell me, brother," Eliab growled, drawing David's face near to his own.

"I have come to fight that man who speaks ill of our king, our country, and our God," David said with a furor. He tore his arm from his brother's grasp, gesturing to the Moabite still calling up to them from below.

"The king has forbidden it," Eliab said, grasping at his brother again but gaining only a handful of fabric, which slipped easily through his fingers.

"That's a good excuse for a coward," David bellowed, getting back at Eliab for the public disgrace he'd offered. "Take me to the king. I will convince him to let me end this insult."

"Is it not enough that you disgraced our family by your behavior to the prince?" Eliab demanded. "Is it not enough that word of your insolence and insubordination lost me my post with Abner? Do you seek now to make a fool of yourself and your family in front of the entire nation of Israel?"

"I would say that you've done a pretty good job of that for yourself." David sniffed. "I am not the author of your shame. It comes not from me. Your shame is born of being forty days behind me at the king's tent to make this offer."

"So you will make a fool of us before the king first?" Eliab accused.

"Lieutenant, you should let the boy make his case to the king," the soldier chided, amusing himself and his friends in the absence of anything but short rations to hold their attention.

"Yes, let's take him to the king," another in the crowd cried out to a spluttering and furious Eliab.

"To the king." The cry went up as others joined in. David was ripped from Eliab's grasp and borne away by a human tide through the camp. The wave deposited him shortly outside the king's tent, leaving Eliab far behind, shouting at their backs.

"Here's the king's tent, boy," one of the soldiers said, ready to call David's bluff. "Tell him you'll dispense with this Goliath for us."

"Faith, yes, go in and show him what you're made of," another encouraged, laughing and shoving David closer.

"Master David," one of the guards at the entrance to King Saul's private tent said. He offered David a bow of respect that silenced the mob. None among them had thought their little joke would go much farther than a safe distance from the king's tent flaps.

"Captain Doeg," David said to the massive Edomite guard, who had recognized him from his days at the palace. "Greetings to you. I need to speak with the king. Would such be possible?"

"Every day here is a slow day," Doeg answered in a familiar tone. "I'm sure that he will be as glad to see you as I am. I hope you brought your harp with you. A little music would go a long way on days such as these we've spent here."

Doeg disappeared into the tent, leaving David and the stunned and silent crowd just outside. He looked over his shoulder at the group of common soldiers who had brought him there to make sport of him. David smiled as he realized that the laugh was his. His anger with Eliab cooled.

"Could one of you go and fetch my servant and my horse and pack mules here to me?" David asked genially. Several of his new acquaintances scurried away to do his bidding. They were unsure of just who his father was and unwilling to chance it making too much difference.

"David, my son," Saul called, coming to the door. To the utter astonishment of those soldiers in his merry escort, the king embraced David and ushered him inside.

"Your Majesty," David said. Taking the hand the king offered with a respectful nod, he allowed himself to be royally led inside.

"I give you men your leave," the king said, dismissing those present in the tent so that he and David might speak. Abner alone remained. It was the custom between them.

The king sat in the simple wooden chair that was his throne in such rude circumstances. Abner took a seat at a table on the far side of the tent.

"Come here, my son," the king offered. He gestured David toward cushions scattered on the broad wooden platform on which his battlefield throne rested. "What brings you here to visit us in the beautiful valley of Elah, the most deadly dull place on God's earth?"

"In truth, Your Majesty, I have come to bring food and the comforts of home to my brothers who are here encamped with you," David said with a respectful tone. He took a place at the king's feet, sitting casually, as was their habit. "But now I'm here, there are two favors that I would ask of you."

"David, you have but to name what I might do for you, after the wonderful gift of health and freedom you have given me," the king said with an expansive wave of his hand.

"I thank you most humbly," David said, inclining his head slightly. "I am glad that my small actions have found favor in your eyes. I hope that they will overshadow any indiscretions which I may have committed against you or your family."

"I know of none," the king answered with an honest shrug.

The king looked then to Abner. The great general only shook his head. Prince Jonathan had assured Abner that the cross words reported between him and David at parting were but a private matter the prince wished to remain between them.

"I am glad to hear it," David said, bowing his head. "I am not blameless, but in my heart I swear that I am loyal to you and your interest as our anointed king. I would ask that whatever I might have done not be held against my brother Eliab, and that he might be restored to his position with Abner, your general, as he took such pride in that duty. I would not have my faults counted against him."

"Abner?" the king asked. He was unwilling to overrule his general but hoped to appease the boy.

"Yes, Majesty," Abner said, half rising and nodding his head. With only the three present, a most informal manner prevailed amongst them. "I can assure you and your servant David that nothing could be further from the truth. I regret if Eliab might think it so. He is one of my best men and a fine leader. I transferred him from my personal service not to disgrace him, but because I needed his leadership in the field, not at heel currying my favor. Where Eliab is concerned, no respect need be earned from me. I will make such clear to him before the sun sets this day."

"There, you see?" King Saul said. Gently he took David's chin in his hand and raised his face so that their eyes met. "I do not know how you think you might have offended me or my men, but the truth is, David, you are held in the greatest respect and highest regard. We all look forward to your company when we return to court, as soon as your respected father can spare you to be at our side."

"I thank you," David said. He maintained a respectful manner before the king, though his heart leapt at the certain knowledge that the prince alone could have willed this. Either the general did not know because the prince had concealed it himself, or he did know and the prince had decreed his silence. He knew Abner was a loyal man and would conceal his knowledge from the king for no one less. Either way, David felt the prince's protection in this, and joy in the possibility of being reconciled with Jonathan. "I am most grateful to you for your words, Your Majesty. And to you, Abner ben Ner, for your actions and many kindnesses on my family's behalf."

Abner and David exchanged a knowing nod between them that each understood.

"I am glad that you have asked me this," Saul said, examining the boy's face. "It seems that just these words have made your spirit lighter than it was when you arrived."

"It is true," David said, his heart glad with relief. His joy strengthened his resolve to justify Jonathan's loyalty and the king's favor. "I have one more request of you, sire."

"What else can I do?" the king asked solicitously. "I can only hope that you will allow me to do more for you than simply to speak a few words of comfort this time."

"In truth, my king, there is something that I wish to do for you," David said, a glint in his eye that intrigued the king.

"How is that a favor?" Saul asked. He tweaked David's chin playfully.

"Because I understand that you will have to rescind your own decree to permit it."

"What is it?" the king demanded with the lighthearted tone David so easily provoked in him. "You vex me."

"I ask that you let me be your champion," David said, rising to his knees, suddenly serious in his tone and manner. "I ask that you let me fight the Moabite, this Goliath, on your behalf."

The king could not have been more stunned if David had asked for half his kingdom. Seriousness creased his brow. He withdrew from David. Rising, he crossed away to another part of the huge pavilion.

"Boy, you cannot ask such a thing," Abner said, taking a cue from the king's manner and rising to take the king's part.

"But to hear the army and the God of Israel spoken of so," David said.

"You cannot begin to understand the reasoning of a king." Abner began a long lecture on the nature of military decision-making. The king kept his own counsel apart from them, appearing to gaze out the opening of the tent into the distance.

Saul was stunned by the boy's request. He had prayed that very morning for a solution to the impasse in which he found his forces. His army was stalled and running low on supplies and morale. The giant's daily excoriations only confounded a problem that was already rotting their spirits.

Looking at the beautiful face, he knew that this treasured boy would be little more than an amusing distraction for the massive and well-armed warrior. The suggestion was as laughable as it was potentially tragic. He loved the boy. He would never wish him harm. Yet, his own feelings aside, he was king and had the good of all Israel to consider.

"So you see, boy, there are considerations that the king must place ahead of the wounded pride and vanity of our men. A bully will always try to bait one into a place of disadvantage by offending the pride of his victim—"

"Yes," Saul said. He turned suddenly to face them. His tone silenced Abner, who was speaking, and David, who could not. "David ben Jesse, I choose you as my champion. You shall fight the great Goliath in the king's armor tomorrow when he comes out to challenge the army of Israel."

And David said to Saul, Let no man's heart fail because of him; thy servant will go and fight with this Philistine.

1 Samuel 17:32

THE REMAINS of the day that followed the king's decision were a welter of preparations.

David, too numb to speak, was sworn to secrecy, bustled off to the king's dressing tent to be fitted with the king's armor, and attended as the king's champion.

"Abner, you need to prepare our forces to be ready for attack by morning," Saul said, wheeling on his astonished general as soon as David was escorted from the tent.

"My king, what is it that you have in mind, sending that boy...."

"It grieves me to allow it." The king sighed, his heart heavy. "But it is the answer to my prayer. I saw in an instant the Lord's plan."

"Which is?"

"I don't know why I have not seen this sooner," Saul explained, withdrawing more deeply into the tent. He took up a place at the table. Clapping for wine to be brought, he gestured Abner to join him. "Perhaps now is the perfect time."

"The perfect time for what, my lord?" Abner asked, taking up the seat beside him.

"We are, both sides, lulled into a sort of sleepy torpor by the heat, the hunger, and the repetition of not only that great ox's taunting but our expectations. We expect to be taunted; they expect our lack of response. If tomorrow I send out a champion, a mere boy, as much to insult as to engage this secret weapon, where do you suppose the entire Philistine army will be focused?"

"On the field," Abner said, smacking his own thigh as he saw the brilliance of the plan.

"Exactly," Saul went on. "Every eye fixed on the irrelevant fight; not one on the army of twenty thousand facing them. It's a gift to us, the element of surprise. They have even given us a way to signal the entire army at once. You must have your men ready to attack, using as their signal the battle's end."

"David's death," Abner said with a sigh.

"Yes," Saul said, already mourning the loss. "He shall truly be the champion of his king and all of Israel."

And Saul armed David with his armour, and he put an helmet of brass upon his head; also he armed him with a coat of mail. And David girded his sword upon his armour, and he assayed to go; for he had not proved it. And David said unto Saul, I cannot go with these; for I have not proved them. And David put them off him.

1 Samuel 17:38-39

"PERHAPS JUST the breastplate?" the armorer suggested as he and his assistants continued what had become David's darkly comic fitting for the serious battle. The king, in his generosity, had provided his personal armor for David to wear as his champion when he faced Goliath. Despite the generosity, the good intentions, and even the gravity of the situation, the armor was forged for a man three heads taller than David, at least.

King Saul stood head and shoulders above other men. David stood a head below. The combination kept the king's aides and armorers tortured on the brink of laughter from just after midday until into the evening.

The helmet was discarded when it completely covered David's head, face and all, coming to rest upon his shoulders. The greaves were deemed to be of little value and set aside when it was discovered that, in addition to protecting his legs, they prevented him from walking. The sword was too long for him to wield. The shield scraped the ground when he walked. The breastplate, similarly laughable, came down to the middle of David's thighs and prevented him bending at the waist, while the straps that held it in place also pinned his arms to his sides.

It was a relief to all present when David gave way to laughter. Unable to maintain a sense of the mortal question, which all present knew he soon faced, he was at last overcome.

"Gentlemen," David said with an awkward bow. "Please thank the king for his gift and a most amusing diversion. I think a good supper will do me more good than all this bronze. Please ask that some food be sent, if you would."

One of the king's aides struck his chest and bowed in salute before departing to see to the order, as the armorers began to disentangle David from the metal shell.

Left alone at last, the enormity of his task came to him. Doubt tightened his chest.

"Do you propose that we have a singer defend the nation?" David heard the truth of Jonathan's words as the tent's interior swam before his eyes. Doubt welled up to sweep away the certainty of David's faith.

"Rather than earning us a victory, they would more likely earn you a place in King Achish's harem," Jonathan's words came back to him. Their meaning stung worse than the slap David had earned at the expense of his friendship with the man he held he dared not admit how dear. Heartbroken and filled with fear his legs gave, unable to hold him up a moment longer.

"Well, my Lord, this is it," David said, falling to his knees on the rich carpet covering the carefully smoothed earth beneath the grand royal tent. "Do you believe in me? I've tried all my life, and nothing I've sought has come to be, for I have sought in pride and overlooked the manifold blessings you have given to me in abundance. I have prayed for your will for me, and I have failed to hear your answer. So here I am. Tomorrow I will step up to defend your name and your people against this giant who thinks you so puny. Is this your will for me? Will you join me in my task? I suppose I will know your answer on the field of Elah tomorrow morning, for I cannot hear you now."

Despite his conviction that a good meal was his best weapon, his appetite deserted him. Sleep was still more a stranger. He lay awake playing his upcoming combat with the giant over and over again on the backs of his eyelids. Oh, that Micah could be there with him. Their bodies fitted together like carved pieces, Micah's hand resting easily on David's belly, his breath warm and comforting against David's neck.

Salty tears stung his eyes. He reached into his robe and clutched Micah's sling, as always around his neck. For a heartbeat Micah was closer. The fear eased. For a breath David felt a flood of relief. He gave tomorrow to the Lord and took his ease in the cushions of his bed.

"Micah," he sighed, clutching the sling tightly.

His fingers brushed the lion's tooth wound into the braided leather lanyard. On a long-ago morning, David had used the weapon to bring down an estimable foe, from whose fearsome smile the fang had been won. In an instant he drowsed not in a tent in the hills above the plain of Elah, but on that ridge above the Wadi Asad on a lazy day, tending his father's sheep. Suddenly a rabbit broke through into the open, making a mad dash for the wadi and safety, the lion fierce in pursuit.

A smile spread across David's face. He understood. Sleep came as easily and soundly as it had those nights with Micah in the hills above the karmel, when all his enemies had been as insubstantial as smoke. When playing soldier was only a game for boys and victory but the chance to play again yet another day.

Part Two

The Covenant

CHAPTER EIGHT
THE VALLEY OF ELAH

Then Jonathan and David made a covenant, because he loved him as his own soul.

1 Samuel 18:3

GOLIATH RAISED his mighty sword to strike the fatal blow. David lay writhing on the ground before him, his ankle twisted and useless.

Jonathan was unable to look away. He fought his desires. His feelings of longing and betrayal were too strong to overcome. A sense of guilt and responsibility roiled his gut as he braced for the inevitable. Still, he wanted to be a part of what life David had left.

The king held his breath as he beheld the brilliance of his plan reach its tragic apex. His heart ached for the lovely boy, but his years on the battlefield had dulled the pain of losing those he cared about. David was far from the first.

Eliab knew his orders. He longed to disobey. Nothing, not his career, his inheritance, not anything he ever valued seemed to him more important than breaking cover, dashing onto the field, and taking the blow for his little brother. Wasn't that why he'd come here in the first place? Wasn't keeping David and those he would protect safe from harm the point of all the bloodshed and horror of making war?

Goliath glowed with sweat and triumph. He raised his arm and the fearsome sword he held, celebrating his victory as he prolonged Israel's defeat.

The Philistines at his back cried for blood. His sword poised to strike the fatal blow, Goliath approached the fallen David. His massive helmet and mighty shield were still with his armor-bearer, by then far from where the two men would end their engagement. He reached out with his free hand, leaning down to David. He thought to get a handful of the golden curls with which to hold up David's head as a trophy. As Goliath drew near enough to strike, David was up and away again, the stone already loaded in the sling. He fingered the rough edge of the lion's tooth. His breath was easy and calm. His heart seemed to slow.

Goliath hesitated, surprised. The boy paused, just a few steps farther than his sword could reach. The blade passed through the empty air before it. The crowds on both sides, cheated in the final instant of what they expected, fell strangely still.

The sling whirled so fast at David's side that it was invisible. There was only the twanging sound it made as it cut the air. Micah's sling appeared, too late to be perceived, only once the stone was launched.

David alone was near enough to hear the skull of the giant before him crack. The smooth dark river rock, chosen as carefully as a ring for a lover, struck Goliath between the eyes. It killed him where he stood, still facing David, never once seeing him as a threat.

The two seemed to regard one another. Both sides stood silently wondering, watching in awe and uncertainty. The sword fell from Goliath's hand. David knew his task was complete.

With a groan of metal, in a cloud of dust, Goliath fell, face first, at David's feet.

"Oh Lord, you do believe in me," David said in a shocked whisper that only the fallen Philistine and the God of Israel could hear. Then, even before those who looked on could react, David stepped forward to his defeated foe. He took up Goliath's own sword and hacked off the giant's head. Warm blood splashed down his arm as he held the gory trophy aloft for the forces on both sides to see.

"The Lord of Israel believes in me," he shouted to the Philistines, waving the head of their champion in their stunned faces.

Victory revealed, the army of Israel exploded from the thickets all across their side of the valley. They advanced as one toward their Philistine rivals still frozen with disbelief. Completely unprepared for the defeat of their champion and unarmed for full-scale battle, the Philistines turned and took flight, leaving their camp and most weapons behind as the Israelites overran them.

Prince Jonathan was the first onto the field, for reasons far more important than war. As a result he and his men led the charge by default more than design. Even his men fell far behind as the prince rushed toward his true goal that day. He was the first at David's side. He swept David up in his arms and whirled him and his horrific prize into the air. Vaulting David onto his shoulders, together they led the charge across the plain of Elah, closing the distance between the Israelites and their terrified opponents.

Once they arrived at the abandoned Philistine camp, Jonathan sent his men on ahead, exhorting them to take up the pursuit. Only then did he allow David's feet to touch the ground, though only just. He crushed David against him, as though terrified that he would be snatched away.

"David, oh my David," he said as he rocked the great hero of Israel like a child in his arms. "Nothing that awaits me, even the gaping jaws of death, will compare to my fear this day. I thought I'd lost you to my own stubbornness and arrogance. I said what I said to you at Gibeah to try to take the fight out of you. I said it so you would go home to Bethlehem, where I knew you would be safe. You were right. It was selfish, and where you are concerned, that will never change. But I will never let you go again."

David could not speak but only nodded his head against Jonathan's shoulder, his silent assent to the unspoken request.

The bulwark of the army approached with supplies, weapons, and help for the wounded. As Paltiel drew near with the prince's horse and shield, the prince eased David down onto the soles of his feet.

"David, my prince," Jonathan said plaintively. He looked deeply into the clear green eyes in which he had thought, only a heartbeat before, never to see his own reflection again. "Will you do me a great service?"

"You have but to name it, my prince," David said hoarsely, finding only a shadow of his voice.

"Please return to camp with my man Paltiel," Jonathan explained. "You have done great service today. It will help me to do my own duty now as I put an end to these Philistines you have routed, if I know you are safe and resting as you await me in my tent. We shall feast and celebrate together when I return."

"Yes, my prince," David answered, the smile spreading across his face as he understood the prince's meaning. "I promise it shall be so. But only if you promise to return to me unharmed."

"Always terms with you," Jonathan said with a little laugh. He brushed the back of his knuckles across David's downy cheek. "I cannot fail to." Drawing himself up to the height of command, he turned to address Paltiel, who had come near enough to hear his prince's words. "Palti, this you know is David, the greatest hero in all of Israel and Judah. Take him back to my tent. Bathe him. Perfume him. Dress him in my finest robes. Alter them to be his. He is to be dressed as a prince of the realm from this day forward. You are to answer to him as though it was me speaking."

"Yes, my lord," Paltiel said with some reverence for the occasion. He too had witnessed David's victory and understood its implications. He handed over the reins to the prince, wise enough to serve his duty before his own feelings. "It will be my honor to serve one who has served all of Israel so well this day."

In parting that day on the southern hill of the valley at Elah, only a look passed between David and Jonathan. Yet in all the time they would ever spend together and all the words that would pass between them, nothing more was ever added to all that, in that fleeting glance, was so eloquently unsaid.

The soul of Jonathan was knit with the soul of David, and Jonathan loved him as his own soul.

1 Samuel 18:1

"ISRAEL WAS saved by a hare," King Saul shouted, pounding the feast table at that night's victory celebration. Choked with laughter, he and all present listened again, rapt, to David's hundredth retelling of the story of his battle with Goliath. "Battle strategy from a simple flop-eared saphan? Genius."

The Philistines had been crushed, driven back to the gates of their own cities in a single engagement. It was a feat unprecedented in the brief history of the kingdom of Israel. David received full credit, though he acknowledged the rabbit he'd seen defeat a lion as the true author of his strategy.

"This is the very lion's tooth," David said earnestly, holding it up from around his neck where it still hung. The simple sling that had served him so well gave him the feeling that Micah was somehow a part of all that had happened. "I brought the beast down with this same sling that I used to best Goliath today. But I'd never have gotten close to either were it not for that rabbit."

"Well, the laws of the Levite judges preclude us from feasting on the saphan, but there is nothing in the books of Moses that says we can't follow one to victory," Saul proclaimed, filled with wine and the high spirits of such a crushing victory. "To the saphan."

All drank to the rabbit, but in every heart in camp that night, it was really just another way to salute David.

He had been borne in to the encampment a hero. Goliath's body, armor, and sword—David's trophies—followed him on a humble mule cart. The feast that ensued upon the triumphant return of the king and his army was as much tribute to David as celebration of victory. David sat at the head of the table between king and prince. Jonathan, at his side, hung on David's every word. He was unable to stop himself from reaching out to stroke David's hair or to drape his arm possessively around David's shoulders.

"So I must ask, my prince," Jonathan began sincerely. "How is it that you can kill a lion and a giant with a mere pebble and a patch of leather, but you cannot hit a man as broad as an oxen's double yoke with a spear?"

"It was my plan to throw his spear into the wood," David answered over the laughter, but only inspiring more and louder gales. "I needed him to come at me with the sword so he would be within striking distance of the sling."

"It is easy to say that now," Jonathan teased.

"I once killed a charging bear more than a hundred cubits away with a spear," David said with certainty and authority. "But a bear is not a man. You saw it for yourself today. One has only to step out of the way, as I did, to avoid a spear at that distance. I had no desire to rearm my enemy."

"A charging bear? With a spear?" Jonathan marveled with a low whistle. "Had I not seen you topple that great beast Goliath with a single stone, I might doubt your word. Since I've met you, I come to believe more each day that there is nothing you cannot do.

"I give you David ben Jesse, the hero of Israel and Judah," the prince toasted. He was answered by cheering that swept through the camp, reaching even to Eliab, who feasted with his men. He gladly raised his glass not only to his brother, but also to the second chance he'd been given to make all right between them. Though his table was not even in sight of the place David occupied, he knew his day would come.

David and the prince held each other's gaze amidst the cheering crowds. They turned with difficulty to acknowledge, certainly the tributes, but also that they were not alone.

"Father, a word," Jonathan asked the king quietly behind David's back.

Saul acknowledged his son. He rose unsteadily to his feet as they stepped away.

"Father, I know that David has been in your service, but I ask that you allow him to come to me now, and that his place with me be permanent," Jonathan asked quietly.

"It shall be so," Saul answered his son. He clapped him heartily on the back with the warmth of the two skins of wine already in him, oblivious to Jonathan's meaning. "I will send tribute to Jesse and grant his family royalties enough to compensate them for the loss of such an asset. Like you, my son, David shall be my captain, but it shall be you he serves. I see a great future between you."

"As do I, Father," Jonathan agreed, catching David's eye and sharing a secret smile. "As do I."

The celebration lasted long into the night. The moon had set by the time they were at last alone.

It was awkward at first between them. They were together on their own in Jonathan's grand tent. Neither needed more wine to heighten their spirits. Being together was the headiest vintage that either could partake. Yet despite what had passed between them, neither knew how to begin anew.

"Come, let's walk for a bit," Jonathan said after they had paced about the tent. Both were too skittish and filled with the day's excitement for bed, yet too anxious to think of anything else but the obvious.

"Yes, that would be pleasant," David agreed, nodding.

They climbed silently away from the firelight of camp and into the hills above, as if they were on a scouting mission. The infinite stars of the moonless night sky above them went unnoticed. At length, and with no real plan on either part in the unfamiliar woods, they broke through the tree line onto a clear rocky ridge. There they paused, side by side, surrounded by the stars. The firelight of camp was far below. The smoldering ruins of what had been the Philistine encampment glowed in the distance across the valley.

Jonathan took David's hand in his. They stood in breathless silence for a time, content simply to be together.

"David," Jonathan said, his voice raspy at first from disuse.

"Yes, my prince."

Jonathan's smile was unseen in the darkness. He squeezed David's hand.

"You must only call me Jonathan when we are alone together. I find I am as much your subject as you will ever be mine," Jonathan said. He sighed with relief, glad to be able to speak his feelings at last. He drew David nearer.

"Yes, my prince," David agreed. He laughed nervously, realizing. "Jonathan."

"David, you must know how I feel about you," Jonathan said, his voice stilted and thick. "I mean, I think perhaps—I hope—that you might share my feelings? At least, that is…." He trailed off. He stepped back and stood at David's side. Being free to say what he felt did not take away the challenge of finding the words to say it. They stood in silence as Jonathan, who had faced down the entire Philistine army alone, searched for the courage to speak his own heart. He took a breath, as though about to dive into deep water, and began again.

"David," he said, turning to face him. He took David's other hand in his so that he held both small hands in his larger ones. "I love you more than I love my own soul, more than life itself. This time apart has taught me just how much. I cannot bear that we ever be parted again."

"But how can that be?" David answered with a gentle smile.

Jonathan winced at his words, unable to see David's smile in the darkness.

"You cannot love me more than your soul. Our souls are knit together as one soul. We are as one."

"I pledge that we always will be," Jonathan said, relieved and ecstatic. He kissed the backs of each of David's hands to seal the covenant between them. "If you'll have me."

"I am already yours," David answered. He fell into Jonathan's arms shivering, more from anticipation than the cool mountain breeze.

Jonathan threw his cloak and his arms around David. They held on to each other for a long time. At last, pausing, they drew back only enough to look into one another's faces.

They kissed.

It was as though they had been starving for one another, and with the words of their covenant spoken, their feast began. The distance between the mountain clearing and the prince's tent disappeared. They were soon naked in one another's arms on the cushions of the prince's bed, now theirs, satisfying appetites for each other so long denied. Their bodies became joined as their souls and were one.

And it came to pass as they came, when David was returned from the slaughter of the Philistine, that the women came out of all cities of Israel, singing and dancing, to meet king Saul, with tabrets, with joy, and with instruments of musick.

1 Samuel 18:6

"David! David! David!" the crowds chanted as the procession bore him through the streets of Gibeah. It was a vision out of a dream. His heart fluttered as it had not before, even when he was facing Goliath, whose head now lay at his feet. Looking over his shoulder, he caught Jonathan's eye. He stroked his chin, a secret sign between them.

Since their first night, being alone together had been a challenge.

The Philistine defeat meant that the king's campaign was ended. The army broke camp as they prepared to return to Gibeah.

Jonathan's duties as prince and commander were many and varied. He secured the plunder of the Philistine camp for his father's treasury. He then saw to the dispersement of the men who served under him as they made ready to return to their homes for the winter.

David, too, had new and unexpected duties, not the least of which was his sudden and newfound acclaim. The battle had made his name legend. The king, mindful of the effect such tales had on raising support and wresting tributes from his people, set about to make the most of David's achievements.

David was borne into Gibeah like a sacrificial bull. Carried by captive armored Philistine soldiers on a golden bier, he rode along with the gory trophy of Goliath's massive head and his equally outsized shield, spear, and sword. David stood, half-naked, draped in animal skins, his hair loose and wild in the wind. He was presented as the simple rustic shepherd he had never been. It was a truth more of his heart than his life. David was proud to be regarded throughout all of Israel as such, a man of his people, from that day forward. The story was an asset to the king and deepened the legend that David was rapidly becoming.

Jonathan was nearby on horseback. He led his men back into the city to receive their victory tributes before disbanding for the season. Each longed to share that amazing day with the other. Instead, they spent it searching over the heads of the crowd to steal a look or to share a private laugh at some absurd new tribute or accolade in a day choked with ceremonies, each more overblown than the last.

Jonathan's mother, Ahinoam, and his sisters, Michal and Merab, awaited them at the palace gate when the procession at last brought them home. Even then there were duties, ceremonies, and the leaders of the country to be greeted and acknowledged. Elders from all the cities and regions whose alliance made up the emerging nation gathered for a huge feast.

Everyone wanted to meet this David who had saved king and country and routed the Philistines with his faith and his courage alone.

For his part there was but one face David truly wanted to see. Still, he was thankful for his good fortune and tried to bear it all with a measure of good spirits and humility. It helped to remind himself that on that night, he would sleep in Jonathan's arms.

"Jonathan, I...," David managed to say as the prince helped him down from the golden sedan that had carried him and his spoils through the streets.

"My prince, you are needed for the investment ceremony." Paltiel interrupted their only time together so far that day. "And David, you should go with the priests to be presented at the ceremony."

The two smiled wanly as they took their leave.

Owing to the miraculous nature of David's victory over Goliath and the Philistines, it had been decided that the sword, shield, and javelin were to be invested as holy instruments of the Lord. Even Micah's sling was to be enshrined, though David kept the lion's tooth as a talisman of his old friend. Following the ceremony they were to be moved to the priestly enclave at Nob. There the Ark of the Covenant was watched over by the holiest men in all Israel, short of Samuel, who had installed the ark there among them himself.

The ceremony was held in the great hall of the palace, where the king sat on his throne to preside over the important rituals of state. David had been in the throne room before, but only to play in accompaniment to what was unfolding there. He was deeply aware of the distance he had traveled, to be the focus of the important rite rather than its accompanist.

Still, the act that truly made his heart swell and his eye fill with joy and pride was when Jonathan escorted his father Jesse to the stage. He joined David and the king to take part in the service where David was to be officially declared an instrument of the Lord.

"Well, my son, I can't say as I'm the least bit surprised by all this where you are concerned," Jesse said quietly into his ear as they embraced. "Is this the secret that Samuel whispered to you?"

Stunned, David thought of the high priest's words, so very long ago. Was this the Lord's will for him all along? Was he done? Was there more to do? A wave of anxiety overcame him, only to be replaced as quickly by peace and an easy smile when he remembered the old man's sunset lesson of faith.

"Father, I am, as always, unsure of the thoughts and plans of the Lord," David answered softy. The priests prepared to make sacrifice before them. "I know that if you are proud of me, then I have at least fulfilled one of his most sacred laws and my loftiest goals."

"My son," Jesse said, surprised by the thought of it. "I have never known a breath of your short life when I have not been proud of you. Today is but an outward expression of what I have thought of you all along."

The two embraced again heartily as though they were alone. The habit was quickly becoming David's, as his days of privacy seemed largely over.

The sacrifice and the ceremony were completed. Following was yet another formal observance where David's entire family was presented to the king. David was, to his surprise, named a prince of the realm and, as such, his family granted royalties over the wine and oil from the hills of Bethlehem. The tribute would bring great riches to the house of Jesse. To accept it, though, would make David Jesse's heir over Eliab. To refuse it would insult the king.

David worried for his brother. Yet none was happier than Eliab for his brother's good fortune. He knelt at David's feet when given the chance. He took David's hand and held it against his face as a dog might seek forgiveness from its master.

David would not have it. He grasped Eliab's hand in his and struggled to drag him to his feet that they might stand together as equals. "Eliab, I would not be standing here were it not for you," David said. He stood on his toes to wrap his arms around his brother's shoulders, and still he missed the mark. "You must surely stand here beside me."

"I suppose that now I shall have to stay home and learn to run your farm for you, little brother," Eliab said to him at the feast that followed.

"You will have to find another brother for that," Abner interrupted. "I cannot spare the service of such a fine captain to stomp grapes and press olives."

"Hear, hear," David said. He raised his glass to make a toast. The room fell silent at the gesture. "To my brother, Eliab ben Jesse, lieutenant in the king's army."

"Captain," Abner amended, adding cheers to the toast.

When at last the long day was ended, David bid good night to his parents. They were to leave at first light on the morning following, a sight David did not intend to witness after his labors of the previous few days. Only three mornings ago, he had been facing Goliath at Elah. Four, he had awakened on his father's farm. Now he was bidding farewell to his parents at his new home with Prince Jonathan in the king's palace.

Nitzevet had taken supper with the queen and her daughters. She was all aflutter and giggling like a young girl when he met with her.

"Oh, my dearest boy," she said, kissing his cheeks again and again.

"Mother, you have enjoyed yourself, I hope?" he said, embracing her.

"My, yes." She sighed, resting her head on his shoulder. "Ahinoam is a most gracious hostess."

"First names with the queen, is it?"

"And I cannot decide which is prettier," Nitzevet went on, oblivious of David's grinning pose of disapproval. "Michal or Merab? Which do you think?"

"It is too hard a puzzle to solve," David agreed good-naturedly.

"No matter, as both are smitten with you," Nitzevet said, tweaking his cheek playfully. "When shall I hear that one of the princesses will be my new daughter? Soon, I trust."

The idea had never crossed his mind. He did not know how to speak to her of the great love that already filled his heart and the covenant he had sworn with the prince.

"I think you will be very much surprised, dear Mother," David said obliquely. A flash of darkness flickered over his fine features.

She took it to be mischief and smiled as she touched his face lovingly.

"Come, woman." Jesse sighed, taking her arm. "Let the boy get some rest. Is it not enough that he has defeated the Philistines? Must he now face the she-dragons?"

"He is the perfect age to marry," Nitzevet scolded Jesse even as she yielded, allowing herself to be guided away. "Good night, my son."

"Good night, David," Jesse said. "Don't let your duties keep you always at court. We will keep a fatted calf at hand for the prospect of your visit."

"I'll not be too long away," David said, forcing a smile. "Good night."

"May the Lord watch over you, my son," Jesse said as they parted.

David stood. He watched their backs recede along the corridor. His mind was lost in the reality of the promises he and Jonathan had made together. What would it mean for his life? He smiled in answer. When he thought of Jonathan, the weight of such heavy thoughts fell away. His heart leaped when he realized. He was at last free to take his questions to the prince directly. They would finally be alone to discuss such matters or just to sit, silent but together.

Walking turned to running through the grand palace halls and passages. Several people late of the feast, making their way to their rooms or to home, called out to him. David only acknowledged them with waves and shouted salutations. He could not stop as he rushed to be at Jonathan's side. Only servants were about as he passed the guard for the royal quarters.

Music and laughter greeted his ears as he stood outside the doors of Jonathan's apartments. The guard, posted outside, held the door open to him as he stepped foot just within.

A fire reached again and again toward the opening in the ceiling in the center of the main room. Crazy shadows danced across the muraled walls. Musicians played pipes and lyres in accompaniment to the prince's festivities. With the drapes drawn aside, David could see Jonathan in the pool of his private baths attended, very closely, by a number of women. All were as naked as the prince was himself, all visible from the door where David stood.

David and Jonathan's eyes met across the room.

Jonathan smiled, glad to see David at last.

"Hello, David," Paltiel said, approaching. "What an unexpected surprise. Have you need of the prince just now?"

"I see that he is more than occupied," David said, not looking at Paltiel. "I am sorry to have disturbed."

"David," Jonathan called as David turned and vanished. The massive doors closed behind him with a deep echo of finality.

David ran to where his old quarters had been when he attended the king. His things were there, piled on the unmade bed. The lamps were unlit. There was no water in the basin. He had not bothered to consider where he would be that night. The day had not permitted him a breath to prepare.

He sank onto the rough upholstery of the naked straw mattress. Suddenly he was afraid and unsure of his place or of who or what he was. His mother's question about the princesses rang in his ears.

"What are you doing in here?" Jonathan asked from the doorway, still dripping from his bath, robes draped loosely about his shoulders.

"This is my room," David said with a shrug of uncertainty.

"No, it isn't," Jonathan said, sitting beside him on the bed. "You live with me now."

"It didn't seem so," David said, still facing away.

"That was only Paltiel's idea of trying to make me happy," Jonathan said, stroking David's hair gently. "I was a bachelor when we left the palace."

"And what are you now?" David said, turning to look into Jonathan's eyes for the truth he could not find in his own heart.

"I am yours," Jonathan answered with sheepish shrug.

"Like those women who attend you?"

"No, those are servants," Jonathan answered sharply, withdrawing his hand. "You are not a servant. You are mine as I am yours. I belong to you as much as you to me. Or I thought it so."

"And my room?"

"Is my room."

"Then may we please not have all those girls in our room?"

Jonathan laughed as he drew David up and into his arms. "Paltiel is making things more to your liking even as we speak," he said, kissing David's face playfully. "Come with me. There is something I want to show you tonight. Tomorrow you can begin renovating our apartments to suit you."

Like thieves in the night, they stole through the palace to ensure that they might breach the walls without guards or attendants.

Making their way into the hills and some distance beyond, they came at last to a great rock. It rose dark and obdurate against the sky on the far side of a peaceful meadow. The moon was long set. Only starlight illuminated the place.

David followed as Jonathan led the way up onto the great rock. Climbing, they reached a small flat place near its peak, hidden from the ground below.

"Here, sit," Jonathan said, spreading a blanket that he kept concealed, along with candles and a few other odds and ends, in a small sheltered crevice adjacent to their perch. "This old rock is called Ezel. This is my favorite place. No one else knows it is here. I have come here in secret since I was a boy and have kept it only for myself until this night. Everything I have is yours now, David."

"Even this?" David said.

"I have no secrets from you," Jonathan said. He put his arm over David's shoulder and drew him nearer.

David put his arm low across Jonathan's back. They sat comfortably in silence for a time. The view and their nearness was enough to fill the vast night sky.

"Look," Jonathan said, pointing into the heavens. "There, Lyra is rising. That is surely a sign for you."

"What?" David asked, uncertain of Jonathan's meaning.

"Lyra, the constellation of the lyre," Jonathan explained. "Surely that must be a sign of your recent ascendance and victory."

"It is easy to make that prediction now that it's already happened." David laughed.

"Well, strictly speaking, it is forbidden to tell the future from the stars," Jonathan said with an air of confidential gravity. "At least according to old bags of wind like Samuel. The ancient knowledge of this dark art was imparted to me by Egyptian captives on one of my more exotic campaigns. If you promise to keep it our secret, I will try to predict your future."

"Oh, will you, my prince?" David smirked, his eyebrow raised.

"Shhh, let me concentrate," Jonathan said ominously. He took the towel still draped around his shoulders. He wrapped it around his head like the exotics of the east, trying not to laugh along with David, who was making no such effort. "There," he exclaimed, pointing heavenward. "There is the great and powerful constellation of Saphan."

"That's the great dipper," David scoffed, shoving Jonathan's shoulder playfully.

"No, not that." Jonathan grunted. "There, above and to the left. You see? One ear is straight up and the other is a little crooked? And those four stars there below. That's the little fluffy tail, the two paws, and the pointy nose."

"I see, oh wise one." David laughed, playing the foolish seeker. "What portents does the Saphan hold for my future?"

"Well, as you know, Saphan presides over young lovers and great heroes. Since you are both, it is your ruling house. And just there, you see? It is about to be pierced by the arrow of the archer."

"So tell me, great mystic, what does the future hold?"

"I can hardly believe that you can't see it for yourself." Jonathan harrumphed. "It is as plain as the ears on a rabbit."

"Enlighten me."

"I predict that soon, no, this very night, you will be pierced by the arrow of the true love of your life, possibly an archer of some note."

As if to make it come true, a shooting star appeared in the sky above them and passed as though from the archer's bow into their fanciful saphan constellation.

"You see?" Jonathan said, laughing in shock at kismet. "The archer and his arrow are near at hand."

"An archer?" David laughed. "Well, I know an archer, but noted? And his arrow? Hmm, let's just say I'm not sure it's quite celestial."

"Perhaps you need to take a closer look in his quiver." Jonathan grinned, falling on David. Their laughter was soon drowned in the passion of their moans and kisses.

"I think I may have been mistaken about that arrow," David murmured. Their bodies pressed together with force in measure to the intensity of their rising ardor, as though they sought literally to become one. Jonathan made his prophesy a reality, and they were united as one for the first time under the stars in a constellation of their own making. Both cried out to the heavens, tributes to their love, unheard by any but each other and the God who had brought them together.

But the Lord said unto Samuel... man looketh on the outward appearance,
but the Lord looketh on the heart.

1 Samuel 16:7

"PRAISE BE to the God of Abraham," Samuel cried out elsewhere under the same stars. "You have sent the one. He has shown himself by his actions on the field at Elah to be anointed by your hand."

Word of the celebration in Gibeah and the reason for it quickly reached Samuel in Ramah. He had taken his celebration, as was his custom, to a special Naioth. The tent city shimmered in the desert night. News of David's deeds and appointment made clear to the old priest the will of the Lord and the vision revealed to him at Bethlehem. As the spirit took him, he chanted by firelight. New images came to him, and the future unfolded before him.

Tears coursed down his cheeks as he saw what he knew must be, even as it broke his heart.

"Your will be done," Samuel said as he collapsed in the dust.

CHAPTER NINE
THE VILLAGE OF SHIN SHARON

And David went out whithersoever Saul sent him, and behaved himself wisely: and Saul set him over the men of war, and he was accepted in the sight of all the people, and also in the sight of Saul's servants.

1 Samuel 18:5

DAVID HAD never actually been in a battle when the time came for him to lead his first company on campaign. His victory over Goliath was already a holy legend, thanks almost as much to Saul's wily promotion as David's triumph. The king and fate, if not God himself, had given him the opportunity to follow his boyhood dreams of adventure. Though he was determined to be at Jonathan's side in battle, David knew he could not face a real enemy with a legend.

Their first winter together, following the covenant of Elah, had been long and cold and rainy. David still kept track of the day-to-day business of his father's karmel in Bethlehem. The wheat and the barley crops promised to exceed any before in their bounty. He relied on his brothers and most trusted and best-trained servants to see to his former responsibilities, so that the season's profits would match the potential promised by the rains.

David and Jonathan spent the season together barricaded in Jonathan's rooms, where David was "undergoing intense combat training." Or so they said. In truth, when they weren't making love and the weather permitted, Jonathan did devote himself to helping David train. Many were the times they appeared at table, wet and muddy from spending an entire day out in the soggy fields, practicing hand to hand. Often they missed supper altogether, staying out on clear nights to study scouting and survival in the wild and to make love under the stars.

David proved an apt pupil for the skills of war but also for the strategies. On days too rainy or cold to train for combat, Jonathan instructed David in the ways of battle using small wooden toy soldiers, archers, and charioteers to recreate Saul's great battles. They played out the king's strategies in heaps of sand and bits of brush on the polished tile floor of Jonathan's sitting room.

"Here, you see, by forcing the strength of a greater number to face them in this narrow valley, the army only fought a front with numbers equal to their own," Jonathan explained, as David took in the tableau Jonathan and Paltiel had so carefully laid out for his education.

"But wouldn't the thing to do be to come from behind them through this pass here, trap them, and make them fight on two fronts?" David asked, looking over the wooden pieces.

"But that would have divided our own forces," Jonathan explained with practiced patience. He had found that, while David was a good pupil, he never took anyone's word for anything. "We would have been diminished."

"No, you'd have been doubled," David exclaimed, trying to make his point clear, though Jonathan was already shaking his head. "And otherwise, you risk the enemy using their far greater numbers to circle around here by the same route to swamp you."

"David, you know my father won this battle, right?" Jonathan pointed out pedantically.

"All I'm saying is—"

"That you would have done it differently?"

"Well, yes," David agreed, bobbing his head.

Amused and annoyed, Jonathan tackled David to the floor and pinned him, facedown, lying across David's back as he held his arms behind him.

"Well, when you are the king and you decide to fight the third battle of Jabesh again, then you divide your men as you see fit, sweet boy," Jonathan hissed into David's ear. "But king or no, when you divide your total number of men in twain, you decrease them. Multiplying doubles men, but as you and I have more than proved this winter, men cannot multiply themselves."

Their laughter ended the argument and the lesson, as wrestling led to other rainy day activities.

Saul and the rest of his family loved David almost as much as Jonathan did himself. His wit, his charm, and his talents added much to the feasts and festivals of winter. David's family joined them when the weather permitted travel from Bethlehem.

During the long winter evenings' entertainments, and at family dinners, David saw that his mother was right; both of Jonathan's sisters were hopelessly smitten. Michal was the more ardent of the two. Like a woman possessed, whenever David was in the room she sought him like a lodestone finds iron. Though her attention troubled him, he did his best to be kind and brotherly to the two women.

It was one thing to take a wife, but another entirely to take the sister of his lover as a wife. He felt about the prospect as he might if his own sisters were suddenly offered to him for marriage.

Rather than speak to Jonathan and get answers he could not stomach, David swallowed his own thoughts about such confusing matters. Their covenant and the true depth of their feelings for one another were their secret. Everyone at court knew them to be as alloyed as the copper and tin that made bronze. That suited. Their places were always set together at table, their rooms adjoined, and their names more and more were spoken as one. Most often, they were called simply "the princes." Though they had never yet discussed it, the rest of what was between them remained between them.

It was all well until David thought too much about it. Then his heart raced, his head swam, and his breath grew short. What place was there to be for him? It would not be thought at all odd for Jonathan to take a soldier's boy. But that would make David more servant than peer. It was well-known that men took their pleasure with one another when they were on their own. Some chose each other even though their choice was not limited. There was a tradition of warrior-lovers, men whose friendships transcended just the bonds of soldiers and lasted long after they had quit campaign and battlefield.

So, instead of worry or discussion, David focused on preparing for their departure the following spring on campaign. He redesigned his armor, plating leather with iron rather than hinging metal plates together. The result was lighter and easier to move in. Jonathan scoffed at first, but after David bested him repeatedly at armored combat, he secretly commissioned similar battle wear for himself.

Following heated arguments over strategy, he also convinced Jonathan to create an entirely new division of their forces. The new cadre's sole job would be to establish and protect supply lines to wherever the army might be.

"But how can I spare men I need to help fight battles that they might instead spend their labors defending herds and grain shipments?" Jonathan demanded as David tried once again to convince the prince of his latest idea.

"Well, my lord, they will be the same men who would otherwise be commissioned with lugging along a year's store of food and supplies in order to feed and arm your troops," David said with a tone that suggested he was addressing anyone but his lord.

"So six here or six there is still a half dozen, is it not?" Jonathan insisted. He folded his arms and turned away onto his side in the hope of getting some peace, since lovemaking was clearly not to happen in their bed that morning.

"When I am tending my herds at father's karmel, I do not send the shepherds out dragging an entire summer's supply of food," David explained. "Instead, as they move from field to field with the flocks, I send food there to meet them. In this way all they need be concerned with are my father's sheep. They can stay out as long as the grazing is good and need not return simply because they are out of food for themselves or go hungry because their task is not at end."

Jonathan hid his smile in his pillows as he faced away. He was both charmed and convinced by David's argument and passion, though he did not give him the satisfaction just then. He knew he would only be treated to a new argument on a new topic if he relented. Instead Jonathan remained silent and waited to be further convinced by other forms of persuasion, more appropriate to the prince's bed, when David's words on the subject ran out.

Well-persuaded in the end, Jonathan added the new supply corps to his armies.

At last David was fully occupied. Creating, organizing, and equipping the troops for the new division, training for combat, and spending any time he could wrest from duty alone with Jonathan kept his mind off the topics that weighed on his heart.

Spring arrived unaccompanied by any great armies to be faced. The season's campaign instead offered the promise of advancing and strengthening the causes and the borders of the expanding Israel. The Philistines, following their crushing defeat at Elah, offered no imminent threat.

Having created his new supply corps, David's latest objective was to "enlist" as many Philistine metallurgists—by force, or by more pleasing enticement—as was practical. He longed to add command of the Philistine secrets of iron to the Israelite arsenal. On this point there was no argument between them. Jonathan took an active role. They commenced at once to try to communicate with those smiths of David's acquaintance who might open the gates for them. Through these men they began to recruit others of the trade for a new life under less despotic rule. Between them a plan for a more peaceful mission emerged.

With no major battle to face, King Saul elected to remain at the palace with his standing contingent of royal guards, to attend to domestic affairs and those of state. The skirmishes and raiding parties he gladly left to his captains, Jonathan and David. The king did launch the expedition with great spectacle and fanfare.

In honor of the occasion, Jonathan presented David with a chain of gold specially wrought at his command to hold the lion's tooth David always carried "for luck."

Following a grand procession through the streets of the city and great public sacrifices and prayers for success in battle, there was a lavish dinner. The banquet was attended by both families' houses as well as all the elders, high priests, and chieftains of Israel and Judah, emissaries from the neighboring kingdoms of Moab and Edom, and leaders from the highest ranks of Saul's armies and government.

Conspicuous by his absence was Samuel. Those closest to the king, Jonathan among them, took note of the extravagant lengths to which Saul had gone in order to appease and court the grace of God in his preparation for battle without Samuel still at his side. Many in a position to know were dubious of the king's decision to surrender his place at the head of the army and remain at court. Jonathan wondered if his father had lost confidence in himself and his ability to lead the very army he had created.

Still, if the king was tense or in bad humor, it was not apparent during the elaborate proceedings of the day or beneath the vast quantities of wine Saul had consumed during the festivities.

To his amusement and mild dismay, David found himself seated between Merab and Michal in the procession for their official public presentation. Jonathan was presented next to Azia, an Edomite noblewoman and sister to Doeg, captain of the king's guard. They put on a brave face for the presentations, but both were relieved when the time came for the banquet and the women left them on their own again.

"Shouldn't we wait until there is a victory to celebrate?" David asked Jonathan in a whisper, with more mirth than disapproval.

"Father will have his fun," Jonathan confided with a laugh. "He has as much a knack for making merry as for making war."

"And for winning people's hearts," David agreed. The shouts, songs and accolades of his first public appearance since their return from Elah overwhelmed him. "Did you hear? They've written songs about me. I feel like a virgin facing the attentions of an unwelcome suitor."

"You are a hero," Jonathan explained, laughing. "And an asset. A king must not only raise an army but the gold to make war. There is no one more skilled than my father at inspiring the generosity of his most tight-fisted subjects. To do that, one must do the most with what is at hand."

"You will be a great king, I think," David said, placing his hand on Jonathan's and smiling up into his face.

"As will you," Jonathan said, turning his hand over and clasping David's in his own.

Once the speeches were made and the music faded into memory, the true adventure of being alone on campaign together began. David's youthful playacting with Micah was made real at last. By day they made their way through the hills and frontiers of the country they were helping to make. By night they lay in one another's arms and schemed of their future together.

The dreams at first were of Jonathan as king and David as his great general, not unlike Saul and his cousin Abner. More and more, though, they spoke of *their* rule. Their words foretold of when *they* were king.

"I think that a king must be guided by laws and not simply act as he sees fit from one breath to the next," Jonathan said as they lay side by side at supper one night in their tent, when the topic had turned to the politics of governing. "In Egypt the king is thought to be a living god, and like the will of God, his word is law. But here we have a God, and it is not my father."

"Praise be," David said, laughing and raising his cup in salute. "Lord protect the king, but yes, I am pleased that your father is not in charge of the weather when he is in his cups."

"Praise be," Jonathan agreed, laughing easily. "There is much primitive about our state and religion that needs attending. We are advanced beyond the ways of the primitives who see spirits in the campfire."

"You will be such a fine king," David said. Lying back, he looked up at Jonathan with love and admiration in his eyes.

Jonathan returned his gaze steadily. David set aside his wine cup, thinking the prince was done with supper and talk of politics.

"We must rule together, you and I," Jonathan said at last. "As equals."

"How is that possible?"

"We shall make it so," Jonathan said with a smile, took up David's hand, and kissed it. "How could I rule with only half a soul? Half a mind? Half a heart?"

"Or I?"

"So, then, it is done," Jonathan said with an air of finality. "This is between us, as so much is just now, I know, but you of all people must know my heart. I would rule with you as Amenhotep and Nefertiti ruled together in Egypt."

"And which of us is to be the queen?" David asked to soften the sharp edges of their dilemma.

"Well, you are the more beautiful. Everyone says so," Jonathan said, smiling and stroking David's hair as his slid an arm behind his head. "Still, I think we shall have to find a way to be kings together. If men and women may rule as equals, I must believe that our path lies there. I cannot believe that the Lord has brought us together as one, as he has done, and does not want us to be together always in this as in all things."

"I love you, Jonathan," David said, rubbing his head against Jonathan's cradling arm. "That is enough for me."

"Yes," Jonathan said, leaning down so close that their noses touched. "I look forward to being old with you and every day until then. But if you don't mind too much, I shall have to die first, for I'm not sure I could bear to live without you."

"Then we shall have to die together," David said, lifting his head and nipping at Jonathan's lips.

"But first...," Jonathan said, leaning down and putting an end to the morbid conversation.

Living in such close quarters and always accountable to one another, as men on military patrol must be, it was clear to even the most casual observer that more than friendship united David and Jonathan. Many were the officers who took their pleasure with the armor-bearer or slave boy they had brought along for such purposes. Nor would it have attracted much notice for foot soldiers to seek companionship in their own ranks. So, though what passed between Jonathan and David occasioned little in the way of comment, it left less doubt.

For one thing, the prince's tent was theirs together. There was a second smaller tent that shared the prince's fire, but no one had ever seen it used, and often it never quite got pitched. More still, they presented a united front. The prince often deferred to David or asked his opinion when there were decisions to be made or strategies to be designed. Out of respect for Jonathan, and for

David's own heroics at Elah, David was treated with deference by the officers around the prince, yet his word was never the last.

David understood. He respected Jonathan's command and knew he would have to earn his place at the planning table.

His only open conflict was with Paltiel. Accustomed as Palti was to the prince's company, ear, and favor, he found himself suddenly adrift in unfamiliar waters. He alone had been fully aware of the true nature of the relationship between David and Jonathan since before their winter at the palace. He had been determined from the start to keep the prince's confidence by keeping the prince's confidence. Despite his less than cordial start with David, and their often prickly relations since, Paltiel was wise in the ways of the court where he had grown up.

After their first night back at the palace from Elah, when the prince had run dripping from a bath filled with all that a man might ask to pursue David into the night, never to return to his own bed, Paltiel understood. Determined not to sacrifice all that he had earned in the prince's service by competing for the prince's heart, Palti made himself attendant to both men. He had watched others mistake familiarity for more in royal service and was resolved not to sacrifice his ambition on the altar of his pride.

It was no different, he reasoned, than if the prince had taken a princess, and he would act accordingly. In the end, though, Paltiel could not scheme his way around the fact that, as a man, David was not so easily dismissed as a woman would have been. He ate with the prince, rode with the prince, campaigned with the prince, and slept with the prince. More and more, Paltiel feared his influence was slipping away.

There had been little signs along the way. The need for privacy necessitated Palti's waning access to the prince's private rooms. Paltiel persevered, remaining ever the faithful servant and second to his prince.

More and more, he felt just that: a servant to his prince. The prince turned to David as friend, confidant, and the lover Paltiel was neither suited nor disposed to be. He simply could not compete. Yet he could not bear to surrender. Too much was at stake.

"Palti, could you leave us alone so we could talk?" Jonathan said to Paltiel one night, when they were all still at the palace.

He knew.

From that time on, Paltiel had begun to look for a new position at court that would more surely advance his cause. Stung, he kept his own counsel and remained loyal to his prince. Palti counted still on his old friend Jonathan to ease his way forward, if not up.

The tenuous place Paltiel had come to occupy at court was a harder position to maintain in the field.

Ironically, Paltiel's undoing was that everyone knew what was going on between David and the prince. Spoken or not, the common knowledge took away the base of Paltiel's power as chief keeper of the prince's secret. David assumed the role Paltiel had always played. After years of service and friendship, Paltiel found himself usurped.

"I think the prince would prefer that we break camp later in the day," Paltiel said in his accustomed manner, giving orders by conveying them to men who were technically his superiors but who had deferred to him in such matters in the past.

"I'll ask David to be sure," the lieutenant said, without thinking, as he took brisk leave of Paltiel. In the simple remark and manner, Paltiel heard the eulogy for his former life. Speaking on the prince's behalf no longer afforded him the same authority it once had. He was born as a new man a little more with the affront of each new reality.

For his part, David found he was faced with elevating himself from Paltiel's servant status. Though generals might take David's word on what the prince would like for supper or whether or not he would be sleeping in or rising early, when it came to matters of warfare, even the lowliest foot soldier regarded David not at all. Equal to David in this at least, Paltiel found some balm for his wounded pride, though not enough to quell his struggle to remain civil in his dealings with David or to staunch his newfound longing for escape.

The company's progress was quiet for several weeks. They fell into the ease of men on a very well-attended hunt as they patrolled the borders that Israel claimed. David's logistical wizardry worked brilliantly. They moved much more swiftly without the stores to transport, yet they were always more than adequately supplied.

The patrol was uneventful. The ceremonial show of force was well received as they made their way from village to village along the country's frontiers, but little else was required.

Freed of the brute necessity of battle or even bandits, David privately urged Jonathan toward his, and ultimately their, more secretive campaign objective—iron.

With no enemy to track, they followed David's own experience and contacts from running and equipping the farm. To the north, through the valley of Shiloh, near Ebenezer, lay the shortest route to the plain of Ono. There the metal craftsmen of Philistia were as thick as the wool on a sheep's back. In pursuit of the secrets of this precious new metal, their patrol made its way to the Philistine city of Aphek. Blessed with essential fuel and metal ores nearby, the city was known for its armorers. Their skills in equipping the Philistines had been in large part responsible for the massive defeat of the Israelites, and the loss of the Ark of the Covenant, at Ebenezer when Samuel was a young man still.

The ark had been recovered. Neither the lesson nor the Philistine advantage had been lost.

David had purchased iron plowshares and gotten other metal tools and implements forged, repaired, and sharpened at Aphek. Though the Philistines were happy to make a profit from their neighbors in Israel, they jealously guarded their superior knowledge of the secret of iron. It not only kept people like David coming back each spring with wheat and shekels to bargain for the edge they needed to keep their farms competitive, it kept the Philistines the masters in the battlefield.

David had long been cultivating a network of such skilled craftsmen. He hoped eventually to convince several to return with him to Bethlehem to set up shop at Jesse's karmel. Through their skill David planned not only to supply the farm directly with the hard edge of iron technology, but to expand the family business into the manufacture and sales of the fruits of the proprietary knowledge.

Old plans, and David's fortunes, had changed. His offers to tempt those who possessed the skill away from their Philistine masters had grown richer and riper but riskier than before. Most of the craftsmen with whom David had bargained kept shop near Aphek.

The town was at the eastern end of the Shiloh Valley, at the head of the Yarkon River. The location provided direct and easy access east to the smiths' needed resources from the valley and the hills beyond, but also west from their ironworks to the key trading port of Joppa. Arriving at such a strategic target with the army of Israel would have made their task more difficult. A more left-handed approach to the problem had been decided.

"I have been in contact with a network of these craftsmen," Jonathan explained to his captains. As they drew nearer to their goal, it became necessary to include his closest advisors in the more secret details of the clandestine plans David and he had forged. "They will meet us in the village of Shin Sharon, west of Ebenezer. I will signal them by veiled message once we have arrived."

They had agreed it would be best to present David's ideas and covert plans as Jonathan's, to give them the added credibility of coming from the prince.

"And what of the Philistine army?" Sarek, Jonathan's most senior advisor, asked seriously. "We can hardly expect to escort their most prized possession from the valley without resistance."

"A very real possibility," Jonathan agreed, unfurling a skin on which was sewn a map of the region. "I hope to avoid direct conflict, but if such is impossible, the Ebenezer pass—here—seems the most defensible point from which to make a stand. The narrow neck of the pass will force them to fight us in smaller numbers and level the field, if not give us the advantage."

"Unless they make their way around and trap you in the valley," David said. He was really only thinking aloud, as they so often did in the privacy of the prince's rooms.

No more than a look passed between the men gathered to hear their prince's plans, but all were uncertain of the outcome of a direct challenge to the prince.

"I hardly think that likely," Sarek spoke up in Jonathan's defense. He sought, in part, to cover the awkwardness by making the argument between him and David. Moreover, short of the prince, his seat was at the head of this table, and he wanted to remind David of that without offending the prince.

"How so?" David replied, undaunted by Sarek's authority or, truth be told, anyone else's. "This is the Philistines' realm far more than ours. To think that they would not simply make their way around these hills—here to the north—through the Kanah Wadi and trap us in the narrow pass seems ill-advised."

"Tell us, general, how would you command this assault?" Sarek said, getting a gentle laugh, but a laugh nonetheless, from the more experienced military men present.

"I would hold back half the men from the force. Since we'll only be fighting on a narrow front, our numbers will be the same," David explained, impervious to the laughter at his expense. "If we fall back and then circle around behind them, we can double our forces by fighting on two narrow fronts and maximize our advantage."

There was a silence, and then broad laughter.

"Thank you, David," Jonathan said with parental patronage. "It seems we shall have to get you a tutor from Arabah or Egypt to instruct you in the finer points of arithmetic. My prince, as I have pointed out to you before, you cannot double the size of our forces by dividing them."

The laughter increased.

"Perhaps if you would let me explain it to you so you could understand," David suggested. The laughter stuck in the throats of the commanders.

"No, let me explain," Jonathan said, more firmly. "It is my decision and it is made. Is that clearer?"

David looked around. He saw his response reflected as disrespect to the prince on the faces of all present. Love and respect overcame his impulse to argue.

"Yes, my prince, of course," David said. Once done, the effect in him was manifold. For perhaps the first time in his life, he was more injured by the thought that he might have embarrassed Jonathan than by any concern for his own foolish pride. "I meant no disrespect to you or your commanders. Forgive me. I am unfamiliar with the ways in which such meetings are conducted. In future I will keep my own counsel until it is asked."

Jonathan's look to David was one of love, gratitude, and not a little admiration. He knew the cost of such a bow from his fierce and proud lover as well as he knew the importance of maintaining the authority of his command.

Sarek and his cohorts smiled with a smug satisfaction at seeing the upstart relegated to his place among them. None were more pleased than Paltiel at witnessing David find the boundaries of his own respect and power.

Plans for battle were days from execution, and then only as a last resort. Stealth was their primary strategy. They made their way to the swampy woodland just east of the small village of Shin Sharon on Israel's side of the Ebenezer pass.

Jonathan, David, and a small band of men made their way on foot, in the guise of Israelite farmers passing through town to make their way to market at Aphek.

What they found there forever changed David's heart.

They saw the smoke rising as they approached and assumed it was merely the cooking fires, as the time of day was right. As they drew nearer, they saw instead a village laid waste. The breath caught in David's throat. He beheld the bodies of a mother and her children, their throats cut, dead where they had fallen in front of the smoldering ruins of what had been their home. Carrion birds picked at their flesh.

Again and again the scene and scenes like it were repeated as they made their way cautiously into the lifeless village. Old women, boys not yet reached manhood, the rich, the poor, and the holy lay in the streets with their slaughtered livestock where they had fallen to the indiscriminant sword of the Philistine enemy.

"David," Jonathan said, grasping his arm and shaking as if to awaken him. "You should return to camp," he urged, alarmed by the haunted look that had overcome his beloved companion since they'd first come into the murdered town.

"This is what war is," David said in a flat and emotionless tone. "This is what all the rousing and romantic psalms are about. This is what young men long for, playing at soldier with their wooden swords." His heart was filled with thoughts of Micah's death and the darkness that had settled on his own brother Eliab upon his return from his first battle; how determined he had been that David would not join them.

"Yes," Jonathan said simply with a somber nod. "This is our enemy. They do this to our villages. This is why we fight."

"Yes," David said, understanding the brutal necessity. He knew what was being asked of him as if he could see his own future. He prayed for the mettle to face the certainty that this kind of savagery would be expected of him. His only defense against this cruel eventuality was his youthful vow that such callous disregard for the Lord's greatest gift would not be taken lightly. This, then, would be his course of last resort. "We must see to it, then, that they are no longer our enemies."

"Over here, sir," one of the small band of their guard called to the prince before he could respond.

David's heart sank as they made their way around the bend and the gruesome scene came into view. There, nailed to the side of the village's crude little temple, was Tunc, the metalsmith with whom David had been secretly communicating. Written on the wall beside the body was a warning to traitors and those who would tempt them to traitorous acts.

"This is my fault. I got this man killed," David said, frozen at first by the sight before him. And then, rushing to the man's side, he began screaming for assistance. "Get him down. Get a ladder and get him down from here. He has deserved better than this. This is my fate, not his."

Startled by the outburst, the others in the party looked to Jonathan for guidance. Should they get a ladder?

Allowing David to scream himself out, Jonathan held back at first. Gently, then, he made his way to David's side. Taking him forcefully into his arms, he dragged him away from Tunc's lifeless and desecrated body.

"He was a man, David. He was doing what he thought was right," Jonathan said, holding him and trying to calm him. "You are not to blame for his decisions."

Jonathan held David's head as he emptied his guts onto the bloody stones of the ruined temple's courtyard. "Burn it all," he said out of David's hearing, signaling his men. He helped David to a nearby stream. With the care of an artist tracing the delicate lines of a sculpture, he washed David's face and hair. Drying him on his cloak, Jonathan then held David as he sobbed in grief for the innocent who lay dead, sacrificed to his plans for greater glory.

"How can the Lord allow such things?" David asked at last, calm and resting against Jonathan's strong chest. His head nestled in the crook of Jonathan's arm.

"What has the Lord to do with this?" Jonathan sighed. His heart was heavy with what war had shown him and his faith tempered by Samuel's meddling in politics and his father's fate. "These are the ways of man, not the Lord."

They lay together in silence for a time before the answer came to David.

"The Lord will make us victorious," David answered.

"What?"

"That's how the Lord can stop such things," David said, sitting up, filled with a renewed energy, born of a force that burned within him almost without his understanding. "By making us victorious in our quest. By allowing us the opportunity to be benevolent in victory."

"Make the Philistines our allies, you mean?" Jonathan asked, puzzled. He wondered at the idea that David raised again, even in the face of such heartless brutality.

"Isn't that what we were trying to do here?" David answered, up and ready to begin anew. "Isn't that what Tunc died for?"

"I guess it is." Jonathan nodded. He rose and brushed the leaves and dirt from his cloak on which they had both been lying. "How do we do that now?"

"With Tunc's help." David beamed. He was already possessed by his idea.

"My own." Jonathan chuckled, engulfing David in a huge embrace. "First you would double troops by dividing them. Now you will enlist the dead to fight on our side. Either you are a wise man or a madman, but I'm afraid I shall never understand you."

"It is easy," David said, struggling unsuccessfully to escape Jonathan's grasp. "We do not need to sneak into Aphek. I have been many times before on shopping trips. Once we are there, do you suppose that the news of Tunc's fate at the Philistines' hands for seeking his own fortune as a free man will inspire greater loyalty to a cruel master? Or greater interest in a new life with us?"

"You are a wise man," Jonathan said, squeezing tighter before letting David go. "And a madman. And I am madder still, for I will follow you forward, my prince."

"And I will walk at your side, my lord," David said. Taking his hand, they made their way back to join the rest of their party, whose gruesome work was done. Fire consumed the last of the village and its still and silent residents as Shin Sharon disappeared from the map and the pages of history.

"What now, my lord?" the captain of the guard asked of Jonathan as they rejoined them.

"On to Aphek for a little shopping I think," Jonathan said, exchanging a look and laugh with David.

Now there was no smith found throughout all the land of Israel: for the Philistines said, Lest the Hebrews make them swords or spears: But all the Israelites went down to the Philistines, to sharpen every man his share, and his coulter, and his axe, and his mattock.

1 Samuel 13:19-20

TO JONATHAN'S astonishment, David was welcomed to the city of Aphek like visiting royalty. As a scion of Jesse the elder, principal landholder of the prosperous city of Bethlehem, David's arrival at the markets of Aphek was always notable. His frequent and substantial trade with the merchants of the city held him in good stead and high esteem with both businessmen and government officials. It was a unique and unexpected experience for the prince to be simply a nameless member of David's party.

As quickly as word of their arrival spread, David managed to put out the news that the Philistines, technically the city's masters, had murdered Tunc for being a free man and trading with whom he wished. These trade restrictions were already a source of great tension between the locals and the representatives from the kings of the five cities.

Philistia was less a country than five overlapping Philistine city-states on the coastal plain, west of the hills that were home to the tribes of Israel. From their pentapolis of Gaza, Ashkelon, Ashod, Gath, and Ekron, the Philistines ruled over the other smaller cities, towns, and villages of the region, though many were inhabited by peoples other than the Philistines. Tunc had come to Aphek from the north, near Damascus, and his family from even farther away. He had come to Aphek to learn a trade that would earn him a better living and a better life than he had known before.

Under the repressive rule of the Philistines, Tunc, like so many of his peers, could only rise so high. The fact that the richest trade route in the world passed within walking distance of his shop made his Philistine muzzle chafe that much more. He ached for freedom long before David had tempted him with it. His trade was restricted and his market controlled, though until his death, it had not been treated as a capital crime.

His yearning brought Tunc together with David. His death made up the minds of many others who shared his beliefs and feared his fate. They would follow David to the east and freedom.

Jonathan could not detect the plan being set into motion, though he spent the day at David's elbow. He watched as David bought gifts for both their families while he chatted amiably with various merchants and artisans.

"I cannot take these with me now. Would you deliver it?" David asked the merchant Vosgi after purchasing table cutlery for his mother.

"But of course," Vosgi said with a short bow. "When will you break camp?"

"Just at sundown tomorrow," David said genially. "We are camped a few steps beyond Shin Sharon at the mouth of the Ebenezer pass. There is a little creek there."

"I know the place well," Vosgi said, nodding and taking David's hand. "How could I not? You have camped there often enough in the past."

"Good, then," David said, still grasping the man's hand. "So I may depend on seeing you there? I hope you will bring the family that I may see them as well. If time permits, come early. Several others, with whom you are acquainted, will also be there with their families. We shall make it a celebration for old friends."

"We will be happy to join you, David ben Jesse," Vosgi said, relinquishing their grasp only to bow stiffly again, as was his custom. "I am only sorry that Tunc will not be able to join our party."

"Indeed, my friend." David nodded sadly. "We shall raise our goblets in his honor. Feel free to invite any who you think would want to join us in tribute to Tunc."

The two men embraced warmly before taking their leave.

Jonathan followed along silently as they made their way out of the city.

"Are we leaving?" the prince asked

"Our work here is done." David shrugged. "All that's left is to plan the party."

"The party?" Jonathan asked with an odd grin.

"Yes, when the Philistines come, they will expect to see a party," David answered with a confidence that surprised him.

"The Philistines?"

"Well, of course." David smiled, taking his hand as they walked along out of the village. "We shall escape by attracting the most possible attention to ourselves."

"Madman." Jonathan chuckled.

Just as David predicted, a small guard of Philistines arrived as their party was in full swing. David had invited a goodly number of merchants to join them in the festivities. The veritable caravan of wagons and mules bringing goods and materials to their camp was anything but secret.

"Officer," David called to the captain of the Philistine guard. "Please join us. There is bread and good wine for you and your men."

To Jonathan's amazement, the Philistines joined the party. The guardsmen heartily thanked David as they departed to return to the city and their duties along with many of the merchants.

Most of those invited to the celebration departed, leaving only five families and their wagons behind, their absence unnoticed in the crowd. The patriarch of each who remained was a master metalsmith. Each had come with only his family, his tools, and the barest possible personal possessions. Each man was leaving his life behind.

"You have done it," Jonathan said to David as they quickly began to break camp to effect their escape.

"Not yet." David smiled. "By midday tomorrow they will come in pursuit of us. But they will not be expecting the army of Israel. We must get our guests out of harm's way, so that we may meet the local garrison in full force once they realize."

David sighed as he looked back down the road toward Aphek.

"You have all but succeeded. Why so sad?"

"It will be a very long time before I can shop here again," David said mournfully.

Jonathan laughed until he realized that David was not joking. He made as if he was clearing his throat, clapped David sympathetically on the back, and stole away in haste to laugh apart from David's hearing.

Their party made it safely back to the army's encampment under moonlight.

"We must make ready for attack," Jonathan instructed Sarek upon their arrival. "The Philistines will come for us by morning."

"The Ebenezer pass?" Sarek confirmed.

"As we have planned." Jonathan nodded. "Can you have the men ready and at arms in time?"

"It shall be so," Sarek answered with a crisp nod of ascent.

"David, I want to you to prepare to move east with our guests," Jonathan ordered, resuming the command he had set aside in Aphek.

"My lord, I can be of more use to you…," David began but got no further.

"You will be of most use to me by following orders," Jonathan said firmly.

Sarek busied himself and tried to look as though he did not hear. David alone caught the grin on Paltiel's face when the armor-bearer thought no one was looking.

"Our mission here is to get these people away safely," Jonathan offered, though still in the same commanding tone. "I need you to make sure that happens."

"And the people of Shin Sharon?"

"Are dead."

"Yes, my lord, they are," David said with a stiff bow.

Where no counsel is, the people fall: but in the multitude of counsellors there is safety.

Proverbs 11:14

JONATHAN AND his men were in place at the Ebenezer pass by sunrise the following morning. The dust of the advancing Philistines forces was visible before midday. He took comfort in knowing that David was safe, well behind the line and on the way to the security of his father's home.

They had agreed to install Israel's newest citizens in Bethlehem under the care and protection of the house of Jesse and thus the house of David. The resources needed for the work of armoring and weapons manufacture were plentiful and easily accessible in the nearby hills of Judah. The Ridge Road provided ready access to outside trade and left the craftsmen free to make their fortunes from the sweat of their own brow.

Jonathan was to meet David there. They planned to remain for a time after. David could be with his family as they tended to beginning the business of smelting iron and properly arming the soldiers of Israel. First, though, there was the Philistine guard from Aphek to be dealt with. Already the calls of Jonathan's commanders brought the troops to ready. They manned a line across the narrow pass and braced for the assault.

The Philistine commander rallied his troops to battle formation. Jonathan and his troops held fast, prepared for attack. None came. The Philistines held, inexplicably. The two forces stared at one another across the narrow isthmus that divided them. The strange silence chilled and unnerved Jonathan's men.

Jonathan, poised just behind the front lines, felt a bead of cold sweat run down his spine as they stood, arms at the ready, in the midday sun. Should he strike the first blow? Or hold his strategic advantage in the narrow pass?

"What do you suppose they are waiting for?" Sarek said at last, exasperated by the maddening pause.

As the prince considered the question, an answer came.

A cry went up. A second Philistine force appeared behind Jonathan's men, just as the first line charged. The Israelites fell to chaos as they scrambled to fight their enemy on two fronts, dividing their forces in two as the Philistines doubled their small company.

Causalities were heavy at first, as the prince's forces fell over one another to throw themselves against the rear guard attack. The rout was quickly stemmed, and the battle returned to a virtual stalemate as the Philistines hurled themselves relentlessly at the two lines of the Israelite army. They fought, trapped in the middle of the inescapable Ebenezer pass, walled in on two sides by Philistines and by the wadi cliffs on two others.

As officer and foot soldier fought shoulder to shoulder to hold the two lines, none who were present at the strategy session could keep David's words far from their minds; no one more than Jonathan.

They heard the trumpets even before they saw the cloud of dust. The supply corps, with which David had been ordered to make camp at Bethlehem, attacked the rear of the Philistine forces on both sides of the pass. Trapped between Israelite forces on both sides and forced to fight suddenly on four fronts, the Philistines quickly crumpled. In the chaos, their recovery was slow. There was a surge in the forces fighting under Jonathan. The rescue brought new hope and new heart on their side.

The outflanked Philistines were quickly undone, though they fought on to the last man. Before the sun was half down the westward sky, Jonathan's forces finished them, with not a Philistine standing in the aftermath.

In the shock that followed, what had seemed a crushing defeat for Israel became a slaughter of the same Philistine forces that had swept Shin Sharon from the map. Jonathan stood dazed amidst the mayhem, unsure of which way to proceed. He wanted only to find David, whom he was more than certain had authored their rescue with his insubordination.

Around him the moans of the wounded and the dying filled the air. He could no longer make out which direction they had been heading. A horse galloped to where he stood, with a familiar figure at the reins. Barely tall enough to see over the horse's head, unruly golden hair protruding from under the leather and iron helmet, his prince arrived.

"So," Jonathan said as David dismounted and rushed to his side. "I thought I ordered you to Bethlehem. What do you have to say for yourself?"

"That, sire, is how you quadruple your forces by dividing them into thirds." David smiled, reaching up to wipe the dirt from Jonathan's brow. "And I will be happy to explain it to my Egyptian numbers tutor as soon as he arrives."

Iron sharpeneth iron; so a man sharpeneth the countenance of his friend.

Proverbs 27:17

THE ARMY was soon united outside Bethlehem and the planning underway for the establishment of iron smelting and armament manufacture. In return for safe passage and the resources to begin again in their new home, Vosgi and his associates agreed to oversee Israel's first steps into the new age of iron that was reshaping the old world.

Jonathan and David stayed at Jesse's house. They were treated to the sort of welcome they might have expected after being lost for many years in the wilderness. Nitzevet fed them so well that they spent extra time in training to avoid becoming too fat to wear their new armor.

Eliab surrendered his place at the head of the table opposite Jesse to David. In turn, David insisted the honor go to Jonathan and that the brothers remain at Jesse's right and left, equals in all things. It was a loving and peaceable gathering. Jonathan was welcomed and treated like a member of the family. A prince he might be, but in Jesse's house, Nitzevet's word was the only law. He took his lead from David and his brothers while in residence.

His place with David was never questioned. He was taken into the family much as Micah had been, though he did not know of his predecessor. He shared his room with David and was, in all things, at his side. Seeing them together, Nitzevet at last understood her son's feelings for Micah's loss more fully. She treated Jonathan more tenderly, thankful for the joy she could see he had brought back into her son's eyes.

One warm summer day after the midday meal, David was called away on some crucial matter about the foundry. Forced to cancel their plans, Jonathan found himself at leisure. Nitzevet asked him to keep her company as she did her spinning.

"David used to practice the harp by playing for me and my daughters while we spun," she said, imploring him to join her.

"I can't play the harp," Jonathan said by way of acceptance.

"Good." She laughed. "I love his playing, but it will be nice simply to have a conversation. I sometimes feel he's singing at me—trying to convince me."

"I see that." Jonathan chuckled, nodding in agreement. "Though the singing does cut back on the nagging and limits the yelling."

"Oh," sighed Nitzevet. She smiled at him with a twinkle in her eye as though they were sharing fond and secret memories. "You should hear some of his earlier work."

They laughed together as she took his arm. She guided him into her sewing room, empty that day as both her daughters were attending their own families.

"Maha," she called to her serving woman. "Bring us something cool to drink, would you?"

"Yes, my lady," she said, leaving to go and crush some of the mint that her lady preferred with cool water, honey, and a taste of pomegranate syrup on hot days.

"I love it here—your home, I mean," Jonathan said, standing in the archway. He looked out over the fragrant gardens in the courtyard as she took up her place on a cushion to begin her spinning.

"It is as nothing compared to the palace at Gibeah." Nitzevet shushed him, adding a wave of her hand for emphasis.

"It is so much more than the palace," Jonathan said, turning to her. "This is a home. I am very comfortable at the palace and grateful for the blessing, but one gives up a lot to live there."

"I suppose there is duty in everyone's life," Nitzevet agreed, nodding as she took up her distaff and began twisting at the wool in her basket. "The wisdom is in how you carry it off."

"Well, you dispatch your duty so graciously that one would hardly know you have any," Jonathan said, smiling at her as she devoted herself to her work.

"Oh, blessings on your silvered words." She giggled like a young girl. "I'm an old farm wife with eight unruly sons and two shrill daughters. It's a nice farm, but it's a farm. I am blessed. We both are."

"Yes, we are," Jonathan said. "Or at least I used to be."

"Have you misplaced your blessing?" she asked archly, looking up from her work.

"Perhaps." Jonathan sighed, looking off into the distant hills beyond the garden. "Or perhaps it's just politics. It's hard to tell the difference between blessings and politics in a palace."

"Whatever does that mean?" she asked, genuinely troubled, dropping the distaff into her lap.

"Samuel and my father are not getting along of late." Jonathan shrugged. "The great judge got mad, went home, and took God with him."

"Oh, dear boy, you do sound like David." She smiled, taking up her spinning again. "No wonder you are so good together. The Lord hasn't gone anywhere. He's right there waiting to take your hand."

"What makes you so sure?" he asked, drawing nearer.

"What is it David always says?" She raised her face and closed her eyes as she thought and then spoke again without opening them, as though she could see the words on the backs of her lids. "How do I know that the Lord believes in me?"

"I've never heard him say that," Jonathan said, puzzled.

"Yes." She smiled, reaching up and taking his hand. "I expect that that's because you are the answer to his question."

"I… do you think?" he faltered.

"Here, sit next to me," she said, drawing him down with one hand and patting Abigail's cushion with the other. "Here is Maha with our drinks, at last."

"And some bits of sweet fried dough," Maha said. She put the plate down on the low inlaid table before them, along with their drinks. Fresh mint sprigs from the garden peeked invitingly over the rims of two of Nitzevet's best cups.

"She must like you," Nitzevet confided, though Maha could hear her well enough. "I'm lucky to get a glass of water."

"Well, my lady, he is the prince of Israel." Maha sniffed as she wiped her hands on her apron. "I'm just trying to keep him happy so he doesn't burn down our house and take all your goats."

"That is most thoughtful of you, Maha," Nitzevet said with a hint of a laugh. "And these are delicious. If you could subdue the Philistines and check on supper, I'm sure we'd both be most thankful. Jonathan might even make you a princess."

"I'll leave that job to David," Maha said with a flourish as she exited.

Nitzevet could not stop laughing, and Jonathan could not help blushing.

"My lord, please don't fret," she said when she saw his discomfort. "Your arrival on the scene may have made the title more official, but David has always been the reigning princess in this house."

Jonathan laughed though he blushed still, feeling exposed.

"Whatever the case between you, I know your arrival is a great blessing in my beloved David's life," she said, taking his hand. "Perhaps you are even the destiny that Samuel himself predicted."

"What?" Jonathan asked, confused but supposing it merely a reference to some commonly held prophecy.

"He came here to see David for some reason." She shrugged.

"Who did?"

"Samuel," she said, turning her palms skyward. "Very mysterious. Showed up unannounced, right after First Fruits, three Passovers ago. We were never really sure why. He spoke with David, but I don't think even he knew exactly the purpose of the visit. At least, he never mentioned it again. After, no more than the days of Omer had been counted and the summer barley harvest brought in before your message to him arrived. He was off to sing for your father and to meet you."

"Samuel?" Jonathan remembered all at one as the conversation brought to mind overhearing the words of Saul's spy describing the priest's visit to Bethlehem. He had long forgotten the substance of the espionage as he'd been more concerned with Saul's state at the time.

"Samuel put oil on the boy's head after wrinkling his nose at all seven of his brothers, as though they were unworthy somehow," she said. She saw the strange evening as she recalled the story, then looked up to discover

Jonathan beside her. "It seemed such a blessing when you sent for him. He was so heartbroken then. His friend Micah had just died. But that was nothing compared to when you sent him home before Elah. He would not even play the harp. Nothing but work. I thought his spirit was broken beyond repair until I saw the two of you together at the palace for the victory feast."

"The two of us?" Jonathan smiled and looked away. He was too shy to admit more than his expression gave away, and too swept up by her words of the depth of David's feelings to hide his.

"Take good care of him," she said, smiling without looking up, coming at last to the purpose of their visit alone together. "I love all my sons and my daughters. But my David is something special. His spirit can fill the house, the city, and the hills with joy and laughter."

"Yes," Jonathan agreed. "And yes, I will take care of him for the rest of my life, I promise."

"I know," she said, pleased with their little talk, having assured herself of the prince and said what she needed to say. "You are family now."

The time never seemed right to speak with David about his conversation with Nitzevet.

For the remainder of their visit, and whenever they were under Jesse's roof, David knew something was different in Jonathan's manner. He took David's hand more on impulse than stolen opportunity. He surrendered the table head again to Eliab and always sat on the same bench with David at Jesse's table, so that he might drape his arm possessively around David's shoulders.

As if in answer to Jonathan's greater ease, Jesse and all his sons treated the prince more as another brother added to the family, just as the husbands of their sisters had been. They chided and teased him but were always glad of his protection of, and affection for, their David.

Nitzevet led the way in this, referring to Jonathan as *my son* once she was sure of him. She was as likely to smack the prince with a wooden spoon for some infraction as kiss his cheek for no good reason.

"A foolish son is his father's ruin and a quarrelsome wife is like a constant dripping," Jesse said with a genial roll of his eyes. "A good son keeps his mother happy so his father's life is easier."

"You are a wise man." Jonathan laughed. He saw the affection with which Jesse said such things. It was clear to him, after only a few days in residence, that Jesse relied on his wife's firm hand and strong will as much as he did his sons to run his considerable estates, groaning under the additions of David's growing fortunes.

The arms business was a further extension of David's properties, though he himself hardly thought of it as such. Jonathan and he felt that they were really building their fortunes together, just as Jonathan felt that the palace in

Gibeah was to be as much David's as his. Such was the covenant between them. There was no argument because there was nothing to be divided.

Too soon, the making and shaping of iron was underway. The road called them to return to their duty. They left the city well garrisoned to protect their valuable new resource.

A planning counsel of Jonathan's commanders was called as they prepared to resume their patrols. Though they met in the hall at Jesse's house, David took a place on a bench near the door, mindful of his last staff meeting.

As if his place was not clear enough to him, Jonathan opened the meeting by admonishing David for going against orders, though praising him for bringing them victory by his actions. David, as they had agreed before the meeting, begged the prince's pardon and agreed that for the safety of all concerned, orders were to be followed without question by all, himself included.

There were a few raised eyebrows, and Paltiel looked as though he'd won a handsome bet, but the meeting proceeded without further comment on the matter.

The discussion progressed quickly to possible routes and directions as they resumed their original plan to make a circuit of the borders King Saul claimed as the boundaries of Israel. News of Amalekite raids in the southern villages of Judah brought discussion of how best to smash the insurrection at the least cost to their resources. The prince invited debate about whether to pursue the Amalekites or take the battle to their strongholds. David observed quietly from the sidelines; he had given the prince the benefit of his best thinking privately.

The decision was made to take the battle to the Amalekite center of Tel Masos just east of Beersheba, the southernmost city under Israelite influence.

"It seems sound," Sarek said as they agreed upon the route and began to turn their attention to planning the strategies and logistics of the operation. "But I, for one, would like to hear David's thoughts before we advance this plan any further."

Only Paltiel was stunned, abruptly remembering business elsewhere. The rest turned in anticipation to where David sat quietly to the side. Palti offered him a raised eyebrow as he departed. The officers looked to David as though waiting to hear from an old and trusted colleague who regularly joined them in such discussions, as he did from that point forward.

CHAPTER TEN
THE CONSTELLATION OF SAPHAN

And the women answered one another as they played, and said, Saul hath slain his thousands, and David his ten thousands.

1 Samuel 18:7

THEIR TRIUMPHANT return to Gibeah at the beginning of the high holy days marked the vaunted conclusion of the longest campaign in the history of the young nation. The army, clad in their new iron battle gear, with weapons never before seen in the hands of any but kings, struck awe into those along the celebratory route through the city. The first iron chariots of Israel actually caused some to cry out in fear as they rumbled through the streets.

Cheers went up as David came into view. The story of his rescue of the prince had beaten them back to the capital by many months. His legend grew, at first with King Saul's collusion, and then in spite of it. For Saul, who had at first used David's victory over Goliath to benefit his cause and to raise tribute for his army and his kingdom, began to see David's rising popularity among the people as a threat to his line.

Samuel's continued silence and lack of response to Saul's ever more elaborate gifts only heightened the monarch's growing fear and suspicion. His fevered mind found more evidence each day that Samuel's prophesy at Amalek was true. Each day he was more convinced that the Lord had forsaken him in favor of another. Saul was afraid to return to the battlefield to surpass David's achievements but equally afraid that David would surpass his own. The demons that David had helped drive from his head were upon him again. His fears and dark dreams seemed more real to him than the world he could see with his own eyes. That fear told him that without the Lord's help, the people would abandon him and choose David as their king.

He sought proof of his suspicions in the least sign. If a cloud fell over the sun during a sacrifice over which he presided, Saul took it as an ill omen. So when David returned to Gibeah, hailed as the great hero he in fact was, Saul saw only dark signs.

The crowd began to sing as Jonathan and David rode together, at the head of the army, toward the raised platform before the temple. The king stood waiting to greet them there, so that together they might make sacrifice to the Lord for their many victories and blessing.

"Praise be to David and to our king for their many victories and the many blessings to us they bring. Praise to Saul for the thousands he has slain by

his skill, and praise be to David for the tens of thousands he has struck down, weapon of the Lord's will."

"The people sing your praises, my prince," Jonathan said. He reined in his mount to allow David to precede him and receive his due praise. He joined the tribute, offering David a jaunty bow from on horseback.

"Don't be absurd," David said, pulling his horse up short so that Jonathan moved ahead. David stood in his stirrups and chanted. "Prince Jonathan, Prince Jonathan, Prince Jonathan," until the crowd stopped singing and joined him.

But as they resumed their pace, the song began anew.

"Thank you, my lord, but you cannot change their hearts," Jonathan said, smiling and reaching out to take David's hand, first to squeeze it affectionately and then to raise it above their heads in triumph. "They love you as I do and cannot help themselves, as I cannot."

"Well, the Lord loves a fool as well as I," David said, struggling to free his hand without success. "Truth be told, though, if the count of our fallen enemy has risen, it is due to being in the field longer because we were better supplied. Our causalities are down and our victories are more substantial because the army is equipped with more iron armor and weapons than before."

"As your father says, 'The way of a fool seems right to him,'" Jonathan quoted. He laughed as they approached the king outside the great temple of Gibeah. "Still, can a man be said a fool for giving credit where it is due?"

King Saul fought to maintain his composure as he heard the songs hailing David for killing his tens of thousands, with only thousands attributed to their king. The demons whispered that David would soon replace him on the throne. When he saw his son and heir bow down to David before the crowds and hold his hand raised as the victor, taking no credit for himself or the house of Saul, he could no longer argue. It was all he could do not to strike David down with the sacrificial knives as he joined Saul on the altar.

Though his hand found the dagger, the demons hissed their darker plan, and Saul complied. Angry though he might be, Saul was no fool. He took full credit for his beloved new commander. He embraced David and kissed him repeatedly on both cheeks before holding his hand aloft and leading the crowd in shouting out David's name.

"Your Majesty," David said, slipping his hand away from Saul's more powerful grasp as soon as it was possible to do so and bowing at the king's feet. "Thank you for allowing me to carry your colors into the field. I am honored to stand here with you."

Graciously the king placed his hand over David's head, as though conferring a blessing. Slipping a finger under David's chin, Saul then raised him up to face him. The king and his son still towered over Jesse's youngest. David looked but a boy beside them, a fact not lost on the king.

The sacrifice made and the public obligations met, the army was encamped outside the city before their seasonal separation allowed them to return to their homes and farms for winter planting. Many soldiers and officers stayed on, joining those already garrisoned at Gibeah as part of the growing standing army, against the unlikely event that their enemies might overcome the rain and mud to mount an attack.

Armories were already being built to accommodate the enormous flow of iron weapons fresh from the forges of Bethlehem. Those soldiers returning home for the season stored their armor and weapons there, awaiting their return the next spring. New weapons and the prospect of new and greater victories inspired ever greater numbers to come forward and fight in the king's army. Training camps had sprung up around the capital to prepare the new recruits in the ways of modern warfare.

The charioteer was the latest of the king's strategies and the talk of the kingdom. The sons of the wealthiest families, who alone could afford the costly iron chariots, had begun to emerge as an elite fighting force. In return for their huge investment, the king granted lands and titles to those who undertook to commission, equip, and man the new rolling juggernauts of destruction.

There was much to celebrate by the time all converged on the banquet hall at the palace, in preparation for the more somber high holy days' observances. The king was well along in his cups before anyone took a bench in the hall. The mood was festive and carefree for all.

Alone together after the festival, Jonathan and David took great delight in bathing and grooming one another in the luxurious privacy of the princely quarters they shared.

"I think this is the best bath I've ever had." David groaned as Jonathan worked rich olive oil and lanolin into his skin.

"It always seems that way after campaign." Jonathan chuckled, taking up the gleaming blade and dragging it against the leather strap to hone it. "After life in a tent six moons passing, a bath and a clean bed are like food to a starving man."

Jonathan guided David's head back, his moist curls resting on the prince's thigh. He brought the blade to David's neck and, with the care of sorting sparrows' eggs, began to shave him.

"And we were at my father's house only three moons back," David said, trying not to move his face too much. His muscles unwound against the warm smooth tiled step of the bathing pool where he sat, only his head and shoulders above the water. "It makes you appreciate what's being celebrated at Sukkot."

"Be still," Jonathan said with a smile. "I'm just glad that after tonight, we can pile the furniture against those doors and stay in this room until spring, if we want."

"And we do." David sighed. He was at perfect peace. It was every dream of their covenant made real. Together they were building a nation they would rule and a life they could share. Everything they had fancied seemed within their grasp. They had only to live out those dreams and meet the future as it came.

David took his turn, shaving Jonathan as he lovingly held his prince's head. Taking full advantage of Jonathan's silence, David spoke of his plans and ideas on every imaginable topic from decorations for their rooms to reorganizing divisions of the army. Jonathan, glad that he was not expected to respond, enjoyed the shower of words as one appreciates favorite music. All was as he wished it would be.

Clean and shaved, they rubbed each other's bodies with scented oils and fine perfumes.

Clad in their finest robes, they made their way arm in arm to the banquet hall to receive the tributes and accolades that were their due after such incomparable success. Theirs was a private celebration in the midst of the great one all around them.

The king was drunk and rowdy already by the time they arrived in the hall. Queen Ahinoam and Jonathan's sisters made a brief appearance early on and then retired to the queen's dining room for their own, less raucous festivities. They left word of their favor for Jonathan and David along with gifts and tokens to welcome them home.

The two heroes made their way to their place at the head table. They paused often to accept greetings and praise from those they had left behind and many who had accompanied them on campaign. All were in their thrall. Though the victory and the celebration were for their country, it was clear the evening had come to be in their honor—particularly David's.

The crowd turned from the king and his antics as soon as the two young princes arrived. Saul soon realized he was playing to the backs of his own party guests. Unsteadily he climbed onto the table, kicking aside the plates and platters there. Raising his glass to the heavens, he silenced the room with a rueful cry.

"To the prince and my harp player, the heroes of Israel," Saul shouted with a mocking tone.

Oblivious of the slur, the crowd cheered them wildly. They raised their glasses to the two young men, who hastened nearer the king as much to catch him should he lose his perch as to accept his barbed salute. Both easily set aside the nasty edge of his toast as the sour sediment of the wine.

"Ignore him tonight. He's in a strange mood," Jonathan said for David's hearing alone as they drew near to their places.

The king's vitriol toward David continued as the crowd looked on, bewildered.

"Truly we should drink to this country of ours, the land of opportunity," the king bellowed, continuing his broad performance. "Where else could a shepherd learn to play the harp and use his music to elbow his way to the king's table, a hero to the people? To Israel," the king proclaimed, lofting his goblet.

Well, who couldn't drink to that? David and Jonathan raised their glasses and drank too, but it was a bitter vintage they swallowed as Saul's rampage continued.

"Truly the Lord has blessed this boy. He himself admits that his greatest strategy was borrowed from an unclean animal," the king wheezed with drink and laughter. "Only the Lord could bestow victory on such a simpleton. Praise be to the Lord."

Once again, who would not be seen praising the Lord? Once again, Jonathan was forced to drink with David to his own derision.

"My king," David said, tugging humbly at the hem of Saul's robe as he stood on the table still. "Please, my lord, if I have done something to harm you, tell me that I might make it right. Or banish me, that my sight might not offend you. But abuse me no more, for I am miserable if I am not in your favor, whom I serve most humbly with my every thought and deed."

David's words and the emotions implicit moved all those who heard his appeal. Every eye turned to the king, as much for explanation of his denunciation of Israel's great hero as to witness their reconciliation, for who could turn from such a plea?

"Well," said the king, touching David's forehead with the toe of his sandal. "It is good to know that you remember that I am your king. To hear the songs your followers sang today, one would think it is the other way around."

Paltiel could hardly suppress his delight in seeing David returned to his proper place. In his heart, though, he held out little hope of ever restoring his place within the prince's household.

"Father, you forget yourself," Jonathan said, rising and grasping his father's foot, nearly toppling the drunken king.

"I clearly remember that I am the king," Saul said, kicking at his son as he struggled to maintain his balance. "Perhaps it is not I who needs reminding? As I recall, for instance, this man who is being hailed as the greatest hero in the history of Israel and the Lord's chosen is in fact my court musician and assigned to see to your, um, needs?"

The color boiled up Jonathan's neck and across his face. He fought the urge to strike his own father for impugning his beloved, cheapening what was between them, his slurs and slanders accidentally striking too near truth.

David, who still knelt below the king's feet, arose and backed away, bowing reverently. He made his way to the musicians nearby, who had long since stopped playing. No music had seemed well chosen to accompany the spectacle. Taking up the harp, he began to play and sing in tribute to his king.

"Some trust in chariots, and some in horses: but we will remember the name of the Lord our God. They are brought down and fallen: but we are risen, and stand upright. Save, Lord: let the king hear us when we call."

Despite David's words, they inspired only the king's fury when he observed the effect they had on all who listened. The room, transfixed by Saul's cruel words only a breath before, again turned their backs to their true king to hear David's sweet ones.

The demons were upon him. Saul's eyes fell on the long battle spear, loosely held at the side of one of his personal guards. Enthralled by David's beautiful voice, the guardsman grew too forgetful of any threat to hold his weapon firmly. From where he stood on the table, Saul grasped the upper shaft of the spear. Quickly shouldering the javelin, with skills learned on too many battlefields to number, the king aimed for David's heart and launched the newly forged iron shaft before anyone noticed.

"*Lord, save the king,*" David repeated, rising in tribute to Saul. The spear, off its mark already from the quantity of wine the king imbibed pierced David's flowing robe, where his cheek would have been had he still been seated. The fine linen garment pinned him to the wall panels behind the stage.

The uproar that followed was overwhelming. The king's drunken laughter rose above the fray. In the confusion, Jonathan, unnoticed, overturned the table on which his own father stood. He leaped into the roiling crowd in an effort to reach David and free him before another attack.

David tore away most of his robe to escape. Barely covered by what remained of his finery, he escaped the hall, reduced to little more than rags at the whim of his king.

Unable to reach David through the crowd, Jonathan wheeled on his father. Saul staggered to his feet, fighting off all offers of assistance in his drunken rage.

"Father, what have you done?" Jonathan said, grasping the front of Saul's robe. Struggling, Jonathan held him in an angry embrace, afraid that the darkness was again upon his beloved father.

"Let go of me, you fool," Saul said, striking out at his son. The two men struggled. No man was sure enough of himself, or his place, or the outcome, to risk restraining either man. "Do you want to give away your throne to that, that, sheepherder?"

"What are you talking about? Have you taken leave of your senses?" Jonathan demanded, ignoring the slaps his father rained on his face as their struggle continued. "David is part of the family. What threat can he be?"

"Do you suppose I would be king if I had given the credit for all my victories to your Uncle Abner?" Saul shouted within hearing of his own general.

Jonathan fell silent. He longed to tell his father that David could no more be a threat to his prospects or his kingdom than Ahinoam could be to Saul's. He looked at the pathetic drunken wretch. Saul clawed at Jonathan's hands to try to escape his grasp. He wondered if there would ever be a time or place to speak of such matters to a man on whose reaction he could never depend.

With a wave of disgust and a mighty heave, Jonathan threw his father into Abner's arms. Glaring a warning to both men, the prince stormed out of the dining room. The hall was in such disarray and chaos that the queen and her party stood outside the door, trembling in fear for the lives of those inside.

"Oh, Jonathan, what has happened?" Ahinoam pleaded, hanging on his robes as his father had only just done.

"Your husband is drunk, my lady, and has mightily offended me and my beloved David," Jonathan said, taking and removing her hand firmly from his robe. "See to him, and see that he finds the words to ask for forgiveness, though he should not expect it. We will remain in my rooms and await the king's apology."

With that Jonathan left his mother to weep in his sisters' arms. He raced back to his rooms in search of David. There was no one aside from servants in their apartments. David's clothes and harp remained behind. Jonathan felt pale reassurance that David had not left the city. Still, he could not be certain, and waiting for David's return proved impossible. He stormed out of the rooms and strode down the hall when a thought stopped him short. Returning, he located a small bundle hidden behind an old decorative shield that hung on the sitting room wall. Concealing it in a pouch under his sash, he went out again in search of David.

Jonathan roamed the halls. He pounded on doors and shouted David's name to the unexpressed dismay of many whom he encountered. Those who offered him words of comfort or conciliation toward the king got a sound beating. Reports spread quickly that the prince was on a rampage through the palace in search of David.

News reached a guard at the back gate, who had seen David leave and observed the direction in which he'd gone. He begged his commander to allow him to go briefly to the prince to impart the information and, he hoped, stem the growing tide of discord that was sweeping through the palace. Granted leave by his superior, equally dismayed by the prince's uncharacteristic behavior, the guard bravely ran toward the noise and shouting. He found Prince Jonathan in a formal reception hall, wailing for David's return as he tore a tapestry off the wall that had been a gift to his father from the city of Jezreel.

"My prince," the guard said, dropping to one knee in a low bow before Jonathan. "I have news of the whereabouts of him you seek."

"Speak, then, and be quick," Jonathan shouted, tossing aside the torn remnants of the fine weaving.

"He has gone out into the wilderness to the east, my prince," the guard said, his voice shaking with fear for his own safety. "He left through the gardens by the private royal gates, as you sometimes do late at night."

In an instant Jonathan knew. He swept up the terrified man and kissed him on both cheeks. "A blessing on your house always," Jonathan exulted, holding him at arm's length like a treasure he wished to admire. "See me tomorrow—late—and we will discuss your promotion for your exemplary service to me this night."

"Thank you, Your High—" the man managed to stay before Prince Jonathan tossed him to the floor, bounding from the room as though fleeing for his life.

For I have said, Mercy shall be built up for ever: thy faithfulness shalt thou establish in the very heavens.

Psalms 89:2

ONLY THE stars of the night sky beheld David's tears. He sat weeping for his lost dreams. His hopes had been dashed before, but somehow it hurt much worse to fall from such a height than simply not to have reached it at all.

It was the sound of his crying that told Jonathan his guess was right as he approached the great rock Ezel. Silently he climbed to their secret place. He took his lover into his arms without a word. He held David as his sobs shook him with renewed vigor. Tears wet Jonathan's eyes, but so long as he had David in his arms, there was no loss that could not be borne. His only thoughts were of how to bring David comfort.

For a time the easy silence between them was more soothing than any words. The intensity of David's sorrow soon flared into blazing sexual passion. But the prince stayed David's ardor, though he too was near to surrendering to David's loving fervor when he tore himself away.

"No, we have been too long in the field for me to forsake the comforts of sharing a proper bed with you tonight," Jonathan said, holding David's hands above his head to contain him.

"I need you now," David pleaded, struggling in vain against Jonathan's advantage.

"And I long to take you tonight, but in our bed, under our roof," Jonathan insisted.

"What roof might we share tonight?" David said, surrendering, falling slack in the prince's grasp. "I am surely not welcome in the palace. The king has denounced me. Who would take us in?"

"Shhhh," Jonathan said as David fell weeping against his shoulder. "The palace is your home. My father behaved shamefully, and I have made it clear in no uncertain terms that we will remain in our rooms until he has apologized to you and to me for the disrespect he showed you."

"Our rooms?" David asked, looking up.

"Yes, ours," Jonathan said, kissing him on the top of the head. "This is your home. I cannot guarantee that you will have no fights with my father—our father. I can tell you that I've had twenty and nine years' worth, and it is still my home."

David managed a weak laugh.

"I have something for you," Jonathan said, searching in the recess of their secret place on the great rock for a candle and flint. Striking a spark, he managed to ignite a little straw that he touched to the wick. "There, now we can see each other. Gods, you look a mess."

"You are too kind, my lord." David sighed, holding up his arms to hide his face.

"Here, let me," Jonathan said, wiping David's face with his fine robes and smoothing his hair with loving hands. "As for that little bit of robe barely covering you, I would consider it a gift if we might save that for future private uses."

"I can read that story in your mind," David said with folded arms. He could not hide his smile, even in the darkness.

"A blind illiterate could just now," Jonathan said, pressing himself against David to make his point.

"Are we to save that gift for future uses, as well?" David asked with a playful growl as he melted into Jonathan's grasp.

"No, my prince; though that too is your intended tribute, I have another gift yet in mind for you," Jonathan said with a hoarse gasp, once again fighting his own nature and setting David aside. "It is but this."

He produced the bundle from his sash and unraveled it to reveal two small soapstone boxes. One he placed in David's hand.

"How lovely," David said, turning the box over, curious.

"Funny," Jonathan said, eyebrow arched. He placed his hands over David's smaller ones. "The lid slides."

The breath caught in David's throat as the candle and starlight mingled to illuminate the box's contents.

"Oh, Jonathan, it's...."

"It's not the sun and the moon, but it is our stars," Jonathan said, taking the gold signet ring from the box and placing it onto David's finger. "See how the jewels are set just as the stars in our constellation of saphan? I had them made while we were away."

"Them?"

"Yes, one for me too," Jonathan said. He fished the second box out of his robes and gave it to David. With newly practiced fingers, he slid the lid aside and removed the identical, if larger, ring. He knew instinctively to put it on Jonathan's finger.

The prince took David in his arms.

"So long as those stars are in the heavens, my love shall last for you. This is your home. This is our home."

David was crying again, but there were no sobs, only joy as his dreams rose higher than he'd ever dared dream them.

"Come," Jonathan said. He rose and offered his hand. "Let's go home."

Faithful are the wounds of a friend; but the kisses of an enemy are deceitful.

Proverbs 27:6

THE KING'S apologies were swiftly made. Still, the evil spirits of pride, envy, greed, and wrath remained upon him, not so easily assuaged as hurt feelings after a drunken fight. The winter passed in a tense peace between prince and father.

David and Jonathan devoted themselves to training in good weather. Otherwise they remained in the prince's rooms. Alone in their own private world together, they were shy of the public life of the palace and its ceremonies. Though careful to do their duty, they remained absent from all other view.

It was thought by all that their estrangement was due to the king's vicious public attack on David, which was, in part, true. In many ways, though, the supposed animosity proved a great blind for their joy in being alone together. They were heedless of others' perception of their feelings for each other and their delight in their own company. Time and their private happiness tempered any harsh feelings they harbored. Both loved and respected the king too much to count him out for the careless words of a wine-soaked tongue.

Paltiel, crowded from the prince's company, was eager to find a new place and a new future for himself at court. At his first opportunity, he asked Jonathan for his blessing and influence in attaining a post working for the minister of the king's treasury. He had observed that the post would put him into greater contact with the king, as well as gain him the power and prestige that came from the control of the king's treasure. When the wealthy youth who had held the post became a charioteer through his rich father's patronage, the timing seemed to Paltiel to be right to plead his case to the prince.

"Well, of course, Palti," Jonathan readily agreed when his old friend asked for his help in getting the new job. He hoped his true feelings were not evident to Palti. "I had no idea you had interest in such things as the coin of the realm. Other than spending it."

"Surely you've noticed I'm not much one for the battlefield." Paltiel laughed, both pleased and stung by how effortlessly the prince could let him go.

"What I have noticed, old friend, is how easy you have made it for me to live on the battlefield all of our lives," Jonathan said. He knew the parting was best, but he did not look forward to finding and training a new armor-bearer he could trust as he did Paltiel. "It will be my great loss, though, I hope, a gain for you."

"You do me honor," Paltiel said with a bow to the prince.

"Let us go at once to speak with Father about your new post," Jonathan said, throwing his arm over Paltiel's shoulder. Sweeping his friend along, the prince drew him toward the great hall where he knew his father was doing the business of the kingdom.

David was glad to be freed of Paltiel, ever underfoot and lurking behind any available arras. He had seemed a friend and confidant to the prince, at least, but David did not trust him.

"I am sorry you will not have your friend at hand," David said of Paltiel's departure, during an awkward supper in their quarters with a strange new attendant.

"Really? I did not think you felt at all warmly toward my old confederate," Jonathan mused, catching David short with his piercing dark gaze and insightful grin.

"I find that my first thoughts, in this and all things, are not of myself," David said, drawing himself up to deflect the inevitable teasing he knew would follow.

"That is most selfless of you," Jonathan said, nodding and resuming his meal. "I welcome the change. Palti was a part of my bachelor life. I am a bachelor no more."

David blushed at the unexpected tribute.

"Palti and I had a lot of fun. We got into a fair amount of trouble and helped each other to grow up," Jonathan said, smiling at the pleasant memories. "We were very, very close. Now that you are here, it was hard to dismiss someone to his own rooms who almost always slept in mine."

David looked up sharply.

"Not as you and I spend the nights together, but as something more like brothers," Jonathan added quickly, to avoid any further confrontations with David over his former intimate. "Still, the time has come to put away childish things. It is a blessing to my old friend and a relief to me that Palti has found a new place on his own. I'm not sure I could ever, in good conscience, have asked him to go."

David's sigh of relief was a silent one but no less real.

"Well, then, I'm glad it's worked out so well for you both," David agreed, toying with the uneaten food at his place. His appetite eluded him.

"Yes." Jonathan nodded, chewing a bite ruminatively. "That and the fact that I won't have to live with you two wildcats pacing each other off, circling the same cage day and night for the rest of my life."

"Yes, my lord," David said. "There's that."

The two fought back their laughter as long as they were able, which was not long.

Inspired by candor and relief, David offered an impersonation of Palti's officious greetings upon his arrival at the palace and his instructions to David later when he first met Jonathan. Their laughter grew as Jonathan chimed in with his own interpretation of the saucy boy from Bethlehem, who had made short work of Paltiel before he turned on the prince to dress him down and win his heart.

Neither knew that Paltiel, who had returned for some of his things, overheard their laughter and impersonations from where he stood, as he so often had, just beyond their sight but not far enough to be out of hearing. Any remaining loyalty

Palti felt burned away in the blaze of his anger. His heart went dead cold where the two were concerned. He made swiftly away, vowing to regain the power he had lost and resolved to erode whatever footing David held.

These were not the only feelings at court to be considered following the king's unfortunate showing at the banquet.

Eliab and Joab both were still in service to Abner and in the king's elite guard. Both privately expressed their feelings and their loyalty to David as soon, following the incident, as was discreet.

"Saul may be the king, but it is you, David, who we truly follow," Eliab blurted out as soon as they were on their own in the prince's apartments when court business took Jonathan away. "I speak for the other brothers as well."

"And for me and mine," Joab added. "To put such shame on the house of Jesse, when you have served him so well, cannot be forgotten."

"The king has apologized," David said firmly. Such a declaration of respect from two elders, who had recently regarded him as little more than an ornament in their father's house, touched him deeply.

"Well, he has not apologized as publicly as he insulted you." Joab sniffed.

"In truth," Eliab agreed. "We do not mean the king any disloyalty; we simply wanted to make it clear that we are loyal to you and to the king because you follow him, not the other way around."

"I thank you, brothers," David said, embracing each in turn. "Though you are my nephew, Joab, you have been as much an older brother to me as the seven others to whom nature granted the title."

"Thank you, David," Joab said, stepping back from the embrace and striking his chest in salute. "I am honored that you would think of me so."

"I would be further honored if you would both remember Prince Jonathan as a brother as well. Offer to him the same loyalty you would offer me," David said earnestly, looking each man in the eye until he had so sworn.

Both easily granted the request, forgiving Jonathan's blameless affiliation.

David was touched and amused. Both, Eliab especially, had said far worse to him in front of their father than the king had implied before the rabble in the hall, though, in truth, neither had tried as hard to kill him.

For David, the gravest aspect of the event had come in the form of his own slight, turning and leaving Jonathan without explanation or consideration.

Though Jonathan assured him that it was of no consequence each of the thousand times David apologized for it, he also was glad of the depth of David's feelings each time.

In the end they agreed on a new sign to express their feelings when words were not possible: each would hold his clenched fist over his heart. With the other hand, they would touch the matching signet they both now wore. The sign was to remind them of that night, to reaffirm the love and the oath they had sworn to one another under the stars of their constellation.

Chapter Eleven
The Megiddo Pass

Therefore Saul removed [David] from him, and made him his captain over a thousand; and he went out and came in before the people.

1 Samuel 18:13

"FATHER, YOU cannot mean this." Jonathan railed at Saul's unexpected decision just days before the prince was to lead the army on spring campaign. "What advantage is there in dividing the army?"

"Oh, hardly that," Saul scoffed, slopping wine from his goblet in a comic little salute. "I'd scarcely entrust half my army to that overrated novice."

"Please do not speak ill of him to me," Jonathan said, putting his hand on the hilt of his sword without thinking.

"Or what, you'll strike me down?" Saul bellowed, throwing the remainder of his wine in his son's face. "Do you choose loyalty to David over your loyalty to me?"

"Do you test me in this, Father?" Jonathan said, wiping the dregs from his face fiercely. "I cannot be sure of my heart in this. You would do well not to gamble on it."

"How can you speak to your own father thus?" Saul wailed, surging forward until their heaving chests were touching.

"I would say the same to David should he ask me to make such a choice," Jonathan said, undaunted by the king's wrath. "Yet I know in my heart he never would. I would have thought the same of you. Is it you, Father, or the spirits that speak to me now?"

They stared in angry silence for what seemed an eternity to those who witnessed their enmity.

"Keep your pretty words," Saul said, turning away. "My decision is made. You may tell your boy yourself if you like, but he leaves tomorrow for the north with a thousand new recruits."

Jonathan could not speak. Heartbreak at again losing the father he'd seen restored swept over him. He stormed from the throne room vibrating with rage and sorrow, leaving his father and his ministers to their palace intrigue.

"Your Majesty, allow me," Paltiel said, taking Saul's arm. He helped the king into a private chamber nearby. Away from public view, he spoke soothing words as he helped the king off with his wine-soaked robe, even as he pressed a goblet, freshly filled, into the king's hand.

With just such simple yet solicitous acts, Paltiel had found his way quickly into the king's favor. Once installed in his new post, he took every opportunity to flatter and appeal to the king's growing pride and vanity. Whenever duty brought him into the royal presence, he skillfully fanned Saul's envy and anger toward David, even as he made himself indispensable.

In fact, Paltiel had become so essential in the royal chambers, the minister of the treasury had been forced to select an aide to Paltiel to fulfill Paltiel's actual duties to the ministry. The minister could not afford to offend the king and would not sacrifice the influence with the throne he believed Paltiel earned him.

"Palti, can you account for it?" the king asked as Paltiel helped him on with fresh garments. "You know the prince better than anyone. You were boys together, grew up together. What has become of my son?"

"I cannot truly say, sire." Paltiel shrugged, choosing each word carefully. He had refrained from making clear to the king the nature of the prince's most intimate relationship, though many at court already knew. He chose to save the revelation for his most opportune moment. "I have not enjoyed the prince's confidence since David's arrival."

"David, David, always David," the king railed. "There is the root of so many of my worries."

"Well, when the prince marries, his priorities will change," Paltiel said in a soothing tone. "I'm sure that once Your Majesty had a son, your thoughts turned away from the pursuits of young men." Paltiel hid his smile.

"Well, I suppose." The king chuckled, slurping some of his wine as Paltiel redraped his robes. "Though being chosen king killed my youth like an old man turns to stone—in an instant."

"So, too, will the responsibilities of marriage and the weighty prospect of the crown bring the prince's head down out of the clouds," Paltiel said with loving patience, smoothing the king's cloak and topping up the king's goblet. "Now, sire, you look your best. Your ministers await you."

"Yes, a wife would do the prince a world of good," the king mused as Paltiel, grinning, led him back into the ministry hall.

And Saul was afraid of David, because the Lord was with him, and was departed from Saul.

1 Samuel 18:12

"HE WISHES you ill," Jonathan insisted, as if David was arguing.

"Your father is doing what he thinks is best." David sighed, trying to calm Jonathan. Though he too was troubled, he knew there was no changing their fate. His heart had shattered on hearing of the king's plan, but the challenge strengthened his resolve. "No man is a hero to his lover's father. This is an opportunity for me to prove to your father, the crown, and all the skeptics at court, once and for all, that I am a loyal and capable commander, worthy of his trust."

"What else do you need to do to prove that to him?" Jonathan shouted, leaping to his feet and stalking across the room. "You have swept the Philistines from the field, stolen the secret of their supremacy, and enriched our own trade and commerce. In the process you've raised our army of farmers, armed with ornamental bits of sharpened bronze, stones, and sticks, into a formidable modern force."

"I am a farmer, and I defeated Goliath with a stone." David laughed. Jonathan knelt and rested his head in David's lap. David twirled the dark curls around his fingers. "My sweet prince, I am glad of the opportunity that your father offers me to stand on my own. I'm youngest and slightest of eight brothers. Sometimes it feels as if I have traded their protection for yours, gratefully. To be entrusted with my own command is an opportunity for which I am equally grateful.

"Though if you could see inside me you'd know," he added, stroking Jonathan's hair. "My heart breaks that I shall be separated from you for the season."

"Well then, wise prince, we had best make the most of the time we have left," Jonathan said, sweeping David from the stool where he sat and falling upon him.

THE TWO lovers parted, tearfully in private and bravely in public. Jonathan set out with the full force of the army to patrol the tranquil southern provinces of Judah and the Negev that the two had spent the previous season subduing. David and his band of a thousand raw recruits were off to the incursions and raids of the north. Eliab and Joab had been unable to free themselves from their commands and obligations to Abner. Though both had threatened in private to resign their commissions, David insisted that they were too valuable to Israel to forsake their duties over the perception of a slight.

"Not many men I know have been given a thousand men at arms and sent off to make what they can of their reputation," David pointed out. In the end, his kinsmen and a growing number of commanders within the army relented. They let David go alone, more in obedience to his private wishes and respect for the prince than any loyalty they felt to their public duty.

The king celebrated, he said, in anticipation of the victories to come, but in truth because he thought he had put an end to his David problem. To see David die a hero's death in battle would not only suit the king's purpose but free him of responsibility for a loss he did not want on his hands. Instead, David's popularity and the resulting grief would assist the king, he thought, in raising more funds and more men with which to wage his wars and make the country whole.

The king's plan turned out to be far more brilliant than he could have imagined.

Fist over his heart, touching the golden signet, David bid farewell to Jonathan, who mirrored the gesture—their private sign of fidelity and promise. He felt his heart race in his chest but smiled in spite of his feelings. Exhilarated by his fear, his sights set on Shechem and the fertile and much disputed Jezreel Valley, David embarked on his first command. Leaving home, security, and all he loved behind, he led his company north.

They followed the Road of the Patriarchs first to the holy city of Ramah. Their arrival was met with the kind of triumphal celebration better suited to a conquering army returning from campaign than an unproven brigade just setting out. David was unprepared for their reception. Their camp was prepared for them. The city fathers offered up a feast in their honor. A sacrifice to victory was made at Samuel's own temple, though the holy judge was away in Shiloh.

Returning to his tent, David found a line of petitioners awaiting him.

"What is this about, Ami?" David asked his lieutenant, calling him aside.

The boy was not much older than David had been when he first came to court. Ami had seen no more of the world than one could spy on the way from his home in Anathoth to Gibeah, little more than a morning's walk. He seemed terrified of most everything, despite many months of training in one of Gibeah's finest new training camps. Ami was proficient with a sword, a bow, and a spear; it was the world and the people in it that unsettled him.

"I'm uncertain, my lord," Ami stammered, falling in behind his legendary commander. "They have all come demanding to speak to you. Many are armed with fine iron weapons. We have kept close watch on them, but so far there has been no incident."

"I see," David said, looking over the decidedly unthreatening line of farm boys. "Well, I shall try to see as many as I can, but the sun is low and I must rest, for we leave tomorrow."

"Yes, my lord," Ami said with an awkward bow.

"Ami, call me captain or sir," David said, a reassuring hand on the boy's shoulder.

"Yes, my lord," Ami said without a trace of humor.

David held his laugh until he was alone in his tent, but only just.

"This way," Ami said from the open flaps of David's tent. Sword drawn, he warily escorted the first of the petitioners into David's presence.

"My great captain," the first boy said, falling to his knees at David's feet.

"Well," David said, still startled by the tone of his reception at Ramah. "What is your name?"

"I am Felix ben Ibrahim," the young man said, his face turned to the ground still.

"What business have you here at the king's encampment?" David asked. Reaching down, he cupped the boy's chin and raised his face so their eyes could meet.

"I would fight at your side if you would have me, great captain," Felix said, raising his face without resistance and raising no hand to touch David's. "It would be my honor to die in your cause."

"Well, Felix," David said, startled. He took his hand away. The boy did not look away or blink. "I hope it won't come to that. Wait outside and I will speak to Ami about getting you assigned.

"Ami," David called out.

The lieutenant came bounding in, his sword drawn, ready for battle.

"Ami." David stayed him with a firm tone. "Put your sword away until I command otherwise."

"Yes, my lord captain," Ami said, really only obeying when he saw that Felix still knelt at David's feet.

"Ami, this is Felix," David said, taking the boy's shoulder and urging him back to his feet. "He would join us. See to him for now. Find him a place to wait. I will deal with him presently. Bring in the next petitioner."

"Oh, if I may, my lord captain," Felix said, adopting Ami's address.

David winced; he knew he had not heard the last of this. "Yes, Felix?"

"All here seek to join your army," Felix said, gesturing to the line of men outside the tent. The man at the head of the line nodded vigorously in agreement. "We would follow you into battle or wherever you would lead us."

David's brow knit as he followed the two outside and addressed the group.

"Who here would join us as we go north on behalf of our king?" David shouted.

Sword, fists, and voices raised in assent.

"Well then, we welcome you," David answered, choked by the sentiment. "We do not have food, weapons, or accommodations for you all, but we will do what we can to help and share what we do have now."

"My lord captain," Felix said, falling to his knees again. "We have brought our own tents and supplies. I for one have money for iron weapons, if you can supply them."

"Aye, my lord captain," another from the line said, falling to his knees. "I do as well."

"As do I, my lord captain," said another and another.

"And I, my lord captain," man after man said until most of the few score men there were kneeling where they had stood.

"I shall send word to Bethlehem for weapons and armor to meet us at Shechem," David called to his new conscripts. "We march at dawn. Get supper and get rest. Stragglers are not tolerated in the king's army."

Accompanied by cheers, David returned to his tent. He fell to his knees with prayers of thanks for this auspicious start to his campaign command.

It was the same the following day when they arrived in Mizpah. There they were met by several hundred men. They had heard that David was leading a campaign to the north and needed no other reason to volunteer. More than a thousand awaited them at Ai and more still in Bethel.

David's fame preceded him in each town and village of Israel he passed. The young men fell in step behind him. Training as they marched, they acquired what armor and weapons they needed at their own expense, for a more modest cost than had been true a year before. The advent of iron from Bethlehem was changing the trade and building a new age.

Charioteers, eager for adventure and the chance to try out their metal-tipped arrows from the backs of their iron chariots, rode out to join David, adding their fearsome presence to his corps.

By the time they met their first enemy, a siege force of Philistines plaguing Jezreel, David had built his army of a thousand into ten times that.

Though the reception at Jezreel lacked the festivity of many previous cities on their tour, it was no less sincere. The elders held council with David to advise him of their plight and to plead for his assistance.

"Most of our wheat and barley harvests are stolen." Ethan, their leader, spoke for the council, though many echoed his words to affirm them. "Their raids have all but ended trade. We have not gotten a single shipment of grain south of Shechem."

"Who is doing this?" David asked, hoping it was merely bandits and wondering if his men could face the challenge of a true army.

"It is the Philistines." Ethan sighed. "So long as they hold the pass at Megiddo, they control the road to Damascus and the sea road to Egypt."

"And they can raid the whole of the valley at will," Abiram interrupted, grandly, earning a look from Ethan. He raised his shoulders in reply. "It is the truth. This has been their way so long as they have held the pass."

"Dislodging the Philistines from Megiddo is more than we need or can ask," Ethan said, trying for patience but not very hard. "Perhaps, my lord Captain David, you could take a message to the king, that the bounty of the Jezreel Valley could be secured."

"I thank you all for you wise counsel," David said, nodding thoughtfully. "I wonder if there are maps of the area that might guide me in a survey of the valley?"

"Indeed, yes," Abiram answered boldly. "My father's library has the finest charts of the valley, made during his days as leader of this council and preserved there on the council's behalf to this day. They are yours, as well as the best supper my humble kitchens may offer you, my lord captain."

David surrendered correcting the title he'd been granted by his high-strung lieutenant. "I would be honored if you would entrust your treasured legacy to me as I would be to take a meal at your table."

This also meant dinners with Ethan and all the other members of the council. It was an obligation David took gladly. The Jezreel Valley was called the breadbasket. The fertile province was the most productive farming region in all of Israel, and the tables of its wealthy first families groaned in agreement. David was well fed and his nights well spent. He was feted, entertained, and presented with the eldest single daughters of all the first families of the valley tribes of Issachar and Zebulun.

His days were filled with a careful assessment of the region aided by the excellent maps from the house of Abiram.

His men, too, were well fed, both from the supply lines David had built on his way there and the generosity of their hosts. Their days, though, were harder. They spent hours in the summer sun in intensive and much-needed training, though for what, they were not yet certain. It mattered not. So long as their beloved captain commanded it, they were unstinting in their compliance.

David spent time in prayer and map study. He looked to both for guidance to find a strategy that might secure the Jezreel Valley for King Saul and the lives of his men.

Abiram was right. The pass at Megiddo was the key. David knew if he could take and secure that, he could take and hold the whole of the important valley and the rich trade routes that ran through it. It was clear to him why Megiddo was called the crossroads of the world. If all nations were to make one great final war, they would surely meet at Megiddo, he thought.

In his heart, though, he knew that Ethan too was right. Victory against the Philistines' skill and numbers was too much to ask of an untried commander and inexperienced troops. Should he just do what he could to protect these people and seek the king's advice and intervention?

David longed for Jonathan's counsel as much as his embrace. He was much tempted by the wiles of the local women, who were brazen in their flirtation. In fine homes he had more than once "accidentally" seen the ankles of daughters and serving women. In the streets and markets from Jezreel to Tanaach, the women were so forward they would have made Anah blush. He smiled fondly as he thought of Anah and Korah and the little souk at Bethlehem.

The market at Megiddo took his breath away. It was not only the largest he had ever seen, but there were goods he had only heard of, bound to Cairo and Damascus. He came in the guise of a peasant farmer and actually sold the ephah of barley he'd brought with him as part of his disguise.

More impressive than the market was the Philistine force that held the pass. Spread across the valley and along the Kishon River, they could easily fall back to defend the pass or advance their line forward to defend the town and villages scattered across the valley floor. Their numbers too were impressive, more than twice the ten thousand that now followed him.

David was up by lamplight, poring over Abiram's charts, copied and amended to include the details he had scouted from the region.

"My lord captain," Ami said, striking his chest and raising his hand in salute as he entered. David smiled. Ami always made the salute with such vigor, it looked mildly painful, though the lieutenant's zeal never failed to charm. "I waner fi miget du nfing," Ami yawned broadly, flushing in embarrassment even before he'd got his breath back. "I'm sorry, sir. I was just wondering if I might get you anything, my lord captain, sire." The words poured out of the young man, his ears and face scarlet.

David hid his laugh behind his hand as Ami began fussing about the table where David worked.

"Perhaps some more wine or water," Ami offered, knocking over the ewer and spilling its contents across the chart David was looking at. "Oh, my lord, I'm, I, I mean…. My lord, forgive me, I…. Captain, it's just that, I was only trying to…."

David dissolved into fits of laughter as the lieutenant trailed off.

Ami rushed around to try to mop up the disaster and save David's work.

"Ah, Ami." David sighed, spent and lighter of heart. "I thank you for that. Ah, look."

David pointed at the stitching on the hide chart.

"You've washed the Philistines away," David said with a note of triumph. "I'd put them in here with a bit of kohl, and now they're gone. If only it were that easy in the real valley."

"I'm sorry, my lord," Ami said, putting his hands behind his back to defer any further disaster. "I was only trying to, well, it's so late, sir."

David only stared at the map.

"If there's nothing else, my lord," Ami said, growing uncomfortable with David's silence.

Still David did not respond. He threw the chart down on the table and began furiously drawing on it with a stick of kohl.

"By your leave, my lord?" Ami said. A note of pleading began to creep into his voice, as it often did when he was scared.

"That's it," David said. Leaping to his feet, he embraced the terrified lieutenant, who winced for fear that David would strike him.

Instead Ami's idol, the man he admired above all things, whose life he prized above his own, whom he would gladly follow into the jaws of the enemy and death, kissed him on the lips.

"That's it," David cried again, releasing the now dazed young man. "You did it, Ami. You did it."

Ami did not hear much else that night. His heart was beating too loudly to make out much else of what David seemed to be celebrating. There was not a second kiss, and David showed no signs of remembering the first one. But Ami never forgot it.

"We begin tomorrow," David said. "Good night, Ami."

"Good night, my lord captain," Ami said as he drifted out of the tent and back to the one he shared with another lieutenant. Unable to express what he truly felt that night, Ami fell on his tentmate, and the two spent a night together that almost made Ami forget what had put him in such a mood. Almost.

The only thing David remembered the next morning was the answer to his prayers and plans.

He assembled his lieutenants, laid out his strategy, and gave orders to muster the troops at dawn of the next day.

The Philistines were aware of the presence of David's forces outside Jezreel. They had no interest in attacking them there. Their interest was in allowing the locals to bring in their crops without destroying them. They planned to appropriate the harvest for their pentapolis and their own purposes. But when David's small band of soldiers launched a frontal assault on them at Megiddo, they were forced to respond. Like ants from their hill, they poured onto the plain first to attack and then give chase to the surprisingly small force David had sent to take such a valuable and well-fortified stronghold. The Philistines easily took the upper hand and were quickly in pursuit of the raiding party that presumed to take the prized pass the city straddled.

Confidently the Philistines drove the small but valiant army of Israel north to the swampy banks of the Kishon River. Victory eluded them there. Rafts awaited the small Israelite corps. They were halfway across the river before the Philistines realized too late that they were trapped.

Ten thousand men at arms cut off their escape. David had simply led the Philistines to their doom. Driving them to the river would have been costly of both lives and resources, and he had other plans for both.

What his men lacked in experience, they made up for in spirit. Though they were outnumbered more than two to one, they backed the Philistines into the swamplands along the river. More of the enemy drowned than were harmed by his men. Those who survived escaped through the pass. David secured Megiddo and the trade routes to Acco, Galilee, and Damascus, as well as the whole of the rich Jezreel Valley under Israel's control. He even captured the Philistine granaries, returning the harvest to the control of the elders of the valley.

David spent the remainder of the summer building outposts to secure and sustain his victories there. By his return to Gibeah for Rosh Hashanah, David had expanded the size of the army of Israel, cemented the northern provinces, secured their borders as never before, and filled the king's treasury to overflowing.

Both Ami and Felix remained behind to command those who defended the pass and ensure that the fall harvest of Jezreel would be delivered to market. David was sad to bid them farewell but only too happy to return to Gibeah and his prince.

Jonathan's tour, aside from ridding the countryside of a few scrofulous bandits, was quiet and uneventful. David's victories and accomplishments were among Israel's greatest.

The king was beside himself.

Jonathan and his southern army had returned early for want of engagement. To Saul's dismay, the prince was waiting with those who had flooded the golden capital to witness and celebrate David's triumphant return.

Saul, too, had been busy in the absence of his perceived nemesis. Infuriated as he was by Jonathan's humiliating fawning over David's victorious return, Saul held his tongue and his fangs for a more propitious moment in which to strike.

Once all were safely ensconced within the palace walls, the king had Jonathan called away on a fool's errand, attending the meeting of the council of elders of Gibeah. The king ruled in Gibeah. The elders were purely ceremonial positions appointed by the king. It was in fact presided over by Saul's brother-in-law. Though he didn't realize it, Jonathan's mission was accomplished as soon as he was outside the palace walls. The king sent for David once his spies assured him the "little general" was alone.

"Well, my son," Saul said, as David knelt at his feet. "You have made a triumph of a trial and proved yourself to all but your most severe skeptics. I congratulate you."

"I thank you, sire," David said, still prostrate before the king. He was unable to see the king's pointed glance at Paltiel as they shared their amusement over the barbed compliment. "Your thanks and congratulations are unnecessary, as such is my duty to the throne and to you as the anointed of the Lord."

"Yes, how kind of you to say," the king sneered, still not offering David leave to arise. "Surely, though, there is some reward we might offer in return for your service?"

"There is nothing more that I need, Your Majesty," David said, prone on the cold stone floor.

"Are you going to stay down there all day?" Saul asked, nudging David's shoulder with his toe.

"I did not know I had your leave to do otherwise," David said, sitting back on his calves and looking up into Saul's eye.

"Why so formal with me now?" Saul accused, without kindness or censure.

"You called for me to appear before you in the throne room," David answered. "I owe such respect to you, to the office that you hold, and to the people of Israel who gave you that office."

"It was the Lord who chose me for this office," Saul said, rising and fighting to keep his temper. "But no matter. I have called you here for a purpose, not to have you grovel at my feet."

"I await your pleasure," David said, rising to kneel.

"I have thought of you as my son for long enough," Saul said, teasing at his true meaning. "I have decided you will be a son of mine in fact as well as in my bosom. It is my will that you marry my daughter Merab and become part of the royal family."

David again sat back onto his calves, dizzied by the immense and unexpected offer. He wished he had overcome his own fears enough to discuss and decide with Jonathan the matter that was at hand. The question had been very much on his mind, long before the royal audience or even his mother's suggestion that such a marriage would be forthcoming. Could he continue to be with Jonathan and married to his sister?

Jonathan, as the king's heir, would be required to marry to carry on the royal line. It was an inevitability David had long ago accepted without much joy. It was an undeniable duty. But his own marriage prospects were far from a certainty. He knew that he might well be expected to marry for the purposes of carrying on his father's line. But it was a duty he could find his way around. He might simply choose the son of one of his brothers as his heir, or even a son of Jonathan's. Such was not outside tradition. These were thoughts he had kept to himself. He feared that to speak them to Jonathan would only make them come true and end what they had together in that perfect season of their lives.

"Your Majesty," David said, bowing low before Saul. "I am honored by this generous offer, the beauty of Merab, and the prospect of joining your august family."

"Good, then, it is settled," Saul said, rubbing his hands together.

"But, Your Majesty," David continued as though the king had not spoken. "It is because your family is so august and mine so humble that I must decline the hand of the fair and lovely princess. Surely there is a king or emperor more worthy than I to take up the place beside the king's daughter, and in so doing secure greater glory for the king's court and all of Israel. I can offer you only the loyalty of Bethlehem. That, I'm sure you know, you have already. Moreover, that it is not mine to give. I am not even Jesse's eldest son."

The king beheld David for a moment. He wondered what the boy could be about. If David was truly the grasping power-seeker the king believed him to be, then he would hardly decline such a propitious offer. A royal marriage would bring David that much closer to the throne. Why then? Had he misjudged him? Or was there a scheme he could not yet see?

As far as David's arguments, the king and David both knew that David's birth had been nobler than Saul's. Saul's royal lineage began with Saul. He was born to be a mule trader and elevated only at the behest of the wellborn of Jesse's class by way of Samuel and the God of Abraham. What's more, David had been designated the heir to Jesse's growing fortunes because it was David's success and service to the king that was enriching his family.

Still, Saul could not see around this corner. It was true that Merab could make a better match for him with some neighboring king or warlord, expanding Saul's influence peacefully. But David could hardly make a better match short of marrying the king himself. What then, Saul wondered, did David hope to gain by this? So twisted were his own thoughts and motives that it hardly occurred to the man to take David at his word.

David waited silently, longing for and dreading the king's answer. The words he longed to scream out rose in his throat: "I am already pledged to your son." But theirs was a pledge of the heart and not the law. The ways of man made no allowance for their love. The foolish rules of law sought to deform their natural desires and distort them as one might prune a tree into an odd shape to suit one's fancy more than the tree's purpose and potential. Pleasing to look at, perhaps, but cheating the Lord's will by denying the tree its natural beauty.

"As you wish," the king said at last. His eyes still squinted in concentrated thought. Though he was certain David was getting the better of him, he could not figure out how. "We shall yet find for you a prize that suits your heart's true desire."

"I assure you, Your Majesty," David said, bowing low again. "Your thanks added to the life I already have is all that I desire. I could want nothing more."

"Then that is what you shall have," Saul said with a tone of irony. Unsatisfied by David's explanation, he could not discern the flaw in his answer. "Your humility is duly noted. You may leave now."

Paltiel's disgusted sigh was audible. David looked up. The two exchanged a knowing look. As Palti smiled, David feared he understood Paltiel's part in the king's decision. He dreaded the king's motives, unaware that Paltiel had kept their confidence, though for less than noble reasons.

"Thank you, Your Majesty," David said, bowing. Unaware of Paltiel's silence in his favor, he supposed the king understood his meaning better than he in fact did. "I can tell you that you have already given me the best gift that I could ever hope to earn from you in a lifetime of service."

Bowing again, David took his leave of a silent and baffled king.

But it came to pass at the time when Merab Saul's daughter should have been given to David, that she was given unto Adriel the Meholathite to wife.

1 Samuel 18:19

"JONATHAN?" DAVID whispered that night, unable to sleep. "Are you awake?"

"No, I am not," Jonathan answered, hoping his tone would be answer enough.

"Good," David said, taking a deep breath in preparation. "Your father called me before him in the throne room today while you were attending to the elders' meeting."

"I'm up," Jonathan said, sitting up. "How bad is it? Must we escape to Egypt at first light?"

"He offered me Merab in marriage," David said by way of answer.

"But she is in love with Adriel," Jonathan said, laughing.

"And I with you," David said, so seriously that Jonathan stifled his laughter.

"Always," Jonathan said, taking David's chin between his thumb and forefinger.

"But will you always be with me?" David asked, reaching up and taking Jonathan's hand.

"How can you ask me such a thing?"

"How can I not? You are the prince and the heir to the king," David said simply. "You will have to marry and produce heirs to the throne."

"And duty is the only reason that I shall," Jonathan said. "I cannot yet change the foolish beliefs of twisted old men like Samuel and his hateful Levite laws, but I will be king one day. We shall show the world what we have, you and I, and rule Israel together."

"And me?"

Jonathan was silent for a while as he tried to imagine the unimaginable prospect of sending David from his bed, which only made his answer the easier.

"What queen I take for a wife will sleep in her own quarters, as my mother does. My wife and I will do our duty together to make an heir," Jonathan said, turning to David and throwing his arm over him. He drew him near and nestled against his back. "You, my prince, you will share my bed with me until the end of time."

"So it will not bother you if I marry?" David asked, making himself clearer. He felt Jonathan tense against him.

"No," Jonathan said, clutching David more tightly. "It will of course bother me. But I will forebear until such time as you and I can put an end to such foolishness as rules about who you can or cannot love or marry."

"You would marry me?" David asked, fearful of the answer but needing to know.

"I already have," Jonathan said, turning David onto his back and pressing himself against him. "I swear to you before the Lord who has brought us together, when we are kings and not just princes at the mercy of antiquated tyrants and old fools, I shall marry you in the palace in a full ceremony before the one true and just God and his genuine representative."

Neither felt much like sleep after that. It was a night to make their covenant flesh and to enjoy each other as fully as any couple might in their marriage bed.

The discussion was not at end between them, but it had lost its teeth and the ability to wound. From then on the two spoke easily of their duty to marry. They discussed their best prospects for advancement through as many marriages as might be beneficial, with no sense of threat to the bond between them.

Merab did marry her love Adriel, a wellborn young man from Abel Meholah in the northern province of Manasseh, though hardly an eastern potentate. Abel Meholah had some minor strategic importance. It did secure a fording place at the Jordan River south of the important trading city of Beth Shan and strengthen access to the essential trade route from Megiddo to the Transjordan Highway. In truth the region was already the king's prior to the marriage, so it added little to the prestige or influence of Saul's reign. Adriel, on the other hand, added many grandchildren to the king's line and great joy to his daughter's life. Though neither fact meant much to the king in his lifetime, both were to his credit.

Merab's sister Michal was another story. She, like her brother, had eyes for David since he'd first set foot in the palace. It was a fact she shared with Jonathan, whom she knew to be David's closest friend, at her first opportunity—the moment her older sister was married.

"Is your friend David spoken for?" she managed to ask, a bit awkwardly. She was next to Jonathan during a part of Merab's wedding celebration where the men and women were together.

"Spoken for?" Jonathan asked, amused at her old-fashioned tone.

"He is such a fine man, and yet I never see him with a woman or hear of his name linked with any," she said, giving her brother's shoulder a playful and useless shove, as one might jostle a stone pillar. "Does his heart belong to some girl back in Bethlehem?"

"And if it does not?" Jonathan grinned, taking delight in his gentle torture of a beloved but often quarrelsome sister.

"Perhaps you might guide him in my direction." Michal sighed, exasperated.

"Why?" Jonathan asked, knitting his brow comically. "Is there someone you'd like to introduce him to?"

"Jonathan, oh, never you mind." Michal huffed. "I'll just be an old maiden aunt, hanging around your court and at your elbow for the rest of your life. A burden to you and your household until my death, many, many, many years in the future. Think of it. It'll be just like having Mother living with you and your wife, if anyone is ever foolish enough to marry you."

"Have mercy, sister," Jonathan wailed, covering his head. "I will speak with him. I believe, though, that he may have given his heart already. So keep your eye trained on the horizon for other sunrises. For I warn you now, before I take you on as an extra mother-in-law, I'll put you on a farm in Ramah near to Samuel and his successors, to tend the scapegoats and grace every trifling religious ceremony on the calendar for your only sport."

"We have a bargain, then. Only let me know as soon as you find out," Michal said, abandoning her brother for the more agreeable company of other women, her mission complete.

Jonathan was still laughing at his sister's girlish crush when he brought the matter up to David later, as they bathed and made ready for bed.

"My sister Michal is quite in love with you," Jonathan said while David was scrubbing his back.

"Do you not live here at court?" David asked, pouring a pitcher of water over Jonathan's head. "Blind beggars in the street in front of the palace know this about your sister."

"And you?" Jonathan said, turning suddenly and grasping David by the wrists. "You know of my sister's feelings and yet you let her suffer on?"

"Yes," David said, laughing as he struggled to free himself.

"I think I need to give you a thrashing for treating my sister thus," Jonathan shouted as the two splashed in the water of the bathing pool.

Wet and slick with scented oils, David almost succeeded in freeing himself. The prince took the uneven match in the end, pinning David against the tiles and polished stones at the edge of the pool.

"Is that how you intend on thrashing me?" David panted, their bodies pressed together.

"Perhaps thrashing isn't exactly the word," Jonathan said, hauling David from the water and tossing him into a heap of cushions and towels nearby.

"Maybe it's not such a bad idea." David sighed as they dried one another.

"I'll say it's not," Jonathan said with a sneer and a laugh to match.

"I mean marrying Michal," David said. "It would make me a part of your family. Maybe it will bring me back into your father's favor. I only fear what it would do to us. Perhaps it has become worth the risk. Did you see how your father looked at me today? If he'd had another spear at hand...."

"Enough," Jonathan said, waving his hand. "My father has nothing but the highest regard for you. You gave him the Jezreel Valley and made him the richest king east of Egypt. He offered you his daughter's hand in marriage."

"He did it because Paltiel told him about us," David said before he'd thought.

"What? Palti? Don't be foolish," Jonathan scoffed, snapping his damp towel at David. "Palti is a dear friend as well as my second for all the years of my youth. We grew up together."

"Then you cut him free in an instant in favor of me," David said, catching Jonathan's eye with an even and serious gaze. "Now he is ever at the king's side."

"You have been at court too long," Jonathan said, shaking his head. He wrapped David in a soft dry towel and his arms. "You imagine phantoms and conspiracies. I know Father is a lot to take, but it's usually the wine talking when he speaks ill. Do as I do and just avoid him after sundown."

"I will try to see it with your eyes," David said, eased by Jonathan's strong embrace. "But have a glance or two through mine, if you would. See what I see."

"I will, my prince," Jonathan growled into David's ear, making him shiver from the closeness and the deep rumble of his voice. "So should I tell my sister that you're seeing someone else?"

"You know that I am," David said, leaning against him. "If you see no profit in it, then it's not worth the risk to us that marrying into your family might present."

"What risk is there to us?" Jonathan said, rocking David gently as he considered it, his eyes half closed.

"I can't help but fear that a marriage so close would either cause family conflict or cool feelings between us or both," David said in a rush. "How would your sister feel if she were to find out about us? Could you help but try to protect her? I do adore her and would not wish to hurt her."

"Whoever we marry will be a part of the family and close at hand." Jonathan shrugged. "How would it be different than if you took a second wife? Or acquired a concubine? I know my sister, and while there would be conflict, I'm sure, it would be more on account of her querulous nature than our alliance. She seeks to marry you. But a woman, no matter how strong-willed, cannot own a man."

"So you think it's a good idea?" David asked, still not entirely convinced.

"I can't say marrying my sister Michal can ever be entirely a good idea," Jonathan said with a little laugh. "I can tell you that you need never fear me finding a need or desire to protect her. If anyone will need protecting in such a match, it's certain to be you. Anyway, the decision is neither hers nor ours to make."

"Talk to your father about it," David suggested reluctantly. "You might kill both birds with the same stone."

"I think I see the true conflict now," Jonathan said, feigning seriousness. "It will be over who gets to wear the bridal veil, you or Michal. And I'll warn you now, she's solid and scrappy as a vixen."

"That's it," David said, pushing Jonathan, towel and all, back into the pool and stalking out of the chamber.

Jonathan was amused and annoyed that David slept far away from him in their bed that night. Not long after, his skepticism of David's phantom plots turned to suspicion. He spoke with his father several days later, at his archery range near the great rock Ezel. The prince liked to practice there, and the king was glad to join him on the warm yoreh day when the tamarisk leaves had turned to gold.

"Father, did you know that Michal is in love with David?"

"This week," Saul said with a dismissive snort of laughter.

"She has spoken to me about it, and I think David might be so disposed," Jonathan said, taking aim and striking his target at the center.

"He turned down your sister Merab right enough," Saul said, taking up his bow and laying an arrow across it. "Arrogant, I tell you. It's not often that a king's daughter gets turned down when offered in marriage from her father's royal hand. What makes you think this would be any different?"

"He told you he was just not sure of himself, Father," Jonathan said, noting the tone in his father's voice with concern. Still, he could not see the continued enmity that David perceived. "Perhaps if you gave him a title or promotion, so that he might feel more a peer to the princess."

"Of course, that's his game," Saul said, letting his arrow fly and missing the mark altogether. "It makes perfect sense to me now. He wants a better title. Prince of the realm is not good enough any longer."

"Oh no, Father, that was my suggestion, not his." Jonathan tried to assuage him as they paused to allow the attendant to run out and pick up the arrow from where he had overshot the target.

"Just like him to get you to do his dirty work and make you think it was your idea," Saul said, shaking his head and speaking more about his son than to him. "He is a clever gamesman, I'll give David that."

"Not a bit of it," Jonathan said, trying to lighten the moment and untangle what he'd woven. "Though in truth a medal is what he deserves, if he marries that hellion."

"She's better than he'll ever merit," Saul said, throwing down his bow and stalking towards his horse.

"Father," Jonathan pleaded, pursuing. His father shook him off like flies on a mare's flank. "I have handled this badly; please do not be angry with David."

"Why do you defend him to me?" Saul demanded, wheeling on his son. "What is between you?"

They regarded one another a moment. Jonathan caught a glimpse of what David thought he saw there. What was his father asking? More to the point, how was he to answer him? Had Paltiel betrayed their trust? Or would he give the game away if he assumed too much in answering? Was there even a game to give away? His father would hardly be upset if he took his pleasure with one of the boys or eunuchs in his harem. His mettle left him, and he settled for a reflection of the truth.

"The greatest love and trust," Jonathan said, simply and sincerely. "I would lay down my life for him, as I'm sure he would for me."

"Then I shall take your word on this," Saul said, mistrustful of Jonathan for his declaration, baffled that his son was unable to see what he saw. "I will give it some thought and try to come up with a way to make this possible."

"Thank you, Father," Jonathan said, helping him onto his horse. "I'm sure that given time, you'll see that David is a fine son-in-law to you and a great addition to our family."

Saul answered him with the dust of his departure. Jonathan did not bring up the matter again. Several weeks passed. He decided not to mention the conversation to David. He did not wish to fuel David's imaginings of court plots and intrigue, though his own doubts had found a foothold. The matter of David's marriage to Michal, on the other hand, seemed concluded.

Jonathan did find occasion to ask Paltiel of his confidence with the king.

"Oh no, my prince," Paltiel answered, truthfully and with a great show of offense. "You overestimate me. Do you suppose that I am such that the king and I sit around and gossip about you? But you may assure David that even was I on such terms with the king or any man or woman, I would no more break the confidences you and I have shared together than I would now breach those I have shared with the king."

"I'm sorry, old friend," Jonathan said, clapping him on the shoulder. "Be assured it is not David who sent me to you with this. It was something my father said to me the other day that made me think that he knew more than I have found the right time or the courage to tell him."

"You must not keep things from your father," Paltiel said with a warmth that hinted at their former friendship. "But neither should you burden the king with every tryst and liaison. You intend to marry, do you not? And give him heirs?"

"I do, of course," Jonathan said.

"So just as a man may have many wives and a king many concubines," Paltiel said with a little shrug, "who's to say that one of them should not be named David?"

The two laughed heartily, as they had so often in their years together.

"It is good to talk to you, Palti," the prince said, embracing him. "I have missed your counsel and feel better for it. Forgive me any offense I may have given."

"It is not possible for you to offend me," Paltiel said, his meaning masked with clever words and a friend's smile. "You may call on me at any time you need an ear. My loyalty to you is as it was the day that I left your service to take up my work with the minister."

"It is good to know that. I thank you as always for your good counsel and your friendship," Jonathan said as they parted.

Despite his clever and misleading assurances to Jonathan, Paltiel's agenda had not changed. He was soon serving his poisoned words with the king's wine.

In his deliberation over the matter, Saul called Michal in before him, and Paltiel had an opportunity to overhear their exchange. He was still at hand when the princess departed, excited and hopeful that David might soon be hers.

"More wine, Palti," the king called when they were alone in his chambers. "My daughter seems quite taken with that young man. Everyone does. Can they not see him for the schemer that I see?"

"You will forgive me, Your Majesty," Paltiel said as he poured wine from the ewer into the king's upraised goblet. "I hope that the princess will proceed cautiously where affairs of the heart are concerned."

"Do you know something, Palti?" the king urged. "We speak of my daughter."

"It is nothing," Palti said with a practiced tone of reluctance. "Nothing certain, that is. Only.... Well, I have heard that where David is concerned, women are not his first choice as bedmate."

"That foolish boy of mine," Saul said, shaking his head. "Such a son of Belail. To befriend and trust such a man as he does."

"The prince's heart does sometimes cause him to turn a blind eye," Paltiel agreed, nodding solemnly.

"Still, your words put me in mind of just the bride price to ask and the means to be rid of David once and for all and all at once." Saul laughed heartily.

"I'm sure Your Majesty will do what is best," Paltiel said, beaming as he withdrew from the room.

And Michal Saul's daughter loved David: and they told Saul, and the thing pleased him.

And Saul said, I will give him her, that she may be a snare to him, and that the hand of the Philistines may be against him. Wherefore Saul said to David, Thou shalt this day be my son in law in the one of the twain.

1 Samuel 18: 20-21

JONATHAN WAS beaming with pride over his cleverness. He and David were called to appear before the king to discuss the matter of David's marriage to Michal.

David, still reluctant, at first resisted the king's call. "It is not a small matter to become the king's son-in-law. I am a poor man compared to kings."

The king's reply was swift. He had in mind a plan to make David worthy.

"You see," Jonathan said as they made their way to the official audience. "It is as I suggested. Father will literally entitle you so that you may be married into our family. He wants nothing more than to have you as his son."

David only nodded thoughtfully in reply.

"David," the king said, rising from his throne as they entered. The chamber was filled with many important men from throughout the kingdom. "I'm pleased you could come. Jonathan, my son and heir, I'm glad that you are here as well. Come and stand beside me, as such is your right and place here."

Jonathan gave David a shrug as he took his place beside his father.

"Your Majesty," David said with a low bow. "How could I be anywhere else when my king wishes me here?"

"Yes," Saul said with a sour tone. "Ever the show of obedience when I see you before me."

Jonathan was discomfited by his father's tone and words to David. Still, it did not seem definite proof of the animosity of which David was so certain.

"I have received, and been duly flattered by, your protestations of humility in the matter of taking my daughter's hand in marriage," the king explained, launching into the discussion without formalities or pleasantries. "True. You are a humble man, rudely born, but then so am I, your king. I know that it seemed to many that conveying a title upon you would make you my daughter's equal, but as I know better than anyone from my own experience, it is the deeds of a man, what we do, that makes us who we are.

"And so with this in mind, David, my humble servant and valiant soldier of the army of Israel, it seems to me that it is only right that I ask a bride price from you that reflects your strengths—what you do best. With your noted and well-known qualities in mind, then, as a price for my daughter the Princess Michal's hand in marriage, I ask you for the foreskins of one hundred Philistines and nothing more."

There was a shocked silence in the room.

Jonathan's face was red. He trembled with rage but could not, from where he stood, do or say anything to redress the insult without bringing his own reputation into it. Like the others in the crowded room, with the notable exception of his old friend Paltiel, the eyes of all who had heard the humiliating request were fixed on David.

"Then it shall be so," David answered, with a bow and a strange expression on his face. His lips seemed to tremble in a way more akin to a smile than the looks of shock and horror that painted the room.

With a sweep as regal as one might have expected from a visiting monarch, David saluted and left the hall. The king turned his attention to other business as he might have had his request been an ordinary ruling.

Jonathan was stunned and looked around the room at the shocked, silent, and bemused faces that surrounded them. He was jolted when his gaze met Paltiel's. His old friend smiled at him warmly, as though they had seen one another across the room at a pleasant social gathering.

"Good of you to stand up for your friend, son," Saul said with a dismissive pat. "If you'll excuse me, I've other matters to attend, though you are, of course, welcome to stay if you like, as is your right."

Jonathan said nothing. He departed the hall the moment his father's back was turned. He found David seated on his cloak, removing his sandals in their rooms.

"Are you all right?" Jonathan asked tentatively. He felt certain at last that David's suspicions of his father were confirmed. He remained unsure how much the king knew about their relationship and of Paltiel's complicity. His old armor-bearer had seemed oddly unfazed by the king's bizarre request.

"I believe, my lord, that I may have injured myself," David said, looking up, his face a mask.

"How so?" Jonathan said, rushing and kneeling at his side.

"I believe that I might have strained something inside trying not to laugh," David said, rocking back on the bench on which he sat, howling heavenward.

"How can you?" Jonathan demanded in horror, rising.

"How can you not?" David said, tossing his sandal playfully in Jonathan's direction. "I could not even decide if the king was serious at first. He asks me for a bride price that reflects my skill, and then the price consists of dead Philistines and penises? At least it puts an end to our argument about his feelings for me and how much he knows."

"But Palti assured me…," Jonathan began and then trailed off.

"And he was grinning like a fox in the vineyard," David said, laughing again. "To be fair, perhaps he just found it as funny as I did."

"David, my father was insulting you," Jonathan insisted.

"He was, but am I to be insulted? He asserted to me what I am," David said, a little more serious in his tone but not greatly. "What the Lord made me to be. If he'd asked for a lock of my ruddy hair, he'd have hit no nearer the mark."

"So, you are not insulted?"

"My prince," David said, taking Jonathan's hand. "You are my commander both in the field and in the bedroom. You know my skills better than any man. Does this request not seem to play to my strengths? Though I do admit I have no experience with the uncircumcised."

David grinned up at Jonathan, who slowly dissolved from rage into guarded laughter.

"What will you do?" Jonathan asked, reaching down to tousle some of those God-given reddish-blond locks.

"Tomorrow I'll put together a small squadron of good men and go out Philistine cock-hunting," David answered with a shrug.

"So you intend to go through with this?"

"We agreed that this would help knit whatever wounds are between your father and me," David said, grinning up at him. "Perhaps the best part of this is that you will no longer argue with me about how your father feels toward me. Well, that and the fact that I get a beautiful princess, and he gets a bag of Philistine cocks."

"All right, then," Jonathan said, folding his arms seriously. "But you are only allowed to touch the unclean parts of those hundred men to cut them off."

"I assure you, my lord," David said, kneeling before his prince and drawing aside his robe, "you are the only man and these the only parts that hold any interest for me."

And Saul said, Thus shall ye say to David, The king desireth not any
dowry, but an hundred foreskins of the Philistines, to be avenged of the king's
enemies. But Saul thought to make David fall by the hand of the Philistines.

                                                                    1 Samuel 18:25

DAVID PLAYED out the charade with complete sincerity. He even exchanged lover's tokens with Michal before he departed the city with a dozen men, Joab and Eliab among them, to go on his grisly quest to win her hand.

The king smiled with satisfaction as he waved good-bye with the rest of the crowd, certain that he had seen the last of David. He hoped the Philistines would do for him what he had begun unsuccessfully with a spear in the feasting hall.

But the royal smile turned south. David returned little more than a week later with a leather sack containing over two hundred Philistine foreskins, still attached to their Philistine members. He emptied the bag's contents at Saul's feet. He had made himself more than hero for the ease and dignity with which he'd acquitted himself of the odious task. David's wedding was celebrated swiftly, a joyous event of state and family, and the acknowledgement still more of David's growing legend.

Michal beamed with pride all through the ceremony, as did her brother Jonathan. When the long day was at end, husband and wife were left alone together in the bridal chambers, hung with sweetly scented flowers and garlands. David made Michal scream with joy in service to his duty.

But as soon as she had drifted off to sleep, a smile on her face as sweet as the flowers that hung above them, David slipped from under the covers and returned to the bed in which he truly belonged.

CHAPTER TWELVE
REFUGE IN RAMAH

Wherefore David arose and went, he and his men, and slew of the Philistines two hundred men; and David brought their foreskins, and they gave them in full tale to the king, that he might be the king's son in law. And Saul gave him Michal his daughter to wife.

1 Samuel 18:27

MICHAL AWOKE aglow and smiling. The blissful feelings of her lovemaking with David were still upon her from the night before. She reached out for him in the gentle feelings of early morning, but he was not there. It was a rude awakening to which she had grown accustomed but not easy.

Why would he not pass the night with her?

That morning the hundred little hurts of David's habitual abandonment were too many. She arose and summoned her servant. She began to dress, and then, thinking better of it, she switched clothes with the serving woman so that she might be about in the palace without calling attention to herself. The servant was smaller than she, and the clothes revealed Michal's fine figure. She thought little of it, as it was too early for there to be anyone about.

Uncertain of her plans, she made her way through the royal wing to where her husband kept his rooms adjoining those of her brother. Letting herself into David's rooms, she stole silently into the bedchamber in order at least to be beside him when he woke up. But her stealth was in vain, as she found his bed empty and snugly made.

Curious, she lighted the lamps and looked around the rooms. Strangely empty, they held little evidence of her husband's presence. Like rooms kept for guests, his were well but stiffly appointed. She emerged into the early morning light, wondering at her husband's whereabouts. Looking up and down the passage as though she might see him, she found herself facing her brother's former manservant, making his way on some predawn errand.

"Paltiel, is it not?" she said softly, her voice respectfully low in the early morning.

"Yes, girl…. My lady?" Paltiel said, pausing as he realized who she was. He was fooled at first by her form of dress, which he found, on closer inspection, most flattering. He was taken with her beauty, as always, and rueful that such a confection should be wasted on a man who did not have the palate to savor it. He wondered at her purpose. "Forgive me, I did not recognize you at first."

"May I trouble you to ask if you know the whereabouts of David, my husband?" she asked, bold and untroubled by who she was and what she was about. Michal, more than any of Saul's children, knew her father was king and exhibited it in her every word and action. "I thought to surprise him as a wife might awaken her husband but find he is already out for his day so early. I suppose it is an old habit of farm life, made worse by life as a soldier."

"Yes, my lady," Paltiel said, eyes downcast. "I am sure that is so."

"But what duty does he perform this early?" she asked again with an impatient air, intrigued by Paltiel's odd reaction. She had met the man many times before and found his manner that morning strangely muted.

"I cannot say precisely," Paltiel answered haltingly, making the hedging in his voice as plain as an oak tree in the desert.

"In truth, I do not care what he is doing so much as I ask where he might be," she said, folding her arms beneath her breasts in a way that made Paltiel turn away slightly to maintain his decorum with the princess. "Do you know where he is?"

"My lady, I do not like to say," he said acting out a reluctance he did not feel.

She knew. At last she understood. In an instant it made sense: his behavior, his departures, his exquisitely precise lovemaking and dutiful husbanding. He was perfect when he was there, but he was almost never there. It was a relief.

"Who is she?"

"Who is who?" Paltiel asked with unmistakably feigned innocence, secretly gleeful for the unasked opportunity in his own cause.

"The woman whose bed my husband keeps," Michal shouted.

"I assure you, my lady, there is no woman," he went on, as though trying to calm her with his maddeningly provocative and obviously false words.

"I demand that you tell me where my husband is at once," she bellowed with no regard for those who slept nearby.

"Let me help you back to your apartments, my lady," Paltiel said, taking her arm as if to lead her away. "I think this is a conversation best had with your husband," he purred, thinking that his work was done.

To his delight she took matters into her own hands in a fashion superior to any he could have crafted, had he written the story with a stylus in wet clay and baked it in the sun.

Tearing her arm from his grasp, Michal stalked to her brother's doors and began pounding on them. "Jonathan? Jonathan," she wailed. Unanswered and enraged, she wheeled on Paltiel. "We'll see what you know and what you do not. My brother will get an answer from you if I cannot."

"My lady, please, for your own sake," Paltiel said without much conviction.

"My sister, have you departed from the land of your senses?" Jonathan demanded, opening his doors, tousled and wrinkled with sleep. "What tragedy has befallen you?"

"Where is my husband David?" she demanded of her brother, as though they had been arguing about it for some time. "This man of yours here will not tell me."

Paltiel exchanged a look of tacit complicity with the prince as if to assure him of his earlier promises of confidence.

"My dear unhinged sister," Jonathan said, putting an arm around her shoulders and leading her the few steps down the hall to David's door. He knocked gently. "David's rooms are here next to mine."

"But brother dear, I have already—"

"What is all the fuss out here so early?" David said, emerging from his rooms, as sleep-worn as the prince. Agape, she beheld him.

He wore a sleeping gown she and her sister had embroidered and given to her brother as a token upon a recent feast day. "Beloved wife, why do you call at my door when the morning is yet so raw?"

Michal recoiled as David reached for her. Her look went from him to her brother and back again. Her eye then fell on Paltiel, who smiled weakly, as if to say *I told you not to ask.*

She turned and left them at a run.

David threw a look over his shoulder to Jonathan and then took up the pursuit.

"My prince," Paltiel said with a vague shrug to cover his unbridled joy at the turn of events. "The bliss of the newlywed is soon lost to the truth of marriage, is it not?"

"Yes, my friend," Jonathan said, managing a blustery tone. "We are lucky men to have our freedom still and to wake up to more peaceful morning greetings."

They laughed and took each other's leave. Jonathan closed his door from the inside. Paltiel continued on his errand, though both ached to follow the chase and discover its conclusion.

It would have been a disappointment to them had they followed, for Michal beat David back to her rooms and barred the door against him. Given the time of day and the circumstances, he only knocked softly. When he was not admitted at once, he gave up his appeal and retreated to his rooms and Jonathan's arms.

Michal wept on the floor. She understood the truth of her marriage and her life. It was one thing for a husband to keep his own bed or even to keep another woman's bed. Her own father had children by women other than her mother. They lived at court and attended feast days with the rest of the family. But for her husband to keep her brother's bed was something she did not know how to countenance. The betrayal and dissembling of them both was almost more than she could bear.

Why had they foisted this fraud upon her? The only answer she could surmise was that she had been deceived so that David could marry his way into the royal family. It seemed an inevitable conclusion, but it left her feeling ill-used and unloved. Even if there was no more plot than to use her to conceal the truth of their relationship, she felt no more than a convenience to a man she had thought she loved.

Something in Michal died, burned away in that bitter dawn. Her love for David fueled the rage that her tears could not extinguish. It was a softness, perhaps her youth, that left her. In the harsh morning light, she could see her marriage to the man she loved for what it was, or at least what it was not. She had no need that it be more, that she be more.

They never spoke of that morning. David was welcome in her chambers but not encouraged. Her response to him in the marriage bed became so perfunctory that he all but ceased his visits there. His relationship with her brother was silently understood between them.

In her immediate grief, Michal sought out Paltiel to discover just how much he knew and who else knew of her husband's alliance, that she might understand the extent of her humiliation. Their liaison, far more dangerous than that of her husband and her brother, began as a noble lady speaking in confidence to a servant.

"My lady," Paltiel soothed, stroking the back of her hand in the privacy of her chambers at the palace. "I know because I was your brother's armor-bearer. I slept at his feet until David arrived. He sent me away from your brother, my dearest friend. As for the men who've campaigned with them, there is some understanding, but men in the field often seek such comfort. I do not know if their comrades are aware that they remain together on their return."

"I suppose that is some consolation." She sighed.

"My lady, if I may speak freely?" Paltiel asked, kneeling before her.

"You are already privy to my most humbling secret. What could you ask or say to me?" she said with a sting of ironic laughter.

"I only wished to say that no one who beholds your beauty could ever believe that your husband has eyes for another," Paltiel said. He looked away shyly to strike a more genuine pose, sincere in his appreciation if not his affectation. He hoped for more than the princess's confidence.

In the spring she asked David for a house of her own, and he had it built for her. It was a lovely villa on a hillside near the palace but far enough to offer privacy from the prying eyes of court. He kept her company there as duty dictated, but he resided at the palace.

In her more private rooms there, and in the absence of a husband on whom she could rely, Michal turned more and more to Paltiel for advice and companionship. Her meetings with Paltiel grew more frequent. Their words grew bolder. By Paltiel's design and constancy, her confidence in him grew along with her affection. Together they savored the bitter tastes of anger and revenge on their tongues. They whiled away their time scheming ways to deprive Jonathan of David, as they had each been deprived.

Then they acted.

Saul was the perfect dupe and instrument through which to realize their designs.

Already salted with Paltiel's words of jealousy, simmering with his own anger toward David, and marinated in his wine, the king had the power to punish at a whim. It took only a little heat and stirring to bring the king's rage to a boil.

"Father," Michal confided in a private audience she had mulled in her heart for days before. "I have something that I need to tell you. I am only a woman and do not know what to do in this matter, and yet it is such that I cannot discuss it with my mother, for I do not think that she would understand."

"My beloved daughter," Saul said, extending his hand. "Come and sit here at my feet, as you used to when you were a little girl. Let me stroke your lovely hair and listen to your troubles, that I may do my joyous duty as your father and take them away."

"Oh, Father," Michal said, resting her head on her father's knee as she took her place. "I hardly know how to say it."

"Daughter, I have seen too much in my life to be shocked by anything you could imagine," he assured her gently. "Speak as though I was not in the room."

"It is my husband," she said, turning her face into his robes. She wept, for though her purpose was false, her heart was truly broken.

"David," Saul rumbled. The name burned his throat as he spoke it.

"Yes, David." She nodded. "He has a lover over me, his wife."

"Oh, my dear," Saul said, stroking her hair patiently, ready to forgive even David for such a trifle. "That is the way of men. You need not take it to heart, for it is no reflection on you. He will tire of her soon enough and replace her with other women, other distractions. But he will always return to you, his wife. It is men. You must not fret yourself, for nature is master to us all."

"Oh, Father, I wish that it was another woman," Michal said, looking up into his warm eyes with her wet ones.

"I don't understand?" Saul asked, confused.

"It is a lover he had before he was with me," Michal said to build the case. "It is another man." She and Paltiel had agreed it would be best for their aims not to implicate Jonathan at first.

"Another man," Saul said, not surprised but unsure of his footing. He had been on campaign often and long enough in his career to know what men were like together. It was not the act that bothered him particularly. In point of fact, it only served to confirm his earlier suspicions, and it helped explain much. Such men typically made better soldiers, and David was the best. Had it been any other man in his service, he would have thought no more of it than of any married man with a concubine. But this was his son-in-law. For David to choose another man over his daughter gave him feelings on a topic he might otherwise have ignored.

"Yes, and he has never, since our wedding, passed the night in bed with me," Michal stuttered through her sobs.

"Your marriage is not consummated?"

"No, he has done his duty, but not one thing more," she wailed. "Now that he has built me a house of my own, I never see him at all. He keeps his rooms here in the palace. He comes to me only on feast days and special occasions. Or when I'm forced to… ask." She broke down again, almost as humiliated by her fate as she was enraged.

"My child," Saul said, taking Michal's hand and lifting her up so that she sat on his knee like a little girl. He held her as she cried. "How have I clutched such a viper to my breast?"

"Oh, don't blame yourself, Father," she said, softly. "I was in love with him and begged for the marriage."

"And your brother, Jonathan, convinced me," Saul mused, rocking his daughter gently. "How could your brother not know? They are best friends."

"We see what we want to see in the people we love," Michal said in a vacant, flat, worldly way that made Saul feel as though he was sitting in a cold draft.

"I suppose," Saul said, holding her more tightly.

"When Jonathan marries, he'll come to his senses," Michal whispered into her father's ear. "For now he's just a great boy and David one of his playmates. Besides, it's time you had a grandson to carry on your line after Jonathan. You should pick out a wife for him."

"It is indeed time, my daughter," Saul said distantly, his mind far away, mulling over plans for revenge, retribution, and assuring his dynasty. "Put this out of your head. Let your father worry about a solution for you in this."

"Yes, Father," Michal said, resting her head peacefully on Saul's shoulder. "I'll try my best, but it is hard to forbear."

"Focus your mind on finding a suitable wife for your brother, then," he said with a tense laugh. "That should lighten your cares."

"Oh, Father, as if you would let me make such a choice for you," Michal said, laughing despite her tears. "I'll let you know my thoughts by Seder."

"Pesach it is, then," he said, delighting in her laughter. "You can whisper it in my ear as you serve the family table. Meanwhile, you let me worry about that husband of yours."

"Thank you, Father," Michal said, girlishly kissing his cheek, glowing in triumph. A grin spread across her face as quickly as her back was turned.

She no longer cared whether or not David returned to her. She wanted only to expose him for what he truly was instead of the noble hero everyone thought him to be.

Paltiel took her hand as he helped her into her royal palanquin and held it even after the four powerful Nubian servants raised the sedan chair from the ground and bore her toward home. Such daring secret acts of affection were becoming more frequent between them. The fatal consequences of being found out made their trysting more exciting. They exchanged only furtive looks as Paltiel ran alongside the sedan chair, returning to the house of David. There they could more easily find stolen tastes of privacy. Her husband was, as ever, in the palace at her brother's side.

Saul made two decisions as his daughter left him. The first was that Jonathan must, at once, make a good first marriage. The only delay Saul would accept was the time it took to engineer a beneficial alliance for his kingdom. He could marry for love later if he wished, but first for state, and sooner than later. The second decision was that David must die.

As those closest to them plotted and celebrated the anticipation of their demise, Jonathan and David were planning that summer's campaign. They did not notice the growing enmity around them. They were deeply involved in their strategies to expand and fortify the borders, closer than ever before to fulfilling the promise of the patriarchs and the Lord. Their focus was, as with all people who are content in love, on other matters and bettering the world around them. The hunger of their loneliness so richly sated, and the warmth of their hearts so generously shared, they could not see the baser thoughts and pursuits of others who did not view the world from the same flattering angle. So when Jonathan was summoned to his father's chambers the next day, the conversation would have never occurred to him.

"Father," Jonathan said, embracing Saul, pleased. He knew that, since their meeting was early in the day, he would be speaking more with his father and less with Saul's favorite vintage. "I am so pleased to have the chance to speak with you. I have many ideas for this year's summer campaign, which I know would benefit from your wisdom and for which I ask your blessing."

"Jonathan, my boy," Saul said, slapping his son heartily on the back as he broke their embrace and stepped back. "I look forward to hearing all about your plans. But I've called you here to discuss a few plans that I want to set in motion closer to home."

"Excellent," Jonathan said, taking a seat without being bidden, a privilege he shared with no one else in the kingdom. "It has been so long since you and I have planned anything together. I remember by teaching your battle plans to David now."

"Really?" Saul said, amused and pleased by the idea. "So he's really just using my old ideas to make his new victories."

"Father," Jonathan laughed. "We would not even have a kingdom to defend if not for your *old* ideas."

"Nice to know you remember that," Saul said, rubbing his son's shoulder. "My faith in you never wavers, my son. Though I do sometimes worry about your judgment."

"Father?" Jonathan said quizzically, turning toward Saul, who stood behind him.

"It is past time you married," Saul said, abruptly, startling and amusing his son.

"Oh, Father," Jonathan said with a dry laugh of relief. "I was worried. I have only awaited your decision in this. I did not think, as heir, that marriage would be my choice. But if you prefer, I'll begin—"

"No, no," Saul cut him off. "I will look to it, but you should plan on a wedding when you return from campaign this next fall. That'll give you the length of the winter rains to get her with an heir before you're off adventuring again."

"More strategy advice?" Jonathan teased, smiling to keep his own anxiety on the topic to himself. The truth and implications of marriage, and its impact on his life with David, closed in around him. They had discussed it between them until they'd made it comfortable. But now there was a date. It made it more real, somehow, and more fearful.

"You'd think your sister would have got me a grandson on the way by now," Saul snorted derisively, pouring himself some wine from the ewer on a nearby chest.

"But, Father, Merab is already—"

"Michal," Saul snarled. "I was talking about Michal. But you know that. You are already seeking to defend him to me, but it is too late, my son. For the other matter I have brought you here to discuss is an end to that ill-fated and ill-favored alliance."

"If you think best, Father." Jonathan shrugged, indifferent to the fate of his sister's marriage to David. Despite what he had thought going in, he was glad he would not have to share him any longer. Better still, it would make his own marriage easier to manage. "But there's Michal's feelings to consider—"

"It is for her feelings that I make this decision," Saul said, and then thought better of it. "I mean, I know that she wants to be a mother, and David does not seem to have either the manhood or the inclination to accomplish the task."

"Father, they are still newlywed," Jonathan said with a sympathetic tone.

"And they always will be," Saul said with a knowing laugh. "For it is a permanent solution I seek to their badly made marriage. I have only just given my men orders to bring an end to the David problem once and for all."

"Father, what are you saying?" Jonathan asked quietly, rising.

"I am certain, now, that David only married your sister to advance his cause and draw nearer to my throne," Saul declared. He searched his son's face for some sign of indignation, if not rage.

"That is not true," Jonathan insisted. "You cannot believe this."

"I can and I do," Saul said with a dismissive wave of his hand, disgusted by his son's complete unwillingness to defend himself, if not his father, against this unbridled usurper. "I have it on good authority; he does not even care for the company of women in the ways of marriage. For those pleasures that most men find with their wives and women, he seeks out the company of men."

"Is this the reason that you would condemn him?" Jonathan asked, bereft. His heart and his spirit fell to his feet as he understood his father's feeling toward his own unspoken truth. He longed for the courage to tell his father all that was in his heart; to put an end to the insane speculations and fears about David's designs on the throne. If only he could simply tell his father. David could not take what he would already gladly give him as any husband would his spouse. But his father's true feelings in this were revealed in his censure. Jonathan could not, would not, risk losing everything to end a foolish argument.

"Is his plan not clear to you? Why else would he marry your sister?" Saul demanded, reeling on him. "Will you not now defend the throne that another seeks to take from you?"

"I can only tell you that I know nothing could be further from true, Father," Jonathan said, shattered by his father's unintended denunciation. "I wish that you could take my word."

"Well, the matter will be at end soon enough. We need never discuss it again." Saul sniffed. "I shall make a present to you of his family's holdings in Bethlehem as soon as he is dispatched."

"You must not do this thing, Father," Jonathan said, grabbing the front of his father's robe to plead.

"And you must not tell me what to do," Saul said, tearing himself away from Jonathan's mighty grip with some difficulty. "My mind is made up."

"Then I must take my leave of you until you have returned to your senses," Jonathan called as he quit his father's room. He made his way through the palace. His heart raced, spurred by his pace and the mortal fear that he would not arrive at David's side in time to warn him.

"David," he called out, bursting into his own apartment. "David."

When there was no immediate answer, panic overtook him. Seizing the sword from the scabbard of the guard who stood outside his door, he advanced into his own rooms, blade extended at the ready.

"Jonathan, what do you…? God's breath, what is it?" David said in fright, almost skewering himself on Jonathan's sword as he rounded the corner from his adjoining rooms, where he'd been retrieving a scroll.

"We must leave at once," Jonathan said, not lowering his sword.

"Did you think I would put up argument enough to warrant this?" David asked, guiding the sword away with the dowel of the scroll. "Where do you want to go?"

"Ramah, to see Samuel," Jonathan answered, his eyes wild.

"Oh," David said, guiding the blade back nearer his heart. "In the name of the Lord, why?"

"Because he is the one man Father may still fear," Jonathan said, tossing the sword aside and advancing into the room. "Grab what you need, but we must ride."

"Your father?" David said, trying to catch Jonathan's arm. "What has happened?"

"Do you love me?" Jonathan said, turning suddenly and taking David in his arms, more to still him than to embrace him.

"Yes, you know that...."

"And do you trust me?"

"With my life," David answered, relaxing in Jonathan's grasp.

"Then get as much coin as you have at hand, your sword, and your cloak, and let us be gone," Jonathan said, releasing him. He turned away in haste as he carried out his own commands. "I will explain on the road or when we get there."

"My prince." David nodded in a small bow of acquiescence and then set silently about following orders.

Before the shadows in the courtyard had advanced a footfall to the east, two cloaked and hooded figures left Gibeah at a gallop. They rode in silence down from the hills into the small valley of the holy city of Ramah, just a morning's ride.

There Jonathan took David at once to the temple in search of Samuel. They found the great priest was away for the day to make sacrifice in the holy city of Shiloh.

"Wait here," Jonathan said to David, having spoken little more than grunts and commands since they'd left the palace.

"Jonathan, are you going to tell me what is going on?" David said softly, placing a gentling hand on the back of the prince's arm. "I do trust you; I am concerned for your safety and for what I might need to do in this situation."

"There is something I must do," Jonathan said, taking David's hand firmly. "I think you will be safe here. Do not trust any but Samuel, and do not leave until I return."

"I will do as you ask," David said, squeezing Jonathan's hand. "But only on the assurance that you are not in danger."

"There is no danger to me," Jonathan said with a smile, moved that David's concern, even then, was for him.

"Then I will await you here," David said, resigned though baffled by Jonathan's unfounded behavior.

David remained with Samuel's servants and novices. Jonathan made his way into the city in search of refuge. Fortune was on his side. He chanced upon a wealthy merchant in need of funds. The merchant, desirous of moving to the ever more prosperous trading center of Jerusalem, sold Jonathan his fine home with servants and all its contents. Better still, Jonathan was pleased to find that it was not far from the place where Samuel dwelled and worshipped.

The transaction was accomplished in secret so that those who lived nearby might still believe the house belonged to the merchant, should any come seeking David or the prince himself. Pleased with his good fortune at having found not only safe haven for the night, but also a retreat that he and David might use to meet in private in the future, Jonathan returned to the temple. Finding that Samuel was still not there, he brought David to their new home.

"Here we are," Jonathan said as he closed the large heavy gate of the walled and sheltered courtyard behind them. "Our new home in Ramah. Do you like it? The stables are just here. Bring your horse."

"Jonathan," David said, following, as they stabled their horses with the groomsmen who already worked there. "I believe I have been most patient with all of this."

"This is our master, Asad," Jonathan said to the groomsmen. "We all work for him."

"Master Asad," the groomsman said, kneeling as he took the bridle.

"Good man," David said, patting the top of the groomsman's head and then scurrying to catch up with Jonathan. "Jonathan, will you wait?"

"Come and see your new house," Jonathan said, opening and holding the heavy front doors for him.

"My new house?" David said, amused and impressed by the fine home. "Have you brought me to Ramah at a gallop on an emergency house hunt?"

"In here is the sitting room," Jonathan said, grabbing David by the arm. He dragged him into a small room. Filled with casks and jars, it was clearly not the sitting room. Once inside he pulled the door behind them.

"It's lovely," David said of the small dark storage pantry. "So dark and airless. Perhaps chairs?"

"David, I do not want the servants to know who we are, so that they cannot betray our secrecy when we are here," Jonathan said in a low rumbling voice that amused and alarmed David.

"You bought us a hideout where we have to hide out?" David said, starting to laugh.

"This is no laughing matter, David," Jonathan said, urgently. "My father wants to kill you."

"Again?" David said, laughing heartily.

"No, my prince," Jonathan said, gripping David's forearms. "This is not drunken spear-throwing. He has given the order to his men that you are to be killed. You are a fugitive and a wanted man in the kingdom tonight."

David stopped laughing.

"You should be secure here," Jonathan said, releasing David only once he was certain he had conveyed his sense of urgency. "The servants believe you are a wealthy trader's son from Judah who holds his privacy so dear that he has a secret place to rendezvous with his lover."

"My lover?"

"A rough Benjamite who for all intents and purposes appears to work for him."

"I like that story," David said with a roguish smile in spite of the hurt he felt. "But Jonathan, why has the king turned so violently against me this time?"

"I am not sure," Jonathan said, taking him in his arms when he heard the tone of David's voice. "He called for me this morning and told me that I would be marrying when we return from campaign, and that he had ordered your death."

"He gave no reason?" David said, holding onto Jonathan more tightly.

"Only that somehow he has gotten it into his head that you married Michal only to place yourself nearer to his throne," Jonathan said, stroking David's head.

"I hoped that when we married, he would stop feeling threatened." David sighed, too overwhelmed to speak of the balance of Saul's other edict. "I only hope Michal gets no word of this. I have no wish to hurt her. Though my heart is yours, I would not have her think that I married for power. I will always be her loving and devoted husband."

"I will try to get word to her when I return," Jonathan said, releasing him.

"Return? When?" David asked, again tightening his embrace.

"Now, at once, tonight," Jonathan said, patting David on the back in farewell. "I have hired bodyguards for the house here to protect you. I must go now to try to find the source of this treachery and to change my father's mind in this."

"Your marriage?" David asked before thinking, at once regretting his selfish candor.

"No, that I must do," Jonathan said hastily, taking no notice. "But he must know you are a loyal and valuable soldier and son-in-law. Remain here. I will try to get word to Samuel, but do not venture from here until you have word from me that it is safe to leave. Trust no one."

"Yes, of course," David said, his concerns for Jonathan helping to mask his feelings about the king's other decree. "You are sure it is safe for you?"

"He can hardly be arranging my marriage in the fall if he plans to slit my throat in the spring."

"I suppose you are right," David admitted, again embracing him. "May the Lord guide and protect your every step, my rude Benjamite."

"I am not saying good-bye to you in a storeroom," Jonathan said, opening the door and leading David back into the fine limestone entryway. "Let us examine your private quarters before I must take my leave."

Jonathan returned to court in the cover of night. He found that Saul had already retired. Sleep was fitful, and Jonathan rose early to make the case to his father even before they had eaten. His heart was troubled. He wondered if he would be able to sway Saul's conviction. Jonathan was heartsick, anticipating a life lived in secret with David hidden away guiltily in Ramah until his father's death.

Fortune favored his cause. News of another sort had beaten him to the king's door, smoothing the way for his petition.

Though early morning, he found his father's chambers abuzz with activity and crowded with his most important and trusted councilors and generals.

"Ah, Jonathan, good, you are here," the king called to his son, spying him at the door. "My foolish houseman said you were away on an errand. I need your help. Come join me."

"Father, what has happened?" Jonathan asked, taking the place that was made for him at his father's right hand.

"We have had news that the five cities of Philistia are again massing their forces to counteract last spring's progress in the Jezreel Valley," the king said, pointing to the map spread on the table before him. "Our scouts tell us that they have begun building up their forces here, just south of Mount Carmel, west of the pass at Megiddo into the Jezreel Valley. It is thought they hope to cut off and regain the new supply routes that have brought us this torrent of new trade."

"Yes, Father." Jonathan nodded. "David's strategic advances last spring have been an undeniable asset. Surely the series of fortifications he has built and manned along the Damascus Road and the Transjordan Highway should put us ahead of the Philistine forces before we've even begun to counter their buildup. Where are you thinking of centering our response? I know so little of this area recently."

"It is true, Your Majesty," Sarek agreed. "Perhaps we should wait until David has joined us. His will be the best understanding of the region."

A silence fell over the room. Someone took Sarek's arm. He was pulled hastily aside. Quick words were whispered into his ear, news of David's fate.

"Father, perhaps we may speak privately?" Jonathan suggested pointedly.

"I don't think that's at all necessary," Saul said haughtily. "I have serious work to do just now."

"Fine, then," Jonathan said, rising and striking the table. "My king, you can ill afford to lose David. You are a fool who is putting his pride above the good of the country if you do not immediately cancel the reward you have offered for David's death."

Saul erupted out of his chair, overturning the table before him. Food and wine and ink and charts flew over the room and those before him. His guests beat a hasty retreat, silently closing the doors behind them as they left the two men to keep each other's company.

"I told you we should speak alone," Jonathan said, a hint of a smile on his lips.

His face burned from the slap that his father delivered; not unexpected, it did nothing to dampen Jonathan's resolve.

"Don't call me a fool in front of my men again," Saul said seriously.

"Don't act like one," Jonathan countered, matching his father's tone.

He caught his father's arm in midflight, precluding a second slap.

The two men struggled until they found themselves at stalemate.

Saul tore his arm from Jonathan's firm grasp, rubbing the sore skin at the wrist where the bruise of Jonathan's fingers was already blooming.

"You will be a good king." Saul nodded grudgingly.

"I will be a great king," Jonathan answered back. "And do you know why?"

Saul only glared at him.

"First, because David will be at my side," Jonathan said with a mighty conviction. "He has been, from his arrival at court, an asset to this kingdom. He saved your life and your wits with his music. He then stepped onto the battlefield when no one else could and struck down the Philistine in a single blow that defeated and destroyed the entire army of Philistia and earned our armies three years' unimpeded progress. It is no accident that the souvenirs of his victory are kept as holy artifacts at Nob with the Ark of the Covenant. He himself has become a sacred symbol to the people, not to mention an asset beyond measure to you and your cause. He has won every challenge you set before him, no matter how unreasonable or unfair or insulting you have been to him, swearing ever his allegiance only to you.

"Do you know what he said when I told him your latest ludicrous charges that he had only married Michal to get closer to your throne and that you'd ordered his death?" Jonathan demanded.

Saul only stared at his son, debating whether or not to tell him of Michal's own accusations against her husband.

"He said 'I hope that Michal does not hear of this and doubt that I am anything other than her loving and devoted husband,'" Jonathan repeated, his voice trembling. "So he is even a fine son-in-law to you and a good husband to my sister, who you know to be a fractious and obstreperous woman who could drive away nettles with her whining and fits.

"So, yes, I think you are a fool in this today, or any other, to throw away a man of such value to you, your army, and your kingdom. I know that, standing at my side, he will make me taller among men and a great king when I might only have been a good one," Jonathan said, readying for another slap and unafraid of it. "No one knows the situation at Jezreel as he does, and he will doubtless save many lives, if not the region, but only if he is at your side."

The two men were silent for a breath. Saul righted his chair and retrieved his goblet. He poured himself some wine, his eyes focused not on his son or the room around him.

"And, Father," Jonathan added more softly, resuming the seat beside Saul's. "The other reason I will be a great king is that you are my father, and I learned to be a great king from you."

And Saul hearkened unto the voice of Jonathan: and Saul sware, As the Lord liveth, he shall not be slain.

1 Samuel 19:6

IT WAS all David could do to remain in the townhouse at Ramah, though the shadows had scarcely turned east. Samuel was still not in residence, and each message sent for his hand only was returned with the seal unbroken. David could not take a meal or rest himself. He spent the night staring at his new ceiling and was no less fitful upon arising.

It was not so much that he was concerned about the arrival of the king's assassins; his concerns were for the prince's fate. He agonized through the night over neglecting to insist that Jonathan send some kind of message or signal confirming his safe return to the palace. It vexed David that he could ill afford to send a message to Jonathan.

All he could do was wait.

Alone with his thoughts, he found his mind wandering to the news of the king's decision that Jonathan marry. He saw for the first time how much he was costing Jonathan. He had driven a wedge between son and father, perhaps even endangering Jonathan's ascension to Saul's throne. It grieved David that his wife Michal, whom he loved in his own way, suffered for his inattention. There was no comfort for him in the knowledge that most men of his station divided their time between many wives and mistresses. Indeed, Saul's mistress Rizpah lived at court with the two sons she had borne him.

Such was the right of a man. Still, it pained David's heart to think that his dishonesty might bring sadness to Michal, whom he cared for, respected, and was proud to call his wife. He resolved to make clear to her the depth and breadth of his affection for her at the first opportunity. She had been his friend and ally at court long before considerations of marriage, even before he and Jonathan had found their way into each other's arms.

Was it time to take his leave? Should he exile himself, no matter the pain it would cause him or those he loved, for their good? Was it selfish to stay, no matter how happy it made him or them? Or cruel to leave only to soothe his own guilt? No idea or argument could defeat the ache in his heart for those he cared about so deeply.

"Ah, Micah," David said, touching the lion's tooth hanging, as always, next to his heart. "Life's blessings give birth to its curses. Our make-believe was so much simpler than the truth of my dreams. Who knew the price that must be paid for happiness?"

"My lord."

David started at the unexpected voice.

"I ask your pardon." One of the bodyguards Jonathan had hired spoke softly from the doorway.

"Please enter," David said hopefully. "I was only talking to an old friend who's no longer with us. Is there news?"

"There is this, from a messenger." The guard knelt as he offered the small parcel.

"Thank you," David said with a nod of gratitude. "I will let you know if there is a reply."

"My lord," the guard said, bowing and backing out of the room.

David smiled at the eastern formality of the guards and servants in the house. Their former master had been from lands beyond the Arabah, and their manner with him was like an elaborate dance to music he could not hear.

He held the thick parchment package, bound with black silk ribbon, aware that he held his fate in his own hands. Stay or go, exoneration or exile, life or death, the decision had been made for him. Anxious to know and fearful of the knowledge, it exacted as much courage from him to pull the ribbon as it had to face Goliath. The package fell open. The ribbon was attached at one end to the signet ring that matched his own and at the opposite to a tiny bit of parchment that bore the prince's mark and his words. "Come home" was all it said.

And he knew where he belonged.

And there was war again: and David went out, and fought with the Philistines... and they fled from him.

1 Samuel 19:8

MICHAL WEPT as she bid her husband good-bye.

"The Lord's justice be yours," she said as he held her close.

Their reunion upon David's return from Ramah had been unexpectedly intense. She seemed genuinely surprised to see him when he arrived at their house. In light of the fact that she'd done all she could to arrange his murder, she truly was. She was even more astonished when he stayed the night with her, the first under theirs or any other roof spent together.

Michal had only just managed to restrain her rage the next morning when she discovered that Jonathan had been away the night before. He'd gone with Saul to make sacrifice with the priests at Nod. Samuel still refused the king's many gifts and entreaties, and Saul was ill at ease starting any venture or campaign without first seeking the Lord's blessing. Michal bit back her anger when, in a flash of lightning, she saw that the only nights she would share with her husband were those when her brother was away. The depth of her feelings for David gave birth to the fire of her hatred for him.

In her fury she called Paltiel to come to her as soon as David had returned to the palace to be with Jonathan.

"Why is he still alive?" she wailed, throwing herself into Paltiel's arms, heedless of the risk if even one of the servants were to see them thus disposed. "Must I kill my own brother to bring my husband back to my bed? Or must I kill my husband, that I might marry again someone who prefers my father's daughter to his son? How cruel is God to hang the door to my happiness on such evil hinges."

"There, there, my dear princess," Paltiel soothed, stroking her hair as she cried. "Fear not, and have faith in a just God. Perhaps the Philistines will do the work for you. Let us wait and see who returns from this battle. It promises to be more fearsome than any your errant husband has fought before."

"It is so unfair, the Philistines so incompetent," she screamed, tearing herself free from his grasp, her rage welling up in her like bile from bad food. "A man may have as many wives as he may need to satisfy him and mistresses beside. But a wife must be content with the husband she gets whether or not he is all that she desires. There is no justice in that."

"My dear and beautiful majesty," Paltiel cooed. He held the distance between them to entice, as a taunting aroma may call one to supper faster than a bell. "Who is to say that is true? Are you not a princess? Do you not make the laws?"

Her tears stopped. She beheld him as though for the first time. A broad satisfied smile split her face when at once she understood, and the horizon of her freedom emerged from the mist before her. She could do as she pleased and seek what she needed. She was a princess, and the wife of a man who had set her free from the bonds of matrimony by his own actions.

Like a predator striking in the wild, she was on him. Before either had the chance to reflect or consider the consequences, they had begun down the most dangerous path available to either. That she was a princess only made their choice riskier. Paltiel fought his own nature and allowed her to be the aggressor to the point where there was no return and no doubt of what she wanted or his willingness to give it.

With furniture reduced to twigs and crockery in shards, their union was born more of rage than of love. They exacted their feelings of loss and abandonment like capital punishment upon each other, deeply, violently, and with an intensity from the depths of their pain. They healed one another, one blow, one bite, one cry at a time.

Finally, lying spent on the floor amidst the remains of the room she shared with David on the rare occasion that he was in residence, they found peace in one another's arms.

They stood dangerously near as they waved good-bye to her husband and his master. Each secretly wished the Lord's justice upon David and Jonathan, that they might be together, triumphant in their betrayal and revenge. Paltiel was not only the princess's lover. Thanks to her influence and the help of her powerful brother, Paltiel was the new minister of the king's treasury. His influential new post gave him and his lover full and unchecked access to the growing resources of the prosperous nation. Michal was free of the bonds of womanhood. Free, just as a man, to find the love and the comfort she had been denied by cruel fate, in arms she chose for herself.

It was a bitter victory, as is all revenge, and not without its risks. But it was better than what either had known before. It was love, or something like it.

CHAPTER THIRTEEN
THE PRINCESS OF EDOM

How long wilt thou forget me, O Lord? For ever? How long wilt thou hide thy face from me?

Psalms 13:1

DAVID'S SKILL in the art of warfare was easy to mistake. Though he possessed a genius for strategy and a sixth sense for outmaneuvering the enemy in the field, he abhorred the death and destruction the wars of great men wrought on the lives of simple people.

No matter how worthy the cause, the cost never left him. It was always as close as the lion's tooth.

It was a bond he shared with Jonathan. Both men delighted in finding solutions and victories that met their ends and spared the innocent to live their lives. However reluctant, both were equally possessed of a flinty resolve to visit the brutal reality and consequence of war only on those who posed a threat to their countrymen and their plans to unite all the tribes into one Israel.

Both men were at once somber and ecstatic as they set off to quell the Philistine uprising in the Jezreel Valley. Serious about the nature of their duty, jubilant for being once again alone together in the field after so a long an absence.

Their only dark clouds caught up to them a few days after they'd arrived in Jezreel to begin scouting. A messenger arrived at their camp with news from the king. A bride, an Edomite princess, had been chosen for the prince. He had met her before—they both had. Because of the strategic importance of an alliance between their two neighboring nations, there had been prior talk of such a marriage.

The red hills of Edom, for whose sanguine hue the country had been named, were south and east of Judah, separated by the strange lands beyond the salty inland Arabah Sea. Since the time of Moses, the two peoples had disputed trade routes. Both claimed dominion over the passages through the Wadi Hisma to Arabia in the east. To the west and south, they disputed routes to Egypt, both on land and across the red southern sea the Lord had parted for Moses.

Thousands of years of animosity were to be solved by marriage to a princess named Azia. As David and Jonathan had agreed, both men were openly celebratory of the news. David offered hearty congratulations on the announcement of Jonathan's marriage to a woman known at court and beyond for her beauty.

In spite of their firm resolve, they soon fell into thoughtful silence with each other as the day wore on. Each in his own way contemplated what the prince's marriage meant for their life together. By the time night fell black around them on the featureless plain of the Jezreel Valley, they sat wordless, eating their evening meal together by the fire pit outside the tent they shared.

The silence eventually became more painful to them than the words they were avoiding. Jonathan was too careful of David's feelings to risk anything. It fell to David to end the drought.

"Azia should be a good wife," David said, toying with the uneaten food on the plate before him, grown cold along with his appetite. "She has always been of the most agreeable temperament. Michal says the princess is too docile, which any man who's met my wife will know is high praise from anyone else."

"Yes, she seems nothing like a Benjamite woman." Jonathan laughed, thinking of the proud and argumentative women of his family. "I hope she is not too quiet."

"Oh, Edomite women may be subservient in public," David said with a knowing chuckle. "But they are as fiery as the red of the hills they come from in private."

Jonathan laughed loudly and without ceasing.

"Why, my lord, is that so amusing to you?" David asked. The firelight hid the red rising across his face.

"David, you sounded so worldly," Jonathan said, trying to stifle his laughter and failing. "What would you know of *women*? I mean in the sense of plural, not the sex in its entirety. I know you have married my sister." He reached out to touch David's shoulder in some small show of affection, still wary of David's feelings.

"Do you think me so inexperienced?" David said, pulling away.

"I do not think of you as a man of great experience with women."

"Well, in truth there was only one other woman, an Edomite, before your sister," David admitted. "But there was the one, and I know from which I speak."

"I see." Jonathan nodded solemnly. "If she was as fiery in the bedroom as you say, perhaps then that is where you learned it?"

David found another use for his cold supper.

Before the fire had fallen to embers, the two were smeared with food and sleeping peacefully in each other's arms on a rug beneath the spring sky. So it was, day by day, that the two navigated the tension of their uncertain future together. Neither felt that another marriage would end them, but each worried that they would be separated by the duties to which they were called.

Saul took a more active interest in their progress with the Philistines. Daily reports of their scouting of the enemy positions and possible strategy were dispatched to him at the palace. Though David laughed it off, Jonathan found that Saul always answered the reports with orders that sent David into the most dangerous situations.

"He is right," David said, as much to cover his own suspicions as to reassure Jonathan. "I am more familiar with the area just now. The men here are my recruits and accustomed to following me. I did well enough last season on my own with less."

Whatever Saul's objectives, the result was always the same.

Whether it was, as Samuel said, that the Lord was on David's side or, as Jonathan maintained, that David was their greatest general, the outcome of his every encounter with the Philistines all through the summer was victory.

With each report of more success, more land reclaimed or reinforced, the king's daring on David's behalf grew. Each new royal assignment was riskier than the one before. Each was another triumph. The Philistines were pushed farther out of the valley, down the coast, and into their own territory. It was as though David could not fail. Hence the king could have whatever he asked for, no matter how extreme. Each success made David more famous and revered, each a blessing to the king—and a curse.

By fall the Philistine forces were decimated. Victorious, the two commanders and their troops returned to the palace for holy feast days and the onset of the rainy season of winter. David was undisputed as hero, the greatest leader in all Israel.

Saul's rage swelled to match the nation's pride. The songs of victory in the streets no longer mentioned anyone but David. The king had, through his own contrivance to destroy his son-in-law, built David into a legend with which Saul feared he could no longer compete.

More frustrated than the king was David's beloved wife, Michal. She had grown comfortable in her own house with a lover she could easily command. Whatever she was, though, Michal was no fool. She knew that each stolen kiss, each touch, each night with Paltiel raised the chance that they would be found out. Discovery meant death.

Palti's end would most certainly be swift and brutal, his head falling at his feet, the expression of surprise at being caught still on his lips. Her fate was harder to divine. Because she was a princess, perhaps she would simply be banished to some prison existence far from court and comfort for the rest of her life. But it was equally likely that her rank would force her father to make her an example. That meant public stoning, battered to death by the vengeful and fleetingly superior.

Her fear and her newfound taste for freedom and fulfillment made her yearn for the safe haven she could find only in word of David's death. With news of each dangerous assignment, her hopes grew. Each victory celebrated dashed them again. The days grew shorter and her husband's return more imminent. Michal decided, with Paltiel's counsel, that the time had come to reveal the secret she hoped would put an end to her husband and possibly, she feared, her brother.

The return of the two heroes was planned with a triumphant parade into the city. There was to be a series of ceremonies, sacrifices, feasts, and celebrations to culminate in Jonathan's wedding. Fully apprised, David and the prince made camp with their forces just outside the city to make ready for their tribute. They sent word ahead, once their arrival was certain, so that the final preparations could be made.

Michal, who had played a key role in planning the festivities, received word that her husband would be returning to her the following morning. It was the news that decided their course of action.

"Wish me well," she said to Paltiel as she awaited a sedan to bear her to the palace. "I hope that I can find the words to conclude my marriage, yet still allow us to claim his royalties and properties in Bethlehem."

"You will be his widow," Paltiel said with a smirk.

"I'll still be a woman," Michal said sourly. "I'm likely to lose it all to Eliab or any one of all those brothers."

"Not if you discredit his name and his family," Paltiel growled in her ear as he smoothed her robes, ever the valet.

"I'll do my best," she said with a shrug. "He has done nothing to wrong me other than what bed he most chooses. That is blessed little claim for a wife who lives as well as I do, or any other, in truth."

"But the bed he chooses belongs to the king's son and heir," Paltiel encouraged. "That smells more like treason than infidelity, if you tell the story right."

"And I am a good storyteller, after all." She laughed, turning to steal a good-bye kiss from him as her palanquin arrived.

Saul was in high spirits, despite his feelings about David's growing fame and reputation with the people. No one benefited more directly from David's many victories and the expansion and advancement of the kingdom of Israel. The treasury overflowed. The lavish celebration was a tribute to Saul's reign, earned on David's back.

Filled with wine and good cheer, Saul was already celebrating when his daughter arrived asking for an audience. Thinking her visit would concern details for the next day's festivity and would detain him only briefly, Saul begged his guests' indulgence and left his private party to attend to his daughter.

"Father," Michal said, rising and bowing as he entered the chamber where she awaited him. "I am sorry to take you away."

"My child," he said effusively, opening his arms to invite her embrace. "Get up and kiss your father. Why so serious and formal?"

"You are right," she said, rising and moving to him. She brushed his cheek with her lips, delighted to find him sentimental and, not coincidentally, reeking of wine. "Now is not the time for worries. I'll leave you to your guests."

"Michal," Saul said, catching her elbow as she turned to go. "I am never too busy to speak with you, my daughter. What would you have of me? Some concern over tomorrow's banquet? The wedding, perhaps?"

"Oh, my lord," she said, sinking to her knees. Her eyes filled with tears as she choked out her words. "I would that I came to speak of such joyous events. I should not be here."

"Daughter," Saul said, kneeling to meet her face-to-face. He took her into his arms. "What is it?"

"I have argued myself sick over whether or not to speak with you," she said convincingly. "I know what tomorrow means to you and to the whole country. I don't know which is the better course for me. I have needed wisdom and guidance in this, and I have not been able to ask my father." She trailed off into hysterical sobs.

"Shhh, I am here now," the king assured her. "I cannot help if you do not tell me what troubles you. Come now, let me decide for myself. That is why I am your father and your king."

"I cannot."

"Daughter, enough of this," Saul said firmly but with an equally firm and reassuring embrace. "Nothing can be so bad."

"I have deceived you," she said suddenly and with a cry of pain. "I have kept something from you to protect you. I fear that I may have done more harm than good."

"I know full well that you and your mother and sister have overspent for tomorrow's celebrations, and I am little concerned." He chuckled, rocking her in his arms. "I only set the first figures I gave you because I knew you'd overspend by less than if I'd told you how much I was truly prepared to pay."

His laugh echoed alone in the room over her quiet sobs.

"In trying to protect you, I fear I may have betrayed you," she said starkly, sitting up suddenly. She looked him straight in the eye.

The laughter died in his throat.

"Betrayed?" he said, sober suddenly. "Daughter, what have you done?"

"We have spoken before about my husband's *tastes*," she said, pulling away and pronouncing the words as though they burned her mouth. "I know you have reassured me that a man will find his own comfort. That it is nothing to his wife, so long as he is kind and supportive. And he is both. I want for nothing."

"I don't understand how you have betrayed me in this," the king said, regarding her with more confusion than concern.

"I have told you that my husband has a lover, a man. That they have been together longer than he and I have been married," she said, half whispering, turning her face to the shadows. "What I have not told you is that the man he shares his bed with each night is your son and heir, the prince, Jonathan."

It was as though the air had left the room.

The king sank to the ground, overwhelmed by the enormity of it. In many ways it explained so much of what had transpired. But the infamy and the betrayal of all of it was more than he could bear. At last he saw and understood David's scheme completely. David would take control of the country through Saul's own heir, and he had been too blind to see it.

"Father," Michal said, rushing to Saul's side when he collapsed before her.

"Go, leave me," Saul said, pushing her away so violently that he knocked her to the ground.

"Father, no," she wailed as he crawled across the floor away from her. "I have come to you for counsel, and I have hurt you. I should have carried this burden alone and spared you."

"Guards," the king bellowed.

Michal was truly terrified. She could not tell if she had achieved her aim or overshot the mark.

"Forgive me, Father," she pleaded, weeping in earnest.

"Guard," the king said hoarsely as several of his personal retinue rushed into the room and to his side, alarmed to find him on the floor.

"Majesty, how may I serve you?" the captain of the small detail asked, trying to help the king to his feet.

"See that my daughter gets home safely," he hissed, shoving the man angrily away. "Bring me some wine and my sword."

"Father, tell me that I've done right," Michal begged as she was dragged away. She withheld her smile until she was safely on her way home to her lover.

And the evil spirit from the Lord was upon Saul, as he sat in his house with his javelin in his hand: and David played with his hand.

1 Samuel 19:9

THE FOLLOWING morning found the king so much changed, Michal worried that his wine had washed away their conversation. When she arrived to join him on the reviewing stage built in front of the temple for the day, he smiled and welcomed her warmly with no sign of his previous mood. From their vantage there, he was to acknowledge the troops as they returned.

She would have been left entirely to wonder, had he not taken her hand as she stepped onto the platform and whispered into her ear. "You have done well, my daughter. Your loyalty will be remembered." Michal smiled and kissed his cheek. Still mystified by his behavior, she was secure at least of her own place in the king's favor. She shot Paltiel a reassuring look and a nod as she took her place with her mother and the women to watch from the background.

The triumph was embarrassingly extravagant. By the time David and Jonathan came into view at the end of the procession, the crowd was frenzied with excitement and spectacle.

Jonathan was presented to the crowd with his bride-to-be. They received heartfelt cheers and accolades. When David was announced and made his way onto the platform to take part in the sacrifice, there was a near riot of acclaim.

Saul stepped back and joined his son Jonathan and the rest of the crowd in their applause. The intensity of the accolade overwhelmed David. After acknowledging the crowds who chanted his name with growing hysteria, he stepped back with a humble bow. Taking the hands of Jonathan and Saul, he held them aloft in a show of victory and solidarity.

The gesture was met with thunderous response. Once again the king demurred and stepped back to be among the admiring, applauding David's accomplishments on behalf of the kingdom. Jonathan was so moved by Saul's show of support and generosity to his beloved David, he was stirred to embrace his father warmly.

The day continued in the same joyous vein. David stood up for Jonathan at the wedding. The subsequent feasts and banquets were filled with an elation born of great hope and relief that the kingdom was safe, sound, and prospering as it grew. Anything seemed possible. Tears and kissing were tempered with prayers of thanksgiving and shouts of joy as the day unfolded, undimmed by care or worry, as in some beautiful dream.

"My son, David," the king called out, silencing the revelry of the wedding banquet for a breath. "Only you have the power to make this night more than perfect. Give us a song in honor of the occasion of my son Jonathan's wedding to this beautiful woman, of this fine family directly descended from King Esau.

I know, as I suspect do others here as well, that as fine a general as you have grown up to be, you are an even finer singer. I can bear witness that your voice is so clear and your playing of such beauty that you have the power to heal with your art. Pray, indulge your king."

The cheer went up. No show of modesty or reticence would deter the crowd or their king's demands for a song from their hero.

David was overwhelmed. It had been hard enough to stand at Jonathan's right as he married the Princess Azia. In truth, it was more melancholy than modesty that caused him to eschew the king's request. He could hardly imagine a psalm that expressed all he felt upon the faceted occasion. After his overwhelming greeting, it was enough that he sit through Jonathan's wedding to another. Spent, he could not muster unfelt praises for an event that burned like an arrow in his heart. But one could not say no to the king. It was to much acclamation that he rose and made his way to the platform. The musicians stepped aside to make a place for him.

He accepted the offered harp. Taking a breath, he stilled his heart and said a silent prayer that the Lord give him strength enough to bring tribute to the man he loved. His eyes met Jonathan's. They shared a smile, and David found the inspiration he'd prayed for there. With resolve and joy, he stroked at the familiar strings. Silencing the crowd with a nod, he began to play. And then he sang.

My heart is overflowing with joy and goodness
as I recite my verses for the prince and his princess;
my tongue is the pen of a skillful writer.
You are fairer than the sons of men
and your lips have been anointed with grace,
since God has blessed you forever.
You love righteousness and hate wickedness;
therefore God, your God, has set you above your companions
by anointing you with the oil of joy.
Your sons will take the place of your fathers;
you will make them princes throughout the land.
And I your humble servant will make your name to be remembered
in all generations: therefore shall the people praise you forever and ever.

It was clear that David was singing the song to Jonathan. Their eyes locked across the room. Few in the hall understood it as more than a sentimental tribute from a subject to his prince. Paltiel stood nearby the women's table. Michal's hand secretly found his. Taking it, she clutched so tightly that his knuckles turned white. Despite the cold that had come into her heart, its season had not changed. It was still David's hand she longed to hold in her own. He had grown from a boy of exceptional beauty into a man still possessed of his youthful charm. However slight, his stature had weathered into the powerful king by whom she still ached to lie. She beheld him in his finery that night. His beauty and her love for him inspired the bitter words of longing for his destruction, caught in a ceaseless refrain playing in her heart like a tune she could not stop humming.

Whatever the reaction, all were enthralled by the evocative scene and David's moving and heartfelt performance of the wedding psalm he had invented. None noticed as the king left his place. He stole behind the elaborate drapes that had been hung all along the walls for the occasion. When he emerged suddenly on the stage, behind David, no threat was at first perceived and none present were prepared or inspired to act against the king. Lunging, Saul came at David with the iron-tipped pike he carried.

"David," Jonathan cried out. He rose helplessly from where he sat at the banquet table. Only a heartbeat before, his father had sat beside him. "Behind you, there."

Without pausing to look, but only reacting to his habit of Jonathan's command, David dropped and wheeled. Using the harp he was playing as a shield, he deflected the king's assault. The spear plunged into the panels that covered the wall behind them.

As the room erupted into confusion and chaos, David's eyes met those of his king. He knew it was finished. He knew that the happiness that had been his ended that day. He knew that he would never again be safe in the king's company.

The two stood frozen facing one another.

"I will always be your humble servant, my king, for you are the Lord's anointed," David said to Saul, though only they heard.

David could easily have plucked the spear from the wall and plunged it through the king's unjust heart, had he chosen. Such befitted neither the man he was, nor the covenant he had made with Jonathan. Instead, with a fleeting and, he feared, final look upon his prince, David turned, placed one hand over his heart, and with the other touched the ring Jonathan had given him. It was their sign. Jonathan mirrored his pose where he stood across the room. David flew from the hall, through the passages and corridors of the palace, and past the guards, unaware of what had transpired and more interested in the confusion.

In the confusion that followed, Jonathan knew he would be of more use to David at hand than in flight at his side, though it was where he'd rather have been. Unable to reach David before his departure, he instead made his way to Michal.

"Go, follow David," he said, grasping her arm and lifting her from her seat at the table. "Get him to go to your house. Wait with him there until I can sort this out with Father. I cannot think what this is about. Be assured—assure him—that I will make this right. Know that all will be well."

"I will take care of him," Michal said with strange calm. She rose from the table as though it was simply the end of the party and time to go home.

Jonathan shoved his way into the crowd without a backward glance. Michal signaled to Paltiel to follow her out.

"I'm going to follow David and take him back to the house," she said softly into his ear. "Tell my father to send his men there to collect him. We shall end this tonight."

"My lady," Paltiel said, bowing and kissing her hand.

"Fetch my sedan and bear me home," she shouted to the groomsmen in the courtyard. Before they could get underway, she spied David attempting to make his way to the street before the palace among a group of musicians.

"Come," she ordered, catching his arm. "I am ready to go. Come and bear me away."

With a formal nod and a smile of gratitude for her quick thinking, he joined the men who carried her palanquin into the street and home.

He spoke not at all to her as she chattered nervously that all would be well and that Jonathan would fix everything. She too was soon at a loss for words when clearly none were adequate. They proceeded in silence.

David released the sedan as they entered the courtyard, before they had even stopped. He bounded into the house and up the stairs, in darkness, to their room. Without lighting so much as a candle, he threw himself upon their bed and wept for what he knew must soon be.

"Oh my Lord, where are you?" he said. "Do you not believe in me after all? I thank you for the glimpses of joy and love that you have allowed me, and I ask only that you keep Jonathan safe."

Michal stood silently outside the open door to her room in the darkness, listening to her husband's prayer. "Amen," she said bitterly and turned to go.

Saul also sent messengers unto David's house, to watch him, and to slay him.

1 Samuel 19:11

PALTIEL MOVED swiftly. He knew that in the end his life depended on it. His time with Michal had been stolen, and the theft would be discovered sooner or later. David's death was not only desirable, it was essential to save his own and, not incidentally, Michal's. More than her well-being was at stake. She was the key to all his plans.

Having worked as a servant in the palace, Paltiel knew the fastest means to get around. He easily beat Jonathan to the king's side. With familiar words of comfort, he was quickly able to gain the king's confidence. Guiding Saul into a servants' passage, they moved swiftly away to the royal quarters by means unknown to the prince.

By the time Jonathan arrived at the king's doors, there were guards posted.

"I'm sorry, my prince," one of the guards ventured timidly, observing his mood and well aware of the evening's events. "The king himself has given us orders that no one is to be admitted."

Heedless of the danger and daring the guards to do anything about it, Jonathan began pounding on the locked doors.

"Father, Father, let me in," Jonathan bellowed. He hammered with his fists and then his sword. "I demand that you see me."

The door opened, but only wide enough for Paltiel's face to emerge.

"My friend," Paltiel said, in a soothing tone he'd used on the prince many times before. "Your father does not wish to see you. He bids you to go to your bride and do your duty 'for a change'—his words it pains me to say. Let me talk with him. I'll see if I can calm him and get him to see reason."

"Thank God you are here, old friend," Jonathan said, taking Paltiel's hand. "I will do as my father bids and rely on you to make things right. I know you of all men to be the ideal ambassador for this treaty."

"Trust me, my prince." Paltiel smiled broadly. "I know just what to do."

Michal David's wife told him, saying, If thou save not thy life tonight, tomorrow thou shalt be slain.

1 Samuel 19:11

MICHAL GREETED the king's guard when they arrived. Paltiel's instructions had preceded the soldiers, though only by long enough to be read and destroyed. She was ready with his words.

"I'm sorry," Michal said with the confidence of a princess. "My husband is ill. Tell my father that David is in his bed and cannot come to the palace now."

She slammed the door in the captain's face before he could speak. As only she could have, she left the armed men in the courtyard afraid to knock again. As Paltiel had calculated, in deference to her, the guardsman had no choice but to post a sentry at her front door and return to the king for further instructions.

Using the time the scheme had earned her, she carried out its next steps. Rushing upstairs with a candle, she began to light the lamps.

"My husband, you must flee," Michal said urgently as she burst into their bedchambers. "The king has sent his guard to collect you."

"His guard," David said groggily. "What of Jonathan?"

"I don't know, my husband," Michal said, pulling some few things into a leather sack. "I've called for some bread and wine to take with you. Clearly Jonathan has not yet succeeded. You will be better off elsewhere until he does."

"Why has this happened?" David asked, still unable to untangle the knot the day had become.

"There is no understanding the riddle that is my father," Michal said, seating herself on the floor. Taking bed sheets from a chest at the foot of their bed, she began tying them together. She hurried in her task as though she might escape the knowledge that she was the author of her husband's fate. "There are guards waiting for you out front. I have told my father's captain that you are ill. That will only last until the king's next orders, which no doubt will include splintering our front door. You must use these." She handed him the knotted linens. "Climb out the window. Escape into the hills just beyond. It seems we got more than just a good view with this house."

"What of you, my wife?" David said, surprising her as he took her in his arms. "I cannot leave you here to face this without me."

"Oh, my husband," she said, stroking his beautiful hair with motherly tenderness, though she longed to tear it out by the root that she alone might always possess it. "I am his daughter. He will not harm me, no matter how angry he is, or what he is angry about."

"I can't bear to abandon you to face this," David said, sinking to her feet. He embraced her at the knees, his face pressed just below the sash at her waist. His hot breath there weakened her resolve, so that she tore herself away by sheerest will.

"You must go, my lord," she said, troubled by the first doubts she'd felt since the day she'd begun the journey to that dark destination. Turning and falling to her knees so that they were again face-to-face, she embraced him with all the love and passion that fueled her hatred. "If you love me, you must go."

"Then for the sake of that alone will I leave you," he said, taking her in his arms.

Racked with guilt over the horrible bargain he had made at her expense, he kissed her as she had only ever dreamed that he would. His passions shattered her jagged heart as she knew that he loved her brother as he could never love her or any woman, but felt in his embrace the truth of his love for her.

"The food, my lady." A serving girl from the kitchen interrupted the kiss, clearing her throat at the door.

Reluctantly Michal pulled away. Taking the food, she shoved it into the bag with the other few possessions she had assembled.

"Here, you must go now," she said. Thrusting the bag into his arms, she kept it between them to protect herself from her own feelings as she let him go. She tossed the ladder of sheets out the window and secured the other end to a rafter with a stout knot.

"I will send for you as soon as I can," David said as he leaned in for one last kiss.

"Go now. I cannot bear it," she said, shoving him away.

"Forgive me for whatever it is that I have done to cause such trouble and for bringing any of it to you, my dear and beloved wife," he said, grasping her hand in his and kissing her knuckles hungrily, aware this might be his last night and this their last meeting. Then turning, he scaled down the back of the house with the crude rope.

Unable to stop herself, she stole one last glimpse of him from the window. With a clipped wave, he disappeared into the night.

The tears that flooded her eyes for once were genuine. Perhaps he wouldn't be caught and killed, she consoled herself. Perhaps he would simply never be found. In her heart she knew that this could not be so. For her sake, and the sake of her plans with Paltiel, David must die. She could hardly see to finish her task, but she soldiered on. From just outside the door where she had concealed them, she brought in a bag of pale goat's hair and a winged teraph. The idol, a strictly forbidden god to whom she had been praying for her freedom, was but a further strand in the web she had spun to catch her long and recently absent husband. She placed the idol in their bed. Arranging the bedclothes and the ruddy goat's hair, she gave the pale illusion of her husband in his bed in the lamplight. Her design was intended less to deceive than to give the impression of his contrivance to escape and the inference of his idolatry.

Drawing the bed-curtains and taking the lamp, she left the room in darkness. She took up a place in the first floor sitting room to wait for the soldiers' return. There, alone, she wept for the love she could never have and would never stop wanting.

When the pounding again came at her door, she dried her eyes. Shooing away a servant who typically would have seen to such a lowly task, she opened the door herself.

"Captain," Michal said in terse greeting as he shoved past her and up the stairs.

"Where is he?" the solider demanded of her.

"Why, upstairs in his bed, ill, as I have told you," Michal answered, pursuing him and his men halfheartedly.

"The king says we're to fetch his bed with him in it and bring it to the palace," the captain explained as gently as possible. "No offense intended, my lady, but the king's orders, you know. And if you'd be so kind as to accompany us."

"I will not let you," she cried out. Pushing past the captain, she dove through the curtains and into the bed with her husband. "I will not be parted from my husband."

"Let's go, men," the captain ordered. "Get a good handhold. We've a long walk ahead of us, and it will the sooner be over once we've begun. And heave...."

"Ho," the men answered.

The soldiers carried the bed through the street as they found it. Because it contained the princess, they dared not examine their burden too closely.

The night was more than half over by the time they made their way, with their absurd burden, into the throne room at the palace.

"Father," Michal cried out, stepping through the bed-curtains and running to him. "I'm so sorry. He told me he would kill me if I did not do as he asked."

"Oh, did he?" Saul said, stepping forward. He drew back the curtains and tore off the blankets to reveal the obscene and blasphemous idol. "Where is he?" With a great cry, he hurled the statue against the stone wall and shattered it.

"God and all my ancestors," Saul shouted, waving his fist heavenward. "Shall I never be free of this man?"

CHAPTER FOURTEEN
THE ROAD TO NAIOTH

So David fled, and escaped, and came to Samuel to Ramah, and told him all that Saul had done to him. And he and Samuel went and dwelt in Naioth.

1 Samuel 19:18

UNDER COVER of darkness, David borrowed a horse from the army's encampment outside Gibeah. He rode all night, reaching Ramah ahead of the royal decrees calling for his capture and his death. In the darkness he slipped into the refuge of the townhouse. He was welcomed by the servants, who were still unaware of his true identity. Giving them instructions that he was not at home to any but Jonathan or the high priest Samuel, he immediately dispatched messages to them both, though Jonathan's had to be sent more circuitously, through Joab.

News that the king had declared him a traitor, and a warrant issued for his head, reached him before replies from prince or priest. He was devastated by the hopelessness of his position. Worse was the prince's silence. He could not understand what had happened to Jonathan. What had become of Jonathan's intercession with the king? What had brought about the turn of events that led to this? Had Jonathan's words on David's behalf been his undoing? Could Saul harm his own son?

David prayed ceaselessly for Jonathan's safety even before his safe return to David's side. For two days there was no word from outside. For two days David waited, sleepless. He took only water and some little bread and oil to sustain himself, watching the horizon from the roof by day and night.

As the sun reached its height on the third day, the servants arrived at the point of distraction with worry over their master. His sudden arrival in the night and strange behavior since had thrown the household into an uproar. At first they had thought their master simply tired from his journey and late arrival. When he refused food, they worried that he was ill and plied him with cures and remedies, which he also declined. By the third day, they were terrified some sort of plague had come into the house with David and argued over who would attend him for fear of contracting the complaint. The mood was so taut that the houseman cried out when there came a knock at the door.

"The judge of the kingdom of Israel, Samuel, come to call upon your master," the young priest announced to the servant at David's gate. Warily, David's houseman looked out. The curtained sedan chair rested on the shoulders of half a dozen or more men in temple attire. Longing for any change and hoping for a cure for his master lest his malady kill them all, he allowed them into the courtyard. After a halfhearted attempt to help as Samuel himself emerged, he dashed inside to announce the arrival of his master's long-awaited visitor.

David, as if suddenly and miraculously cured, leaped to his feet and raced to greet his guest.

"Samuel is here? Not just a message but actually here?" David demanded of the servant. They ran to greet the judge, the servant following. "Prepare a feast and open the sitting room. Bring wine and cool water and cakes and whatever we have to make him comfortable."

"David." The old man's voice brought him up short. There had been many harvests since they'd last met. David, who'd made light of the judge's last visit, knelt at the feet of the holy man.

"You do my house honor," David said humbly. "I had not thought to expect to be granted more than an audience."

"It is I who should kneel before you," Samuel said, making his way forward as best a man of his years might. Extending his hand, he reached as if to help David up. "Alas, given my age, you will have to settle for my intention rather than my supplication. I fear if I were to bow down to you, you would then be forced to suffer the indignity of helping me back up."

"Why would you bow to me?" David asked, arising. He smiled politely, puzzled at what he took as the old man's mirth. Taking Samuel's arm, he led him into the grand sitting room.

"I am but your humble servant," Samuel said, a twinkle in his eye as he beheld the man before him. David had been on the sunny side of manhood when they'd last met. "I thought I had made that clear the last time we met?"

"My mistake, I'm sure," David said, truly amazed at such a statement from the spiritual leader of his people. Deference hardly seemed his due from a man who answered only to the Lord and the king. From what he understood from Jonathan, perhaps not even the king made that list.

"How may I serve you today?" Samuel asked as David helped him into a chair carved of find black wood from the east, polished to a watery glow.

"I don't know," David confessed, taking a seat on the cushions at the old man's feet. "I only know that Prince Jonathan bought this house because it was near you. He told me that he knew you could be trusted because you were the only man in the kingdom and perhaps the world whom his father still feared."

"The king has grown arrogant, but he was a fine man once." Samuel sighed sadly. "I don't know that he fears me. He has not killed me yet, though I've been prepared for it since you and I last broke bread together."

"He has issued a warrant calling for my death," David said, relieved at last, in Jonathan's absence, to be able to trust and confide in someone. "I come to Ramah seeking your advice, if not your protection."

"Then he knows," Samuel said, nodding as though he were speaking with someone other than David. Closing his eyes, he spoke words that were too soft for David to hear or understand. The servants arrived with trays of food and ewers of drink. David held them at bay with a gesture. Rising, he closed the doors silently so as not to disturb the holy man in his reverie.

At last Samuel opened his eyes and began to get himself back onto his feet.

"We must leave at once," Samuel said, taking the arm that David offered. "Your message to Joab for the prince has been intercepted. Though he will not know your exact location, the king will soon know you are in Ramah."

"What shall we do?" David asked, too stunned to question Samuel's knowledge of things to which he was not privy.

"I think it's time we went to Naioth," Samuel said as the two moved to the front doors. They passed the baffled servants, their arms laden with the food David had ordered.

"Naioth?" David said, unfamiliar with the place.

"A vision quest," Samuel answered simply as David helped him into his sedan. "We shall make camp in the desert highlands, fast, and seek the Lord's protection and guidance—Naioth."

"Naioth, then," David said, nodding, still unsure of the idea. "Shall I accompany you?"

"It is for you," Samuel said with a kindly laugh. "Saddle a horse and let us go at once. I shall send my men on ahead to prepare what we need, that we might go at once into the desert. We must make haste, for the king is receiving the news of your whereabouts just now."

And it was told Saul, saying, Behold, David is at Naioth in Ramah.
1 Samuel 19:19

"RAMAH?" THE king gasped as his spies brought him the news. "What is he doing in Ramah?"

"The message said he is seeking an audience with Samuel," the messenger explained. The king's goblet clattered to the stones at their feet, interrupting the man.

"The Lord is turned against me, then," Saul railed, shaking his fist at heaven. "What have I not done for you that you would shelter this traitor from justice?"

"Your Majesty?" his captain asked, unsure of how to proceed.

"We shall beard the lion in his den, then," Saul said, suddenly energized and decisive in his resolve. "Samuel is just a man, after all. We shall take this news as a sign from the Lord that he is on our side. Go to Ramah. Find Samuel. If David is with him, arrest him and bring him back here to me. If he resists, kill him. There shall be rich rewards to the men who bring me David's head, whether or not it still sits on his shoulders."

"What of the judge?" the captain asked.

"No man in Israel is above the Lord's anointed king, not even Samuel," Saul declared in his furor. "No argument from Samuel is to take precedence over the king's word. I don't want him killed. It would be too much trouble to me. But I no longer care what he thinks. If he is sheltering those who plot against me and my line, then he is as a traitor to me. Enough talk. To Ramah."

"To Ramah," the captain and his guard said, striking their chests in salute before bowing to the king.

"To Ramah," Jonathan said softly to himself, smiling. He remained behind the tapestry that overhung the open doorway of the little used office. As his father's rage descended into incoherent rantings, he listened sadly for a breath more, then departed for the holy city.

My voice shalt thou hear in the morning, O Lord; in the morning will I direct my prayer unto thee, and will look up.

Psalms 5:3

THE SOLDIERS rode along the Ridge Road through the night to Ramah, seeking their fortune even as they sought word of David.

The news of David's unnamed treason swept through the country, with promises from the king of great riches in reward for his capture. Speculation about the nature of David's crimes ran wild, as no whiff of scandal or guilt had been in the air a sunrise prior to the shadows that fell upon his character.

Word of David's fate tormented and scandalized Jesse and his sons. Helpless and terrified, they were unable to confirm or deny the truth of it as Eliab and Joab, who were still attached to Abner's army, had no more information than could be had in Bethlehem. The family closed the city house early. Taking refuge at the karmel, they waited, as uncertain of their own fate as they were of David's.

Jonathan made his way through the hills to the east of Gibeah. It was early morning when he rode into Ramah. His horse limped from the stones on their path. Arriving unnoticed, he made his way to the townhouse in hope of finding David still there.

The servants, accustomed to having the house to themselves most of the time, were becoming wary and adept at dealing with the strange goings-on.

"Have you seen our master?" Jonathan asked without greeting. Handing over his horse's lead, he made his way across the courtyard to the door of the house.

"He's not at home, but he has left a message to you," the houseman said less than respectfully, still believing Jonathan was nothing more than their master's plaything. "He said, 'If you rest your head, you'll know where.' Perhaps it's writ on the ceiling above the bed," he called rudely over his shoulder as he led the lamed animal to the stable, chuckling to himself.

He was still laughing at his own wit when he found himself in the watering trough.

"See to the horse, won't you?" Jonathan said, genially patting the man on the shoulder, his hand making a wet smacking sound. "He's got a stone bruise from the ride, I think. And mind how you speak to me in the future."

"Right you are, sir," the houseman nodded with a stiff wave. It was odd, but of late, he reasoned, what in that house was not? In truth, the man was even uncertain of the master's father's name and had only ever seen him on two occasions. Still, if the great priest came to call and bowed at the master's feet, he must be a very important man.

Jonathan lit a candle and found his way to the chambers they'd shared their one night in residence together. He looked around the room. Uncertain of what he was looking for, he searched for sign of the message from David. He could not resist lying on his back to look up to the ceiling and laughed at himself when he found nothing there.

He looked under the pillows on his usual side of the bed and the mattress and the bed on that same side. And then on David's side. It was midmorning by the time he finally, frustrated, lay down on the bed to rest his eyes. When he woke up it was early evening. He despaired of finding David's message or, more important, David, in time to save him from his father's men.

Tears welled up in his eyes as he considered the possibility that he might never hold David in his arms again, or see him, or argue with him about some trifle. Moved by his own sense of desperation, he fell to his knees at the side of the low bed and cried out as he had never done before, in prayer to God.

"Oh Lord, help me," he managed, racked with his own emotion. "I have never asked you for anything, Lord. I have been too proud. Now I beg you only for David's safety. Return him safe to me, or put it in my way to keep him safe. Please, oh Lord, don't let it end like this, but if one of us must go, let it be me. You and I both know he is the better man. I could not bear to live in this world if he was not in it."

He lay for a while in that position, unable to find the strength to move or go on. As he lay there, his eyes traced a couple of cracks in the plaster over the stones in the wall, seeking a pattern as the eye will find faces in the clouds. He looked at the *v* formed by the two cracks. It reminded him of the ears of the rabbit that formed their imaginary constellation. Like a saphan, he was up and across the room to examine his sign. He noted that not only were they like the rabbit's ears but also an arrow pointing straight down. Trying, he found one of the tiles loose—and writing like David's hand in charcoal on the smooth back.

"*J—S has come and we are in Naioth where the Lord or at least S can protect me. I will return to you as soon as I can. Yours now and always—D.*"

"Naioth?" he said aloud, trying on the unfamiliar village name.

Rising and going through the empty public rooms of the great house, tile in hand, he made his way across the central courtyard to the kitchen. He found the staff huddled around the table and more than surprised to see him.

"Where is Naioth?" he demanded, again without greeting.

They only looked at him.

"Have you heard of a place called Naioth?" he asked again.

"Perhaps if you ate something," the houseman suggested cautiously.

And Saul sent messengers to take David.

1 Samuel 19:20

"NAIOTH?" THE captain asked of the young novice who greeted him at Samuel's temple. "Where is this Naioth? Is this a city near here?"

"Something like that." The novice smiled. "It is the priest's retreat in the high desert. A city of tents, really. I've no idea exactly where. No special place. The only way to find them is to go into the desert at night."

"At night?" The captain scoffed.

"Unless you went with them in the first place, it is easiest to find then," the novice said agreeably.

"Perhaps you could show us how this is true?"

"Do you wish to go on Naioth?" the novice asked, most pleased and surprised.

"Yes, please." The captain nodded.

"God be praised," the young priest said, taking his hand.

"God be praised," the captained echoed brusquely. "When can we begin?"

"Well, you must fast for three days, without food or water," the novice explained. "Then you must strip off your armor, your sandals, and your weapons and clothe yourself in goat's hair."

"Why don't you take me today as I am?" the captain suggested harshly, rattling his sword for emphasis.

"Naioth isn't a place." The young priest laughed. "It's a state of mind. You can kill me if you like, but then you'll never know Naioth."

It was maddening, but the priest would not relent, and no man among them would harm a priest. So the men who sought David, and the riches that awaited them in reward for his capture, found that they must also seek Naioth. It was just as Samuel had foreseen and instructed.

Their fast concluded and their journey underway, the captain and his men were dizzy from hunger and thirst. Their feet were raw and burnt from climbing into the hills and trekking across the desert without sandals. Their skin was on fire from the itchy goat hair in the heat, as they followed the young priest through the high desert night. In their state they began to imagine shapes and demons where there were none, to feel strange presences brush cold against them, to hear voices unspoken whispering the truths of their hearts in their ringing ears.

The captain was disoriented. He had taken to holding on to the rope around the young priest's waist so that he did not wander off into the night. The man behind him did so as well, as did the one behind him, and so on. No longer thinking of his destination but only of following the priest, the captain began to listen to the whispers and to hear the voice of truth.

"Yes," he cried out suddenly as they came over a ridge. "Yes, of course. The riches mean nothing. I see now. There, look; it is a sign. We have found our way."

As the others came awake from their own personal reveries, they beheld the amazing sight. Glowing like lanterns in the night, sprinkled together across the desert floor below, were the tents of Naioth.

"We are there," the young priest said with a mixture of joy and relief.

"You can see it, then?" the captain asked, laughing, almost childlike with delight.

"You have found Naioth," the priest said gently, embracing the trembling man.

With shouts of joy, the captain and his soldiers plunged headlong down the hill from which they beheld the lustrous sight. They ran toward the light with a sense of freedom none had known before. Many stripped off their goat hair robes to increase their sense of liberation and release.

"Welcome, welcome," Samuel called from the entrance to the large main tent. The soldiers rushed to greet him, bowing down before him, cleansed by their quest of the motives that had brought them. Inside, the chanting called to them. The sounds of many voices raised in song, prayer, and arcane language blended into a strange harmony that soothed their bodies and excited their souls. They rushed past the judge and fell to chanting with the others, finding and inventing their own music and words with an enthusiasm Samuel knew could come only from the presence of the Lord.

"Thank you, Lord, for your protection," the old priest said softly. A gentle smile crossed his weathered face as he watched the soldiers become followers before him.

Twice more Saul sent men in search of Samuel. Twice more they were lost to Naioth, never again to return to the king's service.

Finally the king's rage was greater than his fear of facing Samuel. Choosing an elite group of his best remaining men, Saul set off in search of Samuel and David, willing at last to face his fear and end his torment.

And when it was told Saul, he sent other messengers, and they prophesied likewise. And Saul sent messengers again the third time, and they prophesied also. Then went he also to Ramah, and came to a great well that is in Sechu: and he asked and said, Where are Samuel and David? And one said, Behold, they be at Naioth in Ramah.

1 Samuel 19:21-22

WHEN THE king and his guard arrived at the sacred temple of Ramah where Samuel worshipped and sacrificed, they came heavily armed. Saul came prepared to demand the whereabouts of David ben Jesse and his own lost legions. He was prepared to deal with the dissembling and trickery he had been warned about. He was even prepared to face armed resistance and his own possible death. He was prepared to face down the only man in the kingdom who was prepared to stand up to him.

What he had not prepared for was the cheering adulation that greeted him as he rounded the corner of the narrow dusty street into the broad court before the temple.

"Welcome, great king," the priests shouted from the steps of the temple.

"Long live King Saul," and "Praise be to the Lord's anointed," shouted the people who thronged him at this, his first visit to Ramah in a lifetime and his first appearance outside the palace forecourt in Gibeah for several years. Saul had become so lost in the schemes, whispers, and gossip of court, and his own jealous demon poisoning him against David's popularity, he had forgotten that he was in fact a beloved king.

Waving genially and taking up the extended hands of the crowd as they pressed in around him, Saul acted every bit the gracious sovereign. Songs of praise were raised to him as he dismounted his horse and made his way up the steps of the very temple he'd come to storm.

"Where is Samuel?" the king asked, trying to make the request sound as cordial as possible. "I understand that he might know the whereabouts of David ben Jesse."

"Indeed, they are together, Your Majesty," answered one of the priests gathered, bowing in greeting to the king, just outside the doors of the noble temple. "Have you come to join them in Naioth?"

"Naioth?" the king asked, tormented again by the strange word. "So, they're not here, then?"

"No, my lord," the priest said, still bowing.

"Can you direct us to this Naioth?" the king asked. Unfamiliar with the village name, he did not want to seem as though all the villages in his kingdom were not well known and important to him.

"You would join them in Naioth?" the priest asked excitedly, daring to look up from his salaam.

"Yes, that would be my great pleasure," the king answered in a booming voice, waving to nearby members of the crowd. *Never send a boy to do a man's work*, he thought smugly, deeply self-satisfied at the ease with which he'd gained David's location and a guide to take him there.

"Who will join the king in Naioth?" the priest called out to the crowd gathered still at the foot of the temple steps.

A great cheer went up. The king waved and smiled. He basked in the return of the attention he had come to love from his people during his long and storied career, unaware it was he who had been absent and not the love of his people.

"Excellent," the king said. Less than thrilled by all the witnesses, he was easily resigned, as all he'd planned to do was to take David into custody. That he could surely do in private once they arrived.

"When would you like to begin?" the priest asked the king earnestly.

"Oh, right away," Saul answered without hesitation. "I've come all this way, and I am ready to start at once."

"Let the fasting begin," the priest called out to the people, who shouted joyous responses. "We shall meet here in three days, time enough before sunset to reach the road to the high desert ahead of the fall of night. Remember, as I'm sure you know, no weapons, no sandals, and robes of goat hair only."

"Three days?" the king inquired tensely. He realized, too late, what he'd inadvertently agreed to only as he heard it from the priest's lips, but he was still well aware that he was being watched.

"In three days, your king will lead you on a pilgrimage of faith," the priest called by way of answering and trapping the king. It was as he'd been instructed by his master Samuel who had been instructed by his own master.

"*Is Saul also among the prophets?*" the people sang happily as they scurried homeward, honored to be taking the sacred journey with their own king.

"Your Majesty, you are welcome to prepare for your quest here with us," the priest offered, gesturing toward the temple doors. "We would be honored to pray with you. There are goat-hair garments enough for you and your men. Of course, you may be sure of their safety if you leave your weapons and armor here."

"Yes, that was just what I had hoped," the king said, grinding his teeth to conceal his rage at ensnaring himself in some sort of religious excursion. He was unable to think of a way out without revealing to his people the disrespect and suspicion he felt in his heart for what he was certain was some ploy of Samuel's. Still, he reasoned, what would be the harm of three days' prayer if it led him to David in the end? He'd prayed for that often enough. "Lead on, my good man, lead on."

When, three days and a night hence, the king found himself lashed by the hot sirocco winds of the desert, delirious from hunger and thirst, and delusional for want of wine and rest, the city of tents appeared like a magical oasis of light in the desert blackness. Fear and reason both forgotten, Saul cried out as he ran toward the tents, tearing at his garments.

"Samuel, Samuel, I am home," the king's voice rose. Those who still followed took up his pace and shouted in chorus with him. His task and his hatred were left in the city behind him. All he could see before him was a joyous reunion with the man for whose faith and guidance he had longed since their angry parting.

"My son, my son," Samuel answered, stepping into the lighted opening at the side of the great central tent.

Naked, the king threw himself to the ground at Samuel's feet. He wept for joy and kissed the hem of the priests robe. "Forgive me, forgive me, forgive me."

"Arise, my king, and come inside," Samuel said, placing his hand on Saul's bowed head. "You are forgiven, and at one with the Lord."

"The Lord our God has delivered us to this place," Saul cried out, still on his knees but throwing his hands heavenward. "I rejoice that he has seen fit to make me his instrument in bringing his chosen people to their destiny. Tonight we are all witness to his healing power. I celebrate my deliverance from the torment of my soul, and this vision of the Lord."

"*Is Saul also among the prophets?*" sang the people, who were witness to his prophesy that night and for many days after.

David, too, was moved by the king's genuine expression and testament to his faith and his joy at his reunion with Samuel. He had heard the old psalms and chants that claimed that Saul was among the prophets, but he truly understood that night. He saw how the Lord had come into the man to replace the evil spirits of pride, jealousy, and anger that had ruled Saul since their return from Elah. He bore witness that, through this grace, the king's true spirit was liberated and returned to the man David had first come to know and love.

As the king embraced Samuel, the priest nodded to David over Saul's shoulder. With a gentle smile, the judge assured him that it was now safe to take his leave. *And perhaps*, David thought as he made haste to comply with the priest's unspoken wishes, *it is unwise to stay.*

David nodded back from the shadows at the edge of the camp where he had waited. He was as ready to run into the dark desert wilderness as he was to follow the road back to Ramah, had the Lord been unable to free the king's true heart. Samuel, though, had never had any doubt that Saul would truly come to Naioth.

With a skin of water, a scrip with some bread, bedding, and a lamp to light his path, David set out on what was in fact the rather short journey back to Ramah. There he would try to reach Jonathan, or get news of him, and plan his next move.

It was, of course, no surprise to the servants that David arrived in the middle of the night. In fact, they would have been more shocked had he arrived in daylight after sending word ahead.

David was unable to rouse anyone at the gate and unwilling to call too much attention to his arrival. Instead he chose to climb over the wall, with the help of a nearby mimosa. From there he managed to make his way across the roof, onto a balcony, and into the house through the open shutters of a second-floor window.

Tumbling exhausted into his bed, he literally fell onto Jonathan. Startled awake, the prince threw him across the room and raised an alarm that at last succeeded where David had failed and awakened the entire household. Darkness concealed them from each other. Uncertain of the identity of his supposed enemy and cautious of revealing his own, neither man spoke beyond the grunts and shouts of combat. The battle was titanic and room-destroying. Jonathan had just managed to pin David to the floor when the houseman entered. Terrified, he held out the lamp to see what demon had come in the night. Instead he found only his master and his lover, though his lamplight did serve to allow the two combatants to recognize one another.

It was all the feast days rolled into one for David to find Jonathan waiting there for him. Jonathan fell on David, kissing him with such passion that the servants simply withdrew, closing the door without comment. Rolling their eyes, they giggled and gossiped their way back to their own quarters, thoroughly baffled by the strange appetites of their new master.

"You're safe, you're safe," David kept saying breathlessly as he kissed and embraced the very reason he'd found strength to survive his recent ordeal.

"Praise be to the Lord," Jonathan said, lifting David up into the air and spinning them both around before falling back onto what remained of their bed. "My prayers have been answered."

"Prayers? You?" David asked, smiling at the idea. "Have you found the Lord in my absence?"

"I think he was here all along," Jonathan answered, rolling on top of David. The moon slipped from behind a cloud. Its pale light came suddenly through the window. He looked down into David's face in the glow that filled the room. "How else could I have been so happy? Was it not Samuel's prophesy that we would rule Israel? Perhaps I've underestimated him and the Lord."

"Well, it was Samuel who saved my life these past few days." David sighed, reaching his arms up around Jonathan's neck and drawing him nearer. "I have much to tell you. I've seen your father tonight and heard him prophesize."

"My father?" Jonathan said, drawing back to look into David's eyes as near as he might in such darkness. "How can that be? You are alive."

"He is among the prophets," David said, pulling Jonathan to him more urgently. "Later, though. That is a story for tomorrow. I have not been with you since we returned from Jezreel. There is other business to be attended tonight."

And [Saul] went thither to Naioth in Ramah: and the Spirit of God was upon him also, and he went on, and prophesied, until he came to Naioth in Ramah. And he stripped off his clothes also, and prophesied before Samuel in like manner, and lay down naked all that day and all that night. Wherefore they say, Is Saul also among the prophets?

1 Samuel 19:23-24

JONATHAN AWOKE before David. It was early the next morning. He sat for a time watching his beloved sleep. His heart was light and joyous that they were again together. As certainly as he felt David's presence next to him, he also felt the presence of the grace of the Lord. He knew in his heart his prayers had been answered, not just for David's safe return, but in that they'd found one another in the first place. In much the same way as when he and David had first fallen in love, he felt as though he was seeing the world anew.

Stealing down to the kitchen without bothering to dress, he managed to frighten the cooking woman and win her undying love in the same breath. Together they prepared a feast of David's favorites. Jonathan delivered the banquet still wearing the apron the kitchen maid had offered him for modesty's sake.

David awoke to the clattering of crockery and Jonathan's soft swearing as he attempted to manage the huge tray and navigate their ruined room. "If your subjects could see you now," David said sleepily, stirring.

"So long as my wife doesn't find out," Jonathan joked but got no laugh. "Sorry, I guess that's not funny yet."

"That outfit, on the other hand," David said, leaning off the end of the bed to push aside the apron.

"Is this how you are with the serving staff when I'm not around?" Jonathan said, swatting at David's hand as he managed to settle the tray on a trunk. He dragged both nearer to the bed.

"I must confess that if my meal is served to me in bed by someone who looks like you do, dressed as you are, you may have something to worry about." David grinned, hungrily tearing off a piece of the fresh hot bread.

"But then, who looks like me?" Jonathan laughed, smacking David's upturned backside for good measure.

"I'm starving," David said. "I've been fasting on and off for nearly a moon." He devoured all that was put before him and called for more.

"Where have you been?" Jonathan asked, sitting on the edge of the bed and, for the most part, watching David eat. He'd had his fill in the kitchen, unaware it was a crime among true servants.

"I've been at Naioth with Samuel," David answered, his mouth full of warm roasted grain, fresh cream, and fruit.

"Please tell me, where is that?" Jonathan asked, taking up a place beside David on the bed and helping himself to a little more. "None of the servants knew. I must confess, though I've traversed the nation, I'm at a loss."

"I had never heard of it either," David said with a gracious laugh. "It's more a kind of contemplative religious observance than a place, exactly."

"But where?" Jonathan asked.

"I take it, it varies. It seems to be decided by inspiration." David tried to explain, still eating like a starving man. "In tents in the desert, or maybe just the wilderness, I guess."

"A religious ritual in tents in the wilderness?" Jonathan asked with a laugh at the primitive notion of it.

"Sort of a spiritual revival," David suggested, looking for the best explanation. "Samuel said a 'vision quest.' People must find the tents at night, barefoot, weaponless, and clad in goat-hair robes after a three-day fast from food or drink. Your father was beyond delirious by the time he arrived. He tore off his clothes and spoke most eloquently of his faith. I can say honestly that I witnessed his spiritual revival."

"Do you suppose it's changed his heart?" Jonathan said, lying back on the bed beside him.

"He was changed." David shrugged, spreading soft cheese on some bread with a wooden paddle. "The spirit was with him, as they say on Naioth. But will he feel the same when he's back at court? I'm not ready to stake my life on it."

"Perhaps he'll be better able to see reason." Jonathan sighed, uncertain of how best to proceed. "I'll go back to Gibeah and speak with him when he returns. At least I will know you are safe here."

"I don't think he'd tell you the truth," David said, his appetite faded by the topic. "I can't help but think that he knows something of us, if not all. He would not tell you if he was planning my demise, at the very least for fear that it would grieve you."

"My father never does anything great or small without confiding in me," Jonathan insisted. "Why would he hide this from me?"

"Did he speak with you about this latest?" David asked, reaching out to stroke Jonathan's leg. The prince's only answer was silence. "Maybe you could find out what my crime is, that I might atone for it?"

"Whatever you want me to do, I'll do for you," Jonathan said, taking his hand and kissing the palm. "I'm just thankful to have found you. I almost didn't."

"You were asleep in our bed when I got home," David said, laughing. "All you had to do was wake up."

"Who knew what or where Naioth was? Is?" Jonathan scoffed. "I mean, the message; I almost didn't find it. If I hadn't knelt in prayer, I would never have seen those rabbit-ear cracks in the wall. They pointed me to the loose tile."

"What are you talking about?" David asked, confused. "What cracks in the wall?"

"Well, the servant said I'd find it when I rested my head," Jonathan explained.

"Yes, and it's on your side of the bed. I aimed those arrows hanging there on that breastplate to point right at it, see?" David pointed to where the arrows hung still.

"I found it when I prayed for it," Jonathan said, smiling as he realized.

"I suppose you did," David said, stroking his hair. "Let's go out and get some air, maybe a walk in the hills. We need to decide what to do, and I need to think."

"So long as I am with you," Jonathan said, rolling onto his side and pulling David down to hold him.

They bathed each other languidly and at length. After, they dressed in simple robes so as not to call attention to themselves to any who might see them. It was still early when they went out into hills in the crisp fall morning. They were content to share their company in silence as they made their way up to a ridge that overlooked Ramah. There they rested and enjoyed the sight of the valley spread below them, swinging their legs over the edge of the precipice.

"The new moon is in a few days," David said, his eyes focused well beyond the view below them.

Jonathan nodded, thinking at first that he was only passing the time.

"I am still the king's son-in-law, twice if he but knew. There will be a place for me at the table for Rosh Chodesh," David went on, spinning the tale. "I will be expected. You must tell your father if he asks after me that I have begged you for permission to go to Bethlehem for an annual sacrifice honoring my family."

"I will," Jonathan said, thoughtfully.

"If he answers you kindly, then you know I am safe," David reasoned. "If he loses his temper, then you know that I am still out of favor. And, my prince, you must promise me, if you find that I am truly guilty of some crime against your father or the crown, then you may kill me with your own hand. I would prefer it, if it be inescapable."

"I could not," Jonathan said, wrapping his arm around David's shoulder and drawing him nearer. "I have sworn a covenant with you that is sacred to me. The most I could do is warn you."

Jonathan embraced David, resting his chin on the top of David's head. They sat for a while, silently thankful for being together and uncertain that they would be again.

"How will you get word to me if your father answers you harshly?" David asked when at last Jonathan released him.

"I have just been pondering on that," Jonathan answered him, nodding. "If all is well with my father, then I will send for you the day after Rosh Chodesh.

But if you do not hear from me, go the next day to our secret place at the rock Ezel. I practice my archery near there, and if I can get away, I will come to you. But if not, I will overshoot an arrow past the targets. I will send the boy out to fetch it. If it is safe for you to stay, then I'll call out 'The arrow is on this side of you.' But if I call out 'the arrow is beyond you,' then you will know to flee as soon as darkness covers your exit. Either way, we will keep my part in this, and this place, our secret, should we need them again."

"Merciful God," David swore in his pain and grief. The thought of leaving Jonathan, and the life they'd made together, in the darkness like some thief, without so much as a good-bye between them, made his chest ache. "How has it come to this?"

"My beloved," Jonathan said, taking David once again into his arms. "I tell you this now and forever. I will love you come what may. Time or distance may separate us, but nothing will diminish my love for you."

"And so it is with me," David said, resting his head on Jonathan's broad chest. "We have tonight, at least."

"That's all anyone has," Jonathan said, taking him up in his arms and carrying him away.

Chapter Fifteen
The Great Rock Ezel

So Jonathan made a covenant with the house of David, saying, Let the Lord even require it at the hand of David's enemies. And Jonathan caused David to swear again, because he loved him: for he loved him as he loved his own soul.

1 Samuel 20:16-17

SAUL RETURNED from Naioth renewed and hopeful. He spent a passionate night with Ahinoam that surprised them both. He arrived at the family table for the feast following the prayers on the eve of Rosh Chodesh. His spirits were easy and lighthearted as none among his family or intimates there had witnessed in him for some time.

Jonathan was on his guard. Still, even his wary defenses fell to the king's easy manner and seeming delight in his family being together.

"My visit to Ramah was most enlightening," Saul announced at one point. "The people there love their king. We had quite the unexpected reception. Is that not so, Captain?"

"In truth, it is, my king," the captain of the guard answered most casually. The salute he offered from the doorway was unlike his usual formality as he stood guard over the king and his family.

"And Naioth was indescribable," Saul asserted enthusiastically, unfazed by the guard's familiarity, acceptable in the field but unprecedented at court. "You must all join Samuel when next he is in Naioth. I had not heard of the practice before, but I would not miss it again. I'm only sorry that he was unable to join us here today."

The evening passed in pleasantries. David's place remained empty and unmentioned, if not unnoticed by the king. Jonathan dared a sigh of relief. He longed to ride that night to deliver David the good news. Obligations at court, though, prevented his departure prior to the prayers for Rosh Chodesh at sunset the following day. Still, he slept easier that night and rose with a sense of hope.

His sister Michal knew no peace. Not only was her husband not present without explanation, but her father had returned without a single mention of David's fate.

"Where is he?" Michal railed when she and Paltiel were at last able to elude the watchful eye of her family and meet privately at her villa. "The entire night passed without so much as a mention." She could hardly stand the strain of their constant fear of discovery. Her only relief would lie in news of David's death.

"Calm yourself." Paltiel sighed. He was fatigued of the fits and tempers of the princess but not of the privileges and position that their liaison offered him. "I will try to get word through channels at court tomorrow."

"I'll get word, all right," Michal announced. "I'll have my satisfaction from the king himself, and before the second feast tomorrow night. I'll know my husband's fate. It won't be a full banquet for me until his head is served me on a platter."

"Perhaps you should take a more modest approach when you speak with the king," Paltiel soothed, his voice oily with solicitation. "You don't want to call too much attention to—"

"Don't tell me what I want," Michal raged, grasping him by the throat. "It is his head or ours. I have a fondness for my neck, and I know you've a positive passion for protecting yours, my love," she hissed, storming out of the room.

Paltiel sighed again. He took his leave of her house for the night. He knew better than to argue with members of Saul's family. Experience had taught him that the last word was theirs, even if they had to cut one's tongue out to make it so.

As sunset approached the following evening, Saul's family gathered for prayer and feasting in the mood born of the previous night's festivities. Jonathan planned to return to David that night, following the feast. Though he would not make Ramah until the dark of the morning, he would awaken David with the good news of his father's sustained transformation.

"If you would, Father," Michal said. She took his arm following the prayers in the family temple just before they went their separate ways, she with the women and he with the men, for their feasts. "Is there news of my husband?"

"Ah, my daughter," Saul said, stepping aside with her into a private antechamber near the feasting hall. "I had forgotten how heavy this weighs on you. It was for your husband that I went in search. Naturally you would wonder."

"My concern is for you and your safety," she said, squeezing his arm from tension as much as from affection.

"Of course, beloved daughter," Saul said, smiling tightly. He was reminded, for the first time since his stay in the desert with Samuel, of the threat David represented to his crown. "I was unable to locate him on this trip. Rest assured that the matter will be settled just as soon as he can be found. Until then—"

"Well, why not simply ask Jonathan?" she suggested, her eyebrows drawn together in a show of confusion.

"What of the prince?" Saul asked, more curious for her confident tone.

"Jonathan has been away since you began looking for David," she answered with a shrug. "I thought you knew. He spent only one night with his new wife before last night. That sums only two."

"I see," the king said gravely, considering her reason.

"I know from my own experience of the two that it is the rare night that they spend apart," she confided in a whispery tone, patting his hand. "I saw last night that David's place was empty, but Jonathan is back and with his new wife. I can only think that Jonathan must know where David has gone, or he would be with him—or at least in search of him."

"You think Jonathan is protecting this traitor against me?" Saul asked, his mood darkening.

"I had hardly thought of it that way," Michal said, her hand at her breast to show surprise. "I simply assume that he, if anyone, would know the whereabouts of his lover."

"We shall see, daughter," he said, brushing her cheek with his lips as he swept from the room, troubled by his thoughts.

The festivities were underway by the time of the king's arrival in the hall. The mood was light. Laughter and music filled the air. It had been a good year, and the harvest promised to be bounteous. The new moon rose on the holy month with much portent for Rosh Hashanah and the dawn of a joyous and prosperous new year.

Even the king's transformation following his reconciliation with Samuel seemed a sign of a joyous new age.

Saul's mood gave no hint of the cares that creased his brow as he entered. He spoke easily with all he encountered as he made his way to the head of the table. Though less intimate than the family supper the night before, the Rosh Chodesh feast seemed no less informal.

At last, taking his place, the king began his table conversation with pleasantries. Quickly he found his target. He turned to Jonathan, who sat at his right.

"And you, my son? How are you?" Saul asked, warmly grasping the prince's shoulder.

"I am well, my father," Jonathan answered, a twinkle in his eye. "Particularly for seeing you in such good spirits."

"I have hardly seen you since your wedding night," Saul said with a jocular tone of accusation. "I suppose the Princess Azia has taken most of your time. I hear good things of Edomite women."

"So do I," Jonathan said without thinking, remembering his amusement at David's remarks on the topic. "I mean I, of course, don't have any complaints."

"Does she?" Saul asked, arching one brow and lowering the other as he closed in. "Have you not been away from court for all but three nights since you took your marriage vows almost a month ago?"

"I have been away some, yes," Jonathan faltered, reaching for his wine.

"Where?" Samuel demanded. His hand shot out to stop Jonathan's before he could raise the goblet to his mouth. "Where have you been?"

"Well, about the kingdom," Jonathan said, looking around anxiously as if to find the answer. "Taking my leisure after a hard campaign."

"I suppose the real question, the one answer we are avoiding, is, where is David?" Saul shouted, pounding the table and silencing the hall.

"David?" Jonathan repeated, too shocked and dismayed by the sudden reversal to answer at once.

"He is not here, I see, again tonight," Saul said, pointing to the empty place at the table. "We have kept a place for him. Yet he does not have the courtesy even to show his face or send a messenger."

"It is my fault," Jonathan said with a panicky laugh. "I am the messenger. David begged my indulgence and permission to return to Bethlehem to be with his family for a special sacrifice for the new moon preceding harvest."

"Yet his wife does not know and has only just now inquired of me after her husband's whereabouts?" Saul bellowed, leaping to his feet. "How is it that you know more of this man than does his own wife?"

There had been some murmuring through the hall. With the public broaching of a matter so often and privately discussed, all fell breathless and silent as death in anticipation of the words to follow.

"Son of a perverse rebellious woman," Saul said, striking Jonathan's cheek with the flat of his hand. "Do I not know that you have chosen the son of Jesse to your own confusion, and to the confusion of your mother's nakedness? Your preference for this man over your wife and even over your own father, your king, and country brings shame on this family. As long as the son of Jesse lives on this earth, neither you nor your kingdom will be established. Now send and bring him to me, for he must die!"

"Why should he be put to death?" Jonathan demanded, leaping to his feet with such passion that he overturned his bench. "What has he done to you or to any man that he should die?"

Saul's rage overcame him. Taking up a knife from the table, he attacked his own son. Swinging wildly, he tore the linen of the prince's robe and scratched the flesh above Jonathan's heart. Saul came perilously near to achieving the deadly goal of his madness. Fearlessly Jonathan stepped into the way of death. Grabbing Saul's wrist, he disarmed him. He then tossed the knife aside with such force that it stuck upright in the table before them.

"It is true, Father. I am ashamed," Jonathan said softly in the shocked calm that followed the intensity of what had passed. "I am ashamed of you."

Again Saul slapped his son's face. Jonathan shook his head sadly.

"I pity you, Father," Jonathan said, his words stinging more than any blow he could have returned. "You will never know the happiness that I know. For always wanting something more, you will miss the joy of what you already have." Boldly he turned and left the hall, the banquet untasted.

Few could stomach the feast meal that evening. Racked with worry, Jonathan knew he could not go to Ramah without exposing David's position. He knew David would be waiting for word at Ezel rock the next day. His fears that they would never again see each other were too near real to be borne. Agitated with grief, he passed the dark night pacing and retching into the dawn.

He refused all food and visitors, though Paltiel waited all day at Jonathan's door. He would accompany the prince wherever he might go in the guise of friendship, but in truth to report back to the king. The assignment, accepted gladly, offered as much to himself and his lover as to his king.

When the shadows hid underfoot, the prince made ready for what he knew he must do and could delay no longer. He called for a boy and several others to accompany him into the field at Ezel.

"I think practicing my shooting could settle my heart," Jonathan said tersely in pale explanation for his abrupt decision to go to the practice range without so much as a meal or a word to his new wife.

"I think that a splendid idea," Paltiel said, chiming in to announce his presence.

"Palti," Jonathan exclaimed, startled to find his old friend waiting in the hall for him like a loyal hound. "Forgive me for refusing you when you last visited at my door this morning. I was not fit company for civilized man or soulless beast."

"I understood, my prince, and waited," Paltiel said simply and slyly.

"You waited?" Jonathan asked. "All morning?"

"Is that not why they called me your man-in-waiting for so long?" Paltiel asked with a mischievous look.

Jonathan laughed despite his mood. He clapped Paltiel on the shoulder.

"Then you, sir, are the company I most need just now," Jonathan said, shouldering his bow and gathering up his quiver. "I'm off to go shooting."

"Near the great rock Ezel?" Paltiel asked, by way of making it clear to the guards, who were also stationed nearby.

"Yes, an excellent suggestion," Jonathan answered as he bolted from the room. He bounded down the hall, more to give chase to those who would follow—and lose as many as possible—as to hurry to his dreaded task.

With no word from Jonathan, David left Ramah just as the sun began to color the morning sky. He awaited news of his fate in their secret place atop the rock Ezel before the shadows began to reach for the west. Fear gripped him. Though he had brought water and some bread and cheese, he could not eat. As still as death, he hardly moved as he waited.

When at last Jonathan and his party appeared on the horizon, David rose only slightly to get into position, as much to catch what he feared was to be his last glimpse of Jonathan as to hear their coded message. He said a silent prayer that all would be well. He entreated the Lord with all his heart that Jonathan would simply ride across to him, hand extended. When he saw the prince take up a position to begin shooting, a tear fell, unbidden, down his cheek. He knew their fate was cast.

At first Jonathan fired a couple of arrows right on target, to make a show and give the outing a ring of truth to his party. Then he overshot, a move David knew was practiced, as Jonathan was too fine an archer to miss a target unless it moved out of range. David closed his eyes and clasped his hand over his mouth to muffle his own sobs, so that he might hear Jonathan's words confirm his worst fears.

"Boy," Jonathan called out as the young man ran out to retrieve his arrows, his voice almost breaking. "There, you see, the arrows are beyond you."

David put his face into his bag to silence his screams of loss and anguish. He fought to control himself so that he might not lose sight of Jonathan until he rode away.

Jonathan quickly wiped away his own tears but was unable to go on. Trembling, he tried to draw back the bow but found he could not control it.

"I'm sorry," he said, relaxing his bow and letting the last arrow fall to the ground. "I'm not up to this. I cannot shoot any more. I would return to the palace."

"Of course, Your Majesty," Paltiel said. "You seem in fine form, but you hardly need practice for that. If it does not soothe you, then this is folly."

"Yes, old friend," Jonathan nodded haltingly, taking up the fallen arrow. "Folly indeed."

"Take heart," Paltiel said as if only casually, but with an aim every bit as deadly as the finest archer's. "It is only a matter of time until the king has David in custody. His Majesty's men search house to house in Ramah and await him at Jesse's very gates. We shall have an end to this matter, with the certainty of the grave. You can be at peace with your father at last, my prince."

"Yes, that is good news," Jonathan said, looking at Paltiel with new eyes. "And how is my sister doing?"

"Oh, she was in good spirits this morning," Paltiel began before he realized himself, and tried in vain to circle back. "At least that's what I heard from one of her serving girls who was at the palace to fetch something back to… to the princess's villa."

Leaping onto his horse, Jonathan brought the arrow down with a crack against the animal's flank. They galloped away together, disappearing into the amber hues of the drowsy sun like desert rain.

Paltiel cursed himself silently for giving up the confidence. He smiled still, at having wounded the man who had so callously tossed their friendship aside when he took David as his lover. Paltiel knew too that he had won. With his influence over the king and Michal's own suit to her father, he would marry the princess as soon as the king could dispatch David. The king would be glad to rid himself of a widowed and despoiled daughter to his trusted and beloved Paltiel. He knew he would replace David, if not in Jonathan's heart, then at the family table, which counted to Paltiel for much more.

Jonathan concealed himself along the way. He waited patiently, feeding his midday meal to the horse who had affected his escape. He stroked the animal's soft nose and begged his forgiveness in soothing words for striking him so. When his shooting party passed them, Jonathan mounted and headed back from whence he'd come. The horse knew the pace was as lightning without being urged to it a second time.

David lay in the stillness that followed the departure of the shooting party. He wept as he awaited darkness to cover his escape. So great was his pain that he considered simply going back to the palace and surrendering to the king, that he might put an end to it at once. The only reason he didn't strike out for Gibeah was how deeply he knew it would hurt Jonathan.

As badly as David was grieving, he knew Jonathan was being forced to choose between love and loyalty to his own father, his king, and his country. It was an unbearable choice. David resolved to do whatever he could to keep Jonathan from one single more painful and impossible decision.

Lost in his torment, David hardly took note of the sounds of hoofbeats. He half hoped it was the king's men come to take him and end his sadness.

Jonathan was upon him before he'd even bothered to look, throwing his arms around David, who was near hysterical in his grief and misery.

"What are you doing here?" David demanded, tearing himself away and bowing down formally three times, as was the custom before a king. "I hope you have come to take my life, for I cannot bear to live it without you."

"You are my life," Jonathan said hoarsely, falling upon him as if in a rage, tearing at his clothes and kissing him savagely wherever he could touch. David struggled to escape at first and then succumbed to Jonathan's ardor. Their lovemaking was passionate in its intensity. Like two condemned, they knew each touch would be their last. When, at length, Jonathan was done and David had exceeded, they lay silently in each other's arms until night fell and the stars rose around them.

They arose as if from death. Silently they prepared to part. Each was unable to find words to say at such a time.

"Look," Jonathan said at last, pointing to the heaven. "It is our constellation. The saphan is rising." Reaching out, he took David's hand and clutched it to his mouth. He kissed the ring that bore the jeweled map to their personal stars. "So long as those stars are in the heavens—" he said, breaking off, unable to finish.

"Longer," David managed. The two held one another as long as they dared.

"Though you may not be at my side, you will always be in my heart, my prince," Jonathan said, clearing his throat and fighting for control, as he knew David was in need of greater comfort than he. For when they had said their good-byes, Jonathan would return to his family, such as it was, but David would be a fugitive. "You cannot return home to Bethlehem, for my father's men are waiting for you there."

"I suspected as much." David nodded sadly against Jonathan's chest where his head still rested.

"There is a house-to-house search for you in Ramah, so no refuge awaits you there." Jonathan sighed, wishing he possessed any good news to impart.

"I did not pack to return when I left this morning," David said with a thin smile. He did his best not to add further burden to Jonathan by letting him see his despair.

"And I think that Michal is in this with Paltiel somehow. You must not trust her if she gets a message to you," Jonathan warned, numbed by the horrific words he spoke, unable to comprehend their betrayal. "I will try to reach you if I can."

"Do not put yourself at risk," David said, taking Jonathan's forearm firmly to reassure him. "I know that a man of honor cannot choose against his own family. I would not have you make such a choice in my favor."

"The oath I have made to you is more sacred than any I will ever undertake," Jonathan said, tightening his grasp around the smaller man. "Go in peace. We have sworn a covenant together in the name of the Lord. I am yours and you are mine, and the Lord is between you and me and between your seed and my seed forever."

"I will love you above all others until the day I die," David said, throwing back his head and looking up into Jonathan's eyes.

Their lips met once more in one last act of passion. Then, in silence, for there were no more words, they took their leave of one another and went their separate ways.

And Jonathan said to David, Go in peace, forasmuch as we have sworn both of us in the name of the Lord, saying, The Lord be between me and thee, and between my seed and thy seed for ever.

And he arose and departed: and Jonathan went into the city.

1 Samuel 20:42

BY MORNING David had made his way through the hills south of Gibeah to the sacred village of Nob. It was a small family enclave. The only residents were both priests and members of the house of Ahimelech. They were the keepers of the most sacred Ark of the Covenant. Not only was Nob close enough to be reached on foot from Gibeah, it was a place where David thought he might seek asylum until he could determine where best to go.

He had made no plans. He had not allowed himself to consider the possibility that he might not be reconciled with the king, for that would also mean he was to lose Jonathan. That thought was intolerable. So making his way south through the hills of Benjamin toward Judah was the first time he permitted himself to ponder his fate.

He knew he could not go home. He also knew that he would have to do something to safeguard his family before the king could use them and their safety against him. In the early morning, though tired and hungry, a smile spread across his face like the sunlight seeping into the sky above, as the perfect plan arose in him. David knew, with the most meager provisions from the priests at Nob, exactly what to do next and how to accomplish it.

Morning prayer was just ending as he walked into Nob. His appearance much surprised all who dwelt there.

"David? Is it David ben Jesse, the king's champion?" Ahimelech said in greeting, recognizing him. "Arriving at our humble settlement at daybreak, on foot and empty-handed? What tumult is this?"

"Your Grace," David said, bowing formally as he began to recite the words he'd carefully rehearsed. "There is no cause for alarm. I am here on a clandestine mission from the king. I knew I could trust you not to tell anyone that you'd seen me."

"Well, who would ask us?" The priest laughed heartily. "What can the priests of Nob do for you?"

"Thank you, Your Grace," David said, bowing again. "I was wondering if I could trouble you for a little bit of food for me and my few men who are still hidden in the hills above us. And perhaps a weapon, if you have one and can spare it?"

"A weapon?" the priest asked, suspicious.

"Yes." David laughed. "Because of the nature of my charge from the king, I had to leave Gibeah at the last minute and without raising suspicion. So,

I could ill afford to provision myself too well or heavily. We soldiers are used to living off the land and usually benefit from the kind farmers and townsfolk nearby our camps."

"But if you went to them, your secret would be lost?" Ahimelech finished the thought with his question. Though still suspicious, he felt he could trust the country's most sacred hero, even though he was fairly certain there was more to the story.

"Something like that," David said. Careful not to tell the priest an outright lie, he kept his answers to a reasonable approximation of the truth.

"Well, you are of course welcome here, as I'm sure you are throughout Israel." The priest smiled warmly, taking David's elbow to guide him. "I'm afraid, however, that the only food we have here is shewbread. You cannot partake unless you are clean and have not been with a woman for more than three days."

"I can assure you, I have not been with a woman," David answered with a smile as he remembered his parting with Jonathan who was, he was most certain, no woman. "And I am sure the same is true of any who are with me."

"Well, we have only just put out the twelve fresh loaves on the table in the tabernacle," the priest said as they walked along together to the meeting tent. "We will gladly share with you the bread of the presence that was placed before the ark yesterday."

"That would be most generous, Your Grace. I thank you," David said as they neared the tabernacle.

"And here you will also find the only weapon we have," the priest said, drawing aside the curtain at the entrance to the tabernacle tent and motioning David inside. "The sword of Goliath is here, ever since you took it off of him in battle at Elah."

"A weapon indeed." David nodded, remembering. "There is none like it. I thank you for your openhandedness."

"By rights it is yours anyway." Ahimelech shrugged, following him into the tent. "This is my son, Abiathar, in training to be the high priest here one day after me, as my father Ahitub was before me. Son, this is the great hero of Israel, David, here for our help in his current mission."

"Well, I hope you are only in need of prayer." Abiathar laughed. "For we are soldiers of the Lord here, and that is our only armament."

"I will take all the prayers you may offer," David assured him.

"We will also give him five of the twelve loaves from yesterday," Ahimelech said, going behind the curtain to the sacred place of the ark to retrieve the sword of Goliath from its place of reverence. "If you would, be so good as to wrap those in fresh cloth so that he might take them to his men."

"Of course, Father," the young priest answered. "I have only our visitor to assist. Then I may be about it."

"Ah yes, Doeg, one of the king's guards, is here to offer prayers for his sister's marriage," Ahimelech said, lowering his voice as he gestured to the altar. The great Edomite knelt awkwardly before the unfamiliar altar, making whatever prayers he knew to the strange deity on behalf of his sister Azia. "Perhaps you may know him?"

"I do know Doeg, though I'd rather not explain my presence here to him. If you could see that we do not meet," David said, lowering his voice. "Does he not pray to Edomite gods? What does he seek here?"

"He has come to pray his strange prayers to our Lord for his sister's well-being in her new country," Abiathar explained. "As you know, his sister Azia has only just married Crown Prince Jonathan and come to live here."

"I see. How generous," David said. He nodded with an approving smile to mask the twinge of pain he felt at just the mention of the name of his lost beloved. "I would not disturb him. I will wait outside."

Just then Doeg looked up from his worship and saw David with the priests. He only smiled and nodded in greeting before returning to his prayers. Doeg was familiar with David but unaware of the circumstances that occasioned David's visit to Nob. Having accompanied his parents home to Edom following the ceremony, he had not been at court since the wedding. Visiting at home for a while before his return to the king's service, his diversion to Nob on his journey back to Gibeah had been an inspiration. The humble man sought a way to give thanks for his family's favor in this strange land.

Relieved by his good fortune and Doeg's easy greeting, David thought the sooner he was on his way, the safer for all.

Ahimelech returned from the sacred place with the great sword.

"I have found this too." The high priest offered his hand. In it was Micah's sling. David's legs nearly failed him as he beheld it. "It would not appear to be a great weapon, but as you well know, such is not always as it appears."

"It is the finest and most blessed of weapons," David said, gratefully taking the sling and holding it to his heart. He felt less alone; as he had that most fateful morning, Micah stood at his back.

"I hope it again serves you well." The priest offered his blessing. "I will see to our Edomite friend and leave you to my son."

"Thank you, Your Grace," David said, moved by the gift. "Your generosity means more than I can tell you."

"God be with you," Ahimelech said as he took his leave.

The high priest tended the tabernacle and Doeg, while Abiathar left to get the bread. David debated whether or not to stay on and kill Doeg. Though he knew that Doeg would take news of his visit there to the king, out of respect for the priests and the holy place, David decided against taking such action.

When Doeg emerged with Ahimelech, David hid himself until they had passed. He then returned to the tabernacle to be alone with the God he feared had abandoned him.

"Lord, I have served you well," he said, prostrating himself before the altar. "I do not know how I have displeased you that you would forsake me so, but I beg your forgiveness now. I hope that whatever good I have done in this life will count for enough that you will heed me when I ask that you keep Jonathan always safe, that he may have a full and happy life. Perhaps that is your will already, and my fate is only a means to accomplish it. I can only suppose that it pleases you now that I be an outlaw. So in faith I turn to the ways of the road this day, not because it is my choice, but because you have left me with no other. I am here, Lord, your servant still. I await your bidding should you decide that you believe in me again. Forgive me for what unintended wrongs I have committed to earn your disfavor. I seek your grace and forgiveness in all that I undertake."

By the time he arose, the shadows were leaning east and the priests were waiting outside the tabernacle to bid him good-bye.

"A blessing to you and your mission," Abiathar said, walking him to the edge of the compound and opening the gate for him. "We will pray for you and your men in your undertaking."

"I thank you, for I most surely need it," David said with a sad smile he could not conceal.

As he followed the sun west, his fingers found the lion's tooth from Micah's sling hanging from Jonathan's gold chain, and the old familiar leather pouch of the sling that hung around his neck once again. Though the reminder made him feel more alone, the talismans gave him the feeling that Micah was with him and Jonathan not so far away.

His earliest memory of Micah had come to him unbidden that morning. It fueled his plan for refuge against the king's soldiers, who he thought would surely be seeking him while the season still permitted. If he could but reach his goal, the onset of the rainy season would put an end to what search might be in effect. On the other hand, he had much to do before the rains began and only his two hands with which to do it.

"Oh, Micah, I would that you could be here with me," David said, clasping the lion's tooth firmly in his fist. "Watch over me and help me to find my way on this treacherous path onto which the Lord has thrust me."

His eyes blurred with tears, but David's pace never slowed. He arrived at the Jebusite city of Jerusalem by nightfall. Improvising a place to sleep and a fire from what twigs he could find, he made his meager camp, lost in the sprawl of traders and nomads. Myriad strangers surrounded him in the darkness. Their arrival, and his, was inevitable. Jerusalem was a great crossroads. Routes to Egypt, Damascus, Arabia, and the great sea, as well as all of Israel, were met there to create the world's marketplace. The city would make a fine capital, David mused as he lay awake under the stars that night. He laughed to himself at such grand notions from a man who slept on the ground, dined on borrowed bread, and had only memories for comrades.

Awaking before the sun, he made an early start down the road toward the great sea. It was a hard day's walk, but it was almost all downhill. He sang his thanks for a cool sea breeze that met him halfway.

The sun hung low in the sky as his destination rose into view: the Philistine city of Gath. He left the road to find a place to conceal his meager possessions, the sling and the sword of legend, for it would hardly serve him to arrive armed at his enemy's gates. He could ill afford to lose his only weapons should he fail to gain admittance to the city. Shedding his robe and tying a cloth around his groin and between his legs, he smeared himself with dirt and tousled his hair before returning to the highway.

As he approached the gates of the city, he began gathering a bouquet of weeds, which he presented with a grand bow to the guards at the gate. "Your Majesty," David sang, circling like a child overcome with excitement. "I am David ben Jesse of Bethlehem. I have traveled far to meet you, the King of Philistia."

"Oh great," the guard said, chuckling and nudging his comrade. "And just why have you come to see me, great warrior?"

"Why, to swear my eternal allegiance," David declared. Tripping over his own feet, he turned it into an awkward bow as he fell to the ground before them.

"Best call the captain," the guard said to his friend. "I'll wait here with our distinguished visitor."

"I'll be right back," the other guard said with a gentle smile as he left the two. "Tell me if he says anything worth knowing."

"So, my friend," the guard called to David, who remained bowed like an eastern slave before the humble guard. "Have you any words of wisdom for me?"

"What may I tell you, great king?" David asked, sitting back onto the ground with his legs crossed, childlike, seemingly at ease before the armed man and the massive forbidding gates. David had remembered his run-in with the traders in the marketplace in Bethlehem on the day he'd first met Micah. They revealed to him that primitives, such as the Philistines, believed that the insane had been touched by one of their gods. They treated those of fractured senses with a reverence reserved for oracles and priests.

"I don't know," the guard said, considering. "There's a girl I fancy, lives down the road from me a bit. Her father's a butcher. He don't think much of the like of me."

"Does she know you care for her?" David asked, raising his shoulder and hiding his face shyly.

"No, I only ever just said hello and the like," the guard said, eyeing the twisted man on the ground before him.

"Fathers always do what their daughters say," David said, realizing his words' meaning for himself as much as for the guard.

"Brilliant," the guard said, smacking his thigh. "If she likes me, she'll do better at convincing the old ogre than I ever could. Them wives' tales are right about you lot."

David was too stunned by his own sudden understanding of the role Michal had played in his troubles with the king to reply. As he paused to see his most recent encounters with Michal in this new light, he seemed to the guard to have lost the power of speech, unintentionally making his performance the more convincing.

Taking hold of himself when he saw the guard returning with an officer, David rose. Seizing a clod of dirt from the road, he began to make marks on the wooden planks of the gate. Sticking out his tongue in concentration, he drooled on the stubble that had accumulated on his face in the few days he'd been away from the comforts of home.

"Baal's wrath," the captain swore as he arrived with the first guard and saw David. "This is the real article. We'll all be generals by sunrise."

"What d'you mean?" the guard asked, confused by the captain's assertion. "The king can't take no interest in whatever random loony what shows up here at the gates."

"This is no random loony," the captain hissed, smacking the guard alongside the head. "I fought in the Jezreel Valley. I'm sorry to tell you that I got close enough to see their general, David ben Jesse. This, my boy, is him in the flesh. Lost his mind, maybe, but not his face."

"Baal and Dagon," the guard swore. "This is our lucky day, isn't it?"

"Hello, David. I am the king's ambassador, and the king would very much like to meet you," the captain said as though speaking to a small child. "Would you like that?"

"But this is my king," David declared fiercely, falling to his knees and grasping the legs of the guard.

"Yes, of course," the captain said. "But this is his brother. The other king will wish to meet you too."

"Two kings," David said, his eyes wide with wonder. "This must be an estimable city."

"Oh, it is," the captain said, helping him up. He put an arm behind David as he led him through the gates, an honored guest with an official escort to the king. David could hardly keep himself from laughing, but he was too terrified at being found out to risk the possibility. His fear kept him in check until he remembered he was mad and could do as he pleased.

Laughing freely, he kicked the dust in a joyous dance as he followed the guards. They took him to the palace of King Achish, the most powerful of the five great kings of Philistia.

There he waited in an antechamber with plain stone walls and wooden benches. It was the sort of spare place where prisoners were kept as they waited to be led to judgment. David understood how those who had waited on the rough wooden benches before him must have felt. He was as uncertain as any man condemned as to what fate awaited him before the enemy ruler he'd faced and defeated so often. Here he had truly found the perfect hiding place from King Saul. It was only left to determine how final that hiding place might be.

"Thank you, Micah," David said just as though he was speaking to someone there in the room with him, aside from the captain and the palace guards. "Be with me now. We're going to meet the king of the Philistines." He was clutching the lion's tooth as he spoke and smiling to himself. Every so often he would shout one of the words he spoke or let spittle run down his unshaved chin without wiping it away.

The captain rolled his eyes and exchanged a knowing look with the guards.

Those around him kept a respectful distance, as much from fear of what he might do as awe for his divine gifts. He was handled reverently when an aide to the king came in to tell them that King Achish was prepared to see them. The attendant led David and his captors into the throne room through a stout iron-plated door.

"Bow before King Achish of Gath and lower Philistia," an attendant called, pounding the butt of his iron spear against the stone floor. The echo called the room to order. All those around David made themselves prostrate against the stones as the king entered the room.

The king did not notice David at first as he made his way to his throne, but as everyone else was lying on the floor, he could not help it for long. Achish paused. He and David regarded one another for a long breath. David reached out and took hold of a fold on the king's robe. He felt the fine fabric between his fingers, a long trail of spit hanging from where it had collected on his chin.

The king raised an eyebrow at being handled with such familiarity.

"You don't look much like your brother at the front gate," David said, reaching as if to touch the king's face.

"My brother?" the king growled, snatching the fabric out of David's hand as he moved on to the throne. "Is this what you have brought me down here to see? A madman?"

"He not just a madman," the captain of the gate guard said into the carpet.

"What?" the king demanded. "What did he say?"

"Get up from there and ask permission to speak to the king," the aide said, giving the captain a shove.

The captain began to get to his feet. The aide grabbed his robe and pulled him back down. "Up on your knees, idiot," he hissed at the captain, who fell to the ground and then scrambled back to his knees.

David clapped his hands and danced with delight as he laughed.

"Begging your pardon, if I may speak, sir—"

"Your Majesty," the aide hissed.

"I mean, Your Majesty, sir," the captain added hastily.

"How many madmen are here?" the king demanded, losing patience with the assembly.

"It's what I began to say before, Your Majesty," the captain went on, bowing and walking forward on his knees as he spoke. "It's not just another madman, sir, Your Majesty, sir. It's David ben Jesse, if you please, King Saul's right hand."

"At your service, sir, Your Majesty, sir," David said, dancing about to a tune of his own invention, finishing with a girlish curtsy.

"Look at the man! He is witless!" the king shouted so loudly that the captain of the guard began backing away, still on his knees, still bowing. David, by then on the platform with the king, jumped up and down and clapped his hands as he cackled with delight.

"You delayed my supper for this?" the king railed, rising to his feet. "Why bring him to me? Am I so short of the touched that you must bring this fellow here to carry on thus in front of me? Must I suffer this man in my house?"

"Your Majesty, sir," the captain of the guard apologized as he knelt his way backward toward the door. "Begging you pardon. I thought it might be of interest to you, sir. Or that he might serve some purpose of yours, Your Majesty, sir."

"Thank you, captain." The king sighed. "What is your name, man?"

"If it please you, Your Majesty sir, I'm called Juk, sir," the captain said, uncertain if it was wise to offer his name but afraid not to. "Captain of the guard at the east gate, Your Majesty, sir."

"Well, Juk, I appreciate your vigilance, if not your judgment. Return to your post, and we will see that this poor soul is cared for as befits one so afflicted."

"Bless you, Your Honor, sir," the captain said, reaching the door. Leaping to his feet, he ran from there to the palace exit and all the way back to where he knew he belonged. As he came in sight of the gatehouse, he let his pace fall to a swagger. Once he rejoined his colleagues at the eastern gate, the story he told differed from the facts of his harrowing audience. He spoke instead of the thanks of a grateful and generous king.

The king regarded the rest of the party before him a breath.

"Leave me alone with our guest," the king said with a wave. "Let me see if the gods have anything they wish to say to me through him."

"As you wish, Your Majesty," the aide spoke for the rest of the party. All rose and backed out of the room, bowing with some relief, given the previous royal outburst. They were glad to be rid of any further responsibility for the incident.

When the doors closed behind them, David felt a surge of true terror run through him. He began spinning himself around and around in place, near the throne where the king sat. Faster and faster he spun.

A strange sound caught David's ear as the room blurred around him. It was a few spins before he realized it was laughter. Stopping himself abruptly and nearly falling, he saw that the king was rocked with laughter. Uncertain, he only stared for a heartbeat, letting the spit run from the corners of his mouth.

"Oh, for the sake of your ancestors, stop that," the king said, tossing David a kerchief from his belt. "And just for the record, we are not all superstitious simpletons, any more than all of your people might be judged by your sons and daughters of *Belial*—isn't that your expression for fools?"

David only looked at him.

"Oh, come now, David ben Jesse," the king said. "You are not mad. You are fleeing your King Saul's warrant for your head. Yes, of course I've heard."

"I see," David said, wiping his face with the kerchief. "So what do you intend to do with me?"

"I will court the favor of my gods and yours and offer you the hospitality of my house," Achish said with a shrug and a laugh. "Wasn't want of hospitality the sin that doomed your city of Sodom? Besides, you look as if you could use it. A bath, a shave, a clean robe, a good meal? How long have you been on the run?"

"Do you plan to keep me prisoner?" David asked, offering the borrowed silk back to the king, who waved it away.

"I plan to put you back outside my gates after I feed you a hearty morning meal for the road," the king said with a smirk. "I will leave you, well rested and well fed, to your own fate."

"You're not going to kill me?"

"I am still the king," Achish pointed out. "Is that how you speak to yours? Perhaps it is no wonder he would have your head."

"I'm sorry, Your Majesty," David said with a bow. "I came into your home under such pretense, I have forgotten what scene I was playing."

"Better," the king said, pointing to a nearby bench. "Do sit down. No need to overdo it. I ask your respect for the title on behalf of my kingdom more than my vanity. In honesty, I'm more comfortable in the battlefield than I am in this pile of rocks. I feel more a prisoner here than master. To answer your earlier question, though, I'll not harm a hair on your head."

"But, Your Majesty, I am your sworn enemy and you are mine," David pointed out, confused. "I'm sure we have faced one another in battle before."

"That we have, young man." Achish nodded vigorously. "It is from there that I recognized you when that simpleton guard brought you to me. And I must congratulate you on your strategy. It fails you tonight, though. For you see, if I kill you, then you become an even greater hero to your people, and I'm more evil than I was before your death. But if Saul kills you, then, to at least half the people of Israel, I think, he becomes the villain. To the other half you become a traitor. Both of which benefit my cause. So no, I'll only offer you the bounty of my home. I'll let it be widely known that you enjoyed my hospitality. I think that will serve me better, both in the charity of the gods and the petty minds of men."

"It's not foolishness so much as worthlessness, Your Highness," David said with a polite bow.

"How's that?" the king asked, puzzled by the response.

"Sons of Belial," David explained. "Sons of Belial are more worthless than fleas on a camel, like little demons."

"I see." The king chuckled, rising.

"On a night such as this, when I have clearly behaved as though I was the son of such, the distinction seems more important to me," David said with a bow of respect as he rose. "Your Majesty, it is always a pleasure to learn from my betters."

"Come, let's get you cleaned up and dressed," the king said, leading the way. "I would take supper with you, and I'm already starved for the delay."

"It would be my honor, Your Majesty," David answered, following respectfully behind as he knew was the custom on the plain.

"By the way, hiding in your enemy's fortress is actually quite a good plan in this circumstance," the king said with a generous nod. "Though, I must tell you in all candor, acting doesn't seem to be your strong suit. I do hear you are something of a singer."

"So I'm told, Your Majesty."

"Perhaps a psalm in payment after supper?"

CHAPTER SIXTEEN
THE CAVE OF ADULLAM

David therefore departed thence, and escaped to the cave Adullam: and when his brethren and all his father's house heard it, they went down thither to him.

1 Samuel 22:1

ELIAB AND Joab rode through the night. They led Eliab's six brothers, Joab's brothers Abishai and Asahel, and a handful of officers and soldiers who'd fought under David and were too loyal to believe what was being said of him. They made up an impressive company of more than fifty men. Theirs was just the party who rode that night from Bethlehem and Gibeah. Other men, with similar loyalties, rode from all parts of Israel to the valley of Elah.

Eliab had remained with Abner's armies, garrisoned near the palace at Gibeah, long enough to determine that his parents were safe and that the king had not discovered David's location. When the time came, Joab too joined Eliab and Abinadab. They recruited any trained soldiers who, given the choice, would follow David, and gave them the choice.

As the king and his advisers struggled to run down the rumors of David's whereabouts, Eliab used the king's messengers to weave his net of David's loyalists. Through reliable sources, and then a message from David himself, Eliab was able to determine that his brother was hiding in the western mountains of Judah, near the valley of Elah. All that remained was choosing the time to act. With a series of cryptic communications originating from Eliab at Gibeah, word spread man to man to the farthest northern outposts of the Jezreel Valley army that David had built, and south to the strongholds throughout Judah.

All were to meet in the Elah valley where David's legend had begun. From there, they would seek the man whom they would follow. It was a dangerous ploy. They found their greatest protection in the king, blinded by his pride and plans of revenge. Saul seemed hardly to consider the divisive consequences of casting out his most powerful commander for no more reason than he had given. Wild speculations about David's betrayal were rampant, but none were substantiated by fact or witness.

Then the king himself took steps that drove a wedge that further divided public opinion and private loyalty. It started with a meeting in Gibeah that Eliab had attended.

Playing on regional loyalties, the group had been composed chiefly of the king's fellow Benjamites and those considered most trusted and highly placed within his command. Eliab had been included. He had held fast to his post and his duty, even as David took flight, though he practiced to keep himself out of the king's sight as he went about his duties and at the assembly that day. Conspicuous at the meeting by his absence was Crown Prince Jonathan.

King Saul came to meet with his men where they were garrisoned. He spoke to them like brothers, seated, spear in hand, under a tamarisk tree.

"Hear me, men of Benjamin, and those who have been born brothers, and countrymen to me in the blood of battle," the king spoke, raising his spear defiantly. "Will this son of Jesse give all of you fields and vineyards? Will he make all of you commanders? Is that why you have all conspired against me? No one tells me when my son Jonathan makes a covenant with the son of Jesse? None of you is concerned about me or tells me that my son has incited my servant to lie in wait for me, as he does today?"

There was silence as those present looked to one another with as much confusion as guilt. Many had known of the relationship between Jonathan and David. It had been such common knowledge, most had assumed that the king knew but turned a blind eye or cared not. All were reluctant to speak.

David's performance in the field had convinced them of his worth. In truth most in attendance, Eliab and Joab included, had come to hear what, if any, proof the king could present against David. None was brave enough to break the silence and call for it.

At length Doeg, who had come to the assembly as a personal bodyguard and kinsman to the king, stepped forward. He bowed before Saul to be recognized.

"Yes, Doeg," the king spoke, annoyed. "Is an Edomite the only one here willing to admit the truth of this traitor to me? What would you say to me, Doeg?"

"I saw the son of Jesse in Nob, my king," Doeg said, raising his face to look upon Saul. "He came to the priest there, Ahimelech son of Ahitub. David was with them when he first took flight. I did not know of the king's warrant then, as I had been with my kinsmen in Edom since the prince's marriage to my sister. I was only then returning from my father's house to take up my post here with you."

"You are forgiven, Doeg," the king said with a curt nod, his brow knit in thought and consternation. "Tell me what else you know of David's visit with the priest at Nob."

"Ahimelech inquired of your gods for him," Doeg replied, relieved by his own absolution and anxious once again to find favor. Fearful of compounding his offense, he hastened to correct his error. "God, I mean, your God. They also gave him provisions and the sword of Goliath the Philistine."

The king's rage cleared the hall of all but the bravest. He dispatched men to fetch Ahimelech and his entire clan to appear before him that very day to answer charges of giving aid to a traitor. It was a distasteful sight and all that was required for many of those present to make up their minds. A number of good and loyal men took their leave of the king, their service at his court, and in his army.

Eliab and Joab departed to make ready for the gathering at Elah. It was clear there was to be no real proof presented against David or his character.

For those who remained, few were left with any doubts about their loyalty.

Ahimelech and all his family of priests were presented before the king. It was a tribute to be asked to court, and the priests were joyously unaware of the reason for their royal summons.

"Your Majesty," Ahimelech said, bowing before the king. "It is our honor to be here to serve you. I am Ahimelech, son of Ahitub. These are my brothers, sons, nephews, and grandsons, all your priests of Nob, guardians of the ark. What would you ask of me and my family? How may we serve you?"

"Listen now, son of Ahitub," Saul said, rising and pacing before the assembled priests. "Why have you conspired against me, you and the son of Jesse? Giving him bread and a sword and inquiring of the Lord for him, so that he has rebelled against me and lies in wait for me, as he does today?"

"In truth, my king, at the time I thought I was in service to you," Ahimelech answered, concerned for the king's censure but confident that their priestly ephods would protect them. "Who of all your servants is as loyal as David? Or so it seemed at the time. When he arrived at Nob, he was still the king's son-in-law, a captain in your army, and highly respected in your household. Was that day the first time he had come to worship at Nob? Of course not, my king. Do not accuse us, your servants, or any of my father's family, for we know nothing at all about this whole affair."

The king was silent for a long while and then, turning, struck Ahimelech in the face, knocking the priest to the ground. Kneeling, he snarled in the priest's ear. "You will die for this, Ahimelech. All your father's family will die here today."

The king's words shocked those present. Other than the priest and his family, who joined hands and began praying, all there were battle-hardened men, witness to all manner of the atrocities of war. Yet even such men were struck silent.

"Who will turn and kill these *priests of the Lord*?" Saul mocked Ahimelech and the priests who stood unarmed and surrounded by Saul's men. "They have forsaken their vows to the Lord's own anointed king and sided with David, the usurper. They knew he was fleeing, yet they did not tell me."

No one moved.

"Is no one still loyal to the king of Israel?" Saul wailed, striking his own men and spitting in their faces.

Doeg stepped forward, drew his sword, and to the horror of all those present, hacked off Ahimelech's head where he lay at the king's feet. The priest's blood splashed the king's robes and his sandals.

The prayers and screams filled the air. The priests beseeched their God for mercy but received none from the king or the men who served his cruel will. Doeg slaughtered eighty-five men who wore the linen ephod that day. Those few who helped did so in fear for their own necks. The king also put to the sword Nob, the village of the priests, with its men and women, its children and infants, and its cattle, donkeys, and sheep.

Along with those who died that day, and later at Nob, the king also put to the sword his country's unity. He forced the people of Israel to choose between loyalty to their much-loved hero David, of whom the only ills they knew were no more than rumor, and their king, from whose wrath even the Lord's servants were not safe. It became a choice between fear and love, and it cost the king more than he could know.

Even as the night sky was lit by the flames of Nob and the king held his power through fear of his wrath, there were those riding through the darkness to take their place at David's side.

By the time the flames had died and the sun turned the morning sky the hopeful pale purple of the mountain wildflowers of early spring, Eliab found himself in the company of over two hundred and fifty who would follow David. Every man there had left all that he had, those he loved, and traveled like a thief under cover of night to fight on the side of the man he would follow without doubt or question. As Eliab looked up to the light at the horizon, he saw they just kept coming.

"So where is this David?" inquired Isaac, a stranger whose home and family David had helped save from a Philistine raiding party during his command in the Jezreel Valley.

"Nearby," Eliab said with a shrug.

"How do we find him?" asked another.

"My brother has never had a talent for minding his own business," Eliab said with a laugh. "Eat. He will find us."

And the king said unto the footmen that stood about him, Turn, and slay the priests of the Lord: because their hand also is with David, and because they knew when he fled, and did not shew it to me. But the servants of the king would not put forth their hand to fall upon the priests of the Lord.

1 Samuel 22:17

EAST OF King Achish and the Philistine city of Gath, and west of the mountains of Judah, the Shephelah rose from the coastal plain. The low, rocky foothills, matted with trees and brush, offered more in the way of hiding places than farmland. The limestone hills were pocked with caves. Watered by springs and the generous rainfall from storms blown in off the great sea, the sycamores were fruitful but little else.

The no-man's-land separated the plain of Philistia from the hills of Judah and Israel by only half a day's ride. Its indefensibility did more to keep the peace than all the battles fought or treaties sworn between the two bitter rivals. There was little farmable land, and the few villages that did survive in that strange in-between place were built on hillsides, to save what little level land could be put to the plow.

Because of its nature as neither here nor there, the Shephelah was the land of the outcast, the disreputable, and those for whom nowhere else was home. It was there that the battle of Elah was fought, over the broad and easily traveled valley that led directly from Gath on the west to Bethlehem on the east. It was also there in the Shephelah, near the village of Adullam, in a large cave high on a hill and easily defended, that David first took refuge when the Philistine King Achish sent him on his way. The king provided David with a comfortable night's sleep, a full belly, and adequate supplies to set up a handsome camp for himself.

David retrieved the sword of Goliath and Micah's sling, his only weapons, along with his few meager belongings. He made his way to the village of Adullam. There, he thought he might be able to abide unnoticed for a few days. In addition to shelter and supplies, he thought he might perhaps find means to make contact with his family, both to be sure of their safety and to assure them of his.

The rain began on the way. David stumbled on the cave seeking shelter and made his camp there. It reminded him of the adventures he'd shared with Micah. Idled by the rain, he explored the cavern during the storm and found it was as sizeable and extensive as it was formidably and naturally well fortified.

When the skies cleared, he went into Adullam, hoping for more comfortable accommodations. What he found instead was a village largely decimated by bandits who lived in the hills above. Naturally the villagers were most unfriendly to strangers. As a result David found supplies scarce and hospitality rarer still. He left Adullam more thankful for the cave, to which he gladly returned. He began to settle in more fully.

The first new friends David found in the hills were a man and his young son. Burned out of their home, they were run out of their village by a larger clan who wanted the man's land and claimed falsely that he was stealing sheep.

The son was attracted to the smell of the roasting goat David had brought down hunting with his trusty old sling. Boldly the youth came to investigate.

"Boy?" David called, not looking in the direction in which he knew the lad to be hiding. "If you'd like to join me for dinner, I'd enjoy the company."

"How do you know I'm here?" the boy asked, prepared to run.

"Because you make more noise in the woods than a charging bear," David said, tending his fire and his feast. "And because you are talking to me. After we eat I can teach you to move through the forest silently, if you like. You will have to learn to hold your peace on your own."

"Can my father come to dinner, too?" the boy asked, stepping tentatively into the opening at the mouth of the cave.

"What?" David asked, looking shocked. "A big strapping lad like yourself, still with your father? Is he a feeble old man whom you must look after?"

The boy laughed.

"Well, go and get him, then," David said, shaking his head. "You two are welcome to join me, but I make no promise to save any if you're late. And, boy?"

"Yes, sir?"

"What's your name?"

"Matthew," the young man answered.

"Good to meet you, Matthew," David called to him. "I'm David. Now hurry up. Supper's almost ready."

"Yes, sir," the boy affirmed enthusiastically, for he was both hungry and friendless and mightily glad of the prospects of dinner and a generous new acquaintance.

Matthew and his father were the first to join David's army, though not one of the three were aware they were doing anything of the kind. Soon their camp of three grew to six, and then twelve, and soon twenty and more. All were there for different reasons, from injustices to a little too much justice. But they came together for the same reason as the three who sat down to dinner that first night—they were hungry and in need of friends. They spent their days hunting and making weapons from what was available, bows and spears mostly. Then they learned to use them. Their first act as an army was to capture the bandits who'd been raiding the village of Adullam and turn them over to the elders for sentencing. They kept the bandits' bronze and iron weapons and their spoils for themselves.

Local heroes then, they were not only welcome in town, but they were rewarded with tributes of food and supplies. Word spread through the Shephelah. Those who'd lost or been denied their place in the world for being born in the wrong way, or too different from their fellows, or who were just unable to pay their taxes to unjust kings, found their place at David's side. He welcomed them all with a wide embrace, though he remembered the pledges of support from Eliab, Joab, and many others and dared continue to hope for their arrival.

A scouting party brought word back to camp that encouraged David's heart. A few of the party were hunting near the very ridge at Elah where the Philistines had been camped when Goliath fell. They rushed back to David with news of a large party of men camped there under no king's standard. With a prayer on his lips and a full complement of his ragged army, David returned to the ridge.

The morning he and his men crested the familiar hills, they doubled their numbers when they joined the two hundred or more who awaited them with Eliab's in the valley below.

A cheer went up as David led a charge down the hill. He ran into the waiting arms of the men who had come to defend him.

"Brothers," David cried. He was glad for the first time in his life when Eliab snatched him off his feet and tossed him over his shoulder. They embraced and celebrated just the sight of one another, David and all his brothers and nephews and friends, for some time. They returned to David's mountain stronghold. A meal was prepared, and all there feasted as they fell in with one another.

"This is quite some place." Eliab whistled as David walked the perimeter with him and Joab after they had eaten their fill and a little more besides.

"You have been busy, Uncle," Joab joked as he surveyed the defenses. "We all thought you were just taking some leisure time in the country."

"It's been like summers with Micah," David said with a sad smile.

"He would have loved this," Eliab said, wrapping his arm around his brother's strong but smaller shoulders, taking silent stock of the man he had become.

"What of our mother and father?" David asked, putting an arm around the small of his big brother's back. "Are they well?"

"So far," Eliab said. "Our mad fool king has only been railing against you. Though he had called the priests of Nob to trial before him just when we left. The Lord only knows where it will end."

"Let us not speak ill of the king," David said firmly. It was a policy he had begun with the men who already followed him.

"David, how can you—"

"The king is the Lord's chosen," David said, patting his brother on the back. "I know I don't know better than the Lord. I expect you to back me in this and to see that the other men who follow do as well; you too, Joab. We will not be purposed with King Saul's overthrow. I have no interest in anything of the kind."

"As you wish, brother," Eliab said as he ducked to follow David into the great cave. He was glad to find that, once inside, it opened up considerably above his head. "I've told you before, it is you we follow, so lead on where you will."

"Well, as you mention it, there is something I have in mind," David said, leading his brother to the quarters his men had made for him within the cave. "I want to take our parents to safety. I feel now that you are arrived, there are enough trained officers and soldiers to keep this place going while we manage it."

"What will become of the our father's karmel?"

"The women will run it as they always have." David laughed.

Eliab blushed in reply. He was certain that were it left to him at that very day, the karmel would fall at once to ruin.

And every one that was in distress, and every one that was in debt, and every one that was discontented, gathered themselves unto him; and he became a captain over them: and there were with him about four hundred men.

1 Samuel 22:2

RUMOR REACHED the king that David had been seen in the vicinity of Bethlehem. He dispatched men to brave the muddy winter trek from Gibeah into Judah to find him. The sun had set twice, and it had not stopped raining once. Sodden, muddy, and at last, the king's soldiers pounded on Jesse's door.

There was no immediate answer, and so the captain pounded again.

"Open this door or we shall break it in and arrest all as traitors inside," he commanded.

"What is the matter with you?" David's sister Zeruiah demanded, snatching the door open and throwing a pitcher of water over the captain. "How dare you come beating at my door in such a manner? What would your mother say of such behavior, young man?"

"I have no... I come with a warrant from the king," the captain said, fleetingly losing himself and then, just as briefly, recovering his authority.

"And do you suppose that gives you the right to behave like a Philistine at my door?" Abigail demanded, pushing past her sister and tapping the soldier's chest with her pointing finger as his men sniggered behind him.

"Now look here, my good woman," the captain began again.

Zeruiah grabbed him by the ear and dragged him out into the yard. This brought outright laughter and hoots of support from the captain's small company. She was a large woman, and the captain had no great desire to harm the women of David's family.

"Who wants a hot meal, and who came here to rough up women?" she demanded, depositing the captain in a puddle under a stand of oaks in front of the house. "Here now, boys, everyone who wants dinner, get down to the barn and get washed up and dry. There's mutton stew and fresh bread and lentils and a dry, warm place to sleep tonight. Those men among you who came here to strike the mother of your countrymen, come along. Here I am. Joab's mother, I'm sure you know that name. I'll take you on one at a time or in groups, as you prefer."

"To the barn," one of the lieutenants shouted. The small company ran cheering down the hill toward the first shelter and hot food they'd had since they were ordered out of Gibeah in the rain.

"There now, Captain," Zeruiah called back to him over her shoulder, retracing her steps across the yard. "If you knock and ask nicely as an officer who fought alongside my brothers and my sons, you may have dinner at Jesse's table and spend the night in David's own room. If not, enjoy the rain."

The door slammed, and the captain sat for a time in the puddle. His will had deserted him along with his men. The spicy smell of the stew was as sharp and irresistible as daggers in the cold evening air. The warm light that seeped from behind the shuttered windows of the great house, and the rich smell of the smoke from the fires burning inside, defeated him. He rose, crossed the yard once again, and rapped smartly on the door. It opened immediately to reveal the two sisters, standing, arms folded, stern as Levites, wooden spoons at the ready in case of mischief.

"Fair ladies," the captain said with a soggy bow and a wet flourish. "My name is Rehob. I am a captain in the king's army. I am proud to say I served under your brother and your son. I would be honored to take a cold meal here on the steps of their father's house. I hope you'll forgive my earlier presumption."

"Oh, you poor thing," Zeruiah said, whisking him inside, suddenly all featherbeds and motherhood. "Come inside and get dry and warm. Maha, bring some towels and hot water."

The captain later reported at court that he and his men had found the house of Jesse empty and the lands around it barren and abandoned.

Thus in a thousand tiny ways began the rebellion that David never started. It was not big or important. There were no trumpets or marching men or armed conflicts. It was made up of countless small kindnesses and the occasional omissions that people who knew better offered one another. It came with good manners and understanding toward their betters and their lessers. It grew from doing what they knew to be the right thing even when it contradicted the king's laws. In this way, even before the conflict was over, the country began to heal. And all of it was done in the name of David.

And David went thence to Mizpeh of Moab: and he said unto the king of Moab, Let my father and my mother, I pray thee, come forth, and be with you, till I know what God will do for me.

1 Samuel 22:3

AS MISERABLE as the soldiers' march was through the winter rains from Gibeah to Bethlehem, David and Eliab's ride from Bethlehem to the Moabite king's palace in Mizpah was worse. The weather cleared up well enough as soon as they came down out of the hills. They crossed the strange desert lands of the Arabah, north of the great salt sea. They made their way in the relative winter cool to ford the Jordan River at Jericho, then crossed to Gad and on through to Moab. But no matter how clear the day, Eliab and David had "abducted" Nitzevet from her home and were "dragging" her across the country to "abandon" her in a strange land. No storm or invading army equaled what the two brothers endured.

"Mizpah?" she ranted. "Take me to King Saul in Gibeah. I'll take care of this without going to Moab. Oh, God's breath, what is the world come to, Jesse? I remember when that king was a ratty little mule herder from a second-rate clan in Benjamin, knocking at our door looking for money and your permission to have a kingdom in the first place."

Though her rants quieted as they drew nearer to their goal, Jesse then found his tongue and began advising David on how best to strike an agreement with the king.

Eliab and David took turns riding watch out ahead for relief.

"Your Majesty, would you allow my mother and father to remain here with you until I learn what the Lord will do for me?" David asked simply. He had been granted an audience with the Moabite king he'd met over a fine meal in Saul's palace not so long ago. The two had struck up a kinship of sorts when David explained that his family line was late of Moab. David found as gracious a protector for his parents as he'd first met in Gibeah.

The meal they shared was less grand, as neither the king nor David wished word to reach Saul of David's visit. Still, the evening concluded with the Moabite king's favorite rendition of his favorite folk song, one David had remembered and played in his honor when they'd first met. They parted warmly and well met.

David's farewell to his parents was another matter entirely.

With wailing and funereal parental lament, the two brothers left Jesse and Nitzevet safely ensconced in Mizpah, in private royal apartments. Their mission accomplished, they rode for many miles without a word—because they could.

"Oh," David sighed, breaking the long quiet between them. "That poor king."

Eliab only laughed in answer, preferring still the noise of hoofbeats on the road to conversation in any form.

The silence was harder for David. It left him alone with thoughts of Jonathan and the loss of his former life. It made him aware of how happiness hangs by gossamer in the lives of men. A flood, a death, a fire, an illness, or an accusation could take a man's life and all that brought him joy as swiftly as a shooting star can cross the heavens. He treasured the fragments of happiness that his life on the run afforded. But he hoped and prayed with all his heart to be reunited with Jonathan.

Perhaps he would have to wait until Saul died, but it was the certainty of their reunion that kept him going and gave him the strength to laugh. Most of the time that was enough. They made their way up the Jordan to the ford at Jericho. There, as was sometimes the case, the wait grew too much, and David felt weak from the strain.

They had hardly spoken any but the most essential words by the time they made camp that night. Their evening meal was a simple one. Eliab was soon asleep by the fire. Stealing away, David climbed into the hills. He made his way onto one of the serrated cliffs of the Ghor, the strange land that bordered the river. Eroded by the shifting course and ancient flow of the eternal waters, the layered bluffs overlooked the river that sparkled in the moonlight below.

There, under a sky twice bigger than the world, David found the room to cry. He wept for his lost love, his lost life, and his lost faith.

"Why?" he bayed at the sky like a lonely animal calls to the moon.

As he looked up, he saw the stars and remembered the saphan constellation Jonathan had given him, with a promise of forever. The smile that replaced his tears hurt almost as much. He sat at the edge looking off at the river in the distance and the thick swampy forests of the Zor that bordered it. He tried to summon the strength to get up and go back to check on his brother; to return to the life he'd been given. Somehow he could not will his legs to bear him back to the fireside.

"David?" a strange voice croaked in a loud whisper. Startled, he almost fell. "David, speak to me."

Drawing his sword, he was on his feet without a thought.

Silent, he held his ground. He made out the figure moving haltingly toward him in the dark.

"David, I know you are there," the visitor said more clearly. "I can hear you breathing. Fear not, for I have been sent to you by my master. I mean you no harm."

"Who is your master?" David demanded as the dark figure of the man made his way straight to where David stood.

"The same as yours," the old man said with a little wheezing laugh.

"I have no master," David asserted.

"Of whom did you ask 'why'?" the man laughed, stopping just beyond the range of David's sword.

"So you're spying on me," David snapped.

"I've no need," the man said, still and peaceful before him.

"How did you find me?" David demanded.

"I followed the saphan constellation," the old man answered with a shrug.

David's sword clattered to the stones. He raced forward to throw his arms about the old man in joy.

"Jonathan is your master," David rejoiced. "He has sent you to me. What word of him? Is he well?"

"You mistake, my son," the old man said. Cane in hand, he patted David lovingly if a bit painfully on the back, hitting him in the head with his walking stick. "I've never met Jonathan, though I can assure you he is most well. His new wife is with child, a boy who will be born in the late spring."

"Who are you?" David asked, drawing back in horror. "How do you know these things?"

"From my master and yours," the old man said. "To whom all things are known."

"Why have you come to me?"

"My master has sent me to assure you and to tell you that you must leave Adullam by the first new moon after your return. You will find your destiny begins in the Hereth forests to the south and east of your camp."

David was speechless at all the man knew, certain he stood before a great prophet. "Why has our master treated me so ill?" David demanded bitterly.

"You are alive, are you not?" the old man answered. "Is not anything possible from there?"

"Tell me if we will be together again, Jonathan and I?" David begged, falling to his knees and grasping the old man's robes.

"Until you leave him," the old man said.

"I would never leave him," David said, drawing back.

"Ah, how often we do for the sake of those we love that which we've said we will never do," the old man said, in a strange, musical kind of way.

"Well, you can tell your master there is no force in all his creation great enough to take me away from Jonathan, should I ever be so lucky as to have him back again," David declared, rising and turning away.

"Is there any force greater than love?" The old man's voice seemed to trail away.

David turned and saw the man in silhouette against the setting moon. He realized he was using the stick he carried to feel his way down the hillside. Understanding all at once that the man was blind, he rushed to his aid.

"Father, may I help you down to the road?" David offered, taking the ancient elbow.

The man threw back his head and laughed.

"And which way is the road?" the old man asked.

"I—I don't know, but we can find it together," David answered sincerely.

"That, my boy, is why my master has chosen you," the man said, patting David gently on the shoulder with an old and withered hand. "He is my guide and yours. Go to the Hereth Wood, and there you will find your way. For now," he went on, pointing to their left with his cane, "your brother is over there, and if you start now and move quickly, that jackal won't eat all your food for the journey home."

"Jackal," David scoffed and then, thinking better off it, snatched up his sword and struck out in the direction the old man pointed. "Good-bye. And my best to your master."

"He still believes in you, David," the old man called in return as they parted company in the night.

When David got back to camp, the horses were shying and the jackal was sniffing around their packs. He woke Eliab, scaring the beast away.

"What is it?" Eliab said, sitting up and fumbling for his sword.

"Only a hungry jackal," David said thoughtfully.

"Good thing you were awake," Eliab said, drifting off again.

And the prophet Gad said unto David, Abide not in the hold; depart, and get thee into the land of Judah.

1 Samuel 22:5

JONATHAN CRIED out as he sat up in bed.

He had dreamed of jackals menacing David, asleep by some campfire in the wilderness. Thunder rumbled through the clouds with flashes of lightning. It had been raining for days. It was the longest, coldest winter of his life already, and winter solstice was still a moon away.

He had fallen asleep in his own rooms. Out of consideration for Azia, he often kept to his own quarters at night. He did not seek to avoid her, but sought instead to see that she at least might sleep. He had not spoken a word to his father, nor passed a decent night's sleep for worry, since he'd hidden in the shadow of Ezel and watched David go.

No one commented on the fact that he did not attend royal council meetings, as was his usual custom when at court. Since Saul's single-minded order of business was the whereabouts and capture of David, it was understandable, even to the king, that Jonathan preferred to keep away. So far there had been no move to change his status as heir to the throne, though he'd have welcomed the freedom to follow David into the wilderness with the much-rumored and growing number of deserters.

Saul was fully aware that Jonathan remained at court more out of duty than desire. The king was content to leave the arrangements for succession as they were and keep his son under his roof.

Michal had wasted no time. Saul had easily agreed to her petition for a new alliance, glad to offer David the insult and caring little for the fate of a daughter who could no longer make a good match for him. Plans were already underway for her marriage to Paltiel. Jonathan avoided them as he avoided the rest of his family. He refused to participate in feast or holy days or any public or family functions. Privately he counted the sunrises and sunsets until the spring, when he might go on campaign and find David, or at least escape the prison that was his life that winter at court.

Jonathan had tried to keep his moods and his feelings from Azia at first, just as he had tried sleeping in the same bed.

One night his crying woke her, and she would not let it be. He never told her for whom the tears were shed. He admitted only that he'd had a bad dream and that he'd been having trouble sleeping. After that he moved back to his own bed more or less permanently. He paid her steady visits to fulfill his duty as her husband, though, and they came to enjoy their lovemaking as a midday pastime.

One such day, as they lay breathless in each other's arms, she spoke of it, understanding somehow. "You miss him very much," she said, her smooth hands kneading the taut flesh of his chest.

"Miss who?" Jonathan said, tensing, pulling away from her.

"Your friend David," she answered, tugging him back insistently.

He turned his face away to hide tears from her, afraid that their silent confirmation would hurt her.

"I miss my best friend too," she soothed, whispering in his ear as she fitted her body against the curve of his back. "Her name was Batan. She attended me when I was young, and we grew up together. She was married to a minister in my father's government. I don't know if she was as much to me as your David was to you, but I know that not a day goes by that I don't think of her and ache to hear her laugh, see her smile, or hold her hand. We slept in the same bed as sisters until her marriage, and even then often enough when he was away or with a mistress. Some nights, when I don't have you with me, I cry myself to sleep, thinking of the shape of her fingers or the way that she smelled in the morning."

"I'm sorry. I never paused to consider that this marriage had stolen you away from your life," Jonathan said, crying harder as he saw his own loss in hers.

"I'm not sorry," she said, taking his face in her hand and turning him to look at her. "I'm glad that I'm here with you. This is my duty, but it is also far better than the lives of most of the people in both our countries. If there is one less war between our people because you and I marry, it is worth the pain of leaving Batan. I only told you so you would know that I understand, and so you would not hide your feelings from me."

He took her in his arms and crushed her small frame against his, his tears for joy and sadness. The storm raged outside. In a flash of lightning, he fell in love with his wife.

Their time together became more of a comfort to him. They lived like refugees within the palace, in a private world of their making. In his apartments or hers but always on their own, they were never with the family. It was excused as the enthusiasm of newlyweds. The king was most pleased with reports that this was true in part, though he well knew it was not what kept Jonathan from his company.

As such, his family, particularly the king, was more than a little surprised when Jonathan announced he was having a celebration to honor his wife on her birthday. It was to be held in the queen's dining room. The entire family was invited along with many friends at court. The king was there and quiet. Always dubious of social affairs that included women, he was little more than a member of the party. Wary and uncertain of Jonathan's motives, he remained suspicious of some plot and seemed mildly disappointed when none appeared.

Michal and Paltiel were there, though Jonathan never looked directly at or spoke to either of them. Merab's sons were both still too young to do much more than mewl, and there was yet another child on the way. Ahinoam, as mothers will, could not resist making a chiding toast of her prayer that Jonathan and Azia would soon be expecting a grandchild and an heir.

"Mother, be gentle," Jonathan chided. "It's Azia's day. Let us be happy with her. I know that she is my only source of happiness these days."

"Well, it is a birthday celebration," Azia said with a knowing smile. "So perhaps I should tell you, husband, in front of all your family, that we will have another birthday late this spring."

"Azia," Jonathan cried joyously. Sweeping her off her feet, he spun her in the air as he used to do with David.

"Jonathan, be careful," Ahinoam fussed, trying to shepherd her away from him.

"To the son who will succeed my son as king," Saul declared. Rising and raising his glass, he came to life for the first time since the festivities began.

There was a toast and for a flicker they were, as other families, happy to be with one another and for their own continuation.

"Well," Jonathan said as the party quieted down. "I guess that news eclipses my surprise."

With his gesture the doors to the queen's dining room were opened. In strode a compact, dark man dressed after the custom of Edom with his robes tucked up between his legs, followed discreetly behind by a beautiful woman about Azia's age.

"May I present Yavuz, a favorite servant and advisor to the princess from her home, and his wife, Batan," Jonathan announced. Yavuz bowed respectfully at Azia's feet. She only briefly acknowledged the man before running past him, tears streaming down her face, to embrace her beloved friend Batan. "I have brought them here so that my wife might feel more at home in this strange place with all you strange people. Particularly that she might take comfort when I leave on campaign this spring, as it turns out, following the birth of our first child."

"First son," the king corrected with another little toast.

"We will be happy either way," Jonathan said, embracing his wife.

"Oh, my husband," Azia whispered into his ear as she held him fast. "I would do the same for you, if only I could."

"And that is why I love you," Jonathan said, kissing her to great applause.

Then David departed, and came into the forest of Hereth.
                                                    1 Samuel 22:5

THERE WAS much confusion and consternation at Adullam. David announced his abrupt decision to relocate his stronghold and his followers immediately upon his return from Moab.

"I will certainly understand if there are those among you who do not wish to accompany me farther," David concluded his brief speech to the stunned group. Most gathered to welcome him home had spent the time of David's absence building and improving their circumstances at Adullam.

While there was more than slight grumbling, not a man among them elected to stay behind. Perhaps more perplexing was that David did not seem to know where he wanted go. He mentioned only that he would remove himself to the south and east, to a different, more densely forested area of the Shephelah called Hereth.

Some, who were newer to David's entourage than others, found assurance in the certainty of those who had known and followed David longer.

"He has the Lord himself at his shoulder, he does," a soldier from Beth Shan who owed David his life explained to the youth Matthew, whom everyone already called David's first soldier or just First. "You'll see. David has never made a false move or had to retreat, not once since he set foot on that field to face Goliath."

That attitude expressed the sentiments of the growing troops.

So it was of little surprise to anyone when, a few days later, news came that Keilah, the principal city of Hereth, had been overrun by the Philistines— and that King Saul had promised no assistance.

"We will rid them of the Philistines and sleep with roofs over our heads for a change," David said, thinking of the old prophet's words under the moon that night in Gad. Encouraged by the sign he saw in Keilah, he urged haste to ensure they would be gone before the new moon, in keeping with the moonlight prophecy. He needed no further convincing from the old man's master, though he was still uncertain of his own.

On the eve of their departure, a stranger approached their camp. Ragged and bloody though he was, he was not a sight that curried a second look. Such was the way of conscription in David's army of outcasts and deserters. The stranger came into camp most distracted, asking for David.

"He's here somewhere," he was told offhandedly by those too busy with the move and too accustomed to the arrival of the wretched to bother more.

Still the man persisted, following fingers pointed north and south until at last he spotted David talking with Eliab and some of his captains. They were conferring with scouts back from Keilah and planning their attack.

"David ben Jesse," the man cried out, falling to his knees, his arms outstretched.

David looked up at the poor man. He smiled warmly, looking about for some foot soldier to bring the wretch together with some food and water and clean clothes.

"I am Abiathar, the last priest of Nob," the man cried out, falling to the ground face first, weeping, and tearing at the grass.

David was at his side almost before he struck the ground. He took the priest up into his arms, calling for food and wine. "Abiathar," David asked softly, cradling the exhausted and beaten man in his arm. "What has happened?"

"Oh, thank the Lord; it is really you," the man said, gasping and taking a sip from the cup David held for him as he helped the priest to sit up. "I have wandered the hills in search of you, hearing but not daring to believe the tales I'd heard of your survival and of this place."

"I am here," David said with gentle laugh. "Such as it is. It is fortunate you have come to us today, for tomorrow we are moving south. Why have you left your family and your duty to find me?"

"I have left neither," Abiathar said with a deep sad sigh, edged with tears that did not come. "Soon after your visit, the men of my father's family were called before the king. I was left behind to tend to the ark and our duties. The king that day killed every member of my family as traitors, burned the village, and slaughtered even the children and the livestock. I was thrown off a cliff by the king's soldiers who came for the ark. It was my escape, as I landed more easily than it seemed, and they took me for dead."

Stunned, David gasped and sat back, spilling the contents of the cup.

"I am responsible for the death of your family," David whispered, his eyes heavy with tears. "I knew when I saw Doeg there that he would be sure to tell the king. Forgive me," David wailed, throwing himself at the man's feet. "I should have killed him, but it was a holy place, and he had done me no wrong."

"It is not to blame you that I have sought you out," the priest said, placing his hand on David's head. "I am here because I understand that a wanted man might find safety and employment here with you."

"You will stay with me," David said, embracing the man. "You will be safe here."

"Thank you, my prince," Abiathar said, taking David's hand and kissing the gold ring Jonathan had given him. "I will be of service to you in any way that I can."

"In truth, sir, as it turns out, we need a priest," David said, rising and taking Abiathar's hand to help him up.

Chapter Seventeen
The City of Keilah

David and his men went to Keilah, and fought with the Philistines, and brought away their cattle, and smote them with a great slaughter. So David saved the inhabitants of Keilah.

1 Samuel 23:5

"Look, sir," Matthew called, bursting into the chamber. David looked up from his meeting with Eliab, Joab, and others of his commanders. The hall where they met was in the house in Keilah that served as both their headquarters and David's home. "I'm sorry, my lord captain. I didn't realize."

It's the weather, David thought with a smile.

"Well, if it isn't the First," Eliab said, collaring the gangly boy in the crook of his elbow and sanding his scalp with his beefy knuckles. "What's your pleasure, commander?"

David smiled at the brotherly show of affection, more than a little pleased that there was at last someone else on the receiving end. Though Matthew was almost Eliab's height, he was still far too willowy to present him much of a challenge. With the exception of David, all of Eliab's brothers had grown into the challenge of his affection.

"What do we have here?" Eliab said, snatching the rolled-up fabric from the boy's hands.

"No, not yet," Matthew cried, struggling to retrieve his bundle. "It's meant to be a surprise."

"A surprise," Eliab tortured. Holding the cloth away, he rolled back a corner of the fabric and sent the boy into a frenzy.

"Enough, you two," David said with a smile and concern that they might turn on him. "Matthew, is it something very important, or can it wait until later?"

The two had had extensive conversations on this topic. Very important was "There are dust or smoke clouds on the horizon" or "I saw someone strange in the wood nearby," whereas "The cat had nine kittens" or "There's beef shoulder for supper," while important, were not "very" important. Matthew was the youngest of his followers, and David was extremely protective as well as respectful. He'd never had a younger brother. He tried to be the sort of older brother to Matthew he'd wished for.

"It can wait," Matthew said, pausing only briefly from his game of keep-away with Eliab. "I thought you were alone."

"Eliab," David said with an arched brow. "Please give Matthew back his surprise so that we might return to work now."

"Oh, Mama," Eliab whined playfully. He too was clearly affected by the sudden onset of spring weather. The attendant seasonal madness was blooming throughout the city like a plague. The spring malady was aggravated by a winter of worry.

At first Keilah had been as much a blessing to them as they had been to Keilah. David and those who followed him had routed the Philistines. The invaders were not expecting any sort of reprisal during the winter months. It had been a brief, intense, and bloody battle. Only a few of the Philistines in the city had lived to escape.

The city's residents welcomed David and those who fought with him as their liberators. They offered them food, shelter, and showers of tributes, as well as the fine home of one of the city's former elders for David's personal use. To encourage their protectors to stay, the elders, with the city's support, gladly handed over the reins of power in exchange for the continued security David's rule offered. For their part, David and his men had been willing to take on the duties thrust upon them for a roof and hearth in winter. It had begun as a marriage of need and necessity. Alas, as with all marriages made in haste, heart all too quickly overruled head.

Locals soon bristled at the command they had invited. Happy to surrender responsibility, they were less jubilant about giving up authority. Soon they began voicing direct opposition to the order they'd welcomed.

David and those who followed him were too wary of capture to remain in the corrupt and ill-defended city that had invited Philistine invasion once already. Uninterested in becoming subjects of Keilah's former ruling council, they remained only on condition that command and security of the city remain in their hands. Arguments turned into scuffles. Scuffles turned into fights. Warm weather promised riots and insurrection if changes were not soon made. David grew concerned that Keilah's liberators were on their way to being regarded simply as new invaders.

His conversation with Eliab and Joab that morning had been about finding a way to share power with the people of Keilah while maintaining order and keeping the city secure from future attacks should the Philistines return.

"Thank you, Matthew, for your patience," David said, repressing his smile and ignoring Eliab's antics. "Perhaps we can have supper tonight—"

"David, there is a visitor to see you," David's armor-bearer, a local named Yusef, said from the door.

"It is such a lovely day." Joab sighed, sitting heavily on a nearby bench. "Why is everyone inside?"

"Who calls?" David asked, more accustomed than his nephew to the constant interruptions of living at headquarters. He preferred activity to the quiet. It afforded him no time to think of Jonathan. While many had taken comfort among the locals, David had abstained, unwilling to trade love for mere distraction.

"The village elder, Amal," Yusef ventured.

"Well, that is actually fortuitous," David said with a nod and a pleasant smile. "Show him in, please."

"David, we are not yet ready to include them in our plans," Eliab hissed, his spring fever and Matthew quickly forgotten.

"There will be no order here without consensus," David said, raising his hand for silence before Joab could join the chorus.

"Good day, Commander," Amal said, ending the conversation with his arrival. "Thank you for seeing me, though I had hoped that we might speak alone."

"Perhaps there will yet be time for that," David said, taking a seat and gesturing to a chair near his. "Your timing affords me the opportunity to add your thoughts to ours in our present meeting. We were discussing ways we may begin to share the governance of Keilah now that the threat of the Philistines has been brought under control."

"Well then, my lord, the timing is perfect indeed," Amal said with a curt bow before taking his seat. "I too have come with a proposal from the council of elders that we resume many of our old responsibilities and free your men of the burden."

"What areas of responsibility would you want to take on?" David asked, hopeful.

"Well, all areas," Amal said, turning his palms up. "You and your men would of course be welcome to stay on as citizens here in Keilah."

"All?" David asked, perplexed. "What of the military responsibilities? Patrols? Manning of the gates?"

"We thank you for your help, but we are ready to take command," Amal said graciously. "Of course, if you or your men wish to continue as our militia and serve under our commanders—"

"Are these not the same commanders and men who lost the city to the Philistines in the first place?" Eliab demanded, his voice thick with contempt.

"Eliab, this is a point from which we can begin," David said, as much to make his position clear to Amal as to quiet and reassure his brother.

"Oh no, you misunderstand," Amal said firmly. "We, the council, have already decided. I have not come to haggle for our freedom any more than you have come to conquer our city. Or am I mistaken in this?"

David smiled at the elder's cleverness but kept his thoughts to himself.

"I only speak for myself, Amal," Joab said in a tone that was tense but more courteous than Eliab's. "But I must tell you that I would not feel secure as a new citizen of your city, with the same incompetent fools defending my safety who cost you your lives and independence only a few moons ago."

"Our soldiers and their commanders have been training with you," Amal said, clearly controlling his own temper. "They have learned much from their recent—"

"I'm sorry," Joab continued firmly, cutting the elder off. "I was not speaking of your soldiers. I have the greatest respect for those brave and valiant men. I was speaking of you. When do we new citizens of Keilah have the opportunity to replace the kind of fool who would come here to dismiss the commander who saved and liberated the city in favor of your continued trickery and selfish incompetence?"

"I have not come here to be insulted," Amal said sharply, rising from his chair to face Joab fully.

"No, you have come to do the insulting," Eliab bellowed, drowning the argument with his powerful voice. "You have insulted our help and our generosity. Most of all you have insulted David, our commander who, against our wishes and under orders from the God of Abraham, came here to deliver you from your own stupidity. Now you want to assume command of soldiers who do not follow you? You arrogant—"

"That is enough," David said. He rose to end the foolish argument, repeated a dozen times over in the streets each day. "I thank you for your visit, Amal."

"And what is your answer?" Amal hissed, still breathless with rage.

"As you have not come here to haggle, then I will not haggle with you," David said, taking the man and the occasion in hand. "I will give you my response when I have decided. Until then I remain in command of my forces and the city. My first command is that there will be no further meetings of the council of elders until I say so. Tend to your home and your business, Amal, and I will tend to mine."

"You have not heard the last of this," Amal said forcefully as he started for the door, but David held his arm as he made to leave.

"Amal, I have heard the last of this until I bring it up again," David said firmly. "It is your city, but the safety of those who follow me is, just now, tied to the fate of Keilah. I will separate your tongue from your head if you use it to bring disorder that threatens me or mine. Do you understand me?"

"I hear you," Amal said through gritted teeth.

"Then do not turn your back on me or leave this room without showing me the respect that my people have earned," David said, releasing him.

The two regarded each other a breath.

"Thank you for receiving me," Amal said, bowing to David.

"It is always an honor to have the elder of Keilah in my home," David said, inclining his head briefly.

The room erupted as soon as Amal was out of the house.

Eliab looked on his brother as though seeing him after a long parting. He saw no longer the anguished boy with his morose psalms and tortured poetry.

Before him stood a man; a prince. It was not just that his body had matured and hardened, for all that had been expected. And certainly he was no taller. Yet the ease with which he carried his office and commanded the respect of those around him gave David a height few men might hope to attain.

"Enough," David said, waving Eliab and Joab away.

"What shall we do?" Eliab demanded, ready to take to the street and battle those he had so recently risked his own life to save.

"I think," David said with a long sigh, "I think it is time for a surprise. Matthew?"

Matthew had flattened himself against the wall near the door, more afraid to move than to remain during the heated discussion. Swept up in the tension of Amal's visit, it only occurred to him that he should not be there when David spoke his name.

"Yes, sir?" the youth asked, his voice cracking.

"Our surprise?" David asked, smiling and extending his hand to the boy.

"Oh yes, sir," Matthew said, moving forward. "When we fought the Philistines for Keilah, it was my first battle."

"Truly?" Eliab said with a gentle laugh.

"I noticed something as I watched," he went on, ignoring Eliab. "Their men followed the flag of Gath into battle."

"For all the good it did 'em," Joab chortled.

"I know that, being inexperienced, I wasn't much help," Matthew said, unfurling his work. "So I thought I could make us a flag; more, if you like this one."

"What is it?" Eliab asked, turning his head left and right to try to see it.

"It is from the ring you wear," Matthew said, taking David's hand and touching the signet Jonathan had given him. "I connected these points where the jewels are set in the gold."

"Those are stars," David said, moved by the gesture and swept up in thoughts of Jonathan all at once.

"That's it," Joab said of the banner. "It looks like a star."

"I connected here and here and here and so on," Matthew explained as he fingered the points of the two interconnected triangles.

"It's upside down." David laughed, thinking of Jonathan describing the Saphan in the sky. The six stars were the tips of two ears, a pointy nose, a fluffy tail, and two paws, and described a constellation known only to the two of them.

"To you it seems upended," Matthew agreed, nodding. "I thought about that. But it's not what I see—what we see—when we look at the ring. I made the points more even, but it's the same six points."

"It's the Star of David," Eliab said, liking the sound of it as he said it. "It's a noble flag, First. Perfect. I'd be proud to follow it into battle."

David only smiled at the thought and the symmetry of the choice for their standard.

And it was told Saul that David was come to Keilah. And Saul said, God hath delivered him into mine hand; for he is shut in, by entering into a town that hath gates and bars.

1 Samuel 23:7

WORD OF David's victory over the Philistines at Keilah was cause for rejoicing at court in Gibeah. Arriving as the weather permitted, the news came not from spies or official channels, but with the traders arriving in town for the beginning of the wheat market, following the Passover observance. It was gossip about yet another victory from the seemingly undefeatable David, both hero and villain of Israel. The tale was made yet more popular by his outlaw status. Songs of David's latest victory sang of how the lost hero turned outlaw had become liberator. His legend grew as he defended the people of Israel when their own king would not. The song concluded as David raised his own flag, the Star of David, over the city of Keilah, the first in his new kingdom.

Saul beat the minstrel who sang him the news for the affront but then celebrated the knowledge that David had been found. His servant was not building an army of invasion in Egypt, as had been popularly rumored at court that winter, among other outrageous tales. David was in fact little more than a day's ride away in an almost indefensible city that was technically still under Saul's rule. The fact that David had raised his own flag over a city in Saul's kingdom was all the justification Saul needed—had he needed any at all—to mount an expedition.

Gleefully he assembled his men and prepared to march on the city, liberate Keilah from David's rule, and David from Keilah, if not his life, in the bargain.

Though Jonathan still refused to take an active part in his father's affairs, Saul's plans were no secret from him. Jonathan easily slipped from the palace and sent a message to David by private messenger. The man was paid well enough to keep riding after the note was delivered.

Jonathan's words found David still wrestling with the decision over what to do in Keilah. The prophet in Gad had sent him to Hereth. David felt he had managed to do the Lord's will there, but given the prevailing sentiments of those in Keilah that he hand over his command or depart, he was unclear of the Lord's direction.

"Lord, what is your will for me?" David pleaded in his own quiet prayers of desperation. He thought with great appreciation of the burdens that Saul must bear, struggling to interpret the Lord's will and then to carry it out to the best of his ability. To risk his own life was his choice and every man's. But to choose for another? The weight seemed inescapable. If he stayed and remained in command, what price would be paid by the innocent of the city?

If he departed and left those same innocents to their fate at the hands of the Philistines, how much greater the price would those same innocents pay?

What would Saul do? he asked himself.

The answer came to him in a blaze of inspiration.

"Yusef," David called.

"Yes, my captain?" the young man asked, arriving gasping and panicked in response to the tone of David's cries. "Are you well?"

"What? Of course," David answered, confused by the question. "Bring me my priest."

"Who?" Yusef asked, still more confused.

"Abiathar," David said with a tone of annoyance.

"Abiathar is your priest?" Yusef inquired. It was the first he had heard that David had a priest at all, much less that it was Yusef's personal nemesis, Abiathar.

"Yusef? Please, could you tell Abiathar I need him?"

"Yes, captain," Yusef answered even as he turned to go.

Abiathar had been injured and grieving when he'd caught up to them the previous fall. He spent the intervening time recovering, a little elaborately by Yusef's way of thinking. Many of the duties of Abiathar's care had fallen to Yusef, whose days were full already with the tasks of running a household to David's standards. Both men were demanding though David, by far and away the more exacting, was a very busy man. In the end Yusef had often neglected Abiathar when necessity forced a choice between the two. Though Abiathar suffered Yusef's negligence with equanimity, he did admit to it when David asked after his comfort. All of which made David still more demanding and Yusef more resentful of Abiathar's vestigial attachment to David's household.

The relations between the two men were strained, but not half so much as Yusef's credulity at this revelation. He had only ever seen Abiathar in a nightshirt, never a priest's ephod.

"Are you a priest?" Yusef demanded, bursting into Abiathar's room.

"And the Lord be with you," Abiathar said, so startled that he laughed. "I am, in fact, the high priest of Nob."

"Nob?" Yusef repeated, still more surprised with each new development.

"Yusef," Abiathar said with a sigh. "Do you need a priest?"

"God's the one needs priests," Yusef scoffed. "But the captain has called for his priest, and he says it's you."

"The captain?"

"Lord captain it is." Yusef shrugged. "David doesn't like us calling him prince. So we've all taken to it. The First mostly started it out of respect, heard it from some soldiers from Jezreel. Then Eliab took it up, I think only as a joke at first—oh look there, I've made a joke myself."

"David?" Abiathar demanded, leaping to his feet and moving more quickly than Yusef had ever seen him. "David has called for me to come to him as his priest?"

"Isn't that what I said?" Yusef asserted, ready to take up old arguments where they'd left them. Before he could get hostilities started, Abiathar was pushing past, still pulling the linen ephod over his head.

"My lord captain," Abiathar said, bowing before David as he barged into the room at a run, Yusef hot on his heels.

"Lord captain, eh?" David said, looking up from his desk with a weary laugh. "I see that's going to catch on again."

Abiathar lurched forward as Yusef ran into the back of him in the doorway.

"You're supposed to let me announce you," Yusef explained sharply to Abiathar, still looking for a battle.

"Yusef, thank you," David said with a dismissive nod and raised eyebrows that said "Not one more word" most eloquently.

"How may I serve you, my lord?" Abiathar asked, grateful at last to be of use after sitting and waiting for so very long to be called.

"Good Abiathar, how are you?" David asked warmly. "Do you require anything? Wine? Water? Bread?"

"No, my prince, I mean, my lord captain," Abiathar said, bowing again by way of apologizing, amusing Yusef by his awkwardness. "I have done little else but be waited upon since my arrival. I have awaited with great anticipation this, the occasion of your call for me."

"I see. I hope I have not seemed to ignore you," David said, pointing to a nearby chair, which the priest vigorously declined. "I'm more used to the ways of the farm and the battlefield than of priests."

"I am here to serve you," Abiathar said, bowing yet again. "Not the other way around."

Yusef rolled his eyes as noticeably as possible as he turned to leave them.

"Yes, well, as it happens, I've a bit of a dilemma," David explained, standing since the priest would not take a seat. It made him uncomfortable, already being a small man, to have to look up into the faces of other men when he spoke.

"How may I assist?" the priest asked. Uncertain of the protocol and too embarrassed to bow again, he left it with a nod, much to David's relief.

"What is the Lord's will for me?" David asked, sincerely and with the casual certainty that he might ask Abiathar about the weather outside or the time of day.

"The Lord's will?" Abiathar repeated, at a loss.

"Yes." David nodded, sitting on the edge of the table where he'd been working. "I met a prophet in Gad who told me that it was the Lord's will that I come here. It occurs to me that, just as I was about to make that decision final, you arrived and presented yourself as my priest."

"I see." Abiathar puffed his cheeks out and tried, unsuccessfully, not to look flustered.

"It would seem that our time here is up, or nearly," David said with a sheepish little laugh. "They want us to surrender or go, anyway. But should we? And if so, where? Any ideas?"

"I will pray on it, lord captain," Abiathar said with great circumstance.

They stood for an awkward breath, each waiting for a sign from the other.

"Proceed," David said with a wave of his hand, unsure of the protocols of prophesy. "Should I kneel? Shouldn't you?"

"You mean now? Pray now?" Abiathar burbled, his face crimson.

"Is there some reason that you can't?" David shrugged. "Candle, incense, a goat? What can I get you?"

"I, er, I will need time to consult," Abiathar said, throwing his arms out for no good reason other than he'd no idea what to do with his hands. "That is all. I will let you know if anything comes to me."

"One prayer," David said, taking the priest's hand and kneeling. "Come along, what could it hurt?"

"Not a thing, my lord captain," Abiathar said, beaming, swept up in the man's real and practical faith. He knelt beside him.

Together they prayed. Abiathar sang the words of a high temple prayer. David prayed to himself in simple words, as though speaking to a friend there in the room, as he always did unless his petitions took the form of a psalm.

"My captain," Yusef said, scratching at the door, interrupting them.

"Yusef—" David began irritably.

"There is a messenger here from Gibeah," Yusef rushed on, sensing it was important. "He has a sealed scroll that he will give only to you."

"I will be with him in a heartbeat."

"The seal looks like your ring." Yusef said the words almost to David's back, his master was out the door so quickly.

"Yusef, see to the messenger," David said, returning almost at once, rushing in to retrieve his knife to preserve the seal and the message. Yusef and Abiathar shared a look. "Give him food, a fine room, see to his horse. Treat him as an honored guest."

Yusef stood in the doorway, curious.

"Thank you, Yusef," David said. Tenderly he opened his first message from Jonathan since they'd parted at Ezel.

Yusef turned and departed with a great sigh of exasperation.

David sank into his desk chair, suddenly rested and relaxed. A smile spread across his face as he read. At last, with a contented sigh, he looked up to see Abiathar still before him.

"Thank you, Abiathar," David said, rising and crossing to the door. "Excellent work. Really good prayer."

"I'm sorry, sir?" Abiathar said, confused.

"Well done," David called over his shoulder. He left, singing a love psalm softly to himself.

Uncertain, Abiathar stood alone in the office.

And Saul called all the people together to war, to go down to Keilah, to besiege David and his men.

1 Samuel 23:8

"I THANK you all for coming today," David called to the nearly six hundred men who now followed him. "I have news that concerns us all. I thought it best that you all hear it together. We have done great service in Keilah. You can be proud of your work here, as I am proud of you."

There were cheers, which David paused to acknowledge before riding over them to move on.

"Spring is here now. I have consulted with Abiathar here, the high priest of Nob," David said. Turning, he recognized the priest who stood on the platform beside him, wearing the ephod of his office. The news that he was in fact a priest still drew looks and responses of disbelief from many of those gathered before them. "Abiathar has interceded in my behalf, and the Lord has answered."

Eliab gave Abiathar a look of genuine surprise and found an expression equal to his own on the priest's face.

"We leave to move east, the morning of the first day following next Shabbat," David continued to the somber crowd. David never revealed the contents of Jonathan's note or even from whom it came. He did not wish Jonathan thought a traitor to his own father. In truth, David honestly felt the timely arrival of Jonathan's message was in answer to their prayers. "Those who will follow make ready, say your good-byes, pay your debts, and conclude your business here. Let us leave the city in good order. For those who have made alliances here they wish to preserve, you are responsible for your own household, though we will certainly do what we can to help."

David left the stunned crowd standing shocked by the announcement. None was pleased. Many had not lived with a roof over their heads in time out of memory; some not at all. They had fought hard, shed blood. Their comrades had died for the sake of the city. None was anxious to give it up to return to the wilderness.

"I'm as surprised by this news as I'm sure many of you are," Eliab said, stepping up, his big voice booming over the crowd. Many nodded and answered in agreement. "But I know that, only a few moons ago, we were all living in a cave and none too thrilled to leave it. Then we were told that we were to fight the Philistines to liberate a city we'd never even seen. We won. Moreover, we spent the winter warm and well fed under strong roofs."

There were sullen shrugs and nods of agreement. Still the crowd shuffled their feet in the dust.

"I have known David all my life," Eliab declared, striking his hand with his fist. "Well, all of his, anyway."

There was scattered laughter in answer.

"I am his brother, though you'd never guess it to look at us," he went on. "The great difference in us is not that I am taller or broader in the beam. The great difference between David and you and me is that David is not held back by his fear from the best that the Lord has to offer. He has always had faith that the road will appear before him around each turn, no matter how sharp. We are all here following him because of that faith. So for those of you who think this place in the middle of nowhere, where we are increasingly unwelcome, is the best the Lord has to offer you, then I wish you every blessing. For myself, I know that the Lord has more than this to offer, not because I'm so pious or such a good man, or even because I have such faith in the Lord. I have faith in the Lord's faith in David. So, for me and my house, we will follow him."

The crowd broke up cheering that day. All but a few there were standing in readiness just inside the gates of Keilah at the appointed time. They all cheered again as the Star of David was taken down from above the gate where it had caught the breeze that morning. They fell in behind as it was taken to the front of their formation to precede them out of the city and into their unknown but hopeful future to the east.

"Amal, I wish you well," David said, taking the man's hand. "Freedom takes work. I pray that you and your people prosper. Every blessing on you and your city."

"Our thanks to you and to those who follow your star," Amal said, his lips stretched over his teeth in a vicious smile. "We are grateful for the return of our city."

David gave him a humble bow and moved on to mount his horse.

"The Lord help you all," Eliab called from horseback to the people of the city, just as the trumpet blew. With a joyous shout, those who followed David began their journey.

The people of Keilah enjoyed several days of freedom. Without guards at the gate, they could come and go as they pleased. The streets were theirs to run once again. Amal and the council of elders met and resumed their profitable position as arbiters of the city's laws and commerce.

There was alarm when a dust cloud rose in the distance, moving toward them. Panic danced in the streets when it was assumed that the Philistines were returning as soon as news of David's departure from the city reached them. Chaos reigned. Looting and anarchy swept the city in the final desperation preceding their anticipated return to Philistine oppression. Those of David's people who'd stayed behind took what they could and fled the city, headed east in search of David, in the company of many who'd been born in Keilah.

Desperation soon turned to celebration. Calls went up from the local militia, who'd mounted the gates to defend the city, that the standard of King Saul had been sighted preceding their imagined invaders. The gates were thrown open wide, and delight turned to amazement when King Saul himself rode into town.

Amal stood in the square before the temple to greet the great king as the crowd thronged around in hope of catching a glimpse.

Saul rode in through the gates waving genially to the cheering crowds. Spotting the village priests and elders gathered, he rode up to them and dismounted.

"Greetings, great king," Amal said, bowing low before Saul. "All of Keilah is at your command. Welcome to our humble city."

"Where is the traitor David?" Saul asked, already concerned by the lack of opposition to his arrival.

"If it please Your Majesty," Amal boasted proudly, "we have expelled David from the city along with all those who are loyal to him. Just as we have expelled the Philistines that we might better serve—"

Amal's head rolled across the stones of the square before he could finish his boast.

Then David and his men, which were about six hundred, arose and departed out of Keilah, and went whithersoever they could go.

1 Samuel 23:13

NEWS OF Saul's brutal sacking of the city of Keilah reached David's camp in the hills of Ziph, near to Horesh. It was said that the king laid waste to the city in reprisal for letting David escape, brutally killing the council of elders, each by turn when they could not tell him where David had gone.

Some among David's followers received the news with quiet satisfaction, particularly the reports of Amal's head on a pike above the city gates with those of the rest of his council of elders. Word that the gates were the largest structure still standing in the city was sobering, as it revealed the ferocity of the king's determination to put an end to them all.

David took the news hardest, seeing the extent of the king's personal hatred and animosity toward him wrought in flesh and blood, as with the priests at Nob.

They kept to their camp, high in the hills above Ziph. It was more primitive than life in the city, but their location could not have been better. It offered views a day's ride or more in all directions. In the cool of the mountain forests, they were secure in their camp for the summer as David withdrew and contemplated.

After the stories of Saul's wrath at Keilah, David remained apart from the others most of the time. His heart was heavy with the price that was being exacted for each step he took. Yusef, who had elected to follow, brought him food and collected the plates untouched. Concerned, he took his worries to Joab, but neither he nor Eliab were able to rouse David from his lethargy.

Together they shared the responsibility of leadership. They brought David reports of progress in the building of their mountain fortress and other local activity. On his orders they led raiding parties into the hills. They cleaned the nearby wilderness of the bands of thieves and highwaymen who lived there, dispatching some and recruiting others to join them. Their deeds again earned them local support and tribute, as well as a growing legend that directly contradicted the king's charges against them.

David remained alone in his tent.

Meals grew regular and security more certain, though without command there were lapses. Those who followed David became accustomed to his absence and respected his solitude. For a time it was peaceful. Their ranks grew as strangers, seeking a place in the world, found their way to the camp and joined their brotherhood.

One such stranger found his way into camp late on a midsummer day. He was met with no resistance or suspicion as he made his way into their midst.

Those without specific duty were to be found in the shade of trees and tents or naked in the nearby streams. The stranger was warmly welcomed. Those he met offered food and wine, clean clothes, and a place to sleep, as was their custom. Delighted, the man asked how they lived so well as nomads.

"Funny, that," one of the men spoke up in reply. He'd recently joined David's followers after they'd banished the band of brigands he'd run with from the forests of Horesh. "We live as heroes here, on the tributes of grateful villagers and farmers, in return for getting rid of the likes of me. I used to steal what I need, but now they give it me for stopping others from stealing it. It's brilliant."

"Brilliant indeed," the stranger agreed, laughing heartily.

Because of their generosity, or perhaps it was just the lazy summer heat of the day that made them too drowsy to pay attention, none noticed that the stranger didn't really seem to need their help. His hair was clean, as were his clothes. He looked remarkably well fed for a man who'd wandered the hills in search of home and hearth. Nor did it seem strange that he was so curious about the exact location of "this Lord Captain David's tent" so that he might thank him personally. When a fight broke out between a couple of men over some small offense, no one took notice when the newcomer wandered off in the direction of David's quarters unattended. The guards assigned to David's door were more interested in the outcome of the fight Eliab was trying to break up than a stranger's approach.

As the guards stepped away just long enough to get a closer look, the stranger slipped inside, unseen. There he found David, sleeping as he had too often since their arrival at Ziph. Easing forward, the stranger moved silently across the fine carpets that covered the ground beneath the tent to the broad down-stuffed mat where David lay. Leaning nearer, the stranger reached under his cape and slowly drew the sword from his belt.

The shadow of his silent visitor fell across David's face, waking him first slowly and then abruptly as he saw the sword and realized. Rolling out of harm's way, he tumbled to the carpet and struggled to get to his feet. The stranger was on him, pinning him to the ground. Grasping his shoulder, he tried to turn David onto his back. Unable to free himself, David opened his mouth to call out for help and found it covered with the mouth of the stranger.

There was only a twist of struggle before David felt the familiar texture of his attacker's hair in his hands and knew that he was at long last again in the arms of his lover.

"Jonathan," he gasped, choked with tears of joy. "Is it you or just a dream?"

"Who cares now?" Jonathan growled into his ear.

Their reunion was stronger for the time they'd spent apart, their craving so powerful, it neared violence as they satisfied themselves with each other's bodies. When at last their appetites for one another were satisfied, they called for food and drink to continue their celebration.

Yusef was startled to find that his master had company but delighted at the state in which he found his lord captain. He hurried away to prepare a feast after supplying them with wine, bread, and cheese to whet their palates. While they were waiting, David surprised Jonathan, jumping and pinning him to the fine wool rug a little more than playfully.

"What are you doing here?" David said, pounding his chest. "You scared Baal out of me. If I'd had a weapon more at hand, they might be burying us together."

"I wanted to surprise you," Jonathan said, straining his neck to plant a kiss at the tip of his captor's nose.

"I was surprised," David said with a laugh, collapsing onto Jonathan's chest.

They fed one another wine and cheese and, later, supper. Each told the other all the thoughts he'd been saving as they ate and made love intermittently until sunrise. To the delight of his followers, David was himself again. He took Jonathan on a tour of the camp and their operation, introducing him as a comrade from his days in the king's army.

Jonathan marveled at David's growing little band, praising the efficiency of the operation over supper that second night. He called David and his men "Habiru," a word that meant mercenary in their tongue. Yusef, overhearing, misunderstood and later proudly told Eliab and Joab as he served the officer's table that he too was a "Hebrew." Of course, Eliab began referring to them all as Hebrews, both as curse and compliment. Almost before Jonathan's visit was over, those who followed David were proudly calling themselves Hebrews.

"I mark a difference in you," Jonathan said to David, alone that night in the tent after seeing David with those who followed him. "You have not yet lost your boyish charms when I am alone with you. But you seem to age many seasons when we are among your Hebrews."

"Is this a compliment?" David asked, smiling, as he looked up from the tablet he was studying.

"It is the truth." Jonathan smiled at the tone and wit that had lit up his days for so long, and that he missed so much. His eyes played over the sharp planes of the body that had grown from boy to soldier, but he saw more than that. "Command suits you. You will be a fine prince when we rule together."

"I will be happy just to serve at your side again, my prince," David said, setting the wet clay aside. To be respected as a man by the man he respected above all others was the highest compliment to which he could aspire.

Though Jonathan's visit lasted only a few days and nights, the change in David was that of a month at leisure. Too soon their time was at end. After making love more than once on their final night together, neither could sleep. They lay awake talking.

"You know your wife is already married," Jonathan said with as much mirth as disdain. "She pestered Father until he relented."

"Michal?" David said with a shocked blast of laughter. "My grieving widow didn't even wait until I was dead?"

"Nope, she and Paltiel couldn't wait to get started," Jonathan said with a dismissive snort. "On what, I'm not sure."

"Building their empire, I suppose," David said, still stung to see how clearly he'd been betrayed. "I guess I deserved it."

"Not half so much as they deserve each other," Jonathan said, drawing David nearer in the cool of the mountain night.

"How is your son?" David asked.

"You've heard," Jonathan said, pleased.

"I probably knew before you did," David said mysteriously.

"How is that?"

"A seer in the Ghor of Gad told me under the full moon last fall," David said ominously. "He was blind and found me in the dead of night looking at the Jordan and thinking of you. He got everything else right, so I just assumed. What did you name him?"

"Mephibosheth," Jonathan said without conviction.

"Well, that sounds royal enough," David said, rolling his eyes.

"It does, doesn't it?" Jonathan agreed, shaking his head. "I call him Sheth. I tried for Phibo, but I almost got disinherited."

"Sheth is good," David said, trying not to laugh in Jonathan's face.

"What is so funny?"

"Phibo?" David said, howling.

"No good?"

"I'd have thrown you out of the palace myself, but you beat me to it."

They rolled into one another's arms until, sighing, their mirth subsided.

"I miss you," David said softly. "It's been so lonely. When you came I had all but given up. I hadn't been out of the tent since Shavuot."

"I miss you every breath," Jonathan said, tightening his hold. "Azia has been a great comfort, though. You should take another wife."

"You wouldn't mind?"

"Of course I would," Jonathan said, cuffing him playfully. "But I'd rather that than you take a lover. A wife I could bear. I couldn't stand the thought of you with another man. At least with a wife, I wouldn't feel replaced."

"I could never replace you," David said, resting his head on Jonathan's chest. "I have not been with anyone since we parted that night at Ezel."

"It grieves me to know it," Jonathan said with a deep sigh. "And yet, selfishly, it is a weight off my mind. Though I could hardly blame you."

"You need never worry," David said, touching Jonathan's lips with a finger to silence him. "Or feel guilty. In truth, I could have, but there is no one else I want."

"Then marry so you won't be alone," Jonathan said.

"From the selection among my Hebrews?" David joked, trying on the new nickname.

"If you like," Jonathan said, trying to be light about it but aching at the thought. "Maybe the daughter of one of the elders of Judah? If our kingdom is to stretch from Dan to Beersheba, we will need strong alliances here in the south."

"Perhaps," David scoffed. "We'll see how many elders will marry their daughters off to mercenaries. In truth, though, you're the only one for me. No woman, no matter how much I loved her, could compare to what we have."

"Of course not," Jonathan said, softly caressing his face in the darkness. "It is only for duty and comfort. No one expects more than that."

"Except Michal."

They laughed again, happy in one another's arms as nowhere else.

"Not all the daughters of Abraham are princesses," Jonathan answered, cheered by their closeness but aware of how near to its ending they drew with each breath.

They were silent after that. Neither ever really slept. Neither could bear to waste a heartbeat of their time together on such. Too soon the sun brought reality, and Yusef, and one last meal. They bathed together and after took a walk out into the hills. They spoke fitfully of the scenery and weather and the inconsequential.

"Don't be afraid," Jonathan said, taking David's hand suddenly and pulling his body near as if to shelter it with his own. "Saul will not lay a hand on you. You will be a king before this is over. We will rule Israel together. Even my father knows this in his heart."

"I don't really care about that so much," David said, holding tight. "I only wish we did not have to be apart."

"I made my covenant with you, David," Jonathan said. "I have taken a vow to you before the Lord and you to me, forsaking all else. Time and space cannot separate us. Certainly no man can. I am yours, David, and with you always, I swear it."

"And I am yours," David said, burying his face in Jonathan's robe to hide his sadness.

After a time they made their way back down the hill to the Hebrew camp. Before either wished it, the time came. Loaded with game gotten from the camp's larder, to make truth out of the story of hunting he had used to explain his absence, Jonathan made his way down the mountainside alone.

David stood and watched long after he could see Jonathan no more, staring at the place on the horizon where he'd disappeared from view, waiting already for his return.

Chapter Eighteen
The Oasis at En-Gedi

And Jonathan Saul's son arose, and went to David into the wood, and strengthened his hand in God. And he said unto him, Fear not: for the hand of Saul my father shall not find thee; and thou shalt be king over Israel, and I shall be next unto thee; and that also Saul my father knoweth.

1 Samuel 23:16-17

HABAKKUK WAS the leader of the Ziphites. He had been chosen because he was a practical man. The wilderness of Horesh in the mountains of Judah was a challenging place to make a home and a life, and those in the village of Ziph were better at it than most. Their good fortune was due, in part, to a nearby spring that gave them water year round, and adjacent highland meadows for grazing and planting. But mostly they were prosperous because they knew an opportunity when it presented itself.

So when Habakkuk received word that there was no less than a king's ransom in reward for David's capture, he journeyed north to strike a deal with the king. He saw that he could bring riches to his people and rid them of the "Hebrew" band. They had traded the thievery of mountain bandits for the Hebrews' ceaseless demand for tributes. While Habakkuk appreciated the Hebrews ridding the nearby mountains of the robbers and cutthroats who had plagued his people, the miscreants were gone. Weren't there people elsewhere these Hebrews should be rescuing?

With this in mind, he came before his king. He was a proud man. To Saul he offered the sparest of bows and a tone of respect but not of awe.

"King Saul," he began with terse formality.

"It is my throne room," Saul answered, amused by Habakkuk's plain manner.

"I understand that you are offering a substantial reward for the capture of David ben Jesse and these so-called Hebrews who follow him," Habakkuk continued, uncowed by the king's mirth at his expense.

"It depends on how richly you value your life," King Saul answered him slyly. "For I have separated the head from the shoulders of those who would shelter him and aid his escape."

"I have done neither, and I am already in possession of my life," Habakkuk said, nodding as if considering a bargain at the market in Hebron. "So then you have nothing to offer me?"

"As with all camel trades, what I have to offer depends on what you have to sell," Saul answered with growing impatience.

"You will find David and his men camped in the strongholds at Horesh, on the hill of Hakilah, south of Jeshimon," Habakkuk said with his customary directness. "It would be a gift to we Ziphites if you removed him from there. If there is a reward, as I have been told, then it will be all the more blessing to my people."

"Ah now, that is something well worth trading for, if it turns out to be true," Saul said with delight at the man's unpolished words.

"I am Habakkuk of Ziph. I would not stand before my king or any man and speak what is not true," he said sternly but with simple sincerity. "Now, my king, come down whenever it pleases you to do so, and we will be responsible for handing him over."

"The Lord's blessing upon you for your concern for your king and country," Saul said, rising and crossing down to stand beside the man and look him in the eye. "Go and make further preparation. Find out where David usually goes and who has seen him there. He is very subtle. Find out about all the hiding places he uses and come back to me with definite information. Then I will go with you; if he is in the area, I will track him down."

The spirits of anger and vengeance rose up in Saul and gave him new life. Each season since Elah, Saul had remained in Gibeah, content to allow Jonathan and David to face the enemies of Israel. The loss of Samuel's guidance had taken his willingness to lead.

It was a strange turn, then, when Saul once again found the courage to make war against his enemies.

"Shall I take our standing guard to Ziph and bring David to you?" Abner asked, to avoid the discussion of asking Prince Jonathan. He knew that Jonathan would refuse and Saul would take the refusal ill. The end of such an argument was too fearful for kinsman or countryman and might well cost family and kingdom. "The scouts report that David's men number five hundred, perhaps some few score more. They are green at best."

"They defeated the Philistine army at Keilah," Saul shot back, not really looking at Abner. "My concern for David's health is not because of his skill with the harp, though that too is formidable. He is a worthy adversary and should not be taken lightly. That, more than anything, is why he must be taken."

"We could have messengers raise the call for the full army without asking them to work next Sabbath," Abner said, nodding silent agreement with Saul's assessment of David. "Perhaps this Habakkuk will have more word of David for us."

"No, Abner, it will not do," Saul said. "Certainly put out the call for more men, and muster as near the full force as you can manage in seven days. We need more men, but they need a leader who is worthy to face David. You are my greatest general, my cousin, and my most trusted advisor. But you are not David's equal in the field. Jonathan...." Saul sighed. He seemed lost in thought.

Abner feared the battle that would come if the prince were asked to lead the army against David. It would be worse for them than any they might face in the field.

"Jonathan could best him, but his heart would not allow him to raise his hand," Saul said with a bitter smile. "His feelings for David, and his blindness to the usurper's ambition, would defeat him before he stood on the same field. No, it must be me."

"Sire," Abner intoned solemnly, trying to keep his joy from his voice. Abner was well aware of David's genius in the field. Jonathan too was a fine commander. But none were the equal of Saul, whom the others studied to understand the craft of making war.

"You know it is true," Saul said putting his hand on Abner's shoulder. "We have won enough battles together to know that this is a fight that I must win for myself. I wouldst that Samuel was here, but I will be honored if you will be at my side."

"To the end, sire," Abner said, smiling an uncharacteristic smile, glad in his heart for the return of his great friend and fellow warrior. "I will ready an army befitting your return to the field of battle."

Jonathan and Saul were strangers at court.

There had been some restoration between father and son when Mephibosheth was born. Saul had made extravagant welcome of his new grandson. Jonathan felt warmth in his heart for Saul unbidden.

They spoke kindly words when they were near to each other, which began to happen more often. Jonathan could not deny his mother her grandson at family feast days. At these he met his father, and they found a grudging new bond that grew with the number of days that each was separated from David.

The household truce was shattered when Jonathan learned of Saul's plans to raise an army and pursue David again.

"Father, you must not do this," Jonathan demanded, bursting into Saul's chambers unbidden while he was in conference with Abner and his other generals.

"What tumult is this?" Saul demanded. His anger over the interruption at first fell on the guards who had allowed the disturbance. "Oh, my son, what have I done to offend you now?"

"David is not your enemy," Jonathan went on as though the king had not spoken. "He would not raise so much as a stick against you."

"Then let him come to me here at Gibeah and throw himself on my mercy," Saul said, rising abruptly.

"Why?" Jonathan demanded, boldly, for they were not on their own. "So you might treat him to the same hospitality you showed the priests of Nob and the elders of Keilah?"

"I am still the king, you know, young man," Saul shouted, blood in his face.

"And I am still your heir," Jonathan dared him. "But you are free to take my inheritance if you think me unfit to receive it."

The two regarded each other, breathless with rage.

Jonathan would have welcomed the freedom that disinheritance offered. Saul could not bear to lose him.

"Leave me to my generals," Saul shouted.

"Your pride wastes your power and the affections of all of those who love you," Jonathan said, turning back at the door to regard Saul one last time. "None loves you more than David, and he will prove it to you wherever you may find him."

Saul also and his men went to seek him. And they told David; wherefore he came down into a rock, and abode in the wilderness of Maon. And when Saul heard that, he pursued after David in the wilderness of Maon.

1 Samuel 23:25

BEFORE THE next new moon, Saul and his forces were marching south to surround and apprehend David and to visit swift and immediate justice upon him. Yet even as Saul felt the resistance of his enemy's neck against his sword, David was rewarding other practical Ziphites for word of the king's imminent arrival.

By the time Saul marched into Ziph, Habakkuk had news that David had moved south, into the desert of Maon. The king left Habakkuk counting his gold. That same day Saul embarked in pursuit with his full forces so that the trail would not grow cold.

The Hebrews were anxious at leaving their summer stronghold in Horesh but faithful as always in David. Their faith wavered as he moved them into the desert of the northern Negev. They encamped there, south of the city of Moan and the mountain for which the city was named. David posted men at higher elevations around the peak of Mount Moan. Runners fetched and delivered reports throughout the day and the night.

"What are we to do here?" Eliab asked, brushing the grit from his bread as they ate a hastily prepared supper. "If we are to fight the king and his army, who outnumber us many times over, we cannot do it from tents in the open with our supplies and weapons stored still on the mule packs."

"We will never fight the king or his army," David said with a quiet fierceness. "We are not traitors to Israel. We will never raise a hand or a weapon against our own. Saul is our king and will have only our respect."

"That seems overly hopeful, David," Joab cautioned. The three spoke alone together around their small fire, unheard by the rest. "I admire your resolve, but I think if this persists, we should be prepared for the possibility of defending ourselves."

"We will see," David said pensively. "Samuel warned me at the beginning. He said that when he was ready, the Lord would deliver my enemies into my hands to deal with as I wish. It was clearly a warning, not a blessing. It may become a blessing to us, but only if I choose wisely. I did not understand then, and I am less certain today. I do know that I seek strategies from my advisers that move us away from the possibility of direct conflict with Saul. I do not believe him my enemy. Though he may think me his I will not prove it to him."

His tone was even, but David's message was stern and unclouded. Hearing it, Joab gave up the conversation and tried to make the best of a bad meal.

"So, what does that mean, David?" Eliab said, venturing where his nephew was too cautious to proceed. "Are we to live as rats in the desert to avoid having anything for ourselves that this selfish king will want?"

"Wit is not best wrought with a hammer," David answered his brother with a smile. "And wisdom is not measured with a scale. For now let us see how we fare. If the king captures me, then we can speak through prison bars of how you told me so."

Eliab could not defeat a smile. He put a reassuring arm around his brother's shoulder, reminded that his was not the head the king sought. "We will never have such a conversation, little brother, for I am sworn that my death will precede any such event."

"I am not convinced that would silence you," David said, leaning into Eliab. It pleased him that he was not without family in such dire days.

In the end the conversation proved to be wasted breath.

As David had planned, word from his lookouts on high kept him constantly apprised of Saul's position at the mountain's base. Because his forces were small and mobile, David countered Saul's every move, remaining always on the opposite side of Mount Moan from the king's circling army.

Saul's rage grew as he found that no matter how quickly he traveled, he always arrived where David had been, never drawing nearer his prey.

Eliab could not stop from laughing. The strategy was as simple as David putting the table in their father's house between the two of them, defeating his bigger brother's pursuit. By simply moving counter, he negated the strength and size of Saul's forces.

The simple strategy could not last forever. Saul soon understood the means of his humiliation at David's hands. In response he divided his forces, closing on David from two sides to catch him in his own trap.

"What are we to do now, lord captain?" Joab inquired, expecting that they would at last have to prepare for a fight.

"Say your prayers, nephew," David answered him simply. Leaving him in his surprise with no further answer, David spent his time in prayer and silent reflection.

With no more guidance than that, his men remained packed to leave when ordered. They slept on the ground in turns. For a day they held their ground. Most of the Hebrews were unaware of the impending danger. They were glad to trust in David, who had never failed to protect and provide for them. He gave them strange orders to march south into the Negev and then to return to camp.

"On your return you must leave no trail," David instructed them. Thinking it yet another of their lord captain's endless drills, they practiced again and again.

When the king's forces were reported near on both the east and the west, David gave the order. His smaller and more mobile force went up and over the mountain, again at orders to leave no trail. They moved slowly but steadily, once again, to a position opposite the king's.

King Saul actually charged his own men at first. Mistaking them for David's, he raised arms before he recognized his own standard approaching and realized that David had once again eluded him. Furious, he made camp and sent scouts south, into the forbidding Negev where he assumed, from the massive and obvious trail, David had taken refuge with sizeable forces. He was more furious still when his scouts reported that the trails simply disappeared.

Saul's rage was boundless. He tore his own tent to shreds and beat good servants. David had bested him without ever raising his hand, proving he was the better man more by his refusal to fight Saul than by any battlefield prowess.

Alone with his wine, amidst the destruction of nothing but the fineries that had filled his own tent, Saul could not drink Jonathan's words from his head.

There came a messenger unto Saul, saying, Haste thee, and come; for the
Philistines have invaded the land.

1 Samuel 23: 27

BEFORE SAUL could determine David's location, fate took the day.

Word arrived from Gibeah that the Philistines were once again encroaching on the king's recent fortifications in the Jezreel Valley, raiding Israelite cities east of the pass at Megiddo. In a galling twist, the king broke off his pursuit of David to defend the very gains in the north that David had made on his behalf. Reluctantly Saul left David and his Hebrews at Moan. Not a single act of hostility had passed between them. David, at least, was pleased.

A cheer went up through the Hebrew camp concealed near the summit of Mount Moan as they watched the king's forces retreating north at double time.

"Well, uncle," Joab said when they were apart from the hearing of the others. "I'll have to give prayer a try."

"Pray if you like, nephew." David shrugged. "But it is now clear to me that it is time to follow the goats."

"Goats?"

The cryptic remark turned out to be far less than mysterious, as Joab learned to follow his captain more and question him less. David led the Hebrews out of the hills. They made their way across the strange and treacherous Judean wilderness through the narrow rocky valley called the Crag of the Goats. They came at last to the oasis known as En-Gedi, an ancient name that meant "the spring of the kid." The place and the way there were well named. The steep descent from the mountains to the freshwater springs was best navigated by the sure-footed mountain goats who lived wild there.

David led his company in the heat of summer with great confidence along the sheer cliff faces. Despite its brutal surroundings, En-Gedi was a lush and verdant paradise. The freshwater springs brought life and beauty to the rugged terrain. Palm and balsam trees flourished in sight of the desert waste just beyond. The springs tumbled down the hillside into the oasis itself.

In the many caves along the banks of En-Gedi they made their camp. Though it did not offer the security of their mountain strongholds, what it lacked in natural defenses it made up in inaccessibility. The king would not be physically able to bring his great army to meet them there. The number of men who followed David had grown to nearly eight hundred—more, if you counted their sons and families. Their numbers could not equal Saul's forces, yet under the circumstances, only a small force could reach them through such narrow passes.

"It is no matter," David said whenever it was brought up to him. "Hand-to-hand or a hundred to one, we will never fight King Saul."

They got the chance to test David's resolve sooner than any would have liked.

Saul soon returned from his fight with the Philistines. He had stopped their encroachment and established a defensive line at Megiddo. Upon his arrival at Gibeah, he was met with news of David's flight to En-Gedi.

While Saul prepared to embark with 3000 of his finest, Jonathan managed to get word to David through an eastbound trader a few days ahead of his father's troops.

As it happened, David was again with Abiathar when the message from Jonathan arrived. The two, along with Joab, were sharing a fine midday meal together in the limestone cave where David resided. Yusef, who had been serving them, was called away during the meal and left without explanation. Accustomed to his serving man's erratic behavior, David rose to get the ewer and pour wine for his guests.

"You mustn't serve us," Abiathar said, attempting to rise as David brought the pitcher to the table. "It is we who should serve you."

"Keep your seat," David said, pouring. "It is Yusef who should serve all of us, but apparently something more important has arisen."

"David, I have seen the way you ran your father's house in Bethlehem firsthand." Joab groaned. "I know you and your patience with poor service. The sun neither rose nor set in Bethlehem without David managing it. How do you endure this son of Belial?"

"I think the Lord has sent him to test me," David said solemnly, resuming his seat. "By the law our Lord set down to Moses, we have been commanded not to murder. The Lord asks me if, in this ordeal, I can obey his commandment."

Yusef was so serious when he entered amidst their laughter, he did not ask to hear the joke. "Sir, it is a message for you, with the same seal as the one in Keilah," Yusef said, pressing the folded papyrus into David's hand. "I have already put the messenger up as your honored guest."

"Excuse me," David said to his companions, rising and leaving them mystified at the table, his food half-eaten.

Abiathar remembered a similar message but kept his captain's council. For his part, Joab ate the rest of David's meal, his appetite undimmed by concern. He was certain that David would tell him what he needed to know. Neither was surprised when they were called from the table to join the others on the bank of the oasis for an announcement from their mysteriously absent host.

"We are growing too large a group to gather in one place such as this for much longer," David observed as he stood on a rock and looked into their many faces. "I will be appointing lieutenants and assigning the rest of you to each. In this way I may tell my commanders, they their lieutenants, and in turn you will know as if from me. I regret that it will not always be face-to-face that you hear from me. Yet I am gratified to see our ranks swell and prosper together. I assure you that, however large a company we become, my door will remain open to each of you always. Should we ever again live some place where I have a door.

"Today I call you all together to let you know that this day, while I was consulting with Abiathar, I learned of a vision for our future," David proclaimed.

Joab looked to Abiathar, who only smiled broadly.

"Saul is coming to us," David continued. "It will take him some time, and he will be accompanied by far fewer men, but his intent is more than clear to all here. We must separate into these small cadres of which I spoke, move upstream into the caves in the hills, and leave the oasis for a time. So long as we remain out of sight, we should manage this visit from the king as we did the last."

None had had time to settle in as completely as before, and all were growing easier with living on the move. There was more excitement in the air than grumbling after the lieutenants were announced and assignments made.

"How is the prince?" Abiathar asked David with a knowing look.

"He is most well," David said with a satisfied smile. "And I would not have him thought a traitor to his own father, if I can help it."

"Nor would I." Abiathar nodded sagely. "I am happy to disabuse any of such a false and bruising notion."

"I will look to you for your help in this answer to your prayer for guidance, then," David said, putting a hand on the priest's shoulder before they moved to their quarters to pack for the move. "I thank you for your service."

When Joab arrived, David was packing his private notes and plans. He preferred to conceal them from Yusef, whose ideas on packing revolved around seeking to discover how much one could fit into a single trunk.

"Saul is less than a day away," Joab said, entering without formalities. "He has reached the Crags of the Goat."

"I thank you, Joab," David said. He sighed as he wondered where Yusef might be, daunted at the idea of doing the more mundane packing himself with more urgent tasks at hand. "See that your men are ready to go and out of here by sundown. Then join me with four or five of your best for a forward expedition. I shall leave Eliab behind to see to the men. They are more afraid of him than of me and move more quickly when he commands it."

"They move before Eliab out of fear," Joab said with a gentle smile. "For you they muster out of love."

"Is there anything else?" David asked when Joab did not leave.

"These visions of Abiathar's?" Joab asked elliptically. "He seems a good man, but not what a poet would call inspired. When do these visions and prophesies happen exactly?"

David looked out from the mouth of the cave, at first scanning the banks of the oasis for Yusef, but then only staring. He was mesmerized by the beauty of the waterfall directly across.

"You remember when I was a boy," David began without looking back. "You used to tell me the story of how Moses's mother prayed to save his life. The Lord did not seem to answer her, so she put him in a basket in the Nile. He survived and was found by Pharaoh's daughter and raised as a prince with every advantage and education he needed to lead us out of Egypt."

"What are you telling me?" Joab asked, uncertain.

"Were his mother's prayers answered?" David asked, turning back suddenly with a broad smile. "Sometimes, I think, the Lord's answers are bigger than our requests, Joab. Sometimes it's up to us to discover the answers to our prayers."

"So if you pray with Abiathar...."

"And I get an answer," David said, finishing the thought, "then weren't my prayers answered? Is it for me to question the Lord's choice of the message or the messenger through which he addresses me?"

"I had no idea I was so wise," Joab said, grinning as he moved to leave David's cave. "I'll meet you by the banks of the oasis when the heat of the day has passed."

By the following midday, the Hebrews were hidden in the hills above En-Gedi, and Saul was half a day's journey away. David, Joab, and their small party drew near to Saul and tracked him. They kept to the cliffs with the ibex, and followed in the crags above the king's head. Heedless, Saul and his troops made their way on the narrow floor of the wadi below them. As they got near to their former camp, David and his group took cover in a deep cave near the king's route. From there they could observe Saul and his men as they paused in the shade to hide from the midday sun.

Saul broke off from his party. He sought privacy to cover his feet and relieve himself. With no privy at hand, fate guided him into the same cave where David hid with Joab and his men. It was, fortunately for both David and Saul, a long cavern. David and Joab simply moved deeper into the cave than Saul was interested in going. Hiding in the shadows around a corner, they observed the king discreetly.

"This is it, David," Joab hissed, prodding him in the ribs. "The Lord has delivered your enemy into your hands just as Samuel prophesied."

The king was undeniably at his mercy. David's heart was rent. He felt compelled to advance on him in stealth. Yet his spirit was heavy and uncertain. This was the Lord's anointed king, and the father of the man who possessed his heart. Was it the Lord's will that he slay this man at his most human? Yet the Lord had clearly put Saul in his way and at David's mercy.

At Joab's urging, David drew his sword and advanced on the vulnerable man. In slaying Saul, he would save the lives of countless men, David reasoned. He could be at once with Jonathan, who would forgive him as soon as David's sword divided Saul's royal neck into two. With a single divine stroke, everything would be changed. Every obstacle that stood between David and his heart's desire would be swept away.

David's joy welled at the thought of it and the power the Lord had placed in his hands.

He moved behind the outcropping of rock on which the king leaned as he relieved himself. He was close enough to recognize the hem of robe that the king had cast aside. He remembered helping Saul on with it, when he served him in his chambers. The fringe had been made by his daughters and added by the royal tailor for a holiday ceremony. Old and worn, the once grand robe was the choice for wandering through the Arabah wastes.

The robe and its wearer had survived much to be there. The thought of ending a life that had meant so much to so many, himself included, pained David's heart. How often he had stood as close or closer to the man? He might have snuffed out that life as easily as the flame of a candle a hundred, a thousand times, had it been in his heart.

And so could the Lord, David thought to himself. In battles beyond numbering and the travails of a life so long as the king's, the Lord could have taken back the life he had breathed into Saul a hundred times, a thousand times, and more. Surely the Lord did not send this man, who had survived so much, to David's mercy. Was it left to him to end a life that the Lord himself had anointed and protected for so long? *Can it be my place to decide for the Lord in this?* David asked himself. In silent prayer he sought guidance. He thought of the story he'd told Joab only the day before, of the way in which the Lord answered prayers. It would change so much to end Saul here, but it would not be what David truly wished. His fondest wish was for peace with Saul. He longed to restore all things to their order in the days of his greatest joy.

He drew back his sword as he prayed. *Guide my hand.* The words echoed in David's heart. *Teach me, oh Lord, what you would have me do in this.*

And he struck.

Returning to his men, he displayed his trophy. David met their disbelief with a smile. The trophy, dangled before their noses, was a piece of the fringe from the hem of the king's robe. "The Lord has put it in my way to do his will in this. He would not have anointed Saul King and kept him alive had he wanted me to kill him. Death is the Lord's province, and I will not raise a hand against his anointed."

"What is the Lord's will, then?" Joab asked, incredulous. "How are you to know?"

"Stay and see," David assured him. "Send word up into the hills that all should conceal themselves so that they might keep the oasis in sight in the time before sunset."

When the king had gone, Joab and his men left David. It seemed to Joab that a great blunder had been made, for he knew that it was only necessary to cut the head off the snake to kill it. Still, he and his men accomplished David's task. All eyes were on the oasis as King Saul arrived. Counting on surprise and ready for battle, he found that the surprise was his. The place was empty.

Before his furor could gain momentum, Saul was distracted by a familiar voice. It called to him from the cliffs above. Out of range of spear and arrow, it was easily heard echoing off the stone walls that surrounded them.

"My lord and king," David called, bowing when Saul turned and saw him. "Against whom has the king of Israel come out? Who are you pursuing? A dead dog? A flea? May the Lord be our judge and decide between us. May he consider my cause and uphold it. May he vindicate me by delivering me from your hand."

"You are a traitor to Israel," Saul railed, waving his sword impotently up at David. "You plot my demise, that you may usurp me and seize my crown for yourself."

David waived the fringe of the king's own robe in reply.

"Why do you listen when men say, 'David is bent on harming you?' This day the Lord delivered you into my hands in the cave earlier. See, my father, look at this piece of your robe in my hand! I cut off the corner of your robe but did not kill you. Some urged me to kill you, but I spared you. I said, 'I will not lift my hand against my master, because he is the Lord's anointed.' Now understand and recognize that I am not guilty of wrongdoing or rebellion. I have not wronged you, but you are hunting me down to take my life. May the Lord judge between you and me. And may the Lord avenge the wrongs you have done to me. But neither my hand nor the hands of those that I command shall be raised against you. As the old saying goes, 'From evildoers come evil deeds,' so my hand will not touch you."

The king's hands raced to find and trace the hem of his robe. Quickly he found the gap cut there and realized how near his own death had been. There was silence as the king beheld and understood the truth and the enormity of the act. Falling to his knees, he wept aloud. Raising his arms above his head, he called out to David in the hearing of all who followed both great men.

"I hear your true voice, David, my son," the king managed, overcome by emotion. "You are more righteous than I. You have treated me well, but I have treated you badly. You have just now told me of the good you did to me. The Lord delivered me into your hands, but you did not kill me. When a man finds his enemy, does he let him get away unharmed?"

"You have found no enemy here," David asserted, throwing his arms wide to include all who followed him. "Only men loyal to you and to all of Israel."

"May the Lord reward you well for the way you have treated me today," the king said, struggling to his feet. "I know that you will surely be king and that the kingdom of Israel will be established in your hands. But for the sake of any good that has ever passed between us, swear to me by the Lord that you will not cut off my descendants or wipe out the name of my father's family."

"My lord, I swear to you that your father's name shall live on and your line will continue on the throne of Israel with my blessings," David said, moved by Saul's words. "Prince Jonathan shall rule Israel in his turn with my support and the support of those who would follow me. His son Mephibosheth shall follow after him, and his grandson after that. You have my word and my oath before the Lord of Israel."

Again Saul fell to his knees, overcome by David's oath. Cheers went up from his men, and from David's, as the canyon walls of En-Gedi echoed with joy and peace.

Even as night fell, Saul led his men out of En-Gedi to begin their journey back to Gibeah. Again the two forces had met and parted without violence or bloodshed.

And David sware unto Saul. And Saul went home; but David and his men
gat them up unto the hold.

                                                    1 Samuel 24:22

FOR A time David and his following remained in En-Gedi, bathing in the
Salt Sea and baking in the summer heat in their desert oasis. They celebrated
David's birthday and Shavuot at once, as the days were close to one another. It
was a tradition that carried on long after. They passed their days in peace.

"David, you heard the king. Let us go home," Eliab urged.

"And take these people with us?" David asked, uncertain of his path.

"Can we not disband now that the king has declared his intentions
peaceful?" Joab agreed, speaking up at the council. The commanders were
gathered to hear David's long-delayed word on the matter.

"The way is not clear to me," David said distantly, lost in his own
thoughts. "I know that many who have come to us are here because they have
no place to go. So I am certain that we cannot simply disband. If, after a season,
things remain as they are with the king, perhaps we can sue to merge our forces
into his, but there is much still undecided between us. I am thankful that there
is peace. For now I think we should continue as we are. I have come to believe
that we should move on from this place. I know that all who are with us are
here by choice. Any who feel that their paths diverge here are as free to leave
as they always were, with our friendship and gratitude as ever intact, always
welcome to return."

The choice was carried from commander to lieutenant and from lieutenant
to corpsman. Still, every man who followed David to En-Gedi vowed to follow
on from there, so long as he would lead him.

The time of harvest and the high holy days drew nearer. David moved
to establish a more permanent base. He chose the forested hills of Caleb, near
the city of Carmel, on the eastern route to Hebron. There, as they had done
before, David cleared the land of thieves, brigands, and the warring tribes of
Amalekites and Amonites who plagued the nearby villages of Judah.

It was a great service, much celebrated by the people living in the
hills. They paid tribute to David and his men with food and supplies that the
Hebrews were unable to provide for themselves. In that spirit, David sent
emissaries to, among many others, the home of Jether ben Nabal, an elder of
Carmel, and a wealthy and prosperous man. His shepherds spent summers
grazing his sheep in the hills. David and his men, who camped nearby, had
defended Jether's shepherds and flocks against Amonite thieves. His men
left the flock intact, taking nothing for themselves, even as they spared its
thinning at less principled hands.

When the time for shearing arrived, Jether's flocks were returned to the fold numbering more than had left for higher pasture. David dispatched Matthew, and other men his age and younger, to carry his compliments to Jether.

"Good sir," young Matthew said, dismounting and bowing before Jether in the field near his home. "Long life to you! Good health to you and your household! And good health to all that is yours!"

"Well met," Jether answered tersely. Uncertain of Matthew's intentions, he was unfamiliar with the strange flag with the single hollow star that rode before him.

"I bring greetings from my captain, David ben Jesse, who has lately been of service to you and protected your shepherds and their charges. Now that shearing time is upon us, it is clear that when your shepherds were with us, we did not mistreat them, and the whole time they were at Carmel, nothing of theirs was missing. Ask your own servants and they will tell you. Therefore, be favorable toward me on my master's behalf, since we come at a festive time. Please give your servants and your son David whatever you can find for them."

"Who is this David?" Jether demanded impatiently, though he knew full well the answer to his question. "Who is his father? Many servants are breaking away from their masters these days. Why should I take my bread and water, and the meat I have slaughtered for my shearers, and give it to men coming from who knows where? Be off with you, and tell this David to keep his band of vagabonds away from my lands and my people."

Returning to David empty-handed, Matthew was ashamed and reluctant to convey the disrespectful message.

"Ah, welcome, young Matthew," David called out as the young man and his company slowly approached the fire. "What news of our friend Jether? His tribute too vast to be carried? Is he sending it along?"

"Not so you'd know it, Lord Captain," Matthew said, hanging back from the fire.

David had grown to be a more peaceful man. Experience had made of him a man of wisdom far beyond his years. After passing his second summer in David's service, Matthew knew, only too well, the long slow route to David's anger. He also knew that when the end of the long journey was attained, it was a fearsome destination. Well suited to read the signposts, Matthew could see they were nearing the end of David's equanimity and approaching the vast and terrible landscape of his anger.

Firsthand he had seen David's deep frustration. Winter was coming, and they were still living in tents. Progress on construction of a more permanent camp was slow. The land around them was rich but the tributes were stingy. There was no word, as yet, from the king. Worse still, there had been no word or visit from David's "old friend from the army" whose time among them had brought such a transformative effect at Hereth.

"Well, First," Eliab prodded with a twinkle in his eye. "Did you eat this Jether's tribute on the way?"

The laughter gave Matthew hope. He reasoned that if he just blurted it out while David was still laughing, it wouldn't matter as much.

He was wrong.

"He said what?" David bellowed. Veins stood out on this neck and at his temples. His sword was drawn as if he meant Matthew harm.

"He asked who you were," Matthew answered, afraid not to repeat the words.

"I am the end of him and all that he holds dear," David proclaimed with a ferocity that sent the rest of Matthew's party running into the bushes and brought even the likes of Eliab and Joab to their feet. "Gird yourselves and be ready to ride with me, those whose lieutenants follow my kinsmen Eliab, Joab, Abinadab, and Asahel. We will remind this son of Nabal just whose son I am."

"David, that's four hundred men," Eliab cautioned.

"And so we shall clear out his storehouse and slaughter his sheep to feed ourselves all winter." David's voice echoed down the hillsides as he raised his sword to the heavens. "The Lord take me if, by sunrise, there are still standing any from his household who piss against the wall."

"Are you certain—" Joab began again, cautiously.

"We ride," David declared.

The torches and fires of the camp were blurred by dust as hundreds rushed to prepare to ride with David and cut the house of Jether from memory.

Abigail, Jether's wife, was a fine and sensible woman. Comely, and years her husband's younger, she had been married to Jether by her father, a wise but poor man, in exchange for enough to make him a wealthy man. It was a good marriage if not a passionate one. Jether was the wealthiest and most powerful man from Hebron to Moan. Abigail lived well and graciously. He had given her no children, and so she had found other occupations. Leaving kitchen duties to servants, she learned to read and write. Traveling between their home in the country and the thriving city markets of Hebron, Abigail learned much of politics and the world. Though she could easily have held her own in a conversation with men who might mistake themselves for her betters, she kept her place as a good wife to her husband. In truth, though, her duty was more in tribute to her father than to her husband.

It was the good fortune of Jether, if not all those who worked for and depended upon him that day, that he had married Abigail.

One of the servants overheard his master's arrogant and dismissive answers to the messenger of the great and fearsome warrior David who, it was said, had killed tens of thousands. Terrified, he ran all the way back to the great house and up the stairs to the sewing room of his mistress, Abigail, to relate what he had witnessed.

"My lady, we are doomed. My master has doomed us all," the servant shouted, distraught, bursting into her chamber. "We must run or surely we will all be killed in our beds tonight."

"Now, my good man," Abigail said soothingly. "Tell me all, that I may best know which path to choose for my escape."

"David, the great general, sent messengers from his stronghold in the hills of Caleb to give our master his greetings," the servant babbled, still near madness with fear. He had seen David's wrath firsthand when he had protected the servant and his master's flocks. "Your husband hurled insults at them. But I tell you, these men, though I knew their ways to be fearsome, were very good to us. It is true what his servant said. They did not mistreat us, and the whole time we were out in the fields near them, nothing was missing. Night and day they were a wall around us all the time we were herding our sheep near them. Consider what you can do. Disaster hangs over our master and his whole household."

"Oh, my dear," Abigail said, patting the distracted man's head as she rose. "My husband is not a wicked man, only too proud of the gifts God in his grace has granted him. Come with me. Perhaps I understand the ways of men well enough to mend this wound without a needle."

Losing no time, Abigail gathered two hundred loaves of bread, two skins of wine, five dressed sheep, five seahs of roasted grain, a hundred cakes of raisins, and two hundred cakes of pressed figs. These she had loaded onto donkeys. Helped onto a mule, her skirts tucked between her legs, she left without a word to her husband.

Just after dawn Abigail first saw David down the road from her mule train.

Quickly her attendants helped her down from the mule. Commending its care to the servant who had come to warn her, Abigail threw herself to the ground to bow before David, her face in the dirt of the road.

Brought up short by the sight, David stopped his mount and leaped down to receive the zealous greeting of this lady.

"Madam," David said with a small bow. "Your servant."

"No, good sir, it is I who am your servant," Abigail said, rising only enough to address him. Her heart raced as she dared to address a strange man on the road. She hardly considered the sword at his side or the men-at-arms who attended him.

"My lord, let the blame be on me alone," Abigail pleaded. "Please let your servant speak to you and hear what I have to say. May my lord pay no attention to that wicked man my husband, Jether. He is a fool and should be named such, for folly goes with him. But, as for me, your servant, I did not see the men you sent to my master.

"Now since the Lord has kept you from bloodshed and from avenging yourself with your own hands, as surely as the Lord lives and as you live, may your enemies and all who intend to harm you, my master, be like my husband, whom we shall name a fool. Let this gift, which your servant has brought, be given to the men who follow you. Please forgive the offense for my sake. For mercy befits a man who fights the Lord's battles and for whom the Lord will certainly make a lasting dynasty. Let no wrongdoing be found in you as long as you live. I know that even though someone is pursuing you to take your life, you have kept the peace, for your life is bound securely in the bundle of the living by the Lord your God. But the lives of your enemies he will hurl away as from the pocket of a sling. And when the Lord has done for you every good thing he promised you and has appointed you leader over Israel, you will not have on your conscience the staggering burden of needless bloodshed or of having avenged yourself on this country bumpkin whose name, Nabal, shall mean fool evermore. And when the Lord has brought you success, I pray that you will remember me, your servant, with kindness."

David rocked back on his heels, threw his head back, and laughed to heaven.

"Get up, woman," David said, extending his hand to her. "That was quite some speech. My heart and my passion are both cooled and inflamed, and I am sorry only to find that you are another man's wife."

"My Lord, you are too generous," Abigail said, hoisting herself daintily back to her feet with his help.

"Not at all, my lady," David said, kissing the back of her hand chastely and with great formality. Then, clearing his throat and clasping his hands behind his back like a schoolboy reciting, he answered her in kind. "Praise be to the Lord God of Israel who has sent you today to meet me. May you be blessed for your good judgment and for keeping me from bloodshed this day and from avenging myself with my own hands. Otherwise, as surely as our Lord lives and has kept me from harming you, if you had not come this dawn to meet me, not one male belonging to your husband Nabal would have been left alive by time the day breaks again."

"Are you making light of me, my lord?" she asked, following his stilted speech with some difficulty.

"No, I seek but to be worthy of you," he said with a flirtatious grin. "Was it laughable?"

"A bit, I'm afraid, my lord," she admitted, with a small laugh she hid behind her hand, as though still the girl she had not been for many summers. "Was I? Laughable, I mean?"

"No, no, my lady," David said, laughing in spite of his best efforts. "You were just very, very serious."

"Well, it was a serious errand," she pointed out, still laughing at them both.

"It was," David agreed, joining her mirth as with an old friend. "I was going to kill your whole family and burn your house."

"There, you see," she said, trying to regain her tone but really only laughing harder. "Very serious, both of us."

The men with David looked upon the pair with a combination of amusement and disbelief.

"My lady, I will accept your generous gifts and take my leave of you," David said with a low bow, unable to regain his composure. "Do you need an escort home?"

"No, I thank you, sir," she said with a curtsey. "I'm afraid if we keep each other's company any longer, one or the other of us will become too dizzied with laughter, fall off his mount, and be killed."

"Very prudent, my lady," he managed. "Most serious."

"Most."

The two turned and took their leave of one another giddily as David's men took the pack animals in hand from her servants.

"May I ask your name?" he called, turning back but still walking away, albeit backward.

"Abigail," she said, mirroring him.

"Abigail." He bowed, almost losing his balance as he continued backing away. "As you seem to know, I am called David."

"Yes, I had heard," she said, tripping and falling into the arms of a vigilant servant. "Pleased to meet you, my lord."

"We'll return the asses," David said, backing into Matthew, who stood holding the reins of David's horse.

"That would be most gracious," Abigail said as she was helped up.

"Good day, my lady," David said, bowing as she turned her mule and rode away.

With a girlish wave, she left him, still laughing.

"Are you well, little brother?" Abinadab ventured as David mounted his horse.

"Never better," David answered, wheeling the steed. "Though I'm tired and more than a little hungry. It occurs to me we left before supper last night."

"Yes, we know, my lord," Joab said as he rode to the rear with David to lead the four hundred men and their kingly tribute back to camp.

By the time Abigail reached home, night had fallen. Jether was feasting at a banquet with his friends, to whom he had drunkenly bragged about getting the protection services of the great David without the cost of tribute. Abigail, who knew how much he had paid so that he still drew breath to boast, went up to bed. The servants brought a tray up to her. The following morning, when Jether was still sore from the previous night's wine, Abigail took him to task for his folly.

"And we agreed, after I bestowed your largesse on David and his men," Abigail concluded her diatribe to her pale and chastened husband, "your name shall mean fool, my husband, and I shall introduce myself as the wife of the first Nabal for so long as we live together as man and wife."

Enraged and humiliated by the tale that he knew must be spreading through the hills of Judah like fire in summer, Nabal stormed from her sight, slamming his own great front door—as it turned out, for the last time. As he stalked across his own yard to his great stables, he fell to the ground as a stroke turned his body to stone.

For ten days Abigail nursed and tended to her foolish husband. At the end of ten days, his heart gave up. Jether made Abigail a widow without ever answering her again.

She was dressed in black when Matthew arrived at her door with his master's compliments and his proposal of marriage. Abigail left that same day with five maidservants to accept David's offer.

They took up residence in the palatial home of Jether, which David took as his dowry. He added Jether's lands to his estates in Judah, as the Calebite had no heirs to lay claim. The newlyweds shared a winter wedding feast there that season, easily providing in abundance for David's own from the rich holdings.

"It is a blessing from the Lord that you kept me from burning this house down," David jested as the weather grew colder. "I am never the best author of my own revenge."

"You could hardly have done better than this to avenge yourself on my late husband," Abigail answered him, amused.

Though older than David, Abigail made a brilliant companion and an excellent advisor, holding David's interests paramount. Abigail herself began that winter to make arrangements for his second wedding while they still celebrated his first. It was at her urging that he soon married Ahinoam, a woman from an influential family of Jezreel.

"Jezreel is called *God sows* for good reason," she said. "The valley could easily feed the whole country. Beyond, you yourself know the importance of the region for trade. You should have family ties to strengthen your influence in the north. Moreover, she's younger than us both and can keep up with you in ways I never will."

David was convinced and loved her the more for her wisdom and selflessness. He did not say it, but he was less lonely for Jonathan with her sharp wit and wise council for company. Though theirs was a union of convenience for both, it was no less sincerely held between them. When troubled or in doubt, he sought her council first, an honor that was not typical for a woman and which she did not take lightly. Theirs was a marriage unlike others.

They were as companions first, with separate lives as well as the life they shared.

Though she did not fully understand, she learned to recognize the seal that matched his ring on certain rare correspondence. She became equally familiar with the change in him that followed their arrival.

He did not say and she did not ask, for the same reason that he spoke to her as an equal. It was what made their marriage unique among peers. They offered one another more than love or passion or affection. Respect was what they gave each other most.

CHAPTER NINETEEN
THE CLIFFS OF DIVISION

And Samuel died; and all the Israelites were gathered together, and lamented him, and buried him in his house at Ramah.

1 Samuel 25:1

SAMUEL AWOKE in the night, as he had the first time so many years before. Once again he heard the familiar voice calling to him. The old man cried out on first waking but then was calmed as he recognized.

"Ah, my Lord," Samuel said as delight spread across his face. "Is it so?"

A sense of joy spread through him as his eyes closed one last time. He saw before him the end of all his efforts and a prophecy that stretched to the limits of his own imagination. His heart was filled to bursting.

"Ah, Saul," he said aloud in the darkness of his small room at Ramah.

David also took Ahinoam of Jezreel; and they were also both of them his wives.

1 Samuel 25:43

SAMUEL'S DEATH brought winter's chill into the following spring. There were few of Israel whose lives had not been changed by the life and works of the old man. All were affected by word of his death, but none more than those lives he'd personally touched, two men most of all.

The news moved David more than he had expected. His life was changed profoundly and forever since meeting the old priest as a boy of sixteen. Mourners from all the tribes gathered at Ramah for the funeral rites. David argued vigorously against his advisors and Abigail's strenuous objections to his proposed attendance. In the end he simply took to his rooms at what he and Abigail called the Nabal's Paradise. He refused her company and the comforts of his newest wife Ahinoam, who had come to him as soon as spring permitted travel from Jezreel.

The two women were friends at once. Abigail welcomed the young woman more as a mother than a rival for their husband's attention. In his absence they spoke of David's rare and fleeting interest in asserting the rights of a husband.

"And when he is, he is more attentive to my delight than any man I've heard tell of or known," Abigail joked with Ahinoam as they spoke of it one morning following the news of the priest's death. "He is a most mysterious combination, but take my oath, you are lucky to have such a husband, for few if any are his equal."

"Do you know the reason he never takes that ring with six jewels from his hand?" Ahinoam asked with an air of secrecy. She hoped for some explanation from the senior wife, though neither had known the man a year.

"I have seen it there on his left hand since we met," Abigail said wistfully. "I have also seen its signet embossed on the seal of the rarest and most celebrated of all the messages that are ever received here."

"From whom?" Ahinoam asked, eager for a solution to the mystery.

"I do not know," Abigail said, shaking her head slowly. "It is the only thing he does not confide in me. I take it to be a sign that his heart is elsewhere. Still, he has never given me cause for complaint as his wife, never spoken harshly to me or struck me. He takes an interest in my thoughts and happiness and includes me as no husband is required. So I am proud to be second in his heart. Or with you here now, maybe third."

Ahinoam embraced Abigail for her courage and her kindness.

While David mourned the priest in private, Saul marked the old man's passage more publicly. His trip to Ramah, with a retinue of ten thousand, was worthy of a pharaoh and, he felt, commensurate with the worth of the man.

The grand ceremonies continued for days.

Jonathan was in attendance as part of his father's entourage. Saul was both pleased and surprised, as the two had never seemed close during Samuel's life. Jonathan's love for Samuel, for sheltering and protecting David, was unknown to the king, and the prince thought it best that it remain so.

Saul's tenuous, informal truce with David was far more important to Jonathan than his spiritual enlightenment. Jonathan's faith had begun to flourish when Samuel acted as the Lord's agent in answer to his first sincere prayers. The loss of David had dimmed his belief but not his gratitude.

Still, what faith Jonathan had was a great consolation to him in those, the darkest days of his life. Though Saul had ceased his pursuit of David, his belief in their rivalry for the throne was unresolved. For Jonathan it was almost worse. He had petitioned his father for David's full restoration to court, but as yet his pleas had gone unanswered. Their enforced separation had rent Jonathan's soul. He lived as a man with a wound that would not heal. The hope that one day he and David would be reunited was all that allowed him to endure the pain of his damaged spirit.

Jonathan wrote to David less and less. David could not risk Jonathan by answering, so neither found any peace in it. In the silence between them, Jonathan imagined himself a coward for not rushing to David's side and a traitor for remaining with his father while still loyal to David. He could not be satisfied by either choice.

Jonathan followed his father to Ramah in search of the peace he could not find at court. He secretly hoped that Saul might find the spirit of reconciliation there.

Though Saul had never been reconciled with the man who had made him king, he was beside himself with grief. He wept and wailed as a young widow or a child made motherless. The window to his soul and his fate was closed forever. He felt he could never again know certainty. Though Samuel had not been his advisor for many years, his death ended any hope the king held. The loss of his oldest and most important friend and advisor brought fearsome thoughts of his own mortality.

Overwrought and overwhelmed with anguish, Saul sought the comfort of Samuel's successor at the Ramah temple.

"I am lost without his council and do not know how to be king without his wisdom," Saul confided in the privacy of the priest's chambers, once so familiar to him, though the priest who sat in Samuel's chair was a stranger.

"You cannot hope for success so long as you oppose the Lord's anointed," the young priest chastised the king.

"I do not understand," Saul replied, drawing back in his confusion. "Samuel anointed me."

"And you prepared the way. He was thankful even in his final days," the priest explained. "But Samuel anointed another to be the king of Israel and prophesied that that man would unite the tribes and fulfill the promise of the Lord of Israel."

"Another?" Saul asked in a deathly whisper, rising from where he sat.

"Yes," the priest answered, confused. "I thought, as did Samuel, that that was why you opposed David so vigorously."

"Samuel anointed David to be king?" Saul repeated.

"Is that not why your own son, the prince, brought David here for protection when you called for his death?" the priest answered, though he was by then as puzzled as Saul.

"This is what Samuel thought?"

"Until the day he died," the priest assured him.

Saul left the audience a man in a trance. His bodyguard pursued him as he spoke not to them or to any man. Long into the night he sat, neither eating nor drinking nor speaking to any who tried to arouse him from his waking slumber.

Jonathan lay sleepless in the room at the townhouse that he'd shared with David all too briefly. He dreamed of a time when they would share it again. David's smell clung still to an old wool blanket on their bed. Tears came to his eyes as he found himself longing for his father's death so that they might at last be free. Ashamed of his selfishness, he was certain of what he must do. He arose invigorated, though he had not enjoyed a good night's sleep since last he'd shared his bed with David.

None of it mattered anymore. He was through with pretense. Jonathan knew. His heart was lightened by the certain knowledge. He no longer cared if he was king. So long as he was with David, all else paled. Were they on the throne or in a tent in the hills of Judah, it only mattered that they were together.

As resolutely as he had ever acted in an existence filled with courageous life-and-death decisions, Jonathan made his way to the royal encampment to gather his things, return to the palace, and go to David. David had never asked him to make a choice, and he had.

"Prince Jonathan," Doeg said, stepping into his path. "Your father has been asking to see you. Please come with me."

"Not now," Jonathan said, pushing past the guard who again stepped into his path.

"I'm sorry, Your Highness," Doeg said, more firmly. "I mean you no disrespect, but I must insist."

"Insist?" Jonathan asked, reaching for his sword as other guards closed in.

"Your father, sire," Doeg said quietly, placing his hand over Jonathan's on the hilt of the sword. "He has ordered us to arrest you and bring you to him in chains as a prisoner, if you will not come as a prince."

"I understand," Jonathan said. Uncertain of what mood or fancy had seized his father, Jonathan followed Doeg to the king's tent. He knew, from far too much experience, his father's capricious nature and figured Saul had found him guilty of some imagined crime as he attempted to drink his grief away. To his surprise, not only was his father not drunk, but the tent was a welter of activity in preparation for departure. Many from the palace had arrived with the fittings and trappings of a greater journey than the morning's ride to Ramah. The commanders of the king's armies were also there.

"Father?" Jonathan asked. "What has happened? Has there been an invasion?"

Saul turned and walked to his son. They stood facing one another for a heartbeat. Saul slapped Jonathan so resoundingly that the prince fell to his knees, more from shock than pain. The tent went silent around them.

"Leave us," Saul shouted.

The large company left the tent hastily, but Jonathan did not rise.

"You knew that Samuel had anointed David to be king instead of me?" Saul demanded in a voice hissing with pure malevolence. "Yet you did not tell me. Instead you protected the man who would replace me?"

"Yes, Father," Jonathan said flatly.

"Then why are you not with him now?" Saul demanded, leaning down, his face only an inch or two away from Jonathan's.

"I have no idea," Jonathan said with a disgusted laugh that threw Saul into a rage. "I suppose because I thought I should be beside my father, loyal to him. But I see that I was mistaken."

Saul's heart shattered in his chest. He fell to his knees facing his son.

"How could I expect you to choose between the will of the Lord and your own father?" Saul said, embracing Jonathan, his anger blown cold as quickly as it had blazed. "My son, my son, I have no idea what you must have been through. Forgive me for my hasty judgment. I tell you now that I will put an end to your suffering. We are off to the ancestral lands of Caleb, where Samuel's pet viper lies in wait for me. I will meet David. We will see who it is that the Lord has chosen."

"No, Father, please," Jonathan said, falling onto his shoulder and holding him as if to prevent his departure. "Not now."

"I won't leave you, son," Saul said, stroking his back. "I'll bring you with me. You shall see the Lord's choice for yourself."

Saul rose. He managed to free himself from Jonathan's grasp. He called out for his party.

"Doeg," Saul said as the tent once again flooded with tailors, armorers, and generals, though his son remained on the floor. "Take your brother to his tent and help him to prepare for the journey. See to it that Crown Prince Jonathan is ready to travel. We leave when the shadows turn east."

"Yes, sire," Doeg said, striking his chest in salute. Nodding to his men, they lifted Jonathan from his knees, uncertain of what had transpired. Hearing Jonathan referred to as the crown prince seemed at least to mean he was not a prisoner, and they treated him accordingly.

For his part Jonathan was listless, participating not at all in his own preparation for travel. Strapped into his armor, lifted onto his horse, and led into formation like a statue, the prince found himself at the king's side. Together they set out to destroy the most treasured half of Jonathan's soul.

Then Saul arose, and went down to the wilderness of Ziph, having three thousand chosen men of Israel with him, to seek David in the wilderness of Ziph.

1 Samuel 26:2

THERE WERE no warnings from Jonathan, no visions from Abiathar, but three thousand men raise a dust cloud like a sandstorm in the desert.

David left two hundred at the estate to defend and protect his wives. He returned with more than eight hundred more to the mountain stronghold at Hakilah, which he had been constructing since his return from En-Gedi. He worried at first to leave Abigail behind. As always, she put his head back in his own business.

"My lord," she said, kissing him and pushing him towards the door. "I am more than capable of running this estate and taking care of Ahinoam and myself. I already do. As do your sisters at your estates and armories in Bethlehem. Such are the lives of a warrior's women."

"Are you certain?" he asked, concerned for her and driven to distraction by the lack of word from Jonathan.

"My lord, when I met you, you were planning to burn this house down," Abigail said, putting her open palm lovingly to his cheek and stroking it with her thumb.

"Well, try not to marry the next invader." David laughed, taking and kissing her hand before turning and rushing through the door.

When they reached Hakilah, his thoughts of Jonathan kept him from food and prevented him doing more than awaiting Saul's imminent arrival. His men ready to move at short notice, David remained determined to avoid doing battle with troops he had once led and sworn to support.

Word came to David that the king's forces were nearby. To occupy his mind with thoughts other than Jonathan's welfare, he led a small expedition to track the king's progress so that he might determine their most effective evasive actions.

Late in the day, David caught up to the king's army. Hidden in the hills above the road, he tracked them as they made their way to the great gorge between Hakilah and Maon, known as the Cliff of Divisions, Sela Hammahlekoth. The king made camp on the Maon side. David and his men watched them from the Hakilah side, unobserved. His relief was immediate when he saw the king there. It meant that Abigail and his household were safe, at least.

As David watched, his heart rose with joy in his chest as he saw that Jonathan was in the king's company. He delighted in observing him even in the mundane routines of making camp, eating supper, making water, and retiring for the night. When darkness had fallen and the king's camp was quiet, David turned to his small party.

"Who will come with me into the king's camp?"

The party, brave men all, looked at David as if he spoke in an unknown tongue.

"I will come with you," Abishai, Joab's younger brother, answered him. He was youthful, inexperienced, and anxious for a chance to prove himself.

"No, it is too dangerous," Joab said. Putting a hand on Abishai's shoulder, he held him back. "Our mother has asked that I look after you. I will go."

"No," David said, taking Joab's hand. "I need you here to run things if I don't make it back. I will see to Abishai's safety. Come with me."

Joab's lips moved, but he made no more protest. David led Abishai down through the wadi and up the steep cliffs onto the opposite side where the king's forces camped. Halfway there, on a well-concealed ledge on the king's side of the canyon, David paused.

"Mark this place," David said, making a notch in the trunk of a small tree. "If we are separated, you should meet me here if you can. In that way I'll know where to come back for you."

"Yes, Lord Captain," Abishai whispered, nodding. His heart raced with fear and excitement as they neared their target.

David smiled at his young nephew's formality, remembering too well youth and his own longing to play soldier. He touched Micah's lion's tooth, as always on Jonathan's chain near his heart. The talisman never failed to fill him with courage, and his calm gave Abishai ease as they walked into the jaws of the enemy.

They paused behind some sage to get a sense of the guards' rounds. When the king's tent was dark and they were certain not to be observed, David led Abishai into the camp as confidently as if he was still a soldier in it. They slipped under the back of Saul's tent. David found him asleep. His cousin and chief of staff, Abner, slept nearby. Both rested on cushions scattered over carpets that covered the ground. By the king was his spear, near at hand to defend himself against attack. At his head was a cruse of water.

Giving Abishai the signal, David left him to stand watch. He moved toward the king, certain of his course and sure of its righteousness. Abishai could hardly keep his eyes on his duty as he stole glances, awaiting the king's demise at David's hand. As silent as the moon steals across the sky, David took up the spear and the ewer and made his way back to the place where they had entered. He motioned for Abishai to follow.

"Why did you not finish it?" Abishai whispered as they got a safe distance away.

David answered him by holding a finger up to his lips. He led his nephew back into the thicket of sage where they had concealed themselves before, safely out of the guards' sight.

"Make your way back to the place where I told you to meet me," David instructed, handing him the cruse and the spear. "Take this, camp there. I will join you in the morning."

"But where are you going?" Abishai asked, concerned.

David only ruffled his hair. He departed him with a sly smile that left his nephew to wonder.

Exhausted from the long journey and his own lack of sleep, Jonathan dozed fitfully. His blankets were tangled, and his leg hung off the side of the mat on which he wrestled with sleep. He dreamt once again that David had been captured, and that Saul would kill him unless Jonathan killed his father. Once again Jonathan watched David die, unable to summon the courage to do what he knew he must.

It was a fearsome dream. It kept Jonathan from sleep most nights, until he was too weak to resist, succumbed to sleep, and dreamed the horror into being once again. Just as his father's spear was about to pierce David's chest, Jonathan awoke gasping, a hand clasped over his mouth.

Struggling instinctively, he hoped for a heartbeat that the assassin would be quick, that he might have an end to his torment. Relaxing, he surrendered himself to the dream—or the reality, he knew not which—and to a longed-for end to his torment. The hand that clasped at his mouth began to caress his face. Jonathan turned to find David naked in bed beside him.

Tears burst from the prince's eyes. He sobbed, clasping David so hard that he left David bruises with which to remember him.

"Shhh," David soothed, stroking the big man's hair and trying to comfort him. "Be still or we will have much to explain."

"I wake up screaming every night," Jonathan said, kissing David hungrily, over and over again. "No one will come."

"Why do you wake up screaming?" David asked, a pain stabbing his chest.

"Every night that I sleep, and those are few, I dream that I see Father kill you," Jonathan said, in a voice far away. "I am the only who can save you, but I am frozen and unable to kill my own father even to save you because I am a coward. David, we must run away together, now, this minute. I cannot bear to live like this any longer. Torn between the two of you. I don't care if I'm king or not. We have to run away before my father kills you."

"We are together, here, now," David said, stroking the prince's body to excite and to comfort him. "And your father is nowhere around. Enough talk of killing. Let us speak of love."

In the cool darkness of the mountain night, they met with the tenderness of two youths exploring each other's bodies for the first time, each part touched and tasted as if to memorize every detail, both uncertain if the beloved flesh would be against their lips or fingertips again. Exquisitely they tortured one another, delaying until, able to resist no longer, Jonathan fell upon him, and they brought their lovemaking to a shattering conclusion.

Serene and at last at ease, Jonathan fell asleep pressed against his lover's back, his arm thrown protectively over David's chest. For the first night in too many to recall, Jonathan dreamed of the two of them together. With David safely in his arms, Jonathan was secure in the knowledge that he could convince David to steal away and sleep in peace with him every night until they died old men in one another's arms. He awoke to the sound of David's voice calling out.

Sitting up in bed, he realized he was alone. He looked around in alarm. Was it just a dream? Had David been there at all? His breath caught in his throat when he saw the gold chain and the lion's tooth, there on the pillow beside him. He grabbed it up with such passion, he punctured his hand.

"Aren't you going to answer me, Abner?"

It was David's voice, Jonathan realized. Leaping from his bed, he pulled a robe over his head as he ran toward the sound.

He found many gathered near the edge of the cliff, looking across to David, who called bravely to the king and his general. Jonathan prayed silently that David stood out of range of the arrows and spears of the heavily armed men he taunted.

Abner arrived, bleary from sleep, as were most at such a raw time of the morning.

"Who are you who calls to the king?" the general demanded, squinting to see.

"Abner ben Ner, you are derelict in your duty," David cried out, quieting the stir on Abner's side of the cliffs.

"What game is this?" Abner demanded, indignant. "Who are you to accuse me?"

"Is it not your job to protect your king and to keep your master safe?" David asked, pacing the boundary of the void that separated them.

"It is," Saul answered, joining them. "And here I am well and sound. What call have you to impugn my cousin?"

"If the king slept safely last night, then answer me this," David went on. "Where is the king's spear and the cruse of water that was by his head?"

"I've no time for riddles," Abner snorted contemptuously.

"Here they are," David said, revealing them from behind a nearby boulder. "I have them. Once again I stood close enough to do the king harm."

As David held the spear aloft for all to see, the brilliance of the low morning sun was caught by the ring on his hand and thrown back into the east. The gold glinted in Saul's eye. He remembered the ring, always on David's hand, and saw its twin as always on Jonathan's. He understood. With dawning recognition he saw the breadth of the divided loyalties his son Jonathan had endured. Saul stepped forward and put an arm around Jonathan's shoulder.

Jonathan, unaccustomed to tender acts from his rough-hewn father, particularly in public, turned to look into his father's pleading eyes.

"Jonathan, my son," Saul said quietly as he reached and took up Jonathan's hand and touched the ring on it. Their eyes met. "Is this why David spares my life?"

The tears in his son's eyes were Saul's only answer.

"David, my son," the king said, stepping forward.

"Yes, my lord, it is I," David answered, casting away the spear and cruse. They clattered against the stones in the silent understanding between the two men. "Why do you again pursue me, my lord? What have I done? What wrong am I guilty of? If the Lord has incited you against me, then may he accept an offering. But if men have done it, may they be cursed before the Lord. They have driven me from my life and my place in the Lord's inheritance, challenged me to serve other gods. I live in the wilderness, cut off from my people and my own family, while the king of Israel looks for me as one hunts a partridge in the mountains."

"I have sinned," Saul said, drawing Jonathan nearer. "David, my son, you have shown me again today that you consider my life precious, taking my spear as a trophy instead of driving it through my heart when it was put in your way to do so. I will try to harm you no more. Surely I have acted like a fool and have erred against you greatly. I have misunderstood what I beheld and taken love for malice."

"I will go my way and trouble you no more, my lord," David called. His voice quavered with emotion as he shouted his good-byes to Jonathan across the chasm that separated them. The words of the prophet of Gad spoken to him that night on the banks of the Jordan were bitter on his tongue but no less true for their poison. Holding his fist over his heart, he touched the signet with his fingers even as he spoke the words that he swore he would never say. "For how often we do, for the sake of those we love, that which we've said we will never do. I ask that, in return for my absence, you end this pursuit now and forever. I know now that there can be no trust between us, but I pray that each of us can find forgiveness enough to keep the peace for the rest of our days."

Jonathan held his fist over his heart to say with the touch of his ring what the Cliffs of Division prevented him putting into words.

"May you be blessed, my son David," Saul said, his arm still around Jonathan, who wept quietly beside him. "You will do great things and surely triumph in all that the Lord leads you to do. Fare you well."

David took one last look at Jonathan. With a silent prayer that the Lord would bring them back together one day, he turned and disappeared into the wilderness.

Jonathan's heart broke. He watched David go.

Saul stood by his son, watching with him even after David disappeared into the wilderness. Soon the others left them, and they were alone together. He had thought that David was but using his son's affections to elevate himself within reach of the crown. But in David's willingness to leave behind even Jonathan's affection, in his refusal to fight, in his reluctance to raise his hand against the very anointment of the God of Israel all for the sake of his son alone, Saul saw the truth. David loved Jonathan. He loved him more than power, more than fame, more than life. It was that love alone that had kept Saul safe.

He shivered.

"I am sorry, my son," Saul said, taking Jonathan by his wrists and facing him. "Forgive me. I understand what you have been trying to tell me. How long has it been so between you?"

"I knew from the first, when he came to play for you, but I was certain at Elah," Jonathan said. Relieved, he struggled to look into his father's eyes as he revealed the truth so long concealed. "Faced there with the idea of losing him, I found the courage to ask, and he too was sure."

Saul nodded, silent with his own thoughts.

"Forgive me," Saul said, releasing Jonathan's hands. "I do not know what I might have done differently had I known. He knows, as I know, that he and I cannot exist together. I cannot share my crown or my home with him. You two may decide what you wish. I will not interfere between you now."

There was a silence between them as both looked once more to the horizon where David had departed. Saul spoke at last.

"We've a kingdom to run. We'd best get back to Gibeah, or Michal will surely usurp us both."

Father and son laughed together bitterly, closer than ever before.

"I will be at your side for the rest of your life, Father."

"No man could ask for better, my son."

Part Three

Gath

CHAPTER TWENTY
THE TRAITOR

And David arose, and he passed over with the six hundred men that were
with him unto Achish, the son of Maoch, king of Gath.

1 Samuel 27:2

THE MARCH was as strangely silent as David had been since returning from
the Cliffs of Division. Leaving Jonathan there hurt as it had when he had been
sent home to Bethlehem before the battle at Elah. In his heart he knew that
when Saul was gone, things could be different. Until then David had to find
a path down which Jonathan could not follow him, to spare his love the daily
agony of choosing.

Returning from his meeting with Saul to the Caleb estate, David collected
his wives and the balance of his forces. Fully outfitted with weapons gathered
from his foundries in Bethlehem on the way, he led the march into the Elah
Valley. With a thousand-plus men-at-arms marching behind him, along with
wives, children, servants, and households, it was a formidable assembly who
arrived at the gates of the Philistine stronghold of Gath.

The gateway was barred. The ramparts bristled with weapons as they
approached. Halting well short of the city itself, David and a small personal guard
of heavily armed men rode out from the shank of his troops. They approached the
gates at full gallop. The guard then paused. David alone rode up.

"Captain of the guard," he called out, his horse cantering and turning in
place. "Juk? Are you there?"

Startled, Juk stepped from behind the battlements to have a look at their
visitor. "Aye, sir," he answered. "Who goes there?"

"It is David ben Jesse," David called out, waving as if to an old friend. "I
come to ask for an audience with your king, Achish. If you would be so kind as
to announce me once again, sir."

Bursting with pride at being known by name to a man who was a legend,
Juk stepped out into full view, as if his pride and importance could deflect
Hebrew arrows. "Good general, I will send word to His Majesty that you have
returned," Juk said, trying to sound as though he'd had a glance's contact with
the king since David last arrived at the east gate. "But you must remember that
unless it is to his interest, he may not wish to make the time."

"Juk," David called back genially. "I am here at the gate with more than a
thousand men-at-arms. Surely that earns me at least the king's curiosity."

"True, my lord." Juk nodded foolishly. "I'll send word and—"

"You idiot," Juk's superior hissed at him from behind the battlements. "Let him in. His men won't attack while their precious leader is inside our walls."

"Right, then," Juk said, turning back to his old nemesis and calling out, "My lord David, why not come with me to inquire after the king's pleasure in this?"

So saying, a small door in the great gate opened. David was ushered quickly inside.

Under heavy guard, led by a beaming Juk, David was escorted for the second time to the palace of King Achish. Word preceded him. He was invited inside at once and taken directly into the king's presence.

"David," Achish said, rising from his throne and crossing to embrace his former houseguest. "It is good to see you again. You have been much engaged since last you visited here. Tell me, have you come to overthrow my city with your paltry forces? Surely not. You seem far too clever for that."

"Your Majesty," David said, kneeling and saluting by striking his armor-clad chest with his fist. "I have come here to offer myself and my services and to swear allegiance to you."

"Have you indeed?" Achish said, his voice high with shock.

"Good king," David said, still kneeling but looking up with pleading eyes. "More than one summer has passed since I was last here with you. I have spent the intervening time raising an army and showing my allegiance to my own king again and again. Despite my best effort, he has sought, more than once, to hunt me down like a mangy jackal who threatens his flocks. Never will he forgive me or grant me my rightful place and inheritance."

"I have heard of the troubles between you two," Achish intoned, nodding thoughtfully as he crossed back to sit on his throne. It was becoming a more formal audience than he'd anticipated, and the ceremonial trappings aided him in conducting the affairs of state.

"I come to you, my king, to plead for the second chance that I cannot find in my homeland," David said, following the king with his eyes. "My people are called Hebrews. It is slang for mercenaries. In truth, we are men who would fight and die for a chance at a better life for ourselves and our families. Let us fight for you and earn your trust and respect, that we might be rewarded for our efforts, rather than be hounded forever, as we are where we come from."

And David dwelt with Achish at Gath, he and his men, every man with his household, even David with his two wives, Ahinoam the Jezreelitess, and Abigail the Carmelitess, Nabal's wife.

1 Samuel 27:3

ELIAB WATCHED as David rode out from the gates of Gath alone.

As he approached, Eliab stepped forward to meet his brother and to hold his horse. The men stood ready and braced for battle in the event that David gave the word. It did not come.

"How is it with you?" Eliab asked, his faced lined with worry, troubled by David's latest plan.

"We have been assigned to the city of Ziklag in King Achish's service," David said, dismounting his horse. "Make camp here. We march there in the morning. We are truly Hebrews now, and we fight on the side of the Philistines."

The call went out through the ranks. The soldiers stood down, moving hastily to make camp, near exhaustion after their march and the time spent at full alert while David was in the city.

"This is a dangerous game," Eliab said, following. David made his way to where he knew he would find Abigail arguing with Yusef over arranging his personal compound.

"Brother, we have hardly been tending sheep all these years. At least this king believes we are on his side and is willing to give us a chance to prove it. The last one could not be convinced."

"We are now in the company of the men who have been our sworn enemies all our lives," Eliab persisted.

"So we know where we stand with them as well," David said, spotting the color of his own tents and making his way toward them. "They do not tell us that they love us and call us son and then hunt us down. They hate us and say so. It's honest, at least."

"Yusef." Abigail's voice carried some distance to where Eliab and David approached. "I will not tell you again. I will have the tents facing south so that the night breeze is gentle and the sun is always at our side. Now take it down and start again."

"My lady, I have not time to start again," Yusef shouted back.

"Haven't time?" David and Eliab heard Abigail demand as they drew near. "What else do you have to do? Make policy? Defend us against armed insurrection?"

"Now this is dangerous," David said, turning to his brother with a broad smile. "One wrong word means either cold food or an empty bed."

Then Achish gave him Ziklag that day: wherefore Ziklag pertaineth unto the kings of Judah unto this day.

1 Samuel 27:6

"TRAITORS?" JONATHAN repeated the word to himself.

"That is so, my son," Saul said, still standing in the doorway of Jonathan's quarters at the Gibeah palace. "I wanted you to hear it from me first."

"I cannot believe that of David," Jonathan said, sitting heavily on a broad tufted stool.

"He has sworn his allegiance to King Achish of Gath," Saul said, venturing in a few steps, wary of his son's reaction. "News has come that he and his Hebrews have wiped out three villages of Israelites. He splits the spoils with Gath, enriching himself and his men with the rest."

"You drove him to this," Jonathan said, turning cold. "He was the best soldier you ever had, and your vanity could not accept it. I suppose the blessing is that he has not yet decided to attack us directly, for we will never stand a chance against him. No one does. Certainly not you."

"My son—"

"Get out," Jonathan said, turning away from his father's outstretched hand. "I am here with you. Are you not satisfied? You have my loyalty; do not expect my love. You have taken that away from me."

"I am sorry, my son," Saul said, retracing his steps to the door. "The Lord has chosen my path, and I have no choice but to defend it."

"Don't hide your deeds behind God," Jonathan called without looking back to see his father go.

And it was told Saul that David was fled to Gath: and he sought no more again for him.

1 Samuel 27:4

AS WINTER came on, David's Hebrews at Ziklag were living better than they ever had. Their raiding parties were hugely profitable. They quickly accumulated vast herds of sheep, cattle, and goats as well as gold, jewels, valuables, and riches beyond what they had ever known.

David's home, the finest in the small city, was already being replaced by a palace built by the grateful citizens of Ziklag. They found that under David's rule, their lives were more secure than they had been before and, still more, they were the beneficiaries of the unimaginable wealth pouring into the city. As winter approached, the land surrounding Ziklag was cleared and brought under cultivation for the winter wheat and barley crops, as was David's custom.

King Achish was the talk of the pentapolis. His controversial decision to include David in his service had greatly enriched Gath and her contributions toward the building of the Philistine army the five cities supported. David had become a favorite at court in Gath. He, Abigail, and Ahinoam were frequent guests of the king.

Exhausted from the summer's raids, David was glad simply to take pause and spend some time under a real roof in a warm bed. Only a year away from thirty, he had lived hard and felt older. The thanksgiving feast that year would be vast. He smiled ruefully at the way in which he'd earned the bounty.

David's thanks were not for the bounty. His gratitude came from the knowledge that Jonathan could not follow him here and would have to move on with his life. David was thankful to spare him at his own expense. Seeing Jonathan in such distress on their last night together had hurt David almost as much as saying good-bye. He knew it was in Jonathan's best interest and prayed it would be well in the end. Until that day, though, it was a thorn in his soul that he could not tell Jonathan the truth of his allegiance.

"Good uncle," Joab called from the door to David's office, interrupting his thoughts. David was unperturbed, immune to interruptions. The immense Ziklag residence that served as his seat of government housed David and his wives, as well as Eliab, Joab, Abishai, and the rest of the family who traveled and fought with him. "I bring word from Abigail that Succoth will be served in the garden soon, and your presence is requested or, and I quote from her gentle lips, she'll 'kill Yusef with her bare hands.'"

"It is good for a wife to have a hobby," David said, rising from his desk and stretching. "I would not trade her strife for all the peace and quiet in the world."

"Just as well, for you're not likely to get much here today," Eliab said, darting past Joab and pulling the door behind him before daring to reveal the hot bread he had concealed in his robes. "I bring sustenance at great risk to us all."

"Food," Joab said, tearing into a still steaming loaf.

"I stole these from the kitchen while your wife and the worst houseman in all the land were doing titanic battle over the centerpieces, I think," Eliab said with a full mouth. "Will the food never be ready?"

"The food has nothing to do with it," David said, fondly remembering the old days when the feasts had been his province. He wondered if it had seemed the same to Eliab then. "It is a battle of wills between those two. I fully expect one day to come home and find the house in flames and the two of them hacking at each other with swords."

"Life is good here, Uncle," Joab said, tearing off another bite. "We have much to be thankful for. I did not think this would work at all. And certainly never this well or this long."

"I worry that the price we pay is too high." David sighed, with no appetite for the fresh loaf his nephew offered.

"Who is being harmed?" Eliab said, crumbs flying from his mouth. "King Achish is growing rich. We are doing well and safe at last. Best of all we are slowly wiping out all tribal opposition to Israel in southern Judah. Soon we will have only the Philistines to fight. With us on the inside and trusted, we may be able to do them in from the top down."

"Perhaps it is the villages we are wiping from the face of the earth who are being harmed," David suggested archly. His soul darkened as he remembered the smoldering remains of Shin Sharon and its slaughtered residents. Learning the true price of war had cost him the contents of his stomach. He wondered what he would pay for accepting it.

"We would all be dead if Achish found out that, instead of Israelite villages, we are instead raiding the settlements of the odious and deceitful Amalekites, Ammonites, Geshurites, and Girzites," Joab pointed out. "All tribes the sworn enemies of Israel." In truth he too was troubled by the brutality.

"Do not forget, brother, it was an Amalekite who cut Micah down when he wasn't looking," Eliab said, the brutal vision still fresh before his eyes. "If we left anyone alive, it could cost the lives of all of us here. Those we love and care about and fight for, those who fight for us."

"I am aware," David said, shaking his head sadly. "I know the cost and the horror of war. I pay with unspeakable dreams and the soul-blackening dread of Saul. I have been a soldier in the field since Elah, and I pray to God for forgiveness for what I have done in his name and the name of Israel. But to be thought traitors to our own people wears at my soul."

"Supper is on the table," Abigail announced, bursting through the door at last and catching Joab with the loaf in his hands. "Unless, of course, you've already had your fill on bread, Joab?"

Turning, she swept angrily out of the room with Joab in pursuit.

"No, Abigail, wait; it's not as it looks."

Eliab chuckled, watching them go. Turning, he found David still seated, leaning on his desk, fingers tented before his face, lost in sad thoughts.

"You know, little brother, he will understand and forgive you when he discovers the truth," Eliab said, putting a large hand on David's shoulder to comfort him. "Probably even before."

"I have no doubt," David said, putting his smaller hand over Eliab's. "And we will be years ahead of where we would have been, if I had not spent this time sweeping our enemies out of the south and isolating the Philistines."

"What then?"

"I must live knowing what he must think of me now," David said, tightening his grip as a wounded man does with each throbbing ache. "I have to know how much pain I am still causing him in order to set him free."

And David smote the land, and left neither man nor woman alive, and took away the sheep, and the oxen, and the asses, and the camels, and the apparel, and returned, and came to Achish.

1 Samuel 27:9

DAVID MADE his way to Gath, as he always did, with some worry. King Achish trusted him, and the two had become easy with each other, but each visit held the possibility of discovery. He made his way that day in reply to the king's summons. The prospects for such an enforced reunion were always more ominous than arriving with a treasure train of spoils from their fallacious raids.

He rode accompanied by only a few guards so that the loss would be minimal if there was trouble. The day passed with the familiar scenery. He reviewed the most recent raids and communications in his mind, searching for errors or revealing admissions. His plan had succeeded beyond anyone's greatest hopes, certainly his own. For sixteen moons he had managed to deceive the Philistines. Living right under their noses, he led a mercenary army, sacking the camps and settlements of tribes hostile to Israel, with Philistine blessings. In fact, he'd become something of a hero in Philistia, though his own reputation at home had suffered for the legend.

The rewards had been astonishing. David, his brothers, and his growing band of followers had grown rich beyond imagining, while scouring south Judah of all but Israelite settlements. More astonishing than their spoils was that such a large following as David's could keep the secret. No one had yet found them out. Perhaps vested interest in the lucrative proposition had kept them silent. They were aided most in their secrecy by the fact that King Achish, who received half of their take and assumed none of the risk, was completely uninterested in finding them out. With so much at stake and so many possible leaks, David was sweating more profusely than the mild early summer day might have brought on.

Despite his dread of discovery, he was waved through the gates at a gallop by his friend Juk and received as warmly at the palace as visiting family. King Achish kissed both his cheeks in greeting. He shooed away all but his personal bodyguard, relegating even them to outside the doors of the dining room, where he shared a meal with David.

"Yesterday I heard a song about you on the streets of Gath, David," Achish said as they nibbled candied dates. "You are a greater hero here now than you were in Gibeah."

"If I am, it is because you are authoring the tale," David said, taking a gulp of the bitter pale wine the Philistines favored. "I am simply trying to find a place for my homeless people."

"That may be your intention, David," the king said with a sly laugh. "But you have done so much more. Shall I tell you why I've asked you here?"

"I wore my shortest tunic," David said with a grin. "Is that not it?"

"You are as beautiful today as you were when you stepped onto the plain of Gath to face that great stupid donkey Goliath," the king answered him back in kind. He teased, as they often did when they were alone together, like brothers or old friends. "But if it were your ass I'd wanted, I'd have had it the first time you came in here acting the fool like some artless traveling player."

David laughed in spite of the tension he felt. Though the Philistines were the sworn enemy of Israel, he had liked the man from their first visit. In the time since David's return, they had grown closer and, whatever fate held in store for them, David did have respect for the man's wit and his wisdom. He had learned much of the serpentine art of the getting and keeping of political power from this man, who had been born a king in a long line of kings.

"Well sire, if it's not my great beauty," David said with a smile, "why then have you brought me here to eat your best pheasant, when I could be out making you richer?"

"You've done so much more than make me rich," the king said, reaching from the divan where he lay and placing a hand on David's knee. "I brought you here to share news with you that I think will please you. David, you and your Hebrews have earned the respect of the kings of the five cities of Philistia. Thanks in no small part to the enormous contributions from your raids, we are mounting the greatest army ever assembled in Canaan. We will sweep Saul from power once and for all and bring an end to all the regional fighting by making it all one Philistia."

David was speechless with horror.

"Grandest tidings of all," Achish went on, oblivious to the pale face across from him, "you have achieved such a place of honor that you may leave off the petty village-by-village raids to fight at the side of the five kings. Who knows, perhaps we shall make you king over Gibeah, and there shall be six great cities of Philistia. What do you think?"

The look on David's face transformed slowly from horror to a catlike grin.

"Have you nothing to say?" Achish asked as he looked curiously on David's radiant expression.

"Only that you will see for yourself what your servant can do," David answered, placing his hand over the king's, resting still on his knee.

"Excellent," Achish said, rising to fetch more wine to refill their goblets himself. "I knew you would leap at the chance to revenge yourself upon the king who spurned you and retake what is rightfully yours."

Their goblets rang like gongs against each other as both men drank to victory, though not the same one.

And David said to Achish, Surely thou shalt know what thy servant can do.

1 Samuel 28:2

NEWS REACHED Gibeah almost as quickly as David could return to Ziklag to take the news to his own commanders. At once he began his own plan to betray the Philistine alliance and to end their aggression against Israel. David tried to keep himself from hoping that if he could destroy the Philistines forever by striking from within, he could at last return to Israel, home, and Jonathan—without need of Saul's demise.

Word of the massive Philistine military buildup south of the Megiddo pass raised more curses than alarms in Gibeah. The news was not unexpected, just sooner than expected. The king called his advisors around him and began to marshal the great army of Israel to mount a defense and repulse the inevitable Philistine offensive in Jezreel.

Jonathan, too, was called to be a part of the council. Saul was determined that he might regain his son. The rift between them had persisted since their return from the Cliffs of Division. Jonathan blamed Saul for David's defection. Though Saul understood his son's enmity, he knew that, had David remained, their rivalry would never truly have abated. David's rumored collusion with Gath gave birth to Saul's great hope that Jonathan's heart would one day heal enough that he could make a place in it for his father. Until then Saul forbore the coldness of Jonathan's company in the hope of earning the forgiveness for which he knew he dared not ask.

"Perhaps we have overreached in the Jezreel Valley," Commander Sarek suggested, as ideas for a strategy to defend the lowland were bandied about. "Without the army of David to defend it, perhaps we should adopt more conservative goals."

There was chaos as everyone answered at once.

"We cannot afford it," Abner shouted, his voice rising above the din in the king's council chamber. "If we do not stop the Philistines here, there will be nothing to defend us from their assault from the north but the mountains on which we now sit."

"I agree," the king said, ending both sides of the argument. "But the question is how? Do we reinforce Megiddo or pass through it and attack them where they are?"

"Will David fight with them, now that he fights on their side?" another commander asked. "He planned and built our defenses from Megiddo to Jezreel. That means he knows how to lead the Philistines around them. We may be forced to attack them while they are in Philistia still."

"David is too busy with his raids on our cities in the south," another general said, to dismiss the topic before it incited the king's or the prince's rage.

"I will say this," Sarek pointed out. "The armies of the south have not yet found one Israelite city that has been so much as visited by David or anyone connected to him."

"Not one?" Jonathan inquired, sitting up and taking interest for the first time since the discussion began.

The discussion continued in the council chambers long into the night, but the king could reach no decision then or the next day or the next. In the end the discussion was rendered moot when the Philistine army took Megiddo and swept away all the defenses before them. At once they commenced a massive troop buildup along the Damascus Road in the north of the Jezreel Valley at Shunem.

Attack or defend? Still the king could not decide.

For most of his career, Saul had followed the advice and counsel of Samuel. The priest had offered divine guidance in all things, not least the king's military campaigns. Since their falling out, Saul had done no more than react militarily. David had made the only advances Israel had recently achieved.

With David, perhaps the Lord's chosen, on the opposing side, and Samuel dead, Saul could neither beg for advice nor hide behind another's command. His delay over the decision of Megiddo cost him vitally, and he was still more afraid to decide. Was this the Lord's judgment against him for his treatment of David? There was no one to ask.

He prayed and sacrificed on his own. He consulted priests. No answers were forthcoming.

At last he consulted his best military advisor, his own son Jonathan.

"What do I think?" Jonathan began pensively, when Saul called at Jonathan's quarters late at night to plead for his son's advice. "I think you would have done well to ask me for my advice five years ago or to heed the advice I tried to give you. If you had not banished David from your service, the Jezreel Valley would be safe, and all of Philistia would be under your rule now."

"How does your certainty help me today?" Saul answered hoarsely, too ashamed before his son to argue.

"Father, you could still find David and reconcile yourself with him," Jonathan answered. "I believe it is your only hope."

"David has joined the Philistines," Saul pointed out.

"Whose fault is that?" Jonathan answered. "I will follow you, Father, where you lead, whatever you decide. But my advice, if you want it, is make peace with David."

Saul left silently. Both men knew that the king could not do what Jonathan asked, and that it was still their best hope.

Then said Saul unto his servants, Seek me a woman that hath a familiar spirit, that I may go to her, and enquire of her. And his servants said to him, Behold, there is a woman that hath a familiar spirit at Endor.

1 Samuel 28:7

So IT was, despite the fact that Saul's own laws barred the practice of wizards, mediums, and spirit familiars from all of Israel, the king called for one of his closest advisors to find him a witch through whom he could consult the spirits. The same superstitions that had led Saul to Samuel in the first place led him again to seek primitive answers. It was at Samuel's urgings that Saul had persecuted and driven such people as he now sought into hiding. While his advisor searched, Saul moved the army to Mount Gilboa, opposite the Philistine forces at Shunem and south of Jezreel. Jonathan and all Saul's sons were there to fight on their father's side, for all Israel knew the battle could decide the fate of the nation.

Jonathan wondered if David was at Shunem. He considered riding to meet him there, heedless of the risk. If he died in the attempt, at least he would have been trying to do what he longed in his heart to do.

In secret, agents of the king traveled north to the land of Endor, outside the king's rule. It was rumored the witches and mediums had fled to the distant northern province. There his agents found a woman of repute.

Under the cover of night, King Saul, in disguise and at great risk to himself and his cause, rode north. Accompanied by only two guards, his little party passed hazardously near the very grasp of the Philistine enemy and into the lands of the witch of Endor. He arrived at her abode in the gray before dawn.

"What brings you to my door this unborn morning?" The woman scowled at him through a spy hole carved in its heavy oaken panels.

"I come with rich rewards at hand," the king said, raising a heavy purse into her sight. "If you can consult the spirits for me and call up the one who I name to you."

"Sir, you put me in danger by your request," she said, wary of his suggestion. "You know very well that King Saul has forbidden such practices under pain of death."

"In the name of the living God, you will not be punished for this, I swear to you," Saul said, bending his knee before her.

Her mind was not easily swayed. She had seen the horrors visited by vicious zealots upon those who practiced as she did. Her people had been burned and torn limb from limb for believing differently. She was loath to risk for some stranger what little life had been left to her.

"My lady, I am not without influence," Saul pleaded, still standing in the cold of the early morning like any common man. "I swear to you that, not only will you be richly rewarded, but I offer you my protection from the king and all those who follow him." That said, he poured gold through the spy hole. "Only a token of what I offer if you can bring me together with the spirit whom I seek."

The door opened. With the king's own guards outside to protect them from Saul himself, he went in and began the ritual. As the rite progressed, the witch was possessed by her spirit familiar and spoke to Saul in another voice.

"Who would you call?" the witch asked him in the altered tongue, when it came Saul's time to speak.

"Bring up Samuel, the judge of Ramah," Saul called out, already afraid for what he had seen.

The familiar called out to Samuel, singing and chanting in tongues alien to Saul's ear. "He is here before me," the witch declared, her eyes closed and her words strange and lifeless on her tongue. "Why have you deceived me? You are Saul," the witch demanded.

"Be not afraid, for who is better able to assure you of protection from King Saul than King Saul himself?" Saul pleaded. "Tell me who you see."

"I see a spirit coming up out of the ground," she said, lapsing back into the voice of her familiar. "An old man with a long white beard and hair that grows far back on his head," the witch continued. As she described him, Samuel slowly appeared before Saul, who was too desperate to run away, though he was much afraid.

"Saul," the spirit said to him as the witch drifted off into her trance, muttering. "Why do you disturb me?"

"Oh, it is you, isn't it," Saul said, bowing down before the spirit of his beloved priest and advisor. "I am in great trouble, and I need your help and prophecy."

"Why do you consult me, now that the Lord has turned away from you and become your enemy?" Samuel's voice boomed in Saul's ears. "Your great general is David, and victory rests in his hands."

"But Samuel," Saul begged, hoping that he could find favor with the Lord again. "David has turned traitor and fights against his own people on the side of the Philistines."

Samuel's bitter laughter filled the house. The guards outside took fright but goaded one another into staying, though not too near.

"David is no traitor," Samuel boomed. "David has found the only way that he can fight for you without your persecution. He has pretended to the Philistines to take their side against you. You have made his story believable by hounding your best soldier and the finest of men out of Israel. In truth he still fights for you, Saul, loyal even now. He has used his deception to banish the enemies of Israel from Judah and the Negev. He has blinded the greedy Philistines to the truth with the spoils of his many victories on your behalf."

"Samuel, is this true?" Saul asked, seeing at once that it had to be as Sarek said, since no cities had been destroyed.

"The Lord has done what he predicted through me," Samuel said as lightning seemed to form and strike inside the room they still occupied. "The Lord has torn the kingdom out of your hands and given it to one of your neighbors—to David. Because you did not obey, the Lord has done this to you. Your only hope was David, and you have sent him away. The Lord will hand over both Israel and you to the Philistines, and whatever you do, you and your sons will be with me tomorrow, and the Lord will hand over the army of Israel to the Philistines."

Saul fell weeping to the floor, certain in his heart that Samuel spoke the truth.

He lay weeping he knew not how long, there where he believed Samuel's feet to be. The woman roused him from his vision when she spoke to him again, gently and in her own voice.

"Are you all right, good king?" she said, touching him tenderly on the shoulder. "Have you eaten?"

"I cannot," Saul said. Looking up, he saw that she was there before him alone, and all was as before.

"Look, your maidservant has obeyed you. I took my life in my hands and did what you told me to do," the woman said. "Now please listen to your servant and let me give you some food so you may eat and have the strength to go on your way."

"I will not," Saul refused, weak and distraught. "I cannot."

The woman summoned the guards who were with him. They took fright at seeing the king in such a state. Together they joined her in urging him.

"You must eat, sire," the captain of the guard advised firmly. "There is a long ride before us. You look weakened by what has passed here this night."

The woman had a fattened calf at the house, which she butchered at once. She took some flour, kneaded it, and baked bread without yeast.

"It may not be fit for a king," she said as she set it before Saul and his men. "Still, it should carry you back to such as will."

"You know who I am?"

"Who does not know you, King Saul?" she said, taking his hand and helping him to the table.

"Yet you would help me, even though it was I who banished you and your people from their very homes?" Saul asked, touched by her generous spirit and ashamed of the short sight that had guided him to bow to the will of religious primitives in hope of gaining their favor.

"I am still but a woman," she said with a flirtatious lilt as she waited upon them. "Perhaps now you take the time to look me in the eye, you can see that. Take a meal with me before you go to face the fate that the spirits have shown you. You look as though it was dire."

"You did not hear?" Saul said, sitting unsteadily.

"That is not how the gift works," she said, turning to the pots on the fire to fetch more for his men, who ate with more appetite than their master.

"Do the spirits always speak the truth?"

"What reason have they to lie?" she asked, a wise smile upon her lips. "Lying and deceit are the province of the living. It is why I seek the company of the spirits. I know they can be trusted."

*And the lords of the Philistines passed on by hundreds, and by thousands:
but David and his men passed on in the rereward with Achish.*

1 Samuel 29:2

DAVID DELAYED joining the Philistine forces for as long as was possible
without attracting their attention. He knew that his best chance to strike a fatal
blow would be when the five kings joined forces for the battle with Saul's
main armies. So it was by design that not until they were at Shunem did David
arrived with his men.

Arriving a day before the great battle was planned, David was brought
before all the kings to be presented. He was preceded by rumors of his duplicity
and met with doubt by the council of five kings. There had already been much
discussion of including the Hebrew forces in the battle. By David's belated
arrival, many were already decided.

The moon was on the rise, and torches lit David's way to the great white
linen tent where the kings met. He found them at work planning the battle and
the combination of their forces for the impending clash. Confident of his plan,
but anxious of its likely outcome, he was filled him dread at his reception.

"David of Ziklag," the chamberlain announced his arrival.

"What is he doing here?" one of the kings demanded.

"And what of these Hebrews who follow him?" cried another.

David fought to hide his fear of discovery as he stood before the kings at
their planning table. Before he could speak, Achish rose to his defense.

"Is this not David, who was an officer of Saul, king of Israel?" Achish
replied. "He has already been with me for over a year. And from the day he left
Saul until now, I have found no fault with him."

Still, the other commanders of Philistia would not be convinced by
Achish's passion. "Send the man back, that he may return to the place you
assigned him," they insisted. "He will not go into battle with us. What reason
has he not to turn against us during the fight? How better to regain his former
master's favor than by taking the heads of our own men? Is this not the David
of whom they dance and sing, 'Saul has slain his thousands and David his tens
of thousands'? His tens of thousands were our own men."

"David," Achish said. "I am sorry that you have traveled all this way. I
know you to be an upright man, and I would trust you with my life. But the
others who gather their forces here today have not had the chance to get to
know you as I have. Perhaps over time they will come to trust you as I do, but
not in time for tomorrow's battle."

"But, my master, what have I done?" David protested, more for show
than conviction. He had arrived knowing the chances of his men surviving the
betrayal he had planned were but slight. He was happy to spare them, though he

would himself gladly have risked death for any chance, no matter how slender, to bring an end to this and be with Jonathan once more. "How have I been displeasing in your sight?"

"David, you are as an angel of the gods to me, but we rule here with five heads and not one," Achish said, coming forward and placing a reassuring hand on David's shoulder. "We will fight side by side one day. But tomorrow you will leave with your men at first light and return to Ziklag. Remain there until you hear from me."

"As you wish, my lord," David said, rising and striking his chest in salute to each of the five kings before turning to go.

His men were frustrated and relieved by the news. The plan was a risky one. Even if it had succeeded, there remained the possibility that they would be killed by the Israelites themselves. None wanted to be put in the position of actually fighting on the Philistines' side.

They made ready to ride out at first light for the home at Ziklag that they had come to know and care for as their own.

So David and his men rose up early to depart in the morning, to return into the land of the Philistines. And the Philistines went up to Jezreel.

1 Samuel 29:11

WITH GREAT resolve, Saul returned from Endor to Mount Gilboa, certain of what he must do even that same night.

As soon as he returned, he sent word to Jonathan, calling his son before him.

"Jonathan, my beloved son," Saul said, rising and rushing to embrace him as he arrived. "I have given much thought to what you have counseled. I have decided to heed your words."

"What does this mean, Father?" Jonathan asked stiffly, holding back from his father's warm embrace. He pulled away to look upon Saul with mistrustful eyes.

"I am delaying tomorrow's planned attack," Saul said, still smiling at his son. "I will find a way to make peace with David and to bring him back to our side. He will live at the palace once more. Michal can go over to the Philistines for all I care."

Jonathan held back a breath, too stunned by his father's change of heart to believe it at first.

"Sending Michal to the Philistines may be what finally brings them to their knees," Jonathan said, suddenly smiling and falling upon his father like the sun breaking through heavy clouds.

The two men embraced.

"What has happened to change your mind?" Jonathan said, laughing and crying as he held his father fast.

"I've had new information," Saul said, thinking of it. "David has been secretly fighting on our side all along, only pretending to side with the Philistines. He has been clearing out the Amalekites and Geshurites from the south of Judah and the Negev. He practiced to make it look to the Philistines that he was attacking us."

"That is why Sarek said he could find no casualties among our cities," Jonathan said, nearing elation. He embraced his father and kissed his cheeks. "It is as though my prayers have been answered."

"Mine as well," Saul said, glad at last to be reunited with his son. "Now, my son, while I try to get word to David, there is an important task I need from you."

"Anything, Father," Jonathan answered him with the resolution of the converted.

"I need for you to go to Ramah and bring the Ark of the Covenant here," Saul said with great sincerity. "I want to carry it into battle before us once David has arrived. With you and David at my side and the ark of the Lord before us, how can we fail?"

"How indeed, Father," Jonathan answered, jubilant. "I will leave at first light."

"The earlier the better," Saul said, reaching out to embrace his son once more and to kiss his hands and cheeks. "I am a very lucky man to have a son such as you, my heir."

"Thank you for this, Father," Jonathan said, reluctantly taking his leave. "You will not regret this choice."

"I'm sure I will not, my son," Saul said, taking a last look upon his beloved son. It cost him all his will to smile, determined that it be Jonathan's last memory of his father.

Now the Philistines fought against Israel: and the men of Israel fled from before the Philistines, and fell down slain in mount Gilboa.

1 Samuel 31:1

AND SO it was, at first light of the next day, that David and Jonathan rode in opposite directions out of the valley of Jezreel. Each with his own duty, each was certain in his heart that the time of their separation was coming to an end.

David moved swiftly to the west, for he and his men had far to travel, through Megiddo and up the plain of Philistia, to the place that had become their home.

Jonathan's purpose set his pace. He believed the battle would not commence until he returned with the ark and was reunited with his beloved David. As he made his way across the rolling plain of Jezreel south to Ramah, he appreciated for the first time since his arrival the beauty of the play of morning sun on the golden barley still awaiting harvest. There in the barley fields he heard the call to battle. In an instant he knew his father's true heart.

Wheeling his steed without word or warning, he departed with such speed that he left his guard behind him. Armed with only with his bow and the sword at his side, he rode into the battle at Mount Gilboa.

The Philistine forces were greater than any Saul had faced before. Sweeping the valley of the army of Israel, they made their way to Mount Gilboa almost without breaking stride. Unimpeded, they advanced on the king's position. Saul saw that the spirit of Samuel had spoken the bitter truth, and that though those who fought at his call died valiantly and fought their best, all was lost before it began.

His fate clear before him, the king turned to his armor-bearer and offered him his bejeweled royal sword.

"Take this, lad, and do your duty," Saul commanded. "Run me through or these rude uncircumcised brutes will catch me and use me to humiliate the people of all of Israel for whom I stand. They will run me through as well and abuse me to demoralize those who still believe as I do."

The boy only turned and took flight, too afraid to kill his king and too afraid to remain at his side.

Saul laughed bitterly to himself as he watched the boy go. He looked out over the destruction of his forces on the plain below him.

Jonathan spotted Saul standing unguarded on the hill above him. When he could go no farther without trampling his own men, Jonathan dismounted his horse and ran into the battle. Unarmed, he hurried to reach his father before the Philistines could break through the line and capture him.

Unaware of Jonathan's approach, the king lowered his gaze to the ground. He found a sharp rock buried deep and solid in the cold earth. Bracing the hilt of his sword against the stone, he pressed the tip to his heart. Looking heavenward, he breathed deep and sought words with which to beseech heaven for his soul's peace. A smile split his face as he found them.

"Take good care of my son, King David," Saul cried out.

Satisfied, he fell upon the blade.

"Father, no," Jonathan screamed out, his voice lost in the din of battle and the thousands of screams that rose up from the slaughter on the plain below. As he ran to Saul's side, an arrow pierced Jonathan's heart. Determined, he stumbled the rest of the way, reaching his father too late.

Falling at his father's side, their eyes met. In their final breaths, Jonathan found the strength to crawl close enough to throw his arm over his father's chest, their faces only a whisper apart.

"This is how you planned to bring David back?" Jonathan gasped with a sad smile.

"It was all I could think of," Saul groaned, finding and taking his son's hand.

"I told you I would stay at your side for as long as you live," Jonathan gasped.

"And so you have." Saul struggled to secure the only peace he could between them. "You are a son that any man would gladly die for."

Jonathan wept as the strength went out of the grip of his father's hand and the life left his eyes.

"David," Jonathan cried out with the last of his strength. Then whispering, he spoke again, his eyes turned heavenward as he clutched the lion's tooth on the gold chain around his neck. "David, I am thankful that I will never know what life is without you."

And it came to pass, when David and his men were come to Ziklag on the third day, that the Amalekites had invaded the south, and Ziklag, and smitten Ziklag, and burned it with fire.

1 Samuel 30:1

DAVID AND his men were tired and anxious for home by the time they crested the last hill in their path before Ziklag. Each knew from their many trips away that it would be their first sighting of home.

Wisps of smoke rose where the city once had been. With a renewed vigor, they charged at a full run down the other side to close the distance between where they had stood and the nightmare that rose before them.

The city and all they had possessed was destroyed or gone. Wives, children, and loved ones, slaves and servants, all were gone. Only ashes remained. The grief of the Hebrews was so great that there was even talk of stoning David for taking them away from home and those now missing.

Abiathar heard the dissention in the ranks and went to David to warn him. David's wives were both gone. The pain of their loss revealed to him the depth of his feelings. "Jonathan and now this too, Abiathar?" David railed. "What does the Lord want of me? How is it that he takes from me everything that I care about?"

"David," Abiathar said with a small gasp of surprise. "You of all men? Has the Lord ever let you down before?"

"What do you mean?"

"When you faced Goliath? When you battled the Philistines? When you led your first army? When you bested King Saul?" Abiathar said to him. "When has the Lord not stood with his shoulder to yours? Go. I know as surely as if I was the prophet Samuel, if you seek, David, you will find all that you think that you have lost and more besides. That is always the way with you."

David called his captains together and told them of Abiathar's vision.

"David," Joab said with a small sad smile, having lost much that day. "Enough with Abiathar's visions. We trust you."

"You may choose your own reason to trust in this," David said, realizing how often he had shown his secret intelligence behind the screen of Abiathar's visions. "Follow me for whatever reason you choose, but know that it is Abiathar's vision that inspires me in this."

Leaving four hundred behind to begin the rebuilding, David led another eight hundred into the field to find those who had been taken from them or, at least, vengeance against those who had taken them.

As they headed south into the desert lands of the Negev, Matthew, who rode beside David as his armor-bearer, saw what he thought to be a heap of rags lying in the dust in the distance.

"My lord, look," Matthew said, pointing. "See there, perhaps it is something that our enemy has dropped in their haste that will aid us to pick up their trail."

"Good eyes, First," David said, proud of the young man's progress. "We will hold here. Go and see what you can tell, for too many might spoil the trail if there is one to find."

As David waited, Matthew ran over to the heap and began immediately waving his hands and calling back for assistance. To the amazement of all, Matthew lifted up a man, little more than the rags he wore. With his arm over Matthew's shoulder and the help of those who came to their aid, the gasping wretch was brought before David.

Starved and nearly dead, he was given comfort, food and water. David spoke softly to the man, revived but weak after he had eaten.

"Who are you, good sir?" David asked in tongues of several desert tribes before making himself understood. "How come you to be here?"

"I am Omid," the man said haltingly. "I am Egyptian by birth, a slave of a cruel Amalekite master who left me here to die when I became ill. They were in haste and did not want me to slow them down."

"In haste why?" David asked, his heart at the hope.

"The armies of the kings of Israel and Philistia are away in the north. So my masters raided the Negev of the Kerethites and the territory belonging to Judah and the Negev of Caleb," Omid explained, more lucid as he regained hope as well as strength. "They stripped and burned Ziklag. They could not wait here in the open."

"Omid," David said earnestly, putting a hand on the man's shoulder. "Can you take us to the camp of those who have treated you so ill?"

Omid looked around at the hundreds of armed men and then back sincerely into David's eyes.

"Swear to me before the God of your people neither to kill me nor to return me to my master," Omid said. His voice trembled with fear and hope for his life and his freedom. "Then I will take you to them."

"Omid," David said, kneeling and taking the man's hand. "You are a free man from this day forward. You may live among us until you are well enough to travel. We will give you provisions enough to allow you to return to Egypt if it is your want. Or you may make a life with us, taking equal share to any man here. For we are all of us people cast out from our homes. As such you are already our brother. This I say to you before my God and yours. Join us."

With great joy Omid took them to the creek in the basin of the Besor Ravine. The Amalekites were there, spread over the valley, drinking, eating, and celebrating the plunder they had taken from Judah and Philistia. From their vantage they could see captives held in pens with the animals. Women and children, old and young; they could not tell if their own families were among them, and so they fought for hope alone.

With a vengeance born of men defending their home, David and his Hebrews surrounded and set upon them.

It was as brutal a battle as he and his men had faced in a long year of brutal battles. The sun was low and the Amalekites at supper when they set upon them. They rode down upon them from all sides, slashing and hacking to pieces the guards who stood watch over the captives.

Outnumbered, David and those with him found themselves defending the captives and themselves, uncertain if their own people were among those cowering amidst the cattle. The moon rose on their victory the following night, and the joy of their celebration at finding their loved ones soon lit up the darkness.

David wept as he was reunited with his two wives and household, worn but unharmed from their ordeal. Just as Abiathar had assured him, nothing was missing, not young or old, boy or girl, or a trunk of all their goods. Beyond all that they recovered, there was the Amalekites' plunder of all the south of Judah and Philistia.

The herds his men drove before them stretched to the horizon and required an army to tend them. The wagons groaned under the weight of their loads.

David was thoughtful as they made their way slowly back to Ziklag. They paused at an oasis along the way to water the animals and refill their skins. David took the occasion to share his thoughts with those who had fought at his side.

"We have been given a great blessing by the Lord," David said, throwing his arms wide to include those loved ones who were once again among them and all the treasures with which they were laden. "To show our gratitude before the God of our fathers, we shall take handsome shares of this embarrassment of riches and make tribute to all the great cities of Judah. To Bethel, Ramoth Negev, Jattir, Aroer, Siphmoth, Hormah, Chorashan, Athach, Hebron, Eshtemoa, and Rachal in Judah, and those in the cities of the Jerahmeelites and the Kenites, for they too shall be part of the new kingdom that we are helping the Lord to build. We may not have left those places respected men, but we shall still be worthy of their respect by acting as men who are held in high regard.

"The rest shall be divided equally between us here and those who remained behind," David decreed, to the cheers of those there who heard him. "It shall always be so among us."

With joy at their deliverance and sadness for the destruction, they returned to Ziklag to begin to rebuild the lives there that they had all come to love. News of King Saul's defeat at Mount Gilboa awaited them, but there was no word of Saul's fate. David was left to worry and wonder. Unable to know where to send word to Jonathan, he found himself lost in the details of the Hebrews, distracting himself with work as he had so often in the past.

Tributes were sent with messengers to deliver word of their final victory over the Amalekites, and to disabuse the citizens of Judah of their belief in the deception that those at Ziklag had lived for so long. The truth revealed, the Hebrews of David were hailed as heroes for allowing the people of Judah to live as free men.

Though both richer and more esteemed than any in all of Judah, they were also homeless. They returned to life in tents as they began to raise their city from the ashes. Though there was a call to build a great palace for David and his government in tribute, he refused them. By David's orders, the people were commanded first to rebuild their own homes and lives.

"There is plenty of time to build palaces and monuments," David said after thanking them for their generosity toward him. "Our people lived in tents for generations upon their arrival in these lands. My family will do well in tents for now. We will graciously accept your offer to build a place for us to live only when we know those who have supported us are secure."

His commands stirred the people's hearts and inspired them to remake the city with greater haste. Working into the night and before first light, they restored what they had lost, making it better than before so that they might the sooner be able to show their gratitude to their lord captain.

It was at David's fine tent just outside the new city of Ziklag where the messenger found him.

His face ashen, and without a word of explanation, Yusef brought the man before David. He then fled the tent to find Abigail and Ahinoam, Eliab, and all of David's kinsmen.

"My lord," the man said, falling before David, his clothes filthy, torn and bloody. "I come to you with news."

"From where have you come?" David asked, rising in dread.

"I have escaped from the camp of the Israelites," the messengers said, raising himself up on his elbows.

"What has happened?" David asked softly, still standing, afraid of the answer.

"All is lost. The battle was final," the man said, getting to his knees. "The army of Israel is destroyed, and the king is dead."

"How do you know this?" David asked, with a thrill of what such news might mean.

"I was there at Mount Gilboa," the man said, finding the strength to rise to his knees. "I saw the king as he lay dying, his wounds mortal. He begged me to help him die before the Philistines could reach him, for he was already in the throes of death. I stood over him and killed him, for I knew he could not survive."

"How do I know that this is true?" David asked, his voice cold and clear as he crossed slowly to the man.

"I have taken this crown from his head," the man said, pulling from his robe a simple gold band. David's heart fell. He had seen the circlet upon Saul's brow. It was the one the king wore in the field to be recognized by his men. "And this, from the hand of the man beside him."

The messenger produced the gold ring that matched the one on David's hand and held it out to him.

"I believe he was one of the king's sons," the messenger said.

"Why were you not afraid to lift your hand to destroy the Lord's anointed?" David asked, his voice little more than a harsh whisper.

"I am not of this land," the messenger answered, terrified by David's tone. He had looted the bodies where he found them on the field and deserted his Philistine masters with dreams of rich rewards for the treasure. He had come to David in search of the riches he'd heard rumored but feared he had somehow been discovered.

"Your blood be on your own head," David said rising up and drawing his sword. "Your own mouth testified against you when you said, 'I killed the Lord's anointed.'"

"I did not know," the man tried to explain as he backed away. "Here, have this too. I believe it is a lion's tooth, but the chain is a gold one from around the neck of...."

Those were the last words the man spoke. David drew his sword and swept his head from his shoulders just as Eliab and Abigail stood at the entrance to the tent.

"No," David cried out, until he thought his heart would fail him. "No, no, no, no, no," he repeated, falling to his knees. His sword fell away as he crawled to take the ring from the man's lifeless hand. The ring that Yusef had recognized, and so allowed the man to enter David's presence.

"No, no, no man may kill the Lord's anointed and live," David said, writhing on the bloody rug where the messenger's body had fallen. "No man may...."

His words were lost in his tears as he lay in the blood, tearing at his hair and clothes. Eliab and Joab tried to aid him, but he fought them off.

"Jonathan," he screamed again and again. "Jonathan, not now, now that we might finally be as one."

Abigail understood. A sad smile cracked her face as she saw her husband whole before her and loved him more for the depth and truth of his heart. Turning away, she left Eliab and his brothers to attend to David, knowing that her best service to him would be to manage their affairs at Ziklag until he found the strength to walk again.

For days, as the city and then their palace grew up around them, David would not speak or bathe or eat. Abigail would sit at his side, occasionally getting him to take a sip of wine or water or a crust of bread, but little more. She had to feed him with her fingers, for he would not let go of the matching ring he had torn from the messenger's dead hand, along with the lion's tooth that she recognized as David's own.

Slowly he found the strength to emerge from the darkness that was upon him. Taking up his harp, he tortured it with only sad melodies, wailing his songs of mourning, cursing the Lord with such ferocity that the servants were too frightened to attend him.

"Lord, why?" David bewailed his fate, his faith destroyed. "Now, at the height of triumph? Why now? Why have you taken him from me? It was only for him that I was able to do all that I have done. Where are you, my Lord? Why do you punish me so? What is your will for me?"

It was in such a state that the delegation from the elders of Judah found him. For days they waited, seeking an audience, before he would see them, and then only at Abigail's insistence.

"My lord, they probably only want to thank you for your tributes," Abigail pleaded, the only one still brave enough to endure his company. "You are a great man. You must find it in yourself to behave as such, even if only briefly."

"I am not a great man," David railed at her. "A great man could have saved him. A great man would not have been hiding in the wilderness when such as Jonathan fell on the field of battle, defending our home and our people."

"So this is how you pay tribute to Prince Jonathan?" she said, her patience with him breaking. "You show your respect for this man, whom you say you loved, by sitting here unwashed in your own filth, weeping only for yourself? Then he died for nothing."

Rising, he bore down on her as if to do her harm. She did not flinch or turn her tear-streaked face away from his blow as he drew back. The blow never came. Her truth had pierced his heart as the arrow that had killed Jonathan. He threw his arms around her, weeping. They cried and mourned together until they had no more tears.

Somberly, he rose to his feet. He helped her up and sent her to fetch him hot water and clean clothes, food and drink. Though he was solemn, he put himself together and received the men of Judah who had waited upon him.

"Good sirs, you honor us with your visit," David said with sincerity but without joy. "Forgive me for keeping you waiting. I have been ill, heartsick, and unable to see visitors. You are my first, and you do me much credit."

"It is you, sir, who honor us," their leader said, kneeling before David, even when David tried to help him up. "We have come at the behest of the elders of all of Judah to beg you to be our king."

CHAPTER TWENTY-ONE
THE PRINCE'S PSALM

How are the mighty fallen in the midst of the battle! O Jonathan, thou wast slain in thine high places. I am distressed for thee, my brother Jonathan: very pleasant hast thou been unto me: thy love to me was wonderful, passing the love of women.

2 Samuel 1:25-26

DAVID'S CORONATION was held in Hebron, his new capital city, later that summer, shortly after his thirtieth birthday. Though he was king of Judah, it would be another seven years before he would become king of all of Israel and unite the country from Dan to Beersheba, as he and Jonathan had once dreamed together.

The day of the coronation was a celebration such as the country had never seen before. The feasts and the sacrifices exceeded any that had been witnessed in their history, for their joy and their certainty in their choice was never greater. All men and women of Judah were as one with their Creator in their choice of David as their king.

But for all the joy of the day of his installation, David's mood and clothes were dark as he arrived. He stood before those he would now rule to receive his crown. When it was done, all fell silent to hear his words to them on this, the day the Promised Land was truly deeded into their hands by the house of David.

"I stand before you on this, my first day as your king, because the Lord believes in me. I am but a singer and a shepherd, whom fate and the Lord have made into a king. But I am a man in mourning. There is one who should be standing here in my place, and I at his side. It is, then, the best that I can do to pay tribute to him as I accept, in his place, this his honor that you entrust to me.

"It is with his psalm that I begin my reign. A psalm of mourning for my prince. I commend these words to you and exhort that all who would follow me learn them, to pay tribute to him who has fallen, that we might stand here together today. I give you only this, my prince's psalm."

The beauty of Israel is slain upon thy high places: how are the mighty fallen!
Tell it not in Gath, publish it not in the streets of Askelon; lest the daughters of the Philistines rejoice, lest the daughters of the uncircumcised triumph.
Ye mountains of Gilboa, let there be no dew, neither let there be rain, upon you, nor fields of offerings: for there the shield of the mighty is

vilely cast away, the shield of Saul, as though he had not been anointed with oil.

From the blood of the slain, from the fat of the mighty, the bow of Jonathan turned not back, and the sword of Saul returned not empty. Saul and Jonathan were lovely and pleasant in their lives, and in their death they were not divided: they were swifter than eagles, they were stronger than lions.

Ye daughters of Israel, weep over Saul, who clothed you in scarlet, with other delights, who put on ornaments of gold upon your apparel.

How are the mighty fallen in the midst of the battle! O Jonathan, thou wast slain in thine high places.

I am distressed for thee, my brother Jonathan: very pleasant hast thou been unto me: thy love to me was wonderful, passing the love of women. How are the mighty fallen, and the weapons of war perished!

2 Samuel 1:19-27

ERIC SHAW QUINN, a *New York Times* bestselling author, wrote his debut novel, *Say Uncle*, during his spare time while working as the creative director for an advertising agency and an on-the-air arts and entertainment reporter for his local NBC affiliate. But *Say Uncle*, a comic and celebratory tale of an eccentric gay man who receives custody of his infant nephew after his sister is killed in a tragic accident, took ten years to find a publisher. The idea of a gay man raising a child was deemed so controversial at the time that one editor went so far as to reject the manuscript with the words "You and I just march to different drummers, Mr. Quinn." Upon announcement of its publication, the film rights were snatched up almost immediately following a Hollywood bidding war, whereafter some of Hollywood's brightest stars and legends spent another few years agonizing over whether or not American moviegoers were ready for such a groundbreaking look at love and family. Ultimately, a studio merger prevented the film from being made. As Quinn Brockton, he wrote two original novels (*Never Tear Us Apart* and *Always Have, Always Will*) based on characters from Showtime's hit series *Queer As Folk*. Soon after, he partnered with megacelebrity Pamela Anderson to write two novels based on her wild life. While the initial plan was for Eric to be a ghostwriter on the project, Ms. Anderson outed him to the world as the author of the books during an interview with Jay Leno on NBC's *Tonight Show*. The resulting media blitz took Eric around the world, landed him a spread in the *National Enquirer*, and earned him the title of Amazon's #1 Chick-Lit Author of 2004. Eric has recently published his first murder mystery, *Write Murder*, volume one in a series inspired by his sojourn in the celebrity spotlight. When he's not busy writing novels, he writes, produces, and hosts his comedy/variety podcast, blog, and YouTube channel, *The Dinner Party Show with Christopher Rice & Eric Shaw Quinn* (www.thedinnerpartyshow.com). You can also visit his personal blog at www.ericshawquinn.com.

By Brandon Witt

After a tortured childhood and years of soul-searching, Brooke Morrison has finally settled into a comfortable life. While his sexuality prohibits him from practicing his degree in youth ministry in a church setting, he's found a fulfilling job as a youth counselor at a residential treatment facility in Colorado. He falls in love, marries the man of his dreams, and makes peace with God. He's happy.

Then his buried past drags him back to the Ozarks.

The life Brooke has worked so hard to build is crumbling in his hands in the face of painful memories and past abuse, and his confidence is withering. In El Dorado Springs, where his nightmares come to life, Brooke desperately seeks closure life doesn't offer. Brooke must find value in himself, in his marriage, and in the world around him—and create the hope and perseverance to keep his past from swallowing him whole.

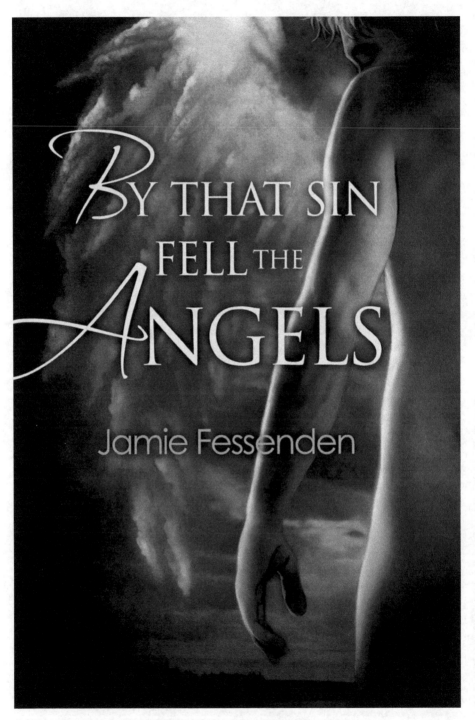

BY THAT SIN
FELL THE
ANGELS

Jamie Fessenden

By Jamie Fessenden

It begins with a 3:00 a.m. telephone call. On one end is Terry Bachelder, a closeted teacher. On the other, the suicidal teenage son of the local preacher. When Terry fails to prevent disaster, grief rips the small town of Crystal Falls apart.

At the epicenter of the tragedy, seventeen-year-old Jonah Riverside tries to make sense of it all. Finding Daniel's body leaves him struggling to balance his sexual identity with his faith, while his church, led by the Reverend Isaac Thompson, mounts a crusade to destroy Terry, whom Isaac believes corrupted his son and caused the boy to take his own life.

Having quietly crushed on his teacher for years, Jonah is determined to clear Terry's name. That quest leads him to Eric Jacobs, Daniel's true secret lover, and to get involved in Eric's plan to shake up their small-minded town. Meanwhile, Rev. Thompson struggles to make peace between his religious convictions and the revelation of his son's homosexuality. If he can't, he leaves the door open to eternal damnation—and for a second tragedy to follow.

By Lloyd A. Meeker

An eye for an eye….

Ian McCandless is a hospice nurse, training to become a shaman. When his mentor orders him to make peace with his estranged family, Ian reluctantly agrees, anticipating another conflict-filled visit. On their way from the airport, Ian's older brother Will interrupts a convenience store robbery and is shot. As he dies in Ian's arms, Will begs Ian to avenge him.

Ian uses his shamanic abilities to track down the killer, but his quest soon becomes a hunt for revenge—forbidden to any shaman. His actions jeopardize his relationship with the spirit-world, endanger the lives of those he loves, and threaten to banish him from the path that gives his life meaning. Ian must choose between vengeance and service to community as the root of his shamanic covenant. Evil or noble, every choice is sacred to the Great Web, and every choice has consequences.

CPSIA information can be obtained
at www.ICGtesting.com
Printed in the USA
LVHW081135211121
704034LV00023B/738

9 781634 768351